A Stone on Their Cairn

Clach air an Càrn

A Cape Breton Saga

Kevin S. MacLeod

GlenMargaret
PUBLISHING

English editor: Grayce Rogers
Gaelic editor: Catriona Parsons
Design: Brenda Conroy
Map: Marc Guertin
Front cover artwork *Eilean mo Chridhe* ("Island of My Heart") by Canadian
landscape painter, Mark A. Brennan <http://www.markbrennanfineart.ca/>
Photograph on back cover by the author, taken from the St. Anns look-off,
looking towards Englishtown and the North Shore

Published by Glen Margaret Publishing
P.O. Box 3087, Tantallon, Nova Scotia B3Z 4G9

Distributed by Glen Margaret Publishing
www.glenmargaret.com

First printing August 2007

Printed in Canada

Library and Archives Canada Cataloguing in Publication

MacLeod, Kevin S., 1951-
A stone on their cairn = Clach air an càrn : a Cape Breton saga /
Kevin S. MacLeod.

Includes some text in Gaelic.
ISBN 978-1-897462-00-3

1. Scots—Nova Scotia—Cape Breton Island—Fiction. 2. Cape Breton
Island (N.S.)—Social life and customs—Fiction. 3. Cape Breton Island
(N.S.)—Fiction. I. Title. II. Title: Clach air an càrn.

PS8625.L456S74 2007   C813'.6   C2007-904164-7

To my parents, John and Norma MacLeod, and their parents
Dan K. and Murdina (Kerr) MacLeod
Norman R. and Ida (Urquhart) MacLeod
who provided me with boundless love and an abiding sense of heritage and faith.
Beannachdan.

CONTENTS

Acknowledgements

A Stone on Their Cairn is both a labour of love and an exercise in team work. There are many players who warrant my deepest appreciation and thanks. At the initial writing stage, the English and Gaelic editors (Neil Kelly, Creative Edge, Ottawa, Ontario, and the late Reverend Murdo MacKay, Grace-Ferguson Presbyterian Church, Millerton, New Brunswick, respectively) provided constant encouragement to keep the story going. It did indeed come to completion but only with my constant taxing of the time, tremendous talents and perhaps even the mental health of both the final English and Gaelic editors (Grayce Rogers, Tantallon, Nova Scotia, and Professor Catriona Parsons, St. Francis Xavier University, Antigonish, Nova Scotia, respectively), who took the manuscript to heart and became its greatest champions. Two outstanding Canadian artists helped bring *Loch Dubh* to life in a way that goes well beyond the written word — Marc Guertin of Ottawa, Ontario, who created the black-and-white map of *Loch Dubh* that is more a photograph than a drawing and Mark Brennan of Westville, Nova Scotia, who painted *Eilean mo Chridhe* ("Island of My Heart") that is the painting portrayed on the book's cover. I stand in awe of your talents. Brenda Conroy of Halifax, Nova Scotia, co-ordinated all elements of graphic design and brought the many pieces of the puzzle together in an absolutely masterful way. And just when all hope was seemingly lost in finding a publisher interested in this project, I had the tremendous good fortune of crossing paths with Richard Rogers of Glen Margaret Publishing, Tantallon, Nova Scotia. An "adopted Nova Scotian," it was Richard who saw merit in making this book a reality. It was a story worth telling given that it spoke about an important and intriguing wedge of Nova Scotian and Canadian history. Words of thanks do not seem sufficient but thank you a million times over for taking a chance on an unknown author. To my family and friends in Nova Scotia, Upper Canada (Ontario) and the "Boston States", I extend my eternal gratitude for your words of encouragement and your patience over so many years for making yourselves available to listen to another possible vignette story line or to read just one more "polished" version of the manuscript. And to the people of Cape Breton, I give you my thanks for being part of my family and providing me with the stories, heritage and pride that make us who we are. *Suas Ceap Breatuinn!*

Foreword

*L*och Dubb does not really exist in terms of Cape Breton geography. There is no such glistening lake surrounded by majestic mountains. There are no farm houses, mill, community hall, school house and Kirk clinging to its shore. There is no road winding down the bluffs to New Carlisle and the North Shore.

Still, it is hoped that readers will follow their own road to *Loch Dubb*, whether prompted by a desire to rekindle memories of their own past or simply to visit a place in a time long ago. Today in the highlands of Cape Breton, there are brooding mountains watching over lakes and the people below whose names will no doubt differ from the fictional characters portrayed on the pages of this book. In this way, *Loch Dubb* really does exist, perhaps not in name but most assuredly in spirit. May it always be so as we continue to place a stone on their cairn.

The Genealogy of the Families of Loch Dubh

(The individuals whose names do not appear in bold-face type
were deceased before 1896.)

FRASER

Duncan (1837 -) / **Jennie** (1856 -)

    - **Alexander** - **Sandy/'*Sandaidh Beag'*** (1886 -)
    - **Matthew** (1888 -)
    - **Emily** (1889 -) / **Christopher** (1877 -) (Hickman)
        - **Duncan** (1912 -)

MACGREGOR

James - **'Mac na poit-dhuibh'** (1868 -) / **Margaret** (1872 -)

    - **Peter** (1888 - 1909)
    - **Charles** (1890 -)
    - **Betty** (**1891** -) / **James** - **'*Mac an Fhìdhleir*'** (1885 -)
                                          (MacInnes)
        - **Diarmad** (1911 -)
    - **Albert** - **'*Rìgh Beag'*** (1893 -)

FERGUSON

Norman (1867 -) / **Rachael** (1869 -)

    - **Morag** (1889 -) / **Elliott** (1883 -) (Cabot)
        - **Jonathan** (1912 -)
    - Harris (1890 - 1893)
    - **Stuart** (1891 -)
    - **Andrew** - **'*Anndra an saighdear'*** (1900 -)

ERSKINE

Neil (1872 -) / **Iona** (1873 -)

    - **Kenneth** - *'Coinneach Bàn'* (1892 -)
    - **Aulay** (1904 -)

GRANT

Angus - *'Aonghas Dubh'* (1818 - 1887) / **Flora** - *'Floiridh Aosda'*
                                                  (1820 - 1899)

    - Annie (1842 - 1853)
    - John (1844 - 1853)
    - **Angus** (1845 -) / **Isabelle** (1854 -)
        - **Iain** - *'Iain an dealanaich'* (1884 -) / **Alexandra**
                                      (1890 -) (Dunn)
        - **Sadie** (1886 -) / **Donald** (see Urquhart)
        - **John** - *'Iain Beag'* (1889 -) / **Christine** (1890 -)
                                     (Matheson)
            - **Flora** (1912 -)
    - Mary (1847 - 1854)

MACDONALD

Archibald -**Archie**/*'Seanair Naomh'* (1820 - 1907) / Hannah
                                            (1823 - 1893)

    - **Malcolm** (1840 - 1897) / **Jessie** (1854 -)
        - **Duncan** (1884 -) / **Mabel** (1889 -) (Taylor)
            - **Catriona** (1909 -)
            - **Malcolm** (1911 -)
        - **Seumas** (1886 -)
        - **Murdina** (1888 -)
        - **Mary** (1891-)
    - Roderick (1844 - 1853)
    - Catriona (1846 - 1854)
    - Kenneth (1847 - 1853)
    - **John** (1860 -) (see MacDonald)
    - **Martha** (1868 -) (see Campbell)

MACDONALD

John (1860 -) / **Ida** (1862 -)

- **Andrew** (1882 - 1900)
- **Roderick** (1882 -) / **Margaret** (1884 -) (Buchanan)
    - **Andrew** (1908 -)
    - **Hannah** (1911 -)
- **Catherine** (1885 -)
- **Daniel** (1886 -) / **Agnes** (1891-) (Bain)
    - **John Murray** (1914 -)
- **Murdoch** (1888 -)

URQUHART

Hector - *'Eachann nan Sgeul'* (1858 -) / **Sarah** (1861 -)

- **Elizabeth** - *'Ealasaid Bheag'* (1883 -) / **Calum** (1876 -)
                                                                    (MacLeod)
    - **Naomi** (1907 -)
    - **James** (1910 -)
- **Donald** - *'Domhnall Òg'* (1885 -) / **Sadie** (1886 -)
                                                            (see Grant)
    - **Blair** (1909 -)
    - **Ewan** (1911 -)
- **Allan** (1886 -)

ERSKINE

Daniel (1823 -) / **Tina** (1838 - 1911)

- **Neil** (1872 -) (see Erskine)
- **Alasdair** (1877 -) / **Kristy** (1878 -) (MacNeil)
    - **Grace** (1906 -)
    - **Fergus** (1912 -)

CAMPBELL

Peter (1870 -) / **Martha** (1868 -) (see MacDonald)

- **Lachlan** (1897 -)
- **Colin** (1898 -)
- **Moira** (1900 -)
- **Ismay** (1903 -)

Glossary

General Terms

amadan	fool/foolish man
athair	father
balachan	little boy
bànrigh	queen
bàs geal	"white death"
beannachd leat/leibh	farewell/adieu/good-bye
beannachdan	blessings upon you
boban	pappa
bòcan (bòcain)	hobgoblin(s)/ghost(s)/apparition(s)
bodach (bodaich)	old man (old men)
bodachan	little old man
bodaich-fhleasgaich	old bachelors
bonnach	tea-biscuit bread/bannock
bràithrean anacuibheasach aingidh	very bad brothers
caileag	girl
cailleach	old woman
canntaireachd	the humming of a tune/chanting/singing
caragan	little darling
céilidh	party
ceòl beag	"little music"/favourite song - airs played on the great highland bagpipe
ceòl mór	"big music"/the classical music of the great highland bagpipe
cridhe	love/heart
deoch	a drink
dorus-siar	west door/door facing the wind
gaolach	beloved/darling
gràdhag	dear little one
gràdhan	little darling
mac	son
mamaidh	mamma
marag	oatmeal and suet sausage(s)/pudding(s)

màthair	mother
mo	my
muileann dubh	black mill
naoidhean	infant/little child
nighean	daughter
òinnseach	fool/foolish woman
rìgh	king
rùn	loved one
rionnag	star/little star
seanair	grandfather
seanamhair	grandmother
seann mhaighdeann	old maid
seud	treasure
sgainneal	gossip
strùpag	tea and a snack
suas	long live/up with
tapadh leat/leibh	thank you
uisge beatha	"water of life"/whisky
ùireach	a clean up

Place Names

A'Choille Mhòr	The Big Woods (a cluster of farms to the east of *Bail'a'Mhuilinn* on Boularderie Island)
An Abhainn Mheadhonach	Middle River (a community north of Baddeck)
An Deireadh	The End (an island off the coast of New Carlisle)
An Toiseach	The Beginning (an island off the coast of New Carlisle)
Bail'a'Mhuilinn	Millville (a community on Boularderie Island)
Beinn an t-Sealgair	Hunter's Mountain (a community north of Baddeck)
Beinn Bhreagh	Beautiful Mountain (a mountain, peninsula and Bell residence near Baddeck)
Beinn-mo-Mhulaid	Mountain of My Sorrows (the mountain overlooking *Loch Dubh*)
Ben Gulicanthe	A mountain in Scotland (birthplace of Reverend Duncan Fraser)
Cobh an Easgainn	Eel Cove (a community on the North Shore)

Cobh a' Ghèòidh	Goose Cove (a community between St. Anns and *Drochaid Na h-Aibhne a Tuath*)
Drochaid na h-Aibhne a Tuath	North River Bridge (a community north of *Cobh a' Ghèòidh*)
Eilean na Nollaig	Christmas Island (a community on and across the Bras d'Or Lake from Baddeck)
Loch Dubh	Black Lake
Loch a'Mhuilinn	Millpond (a cluster of farms to the east of *Bail'a'Mhuilinn* on Boularderie Island)
Sgeir Dhubh ('Skir Dhu')	Black Rock (a community on the North Shore)

Personal Names

Anndra an saighdear	Soldier Andrew (Ferguson)
Aonghas Dubh	Black Angus (Grant)
Banrigh Shalach	Dirty/soiled Queen (Annabelle Calvey)
Coinneach Bàn	Blond Kenneth (Erskine)
Dìleas	Faithful (the MacNeil dog)
Domhnall Òg	Young Donald (Urquhart)
Eachann nan Sgeul	Hector of the Stories (Urquhart)
Ealasaid Bheag	Little Elizabeth (Urquhart)
Fear-brèige an righ	The Puppet of the King (Daniel Erskine's term for the G.G.)
Floiridh Aosda	Old Flora (Grant)
Gnùis a' bhiorain-ghriosaich	Poker Face (Annie-Mae Massey)
Iain an dealanaich	Lightning Iain (Grant)
Iain Beag	Little John (Grant)
Mac an Fhìdhleir	Son of the Fiddler (James MacInnes)
Mac na poit-dhuibh	Son of the Still / Son of the Black Pot (James MacGregor)
Rìgh Beag	Little King (Margaret MacGregor's endearment for Albert)
Rionnag	Little Star (the Fraser cat)
Sandi Beag	Little Sandy (Fraser)
Seud Beag	Little Treasure (Jennie Fraser's endearment for her children)
Seann Chleasaiche	Old Trickster (Diarmid MacInnes)
Seanair Naomh	Holy Grandfather (Archibald MacDonald)
Taghta	Choice / Chosen (the Campbell dog)

From the lone shieling of the misty island
Mountains divide us, and the waste of seas –
Yet still the blood is strong, the heart is Highland;
And we in dreams behold the Hebrides.

Canadian Boat Song
(second verse)
Anonymous

▨ Chapter One ▨

Togaidh mi mo shùilean chum nam beann, o'n tig mo chabhair.
Thig mo chabhair o'n Tighearna, a rinn nèamh agus talamh.
Salm CXXI: 1 – 2

I will lift mine eyes unto the hills, from whence cometh my help,
my help cometh from the Lord, which made heaven and earth.
Psalm CXXI: 1 - 2

*R*ionnag was not amused; that was abundantly clear to anyone who was
the least bit observant or possessed even a modicum of common
sense. It was more than the slight twisting of the head and the turning
back of the ears. Indeed, she didn't even bother to open an eye to confirm
the source of the vile and quite thoughtless irritation. There was simply
no need because this was certainly not the first time she had been forced
to endure such an annoyance. Her indignation was only further heightened by the realization that it would not, in all likelihood, be the last.

It had been the creaking of the veranda floor boards under the chair
that disturbed her sleep after what had already been an extremely long
and busy day. As the sun caressed her shiny black fur, her mind began to
wander and she suddenly found herself contemplating why it was that
a cat's life should be so difficult and yet, at the same time, so grievously
under appreciated by its owner. Owner?! The mere thought had now so
shocked her that she actually came close to opening both eyes as if to
reassure herself that she had not been unwittingly damned to a state of
pure insanity. Of course humans thought they were in control; didn't they
always? It was so terribly tiring to constantly endure commands to do this
or that, being swatted with the kitchen broom or, horror of horrors, having one's delicate ears mercilessly crushed under the confines of a frilly
baby's bonnet. Yet, as she lay awash in the glorious warmth of the late-
afternoon sun, she convinced herself that such issues should not concern
her, certainly not at this moment anyway. She was availing herself of a
well-deserved rest. Whether her "owners" believed this or not, it did not
matter. Even if it did, she knew that she would not much care.

But then, the Frasers were still a fairly acceptable family with whom
to live. She had to admit that; if nothing else she knew herself to be
terribly perceptive and always honest. After all, she had come across
other felines, normally on her routine nightly forays, who were forced to

scavenge for a bit of meat wherever and whenever they could. Oftentimes, this involved theft — something that troubled her greatly given her present living arrangements and the accompanying moral rectitude that would most assuredly condemn such wayward wickedness. As the sun sought a temporary respite behind a wispy cloud, the slight coolness of the air caused her to also think of how these poor unfortunates seldom knew the joy of a large bowl of warm milk fresh from the cow. Even as the sun reappeared and once again cast its warm caress over her, *Rionnag* experienced a sudden memory flash that streaked before her firmly closed eyes and chilled her to the core. For the second time in so many minutes, she had unwittingly succeeded in startling herself and twitching whiskers were a visible sign that she was not pleased. In the most demonstrative act of self-assurance known to her, she curled her body up into an even tighter ball as if to comfort herself in countering the memory that was simply too horrid and still tormented her even with the passage of all these weeks.

It had been an evening in mid summer, early August she thought, as she sauntered across the farmyard in surveying her domain and taking stock of all goings on, which was her normal late-afternoon ritual. Approaching the ashen-grey barn that served as a repository for all manner of pungent odours, she decided to venture inside with the delicate grace that was hers alone and assume a watchful position near the side door. Was this not the very same one that always creaked and alarmed the chickens in the adjoining coop? Such silly animals they are — almost as stupid as the fleece- mottled sheep! In any event, that was when fate would have it happen, when all hell first broke loose. Initially, she likened it to a shooting star, the ones that the children always searched for in the night skies and of which favours were asked. The next moment, she felt the sharp bullet-like sting as the milky comet hit her squarely in the face, very nearly sending her arse over tea kettle. The young Fraser boy was up to his usual tricks as he sat there straddling one of those milking stools whose legs she occasionally used to sharpen her claws. For one brief moment, she gave serious thought to using one of his own legs as an appropriate replacement in the future. However, quickly composing herself in the midst of such a heinous crime, *Rionnag* defiantly fought to retain her dignity. If nothing, she was proud! Now, having gingerly licked the dripping warm milk from her face, chest and paws, she held her head high and clearly remembered giving Alexander Stuart Fraser the stare of his life. With that, the point was made. She quickly turned her back on him as he continued to milk the unkempt-looking guernsey and left the barn with her tail and whiskers held high. As she withdrew, all that remained was the ringing in her ears of the riotous laughter of the *amadan* (fool) who continued to revel in his marksmanship and devious treachery.

She promised herself that *Sandaidh Beag* (Little Sandy), as his mother was fond of calling him, would live to rue this day. That time would come soon enough and she would be there to enjoy it, perhaps even play the role of instigator. But for now, there were other priorities that warranted her immediate attention; the hay field behind the barn that stretched beyond the orchard and up the hill to the spruce trees awaited with its piles of freshly cut hay. No doubt, there would be field mice scurrying about in search of alternative accommodation in the newly built mounds that appeared following the decimation of their own homes by the heinous butchery of the farmer's scythe. She would have a good feed to fill her stomach and to remove both the milk from her tongue and the humiliation from her mind. That night at least, she would be on the prowl and, thankfully, on her own far away from the Fraser children.

Finally, peace was restored to her mind as she remained curled up in the security of a tight ebony ball. All the while, the sun continued to bathe her and, from the direction of the apple orchard, she heard the frantic chirping of birds that was not dissimilar to that of the barn swallows that were forever tormenting her. She could always sense their devilish amusement as they swooped down on her from the rafters like so many shards of glass as she exercised her right and duty to take inventory in the various nooks and crannies of the hay mow. As this newest memory passed as quickly as had the calliope of chirping, she twitched her whiskers and slowly slipped into a contemplation of her life. The things that are sent to torment us! For now, the birds could enjoy a respite from her pursuit and would be free to do whatever it was they did with their time. She didn't much care; right then she had more important things to think about. After supper, she would begin her travels across the adjoining fields and meadows and, if time permitted, to the early fringes of the woods that cascaded down the surrounding mountains. She knew that she must rest in preparation for the hunt and, with visions of edible delicacies flooding across her mind, suddenly began to purr.

The pronounced sound of the cat's contentment caused Duncan Fraser to turn his head and, for that brief moment, the rocking chair fell silent. Upon reflection, he was somewhat taken aback given that it would normally take an important interruption, perhaps from his wife or a visiting elder, to cause him to cease his rocking. At fifty-nine years of age, Duncan was not an old man, and certainly not one who would idle away his time in foolish ways. No, there was something more that drew him to the chair with its curved arms that eagerly enveloped anyone who dared venture near. As his body once again swayed back and forth like a metronome possessed, Duncan knew precisely why he was here on this veranda and in this very chair. His mind was awash with whispers of melodies that his mother had sung to him as a bairn many years ago in the old country. He could hear her dear voice still and it gave him a certain sense of peace. He had always allowed himself this luxury because it calmed him in much the same way that Jesus had calmed the angry waters in the presence of His disciples. He was well pleased with this analogy and thought that it held promise for a future sermon on the need for a pious and humble heart.

The rocking resumed as if to provide validity to both a homily yet to be delivered and a life's course still to be run.

Duncan was forced into the assurance that he was not actually engaging in any musical endeavours. Certainly his rocking bore not the slightest resemblance to what others did at the *céilidhs* (parties) and milling frolics that were still held at the community hall against his will. True, they maintained a musical beat much as did his rocking. However, the difference was that they were seeking pleasure and excitement of the body through their actions while he sought only solace for the soul. With his mind increasingly placated by this subtle affirmation of piety, he suddenly began to hear a faint lilting melody that he realized had caused his eyes to moisten. For that one brief moment, he was no longer in a rocking chair on a veranda but in a small, rudely made bed in a croft on the slopes of *Ben Gulicanthe*. And what he heard was not the purring of *Rionnag* but the sound of his mother's soft voice as she coerced her young son into sleep.

> *Cagaran, cagaran, cagaran gaolach,*
> *Cagaran laghach thu, cagaran gaoil thu;*
> *Dean do chadalan, dùin do shùilean,*
> *Rinn thu cadalan, fosgail do shùilean.*

> (Little darling, little darling, lovable little darling,
> Pleasant little darling, darling of my love;
> Go to sleep, close your eyes,
> Wake up again, open your eyes.)

As Duncan continued to rock, he felt a small stream of tears roll down his cheeks. Few would have attributed such sentimentality to him and even he was uncomfortable with, what appeared to be, a visible display of emotion. After all, he was not merely Duncan Fraser; he was the Reverend Duncan Fraser who preached the word of God from the pulpit, lived it daily through his works and deeds and was forever strong in the faith. Still, he thought it fortunate that he was alone here in his chair. His appearance might well be a source of amazement to others who through time had come to know the Reverend Fraser as a man who wore a constantly stoic, if not stern, face as easily as he wore the black woollen robes and brilliantly contrasting, white tabs of the ministry. No, he was indeed alone and could avail himself of this richness of mind that God in all His wisdom and mercy had bestowed upon him. For this one moment at least, there would be no guilt, no shame. There would only be a sense of loss, of the past never to be recaptured. And yet, there was also a feeling of things yet to come, a future to be built on this land with a true sense of heritage and faith. With God's help, it would happen and he longed to play his full part. He knew that he would; he knew that he must. The past was never to be repeated.

A sound from the direction of the hallway led Duncan to believe that one of the children would soon appear before him. No doubt, it would be Emily who delighted in sharing bouquets of wild flowers that she would gather lovingly and with such great care. Was she not known to spend hours picking them around the orchard and well beyond up in the hills? And if that were not enough, she revelled in giving each one a name and a personality that usually resulted in lengthy stories and equally lengthy explanations. It was not that he would be embarrassed about the presence of tears on his cheeks. No, it was that he would have difficulty trying to make little Emily understand his real need to rock for hours in this chair. But then, could he fully explain it even to himself? Besides, she always had a million questions and was never satisfied with anything less than a million detailed answers, be they fact or fiction. With her, it never seemed to matter one way or the other. Such an inquisitive child! No, it would be best to dry the tears and keep these memories as special souvenirs for him and him alone, as one places valuable possessions in a trunk for safekeeping. It was not selfish he told himself; no, no. It would be easier for everyone, especially the younger ones, who had no memory of the land across the seas. Their home was in a new place now and things were so incredibly different. His memories and his longings were very personal and belonged only to him. This was God's will. It was a sense of heritage; it was a sense of faith. He had no doubt.

Once again, the rocking came to an abrupt stop as his hand reached back for the handkerchief that was always freshly ironed and placed in the right rear pocket. Opening the cloth and wiping the tears away, Duncan recalled the verse in St. John's Gospel when Jesus stated that we must be born of water and of the spirit. This water on his cheeks was perhaps symbolic of his rebirth in this new land and, at that moment, he recommitted himself to his faith and dedication of purpose in building the Kingdom of God here amidst the spruce, pine and maple trees of Cape Breton. While God does indeed work in mysterious ways, it was not a mystery to him. Duncan Fraser understood.

The sounds inside the house had subsided and Duncan realized that his solitude would continue for a bit longer, no visitation appeared imminent, thankfully. As the sun began to disappear behind the western mountain, *Beinn-mo-Mhulaid* (Mountain of My Sorrows) as it was called, he cast his eyes across the placid glen and the waters that gave the community its name. *Loch Dubh* (Black Lake) was now not only his home, it was also his commitment to God. Even with the houses, barns and other earthly manifestations of man that ever-so-sparingly dotted the landscape before him, this was not a community. It was a flock and each one was his sheep. He was their shepherd and, with the Almighty's help, would continue to lead them beside still waters and restore their souls. At that moment, he was overcome with a sense of ownership as well as awesome responsibility. He recognized full well that, while his was indeed a tremendous task, he was at peace with himself and with his God.

In the far distance, beyond the bluff that cascaded down to the broad Atlantic shore, he could faintly make out the gulls and puffins as they circled over *An Toiseach and An Deireadh*, the craggy solitary islands that lay cradled in the coastal waters. To Duncan's mind, the two rocky protrusions had always appeared as abandoned orphans destined to never know the warm embrace of Mother Earth. The expanse of distance between manse and islands prevented him from actually hearing the birds' cries as they nested on these rocks and competed with local fishermen in bringing home a catch of the herring, cod or halibut that frequented these waters. Regardless, Duncan continued to watch the birds as they dipped low over the islands and, just as suddenly, were lifted high above as if they were now having second thoughts and were seeking a more-heavenly resting place. *"Ach iadsan a dh'fhéitheas air an Tighearna gheibh iad spionnadh nuadh; éiridh iad suas mar iolair air a sgiathaibh...."* (But they that wait upon the Lord shall renew their strength; they shall mount up with wings as eagles....) Unknowingly, he was speaking aloud as he quoted the beautiful imagery of Isaiah 40: 31. As if continuing on with liturgical purpose, he began to pray a brief prayer, this time silently to himself, in seeking assurance that he too might be borne up and given strength.

He stood in preparation to go inside the house to ready himself for both the supper that would soon await him and the worship that he would conduct with his wife and children before bed. As was always the case, the time of devotion would end with the entire family gathered in a circle on their knees in prayer of thanksgiving for another day bestowed upon them. In the same movement, as he vacated his chair and now the veranda, Duncan lowered his hand to *Rionnag* and proceeded to rub her delicately under the chin. Her eyes opened ever so reluctantly and he looked down at her as, in a somewhat envious manner, he spoke liltingly to her and about her. *"Nach tu a tha sona, a pheata bhig. 'S ciùin do bheatha 's beag do chùram."* (How lucky you are, wee thing. Such a placid life with so little responsibility.) With that, he finally left the veranda and entered the house through the large screen door with its gingerbread scrolling, passing from one solitude to another.

Raising her head, *Rionnag* looked in the direction where he had gone with only the reverberating sounds of the closing door to now keep her company. She cocked her head to one side and reminded herself that she really must learn to tolerate these people because, in all likelihood, they did mean well. Little responsibility, indeed! With that, she again curled herself into a ball and resumed her well-deserved sleep. Night would soon be upon *Loch Dubh* and she would be busy, regardless of what the Reverend Duncan Calum Fraser might think.

"Mo chaileag, chan eil teagamh sam bith agam. Tha fios aig a h-uile duine gun do chriochnaich thu d'obair-sgoile. Tha thu glé dhìchiollach a ghnàth agus chan eil feum agam air cuideachadh anns a' chidsin an dràsda. Bu chòir dhut cuairt a ghabhail oir tha àile an fheasgair math dhuit." (My girl, I have no doubts. Everyone knows that you have fully completed your school work. You are always so diligent and I do not need help in the kitchen right now. You ought to take a walk; the cool air is good for you.)

Sarah Urquhart's voice was nothing if not commanding as she turned and responded to Elizabeth who already had her hand strategically and quite firmly placed on the knob of the back door. Sarah's words had taken into account a hint of urgency in her daughter's voice and in her desire to be free of the house, for whatever reason. Elizabeth was known to enjoy an afternoon walk; she said it gave her a sense of freedom and cleared her mind after spending the better part of the day in the classroom and afterwards with her books at the small desk in the front parlour. No, it was not the request that surprised Sarah as much as the eagerness with which it was made. Heavens, Sarah had known horses that chomped on their bits less ferociously than this!

She wiped her hands free of the bread dough that billowed on the pantry counter. Thank heavens for aprons. What a state the kitchen floor would be in if you were ever to be found wanting one! Sure enough you might as well be married to the broom since you would be forever sweeping the floury film from the wide boards and gaping cracks in between. But thoughts of bread, aprons and brooms soon left her as she focussed on Elizabeth who continued to stand there across the broad expanse of kitchen. Sarah felt a need to speak to her daughter, if for no other reason than to better understand the sudden urgency for a walk.

In turning about, Sarah noted that Elizabeth was perfectly framed by the old pine door that had welcomed countless visitors to this home over so many years. While she would be the first to admit that she really didn't know all that much about art, Sarah could call to mind the time when she had found herself admiring some wonderful paintings of far-away places that were displayed in a shop window in Baddeck when last she visited the county seat. Knowledge may be lacking but still in all she had a natural appreciation for beauty, whether it was a brooding duck with her ducklings on the loch, the glorious refrains of the Psalms being precented at Kirk, the fragrance of a rain-soaked forest in spring, a feast of hot molasses biscuits with cold milk or the velvety surface of the mare's damp nose. She admitted to herself that she was only a simple country woman and certainly no one would ever deny that. But she was also a woman who could be and was justifiably proud of the beautifully framed picture that now appeared before her.

In that brief moment as she turned and spoke, her wee girl had somehow been replaced by a young woman. She wondered to herself where the years had gone; had it not been only a short time ago that she had been delivered of the most beautiful bairn that ever was? Oh yes, Donald and Allan who came later were special too; all three children were her pride and joy. But somehow, Elizabeth, the eldest, was different and always would be. She couldn't really explain it, even to herself. But then, after all, perhaps there was no need. It was something of the heart and not the mind.

From the very beginning, Sarah had nurtured a close bond with her children and could never envisage the day when they might be removed from her. At this moment, it struck her that the physical distance of the kitchen floor that separated the two of them, with its smoothly worn, spruce boards, must be closed. The symbolism was not lost on her as she moved closer towards the stove on the pretext of placing more wood on the fire. After all, bread needs a good consistent temperature to bake properly and produce a brilliant golden crown. Bread good enough for Queen Victoria to eat she had always joked with the children. If ever Her Majesty were to visit *Loch Dubh*, they would be prepared and have a nice *strùpag* (tea and snack) ready for her. Elizabeth, Donald and Allan would squeal with laughter hearing their mother speak almost personally of the Queen who lived far away on the other side of the ocean, as if her house was just down the road and around the next bend. Would she really ever come here to *Loch Dubh*? What room would she stay in and would they have to purchase a special chamber pot with gold around the edge? Many nights, as they lay in their beds following evening prayers, they would make up stories of how pleased the Queen had been to visit with the Urquharts and the many beautiful presents that she had showered upon them for being such gracious hosts and loyal subjects. There was never any doubt but that she would stay with them. After all, Queen Victoria also had a home in the Scottish Highlands and didn't the Urquharts have a castle, be it ever so drafty, on the shores of *Loch Ness*? Yes, they would make her feel right at home; she would be one of the clan, Victoria Urquhart! The stories and resulting laughter would continue as each one in turn added his or her own embellishments to the growing saga. Oftentimes it went on for what seemed like hours, until only encroaching sleep was able to finally silence them.

As Sarah leaned down to the wood box by the stove, a strand of hair fell from the well-pinned bun that always sat on the back of her head. Almost unconsciously, she tucked it back in place and found herself standing immediately in front of Elizabeth who, for the first time, seemed to take note of the grey hair that had begun to appear on her mother's head. Elizabeth couldn't help but think that a woman of thirty-five years should not be aging so. Perhaps it was the result of all the strenuous work on the farm that her mother was required to do, to say nothing of the many domestic chores around the house keeping the family contented and in good health. At that moment, Elizabeth promised herself that she would never grow old; she would never be a *cailleach* (an old woman) with white hair. Not ever; she enjoyed being the young woman she now was far too much.

Elizabeth had indeed been transformed into a young lady, no longer the freckled-faced girl with hair braided in pigtails, as the fashion was now called. Her height made her look even older than her thirteen years. Her slim figure and long reddish-brown hair so reminded Sarah of her own mother who now, God rest her soul, lay buried in the cemetery behind the Kirk. It was the colour of the hair in particular. What a pity it was that Elizabeth never knew her grandmother. How similar they were physically and temperamentally; they would have gotten on so well together. For Sarah, it was a harmful and bitter truth that her mother had never really accepted Hector Urquhart as an appropriate choice for son-in-law. She had made that abundantly clear time and again and it had been a source of great trouble within the family that abated somewhat only many years after wedding vows had been exchanged. These episodes were now relegated to the past and, thankfully, their sentiments taken to the grave. Even with the emotional turmoil that she had endured as a result of her own mother's rigidity, Sarah believed that the characteristic ambition of the MacGregors was probably a good balance for the level headedness of the Urquharts. She had always maintained that time would tell as her children grew into maturity and, judging by the young woman standing before her, she knew that she would likely not have long to wait.

"Tha gaoth an ear a'gleadhrach faisg air an loch agus tha cnàmhan Floiridh Aosda a' taisbean an t-sneachda. Cuir ort tuille aodaich. Tha an sgeadachadh bòidheach gu dearbh. Ach, cuir ort do chòta. Ma bhios tu tinn am màireach cha dèan mi sailleadh. An eudar dhomh a bhi 'nam bhanaltrum mar an ceudna? Och ma tà; do chòta mas fhalbh thu." (The east wind is blustering near the loch and old Flora's brittle bones indicate snow is in the air. Put on more clothing. The dress is truly pretty but put on your coat. If you are sick tomorrow, I will not be doing preserves. Must I also become a nurse? Oh indeed, a coat before you go.) With reflections now behind her, Sarah was absolutely unrelenting in offering what was more a motherly command and less a kindly word of advice. At least in this case, the bull headedness that she inherited from her own mother was justified, or so she told herself.

Elizabeth took note of and even, to a degree, appreciated the words of concern that had been spoken. Still in all and more than anything else, she was anxious to leave at that very moment so as to be seen walking down by the loch in her lilac-coloured dress, or frock as her mother was still wont to call it. Indeed, was this not the very same frock that caused so many heads to be turned at Kirk last Sunday? She had initially and almost reluctantly admitted to herself that she was pleased by the reaction and noted that heads had pivoted and tongues had waggled in sheer admiration of her appearance and, obviously, how she held herself. It was just as well for all concerned that the truth had never been made known to her. Many of the older people, including Flora, had been absolutely aghast that such a devilish-bright colour should be worn into the House of God and they had lost little time in putting the Reverend Fraser on notice that such practices were not to be tolerated. Did he not know that such things were of the devil and were intended to keep minds off their worship and off their God? With evil temptation abounding and wickedness beginning to flourish, whatever would this younger generation be apt to succumb to next?

Regardless, the dress remained Elizabeth's favourite; she knew it made her look older and feel ever so elegant. The breeze off the water would make it billow and, at the same time, scatter her hair round its high laced collar. She thought this scene terribly romantic and, just by chance, was this not about the time of day that the MacDonald twins, Andrew and Rod, normally went fishing off the bridge near the mill?

"A Mhamaidh, chan eil mi am leanabh. Am feum thu mo phasgadh ann am plaideag? Thig mi air ais gu luath; tha mi luath. Cha ghlac a 'ghaoth mi, no mo chnàmhan." (Mamma, I am not a child. Must you bundle me up in a small blanket? I will return soon; I am quick. The wind will not catch me, or my bones.) Elizabeth chose her words with some considerable thought and expressed them in an almost plaintive tone knowing that her mother always weakened into laughter at such use of imagery. Now, she waited with anticipation and hope that she would be lenient in letting her daughter proceed with her afternoon walk on her own terms.

A slight smile appeared at the corners of Sarah's mouth as she stood there before the stove once again wiping her hands on the now-soiled apron. No words were spoken but Elizabeth somehow knew that she was about to succeed yet again in having her way. She lunged forward, hugged her mother and, as in a flash, disappeared through the door. Suddenly faced with nothing but a stark wooden frame before her now devoid of beautiful canvas, Sarah half-heartedly attempted to reaffirm her authority by calling out yet more motherly words of advice. *"Thoir an aire — tha an t-uisge domhain agus an t-àile fionnar. Fiach nach teid thu ro fhad air falbh."* (Pay attention to the deep water and cool air. See that you don't go too far away.) She knew the words to be completely futile as they bounced off the pine door and flooded back over her. Elizabeth would be fine; Sarah knew it to be the case. After all, she was *her* daughter and didn't the MacGregor blood also flow in her veins?

Turning from the door, Sarah returned to the stove and placed another birch log on the already roaring fire before once again crossing the creaky spruce floor to the pantry. Without realizing it, she found herself speaking to the mounds of rising dough on the coarse wooden counter that were soon to be imprisoned in their black pans. She thought it best to get the dough moving on its way to the oven before it continued to rise all the way to the ceiling. What if Her Majesty were to arrive unannounced and there was no breaded crown? Heaven forbid!

She indulged herself in a hearty chuckle and proceeded to wash her hands in the tin basin immediately adjacent to the kitchen window that faced eastward. In raising her head, Sarah was suddenly seized by a sense of absolute terror that cascaded over her. She was frozen in stark disbelief for there, in the window on yet another canvas before her, stood her mother glaring back at her, motionless. It was her to be sure; there was no doubt. How could you ever forget those piercing eyes? No, wait a moment. Perhaps it was nothing more than the *bòcain* (hobgoblins/ghosts/ apparitions), the ghosties who played hideous tricks on people? Yes, maybe that was it after all. Perhaps if she simply were to close her eyes, they would be gone and the canvas would be made right again, would be cleansed of all unwanted blemishes. Sarah confessed that she should have been more dutiful in saying her prayers. If she had, they might not be here now to torment her so. Finally, with the passage of a few brief seconds that seemed to be hours, she came back to her senses. She realized that she had been doing nothing more than looking at her own reflection in the window. Foolish, foolish woman. She was truly embarrassed by just how silly she had been with her thoughts of the *bòcain*. In an attempt to restore some sense of credibility, she told herself that, once the bread was in the oven, she would turn the wick of the kerosene lamp up higher to dispel these shadows and the frivolous games that light sometimes plays with the un-suspecting vulnerable mind. Such foolishness indeed.

Sarah continued to look into the window and held her hands tightly together, not in prayer but as an act of reassurance. Had she really some-how become her mother? Oh indeed, the facial features were somewhat similar; there was no question of that. What now began to trouble her most was the thought that perhaps one day she might become as rigid and intolerant with her children as her mother had been with her. Was that too part of the MacGregor blood that flowed in all their veins?

As if to dispel such musings, Sarah now made a conscious attempt to look through the window, not into it. The quickened pace of her heart slowed as she began to take solace in the beauty of the closely cropped hay fields that coasted down the hillsides to the edge of the loch. High up near the horizon, one could see that a few of the hearty maples had already been touched by an early frost and were beginning to assume their glori-ous new mantle of red and yellow and orange. Yet, of all the magnificent colours appearing before her, none was more beautiful than a billowy wisp of lilac that moved gracefully towards the road that encircled the loch. In the distance, Sarah could also make out the form of two figures sitting on the edge of the mill bridge. With that, she smiled a broad knowing smile and returned to her bread.

"Geasagach" (enchanting/magical). Without any doubt at all, it would have been perhaps the most apt description to roll off the tongue of any in-truder first chancing upon the scene. The image of the sleigh ride down the twisting hillside from *Loch Dubh* to New Carlisle had a purely magical quality about it. The black horse with its crimson sleigh and two solitary passengers moved gracefully and effortlessly through the snow-capped

evergreens, creating a stark contrast with the ever-expanding blanket of falling snow. Had it not been for the jingling of the bells on the horse's harness, they would have passed in almost total silence, like players making their way through some mystical dream.

Rachael could not recall seeing flakes quite this large before and thought that their lengthy voyage to earth, floating as they did like so many rose petals on an invisible vertical stream, was being greeted most appropriately by a rich symphony of bells. She stared up towards the bluffs where the silhouettes of the black spruce stood erect against the expanse of blue skies as though forming a shoulder-to-shoulder guard around the approaches to *Loch Dubh*. Were they truly soldiers there to protect the people who lived along its shores or simply nothing more than silent witnesses to the ebb and flow of life with all its joys and sorrows? At this Christmas time when families were coming together to rejoice and share fellowship, there would be joy abounding. But Rachael could not feel the exhilaration that others would surely experience. There would be no rejoicing, no fellowship, no joy. All there would be and all that she could feel was a sorrowful void, a devastating emptiness; she thought of Harris.

The sleigh rounded a sharp turn and, in leaving behind its hovering escort of spruce and pine and birch, entered a clearing where the roof tops of New Carlisle first poked their heads up into view. Fiona was somewhat spooked by the sudden open expanse and jerked the sleigh and its runners slightly off the compacted ribbons that had been created earlier in the day by the many sleighs carrying families on their Christmas shopping pilgrimages down to the town. The unexpected movement shattered Rachel's thoughts and brought her back to the reality of the moment. Fiona, the steady and ever-reliable horse; the children had such fun in naming her after that little girl in the picture book they had read in school. They said the horse that Papa had just purchased was every bit as kind and gentle as the little girl who was shown mending the broken wing of a tiny sparrow. She and Norman thought it was as good a name as any and Fiona it was to be for the mare. And yes, as it turned out, she was indeed a placid animal. Morag and Stuart were forever visiting her in the barn, always carrying an apple behind their backs that, with the passage of time, Fiona came to anticipate with obvious delight as her tail knowingly swished wildly back and forth. Rachael was often to jokingly express concern that there would not be enough apples left in the orchard for her to make pies and jellies or to dry behind the stove on lengths of string for use during the winter months. Never once did they take her comments to heart; the slight snicker in their mother's voice told them otherwise and the visitations with gifts in hand continued on unabated. And how those two loved to climb the fence and slide onto the mare's bare back for lengthy rides through the pasture, having coaxed her over with yet another tempting morsel. They would do this every day and for hours on end if you were to let them. Rachael often did precisely that but certainly never ever on the Sabbath. In so often hearing and seeing their pure expressions of joy, she knew in her heart that Harris would have loved to ride her as well.

Rachael's gaze now fell on the spire of the Church of England looming ever higher as the sleigh slowly descended the last hillock in its approach to the town. It seemed to draw her eyes Heavenward and she wondered if there was not a subtle message here as she struggled to create a passage for herself through a constantly changing kaleidoscope of thoughts and emotions. Norman turned his head abruptly to ask her about an item that had just sprung to mind that he thought should be added to the all-important shopping list. From the look in Rachael's eyes, he realized that his wife was elsewhere; he had seen that look before. He intuitively knew that her thoughts were far away and decided it best to leave them be. Perhaps she was planning some special surprise for the children on Christmas morning. There was no particular need for him to know the details, at least not now, and so he would not ask. Besides, he was the first to admit that he was dreadful at keeping secrets from the children and for him to pose any questions to his wife might only lessen the element of surprise. No, he would leave her to her planning and await Morag and Stuart's shrieks of glee in the kitchen tomorrow morning. The Fergusons had so much for which to be thankful.

The town was directly in front of them now as the sleigh coasted down the final incline to the shore road with the buildings just beyond. The melodic lines of the jingling bells intensified as Fiona, sensing a respite ahead, sped up in eager anticipation. Rachael's stare had continued to follow the inverted lines of the steeple all the way to its tip and she was left contemplating the vast expanse of white-speckled skies that now seemed to unite the curving coastline with the vast Atlantic stretching well off to the horizon. Christmas was the holiest of seasons, marked by the birth of a child wrapped in swaddling clothes and lying in a manger. How then was it that the picture in her mind was one of the death of another child wrapped in a whitened shroud and lying in a grave? *"Na biodh 'ur cridhe fo thrioblaid, agus na biodh eagal air."* (Let not your heart be troubled, neither let it be afraid.) She whispered the words softly to herself, the very same words that the minister had pronounced with such measured resonance all those three long years ago — the very same words that she had so often repeated to herself in the damning confines of her solitude. Norman thought he heard a slight sound, as if a sigh, but kept his hands firmly on the tightened reins and his eyes fixed on the approaching buildings. The only audible sound was now that of joyous sleigh bells. He kept his eyes fixed ahead; he knew better than to do otherwise.

By any standard, New Carlisle was not a large community with its one short street that ran from the shore road, along the water and up to the church on the hill. Other than the church, the heart of the town comprised Dunn's General Store, Her Majesty's Post Office, Bain's Apothecary and the recently opened branch of the Bank of Nova Scotia. There was normally a fair bit of activity on the street as the farming and fishing families would travel from up and down the length of the coast to transact their business. It became a major community event on those days when the Bras d'Or Steamboat Company steamer came to call on its prescribed route up and down the North Shore. Its far-off whistle seemed to beckon everyone to the wharf, including the residents of the houses that were tucked in behind the handful of commercial buildings. One could always count on a goodly crowd being in place well before the steamer slid into its berth at the government wharf. Still, it would be extremely difficult to become lost in the town, even for the smallest of children. Everyone knew everyone else, or so it always seemed, to say nothing of both their public and personal business.

Dunn's General Store could not have been in a more prominent location, positioned as it was directly across from the wharf and just down from the church. Its two large windows, one on either side of the double doors, resembled gigantic eyes that stared out to sea in some ever-diligent ritual of taking stock of everyone and everything that dared cross their path. Its proximity to the wharf had made the store a sort of adopted second home for fishermen, especially during the bleak winter months when fishing became as much a test of the soul as of the body. It was itself a safe harbour that provided much-needed company and a comfort from the oftentimes cruel elements.

Certainly, the fisherman were not alone; Dunn's General Store had become a well-known meeting place for those wishing to exchange the "news of the day" and that included the local farmers from along the coast and up the bluffs towards *Loch Dubh*. It was always in the front corner, near the pot-bellied stove surrounded by high shelves on two sides, that they tended to congregate. The proprietor, Allan Dunn, knew full well that they were in his shop more to exchange gossip for entertainment than they were currency for goods. Never mind; it was innocent enough for the most part and they were, by and large, all good decent people just doing their best to make a living for themselves and their families under oftentimes trying conditions. But still, conversation makes men thirsty and they did tend to drink copious amounts of tea, sometimes with the odd buttered tea biscuit or oatcake. Certainly the misses and young Alexandra were always kept busy in the back kitchen, thankfully leaving the running of the business to the responsible menfolk up front.

Allan was proud of the fact and certainly well pleased with himself for having had the foresight to hire Iain, the Grant boy from the loch, as part-time help to assist with those older customers who only had the Gaelic. Iain was a good worker and quick as a squirrel in climbing the ladder to the high shelves. He soon learned where everything was positioned, including the contents of the holding bins. People would watch in amazement at how quickly he worked, especially when it came to wrapping parcels. The roll of brown paper would fly and the cone of string, hanging high above the counter, would sing as he sped into action. One old farmer had nicknamed him *Iain an dealanaich* (Lightning Iain) knowing that it would make the boy blush, especially in front of the girls. From the outset, it was all too clear that Allan had ulterior motives in hiring him; an extra pair of hands would always be of help, especially with the heavy lifting and storing of goods. But as a successful and well-established merchant, Allan also appreciated the need to keep all his customers satisfied including, God forbid, the older Scotch people. He knew full well that he would never get the gist of the strange tongue of the "Gaelickers." And frankly, why should he even bother to try? Would it not soon be a dead language spoken only by these elderly few? After all, English was the language of the Dominion and everyone should learn it or move on to other parts. It was just that simple.

The discussion coming from the gaggle of bodies seemed to abruptly heat the corner every bit as much as the stove itself around which the men now stood holding their tea cups. John Rogers, from the back street up near the church, had been singing the praises of Wilfrid Laurier, the Dominion's newly elected Prime Minister, even though he was still getting his arse warm in office, having been voted in only last June. "It does not bother me a tinker's wit that he is French or even a 'left footer' (Roman Catholic) for that matter. The Sir John A. crowd were only in it for themselves and that includes the Right Honourable Mister Tupper." Rogers then nodded his head briskly as if the movement would somehow validate the accuracy of his statement that had been delivered with such conviction, if he did think so himself. The room fell silent in anticipation of a battle royal that would almost certainly erupt as a result of such vehement and accusatory comments. Several moments passed while the words hung there in mid air, as if they were the epitome of absolute truth and innocence waiting to be savaged. In all likelihood, they would not have long to wait in both anticipating and suffering their fate.

Sitting on a bench to the side of the front window and well hidden from view, old Archibald MacDonald paused momentarily, cagily taking stock of his surroundings and settling himself before proceeding to call out in a metrical tone and melodic cadence as if reading from the Bible itself. "Sir John was a fine man; he was one of us and I will not have any one of you here speak ill of him. This new one will be nothing but trouble, you mark my words as God Almighty is my witness. He is soon off to London to some sort of fancy meeting and Heaven only knows what mischief he will be getting us into. I tell you, if God is just, this man will not last long." His eyes glared in the direction of Rogers as his words took their turn in hanging in the now still air, unchallenged. There were several others, both sitting and standing nearby, who differed strongly with Archie and dearly wanted to say as much. But at seventy-six years of age, the old man commanded a certain respect, regardless of the broad blue stripe that ran down the centre of his back. It was only after a somewhat uneasy pause of complete silence that the talk was eventually restored and mercifully turned to the weather and other more-mundane less controversial matters.

Allan watched as the combatants paused to indulge in yet a bit more tea, a fine way to re-establish calm and, at the same time, confirm the correctness of their views if not the dignity of their person. Although war had not been officially declared, the truce seemed to be holding none the less with things back to a relative state of normalcy. Allan turned and, through the front windows, took note of another horse and sleigh being tied up to the post outside. If he was not mistaken, it appeared to be Norman Ferguson and his wife from *Loch Dubh*. People still spoke in hushed tones about the grief that they bore with such grace and composure. The highlanders' reputation as a stoic and resilient stock was certainly put to the test here as it had been during the terrible epidemic of some forty-three years ago that had taken so many of the younger children around the lake. The number of white grave stones behind the Kirk was exceeded only by the tears that, even with the passage of years, continued to be shed in silence.

With all thoughts of sadness quickly banished from his mind, Allan discretely took one last mighty swig from the jug of moonshine and returned it to its strategically chosen hiding place, tucked as it was behind the pile of seed packets on the top shelf. Even the inquisitive Alexandra, who was known to search out hidden Christmas goodies, would never find his treasure trove. His cache of James Mac Gregor's *uisge beatha* ("water of life"/whisky) was just the pick-me-up he needed to make it through to the end of an extremely busy day. It was a gentlemen's agreement and a fair one he thought — a jug every now and again in exchange for a few extra bags of sugar. None the wiser, most people might well think that Margaret MacGregor was doing nothing more than making several large batches of sugar cookies. Allan laughed to himself at his own imagery as his gaze fell upon Norman and Rachael now approaching the front doors. With treasure once again safely secured, it was time to return to the counter and his work.

Looking back, Peter could never have imagined that he would one day live on the shores of a lake, certainly not one so far removed from everything he had grown up with and knew so well. Oh, it was beautiful enough and he was immensely happy. There was absolutely no doubt about that. It was just that he hadn't planned it this way and he had always prided himself in the belief that he and he alone would be the master of his own destiny. In this particular case, he had had absolutely no say in the matter and the words of his mother's favourite expression, 'God works in mysterious ways', had often come to mind. How true He does and how right his dear mother always proved to be.

After all, Peter was a "city boy" from the coal-mining town of Sydney Mines, clear on the other side of St. Anns Mountain straight down the coast. In some respects, it seemed like a lifetime ago but it was, in actual fact, only a mere two years that he had been offered summer employment with his Uncle Murray peddling iron wares by boat up and down the coast as far as Cape North. It was during a brief stop at New Carlisle, on the North Shore, that he had first laid eyes on Martha, that "vision of loveliness" as he was later wont to call her whenever he wished to see the blood rush to her face in embarrassment. Peter always maintained that the precise circumstance of their meeting would forever be 'as if it were yesterday' and it seldom took much prompting for him to recount the story in the most minute of details and, oftentimes, with humorous embellishments added for effect. He had just completed a transaction involving the sale of metal tubing to that MacGregor man, who appeared so terribly eager to buy every scrap he could lay his hands on. He seemed intent on offering an explanation as to its purpose although none was ever sought or desired; odd jobs around the farm he claimed. It was just then as they were concluding the sale on the wharf that she had walked past them, oblivious to the eyes that were fixed on her every move.

Of all the details, it was the intensely black hair and the brilliantly blue eyes that had pulled him up short. As she walked past and proceeded away from them up the winding road towards the bluffs, Peter knew that he would have to meet her; no, not meet her, woo her. Never before had he been so totally smitten and he knew that, in all likelihood please God, he had just crossed paths with Mrs. Peter Campbell.

If nothing else, he was persistent. Within a year, after numerous subsequent visits to the North Shore, he had mustered up sufficient courage and proposed to Martha Anne MacDonald. As fate would have it, he was not the only one who knew what he wanted for she had eagerly accepted his offer of marriage. If the truth be known, some of the older folk had actually used the term 'too eagerly' in private conversations while publically going out of their way to personally extend congratulations to the beautiful couple. That aside, it did not matter that, at twenty-seven years of age, she was two years his senior. Age was never the problem; life should always be that simple. No, the issue was her father, Archibald or "Auld Archie" as he was sometimes known, especially by the younger people. A widower of two years, he was extremely protective of his only daughter whose earlier years had been totally dedicated to caring for her invalid mother. But there was more. His wee lassie would not be taking a Campbell for her husband. Would not his own father turn in his grave at the mere thought and Archie himself hear the rumbling clear across the Atlantic? And on more than one occasion, he had tried his strong-armed tactics on his two sons, Malcolm and John, to have them concur with his point of view. It was all to no avail. Martha's brothers had seldom before seen the light of love shine so brightly in her eyes and they had finally been resolute in not only standing up to the old man but actually persuading him that his daughter could never find a better man — clan name be damned. Indeed, they had even gone so far as to say that their *seanair* (grandfather) would have no good reason to move about in the peace and tranquillity of his final resting place.

Peter and Martha were very much in love and were married by the Reverend Fraser in the front parlour of the MacDonald home on a fine spring day just over a year ago. Of course, the ceremony had been conducted in the Gaelic and Peter did well enough. His mother, a MacLeod originally from Boularderie Island, had the "Scotch tongue" and spoke it to him as a child, whenever they were out of earshot of his father. No, Peter would have no problem adjusting to life here in *Loch Dubh*, especially as he and Martha had been extremely frugal in saving enough money to buy the old MacAulay place on the far side of the loch down from the MacDonald property. Peter loved to joke that Martha would not have far to go if ever she wished to run away from home and Archie was happy enough knowing that he was close by so as to keep a goodly eye on her. Even he, in time, came to accept the treacherous Campbell as family.

The old farmhouse, located as it was on a hill between the Erskine property on one side and Crown Land on the other, offered a panoramic view across the loch. True, it required a bit of work but it was an ideal spot for them to start their life together and, in time and faith, a family. It was several months later, a clear autumn day during potato harvest as he recalled, that Martha had called him in from the back fields for a bite of dinner. Initially, nothing seemed out of the ordinary as he made his way to the kitchen door. Little did he know that this was to be yet another moment that would be forever committed to his memory. She had just placed a plate of freshly baked date squares on the table near the end of the meal when, as if part of the same movement, she turned to face her husband.

"Peter, I do not believe we should be off to the *céilidh* tonight. Would you mind awfully if we were to stay at home just this one time?" Her voice sounded somewhat forlorn and yet, at the same time, mischievous. A look of surprise came over his face; this was not like her, not at all. In the short span of time since their initial courting and now marriage, he had experienced first hand Martha's love of Scottish jigs, strathspeys and reels; and how she loved to dance.

"What is it really that you are telling me *mo chridhe* (my love)?" Faced with the direct and somewhat matter-of-fact tone of his question, she no longer appeared forlorn or even mischievous. He had seldom before seen those blue eyes sparkle as much as they did at that very moment. Never one to lightly walk away from a challenge, she placed her hands firmly on her hips and proceeded to scold him.

"Peter Campbell, do you not think it improper for you to dance with two persons at the same time?"

During the long, cold winter months, they would lie close to each other under a mountain of multi-coloured quilts and blankets, many of which were made for them by the women of *Loch Dubh* and given as wedding presents. Encased in each other's arms, they would discuss possible names for the eagerly awaited child and Peter often made up silly ones just to force her into laughter. "Horatio" once sent her into convulsions of giggles while "Lucretia" was dismissed out of hand as an obvious townie name. But, even as a youngster around the Christmas season, he had seldom before known a sense of excitement and anticipation as great as this. Their lives would be changed forever with the arrival of the bairn. It would be a new and heavy responsibility but he had every confidence they were prepared. Their child would be the result of love shared between a Campbell and a MacDonald. In so many ways, both real and symbolic, this would, in itself, be a new beginning.

All these thoughts came streaming back across Peter's mind as he stood by the open kitchen window. The fresh spring air danced through and flooded the house as if challenged to cleanse it of the stale lingering odours of winter. Peter was looking at the Erskine house next door — Daniel and Tina's; they had become, in some ways, his surrogate parents and were always present to offer kindly words of encouragement to both him and Martha. And just beyond, he could see Elizabeth and the other Urquhart children playing in the front garden. His thoughts fixed on this scene for several minutes as if they too were in search of a calming rest.

Tina and Sarah were now upstairs in the front bedroom with Martha while he was relegated here with nothing else to do other than stand at the window, waiting. Archie was present as well and both of them had been given strict orders to keep the pots of water constantly replenished and at the boil. With the exception of the roar of the fire in the stove and the odd gust of wind from the window, the kitchen was blanketed in silence. Peter cast a glance over at the old man seated at the end of the table and sensed that he was every bit as nervous, although he did his best to not let it show. It was, after all, his own wee lassie upstairs and he must remain nearby for fear he might be needed. Martha's mother would be pleased knowing he had stayed close. Still, everyone understood; it was simply his way. Peter turned back to the window and looked eastward, now well beyond the two MacDonald houses on the far side of the loch. His eyes were fixed on the crimson-edged clouds that were forming on the horizon as dusk slowly began to fall. Red skies at night, sailors' delight. He hoped that there might be some truth to the words and, more importantly, that this Heavenly display would also bode well for a young farming family on the shores of *Loch Dubh*.

Shadows had begun to appear outside the window, creeping across the fields in the direction of the house as if intent on playing a mischievous game on the unsuspecting souls within. Peter and his thoughts were soon retrieved from this hypnotic entrapment as, from behind, he heard the door to the dining-room open. It was the very same door that gave access to the bedrooms upstairs. It opened reluctantly with a loud creaking as if attesting to the fact that it too shared in some laborious pain. As Tina stepped down and entered the kitchen, Peter took note of the long white apron over her calico dress that was now rumpled and stained with reddish brown blotches. He turned to face her as Archie slowly rose from his seat at the end of the kitchen table. For the eternity that lingered, there was nothing but silence and an excruciating sense of anticipation.

Tina looked terribly drawn and her hair fell askew around her wrinkled forehead like some sort of dishevelled halo. Peter raised his head so that his eyes could now meet hers. He stood there motionless, waiting. Finally, Tina's face, which had so captured the pain that Martha had obviously endured, was suddenly radiating a sense of peace and joy. "Congratulations to you both; Martha has been delivered of a beautiful and healthy laddie. Mother and bairn are doing well. But give them a wee bittie time to rest before going up. Sarah and I will stay close by just in case we are needed." The message, in the English, was obviously meant for Peter as Tina slowly moved across the room and motioned to the old man to resume his seat. She then took his hand in hers and softly repeated similar words in the Gaelic. They would have more meaning.

Peter and Archie looked at each other and smiled broad knowing smiles. Without a word passing between them, they both knew that an ancient chasm has been bridged with the birth of this child. Peter slowly returned to the window and suddenly realized that night has already fallen over the mountains. It was not the blackness that held him captive or even a sense of the unknown. Rather, it was the North Star, shining brightly over the vast Atlantic, that told him that the sailors' delight would also be his and Martha's. Spring, the time of rebirth, had finally arrived and, for the first time, Peter knew that *Loch Dubh* had truly become his home.

⎯ Chapter Two ⎯

*Seinnibh do an Tighearna òran nuadh; seinnibh a chliù o iomall na
talmhainn; sibhse a bhios a' dol air cuan, agus na h-uile a tha 'g a lionadh;
'eileanan, agus na h-uile a tha chòmhnuidh annta.*

Isaiah XLII: 10

Sing unto the Lord a new song, and his praise from the end of the
earth, ye that go down to the sea, and all that is therein; the isles,
and the inhabitants thereof.

Isaiah XLII: 10

Seldom before could anyone recall such excitement being generated
and it was even more rare that *Loch Dubh* had found itself caught up
with something taking place so far away from its own shores. In the early
days of June, the focus of conversation among the children was clearly not
on school examinations or even the exhilarating freedom associated with
their escape that would follow shortly thereafter. No, it was on something
quite different. And such discussions were certainly not limited to the
wee ones; the entire community was actively planning its own celebratory
events. There was no question but that this was to be a time the likes of
which they had seldom before known and there was every confidence that
it would be remembered for many years to come.

There was also no doubt that there were a few persons, mark you only
a handful at the most, who may have been surprised or even aghast by the
tremendous fuss that was being made about the entire matter. After all,
why should so much time and energy be devoted to the celebration of a
little old lady who always looked so dour, dressing as she did in black and
seldom bothering to go out of the house to see people, let alone speak with
them? But in fairness, this was not just any *cailleach*; it was a very special
cailleach — Her Majesty Queen Victoria, Queen of the United Kingdom of
Great Britain and Ireland, Defender of the Faith, Empress of India — who
was about to mark the sixtieth anniversary of her accession to the throne
as the Empire's most gracious and beloved sovereign.

The actual date of the anniversary was June 20. Initially, this presented
a great deal of concern and some considerable anxiety in that it fell on a
Sunday. However, it had finally been agreed, following extensive debate
and consultation with the manse, that any such celebrations should be
held the day before. The word had gone forth: God could and should save

the Queen; but she should not expect Him to share the Sabbath with any celebrity, regardless of their temporal position or power! Saturday would be the chosen day and the residents of *Loch Dubh* were eager to be active participants in the excitement that had been sweeping across the Empire, in every corner of the globe, for months on end. Clearly they were not to be left out and would do their part to show the Queen that they too wished to "send her victorious, happy and glorious." It was up to the Almighty to determine just how long she was to reign over them. But God save her anyway; their celebration would be a grand affair, at least by *Loch Dubh* standards; they were bound and determined to see to that.

John MacDonald, old Archie's son and Martha's brother, lived at the opposite end of the loch from the Kirk, with his wife Ida and five children. Their house had been built immediately adjacent to the one on the original MacDonald grant of land, now occupied by his father and sister-in-law Jessie. It was good that they were so close to Jessie and her children given the tragic death of his brother Malcolm less than a year ago. Such a horrible death he had endured, having been terribly crushed by a large tree that had obviously caught him off guard as it fell, perhaps captured by a sudden gust of wind coming off the water. No one knew for certain. What was known was that he should never have gone off to cut timber far up into the high woods on the mountain all by himself. If only he had not gone alone. Perhaps if he had been found earlier. Maybe something more could have been done to save him. But for all the ifs, there was only one certainty — it was not to be. Jessie had shown a strong resolve throughout the tragic ordeal and both John and Ida knew that this spirit would help ensure that the four children would be well nurtured and cared for under her watch. The grief was upon her but, mercifully, the rest of the MacDonald clan would be there to offer whatever assistance might be needed.

It was partly to help boost the spirits of Jessie and her children that John had agreed to allow his land, high up on the bluffs, to be used as the focal point of the celebrations, a gigantic bonfire that would surely be seen for miles up and down the coast. It would be good for all of them to go as a family to enjoy a fun time together. Still, the same could be said for everyone in *Loch Dubh*. After all, how often do the Dominion and provincial governments encourage their citizens to indulge in some well-deserved patriotic fervour? So much tax money is indiscriminately taken from everyone's pockets; och well, one might as well make the best of it and go through the motions of pretending to take pleasure in being robbed. One never had to dig too deeply to hit upon a healthy dose of cynicism.

As the date grew near, a heightened sense of excitement spread like a giant wave across the loch, inundating every house in its path. Among other things, the children had busied themselves for weeks with drawing paper Union Jacks and affixing them to kindling. Even at school, the mistress allowed them to make as many flags as they liked, on the condition that they took some time to understand and appreciate who and what the three crosses represented. Who were Saint George, Saint Andrew and Saint Patrick and why were they so honoured on our flag? After much discussion of these three saintly men, the children of *Loch Dubh* felt as if they had come to know all three personally and were comfortable in calling each one by name. Of course, Andrew was the favourite by far for obvious reasons. Had the three still been amongst the living, surely poor George and Patrick would have felt shunned or, at least, less valued than that other lad. As it turned out, in addition to Andrew, one of the most popular men was Allan Dunn down at the general store who couldn't possibly keep up with the demand for red and blue colouring pencils. Price seemed to be no object and he was certainly not one to complain about the increase in business.

Even with all the carefully thought-out and well-organized planning that had gone on for weeks, June 19 arrived far more quickly than anyone could have imagined. True, most of the details were already in place; flags were drawn, coloured and dutifully tied to sticks and lengths of twine, meals were cooked and beautifully presented and clothes were washed and ironed ready to be worn. Most importantly, the wood had been gathered by all the residents of *Loch Dubh* and a huge cone had been slowly and systematically constructed on the bluff's edge, looking ever so much like some sort of rag tag pyramid that had precariously hunkered itself there. In the clearing around the cone, the community picnic would be held with ongoing activities throughout the late afternoon and into the evening. Everyone shared in the anticipation and the children, who had diligently decorated every conceivable spot with their colourful Union Jacks, were almost frantic with excitement for the time to finally arrive. Her Majesty aside for the moment, they were bound and determined that Andrew would be done proud!

With milking and other essential chores completed, the entire community began to gather late in the day for the meal, given that the cone would not be set ablaze until 9:30 p.m. or thereabouts when its glow would be best appreciated against the darkening skies. Still in all, the bairns would have to be in their beds at a decent time; were they not mindful of the fact that the morrow was the Sabbath? Still in all, everyone was there, even the older folk including Flora Grant herself. It went without saying that, if the Reverend Duncan and Jennie were to attend with their three children, surely it would be only proper for the entire community to be present as well. Indeed, the only dissenting voice seemed to be that of Daniel Erskine who expressed quite a different view and was adamant that anyone who dared come within ear shot would know exactly what it was, whether they so inquired or not. If the truth be known, was it not Victoria and her ancestors who sat on a golden throne in London while their very own impoverished fathers and grandfathers were being unceremoniously and brutally cleared from their crofts across the highlands? Of course, everyone knew him to be quite correct on the point but, at the same time, they did not necessarily want a history lesson to put a damper on the festivities. This initial fear was somewhat ill founded given that, when all was said and done, even Daniel succumbed and begrudgingly decided to go along. To those who were courageous enough to broach the subject even in jest, he pointed out that to stay away would be disrespectful, not to the Queen mind you but to the people who had gone to such trouble to organize the event. Everyone knew that the truth lay in the fact that he enjoyed a good time as much as the next person and would not be left out. It was only the respect attached to Daniel's advanced age and position in the community that spared him from the well-honoured and finely honed ritual of poking many a rib.

The pasture behind John MacDonald's barn was used as a holding area to tie up all the horses and wagons that brought the families as well as the food, decorations and other items that would ensure a pleasurable evening. John had asked his eldest, the fifteen-year-old twins Rod and Andrew, to do some necessary work in preparation for the cavalcade that would soon descend upon their farm. Buckets of water and small piles of hay were strategically placed under trees in the back corners of the pasture so that the animals would have shaded spots to rest and nourish themselves. From there, it would only be a short five minute walk down the path to the bluffs. Part of the boys' duties was to remain close by to assist any families that might need help carrying items to the site. All their initial grumbling about not being able to spend time with their friends and missing out on the eagerly anticipated fun was quickly abated by their father's promise of a token payment. Clearly, it had the desired effect as they went about their task with increased vigour and speed, like so many bees to honey. Their thoughts had all too obviously been turned to the money that would soon occupy their pockets and be spent any way they liked; in their minds, they were already taking inventory of the shelves in the general store down in the town. And besides, the Urquharts would soon be coming and the boys were both prepared to offer whatever assistance would be required, especially as it related to Elizabeth.

Seated on strategically placed logs forming a semicircle around the cone, everyone consumed the communal supper with great eagerness and delight after so much activity earlier in the day and in anticipation of what was still to come. There had been great gales of giggles and laughter from the children as they ran about playing in the clearing and among the adjoining trees. The wee ones had all been put on strict notice that they were not to go near the bluff's edge and, quite surprisingly, none had tempted either fate or the dreaded kindling stick. Now, as dusk fell, excitement grew as the grande finale came ever closer. With children gathered up and the sitting logs repositioned a bit farther back and out of the path of any errant sparks, the kerosene-soaked cone was lit and virtually exploded into one immense luminous flame.

Suddenly, from off to one side, there came a scream of horrific proportions that filled the air. It was Flora who, with hands plaintively covering her wrinkled and trembling cheeks, cried out as though she were in excruciating pain. *"Tha'n dùthaich 'na teine; tha'n dùthaich 'na teine!"* (The country is on fire; the country is on fire!) Everyone enjoyed the humour in her anguish while those seated closest to her made a special effort to calmly assure her that all was well. As the initial wave of heat licked the faces of the spectators with its fiery tongue, Peter Campbell turned his head away and his eyes peered across the broad expanse of darkened water off to the south. He knew that his parents in Sydney Mines would be watching and, on such a crystal- clear night, would surely see this majestic beacon far off on the North Shore. With similar celebrations taking place in all parts of the Empire, everyone felt a certain honour knowing that they were in communion with the larger and very proud imperial family.

As abruptly as it had begun, it rapidly drew to a natural close. Within twenty minutes, there was little else for the voracious appetite of the flames to consume. As quickly as they had first invaded the night skies, they were now forced to retreat and begrudgingly surrendered to the black domain. Spontaneously as if planned, although it had not been, the crowd broke into a rousing rendition of *God Save the Queen* as a final tribute to the little old lady over the seas who was forever dressed in her mournful black garb. Seemingly, it was only Daniel Erskine who did not join in the singing as he stood and looked off in the direction of the open Atlantic. His thoughts temporarily strayed far from the bluffs and the light whose dance slowly ebbed and began to die; his thoughts were far away on another coast in another time, clothed in a regal robe of purple heather.

Angus and Isabelle Grant were now walking up the path to the hall that pulsated with a multitude of sounds, standing as it did in sharp contrast to the silent black-spruce trees that clustered immediately behind and farther off to the sides. It could have been that the high narrow windows had been thrown open as much to prevent an explosion of built-up energy as to allow the cool late-summer air to infiltrate the warming room. The front doors were also flung open and, as the lamplight cascaded down over the front steps and onto the ground below, extended an enticing invitation to take refuge inside away from the bleak solitary darkness of a September evening. It was a beacon that, along with its musical accompaniment, was seductively coercing them to join in the merriment abounding within the walls.

Even with these joyous sounds bathing her ears like silkened waters, Isabelle had a sudden pang of guilt at having left her children, Iain, Sadie and John, at home while she was off enjoying herself. Perhaps she should have said no when Angus had first inquired as to whether or not she wished to go. Still in all, it had been less a question and much more a general statement of fact. Now, their walk down by the loch, passing as they did in front of the manse and the Kirk, had only served to reinforce her guilt for having so eagerly agreed to attend. But she knew that Angus' mother Flora, the matriarch of the family as she was always wont to title herself, would watch over the bairns. She would be diligent; didn't she always attempt to run the household as if it were her own? Isabelle had found Flora's attitude difficult to accept on more than one occasion but always managed to control her tongue if not her thoughts. She took some considerable comfort in knowing that this would change, in time. Flora couldn't live forever, ... or could she? For now, Isabelle would allow her to rule the roost, as long as she kept her grandchildren well in her care like the brooding hen that she was. As these thoughts passed through her mind, Isabelle tightened her grip on Angus' arm in an act of reassurance and attempted to lessen her own anguish by cooing in his ear. *"Nach truagh leat mo chlann, le té eile 'n an ceann?"* (Don't you pity my children with another woman in charge of them?) At first, he seemed startled by the shattering of the silence as well as the unexpected nature of the provocative question. Eventually sensing the obvious mischief in her voice, his shock soon turned to laughter as he glanced down at her and playfully rubbed the crown of her head. She drew even closer to him and told herself that she would enjoy the evening, regardless.

"Aonghais! Iseabal! Ciamar a tha sibh? Failt' oirbh gu dearbh. Tha oidhche mhath ann an nochd. Tha 'n ceòl cho nèamhail. Tha e coltach ri seinn an t-Salmadair!" (Angus! Isabelle! How are you? You are heartily welcome. It is a good night tonight. The music is so heavenly. It sounds like the singing of the Psalmist himself!) Like an invisible voice emanating from some deranged burning bush, the rousing and quite-unexpected welcome had come from James MacGregor who was standing well off to the side of the steps, dappled by shadows, with a few other men. One could still see that he was busily tucking something back into his hip pocket.

"Fàilte chàirdeal gu deimhinn." (Truly a friendly welcome.) Angus made the effort to shake hands and laughed aloud at the thought of MacGregor serving as the self-ordained official greeter for the community, given that his appearances always seemed to be limited to a few intemperate social functions. And was it not Flora herself who was forever commenting about his absence from the Kirk? More often than not, poor Margaret and the children could be seen sitting alone in the MacGregor pew. James' absence never went unnoticed and without comment even with the passage of the years. It was to be both pitied and spoken about at great length. Now, still reeling from their greeter's blasphemous reference to Heaven and the Psalmist, Isabelle suddenly reminded herself as to why it was he still fumbled with his pocket. Was it not the same reason that he so seldom darkened the doors of the House of God?

She turned to her husband with a certain uneasiness standing, as they were, outside the hall with the group of men that included some from down the hill. Among them, she recognized the store owner, Allan Dunn, who often made an appearance at such festivities, usually staying in James' company. All of them were, no doubt, up to no good as they stood there partying in a way that was particular to them. *"Aonghais, thig a-stigh. Tha mi fuar."* (Angus, come inside. I am cold.) The sharp and somewhat clipped words clung to the intoxicating air that hung about their faces. Isabelle seldom used such abrupt tones when speaking to her husband but her irritation was beginning to show and, of greater consequence, make for an awkward situation. A slight nod of his head told her that Angus fully understood and the stairs were quickly mounted as, in the same movement, he gave a knowing final wave to the men, who remained standing off in the comfort that was theirs in the shadows of the adjoining trees.

As they entered the hall, they were immediately drawn into a tempestuous whirlwind of sights and sounds that erupted before them. The floor boards vibrated with life, providing an accompanying base sound to the music, laughter and frequent hooting that filled the hall. Just inside the door, in the right-hand corner, sat Ida MacDonald, Martha's sister-in-law and John's wife, and Sarah Urquhart minding the tea table. It struck her a bit strange, almost amusing, that they appeared to be the only stillness in a room that swirled around them. For obvious reasons, there were no customers at that particular moment although business was bound to pick up at the next break between dance sets. Isabelle made a point of waving to them in both offering a cheery greeting and acknowledging the importance of their work. She would go over and chat with them a little later on, perhaps even give them a respite so they too could have a dance before the night was over.

On a raised platform, at the very front of the room, sat a solitary figure in a small wooden chair. Isabelle immediately recognized young Jamie MacInnes who hailed from a farm just south of *Loch Dubh* down along the coast. He belonged to one of the most well-known musical families in the area and was renowned for one thing — his fiddle, which was quite obviously his prized possession. It had belonged to his grandfather who had brought it over with him from the old country. Jamie knew the story well and often recounted it in much the same way that one wears a badge of honour: his grandfather could not take much more than a simple wooden trunk on board the vessel. Yet of all his worldly possessions, none was more valued than his musical instrument that was tucked securely under his arm and often used during the voyage to bolster spirits in desperate need of solace. And so it was that the MacInnes fiddle bridged the broad Atlantic and found new life here through its vibrant and consoling music. Indeed, Jamie didn't so much play it as hold it for there was always the impression that it assumed a life of its own; it "spoke" the Gaelic. Isabelle never ceased to be amazed at just how much he loved to sit there, almost oblivious to the crowd in front of him, as his bow flowed over the strings in an utterly effortless movement. More often than not, his eyes were firmly closed as he played. And his elbow! How it bobbed up and down with such vigorous life. She hoped that *Mac an Fhìdhleir* (Son of the Fiddler), as he was affectionately known, would never be stricken with the terrible arthritis that so afflicted the older people like poor Flora. This gift, yes God-given, should never be silenced. She promised herself that she and Angus would soon be on the dance floor.

Unconsciously, Isabelle's eyes were raised high above Jamie's head and settled on the beautifully framed picture of the Queen, located as it was in a place of honour in the centre of the raw pine wall at the very front of the hall. It had been positioned there a few weeks past as yet another tribute to Her Majesty in recognition of the Diamond Jubilee. The photograph had been carefully extracted from a special edition of the Sydney newspaper, **The Record**, and placed in an old frame, which was retrieved from the vestry of the Kirk. How stern the Queen appeared as she sat there glaring down at them. It was more than the possible irritation of the still-visible paper crease that ran across her ample bosom. No doubt, she could never be comfortable in a setting such as this but, never mind, she was far away sipping tea and still dwelling on her beloved Albert. Thankfully, her mourning would not put a damper on the jovial nature of the people gathered here tonight. Thankfully.

"A mhnathan agus a dhaoin'uaisle! Tha an ath dhanns' a'dol a thòiseachadh." (Ladies and gentlemen! The next dance is going to begin.) Angus heard the call of the not-so-subtle message, although he did not seem to recognize the voice. Not that it mattered. He quickly sought out Isabelle's arm and led her to the centre of the room, away from some of the other women seated on the side with whom she obviously had every good intention of sharing a few words of greeting. They were soon joined by Daniel and Tina Erskine and two other couples in forming one of the first square sets. Isabelle had no time to catch her breath or even to place her handbag on one of the side chairs. In a flash, Jamie's fiddle was speaking its Gaelic and casting a magical spell as hands were joined and feet began to assume a life of their own. The dance was now in full flight.

Isabelle laughed with delight as she was swung by Angus and, in turn, by the other three men as she rounded the set. She streaked around the circle like a wild whirling dervish with the music and the sounds of step-dancing feet ringing in her ears. The men of *Loch Dubh* were somewhat timid when it came to singing, except of course for services at the Kirk, but how they loved to "step it off" during the dance. Never mind, they were enjoying themselves after many hard gruelling days of work in the hay fields. It was their time.

The dance went on and, with four square sets on the floor, the onlookers seated against the walls were buffeted by various frocks as they whirled about and blanketed the hall like so many tufted multi-coloured clouds. Isabelle was now almost accustomed to seeing the room swirl around her and thought that she would surely become dizzy. Still in all, she didn't mind. There was such a sense of freedom when she and Angus danced together. The dance went on forever and still, as quickly as it had begun, it was over as the fiddle lay silenced yet still warmed as it rested on Jamie's now-vacated chair. Jamie was taking a well-deserved break and on his way out the doors for a breath of fresh air; he would undoubtedly join the men who continued to stand guard at the side of the front steps. Isabelle could not help but look up once again at the stoic portrait of the old Queen. She had little doubt but that Her Majesty would never approve of the outdoor activities now taking place. However, in their own ways and for different reasons, they both could breathe a sigh of relief and enjoy the temporary stillness that had fallen over the room.

There would be a pause for a *strùpag* and Ida and Sarah would finally have a steady stream of customers. Soon enough, the next set would be announced and the *céilidh* would be on once again. Daniel Erskine would be asked to offer a tune or two on the pipe; invariably he obliged but only after insisting that he would first have to warm himself up. There was a predictability to his modest reluctance that was always greeted with good humour and, from time to time, encouraged with a bit of rib poking. There would also be a Gaelic singalong, including the old well-known songs. On these occasions, they would all hold hands and beat time on the imaginary milling table in front of them. And, as was usually the case, they would be led by Margaret MacGregor who was admired and credited with possessing the voice of an angel. After all, if the English was the language of the shops, surely it was the Gaelic that served as the language of Heaven!

It was several hours later, about 11:30 p.m., that the music reached its final crescendo and began to die away for the night like a flickering candle resting on an open window sill. Everyone knew only too well that it was important to be home before the arrival of the Sabbath. Thus, after numerous words of farewell to neighbours, Isabelle and Angus finally left the hall and headed out for the walk home in the cool night air. Even with the slight chill, Isabelle noted that MacGregor was still standing in the shadows, now encircled by an even larger number of men, almost as if he were holding court. Ever so faintly, she could hear him laugh and then attempt to whisper to the blackened figure standing next to him. *"Tha buaidh anns an uisge bheatha."* (There is a benefit in the whisky.) She and Angus turned and walked away knowing full well that they would see Margaret and the children alone at service in the morning. It was, indeed, a pity.

They strolled arm-in-arm down to the loch and turned left onto the road towards the Kirk and home. It was still a lovely calm night, even with the chill. There was no doubt but that her shawl would come in handy for the walk by the water's edge. She had enjoyed the *céilidh* right enough but was now grateful to be alone with her Angus and on her way back to the bairns. Had they had cause to look up the hill off to their left, they would have realized that, in fact, they were not alone. They would have seen a solitary figure standing and peering out of the manse window as the kerosene lamp in the front parlour was finally extinguished for the night. Gazing down on the blackened figures streaming from the hall like so many tea leaves from an agitated pot, Duncan Fraser shook his head and slowly proceeded to bed. He had just put the final touches to his sermon and vowed that he would preach with increased vigour in the morning.

If one were to have asked Martha to recount this moment, it most certainly would have included no recollection of the wintery weather that had befallen *Loch Dubh* that blustery January morning. The birches bore silent witness to the silver thaw that had occurred the previous evening and crept into the early morning hours. They sparkled like diamond slivers jutting out of the earth and the snow that encircled them was itself encrusted with a gem-like coating that made the fields look surreal in the brilliant sunlight. The wind from the east, off the open Atlantic, had picked up force and was now playing through and around the branches as if it were engaged in a devious game intent on robbing them of their newly acquired riches.

The details of this majestic scene were lost on Martha. She had risen early that morning to watch over Lachlan who was peacefully asleep in his wooden cradle, securely blanketed and protected from the cold by a thick woollen throw. As she gazed down upon her son, Martha gingerly placed a hand on the cradle rail and began to rock it ever so slightly. Her mind was cast back over the years and she recalled how her own dear mother, in her time, had lulled her own three bairns to sleep in this very cradle. And even long after all three had grown, she had kept it in her bedroom, perhaps as a subtle reminder to herself of blessings received. Martha has gone to her father, Archie, and asked if he would retrieve it from the attic where it had been placed shortly after her mother's passing, now almost five years ago. At the time, it almost seemed as if their father was trying to cleanse the house of her cherished possessions, of her memory, of her. Perhaps it was not a conscious attempt to forget her but rather a more-subconscious desire to alleviate the terrible pain of having witnessed her courageous passage through prolonged illness and death as well as the memories of her that seemed to linger everywhere. Of course, the children were a part of her that lived on beyond the cradle and they would be a legacy to her beauty and strength of character. Regardless, such material things that could be expended with were quickly removed from sight, including the cradle, as if banishment would temper the sorrow that seemingly would never be removed from their hearts. Time passed while pain endured.

Martha had understood and was eventually forced to go to the attic herself to collect the cradle. With the expected arrival of a new child, it was based as much on sheer practicality as it was on any notion of sentimentality. Still, she felt that it would bring her mother closer to the bairn who, she believed, bore an ever-increasing resemblance to his grandmother. Oblivious to the memories that his placid face now evoked as he slept, Lachlan would perhaps one day come to appreciate the special bond that his birth had created for a young woman — his mother, who herself sought reassurance in the caress of her mother's arms. As her hand began to rock the cradle, Martha promised herself that her son would know unbounding love, the love that she had always so desperately sought but which was taken from her far too quickly. Now accompanied by her thoughts, she gently raised Lachlan from his slumber and, having carefully wrapped him in a small white blanket, proceeded downstairs to the warmth of the kitchen.

Peter had been up early and laid the fire in the stove, whose heat was even now extending its long temperate fingers across the room. The kitchen was breathlessly quiet as mother and child entered. Only the creaking floor under her feet offered up a welcoming, if not somewhat reluctant, greeting. No doubt, Peter was off doing morning chores in the barn, relieving the cows of their rich repository of milk, feeding and watering the livestock and undertaking other such matters. Martha was pleased that she had a bit longer to be alone with Lachlan to share some thoughts before this important day began to unfold. It would involve the entire family but, for now, she would be selfish in sharing some personal thoughts with her child. For this, she needed a few quiet moments alone.

As she walked in front of the side window, Martha took passing notice of the crystallized beauty that covered the land and the playful nature of the sun on the branches of the trees adjoining the house. Yet, her concentration was very much centered on the rocking chair that, for the past several months, had remained strategically placed immediately beside the stove. Lachlan slept on as she slowly placed herself into the warm clutches of the chair and continued the rocking motion, as if they both were now in a cradle of their very own. She thought how strange it must appear this Madonna and child image before the roaring fire. She looked deeply into the tiny face still full of sleep that rested on her breast, knowing that she would speak and, more importantly, that he would somehow understand. *"Och, a Lachlain Bhig, luaidh do mhàthar. Fad do ré gun robh thu slàn. Móran làithean dhuit is sìth, le d'mhaitheas is le d'nì bhi fàs."* (Oh Little Lachlan, you are your mother's treasure. May you be healthy all your days. May you be blessed with long life and peace, may you grow old with goodness and with riches.) As she whispered these words and drew him ever closer, she knew that she had uttered something that was more a prayer than a wish. At that moment, she recommitted herself to ensuring that her son would indeed be raised surrounded by health, peace and unbounding love.

It was true that the child had suffered from a severe case of the croup shortly after birth and that his health had been frail for the first six months. He had been watched over carefully and, while progress was oftentimes slow, had eventually enjoyed a complete recovery. Throughout the ordeal,

Archie had expressed concern with his grandson's physical health, as did everyone else. However, he was even more anxious about his spiritual state; the bairn had not yet been baptized in the faith. But today, with health restored and numerous assurances from the women of the community that he was indeed a fine robust specimen, the wee Lachlan would be taken to the Kirk and anointed with water and spirit. With a myriad of thoughts continuing to flood her mind all at the same time, Martha looked down lovingly into the silent little face before her and rocked, basking in the warmth of both Peter's fire and her own joy of fulfilment.

"*Mo chridhe*, the time is passing quickly and here you sit making no effort to prepare for Kirk. Your father will be here shortly and we had better be ready to go at a decent hour or suffer his wrath. There must be time to speak with the elders before the service." Peter's sudden entry into the kitchen had startled her somewhat although she attempted to mask it well. In shielding the bairn from the blast of cold air that had followed her husband through the door, she was still thankful that she and Lachlan were finished with their conversation. She rose slowly as if to signal that she was equally adept at making a case with similar conviction.

"Peter, I was just quieting him before the feeding and making certain that he was content. I just hope that he will not decide to exercise his lungs when the Reverend Fraser wets his head. Heavens only knows what people might say about 'that Campbell child'!" Martha made light of her tardiness and proceeded to place the kettle on the stove to prepare the pot of tea that she knew Peter would want and need following completion of his chores. It was not terribly long thereafter, perhaps a mere twenty minutes, that Archie arrived all bundled up in his long black coat, looking ever so much like a lanky sombre stick. His gaze immediately fell on Lachlan who had now been fed and dressed by his mother in a cream-coloured gown that had been made for him by Peter's mother, from remnants of her wedding dress. It was a lovely idea and a thoughtful gift, Martha told her father, that they would treasure always. They could use it for the baptism of all their children, starting a new family tradition! She deliberately emphasized the word all, shot him a mischievous look and winked. The sternness of the face that greeted her attempted humour said it all. Archie did not seem terribly impressed or amused; it was the Sabbath. Proceeding to unfurl himself from the clutches of coat, scarf and beaver fur hat, he now sat with a cup of tea in the rocking chair proudly sporting his MacDonald of Clanranald tie that was worn only on the most special occasions.

"*A bheil thu deiseil? Greas ort, mo nighean bhòidheach. Tha e leth-uair an déidh deich mu thràth.*" (Are you ready? Hurry along my beautiful daughter. It is already half-past ten.) He was speaking directly to Martha but his comments were meant for Peter as well. As he poured tea from his cup into the saucer, something he was always wont to do in order to cool it more quickly, a fatherly look of concern was cast across the room. "*Greas ort. Tha an eaglais a'dol a staigh aig aon uair deug. Falbh romhad; cumaidh mi-fhìn an aire air an tè bheag tacan."* (Hurry along. Church goes in at 11 o'clock. Go about your business; I will keep an eye on the little one for awhile.) Martha smiled knowingly, realizing that, in all likelihood, her father wished to have one last private moment with the wee Lachlan before his baptism. She urged Peter to follow her upstairs.

The sleigh ride to the Kirk was brief enough, given the short distance, but still Martha had Lachlan well bundled under the heavy fur robes and a white blanket taken from the bedroom trunk. Peter glanced over at them and joked that his son looked like an oversized snowball. Archie, who was seated behind them, remained silent and his expression was proof enough that he was not terribly enamoured with the comment, given the day. They moved on at a steady pace and Martha realized just how amused she was by the fact that Peter had no real need to hold the reins since the horse always seemed to know when it was Sunday and was content to set its own course for the Kirk without the least bit of prompting. Upon their arrival, they noted that many other horses and sleighs had already been tied up outside the Kirk as the four of them proceeded to climb the front steps. Just inside the large double doors, they were greeted warmly by Angus Grant and Daniel Erskine. They, along with Archie himself, were the three elders who, years before, had been duly elected by the congregation to represent them on session. As elder, clerk of session and grandfather, there was even greater pride in Archie's face as he escorted Martha, Peter and Lachlan down the aisle to the waiting pew near the centre of the sanctuary.

Made of locally hewn, pine and spruce lumber and adorned with clear glass windows, the Kirk seemed to speak of the simplicity and powerfulness of God's relationship with His people and theirs with Him. This was what Martha and all the children had been taught from their youngest days. Although never the most diligent of students, had they not all committed to memory the first question in **The Shorter Catechism**: "What is man's chief end?" And had they not all dutifully learned and memorized the answer: "Man's chief end is to glorify God and to enjoy Him forever." Therefore, the congregation was to enjoy Him, albeit seated in long narrow pews of pine that ran across the entire width, with an aisle on either side. The seats and backs were at a rigid ninety-degree angle and the odd comment had been made that it was so to ensure that no napping occurred during the sermon. Indeed, the only memorable statement ever to come from James MacGregor's mouth about Kirk, albeit made a long time past, was that, while we might try to enjoy God, we still had to endure the Reverend Fraser's lengthy sermons. In general, the comment had not been well received.

Martha was grateful for the heat that was thrown off by the pot-bellied stove at the rear. It was now at full roar and most effective in robbing the cold air of the safe haven that it enjoyed here in the Kirk for the other six days of the week. With a comforting warmth on her back, she took time to note that every single family from *Loch Dubh* was in attendance for this special service. Of course, both MacDonald families were present: Jessie and her children as well as John and Ida with theirs. The twins, Rod and Andrew, were home for Christmas from Baddeck where they had been sent last September to continue their studies given that the local school provided education only up to level eight. Rod and Andrew were billeted with Ida's cousin who had married a man from Baddeck gainfully employed in the shipbuilding trade. Living arrangements aside, it had not been an easy decision for John and Ida to make, given that help was needed to run the farm. Yet, they wanted their boys to have every advantage in life and, especially for Ida, that meant more education. They finally decided that, with the two younger boys still at home, the family would make do.

Margaret MacGregor sat immediately in front of Martha and Peter with her four children. No sign of James was to be had. Near the front was the clergy's pew that the minister's wife Jennie, along with their three children, occupied each Sunday. It was always so amusing to watch little Emily squirm and the various antics that ensued, especially during the sermon that came near the end of what was a long two-hour service for a small child. And off to the right sat the Grants, Angus and Isabelle, with their children and old Flora, whose head constantly pivoted as if it were a weather vane caught in the most vicious of winter gales. Martha received a smile and knowing nod from Tina Erskine, her dear neighbour, who still made daily trips to visit her and the bairn. She and Daniel had become such treasured friends. Their younger, Alasdair, was still at home while the elder, Neil, lived with his family on the far side of the loch. Martha always sensed that Tina would have wanted a larger family but that was a subject that was seldom referred to and, she knew, best left alone.

At precisely 11:00 a.m., the Reverend Fraser entered the sanctuary and proceeded to climb the high steps to the raised pulpit that dominated the front of the Kirk. Directly beneath sat the three elders who were also the precentors and would lead in the singing of the Psalms from the precentor's box. All three had excellent voices although Archie always maintained, with a fair degree of whimsy, that he had been elected not for his knowledge of scripture but rather for his ability to carry a tune. And directly behind the pulpit, a large window looked out towards the snow-capped slopes of *Beinn-mo-Mhulaid*. Oftentimes, near the end of the service, the sun's rays would stream through the window and bathe the minister in glimmering light. As a child, Martha had often thought that the sun must have made his black woollen robes feel twice as heavy as they were in actual fact. However, nothing ever seemed to distract or deter him from the order of service, to say nothing of its duration. He particularly loved to preach lengthy sermons, which he trusted his congregation would ponder and heed with mindful hearts. Full many a time, it was not that the sermon fell on deaf ears; hearts may have been mindful but backs were terribly stiff from the coarse rigid pews.

Duncan Fraser had chosen the topic of purity of soul for the day's sermon and had just begun to read the New Testament lesson taken from the fourth chapter of I Timothy. Martha was doing her best to concentrate on the reading but was distracted by Lachlan who had awoken and began to fuss in her arms. In rubbing his cheek to offer reassurance, she was momentarily transported back to her own childhood seated in a similar pew, placed as she always was between her brothers John and Malcolm. She smothered a chuckle as she recalled how they would stare at the pulpit fall, the piece of cloth that hung from the front of the pulpit high above the heads of the three elders. Taking the term literally, the children would watch it carefully, waiting for it to drop to the floor. It never did. And that image of a burning bush on the fall; would not the flames soon shoot upwards and set the minister himself on fire? At least then the service would finally, and thankfully, be over! Perhaps Lachlan would grow up to be a more-attentive listener than she and her brothers had been. It was then that she was reminded of the wish she had made with him in her arms before the kitchen fire earlier that morning, that he might enjoy long life and peace. This was the most important thing of all. With the words of Timothy all around her, she once again transformed her wish into a prayer, this time in silence, as they sat there in the Campbell pew.

Immediately prior to the sermon, Peter and Martha were invited to go forward in presenting their child for baptism. The Reverend Fraser was ever so gentle with Lachlan, who now lay cradled in the crook of his left arm. Even with the cool water from Duncan Fraser's hand running down the crown of his head, the bairn remained hushed and still. It seemed strange that he, of all people, should be oblivious to this moment as he was baptized Lachlan Archibald Campbell, *"An ainm an Athar, a Mhic, agus an Spioraid Naoimh. Amen."* (In the name of the Father, and of the Son and of the Holy Ghost. Amen.) Peter glanced over at Archie, seated at the front beneath the pulpit, whose face broke into a broad smile. The choice of middle name had not been shared with him in advance but it was obvious to all that he now basked in the joy of having his name shared with the wee Lachlan, Lachlan Archibald, whom the minister now lovingly returned to Martha's waiting arms.

The baptism was followed almost immediately by the sermon as the Reverend Fraser resumed his position at the elevated pulpit at the front. Martha loved to hear the message in the Gaelic because it spoke to her heart in a way that the English never could. Even though she and Peter often used it at home, she still had difficulty getting her tongue around certain English sounds and always felt great ease and comfort in the language of her people. But now, she was anxious for the sermon, which oftentimes lasted a full hour, to end so she could return home to tend to Lachlan. Martha recalled finally hearing the Reverend Fraser praying for the souls of his sheep. She knew that the benediction would soon follow for there was always a tear in his voice as he prayed the closing prayer. Was it in grateful thanksgiving for another week in the presence of the Almighty or could it be in anticipation of sorrow for those who might linger in another kingdom by the time of the next Sabbath? One was never certain.

She and Peter were to arrive home with the good wishes of the entire congregation still ringing in their ears, to say nothing of the glowing reports of the child's appearance, both in terms of his health and physical appearance. Now at home, they would once again have Lachlan all to themselves. Martha took him upstairs straight away to relieve him from the constraints of the baptism gown while Peter busied himself by placing the kettle on the stove. Were not his first words through the door always the same light-hearted ones? "*S bidh mi deònach air bobhla de 'n tì!*" (I will be wanting a bowl full of tea!) Her "tea granny", as she loved to call him, was nothing if not predictable.

Alone at last with her child in the front bedroom, Martha found herself gazing in absolute amazement as she gingerly removed the gown from the tiny body. Standing rigidly still, she first looked down at her son and then proceeded to gently rub the surface of the silky garment. There, pinned to the inside, just over the heart, was a tiny bow of MacDonald tartan — MacDonald of Clanranald, to be exact. She instantly recognized the faded pattern and knew that the underside of her father's tie had been forced to offer up this tiny bit of cloth. She smiled lovingly down at Lachlan Archibald Campbell and decided that the bow and its story would remain a treasured secret between mother and son.

Elizabeth knew the route well. Was it not just about a year to the exact day that the entire community had made its way through the MacDonald pasture and down this very path for the Queen's celebration? Even as a younger child, she was familiar with the open area that skirted the bluffs because it was here that she and the other children found excitement in each other's company as they so often played among the thick ferns and mosses that carpeted the earth around the towering spruce, pine and maple trees. But now, as she slowly walked down the path towards the bluffs with the warm afternoon sun on her back, Elizabeth knew that she needed quiet time to think and to sort out some thoughts that had been a source of some considerable preoccupation and genuine concern over the past few months. In some respects, she wished that she were here to play with her friends as in previous days. But she also recognized that she had put away childish things because she believed that she no longer spoke or thought as a child. She was now a young woman and must begin to prepare herself.

Emerging from the calmness of the warm tree-arched path, Elizabeth was suddenly confronted by the wind that was in the process of launching a blistering assault on the open bluffs. It caught hold of her skirt and whipped it about her legs as though she had been summarily caught in the act of trespassing on some great private sanctum. Battered by its force and contemplating a hasty retreat from its viciousness, she called to mind a large outcropping of rock along the bluff's edge where a few straggly pine trees would offer some shelter from the irrational and indiscriminate aggressor. Even the pines showed the ravages of previously fought battles given that they stood there humiliated by the scars on their twisted and oddly shaped forms. They did not so much stand as simply exist there given the astonishing contrast with their graceful cousins that grew straight and tall further back in the shelter of the woods. Elizabeth walked in the direction of the rock and wondered what conflicts might lay ahead in her life and which of the pines she would resemble most when her days were done.

Even as a fourteen-year-old child, for she was still a child in many ways, Elizabeth always showed a strong determination to follow those things that she felt were right, regardless of what others might think. Her mother always maintained that it was her side of the family, the MacGregors, that made her so. For her part, Elizabeth had decided early on that it would be futile to analyze the origins of or reasons for her make-up. She was who she was! While proud of being both a MacGregor and an Urquhart, she knew that she was her own person and must inevitably make her own way in life. Still, she now found herself needing time to think. It was for this reason that she had refused, quite skillfully she thought, her mother's request to take Donald and Allan along on her walk. No, time on the bluffs alone by herself was what she wanted and needed. She would make it up to her brothers later by spending time with them after supper and before worship. Fortunately, they were still young enough to be inherently forgiving.

The coolness of the wind aside, the rock was warm from the sun's lengthy embrace when Elizabeth finally made her way to it and positioned herself facing out towards *An Toiseach* and *An Deireadh*, the two islands off in the distance. As a child she had always found the names quite intriguing if not a bit strange. Why should anyone call them so — *An Toiseach* (the beginning) and *An Deireadh* (the end)? It was only Daniel Erskine, their elderly neighbour, who had actually taken the time to offer an explanation in response to a legitimate question, albeit flowing from the inquisitiveness of one so young. Daniel, who was considered by many to be the repository of local history, had told her the story of the highland settlers who had sailed to these shores back in 1840. The creaky ship that had carried them from *Loch nam Madadh*, on the Scottish Isle of *Uibhist a Tuath* (North Uist), had approached the coast after a particularly rough voyage and the people were anxious to have their feet planted on something more solid than rotting planks.

According to Daniel, it was *Aonghas Dubh* (Black Angus) Grant and his wife Flora, standing on the upper deck taking the air, who were the first settlers to actually see the islands through a hovering mist. A man of deep religious faith, Angus sighted the outer island and named it *An Deireadh* to symbolize the end of their voyage and banishment. The one closer to the shore he named *An Toiseach* to represent the rebirth of their lives in the new world. Even with the optimism that came with such a symbolic beginning, it had not been an easy task for them to adjust to their adopted land. This was particularly the case in the context of the nearby and well-established English settlement of New Carlisle, which had been founded as a fishing port by loyalists from the American colonies some sixty years previously. The issue of proximity had certainly influenced the highlanders' decision to approach the colonial administrators for a grant of land further inland, away from the town and its inhabitants.

The area around the dark loch was soon identified as potential settlement land and, according to Daniel, was eagerly chosen as the site of their, as he referred to it, *Ierusalem nuadh* (New Jerusalem). He could still recall quite vividly just how proud they had all been to own their own land even if it was completely blanketed with a thick evergreen cloak that swept down from the mountain tops to the very edge of the loch. It was of no consequence. The land could and would eventually be cleared but they themselves would never again endure a clearance.

These islands, "the beginning and the end," were also part of Elizabeth and what made her the person she was. Her thoughts were seemingly taking her on another type of voyage because, as she stared off in their direction, she wondered what special meaning they might hold for her. Perhaps the inner one symbolized her future while the second one, farther out, now enshrouded in wisps of mist, stood as the greater unknown of her life, to end only where providence would have it end. It was difficult for this fourteen-year-old child to fathom it all. She had the presence of mind to freely admit that it would obviously take much greater thought on her part. In some respects, her voyage was only beginning.

In a matter of only two short months, she would be leaving *Loch Dubh* to take up her studies in Baddeck. Her parents had spoken to the Reverend Fraser who, in turn, had written to the Presbyterian minister in that community; she recollected his name to be Sinclair. He had made arrangements for her to find lodgings with a family in his congregation in exchange for her domestic services around the house. The idea of such work did not trouble her; after all, she was accustomed to helping her mother with household chores including special care in tending to the boys. No, it was something else, something quite different. She would be leaving her parents and everyone here in the only home that she had ever known. Although it would only be a three or four-hour trip by steamer down the coast, through the Great Bras d'Or Channel, past Boularderie Island and into Baddeck Bay, she may as well be going off to Sydney or Halifax, or even Boston for that matter. How would she cope with the loss of her home and the people she loved? Even with MacGregor and Urquhart blood coursing through her veins, would she ever be the same person again?

She thought of Rod and Andrew MacDonald, her friends who had gone off to Baddeck the year before. Her friends. She sensed that they were more to her than mere friends and hoped that the reverse was true; especially Andrew who was the big tease of the two. From her earliest years, she had been captivated by his shocking blond hair and sparkling blue eyes. She could always tell by looking into those very eyes when he was up to no good and, invariably, it would involve her in one way or another. Trickery had always been second nature to both boys and she was forever on guard against their mischievous schemes. Still in all, they were no longer children and no longer played together the way they once did. Yet she wanted to spend time with him, in particular, and was never quite certain how to express it to him or even to herself. She would see them both at the Baddeck Academy and they would certainly be a valued connection to *Loch Dubh*. At least, the three of them could speak from time-to-time in the Gaelic and share news of home since she had heard on more than one occasion that Baddeck was very much an "English town" like New Carlisle. Would she come back to her parents a changed person? Indeed, did she want to change? Was this part of what her mother meant when she referred, much to the chagrin of her husband, to Elizabeth as a real MacGregor? There was still a great deal to think about for a young woman with both the beginning and the end in front of her.

The sun was making its way down the western sky behind *Beinn-mo-Mhulaid* when Elizabeth finally took note of the shadows that were mischievously creeping towards her like blackened tentacles. It was obviously time for her to start back for home and the supper that would be waiting. Later, she would be called upon to help her mother clear the dishes and ready the kitchen for morning, all in advance of evening worship and the eventual preparations for bed. Perhaps a brief prayer would be helpful to assist her in sorting out her many thoughts. If the Almighty had led the people of *Loch Dubh* across the seas and given them a sign such as *An Toiseach* and *An Deireadh*, perhaps He would offer her a glimpse of what He had in store for her as well.

Her long bony finger reached out ever so slowly to touch the window pane as if to confirm whether or not it was still in place. Was the glass truly there, separating the sombre warmth of the bedroom from the chill wind that was blowing up from the loch? There had been a frost last night; you could still see certain areas where the grass had been capped in white as if singed by some cold wintery flame. The summer had come and gone so quickly that it was difficult to ready one's mind for the realities of winter that were now making their presence felt in subtle yet very real ways. How true this was of life itself. The summer of youth is so fleeting and, all too soon, it begins to fade and evaporates into nothingness as if taken by a thief in the night. In the twinkling of an eye, it is nothing more than a mere memory as the coldness of the grave awaits our return to the ashes from whence we came.

Except for such thoughts, Flora was seated alone in her chair in the upstairs front bedroom that looked down and across the loch towards the Kirk. This had been the bedroom that she and Angus had always occupied since the large framed house was first built some forty years ago. Although the original house or cabin now served as nothing more than a milk shed out back, it still occupied a special place in her heart even if the others did not quite understand why. How she and Angus had worked so diligently together during those first years, cutting the mighty trees that soared up to scrape the vast ceiling of sky, squaring the logs with the broad-axe, watching the structure slowly take shape and finally filling the cracks with moss lovingly gathered up from the lush floor of the forest. They were so close then and now, now she felt so alone. In looking around as if to distract her mind from such thoughts, Flora took comfort in the realization that little had changed in the bedroom over the years, quite consciously so. The only furniture was a four-poster bed and a chest of drawers, made of pine, as well as a dry sink, a commode and this table and chair placed between the two single windows at the front. An old wooden trunk sat tucked in the far corner almost as if it were an afterthought although it was anything but. Flora always found considerable solace in the subtle scent of peat that she believed still lingered ever so faintly in its boards. It was a glorious fragrance that took her far back to another place and time. The entire room was dressed with a simple blue-and-white floral wall paper whose flowers were as faded and lifeless as those in the garden near the apple orchard. The bedroom smelled old.

Flora had been shocked when her son Angus and his wife Isabelle had first suggested that perhaps she would be more comfortable in the bedroom on the main floor off the parlour. They had both maintained that it would save her all the trouble of going up and down the stairs, what with her arthritis and all. Without the slightest hesitation and, indeed, with glaring eyes and raised voice, she had put a quick end to that kind of foolish talk. Was there no respect for her feelings or what it was that she might want? And such nonsense coming from her own son. Did he not realize the sacrifices she had made, and continued to make, to keep this family together especially after the grievous loss of the other three children during the time of what the doctor had termed "the terrible sickness"? She never forgot; she could never forget. The answers were painfully obvious to Flora and it was to this window, overlooking the loch and Kirk, that she constantly returned to find peace and consolation, away from the trials and tribulations that were sent to torment her. The words came in a hushed, almost mournful tone and washed over the window pane like a ghostly mist. *"A Thighearna."* (Oh Lord.)

Her eyes were drawn to the Kirk, with its place of prominence at the high western end of the water. Her gaze was now guided more by memory than by clarity of vision given that her sight was not as keen as it once had been. Still, she delighted in discerning the whiteness of the building set against the multitude of greens that was *Beinn-mo-Mhulaid*, rising up from behind. Sun and shadow played the most glorious magical game with the colouring of the trees throughout the day and Flora likened it to a curtain of rich green velvet that God had placed before her. Unconsciously, her hand dropped to the course black material of her frock and her fingers began to caress its texture as if, in so doing, it might somehow be transformed into the velvet that lay before her on the far side of the loch.

With her eyes still focused on the Kirk, Flora cast her thoughts back to the time when the thick forest swept totally undisturbed down to the water's edge. In those early days of settlement, there was no church in which to congregate and no minister to preach the word of God to the people. Had it not been her own dear Angus who served as the catechist in preaching the gospel and teaching the Catechism wherever the flock was gathered? Even now, Flora could see him standing on a milking stool in the Erskine barn, leading the service for those seated on crudely made benches or standing on a carpet of freshly scythed hay. Few people in *Loch Dubh* ever knew that Angus could not read or write; he had committed vast amounts of scripture and portions of **The Shorter Catechism** to memory and could recite them flawlessly at great length. Flora would read to him for hours on end, oftentimes under the light of a candle and later a kerosene lamp. How he loved to hear and absorb the words. If only she could go back to that time. They had been solid in their faith and content in their lives. Now, so much had changed.

"A Sheanamhair, gur e mise tha fo mhìghean." (Grandmother, I am indeed sad.) It was John, the youngest of Angus and Isabelle's three children, who was now standing in the room, quite unbeknown to the unsuspecting old woman. He had come in search of a sympathetic ear to listen as he pleaded his case. At eight years of age, he thought it unjust that Iain and Sadie, thirteen and eleven respectively, would not play with him simply because he was "too wee." Jokingly, they had told him to go see the *cailleach* and that she would surely make it better by sorting it all out for him. In absolute innocence and trust, he had taken them at their word and gone off to seek her out, even though the children had often been warned not to disturb their grandmother, especially when she was in her room.

John stood slightly back and to the side of his grandmother, whose eyes remained fixed on the window before her. He looked up at the towering individual and wondered if the sunlight would fade her long black dress and make it white as snow, if she stayed there long enough. She was indeed a tall formidable figure dressed as she always was in black, which contrasted so sharply with the white and cream of her hair forever pinned into a tight bun at the back of her head. It was true that she was often quite harsh with the young ones but they had been told by their parents that everyone should be patient with her. They said that this was simply her way. Whatever that was supposed to mean, the children had never been certain. John had tried but decided, in the final analysis, that it would be best to simply stay a goodly distance away from her. It was all the more surprising that he now chose to approach her personally to resolve this pressing matter of ostracism from the other children. He was certain even she would understand the urgent nature of the problem and do whatever she could to help him resolve it. After all, she was his *seanamhair*.

Flora's gaze now settled on the cemetery that crept up the hill directly behind the Kirk. Her dear husband had been committed to his eternal rest there some eleven years ago and often she sat here talking to him. Och, she knew it was foolish enough but there were so few of the old people still left with whom she could share stories and commiserate one with the other. From time to time, Archie MacDonald and the Erskines would visit and they would have a grand time together reminiscing about the early days. It just wasn't the same now; things were changing so quickly and people oftentimes didn't even know their proper place. In particular, many of the children were becoming so bold. This would never have been allowed in her day, their day. On this point, she was confident that Archie and the Erskines would surely agree. She looked into the cemetery at her Angus' white stone marker and softly spoke aloud. *"Far an d'fhàg mi mo chridhe air a chàradh 's an ùir."* (Where I left my heart buried in the earth.)

From where he stood off to the side of the chair, John heard his grandmother's mumbling but couldn't quite make out what it was she was saying. It could not be very important; certainly not any more important than his current problem. She had yet to respond to his initial plea and he resolved that, this time, he would be certain to get her attention. Placing his tiny hand on the pleated black material that covered her thin arm, he repeated the very same words only now in a slightly louder voice while, at the same moment, giving the cloth a gentle tug. *"A Sheanamhair, gur e mise tha fo mhìghean!"* (Grandmother, I am indeed sad!) Eternity sped by and remained frozen all at the same time. John's next recollection was of his grandmother's startled face staring down at him as her mouth gaped open.

"A Thighearna! Cuiridh mi thu gu Baddeck air muin mairt!" (Oh Lord! I will send you to Baddeck on a cow's back!) With eyes glaring, she bellowed at her unsuspecting grandson, who stood there transfixed as if unable to move a muscle let alone two legs. There could be no greater threat to a child than this, to be banished to that far-off place in that peculiar way. Was that not where the MacDonald twins and Elizabeth Urquhart had gone? And they were now so seldom seen. There was something terribly frightening about the idea and John had no desire to wait and hear more. Suddenly and quite unexpectedly, his feet assumed a life of their own as they flew down the stairs carrying him out the kitchen door in what seemed like mere seconds. It was only when he had eventually caught his breath and composed himself that he decided he would tell Iain and Sadie

that the *cailleach* was not as good at sorting things out as they might think. He had learned a valuable lesson and certainly would be more careful in the future as to whom he might approach for the sharing of concerns.

Having sufficiently calmed herself from the fright, Flora once again took solace in leaving the present behind by staring out the window into the past, to a time and place that made her feel comfortable and secure. For a moment, she was with Angus again; in this scene, they were seated by the kitchen stove on an early winter day such as this. Dropping his tea cup back into its saucer, he slowly turned his head towards his wife and, in the calmest of voices, asked her a most compelling question. *"Nach cluinn sibh fuaim na pìob' a' tighinn?"* (Do you not hear the sound of the bagpipe approaching?) At that instant, Flora was abruptly transported back and once again found herself seated in front of the window in the upstairs bedroom. Angus had spoken to her from afar and she knew full well what was meant. This time it was her turn to speak. *"Och Aonghais; 'S mi nach iar-radh dealachadh ri 'm bheò."* (Oh Angus; I don't want to be parted from you while I live.) She knew that she would have to prepare herself. The answer to Angus' question had been yes. She had indeed heard the pipe.

'N uair nach 'eil fhios agaibh ciod a tharlas air a' mhàireach: oir ciod i'ur beatha? Is deatach i a chithear ré ùine bhig, agus an déigh sin a théid as an t-sealladh.

Seumas IV: 14

Whereas ye know not what shall be on the morrow. For what is your life? It is even a vapour, that appeareth for a little time, and then vanisheth away.

James IV: 14

For some reason clearly unknown to him, Sandy believed that the hay-filled mattress was intentionally keeping him awake. Why else would it choose to prod and poke him every time he moved? It had never done so before and it was odd that it should choose this night, of all nights, to torment him and keep him from sleep. Indeed, he always found great comfort and security in his bed positioned as it was on one side of the window with Matthew's just across. Now glancing across the room, Sandy could see that his brother was sleeping peacefully as a torrent of moonlight streamed through the glass panes and ghostly white curtains. It was then that he decided that Matthew must surely have a softer mattress and that tomorrow, if no one was looking, he might even switch them. Well, perhaps not. After all, at twelve years of age, Sandy was the eldest boy and had always sensed a natural responsibility to watch over both Matthew and Emily. The others regarded him as the wise older brother to be emulated and, although never relishing the position, Alexander Stuart Fraser took some degree of pride in the fact that, with the exception of his father, he was the oldest man in the family.

Sandy and Matthew occupied the upstairs bedroom just off to the right of the landing at the top of the stairs. On the opposite side was Emily's room that faced the front of the house with the loch off in the distance. Looking out her window, one had a panoramic view of the Kirk and cemetery, as well as the white-shingled school just up from the hall on the far side of the water. Still in all, Sandy was glad that his room faced the back of the house. He liked school right enough; he just didn't need to be constantly reminded of its presence. There was so much to do here on the farm that was a great deal more interesting and exciting than studying books, memorizing text and working at the blackboard, all under the attentive watch of Miss MacNeil, the school mistress. He was also pleased that he and Matthew had their own room separate from Emily who was forever nattering about girlish things that held absolutely no interest for them. He often imagined himself and his brother as saints because, if patience was indeed a virtue as their mother was always wont to remind them, the two of them were surely bound for glory.

Sandy had no way of determining what time it was exactly but something told him that it must certainly be early morning. There were no sounds coming up from downstairs which meant that his parents were most probably asleep in their bed. Late into the night, the only thing that ever dared travel around the house and upstairs from the main floor was the heat from the stove that had been strategically positioned to the side of the staircase in the entry hallway. But even the heat, after a time, would succumb to the onslaught of the cold winter air that always claimed victory in the early hours and whose presence would be expelled only with the building of the fire in the kitchen stove the next morning. There would constantly be a race among the children to see who would be the first to dart from their warm beds, down the stairs, through the chill damp hallway and into the welcoming kitchen with its luxuriating heat.

For as long as he could remember, it had been his father's nightly routine to ensure that the hall stove was well banked after evening worship and just before they were sent off to bed, thus allowing them sufficient time to say their prayers and sneak under the waiting covers without feeling the full effects of Old Man Winter on their bones. Once in bed, Sandy would nuzzle up against the woollen sheets, inundated as he was by a mountain of blankets and, of course, his favourite multi-coloured quilt. Since earliest childhood, Sandy had held the quilt close and always likened this protective mantle to Joseph's coat of many colours — a favourite story of his that had been taught in Sunday School. Often, he would regale his mother with stories about how he would go upstairs and spend long fun-filled hours in conversation with his friend Joseph who, in one dramatic movement, had thrown his coat across the bed much as one scatters seeds to the furrowed soil on the spring wind. He knew that, each time the story unfolded, his mother would laugh heartily, as much with her eyes as with her mouth. Such was never the case with his father.

The stoic face of the Reverend Duncan Fraser was nothing if not constant, whether at church, in the community or at home. The first and only time that Sandy had attempted to share his Joseph stories with his father, the response came back that perhaps he would be better to devote more time contemplating his Lord in the event he was called to his heavenly home before the morning. Sandy still remembered how the very thought had scared him and caused endless bouts of fright as night began to fall. But it wasn't this thought that was now keeping him awake nor was it, he concluded, the mattress. Why would God take him to Heaven before he even got to open his Christmas presents in the morning, something for which he, Matthew and Emily had waited with great anticipation all these months? Sandy wanted to understand his father's rather fearful comments, but was forced to admit that he could not.

Even at his tender age, Sandy realized that he should be thankful for his many blessings. Did not his father remind all the children of each and every one, especially at meal times with grace and at worship each evening with prayer around the Bible? He was truly grateful for his family, even with Emily's constant pestering; he truly was. Sandy reminded himself of the poor MacDonald children who had lost their father Malcolm two years ago in that terrible accident back in the woods. He could still see the tear-stained faces of the four children as they accompanied their mother behind the coffin to the Kirk for burial. With such grievous images flooding his mind, he unconsciously reached out and drew the blankets close, knowing that both his parents loved all three of them very much. It was just that Sandy found it difficult to understand why they showed this love in such completely different ways.

Rolling himself into a ball under the thick heavy covers surmounted by Joseph's mantle, his hands clutched the corners of the luxuriously soft pillow, which had been made for him several months earlier by his mother. She had proposed it as a summer project, a sort of game for the children, to gather up as many chicken, goose and duck feathers as they could find. He remembered the care that she had taken in boiling them on the stove to rid them of all insects and lice. What fun they all had afterwards as feathers were carefully spread out to dry on blankets in the orchard. How Emily had chased the ones that decided to suddenly take flight as if attempting to escape and return to their original masters. And how he and Matthew had laughed and tried to explain to her that a few less feathers would not make a great difference one way or the other. But she was adamant and put them both on notice that these feathers would be destined for her pillow, which would surely be the fluffiest and softest of them all.

As he lay there, Sandy realized that his thoughts of his mother were every bit as soft and gentle as the pillows that she had made with such loving care. Thoughts of his father were quite different however and maybe that was more than understandable given that he was a man of the cloth and was naturally expected to be a pillar of righteousness for the entire community. Still in all, did he truly have to be so terribly strict with his own family? He could never seem to find time to take them for a walk in the woods or go fishing like John MacDonald used to do with the twins and continued to do, even now, with his younger sons Daniel and Murdoch. Sandy desperately wanted to walk, to fish or do any number of other things with his father. With past attempts as a guide, the reality was that he was now not able to bring himself to ask and it was obviously never offered.

Over time and with some considerable amount of thought, Sandy had come to recognize some important truths about his family. His father did not belong to them in the same way that his mother did. His father was the property of the community and that was proven by the fact that he was always away from home conducting prayer meetings, visiting the sick and dying and performing all those other duties that come with being a minister. It was his mother who brought the family together with her special ways. For some reason, Sandy suddenly conjured up a special memory — the magical moment that his mother and the three of them had shared on laundry day just this past week. With clothes strewn across the kitchen floor waiting to be washed, the children made mountains out of the various garments and leaped from one peak to the other, pretending to be eagles in full flight. How the laughter resounded off the walls as all four of them enjoyed their whimsical mountainous escape. It was all so apparent why it was so; the Reverend Duncan was not at home.

There was also the fundamental realization, shared by all three children, that their family was different from the others in *Loch Dubh*. Not that they wanted to be different mind you; they just were. They were the manse children and that in itself was enough to set them apart. Sandy, in particular, found it difficult when people would look at them as if expecting wings to magically sprout from their backs or halos to appear above their heads. Seated in a front pew at Kirk each Sunday, he could feel the eyes of the congregation looking through him. And even at school, he sensed he had to behave even though all the others were free to do otherwise. He was being cheated of something for himself but, most of all, he felt cheated for his mother, who loved to laugh but so seldom was given the opportunity.

Sandy also knew that his family, while rich in social standing, was relatively poor. He had overheard his parents speaking on the veranda late one evening about trying to make ends meet on such a limited income. The *Loch Dubh* congregation was doing its best to support the Fraser family, not only with the clerical stipend but also with the provision of household goods and services. The men of the congregation would help out with plowing and planting in the spring, hay making in the late summer and other major tasks that had to be undertaken throughout the year to keep the farm and, by extension, the family going. The three children had become accustomed to seeing ladies of the community arrive at the back door with baked goods and preserves or even some recently woven cloth. A few of them, whose families were already grown, brought children's clothing that they thought could perhaps be put to good use by the Fraser bairns. All were graciously accepted by his mother who would always thank them by saying that it was far too generous and not really necessary, when in fact it wasn't and it was. She was so appreciative of these acts of kindness and was never once heard to complain. But she was also tired, with so much work to be done at home as well as obligations to be shared with her husband in the congregation. Sandy wondered how it was that she always found time for her children, *mo sheud beag* (My Little Treasure) as she would call each one of them in turn. A constant in their lives, her love was demonstrative; her love was a saving grace.

With his eyes now fixed on the ceiling, Sandy realized that the white fog clinging to the air in front of his face was of his own making. He could hear his words being spoken ever so softly, as if to safeguard Matthew's slumber. *"A Thighearna, sàbhail mo theaghlach. Seo m' ùrnuigh. Bhiodh e 'na thìodhlac iomlan."* (Oh Lord, preserve/watch over my family. This is my prayer. It would be a perfect gift.) He knew well enough that, in the morning, spruce boughs and evergreen vines from the woods would have magically appeared and be hung over the doors for decoration. In all likelihood, there would be a few pieces of hard candy and fruit, some recently knitted mittens or socks and possibly some nuts for each of the children. They would be placed near the fir tree decorated, as it always was, with acorns, buttons covered with tissue paper and empty spools of thread encased in silver paper from discarded tea packages. Sandy was certainly old enough to know that such gifts came by way of Dunn's General Store in New Carlisle and not Saint Nicholas' house way up north beyond Cape Smoky. He also knew that it was his mother who saw to it all. But regardless, he would be thankful for the decorations and presents. Most of all, he would be thankful for family.

A sudden noise somewhere outside the house broke the silence and, as the white fog settled all around him, curiosity compelled Sandy to venture into the chill of the night air to investigate. Pulling back the cozy covers, he slipped from the warmth of his bed and stood bathed in the deceivingly cool moonlight as Matthew slept on undisturbed. The small bedside rug, which had been hooked by his mother from strips of old clothing, was soft under his feet and, thankfully, prevented any creaking of floorboards that might alert his parents to his wakened state. As he pulled back the curtains and peered through the window, he observed how the moonlight illuminated the broad expanse of snow that spread back towards the barn and beyond to the fringes of the forest. All seemed to be in absolute tranquillity when, suddenly, his eyes fell upon the blatant culprit. There in the foreground was *Rionnag* with her head inside a milking pail that she had obviously knocked over on the casement covering the backyard well. Caught in the light, her black fur glistened as she searched for a bit of nourishment following a night forage in the woods. *"Sud cat aimhleasach!"* (That mischievous cat!) The words came to him so naturally. She never really liked him; Sandy always sensed that. His breath had poured over the window pane resulting in the formation of a frosty coat that shrouded his view of *Rionnag*. Although temporarily blinded from the scene unfolding outside, Sandy was struck by the realization that this, of all days, was a time to be at peace with everyone and everything. He must try. Like it or not, she was part of God's creation, regardless of how snooty she always appeared to be or how aloof she remained from the family.

With mystery solved and a resolute determination to give thanks for both presents and family in the morning, Sandy hurriedly returned to his bed and, this time, found himself cradled by the mattress that eagerly enveloped him in its now soothing grasp. Sleep was soon upon him. However, had he managed to linger at the window a bit longer, he would have seen *Rionnag* reappear from the bucket and stare off in the direction of the house. Her thoughts were also of family. She was tormented by the fact that the Frasers had never shown her the attention and appreciation she so properly deserved. The things that are sent to torment us.

⬯⬯⬯⬯

The view from the wooden bench, situated as it was immediately in front of the courthouse, was nothing short of magical. Elizabeth was captivated by the deep blue of the water as it stretched out before her so vast and so strangely still. The gentle rolling slopes of the hills, *Beinn Bhreagh* (Beautiful Mountain) in the foreground and the western tip of Boularderie Island just beyond, were a palate of greens, blues and purples that seemed to change hues continually. She likened the late afternoon sun, now drifting towards its western bed further up the Bras d'Or Lake, to the Almighty's brush touching the immense canvas that lay before her.

In some ways, the water and rolling landscape reminded her of *Loch Dubh*. Oh it was different enough; there was a greater expanse of water here and the mountains were more like hills compared to *Beinn-mo-Mhulaid*. But then, *Loch Dubh* was located a greater distance up in the highlands of Cape Breton and the region, she thought, was aptly named. All the same, there was enough here in Baddeck to remind her of home; perhaps too much, for she often felt remorse or guilt for not being more homesick for her family and neighbours. Yet, even though it was now nine months since she left *Loch Dubh* on that blustery September morning, she had returned home at Christmas and, besides, Andrew and Rod MacDonald were here as well. Still, with the closing of school or the academy as the locals referred to it, she would be back with her parents and brothers, Donald and Allan, in a month's time. She desperately wanted to experience as much as she possibly could before that moment arrived.

The mild May air had invigorated the town after what had been a particularly long and dreadfully cold winter. The wind off the lake, which up until several weeks ago was still garnished with bits of drift ice, had reaffirmed that winter was not about to loosen its grip without a fight. She recalled returning home one day from the academy and meeting an elderly man who was walking towards her with head bowed and talking a blue streak to himself. As she drew closer, she could hear him muttering aloud. *"A Thighearna, an deigh-shiabaidh, an deigh-shiabaidh!"* (Oh Lord, the drift ice, the drift ice!) Even with the coolness of the air against her cheeks, she felt warmed by this unknown *bodach* (old man) whose lamentations confirmed that *Loch Dubh* could never really be that far away.

Even though it was a small village by Cape Breton standards compared to others such as Sydney, Glace Bay or even North Sydney, Elizabeth found

Baddeck to be quite cosmopolitan. Its planked sidewalks offered an enjoyable walk by the row of houses and bustling wharfs that clung to the shore line. From time to time, she would stop to pet the various livestock, especially the horses, cows and sheep in their pens, before they were boarded onto vessels bound for the lucrative markets of Newfoundland and St. Pierre. Still further back along the main street, she was able to saunter along at her own leisurely pace and admire the many interesting architectural styles that were beginning to appear. The local residents were still boastful about their "new" courthouse, even though it was now seven years old. She had been particularly drawn to the numerous churches, some with names that were all so new to her. Of course, she now attended the Greenwood Presbyterian Church and was familiar with the Church of England, the Queen's church, because there was one in New Carlisle. However, she had never before seen a Roman Catholic, Methodist or Congregational church. She was quite amazed when, one day in mid winter, she had been walking past St. Michael's, the Catholic church. As she watched members of the congregation streaming out the front doors following a Saturday service, she overheard several women speaking in the Gaelic. She was both surprised and intrigued because she had always associated her native tongue with the faith of John Knox. However, she was not about to let her guard down by exhibiting the least bit surprise given that she was now conscious of having become more worldly. She was confident there would be many a story to tell when she returned home to *Loch Dubh*.

Whenever she had a moment free from her studies or domestic chores around the MacRae household, Elizabeth would walk along the main street and very purposely absorb as many sights and sounds as possible. It was as if she couldn't experience all of it quickly enough. The shops, including general goods, tailors, photographic supplies, marble and granite works, to say nothing of the doctors and lawyers offices as well as the hotels, provided her with endless hours of pleasure. It was not only the buildings themselves but also the people who owned and frequented them. Why there was even a Chinese laundry and several newspapers! She was also a frequent visitor to the large library in Gertrude Hall and had every intention of attending a meeting of the Young Ladies Club, both of which had been established by Mrs. Mabel Bell. Sometimes she felt as though there was simply too much to take in all at once. Upon her eventual return home, she would have to be discrete above all else. Secretly, she freely admitted to herself that she felt terribly comfortable here.

Her studies at the academy were going well enough, even though all the subjects were taught in the English. She had been surprised and in some ways pleased to realize that there were others, besides herself, Andrew and Rod, who also spoke the Gaelic. They often chatted among themselves on the way home at th end of the day; it served to lessen any lingering sense of guilt by providing Elizabeth with a sense of still being part of *Loch Dubh* even though it was far away. Sometimes, it was also far away in her mind and she would later promise herself that she would never forget where she had come from and that it would always be a part of her. She promised herself that it would be so. It had to be so. Or did it?

And here she sat on the bench admiring the broad sweep of water and mountains, utterly entranced by her own musings. It was for this reason that she was somewhat startled when a firm hand seemed to appear out of nowhere, coming to rest on her shoulder. *"Ciamar a tha thu Ealasaid Bheag?"* (How are you Little Elizabeth?) It was Andrew who had addressed her as he passed by, obviously en route to one of the shops on an errand judging by the list of items on a crumpled piece of paper clutched securely in the other hand. It was apparent that this was one of the many chores that he and Rod were called upon to do for the family with whom they were boarded.

"Gu math, tapadh leat. Tha latha math ann an diugh." (Fine, thank you. It is a fine day today.) Composing herself from the initial surprise, she was determined not to offer any signs of being annoyed with his reference to her as "Little Elizabeth," even though she most certainly was. She was a young woman and should be addressed and treated as such, thus her most proper if not staid response to his more-familiar approach. Yet she longed for him to sit with her, even if only for a few moments. Perhaps they could chat together and, then again, perhaps not. She always became so tongue-tied in his presence and felt, even now, that her face must surely be turning a dozen shades of red.

"Tha agam ri dhol do'n bhùth. Am bi thu aig an taigh an nochd?" (I have to go to the shop. Will you be at home tonight?) Although emotionally convulsed with disappointment and pleasure all at the same time, she was quick to almost calmly inform him that indeed she would. Elizabeth trusted that Mr. and Mrs. MacRae would not mind if she had a visitor come calling even into the evening hours. Now, as Andrew turned and walked away from her with a knowing wave of the hand, she hoped that she could get to know him better, at least to talk to him without becoming the little girl that he still supposed her to be. Perhaps their friendship on the shores of *Loch Dubh* would blossom into something more here on the shores of the Bras d'Or. She hoped that it would and, as he passed through a shop doorway and finally departed from her view, she caught herself speaking aloud ever so softly. *"Tha mo rùn air a'ghille."* (I am in love with the laddie.)

How far she had come over the past nine months and how much she felt she had grown. Had she not left her home a young girl and now become a mature woman? She cast her mind back to that September morning when she bid farewell to her family on the government wharf in New Carlisle. She stood with her parents, along with Donald and Allan, as the steamer of the Bras d'Or Steamboat Company glided towards its mooring. It was on its return voyage back to Sydney, via Englishtown and Baddeck, having just come from Aspy Bay, Neil's Harbour and Ingonish, with many a well-to-do vacationer on board. As people milled about, loading and unloading cargo, the Urquhart family eagerly watched the proceedings and chatted about all manner of things: the black and tan pony's possible final destination; the statuesque lady with the parasol speaking French to her three children; the blue air that hung about the heads of the young and obviously virile ship's crew. Elizabeth knew well enough that the conversation was not entirely spontaneous and that it was nothing more than a valiant attempt to mask the emotions that her imminent departure now incited. She watched her mother's eyes as they filled with moisture and suddenly found herself coming close to tears as well. She was conscious of the need to remain strong, especially for little Donald and Allan who must not be allowed to become upset. Yet, they would miss her and she them.

Neil Erskine, Daniel and Tina's son who lived on the far side of the loch, was travelling to Baddeck with his wife Iona and their small son Kenneth to have the boy looked at by the doctor. Kenneth, or *Coinneach Bàn* (Blond Kenneth) as his grandparents loved to call him, had been stricken five years ago with diphtheria and, unlike poor Harris Ferguson, had survived. Now at six years of age and with much tender and constant care, he seemed healthy and content enough as he stood there diligently holding to the safety of his mother's hand as the whirlwind of activity continued to surround them on all sides. Still, no chances would be taken; the doctor would see him. There on the wharf, Neil and Iona first greeted the Urquharts and, sensing the growing anticipation of the moment, promised that they would stay with Elizabeth all the way to Baddeck where Gordon and Mary MacRae, her host family, would be waiting to greet her. Although Hector and Sarah were relieved and thankful that their daughter would be seen safely to her new dwelling, it would not make the parting any easier.

When the time had come, Elizabeth bent down to hug and kiss her brothers who both insisted that they wanted to go with her on the boat. It took some doing but they were eventually placated by a promise of a special giftie when she returned at Christmas. Her father remained strong as always, simply hugging her and offering advice to study hard and make the family proud. Her voice became noticeably choked with emotion as she clung to him and promised to do so. However, it was her mother, now in tears, who most affected her. Elizabeth had anticipated that parting would be difficult but nothing had quite prepared her for this. No words were spoken between them; it was obvious none would be sufficient even if they could be coerced forth. Elizabeth engulfed her mother in a lingering embrace and kissed her on the cheek before moving slowly towards the gangway. As she looked back at the four figures standing there on the wharf, she felt the tears cascading down her face, the very same tears that she had earlier assured herself would not occur. Through the blur of sadness, she thought she had seen her father's mouth move but neither her mother nor brothers seemed to respond in any way. However, had she been close to him at that moment, she might well have heard the quietest of prayers. "*A Dhé a tha anns na h-àrdaibh, O deònaich sìth air sàile.*" (Oh God who is in the heavens, grant a calm sea.) She stood there on the stern until all that remained visible to the eye was the church steeple set against a vast expanse of blue mountains. The four figures were long lost to her sight. Something deep within told her that a page had been turned.

Even with an overwhelming sense of sadness, Elizabeth still felt strangely exhilarated by the voyage down the coast of the North Shore with both the magnificence of the landscape and the newness of the experience. She began to conjure up stories in her mind of the families whose farms ran down to the shore like colourful ribbons of green and gold billowing in the sea breezes. Approximately two hours later, as the steamer made a right turn into the Great Bras d'Or Channel, she found herself marveling at the immense beauty of the lake that now stretched for miles before her with the setting sun bejeweling its tranquil surface. On the right was the tiny settlement of New Campbellton located on a sheltered inlet at the base of St. Anns Mountain. Across lay the beautiful island of Boularderie whose sloping hay fields cascaded down to the water's edge. She reminded herself of the fact that this was where Peter Campbell's mother, a MacLeod, hailed from as did the Reverend James Fraser who was still affectionately referred to as "the Shepherd of Boularderie" for the many years of devoted service to his flock. Indeed, off to the left, she could now see the white form of St. James Presbyterian Church high on a hill with its mighty steeple piercing the expanse of blue sky. It was here that so many highlanders had come to start a new life. And it was also here that at least one ship had been built to carry the Reverend Norman MacLeod and his parishioners from St. Anns on to yet another new life halfway around the world in Australia and New Zealand some fifty years ago. Already there was such a sense of history to this place — *tìr nan craobh 's nan ard-bheann.* (land of trees and mountains) Time changes everything and nothing all at the same time.

Within the hour, the steamer approached a towering point of land on the right that Elizabeth was soon to come to know as Red Head or the more popular *Beinn Bhreagh*. The mountain was indeed beautiful but her attention was drawn to the magnificent home of Mr. and Mrs. Bell that was positioned high on the point facing westwards up the lake. It was so imposing with its turrets and chimneys, which seemed to rise up and scrape the sky, and the large windows on both floors that looked out in all directions. She had never seen the likes before except of course in books and immediately imagined herself being invited there to some fancy dress ball. She was dancing in the arms of Andrew.

As the steamer rounded the point of land and cruised across the waters of Baddeck Bay, Elizabeth noted a flurry of activity in the fields adjacent to the residence. She could make out a solitary figure with hair and beard as black as a crow who stood in a field near a large display board to the side of an out building. He was wearing a brightly coloured, tartan shirt and, what appeared to be, knickerbocker pants. A black tam-o'-shanter was pulled down over his mop of hair in such a way that it all appeared to blend together in forming one massive dark blob on the top of his head. Elizabeth was intrigued by this person whom she took to be the grounds keeper or perhaps a farm-hand. Seemingly without notice, the figure came to life and began to run downhill towards the shore with a length of rope trailing behind like a monstrous tail. She had no idea what the steamer may have done to upset him so. It was only when these initial questions had passed that Elizabeth realized that this man was doing nothing more than simply amusing himself in leisurely activity as a huge kite rose in the sky behind him. She thought that he must have a most understanding employer to tolerate such idleness in the middle of a work day.

The steamer glided the last half-mile towards the wharf as deck hands suddenly appeared from below and busily readied the ropes for mooring. One young crewman glanced over at Elizabeth and began to watch her closely as she leaned against the railing, intent on observing the activity unfold on the fields of *Beinn Bhreagh*. As he moved forward and sauntered casually past her, he cheekily brushed against her coat. "In case you don't recognize him, that's himself — Alexander Bell. Some say he's quite daft playing as he does all the while with his toys. Myself, I don't mind since he gives work to a lot of people in these parts. He can keep his toys; I just wish I had a bit of his money." With that, he winked at her and was gone. Elizabeth quickly collected her thoughts and then returned inside to gather up her bags where, at the same time, she would thank Neil, Iona and *Coinneach Bàn* for their company.

With whistle sounding, the vessel eventually cut a final path to the wharf as a number of people could be seen streaming down from the town towards the water's edge. Elizabeth scanned each of the faces in turn, attempting to guess which ones might be those of Mr. and Mrs. MacRae. Still, she remained captivated by the images of the man on the hill wearing those funny-looking knickerbockers and tam-o'-shanter. She would get herself settled in Baddeck and perhaps, in time, have an opportunity to actually meet this Mr. Bell and discover what it was that made him the way he was.

John Grant's eyes were keenly fixed on the school bell that rested on the corner of Miss MacNeil's desk at the head of the classroom. His concentration was not broken even by the fluttering of the Union Jack that hung on a pole affixed to the wall at the front along with a picture of the Queen and a large map of the Empire. He had always been intrigued by the fact that Canada and the numerous members belonging to the British family of nations were coloured a brilliant red while all others were portrayed in a drab beige. He thought it only proper that the United States should have such a bland colour; had they not had a revolution and gotten rid of the

King? It served them right. Beige looked good on them!

At nine years of age, John was one of only three students in grade four; the other two being Emily Fraser, the minister's daughter, and Morag Ferguson, whose parents lived next door to "that MacGregor man", the one so seldom seen at Kirk. This was how his grandmother and some of the older people often referred to him, in the Gaelic of course, but John never really took much notice himself and didn't much care one way or the other. His concern was with the ringing of the bell that would be the prelude to his escape from the clutches of the school house into the glorious sunshine of a June afternoon. He hoped that Miss MacNeil would be lenient with the twenty-two students in her care, from the wee ones in kindergarten to the older ones in level eight. Surely she would allow them to leave a bit earlier just this once. It was, after all, the end of the week and hopefully even the MacNeils could have a heart, now and again. *"Seirm an clag; seirm an clag!"* (Ring the bell; ring the bell!) He muttered the words softly in the hope that, somehow, they would magically make it happen.

The bell did ring, eventually, but only at 3:00 p.m. as it always did at the appointed hour. As a consequence, the entire MacNeil clan had just been demoted even further in John's estimation. She could have been more understanding but, nonetheless, he was glad to be free of the school and all things academic. As the students streamed out the front doors and spread out in every direction all the while chattering excitedly to one another, John soon realized that he would be on his own. His older brother Iain was heading off to work at Dunn's store down in the town while his sister Sadie had already made plans to go home with Catherine MacDonald, the younger sister of the twins who were still at the academy in Baddeck. Solitary or not, John was not one to be deterred and decided that he would become an explorer, like Dr. Livingstone, and trek around the darkest fringes of the forest that, for his purposes, would be magically transformed into a tropical jungle. He set a path for himself along the edge of the woods high above and around the head of the loch, behind the hall, the Kirk and the four farms that separated him from home. Perhaps he would stumble across a treasure like the one that had been recently discovered in that odd-sounding place, the Klondike, a few years past. He would be famous and perhaps then Iain and Sadie would finally be willing to play with him more often.

As John approached the back door of the house, he was anxious that the special gift that he had gathered with such care for his mother would be in perfect order. The field high above the Kirk and cemetery had been transformed into a vast carpet of the most beautiful mayflowers and he had lovingly picked a large cluster to grace the kitchen table. Now, he was at the back door with bouquet well hidden behind his back, knowing full well that his surprise would cause his mother to smile with sheer delight. Yet, in an instant, John's life had been dramatically altered and he suddenly found himself trying to make sense of this unexpected turn of events —

this whirlwind of thoughts and emotions that encircled him. All the while, he stood there in the kitchen with treasure in hand, not understanding. He remembered how his nose was enveloped with the fragrance of the flowers while, at the same time, his ears were bombarded by the mournful sobbing of his mother and his eyes by the blank expression on his father's drawn face. He stood in complete silence, not knowing, simply waiting.

John's grandmother, Flora, was dead. Isabelle had found her when she went upstairs to call her to tea just before the noon hour. She was seated in her chair in front of the open window as a soft summer breeze made its way up from the loch. She seemed so peaceful there with her hands folded in her lap and the family Bible in front of her on the window sill, its pages fluttering back and forth as if seeking out the most appropriate piece of scripture. It was only later when he went to his mother that Angus had discovered a small piece of paper clutched tightly in her hands. It contained his father's favourite passage written years past in Flora's own hand. *Tha mi fàgail sìthe agaibh, mo shìth - sa tha mi toirt duibh: cha'n ann mar a bheir an saoghal a tha mise toirt duibh. Na biodh 'ur cridhe fo thrioblaid, agus na biodh eagal air. — Eòin, XIV: 27.* (Peace I leave with you, my peace I give unto you: not as the world giveth, give I unto you. Let not your heart be troubled, neither let it be afraid. — John, XIV: 27.) As he read the faded writing, Angus looked down into his mother's face and prayed that, in death, both she and his father would finally find the peace they had always sought and now so richly deserved.

It did not take long for word of Flora's passing to spread throughout the community given that *Loch Dubh* was little more than a gathering of a few scattered farmhouses. Well before the supper hour, Angus had been visited by Daniel Erskine who asked if he might be given the honour of making Flora's coffin. He felt it was the very least he could do for an old and very dear friend. Of the original settlers, he and Archie MacDonald were the only two left. Soon they too would be taken to be joined with their forefathers in glory. That time would come when God so willed it. But for now, he wanted to offer this tribute to Flora who, along with her Angus, had been such pillars of the community and whose presence would be sorely missed. It was to be the only time that terribly long day that Angus attempted a smile. He understood.

It was truly a beautiful coffin made from broad white-pine boards. Daniel had first laid a bed of soft hay inside that was then covered with Flora's favourite quilt, with the white underside facing upwards. She was laid out in the very same long black dress that she had worn to her husband's funeral long ago. It was strange how it still suited her, so simple and so somber. Around the collar was a small speck of colour — a tiny cameo brooch that Angus had given her to mark their forty years of marriage many years before. She had seldom worn it, claiming that it was far too ostentatious. Strange how it now seemed to suit her so well.

Flora's head rested on a blue flannel pillow that had always occupied a prominent place in her bedroom. In its centre, there appeared a small heart made with two tattered pieces of tartan — one Grant and the other Robertson, which had been her family name before marriage. The reds and greens of the two tartans were quite similar and one had to look very closely to determine which half of the heart was which. At the same time, one could not help but notice the meticulous stitching that had gone into transforming the two worn and faded pieces of cloth into one. Isabelle had always thought that the heart mirrored Flora and Angus' lives that had been drawn together. These bits of tartan, which she had lovingly transported across the Atlantic many years ago, would now offer comfort to Flora on her last journey where two hearts would indeed become one again.

On the first night of the wake, before others came to pay their respects at the Grant home, Angus and Isabelle gathered the children together around the coffin that had been placed in the front parlour on two chests covered with white linen. All pictures had been turned to face the wall and all ornamentation, including the brass candlesticks and coloured-glass vase on the mantle, was taken away. The family was to have a private moment and the children were quite obviously grateful for the presence of their parents, who held firmly onto their hands. As he peered inside the coffin, John remembered thinking how white his grandmother's face was, almost as white as the lady's on the brooch. He was sorry for having thought of his grandmother as a *cailleach* and hoped that she would have forgotten about it when next they should meet. He also recalled looking up into his father's face as he spoke his final earthly words to his mother. *"Beannachd Dhé leat, a ghaoil. Beannachd leat a mhamaidh."* (May the blessing of God attend you, dear one. Farewell Mamma.) Isabelle, with tears streaming down her cheeks, asked each of her children to say their own good-byes to grandmother. When it was John's turn, after Iain and Sadie, he reached forward and ever so gently placed a small mayflower in her folded hands, which still bore the calloused evidence of years of hard labour. In a soft voice that was almost a whisper, he told her he was sorry he had gone to her room and scared her so. He also told her he loved her and always would. With that, he stepped back and the family slowly returned to the kitchen to affix a small ribbon of black crepe to the back door in anticipation of visitors.

The Reverend Fraser stayed with Angus in the parlour throughout the evening and the entire next day and evening as friends and neighbours filed in to pay their final respects. Later, there would be a vigil through the night and Angus was insistent that he would do it alone; the others would need their rest. Isabelle and the children stayed in the kitchen serving a *strùpag* to the neighbours as they returned from the visitations in the parlour. On several occasions, Isabelle turned a blind if not irritable eye to the *deoch* (drink) that was passed about by James MacGregor, even though she strongly disapproved of such practices. It was not the time for words and she as much as anyone realized that some traditions were hard to break.

She countered this annoyance by focusing her thoughts on the gratitude she felt for the other women who had brought baked goods and offered to stay behind to help with the serving and eventual clean up. There in the kitchen at least, Isabelle felt a comfort.

John would always recall the hushed tones as if everyone was afraid of waking grandmother in the next room. He didn't think that was possible but he too spoke quietly, just in case. At one point, John remembered hearing the lovely mournful strains of Psalm XXIII coming from the parlour as the three elders bade their own farewell to Flora. A few minutes later, he noted how Archie MacDonald had departed so quickly without even bothering to stay for a cup of tea. It seemed strange to him that the old man didn't want to join with the others now seated around the large kitchen table. Isabelle took her son aside and told him quietly that she would explain it all later.

By *Loch Dubh* standards, it was a large funeral in the Kirk and Duncan Fraser spoke glowingly of Flora as a mainstay of the community and of the church, making numerous references to the esteem in which the entire Grant family had always been held. Psalms were sung and prayers offered by the three elders. It appeared to be most difficult for Archie whose voice quivered on more than one occasion. The Reverend Fraser then read from the Gospel according to St. John, Chapter XIV, Verse 27 and, with the closing prayer, came close to tears. Later, at the grave side, he committed Flora Grant to her eternal rest beside her beloved husband Angus and their three children. John was standing next to his father near the head of the grave and immediately adjacent to the stone that bore the names of people he had never known, his grandfather, uncle and two aunts. Soon it would have Flora's added as a final testament to the path she had trod in this place and through this time. As the service was ended, John looked down the length of the coffin before him and beyond, across the loch up to their house that sat on the far hill. His eyes were focused on the upstairs bedroom windows and, for a fleeting moment, he thought he had seen something move. He smiled to himself knowing that it was nothing more than the curtain billowing in the wind. The *cailleach*, his dear *seanamhair*, was not there. She was now at another window that was certainly much higher up. He only hoped that she was smiling down on him and would, one day, thank him for the mayflower.

At this particular time of year, the various fragrances of the garden flowers seemed to dance in the air, cascading over the nose like water over a steep precipice. True, some of the early summer flowers had already made their appearance, having bloomed and now passed from view. But still, in late August, there were many joyful delights waiting to be savoured in Margaret's flower garden. In several ways, she was so much like her late mother; she would sit in the garden for hours on end in absolute awe of God's workmanship. Here she lounged under a crab-apple tree that enveloped her in its shade as if she were an honoured guest seated in a royal box. Just beyond the carpet of green before her was assembled the cast of this majestic play: the sweet williams, the wild flox, the tangerine nasturtiums and many others all in their seemingly prescribed places. Off to the side, she could see a great hoard of multi-coloured chrysanthemums eager for their cue to burst onto the stage. However, in this particular play, timing was everything and they would simply have to wait. Theirs was a fall scene and everything had to be done just so. Like so much of life itself, one should always know one's place.

The flower garden, at the rear of the MacGregor home, was located immediately adjacent to the small vegetable patch that Margaret planted each year. It was one of the few conveniences she granted herself in that it allowed for easy and quick access in preparing meals for the family. But now, her thoughts were not on household chores or even family. James had taken the children down the hill to New Carlisle to shop for pens, ink, copybooks and slate pencils that would be needed for the new school year beginning in a week's time. No doubt, they would be gone for several hours; it was always James' habit to engage Allan Dunn in conversation while the children stayed outside, exploring the area around the wharf and, of course, the fishing boats. At six years of age and youngest of the four, little Albert was always the most excited about these trips to town. He had been named after the late Prince Consort and Margaret loved to refer to him as *mo rìgh beag* (My Little King). She was forever spoiling him so and giving him licence that was hardly ever extended to the other three. He was simply her bairn and, besides, Peter, Charles and Betty always took it all in fine form and humoured their mother about the "wee spoiled thing."

For a few hours at least, Margaret was alone and would spend some time here in the garden without feeling any pangs of guilt for such idleness. Seated there on the soft grass, she slowly raised her head as she gazed beyond the flowers that lay before her, across to the manse and the Kirk in the distance. The church was such an important part of her life and she had an abiding desire to ensure that her children were well grounded and nurtured in the faith. If only James would share her concerns with feeding the soul as much as the body. She knew, all too well, that comments about him flew around *Loch Dubh* like so many wizened maple leaves on the autumn wind. She also recognized that there was very little, if anything, she could do about it. This was her lot in life and she would have to do with it as best she could. There was a resignation about it all.

Even with her beautiful children around her, Margaret carried a constant feeling of being alone. In times of doubt or anguish, she had no one to talk to, no one to whom she could bare her true feelings, her soul. Even she, from time to time, needed comfort and perhaps this is what brought her to the garden to think and, on Sundays, to the Kirk to pray. Margaret looked down at the blade of grass whose soft texture she had been unconsciously caressing between her fingers. *'S e chuir mise an diugh fo bhròn, cuimhneachadh air làithean m'òig'. 'S deòir mo shùilean a' ruith gu làr.* (I am sad today thinking of the days of my youth. The tears from my eyes are streaming to the ground.) At that moment, even she was taken aback by both the plaintive choice and tone of the words spoken almost without thought. Never before had she felt so alone. As a child, she constantly dreamed of far-away places, across the water thousands of miles from *Loch Dubh*. She had soon learned to not speak of such things. Her parents were forever chastising her for such frivolous musings and, even when she first began to see the young MacGregor boy, instructed her as to what she was and was not to do. She was told, in no uncertain terms, that James MacGregor was not worthy of her and must not be associated with, especially in that way. It simply would not be tolerated. Even then, she had a premonition that her life was not to be her own.

It had never been her intention to become with child, even though her parents had accused her of willfully going against their wishes and sinning in the eyes of God. Protestations aside, she and James were married in the Church of England in New Carlisle since the Kirk was still without a minister. That was in the time before the Reverend Fraser. They had set up housekeeping and Peter's arrival eleven years ago was, for her, a blessed event. She resigned herself to the fact that she would never visit those far-off places. That was all in the past as she looked down into the face of her beautiful bairn, someone who loved her; someone who needed her. She sensed that her parents finally, although somewhat begrudgingly, accepted her marriage and their grandson. Perhaps Margaret's selection of name, which also happened to be her father's, had something to do with it. Yet it still haunted her that her parents appeared to carry her shame with them for the rest of their days. Margaret was certain that they both had gone to their graves seeking a peace that they never found on the shores of *Loch Dubh*. Guilt was never far from her.

After Peter's birth, James was never quite the same with her. Of course, they had the farm and eventually, with the passage of years, Peter was joined by three others. James seemed to take comfort in other worldy pleasures while her attention was always on the children and providing a nurturing home for them. At times, she thought that perhaps he felt that he had been robbed of his own younger years all too soon. If so, could he not understand that she also had given up a great deal of her youth to say nothing of her dreams? Did he not realize that her life could have, would have, been quite different? No, he most certainly did not. But then, what did it matter. There was a resignation about it all.

Her thoughts were broken by the sound of the horse's hooves and the laughter of the small ones as James and the children returned from town. She hurriedly made her way to the adjoining garden to pick vegetables for supper, which had been the original point of her outing from the kitchen. The sounds increased in intensity as the horse and wagon finally rounded the corner of the house. "Mamma, Papa bought us each some peppermints and the others have already eaten theirs. I am going to save mine so they will last until school begins. And look at the beautiful copybooks and pens that Peter and Charles have. Betty and I each have two new slate pencils!" Albert was so amusing when he came home from town; there were always a hundred stories to be shared, all in the first minute.

"And what did you purchase for your poor dear mother?" There was a mischievous tone to Margaret's voice that she knew, full well, would create a momentary diversion from the endless stream of excited chatter.

"Papa brought you some salt and sugar for baking, some tea and a big jar of Jamaican molasses as well." Betty had quickly jumped to Albert's rescue, knowing that their mother had earlier made a list of much-needed baking stuffs. Margaret smiled broadly in reassuring the children that this was indeed a fine present and one that she would enjoy. Even now, she still thought of far-away places.

With carrots and turnip cradled in her apron, Margaret moved towards the children as they descended from the back of the wagon. She knew it would be best to go inside to peel the vegetables to be added to the water and soup bone, which had been put on the stove to simmer earlier in the afternoon. The family would have nutritious vegetable soup for supper, complete with the fresh homemade bread she had baked following the noon meal. The children would be allowed a special treat of molasses on bread and tea biscuits after supper, just before she led them in evening worship and then off to their beds.

As she opened the kitchen door waiting for the young ones to join her, she looked back over her shoulder towards the barn where James was busily unloading supplies from the back of the wagon. She took special notice of the fact that he was carrying several large bags into the adjoining hen house for safe keeping. No doubt, she would be alone with the children this evening as he headed off to the woods in pursuit of other solitary enjoyment. They entered the kitchen through the outer porch with its ceiling cluttered with dangling bunches of dried plants and herbs held in reserve for the cooking of meals and dying of cloth that was her future. This, the here and now, was her present, her reality. All that remained was the sound of the screen door slamming closed behind them. She moved forward as thoughts once again came back to haunt her. What did it matter.

From the very beginning, she had never much liked the idea of a boat being named after her. It certainly wasn't that she was vain or even that she might worry about what family or friends might think. All she knew was that she simply should have heeded her initial instincts. And now, ever since the incident of last June, she felt so uncomfortable whenever anyone from *Loch Dubh* came to town. She could feel them looking right through her and she knew well enough that, once her back was turned, they would snicker and talk about her among themselves. Of course, they spoke in that God-awful tongue of theirs that no one could ever make head nor tail of. But still, she knew that she was more often than not the object of their ridicule and it annoyed her to no end.

As postmistress of the New Carlisle Post Office, Annabelle Calvey took her responsibilities very seriously indeed. She was of the view that hers was an extremely important position in the town and liked to believe that she would be given the respect that should be accorded her as a civil servant in the service of the Queen. After all, with the exception of John Oliver who worked part-time throughout the year as a fisheries inspector, she was the only permanent employee of the Dominion government along the length of the North Shore from Englishtown to Ingonish. The Royal Mail was a critical part of the life of this community and offered a valued link between the locals and their relatives and friends who now lived in places so far afield. She was always amazed, carefully inspecting the postmarks on incoming mail: Halifax, Boston, Montreal, Toronto and Winnipeg to name but a few, just how far away some people had moved. Why only last week the Erskine woman from *Loch Dubh* had received a letter from her son, Alasdair she thought his name was, who had recently moved away to Halifax. It was all so sad. Still, it struck her as odd how Mrs. Erskine had so quickly stuffed the letter in her pocket as if she were afraid someone might catch sight of it. But then, those people from up by the lake beyond the bluffs were a breed unto themselves. Thank God for the distance between them.

Her husband George had insisted that his new boat be called after her because, he maintained, as long as her name graced the stern, he would be safe from all harm on the water. The fact that he couldn't swim a stroke had never seemed to cross his mind or, if it had, to cause a moment's worry. The name Annabelle would be sufficient to afford him protection and perhaps even ensure a fine catch. He had made such a convincing case that she could do little else but finally agree to lend her name, somewhat reluctantly, mind you. But if it kept him happy and made him feel any more secure on the rough waters, especially beyond *An Toiseach* and *An Deireadh*, then that was not such a hefty price to pay. There again, it was those meddlesome highlanders who had gone and changed the names of the two islands years ago. Obviously someone in authority had agreed because there they were still in a tongue beyond her comprehension and next to impossible to pronounce. Never mind, she would remain adamant in her refusal to refer to them as anything other than "the islands." She saw nothing wrong with the original names, George and Charlotte, that had been given to the two rocky protrusions by the first loyalists who had settled the area around Ingonish following the rebellion in the thirteen

American colonies over a hundred years before. What better names could have been chosen than those of the King and Queen? But the Scots are such a pushy race, always having to have their own way. God help us if they got it in their heads to move down the hill. Who knows what might happen; New Carlisle could become New Mallaig or some such other queer name. It was best not even to think about it; she did not want to upset herself any further.

Annabelle considered herself most fortunate to occupy the position she did. The post office was her domain and she ruled it as if it were her very own private kingdom. Sure enough, there were printed guidelines for the administration of post offices that had been provided by Ottawa and she always abided by them — well, most of the time anyway. On the odd occasion, she had taken some licence in leaving her counter to go in back to make a cup of tea, when no one was about. The post office, while fronting onto the main street, was actually nothing more than an addition that had been built onto her kitchen at the back of the house. The Calvey home was located immediately behind the main street so the extension allowed her to do both her jobs. All she need do was slip around the partition, with all its numbered pigeon holes, and she was at the kitchen table. It made her life so much more bearable; she could bake a pan of tea biscuits and never be far from her other work. Surely what the officials in Ottawa didn't know wouldn't hurt them one iota.

The proximity of the kitchen also allowed her the luxury of always having a freshly brewed cup of tea in her hand as she went about her duties. It helped her get through the day with a cheery disposition that she felt was so important to her work. Not that she cared what others might think, mind you. Indeed, there were days when the tea came in particularly handy, really more of a necessity than a luxury. From time to time, an envelope or two would arrive in the mail that was half open owing to the normal wear and tear of handling. The steaming heat from the tea would allow her to seal it up as it properly should be. It was passing strange that people could never quite understand how it was the Calvey lady was always so well versed on matters that weren't really her business. Ah, but a good cup of tea offered many insights into the life of a small community such as this. She would just go about her job and mind her own affairs. If there was one thing she could not abide it was gossip.

The north-east winds of early November were blowing in off the water and, for some reason, her mind was cast back to that dreadful day in June when the incident had taken place. It too had been a blustery day, she remembered well, because George and the other fisherman could not go out on the water owing to the strong winds and choppy seas. Instead, they satisfied themselves by sitting on the wharf, exchanging stories and smoking their pipes. She could see them clearly enough from her position behind the counter and wished her George would find something a bit more constructive to do with his time. If he wasn't telling fishing stories on the wharf, he was talking politics in the general store. As far as she was concerned, one smelled as bad as the other. If there was one thing she could not abide it was idleness.

As her George was later to recount the story, he had been speaking with several men, including John Rogers from up near the church, about repairs to the boat that he would soon have to undertake once it was taken out of the water for inspection and general maintenance. Unbeknown to him, Archie MacDonald from *Loch Dubh* was strolling close by with his grandsons, taking the sea breeze while waiting for his daughter-in-law Jessie to finish her shopping. "I tells ya boy, I knows my *Annabelle*'s bottom is in an awful state. I loves her dearly but am thinking that I will have to turn her over and give her a good scraping so as to get rid of all the muck that's stuck to her. I's thinking that she has been far too idle of late and a good scrubbing will do her all the good in the world. Then she'll move along so much quicker and easier all rightie. You marks my words; yes indeed." Archie listened in absolute horror and amazement. The name of George's boat was lost on him as he automatically conjured up the most ghastly images of the postmistress' physical condition and what treatment was about to be befall her.

It had not taken long for the story to be put right but, by that time, Annabelle Calvey's name had become the source of numerous hearty chuckles around *Loch Dubh*. At *céilidhs* and milling frolics, many a head had been bowed and knee bent in mock courtesy as the name of the *Banrigh Shalach* (Soiled/Dirty Queen) was mentioned. Word had eventually gotten back to Annabelle who was devastated just thinking about what went through people's minds when they first entered the post office. Still, she would hold her head high and ignore their insolence. She would never give the highlanders any satisfaction in thinking that she was in the least bit embarrassed. No wonder they had been thrown out of Scotland on their ear. Was not England's gain Cape Breton's loss? If there was one thing she could not abide it was snobbery.

She had just completed sorting the delivery that had arrived on the previous day's steamer as well as the regular mail run that had come up the shore road from Englishtown. As was normally the case, most of the letters and parcels were for the town locals. However, she had noted in passing that there was also the odd piece for the *Loch Dubh* people. There she sat with her cup of hot tea strategically placed nearby as she personally inspected each one so as to ensure that any and all broken seals were properly restored. She thought that such diligence should be rewarded somehow by officials in Ottawa. A suitably embossed certificate with her name on it would look so lovely and impressive on the far wall, just above the writing desk with its bulletin board affixed with a listing of postal rates, a calendar and the schedule for the steamers. In due course, she would make the necessary inquiries, subtly of course.

All thoughts of personal recognition were shattered by the ringing of the bell affixed to the top of the front door, announcing the arrival of yet another customer. As she looked up, Annabelle recognized Ida MacDonald from up the hill, the daughter-in-law of that miserable old Archie who had such a blabbering mouth. "Good day to you Mrs. Calvey. I was just in town to do a bit of shopping next door and thought it best to check to see if there was any mail for the family."

"And good day to yourself, Mrs. MacDonald. I trust that you and the family are keeping well and that you are steering clear of the colds that are now on the go." Annabelle was still quite annoyed with the entire MacDonald clan but, as a professional, was determined to go about her duties in as amicable and efficient a manner as possible. Secretly, she could not care less about their physical state of being; the MacDonalds and all the Scotch people for that matter. "Indeed, I believe that there is a piece of mail for you. Let me check." She turned and looked inside box 494, the one with J. MacDonald written below the number, quickly extracting a single envelope that she passed across the counter to Ida.

"Thank you very much and I would be pleased if you would pass along my greetings to your husband." Ida smiled and, with that, turned and departed the post office leaving Annabelle alone with the resonating sound of the bell filling the room.

"Pass along your greetings indeed!" Annabelle's final words came in a huffed tone as she sensed that the MacDonald woman was being far too condescending and had she not slightly bowed her head before departing? Such impertinence! For that she would eventually get hers in return. If there was one thing she could not abide it was someone who didn't know their place.

The postmistress continued to watch as Ida descended the steps and climbed into the wagon that her father-in-law had now pulled up in front of the main door. She could see her sitting there next to the old man as she carefully opened the envelope and began to read. The next thing she observed was the MacDonald woman leaning into Archie, no doubt sharing a good laugh about Annabelle and the muck on her bottom. The absolute nerve!

Once opened, the envelope had revealed a brief handwritten message. Ida attempted to digest each word and, having finally read it through, leaned into Archie's shoulder in search of support.

Baddeck
October 26, 1899

Dear Father and Mother:
    By the time you read this, we will be on bord a ship going from Quebec to South Afrika.
    We both decided that school was important but it was our duty to sign up and help the queen in fighting the boars.

83

The empire needes us. Besides, *seanair* always says that the MacDonalds will be there to do their part.

We promise to be good soldiers and make you all proud.

Dont be mad or displeased with us. It wont be such a long time until we are back home. Give Catherine, Daniel and Murdoch a big hugg for us.

Love always

Roderick & Andrew

ᛋᚷ Chapter Four ᚷᛋ

O'n là thug thu 'n cuan ort
Bha gruaim air na beannaibh.
Bha snìgh' air na speuraibh
'S bha na reulta gallach.
                    Òran Do Mhac Iain Mhic Sheumais (òran)

The day that you sailed off
The mountains were mourning.
Rain streamed from the heavens
For the stars were weeping.
                    Song to Mac Iain 'ic Sheumais (song)

The sound of the clock's ticking had long since been lost amid the laughter and uproarious exchange of stories taking place around the large wooden table that dominated the kitchen. There was a warmth about it on this night as the frigid north-easterly wind outside provided absolutely no respite for any living creature. The snow buffeted the house as if intent on white washing it free from all blemishes of sin. All the while, the wind whistled around the corners of the building and rattled each window pane in turn with its plaintive cry and incessant knocking, pleading for safe haven in front of the roaring fire in the kitchen stove. It was the perfect sort of night to be indoors, savouring the simple comforts of life and giving thanks for blessings received.

Neil and Iona Erskine had wanted to spend *Oidhche na Calluinn* (Hogmanay/New Year's Eve) at home quietly this year in the company of family. The last week had been such a hectic time for them, given this was the first real Christmas that little Kenneth had been healthy and strong enough to join in the festivities. Iona had taken such joy in seeing the excitement build in his face day by day. Indeed, for the better part of two weeks, it had been a major undertaking to lull him to sleep. She would sit on the edge of his bed for what seemed like hours, reading stories under the glow of the kerosene lamp. Even after sleep had finally claimed him, she would rest awhile, looking down into his tranquil face. God had given him back to her and she knew that words could never begin to express her gratitude. Oftentimes, her thoughts were also of poor Harris Ferguson.

Earlier that evening, Kenneth had joined with the other children of

Loch Dubh in undertaking their own holiday revelry. Although they would not be allowed to stay up much beyond 10:00 p.m., they were free after supper to celebrate in whatever way they wanted. Little Betty MacGregor had been the first to come knocking at the back door in search of him. Her mother Margaret had bundled her up to such an extent that all one could see were the blue eyes peering out from behind the knitted scarf that covered the lower part of her face. Iona knew well enough from the voice that it was a MacGregor; the lilt was so strong and beautiful. No doubt, she would one day grow to become a beautiful singer just like her mother. As she quickly beckoned the child in from the cold, Iona wondered what qualities this wee one would inherit from her father. She then thought better of it, knowing full well that it was not her affair. After all, some things were best left to themselves.

Now properly clothed and well insulated from the wintery air, Kenneth was off hand in hand with Betty to join the other children who had been gathering down at the road. From the kitchen window, Iona kept a watchful eye and could see the younger Urquhart children, Donald and Allan, as well as all the MacDonalds and Grants. They were trudging their way through the deep snow drifts to the large field in front of the Ferguson house, where the small grove of birch and maple trees afforded at least some shelter from the winds roaring across the loch. It did not take long, perhaps five or ten minutes, for a major snowball fight to break out. The MacDonald boys, Daniel and Murdoch, had been quick to choose sides, insisting that they were to be the redcoats while all the others were to be "the Dutchmen." However, much to the chagrin of Clan MacDonald, armistice was soon declared when Morag Ferguson persuaded all the other girls to leave the battlefield, proclaiming this to be nothing more than a stupid and hurtful game.

Efforts had then been quickly channeled into maintaining the truce as they began to work together in building a family of snowmen around which all the children would parade three times in offering season's greetings. With batons quickly fashioned from branches taken from the lower portion of the trees and now held firmly in hand, the young ones encircled the stoic figures, tapping each one on the shoulder as they passed by. *"'S e mo ghuidhe 's mo dhùrachd, Bliadhna mhath ùr; Bliadhna mhath ùr!"* (It is my wish and my prayer — Happy New Year, Happy New Year!) Finally, as even their thick woollen coats proved no match for the bone-chilling cold, the children beat a hasty retreat each to their own homes for a hot drink to be followed soon thereafter by a warm bed. It was only when all the others had passed from sight that Daniel and Murdoch MacDonald covertly returned to the silent family that continued to stand there as peaceful sentries against the frigid winds. The boys did quick work on the unsuspecting figures as heads and bodies were savagely dismantled and returned to the very same field of snow that had shortly before given them life. In leaving the battlefield, Daniel turned to Murdoch and boasted. *"Clann Domhnaill!*

Cha bu réidh dol 'nan còir!" (The MacDonalds! Opposing them would be no easy task!) On that night at least, Clan MacDonald had met with complete victory; the Boers had been well and truly put in their place.

Upon his return, Kenneth had been unbundled and plied with a large cup of hot milk flavoured with cinnamon. It was only then that he was taken upstairs by his mother to be put to bed. The wee *Coinneach Bàn* was too tired to stay awake even to greet his grandparents, although the struggle had been an incredibly valiant one. They always made such a fuss over him. Indeed, it was only moments later that Daniel and Tina arrived, covered from head to foot with a thick layer of snow and ice. Iona thought they created quite an amusing sight but dared not say a word, knowing that it would probably not be well received. Although it had only been a short drive around the end of the loch by horse and sleigh, the winds off the water were now causing heavy drifting on the road that, in the end, had forced Daniel to make several unexpected detours into the side fields. Tina, in particular, was grateful for the warmth of the fire in the kitchen stove that now enveloped her as she stood close rubbing life back into her hands and feet.

Even though a *céilidh* was being held at the community hall, both Neil and Iona had wanted a special evening at home alone with his parents. What with Kenneth's childhood illness, they felt it even more important for him to have a strong sense of family and times together such as these were to be experienced as much as possible. Indeed, by *Loch Dubh* standards, the Erskine clan was exceptionally small and, as a consequence, gatherings at key times of the year were perfect opportunities. This was just such a time. As they sat around the table, Neil thought how good it would be to have his brother Alasdair back with them; he belonged here in *Loch Dubh* and not in far-off Halifax. There had been a chair at the Erskine table that was needlessly empty for too long a time. Had it not always been his younger brother who brought such laughter to the entire family, including his father? Now the room felt eerily silent, even with the wind at the corners of the house and the animated conversation between Iona and Tina at the far end of the table. Neil desperately wanted to resolve the issue but somehow knew that tonight was probably not the time; it would only upset his mother and aggravate his father. Yet Neil felt both a need and a desire to reclaim his brother and, as the eldest, realized that he had a responsibility to somehow make the family whole again. He also appreciated that he would have to choose the moment with extreme care. He knew his father all too well.

Over the past few days, Iona had gone to great lengths to ensure that the table would be set with a host of treats for the evening festivities. On the pantry counter rested several plates that would be served with tea before the twelfth hour arrived: freshly made, raisin bread and sweet biscuits laden with butter and cheese, great mounds of oatcakes, molasses cakes with ginger, sugar cookies, strawberry jam tarts and many other sweets that had kept her by the stove for hours on end. She was well pleased with herself and the fruits of her labour that would soon be laid out before them. With stories in full flight around the table, Iona excused herself and moved to the stove to put the kettle on for tea. She knew from experience that, with the approach of the midnight hour, stronger liquid would soon enough be the order of the day.

True to form, the teapot had been drained in a very short time. Indeed, Iona's almost poetic *"Théid tì a bhreothadh is òlair slugadh dhi."* (We will brew the tea and drink a mouthful of it) had quickly been replaced after the *strùpag* by Neil's rhetorical and somewhat-whimsical question to Daniel. *"Saoil nach gabh thu dram? 'S b'fheàrr dhomh e na tì!"* (Will you not have a drink? It's better than the tea!) Amid the laughter and almost as if by magic, four glasses and a bottle of whisky had suddenly appeared from the top shelf of the pantry cupboard. It was a bottle of fine Scotch whisky that Alasdair had given his brother on the day of Kenneth's birth. Neil and Iona had drank from it sparingly, promising themselves that they would finish it only when the bairn was nurtured back to full health. That time had now come and, regrettably, Alasdair was not with them to help drain the bottle and ceremoniously kiss its smooth glassy bottom.

The glasses were poured and, almost without notice, Daniel was standing looking through the kitchen window towards the far end of the loch. He proposed the customary highland toast to departed friends. Although no names were mentioned, the three figures seated at the table knew that his thoughts were of Flora, *Floiridh Aosda*, who had gone into eternity only six months past. Looking up into his father's face, Neil could not help but wonder why it was that the Celts had such a lingering preoccupation with the dead that oftentimes seemed to overpower their concern for the living; why was Daniel now dwelling on Flora and not Alasdair? At that moment, Neil desperately wanted to confront his father but, instead, found himself joining with his mother and wife in rising to respond. To departed friends!

At least two goodly drams had been poured in all four glasses by the time midnight was duly proclaimed by the clock, sheltered as it was in its gingerbread-styled case on a side table near the dining-room door. It was Neil's turn to rise and propose a toast to the new year and, indeed, the new century that was now upon them. He first toasted family and made a very deliberate reference to the hope that the entire Erskine clan would be richly blessed with health and happiness throughout all their days. If the point had been made, subtly or no, it was not apparent by the blank expression on Daniel's face. Almost without pausing, he once again began to reminisce about years gone by. Neil felt such incredible frustration in wanting his father to look to the future while forced to realize that it was possibly too much to ask of him at his age. Perhaps, he was too much like Flora who now lay cold in her grave.

The sudden and somewhat persistent knock at the back door, while startling everyone around the table, at least succeeded in bringing all thoughts back to the present. Tina's natural reaction had been to suspect the *bòcain;* they were real and evil enough to trouble God-fearing people like themselves even on a night such as this. Neil took a final gulp of whisky before putting the glass down and walking towards the outer porch to investigate. In passing the table, he placed his hand on Iona's shoulder as if to reassure her that it was probably nothing more than the wind rattling the unhinged storm door. All eyes remained fixed on the kitchen door with great curiosity as a sudden and quite hearty laugh emanated from behind in the porch, followed by the pronouncement of a rhyme and the sound of footsteps. Neil was obviously returning with company, but whom? Who could possibly be out and about on a blustery night like this and at such an un-Godly late hour? As the door leading into the kitchen finally opened, Tina let out a shriek of absolute horror that reminded Iona of poor Flora's fright at the Queen's bonfire celebrations several years back. *"Mo Thighearna! 'Se bòcan a th' ann. 'Se bòcan a th' ann."* (My Lord! It's a ghost. It's a ghost.) To everyone's amazement, behind Neil stood a tall smiling figure with the blackest of faces that only served to accentuate the contrasting whiteness of the eyes and teeth. The figure continued to smile at them in a way that was mischievous and yet somehow knowing.

"Latha mhath dhuit agus Bliadhna mhath ùr." (Good day to you and Happy New Year.) The *bòchdan* spoke the Gaelic perfectly and with hardly a trace of an accent. They were truly the work of the devil himself. It was perhaps no longer than a few seconds before everyone recognized the *bòcan* as none other than James MacGregor. He was later to recount how, upon departing the *céilidh* on the far side of the loch, he had seen a light at the Erskine house and was determined to be the first-footer across their threshold. Armed with a jug of whisky and a few oatmeal scones pilfered from the hall's tea table, he had prepared himself well by blackening his face with a lump of coal that now rested in his pocket. With dark hair and matching face, he and his symbolic gifts were a sure sign that an abundance of food, drink and fuel would grace the Erskine house throughout the coming year.

As he staggered in, James still had enough wits about him to know that he would have to make three circles around the table; the Trinity would be called upon to bless the good fortune that he brought. As he went along, he made a point of replenishing each of the four glasses on the table from the jug lovingly cradled in his arms. *"Tha buaidh air an uisge bheatha. Òlaidh sinn drama."* (A dram of whisky has influence / is good for you. We'll drink a dram.) Tina shot him a look that, had he been an actual *bòcan*, would most assuredly have put the fear of God into him. Dastardly appearances aside, he was finally offered a polite welcome and a place at the table, even though she still looked somewhat offended, almost preferring that it had been a ghost. By this time, Tina had succeeded in quieting herself and now proceeded to half jokingly scold him as *"A Sheumais, mac-an-diabhoil dhuibh."* (James, Son of the Black Devil) She eventually forced a laugh and an admission that the first-footer was a true and valued sign of good luck and fortune for the coming year. He would probably always be the *caora bhrogach Loch Dhuibh* (The Black-faced Sheep of *Loch Dubh*) but, still in all, should be treated with some respect, at least for tonight.

With the blessings of the Trinity now assured, James joined them at the table and a fifth glass was quickly retrieved from the pantry cupboard. The conversation carried on for quite some time until all agreed that the new year had been well and truly christened. At times, it seemed that the coal dust on James' blackened face disguised something more, something greater. On several occasions in his drunken state, he had mentioned how much it meant to him to be greeted, at least on this one night of the year, as a welcomed guest and friend. He then rose somewhat unsteadily from the table with jug once again securely in hand and wished a final good health and fortune upon the Erskine family. With that, he was gone to once again blend into the dark night from where he had come as if he had never truly existed. Tina looked at the back door through which he had passed and hoped that the blowing snow might rid MacGregor of his blackened face if not his evil habit of overindulgence with the drink. For his part, Neil thought it somewhat ironic that the man had made a determined effort to come and bring greetings to the Erskine home while, in all likelihood, ignoring his own. It was a pity but what could one do. Neil's hope was that health and fortune would indeed fall upon his family in this new year, making it whole once again.

When they took time to stop and actually think about it, it seemed terribly strange to be sitting outdoors in early February in short-sleeve shirts. Both Andrew and Rod were seated on a log just outside the mess tent where the noon meal was being served. It was a well-deserved break from the long days of intense training that the Canadian troops had been undergoing since first arriving in South Africa. They had almost become accustomed to the food, although it had taken some considerable getting used to. They often thought of the meals that their mother served at this time of year around the large kitchen table back home. What they wouldn't give right then for a large plate of *maragan* (oatmeal and suet sausages/puddings), complete with potatoes, carrots and turnip from the storage bins in the root cellar. It was only then that it dawned on Andrew just how long they had been away from home, almost four months. He knew full well that, while the time had gone by quickly for both him and Rod, it must seem like an eternity for his parents and the small ones in *Loch Dubh*. It was just that everything had happened so suddenly and there had been little time for explanations. What thoughts must be going through their minds. Would they be proud or ashamed of their sons and brothers for having gone off without proper notice and farewell? Andrew could not concentrate on his food, if one wanted to call it that. As he placed his seemingly battle-scarred plate on the parched ground before him, he was back by the loch with the brooding and ever-protective *Beinn-mo-Mhulaid* rising up, linking the deep black waters with the bright blue skies. At that moment, he had a greater appreciation of the fact that, at least for him, the mountain of sorrows was such a misnomer. He saw it as a mountain of great happiness. Even here in nothing more than mere memories, it gave him a sense of presence and attachment to something far greater than himself. He knew that that was where he belonged and he desperately wanted to be under its watchful gaze once again. He would not say as much to Rod, at least not now, but he longed to be home.

It had been a mild autumn day in mid-October when Rod first raised the idea with him. He recalled that classes had just ended for the day as they left the academy for home. It was then that the distraction came; the call of destiny as Rod would later call it. From somewhere further, down the hill towards the bay, came the sound of pipes. Both boys recognized *Highland Laddie* because it was a tune sometimes played by Daniel Erskine back home, even though it was quite dissimilar in style and cadence from the step-dancing tunes that he played at *céilidhs* and milling frolics. Still in all, the old man admitted to the fact that he enjoyed its rhythm even if it was, according to him, nothing more than musical concoction for use by the regimental bands of the English Queen. Clan Erskine's royal animosities aside, the tune had become a favourite of the boys' mother who always cried when she heard it. She claimed to have hummed it a million times to her own wee lads in the cradle. She had always maintained that it had been the one sure way of lulling them into sleep, after a time anyway.

Andrew and Rod followed the sound down the hill; the music became louder and louder as they grew closer to the shore away from the main street. Soon enough, they found themselves in front of the Baddeck armoury as the band of the 94th Victoria Battalion of Infantry, Argyll Highlanders, marched on parade before its regimental headquarters. The boys had often heard Daniel Erskine play the great highland pipe on his own but a full band was a new and stirring experience for them. They stood there almost in awe, watching and listening to the band as it marched and counter-marched in front of the building's large wooden doors. Inside on the dimly lit parade square, several young men could be seen standing in a single rank as a uniformed officer, with a sort of cane tucked under his arm, walked back and forth before them. Even to the two boys, it was apparent that these were fresh new recruits in the process of receiving their induction orders. No doubt, they had taken the oath to defend Queen and Empire and were, even now, preparing themselves for duty overseas in the service of their sovereign. Cape Breton was their home and their Queen resided in London but, obviously, their duty lay in the distant veldts of South Africa.

Originally, it had been Rod's idea to approach the recruiting officer, simply to make subtle inquiries as to what "service" entailed. Andrew had been adverse to even this, knowing full well that his brother was prone to romantic notions and, more importantly, that their parents would never agree to such foolishness. But Rod was also persuasive; did not his mother always maintain that he could charm the birds from the trees? It had been only after some considerable discussion later that evening during their studies that Andrew had finally agreed to accompany his brother and speak to the recruiting officer just to appease him and his incessant sense of curiosity. But that was to be all — talk and nothing more.

The office was little more than a large closet whose walls were lined with bits of military paraphernalia, including several illustrations of high-land regiments in full battle formation. As he pointed out each one in turn, Captain Iain Matheson expressed great pleasure in the boys' interest and was somewhat less than subtle in encouraging them to consider becoming "Soldiers of the Queen". After all, the skirmish in South Africa would be over in no time at all and it would be an ideal way for Andrew and Rod to go abroad as boys and return from battle as men, as had their ancestors for centuries before them. It was only by mere chance that the commanding officer, a Colonel Bethune, was passing by and overheard the conversation taking place. Bethune entered the room, introduced himself and, in the course of the ensuing conversation, quite skillfully and purposefully pointed out that his family was a sept of Clan Donald. He said that he would be personally honoured and proud to have his fellow clansmen in the regiment. He then went on to recount how he had just, earlier that same week, welcomed a young John MacDonald from St. Anns whom he described as a fine specimen of a man destined to become a great soldier. The point was as calculating as it was well made; both Andrew and Rod would be in good company. With that, he shook their hands, wished them a good day and, with a clicking of the heels, was gone. However, the smile on his face was unmistaken proof that he believed seeds had been well and truly sown.

As they lay in bed that night, it was Rod who continued to make the case advanced by both the captain and colonel earlier in the day. Why should they not sign up? Others were signing up and they would come back as heroes, especially in the eyes of every girl from Cheticamp to Sydney to St. Peter's. Besides, they would be gone only a few months, back in plenty of time to help their father with the summer harvest and hay making before resuming their studies next fall. They would simply come back and pick up where they had left off. Andrew was not easily convinced by the argument, subtle or no, and for that reason was doubly surprised by Rod's sudden announcement that he had already made up his mind and would return the next day to enlist. That night, long after Rod had fallen asleep, it was left to Andrew to decide if he would allow his brother to go off on his own or whether they would stay together as had always been the case. With the first light of dawn streaming through the bedroom window, Andrew lay in bed wide awake with his thoughts and growing uncertainties.

Both Andrew and Rod were back in Captain Matheson's office the next afternoon to sign the necessary documents that would make them soldiers in the service of Her Majesty. They were to report for duty the following Monday and would be taken, with nine other recruits, up country to a farm at *An Abhainn Mheadhonach* (Middle River) for some initial training and parade drill. It had been an agonizing decision for Andrew whose final decision rested on the hoped for understanding that, even though they would likely be opposed to the idea, his parents would take some comfort in knowing that they had stayed together to take care of one another. And perhaps, after all, Rod was right; perhaps they would be back soon enough to resume their studies and their lives.

The boys had agreed between themselves that they would inform Elizabeth Urquhart that they were needed at home for a week to help their father with the building of a new barn. The story would be a convincing one with a heavy measure of persuasive details added for effect. On Friday afternoon, they made a point of walking Elizabeth home and told her of the plans for the new structure that was to be built before the first snow. From all outward appearances, it seemed that she suspected nothing, having asked a few polite questions in passing and then moving the conversation on in other directions. It was only several minutes later, when she asked if they would be kind enough to carry a letter back to her parents, that they realized just how convincing their fraudulent story had been. Both boys felt badly about lying to her but were forced to accept the fact that it was the only way to ensure complete secrecy. They would write to Elizabeth later and apologize for having taken such blatant advantage. They were confident that, with the passage of time, she too would understand. She was, after all, their friend.

Even during their week of training and constant drill in a farmer's field, Andrew continued to harbour second thoughts and questioned the wisdom of their decision. Would their parents be forgiving when they returned? Would Elizabeth be annoyed with them for having used her in such a devious manner? Would they be considered heroes or just foolish irresponsible boys who chose to ignore their studies while others were at home working diligently on the farm? Andrew was troubled by these and other questions but knew deep down that his greater responsibility rested with his brother. They would remain together and see this through. He hoped Rod was right. He hoped it would all work out in the end.

The morning they were scheduled to leave by ferry for Grand Narrows to link up with the Inter-colonial Railway bound for Halifax, the boys had written a letter to their parents explaining what they had done and trusting they would find it in their hearts to understand. Both this letter and the one from Elizabeth to her parents were posted at the same time. It would take the better part of three days for them to reach *Loch Dubh* and, by then, the new recruits would be long gone. As they departed, Andrew and Roderick MacDonald were both conscious and proud of the fact that they would soon become members of the 2nd (Special Service) Battalion of the Royal Canadian Regiment of Infantry en route to Halifax, Quebec and South Africa. Once in the provincial capital, they were to be joined by other recruits who, Andrew and Rod were quick to discover, may have shared their enthusiasm but also shared their ignorance of military routine and lack of any real training. The ongoing assumption was that this would come in time. For the moment at least, this did not seem to matter a great deal; the maple leaf insignia now emblazoned on their uniforms, they knew they would do both Her Majesty and Canada proud. In those early days of service, there was more than one prayer that their family would see it in their hearts to share this pride.

By the time they reached Quebec in late October, both boys had been caught up in the excitement of the "crusade", as some people now referred to it, upon which they were about to embark. The ship, which would take them across the Atlantic, was the *S.S. Sardinian*. It was a vessel not necessarily renowned for its luxurious features. In fact, Andrew and Rod had been told that the thousand or so men were being transported in a converted cattle boat. As a lark, some soldiers had renamed it "the sardine". Andrew and Rod laughed aloud when thinking about what the people of *Loch Dubh* might end up calling them upon their return; perhaps *sardine na banrigh* (A Sardine of the Queen) and not *saighdear na banrigh*. (A Soldier of the Queen) They knew all too well the sharp wit of their friends and neighbours back home. The MacDonald boys would most assuredly be on the receiving end of many a light-hearted barb and playful quip. In the end, the Sardines of the Queen would take no offence and accept such treatment with all good humour.

Although a lengthy voyage on a cattle boat did not seem to be an auspicious beginning to their military careers, the boys knew that they would be back on solid land soon enough. Indeed, it was the better part of a month later that the *S.S. Sardinian* glided into Cape Town harbour to be welcomed by hundreds of people waving Union Jacks as a brass band played its heart out in attempting to further incite patriotic fervour among the crowd. The sight of the flags made the boys think back to the Queen's birthday celebrations on the bluffs a few years ago. This memory of *Loch Dubh* was somehow comforting and, for the first time, even Rod admitted to being a bit homesick.

The first Christmas away from their family found the MacDonald boys finally receiving the long-anticipated training they would require. At an outpost camp near Belmont, they passed the holiday season being taught drill, rifle practice and all sorts of battle exercises under the constant and watchful gaze of a stern-looking sergeant. The training was rigorous enough but the boys had an advantage in that they were more than accustomed to hard work on the farm. The real challenge was adapting to the weather; during the day the soldiers sweltered in frightful heat and at night shivered in freezing cold. "Belmont dust bin", as it was soon named, became renowned for its poor food, lack of water and endless hordes of lice. Every "Soldier of the Queen" was eager to serve but even more eager to escape the hell hole that had now been their home for two long months. It was, therefore, with a great deal of relief that word had begun to spread throughout the camp in early February that the 2nd Battalion would soon be moved north for its first official engagement with the enemy.

Throughout this time, the boys had been quite faithful in writing home every two weeks or so, taking turns at holding the pen. They dared not mention the dismal conditions of the Belmont camp knowing full well that it would cause their mother no end of worry. Instead, they focused on the excellent training they were receiving along with the other Cape Bretoners who were in service with them. They had grown particularly close to both John MacDonald from St. Anns and his first cousin George Buchanan from *Cobh a' Gheòidh*. (Goose Cove) Together, the four of them had sung Christmas carols in the Gaelic and organized an impromptu Hogmanay *céilidh*, just like the ones that were always held in the *Loch Dubh* hall. It gave them a sense of attachment that they dearly missed, especially at that time of year when families would make a special effort to gather together. One evening, they joined hands and sang several Gaelic ballads, including a North Shore milling song — *Ged A Sheòl Mi Air M'Aineol*. (*Though I Sailed to Unknown Places*) They swung their arms back and forth and beat time as if the cloth was in front of them on a coarse wooden table. The odd perplexing and sometimes disparaging look bedamned, the singing brought them closer to each other and, in a strange sort of way, to the mountains and lochs of Cape Breton. Next year would be different; Andrew and Rod would return to the dark waters and the lofty mountains that were *Loch Dubh*. God would see them home for they were MacDonald men and knew well their clan motto: *Tha mo dhòchas daonnan annadsa*. (My hope is constant in thee.) And so it would be.

✦✦✦✦

The pungent smell of wet wool hung in the air, mixed with the lingering traces of smoke that continued to escape from the pot-bellied stove in the middle of the room. The woollen mittens were long since dried by the heat of the fire that roared throughout the day. Those very same mittens were even now on their way home and, no doubt, becoming drenched once again as their owners engaged in the many pleasures that awaited them in the snow banks and drifts formed along the edges of the road. The odor would bide for many hours yet and it would be only the still cold air of the approaching weekend that would finally drive it from the room. This earthy incense had become a regular routine that was every bit as predictable as the sun cascading over *Beinn-mo-Mhulaid* or, worse still, the icy winds that so often raced across the surface of the loch.

Kristy MacNeil sat behind her desk at the head of the classroom looking down the five rows of desks towards the double doors at the far end. The wooden pegs, which until a few moments earlier had been blanketed with a host of scarves, hats and coats, rested forlornly in the far corner, ignored and all but forgotten until next Monday morning when they would once again feel the caress of tiny hands. The stillness of the room brought home to Kristy the fact that she herself was not unlike those very pegs. She knew that her role as teacher was an important one in the community, almost as highly regarded as the clergy. At least, this was the case from Monday to Friday. It was on weekends that she felt most alone and in need of reassurance. Her students were obviously a large part of her life and now they were taken away from her. They were her link to the larger community in which she so desperately wanted to feel at home. It wasn't that she didn't try or even that she disliked *Loch Dubh* or its people. No, it was not that. Rather, the truth was that she could not escape the realization that, beneath it all, she remained an outsider who seemingly would never be totally accepted by the locals as one of their own. Among other things, she was "from away."

As she rose to tidy her desk before leaving, she picked up her leather-bound copy of Robert Louis Stephenson's **Robinson Crusoe** and slipped it into her satchel. It was her custom to treat the children to a special reading of a chapter each Friday afternoon at end of day. At the outset, it had taken her some time to convince the younger ones that Mr. Crusoe and Mr. Friday were not actually living on *An Toiseach* or *An Deireadh*. Their island was a little further off and she had been diligent in assuring the wee ones that there was really no need for their mothers to make a *bannoch* (tea-biscuit bread) or other baked goods to take to them. Not wanting to ridicule their heart-felt concern, Kristy calmed the children's fears by informing them that the two men were doing just fine. The children had no reason to suspect that, when Miss MacNeil turned her back on them to write on the board, she was actually biting her lip and making quite a valiant attempt to stifle a chuckle.

Kristy placed her pen and ink bottle in the satchel along with some papers that would need grading over the next few days. In so doing, she was reminded of the time that winter day when she had unknowingly left a bottle of ink in the desk drawer on Friday afternoon, only to find it frozen solid on the following Monday morning. She had learned her lesson well and had never repeated the mistake. Her first winter in *Loch Dubh*; was it really possible that it had been more than three years since she first arrived here? It didn't seem possible and yet, as she looked out over the empty desks and chairs, she realized that she had already been witness to children growing up before her and moving on, not only from grade to grade, but also from this school to academies elsewhere, far from *Loch Dubh*. In particular, she thought of Elizabeth Urquhart in Baddeck and the MacDonald boys who were now in uniform much farther removed from this place. She continued to feel their presence here even as she gazed out at the empty seats before her. Kristy promised herself that a special novena would be said that night for Andrew and Rod. The prayer would be carried over the next nine days up to the feast day of Saint Matthias who would be certain to watch over them as well. She had every confidence; if nothing else, she was a woman of faith.

It still seemed strange to Kristy to speak of saints and *Loch Dubh* in the same breath. After all, it was such a Calvinist setting, especially for a woman of the Roman faith from clear across the other side of Cape Breton. As she did a final inspection of the room, now proceeding down each aisle picking up copies of **The Royal Reader**, she thought of her home in Christmas Island, or *Eilean Na Nollaig* as it was still known to the older people. It was so far away in terms of geography and yet even farther in some other respects. She thought it strange that God had brought her to this place of all places and she still wondered, after all this time, what His plan for her might be. But then, she thought it best not to dwell upon it and just let matters unfold as they most assuredly would. No point would be served in troubling herself further.

At twenty-one years of age, Kristy felt as though she has already seen and experienced so much of life. As long as she could remember, she had wanted to be a teacher and her parents had struggled on the farm to skimp and save in order to send her off to the academy in Sydney. It had been a proud moment for her family when she passed her final gruelling exam and was awarded a certificate from the Province of Nova Scotia education officials. She wanted to teach in a small school where she would be able to use her Gaelic as well as English, be it sanctioned or not. Of course it was not but to her it was of no consequence. To her dying day, she would always remember how her father, in sending her off for higher education in the big English city, had begged her: *"Ged shiubhladh sibh deas no tuath, na leigibh suas a'Ghàidhlig."* (Though you should go north or south, do not give up the Gaelic.) She assured him and herself that this would be the case and she was nothing if not true to her word. As fate would have it, only two rural school openings had been identified for her consideration that summer by officials: Dunvegan on the west side of the island near Inverness and *Loch Dubh* on the North Shore. After lengthy discussions with her parents, Kristy had decided on the latter given that it afforded easy access by steamer from Sydney and, besides, there would be distant cousins to visit in nearby Ingonish. It would be an auspicious start to her career, she had no doubts.

She had subsequently been informed by education officials that tentative arrangements had been made for her to be billeted with an Erskine family, who lived relatively close to the school. It was later, in a letter from Daniel and Tina, that Kristy learned that the two Erskine sons were grown, although the younger one still resided at home. There were several spare bedrooms so space was not an issue; they would certainly enjoy the extra company. Tina had even gone so far as to add a special note at the bottom of the letter stating that it would be a welcomed change to have another woman in the house! With room and board secured, the sixty-dollar-a-year salary appeared to be quite an acceptable arrangement. By early August, Kristy had forwarded a notification of acceptance to the authorities and a letter of thanks to the Erskines for their generous offer of hospitality.

On the day that she left home to begin her new life in the teaching profession, Kristy was subjected to a tearful farewell as she and her parents waited for the Sydney coach to pull up at their gate. The wind off the lake put up a valiant effort in competing for her attention but she would never forget her mother's parting words to mind her prayers and attend mass each day. As long as she remained close to God, He would remain close to her. *"Is tìm bhith nas tric ag ùrnaigh agus a' leanadh dlùth ri Dia."* (Now is the time for frequent prayer, keeping close to God.) It was only much later, when she was settling herself in *Loch Dubh*, that she discovered the new crucifix and rosary beads that had been secretly place at the bottom of her carpet bag. She was later to learn that they had been purchased in Antigonish and personally blessed by the bishop himself. Her parents knew that they would serve her well in her new home and that the parish priest would be there to help guide and watch over her.

As the steamer made its final approach to New Carlisle, Kristy stood on the bow admiring the beauty of the church rising ever higher on the point of land before her. She thought how wonderful it would be to attend mass here on the very edge of the Atlantic Ocean. The Isle of Barra was just "over the waters" to the east and, here in *Loch Dubh*, she would have a sense of communion with her ancestors on that distant shore. As the vessel began its final approach, Daniel and Tina moved onto the wharf in order to be well positioned to offer a proper greeting. Shortly after the customary pleasantries had been exchanged, both of them could not mask their surprise when forced to respond to one of their new boarder's many questions. It concerned the times of mass and the hearing of confession. They looked at each other and, following the most pregnant of pauses, very matter of factly explained that this was New Carlisle not *Loch Dubh* and that that was the Church of England, the Queen's church. The word "Queen" had been intentionally emphasized, although for a reason Kristy still did not fully understand. She would always remember the strange feeling in the pit of her stomach as she sat in the back of the wagon while the Erskines rode in the front seat, leaning into each other and softly whispering. In the relative silence that ensued, the clopping of the horse's hooves echoed in her ears as she first folded her hands in her lap and then promised herself she would be happy here regardless. She would. The hushed tones continued as they rode up the bluffs together with *Loch Dubh* drawing ever near.

Kristy clearly recalled the drive up the winding hill and rounding the final bend in the road at the very top. Her eyes settled on the community of *Loch Dubh* that spread out before her for the first time like so many toy buildings plunked down on an immense green blanket. It appeared so peaceful, as if God had intentionally tucked it back here in the hollow of these mountains away from the hustle and bustle of the rest of the world. At the far end of the loch, resting in the shadow of the large mountain, was yet another beautiful white church. This time, as she began to point to its tall steeple, her question was anticipated and greeted with the terse statement that no masses were held there, just the celebration of God and of His gift of salvation to His flock. The rather direct and cold tone of Daniel's response ensured that the remainder of the journey was conducted in absolute silence. It was shortly after their arrival at the house that she was escorted inside by Tina, who introduced her to their nineteen-year-old "bairn" Alasdair. However, as they entered through the porch door, Daniel could be heard informing his wife that he would be off to visit the manse. Whatever that might be, Kristy did not know. She was not at all familiar with the term and would not venture to ask what might well be yet another provocative question resulting in an equally stern reply.

Even now, with the passage of time, Kristy was still very conscious of removing the crucifix from above her bed each morning and placing it back in the carpet bag in the closet. The original plain wooden cross would then be returned to its place and only she would ever be the wiser. With the exception of grace at meal time and the private family worship each evening, religious matters were never discussed. Having said this, there was one particular evening when Kristy had overheard Daniel suggest to Tina that they offer a special prayer that God might save the souls of the lost with the invocation "*Treigeadh an t-aingidh a' shlìghe chlaon.*" (Let the wicked quit his/her perverted way.) Kristy somehow knew that it was she who had figured largely in these thoughts on that particular night. And yet, a counter statement had also been made in the most subtle of ways. Tina's response to her husband had been as brisk as it was telling and comforting. "*Ni sealbh an rud as còir.*" (Providence will do justice.) For some reason, the smile on Kristy's face told her that a special bond was slowly developing between herself and Tina. At the same time, she knew that a Calvinist prayer would do her no real harm, right enough. But still, she would be obedient to her mother's commandment and continue to pray with her rosary every night under the crucifix. Although she longed to attend mass, it would only be on the occasional end-of-week trip to visit her cousins up the shore road in Ingonish that she would receive the sacraments. Surely God would understand her plight of delinquency and hear her confessions regardless of where she knelt in prayer, even in the Erskine bedroom.

It had not taken Kristy long to adapt to her new environment. Most of the highland ways and traditions of *Loch Dubh* were much the same as the ones back in Christmas Island, many of them anyway. She had come to know all the families, through school visitations at report card time and other occasions. Soon she was quite at ease with the community and knew everyone by first and last names. The most stressful time for her had undoubtedly come when speaking with the Reverend and Mrs. Fraser about their children's academic performance. Initially, she sensed that she was being looked upon as a lost soul in need of salvation — *a' chaora bhrogach* (The Black-faced Sheep), which had become an all-too-common expression. However, in time, she even managed to feel a bit at ease with the Reverend Fraser who she discovered shared her love of Gaelic poetry, Scottish history and classical literature. On this plain at least, they were of the same faith.

On one issue, there was never any doubt; Kristy had eventually been accepted by the community as a kind and considerate teacher. All the children spoke highly of her and every attempt was made to include her in their social gatherings, Kirk functions being the obvious exception. In particular, she loved the *céilidhs* and milling frolics that were held from time to time in the hall. She quite enjoyed walking the short distance up the road in the company of Daniel, Tina and Alasdair. While she would occasionally help out at the tea table, Kristy was invariably drawn to the circle of women who would always start in on the milling songs. She and Margaret MacGregor, the one with the wonderful voice, became fast friends and Kristy took great delight in teaching them several songs that were unique to the area around Christmas Island. But more than anything else, she was drawn to the dance floor whenever the fiddle or the pipe began to fill the room with their seductive melodies. How she loved the lilting sounds in her ears as she whirled around the room, more often than not on Alasdair's arm.

Having locked the school doors behind her for the weekend, Kristy crept down the icy steps, glancing at her feet as she proceeded along the channeled path that led to the loch road. There she stopped momentarily to draw in a deep breath of the sharp clear air before turning right into the road in the direction of the Erskine home. Invariably, Tina would be sitting at the kitchen table with a large pot of freshly made tea at the ready. It had now become a bit of a ritual that Kristy looked forward to and enjoyed immensely. There would be a good chat over tea and sweets and the house would be warm and comforting after her brisk walk in the biting cold. And yet, there would still be a coolness to it; Alasdair would not be there. Even with the passage of several months, she realized that her longing for him had not diminished. In fact, it continued to grow in intensity. Tonight, she would say a special prayer for the prodigal son with the hope that he too would eventually return and be welcomed with open arms. *"Och Alasdair, 's tric a chì mi thu nam shuain."* (Oh Alasdair, often I see you in my sleep.) Seldom before had she felt such a coolness on her bones.

Saturday, February 24 was a day that Archie would well remember for as long as God saw fit to keep him here in his temporal home. Not that he was prone to pride of course; was it not well known that the prouder the man the vainer the heart? No, he would recall this time with great thanksgiving for the blessings that the Almighty had showered upon him and he would be glad of it. Even the cold air blowing off the loch would not lessen the warmth of his spirits. Today of all days, he saw beauty in all God's creation and in all things that He in His infinite wisdom and mercy bestowed upon His people. There was indeed an undeniable warmth.

There had been no reason for Archie to believe that it would be anything other than the regular monthly meeting of session. The three elders, Angus Grant, Daniel Erskine and himself as clerk, had gathered with the Reverend Fraser in the parlour of the manse to undertake the important work of the Kirk. As they arrived, Jennie had just finished her task by placing a large pot of tea, cups and a plate of sweets on the front table. She did not linger long given that their business was to be conducted in absolute privacy, as was the well-honoured and, indeed, prescribed way. It was only as the meeting drew to a close two hours later that Duncan Fraser first sought indulgence from the chair in deviating from the established agenda and then requested the permission of members in raising an important subject. Very matter of factly, he informed them that it was an issue that had been brought to his personal attention and warranted the immediate attention of session. As chairman, the clerk proceeded to oblige by dutifully offering the floor to the minister while the other two elders sat back in their chairs, as if somehow fully anticipating what was about to unfold.

The following Monday would mark Archibald MacDonald's twenty-fifth anniversary as clerk of session and also the thirty-second of his election as elder. Reaching behind him to the small table where sermons had been prepared over many years, Duncan picked up a small brown envelope and walked across the room to stand immediately in front of the clerk. On behalf of session and the entire congregation, the minister expressed deepest satisfaction with God's gift to them of Archie's leadership over several decades and prayed that it would continue for many more, guided by the wisdom and strength that his Saviour had seen fit to bestow upon him. He went on to indicate his great pleasure in presenting Archie with a black leather-bound Bible, in the Gaelic of course, that had been duly inscribed by all three men. It had been last September that the minister had first written to the "Ladies of Edinburgh", a missionary society located in the Scottish capital, and they had eagerly and most generously provided a Bible at no cost to the congregation. It was, after all, a momentous time in both the life of the church and this God-fearing man.

Archie rose slowly almost hesitantly and, with tears welling up in his eyes, thanked the minister and his two colleagues for the gift that he would treasure always and for the honour of serving with them. Later, he would recall looking towards Daniel and Angus who had both been aware of the secret and whose faces were awash with broad knowing smiles. Although words of thanks did not seem sufficient, Archie tried in his own understated way to express his gratitude to them for their support over the years in guiding the work of the Kirk. It was only then that the meeting was finally closed in prayer as they asked Almighty God to grant them His providence in the work that still lay ahead.

Daniel and Angus were the first to depart while Archie remained behind for a few minutes longer to have a private word with Duncan. He told the minister that he felt unworthy of such generosity and that he was truly humbled by their kind words about him. He was doing only what he had been called to do and was honoured to serve in the company of such pious righteous men. The minister placed his hand on Archie's shoulder, smiled and asked if they might have a private prayer together, just the two of them. While there was mention made of Archie as a man of steadfast love and faithful witness, there was also a very personal reference to him as a devoted father, grandfather and friend. It was a prayer that would be engraved in the clerk's memory for many years to come, of that he had no doubts. Seldom before had Archie heard words spoken so clearly. On his way through the kitchen, he thanked Jennie for the lovely *strùpag* and she, in turn, extended her sincere congratulations. He recalled the blood rushing to his face as he made his way out the back door to the horse and sleigh that were tied to the casement covering the stone well.

It was a glorious ride by the loch with the sun beaming down on the snow, making the fields appear ever so luminous in the late-afternoon light. He passed the MacGregor children playing in the front field and gave them a knowing wave of the hand. No doubt, he would see them and their mother in Kirk tomorrow. Archie was deep in thought and at peace with himself as the horse continued to pick up its pace heading down the road for home. It was only as he neared Angus and Isabelle Grant's home, the old homestead up on the hill to the left, that his concentration was suddenly and quite unexpectedly broken.

Directly ahead lay the MacDonald home where he still lived, now with his daughter-in-law Jessie and her four children. Dear Malcolm had already been dead for almost four years. As a man of deep faith, Archie had mourned the terrible and quite tragic loss of his eldest son but always sought solace in the knowledge that he was with his mother and other family members in their eternal home. Although there was the odd gust of bone-chilling wind on his face, he felt comforted. And still farther off in the distance was John and Ida's house high up on the adjoining hill. Yet it was not the view that broke his train of thought. It was the sound. He heard the unmistakable sound of the great highland pipe coming from John's place and it struck him as quite odd that Daniel, who was the only piper in *Loch Dubh*, would have so quickly gone home and now be visiting the MacDonalds, especially having just come from a meeting of session. Not that he knew his music well, but Archie thought it reminded him of that tune that Ida had always hummed to the twins to coerce them into sleep. Even with the distance, it sounded so familiar. With curiosity upon him, he steered the horse away from its intended course and continued down the loch road to investigate further.

The pipe grew louder and louder as the horse and sleigh turned off the road into the laneway leading up the hill to the house. After tying the horse to the side of the barn, he turned and proceeded across the yard to the porch door. It was only then that he realized the music had abruptly stopped. There was an eerie silence that was shattered only by the crunching of snow under his feet. Perhaps Ida was serving a cup of tea and Daniel was partaking of yet another *strùpag*. He promised himself that he would tease poor Tina tomorrow after Kirk for not giving her husband enough sustenance at home; he was forced to go visiting other homes in search of sufficient nourishment. As always, she would surely fain horror at the thought and admonish him with a slap on the arm and her well-known yet kindly words of reprimand for the benefit of all within earshot: *Ud. Ud. Nach e a tha dona!* (Tut. Tut. Is he not a mischievous one!) There, in the shadow of the tall steeple, it would all be given and taken in a spirit of good-natured fun.

As Archie entered the kitchen, he found it completely empty except for the young Murdoch who was lying on the floor in front of the kitchen stove engrossed in a picture book. With a look of both delight and surprise, the child ran to his grandfather and hugged one of his gangly legs in greeting. *"A Sheanair, ciamar a tha thu? A bheil thu fuar? Tha teas anns an teine"* (Grandfather, how are you? Are you cold? There is heat in the fire.) Archie looked down into the concerned little face and calmly assured him that he was indeed not yet completely frozen but that he could not stay long, even with the luxurious heat flooding from the stove. He had merely dropped by to check on the family to see that all was well. Hearing the conversation from afar, Ida soon appeared from upstairs where she had been busily readying the children's clothing for the Sabbath. She smiled at Archie, somewhat taken aback by the unexpected nature of the late-afternoon visit, and discretely inquired as to whether anything was wrong. He calmly assured her that there was not and, in quickly concocting a story, said that he had only wanted to speak to John about the horse. It was not urgent and could wait; he would talk to his son after service tomorrow. With that, he indicated that he had better be getting home to oversee the milking and other evening chores that awaited his attention. Beside, would not Jessie soon be having supper on the table?

Once back in the cold air, Archie first stopped to collect his thoughts and then ever so slowly made his way back to the horse and sleigh. Even with the stillness of the air, he was not able to hear the crunching of the snow under his feet like before. Daniel Erskine was not visiting the MacDonalds after all; no doubt, he was at home with Tina and the MacNeil girl sharing a pot of tea. And yet he had heard the pipe, he was as sure of it as he was of the Bible that sat in its brown envelope on the seat next to him in the sleigh. He tried to convince himself that he had been mistaken. He could not have heard the pipe; it was only his imagination and he must banish such foolishness from his mind. As he drove down the long laneway towards the loch road and home, he glanced back at his son's house and prayed that the Almighty would watch over it. *"Na tigeadh gu dillinn ach sìth is sòlas 's an àit' am bi sibh agus bh'ur clann."* (May peace and happiness stay forever where you live and with your children.) He had indeed heard the pipe. He picked up the Bible and held it close.

There was a distant look in his blue eyes, as if he really was not there. They stared out as though focused on nothing and, yet, focused on everything all at the same time. In that split second, the entire world was centred on his eyes. Rod recalled hearing the command to advance while all other senses had gone strangely numb. All he could do was look into his brother's face, his eyes. Time stood absolutely still. Although there was smoke and noise and movement all around them, there was nothing else. There was only he and Andrew. The eyes.

Rod did not advance; for the first time in his military career, he consciously disobeyed a direct order. He was kneeling over Andrew who had fallen back, resting motionless in this filthy trench in this desperate place called Paardeberg. The pitch-black darkness of early morning still blanketed them as they remained there together. Rod gently placed his hand under Andrew's head and raised it towards him. As if guided more by hearing than actual sight, the blue eyes turned slowly in search of his brother's face and, in them, Rod could see both pain and anguish. At the same moment, he could not help but note the ever-increasing circle of blood on Andrew's tunic. Something somewhere from deep inside told Rod that their time together would be short; there was so much he wanted to say to him but the words refused to come. There were only tears. Now, through the intense blur, Rod was no longer able to see Andrew's eyes. In both fear and desperation, he leaned forward as if to protect, now cradling the head in his arms and weeping. Please God, no! This is not happening. Only the old people like Flora are supposed to die, not the young like Andrew. This is not happening. You cannot have him; I won't let You. Please God, please.

"A Ruaraidh. Chì mi Beinn-mo-Mhulaid, tha sios gu bruachaibh Loch Dubh — B' sud dùthaich mo ghràidh. Chì mi fada, fada bhuam i. Gun gléidh Dia thu; thug mi luaidh òg dhuit." (Roderick. I see *Beinn-mo-Mhulaid*, down by the shores of *Loch Dubh* — it is the land I love. I see far, far away. May God now preserve you for I have loved you since my youth.) Rod heard the words that came so slowly and laboriously and yet with such determination from Andrew's lips. These were things that Andrew wanted so desperately to share and, having done so, an obvious sense of contentment now fell over

him. Still, Rod could not find the words or the will to respond. All he could do was struggle to keep hold — to look into the face and eyes of one who was more to him than life itself. For a fleeting moment, they were laughing together, fishing off the mill bridge in *Loch Dubh*. He saw them there together and still, all he saw were the eyes. Andrew smiled at his brother and, as he held him close, Rod felt him slip from his own arms into those of Another.

It was just as daylight was breaking that Rod heard the troops returning in jubilation; the Boers had raised the white flag. The first engagement by Canadian troops had led to a stunning victory. To a man, they were confident that Paardeberg, February 27, 1900 would surely become a glorious battle honour and they revelled in knowing that they had been a part of it. Rod continued to hold Andrew's hand and gaze into the stilled face. There he saw no honour, no glory. This time, there was no look in the eyes. There was nothing and, for the first time in his entire life, Rod felt completely alone.

John MacDonald and George Buchanan found Rod after several hours of frantic searching through the adjoining fields and parapets. Together, they lifted Andrew from the trench but it was Rod who carried his brother to a clearing down by the Modder River that, even then, was being readied to receive the dead. He insisted that he would prepare the grave. It was his duty and it would be his alone. As Rod began to dig, George whispered something to John before quickly disappearing from view over the crest of an adjoining hill. John remained behind to offer whatever consolation he could although he would be the first to admit that he was never one with the words. In fact, very few words were actually spoken between them as the grave continued to take form. There was no need. There was only the muffled sound of the shovel as Rod continued to dig into the dusty red soil. All the while, Andrew lay peacefully, waiting for his final earthly bed to be prepared.

It was perhaps a half hour later that the padre arrived to conduct committal services for each of the dead in turn. Rod had cleaned Andrew with water from the river and gently closed the eyes before lovingly wrapping him in an army blanket. With John's help, the body now lay in the open grave, waiting. As he proceeded up the line, the padre said a brief prayer over each one in turn as he committed their souls to eternal peace. He approached Andrew's grave and, once again, began to invoke the standard committal service, seeking the compassion of Almighty God in taking this soul into His safekeeping with the steadfast assurance of everlasting life and peace. Rod, whose eyes had remained fixed on the blanket throughout, shook hands with the padre and thanked him for his words. Yet something told him that he could not allow his brother to depart from him in this way. It all seemed so cold and impersonal. Rod and John stood on either side of the grave and, as if planned, began to pray aloud:

"Is e an Tighearna mo bhuachaille: cha bhi mi ann an dìth.
Ann an cluainibh glas bheir e orm luidhe sios:
làimh ri uisgeachaibh ciùin treòraichidh e mi.
Aisigidh e m'anam, treòraichidh e mi air slìghibh
na fireantachd air sgàth ainme féin.
Seadh, ged shiubhail mi troimh ghleann sgàile a'bhàis...."

(The Lord is my shepherd; I shall not want.
He maketh me to lie down in green pastures:
he leadeth me beside the still waters.
He restoreth my soul: he leadeth me in the paths
of righteousness for his name's sake.
Yea, though I walk through the valley of
the shadow of death....)

Rod broke down in tears and could not go on. With eyes firmly fixed on the open grave, John was determined to complete the beloved Psalm for Andrew. *"...agus còmhnuichidh mi ann an tigh an Tighearna fad mo làithean."* (... and I will dwell in the house of the Lord for ever.) Then there was nothing but total quiet, a quiet that simply lingered there with an unknown sense of apprehension. It was only after several minutes that Rod looked up and smiled across at John in thanks and, having composed himself, spoke to Andrew. *"Tha thu 's na speuran shuas, fhir mo rùin."* (You are up in Heaven now, my loved one.) Andrew would depart his earthly home as he entered his Heavenly one, with the language of his ancestors caressing him.

As the evocative words of Psalm XXIII dissipated on the mild breeze, George reappeared in the company of a piper from the Ist Battalion Gordon Highlanders alongside whom the Canadians had fought earlier that day. Rod thanked Corporal MacPherson for coming and asked if he would be good enough to play for his brother; it would mean a great deal to both of them. It should not be a lament because Andrew had gone to a place where no more harm could ever come to him. There was one tune in particular, above all others, that Rod wanted to hear. As the strains of *Highland Laddie* filled the air, Rod lovingly placed the first blanket of soil over Andrew, resting in his cradle that would forever be the fields of South Africa. As he worked to fill the grave, Rod's eyes were once again blurred with tears. It seemed strange because he could no longer hear the pipe. All he heard was the soft sound of his mother humming them to sleep. *"Caidil, fhir mo rùin."* (Sleep well, my loved one.)

Later that evening, John and George stayed with Rod to offer what comfort they could. They shared his sorrow but knew that there was little else they could do. As they sat around the camp fire, John and George began to recount their happiest recollections of Andrew: the singing, the practical jokes, the infectious smile, the blond hair forever askew. Rod forced a knowing grin in the realization that they too were experiencing his pain and, at the same time, making a valiant attempt to bolster his spirits. He listened attentively to their stories but his thoughts were not there. Several minutes later, Rod finally excused himself and walked off alone into the darkness towards the river. John and George remained by the fire and it was only the crackling logs that broke the deafening silence. Neither showed surprise nor even made an effort to look up from the flames as, ever so faintly and plaintively, they heard Rod's voice on the still night air.

> *"O chì, chì, chì mi na mórbheanna;*
> *O chì, chì, chì mi na còrrbheanna;*
> *O chì, chì, chì mi na coireachan,*
> *Chì mi na sgoran fo cheò."*

> (O I will see, I will see, I will see the great mountains;
> O I will see, I will see, I will see the lofty mountains;
> O I will see, I will see, I will see the corries,
> I will see the peaks under mist.)

The song was *Chì mi na mórbheanna* (I See the Great Mountains) — *The Mist Covered Mountains*. Standing at the grave, Rod knew that Andrew had walked through the valley of the shadow of death and was somehow by a loch in the shadow of the great lofty mountain — *Beinn-mo-Mhulaid*. And with that, for the first time that dreadfully long day, Rod smiled and again felt at peace.

⁂

The soft early-morning breeze off the loch rustled the leaves in the apple trees as the tall grass below swayed back and forth, still wet with dew. It would not be long before the sun rose high over *An Toiseach* and *An Deireadh*, bathing the western face of *Beinn-mo-Mhulaid* in glorious light. Except for the moist grass, this was her favourite time of day. She absolutely hated the dampness on her paws; it chilled her even more than the piercing wind that often skirted the edge of the woods high up on the hills. As she plodded slowly towards the manse, *Rionnag* was content knowing her stomach was full, following a successful night's outing, and that her paws would soon be free of this God-forsaken wetness. She was also thankful that none of the evil birds were about to torment her, at least for now.

Rionnag came to rest on the steps leading to the veranda where she sat looking down towards the loch and beyond. It was so quiet and peaceful here at this time of day. The Fraser family, especially the children, were obviously and thankfully still in their beds. While she enjoyed the tranquility, she realized that she would not have her bowl of milk until the silence was broken by the sudden stirring inside the house that signaled the preparation of the morning meal. She would have her milk and beat a hasty retreat, well before the little ones could even begin to annoy let alone terrorize her with their rough grasping hands. In her expectant state, she especially did not want to be mauled by those ruffians.

May was also *Rionnag*'s favourite month. It was just the right temperature for her; the bitter cold of winter had passed while the oppressive heat of summer was not yet upon them. But in fairness, it was not only the temperature that pleased her so. There were also many wonderful smells signalling the rebirth that was spring. She intentionally raised her head high in the air so that her nose could catch the fragrance of the early spring flowers wafting on the breeze. As she sat there, she continued to look down the loch in the direction of the bluffs. In the far distance, she could see a solitary figure seated on a rock by the water's edge. *Rionnag* recognized Ida MacDonald who belonged to the house back up on the far hill, the one with the stupid and quite-ugly mongrel of a dog. That aside for the moment, the woman sat there motionless looking across the loch and up at the mountain that was being enveloped ever so slowly by the rising sun. Even *Rionnag* appreciated the grandeur of the scene as the golden rays first illuminated the summit and then began to gently ripple down its facade to the water's edge. Each in their own way, both Ida and *Rionnag*, remained still in watching the great lofty mountain gently come to life.

It was the sound of wood being piled in the kitchen stove that brought *Rionnag*'s thoughts back to her own situation and condition. She would be quick in going to the back door in search of her milk. Only then would she proceed to find a secure resting place under the barn to settle until her wee ones arrived. She would ensure that this was a protected place, preventing the kittens from suddenly disappearing as had been the case following the last three births. They had all been so young and vulnerable — and never to return. *Rionnag* could still recall the scent of each one. She still missed them so.

Rionnag forced herself to focus on her milk and the need to prepare herself to bring new life to *Loch Dubh*. In raising herself ever so gently from the step, she looked down the loch a final time only to see Ida proceeding home along the road. The MacDonald woman walked so slowly and her shoulders were hunched over as if carrying a heavy burden. *Rionnag* wondered what it could be that troubled her so. Whatever it was, it certainly could not compare to her own preoccupation with the birth that was now so imminent.

⟐ Chapter Five ⟐

Feuchaidh tu dhomh slighe na beatha: tha lànachd aoibhneis a'd'làthair-sa: tha mòr-shubhachas aig do dheas làimh gu sìorruidh.

Salm XVI: 11

Thou wilt shew me the path of life: in thy presence is fulness of joy; at thy right hand there are pleasures for evermore.

Psalm XVI: 11

Deep within herself, she knew that she had finally found peace — finally. She tried to recall exactly when the realization came that her mourning had gone on long enough. She had grieved for her son to the point that she often thought that her life no longer held meaning for herself or anyone else. Although the Reverend Fraser had done his very best to offer comfort through his words and presence, inside she had an excruciating desire to confront him as she so desperately wanted to confront God, this so-called God of love and compassion. How could You give this life in miraculous beauty and then, in the twinkling of an eye, steal it away in heart-wrenching pain? What did I do to deserve this — having life plucked from the warmth of my womb only to have it thrown into the coldness of the grave? *"Mo Dhia, mo Dhia, carson a thréig thu mi?"* (My God, my God, why hast Thou forsaken me?)

Thankfully, this anguish was now behind her and she would be forever grateful for having finally been brought to this point in her life — this time of repose. She was confident that the peace that now surrounded her also blanketed her beautiful son. Finally, Rachael Ferguson knew that she could now go forward. After seven years, she had laid Harris to rest in her heart as she had done so long ago in the grave of the Kirk cemetery. In bestowing rest, she was also able to claim it for herself. After such a lengthy absence, she would once again be a wife to Norman and a mother to Morag and Stuart. It was only now that she fully realized how much she had missed them; how much she loved them. She could finally let Harris go because he was already gone. The spirit inside that frail little body had soared with the strength of eagles high above *Beinn-mo-Mhulaid*. This was why she would always find comfort and reassurance in watching the sparrows over the loch, the blue jays in the orchard and even the swallows in the hen house. Harris was with her still but finally there was no more pain. There was just such joyous freedom and peace.

Rachael put her hands on her stomach and suddenly felt the baby move. Every instinct in her body told her that it was a boy just by the positioning. Still, all she wanted was a healthy child, healthy at birth and throughout a long life. She had promised herself that she would watch over this bairn like no other. God had seen fit to bless her with new physical life and she would, in turn, feel forever blessed by her own spiritual rebirth on the shores of *Loch Dubh*. Here the everlasting arms of the God of their fathers embraced and held them close to His heart. In much the same way, Rachael looked out upon the mountains that surrounded her, holding its people close to the water's edge. She gazed up into the infinity of blue sky and smiled; she thought of eagles soaring in high flight. She thought of Harris.

Rachael was seated on the front step of the house facing the loch with *Beinn-mo-Mhulaid* looming just off to the right. She was surrounded by piles of newly washed and dried wool that was in need of carding before the spinning wheel could be coaxed back into its melodic song. A few minutes earlier, Norman had passed by on his way to the potato fields behind the barn, calling out to her as *m'aingeal bòidheach*. (My Beautiful Angel) He said that, from a distance, it appeared as though she was floating among the clouds with the carding comb as her harp. She laughed at his silliness and quickly waved him on his way. Still, she was well pleased to see him so happy, the happiest he had been in a very long while. They both wanted another child and it seemed to bring a new joy to the entire family. Morag and Stuart were particularly excited about the prospect of having a bairn in the house and spent many an hour dreaming up special names. Stuart was especially taken with Skookum Jim and Tagish Charlie — the names of the two Indians who had helped discover gold in the Klondike a few years back. Morag thought these to be quite foolish, saying that they might as well call the bairn *Amadan*. (Fool) Stuart's willingness to give even that suggestion all due consideration only infuriated Morag all the more. "*A' bhalacha!*" (Boys!)

Picking up a large pile of wool, Rachael began to card as the late-August breeze off the loch wafted its way up to the house. Even the trees that lined the front field could not hold it back from its intended course. She suddenly stopped, knowing that this scene held particular meaning for her. It was from the kitchen window, overlooking this very field, that she had watched the children playing on Hogmanay evening. Morag and Stuart had joined with the others in making snowmen and, except for a brief snowball fight, amicably sharing in the holiday spirit. On that occasion, her attention had been focused on young Kenneth Erskine, or *Coinneach Bàn* as some were known to affectionately call him, who had been taken ill with the diphtheria at the very same time as her Harris. One had lived and one had died. For the longest time, Rachael had difficulty whenever she saw Kenneth. Why had he lived and why had Harris died? Och, she meant no harm. It was just that she had asked the question a hundred times, over and over again in her mind, only to find that never once was there an answer.

It was on that very same blustery winter's night that Rachael had finally come to terms with Harris' death. After years of painful torment, the answer had come from the children in the field before her. It was not what they said because she certainly could not hear them. No, it was what they did. Here in the deep death of winter, they had not only found and grasped life but revelled in it. Did the Bible itself not speak of such things? *"...oir tha clann an t-saoghail so'n an ginealach féin na's glice na clann an t-soluis."* (...for the children of this world are in their generation wiser than the children of light.) Totally unbeknown to him, Kenneth had shown her that life was glorious even on a cold stormy night in a field shrouded in snow. It was only then, after seven long years of torment and pain, that Rachael realized that her suffering was over. The new year and the new century would open another chapter in her life, one that would have peace returned to her heart once again. In absolute innocence, a child had taught her a fundamental truth about life, death and the resurrection of spirit.

Rachael was now seated motionless, among her clouds, as she stared out at the very same field seething with life in the glorious warmth of the afternoon sun. Her long sandy-blond hair hung freely around her shoulders and she felt such freedom as the breeze seemed intent on undertaking its own carding. In staring off into the distance, she cast her mind forward knowing that her child would be born in the fall just as the trees began to shed their glorious mantles of colour. For some reason, her thoughts were suddenly of poor Ida MacDonald who had received the terrible news about Andrew last March. Such a tragic death at a time when the smell of spring was in the air and the trees were preparing to burst into bloom. The irony and contrast with her own situation were not lost on her.

While the entire community had shared John and Ida's grief, Rachael realized that no one could fully understand how and what a mother feels unless she had gone through it herself. How well she knew that a part of your very soul is also taken and committed to the grave. In a very strange way, the child who had drawn life from you at birth would continue to do so in death. There was a certain look that defied description. It was the very same look so terribly evident on Ida's face and Rachael suddenly realized that she herself must surely have worn the identical mask for all those years. With her hands now folded over the still carding fork, Rachael hoped that, in some small way, the birth of her child would be a source of comfort to Ida just as Kenneth's "rebirth" had been to her.

It was with a greater openness of heart and mind that Rachael promised herself that she would always heed the wisdom of the children. Little had she suspected that such wisdom would reveal itself to her again so soon and in such a profound manner. It had been an afternoon in late May; she was making her way to the school house for a meeting with Miss MacNeil to discuss her children's progress. As she walked down the road past the Kirk, she happened to notice *Iain Beag* (Little John) Grant making his way home through the cemetery, oblivious to everything and everyone around him. Initially, she had thought it odd for a young child to choose such a route but cast it from her mind as she hurried to be on time for the appointment with the school mistress. It was only on her own return from the school a good hour later that the image of John once again crossed her mind.

She soon found herself walking among the white gravestones, which was a well-accepted routine for the older people to maintain. They trod here often, to linger, to visit and sometimes to speak. Perhaps, in some way, it enabled them to preserve a link and evoke comfort by bringing memories to life. Rachael knelt down and spent time with her parents and Aunt Effie before passing several moments with Harris, who was slightly higher up on the hill. She lovingly touched the side of his stone before rising and slowly walked down towards the gate near the Kirk. This was the oldest part of the cemetery and the most frequently visited, especially by those with the years upon them. It was only as she was about to leave that, out of the corner of her eye, she caught a glimpse of a large bouquet of freshly picked mayflowers on Angus and Flora's grave. Across the generations that spanned life and death, there was a connection that ran deep, even for a small child. Quite intentionally, Rachael stopped and smiled as she corrected herself. It was not "even for" but perhaps "especially for" a small child. The truth resonated across her mind as she conjured up images of *Iain Beag* gathering up the flowers and lovingly placing them here for his grandparents. There was a radiance in her smile as she passed through the gate, speaking the words aloud: *"Gliocas na cloinne."* (The wisdom of the children.)

The horses had long since learned to ignore the irritating sound. It was almost as if it no longer existed. They softly nuzzled each other's necks in greeting as the steam, rising from their nostrils, offered a visible ghostly face to the chill of the November evening. It would be several hours yet before each of them would be directed home to their stalls where a pile of hay and a bucket of fresh water would invariably be provided. They would be thankful for the nourishment and the warmth of the barns after such a long and idle time in the cool night air. For now, they simply waited patiently for their owners to finish whatever it was they were doing. Still, the incessant thumping continued over and over and over again. It was beyond them why the people inside the hall would willingly subject their ears to such a persistent annoyance.

Throughout the late summer and early fall, a symphony of sound had played itself out, filling the air around *Loch Dubh* as spinning wheels were once again cajoled into life with their songs. Soon after, the second overture came with a more-measured cadence as looms clicked and clacked the musical line towards the ever-rising crescendo. The soft coat of wool that only months ago had adorned the sheep on the hills high above the loch had now been transformed into the coarse material that would clothe and blanket the people down by the shore. With the imminent approach of winter, the cloth was still to be shrunk, softened and made ready for the numerous articles into which it would be lovingly transformed.

It was always at the milling frolics that the symphony played itself out with a finale of sights and sounds fit to rival the finest opera houses of London, Paris and Vienna. As with their ancestors over many centuries before, the people of *Loch Dubh* found simple pleasure in coming together in celebration. It was as if the milling of hard twisted threads of cloth into fine nap somehow served to also soften the harsh realities of their own lives. There was an element of fellowship to the gathering that, in a symbolic way, wove their lives together and strengthened their sense of attachment to their home as well as to each other.

As they began to walk in the direction of the hall, Hector and Sarah Urquhart could ever so faintly distinguish three figures ahead of them well off in the distance. In rounding a point of land, the three suddenly became beautiful blackened silhouettes against the water, which sparkled like a carpet of stars in the moonlight. Somehow, they knew it to be Daniel, Tina and Kristy on their way to the milling. With a fair distance between them, Sarah thought that the human forms could well be almost any family from *Loch Dubh*. Had Alasdair been there with them, it would have seemed more like a real family. But he was not and it most assuredly was not. If only Alasdair had not gone away, perhaps things could have sorted themselves out and made them the family that Sarah believed they could and should be.

"A Mhòrag, bithidh céilidh sona ann 'n nochd! Tha mi 'n dòchas gu'm bi do chasan beòthail." (Sarah, it will be a grand time tonight and I hope your feet will be lively.) These words broke both the stillness and her train of thought, something for which she was most grateful given that they offered a release from her ponderous musings. Images of other families soon vanished as Sarah turned to Hector in assuring him that she would certainly see him under the table when it came to the dance.

"Dannsaidh mi air an ùrlar gus an toll mi mo bhrògan. Och, nach ann do Chlainn Ghriogair a bhuineas mi?" (I will be dancing on the dance floor until I wear out my shoes. Oh, am I not a MacGregor?) She laughed and grabbed him tightly by the arm. He looked down into her eyes, the eyes of the mother of their three children, and freed himself from her grasp as his arm quickly encircled her waist in offering a knowing and comforting presence.

"Gu dearbh, tha thu fada 'n ad bheachd féin mar Chlann Ghriogair, m'eudail." (Truly, you are head strong like the MacGregors, my darling.) Even with the obvious and quite mischievous tone in Hector's voice as he gently tapped her on the head, Sarah feigned shock and poked him in the ribs for both the unkindly act and accompanying comments. Their laughter carried across the water to their right while, on the other side, it crept

up the steep hill to where the Campbell house stood with its large vacuous windows gazing down upon them. No doubt, Peter and Martha would remain at home tonight with the bairn. The bairn — it was so difficult for Sarah to believe that it had already been close to four years since she and Tina had assisted at Lachlan's birth. He was growing into a fine-looking lad and, with the passage of time, she maintained that he was becoming more and more the spitting image of his grandfather Archie as a young man. As she drew close to Hector, she chuckled to herself in thinking that perhaps the MacDonalds would be victorious over the Campbells in the end, if not in name then certainly in looks.

It was as they approached the darkened school house that the wave of sound first rolled across the tranquil night air to envelop them. It was obvious that the milling frolic was well and truly under way and, as they walked on at a faster pace, the words of the songs became louder and clearer. Hector was certain that the voice of the soloist, so dulcet and pure, was that of Margaret MacGregor. Now with the hall in clear view, they quickly passed the horses tied to the trees off to the side, and climbed the front steps. It was just as they appeared inside the doors that they were met with a greeting from Kristy who was in the process of hanging up her coat near the tea table. *"Eachainn! A Mhòrag! Ceud mìle fàilte do' n chéilidh."* (Hector! Sarah! A thousand welcomes to the *céilidh*.)

Hector and Sarah turned to respond to the words of welcome but, without the least bit of warning, suddenly found themselves struggling for their voices. At that very moment, the entire hall suddenly erupted into the melodic chorus of *Hé Mo Leannan* (*He's My Darling*) — a favourite milling song of the North Shore.

> *"Hé mo leannan, hó mo leannan,*
> *'S è mo leannan, am fear ùr,*
> *Hé mo leannan, hó mo leannan."*

> (He's my darling, o, my darling,
> He's the new man that I love,
> He's my darling, o, my darling.)

All Sarah could do was laugh as they responded to Kristy's greeting with a simple wave of the hand; there would be no point in competing with the boisterous singing. She recalled feeling the lilting words cascading around her in all directions as they flooded out the door and down the steps like some gigantic wave in search of the shore. It was as though the singing could no longer be contained by the walls; it needed to flow unabated, back to the freedom that was the broad open loch.

With great delight, Hector and Sarah simply stood there in the doorway watching and letting the words and melody wash over them. This particular song had always been one of Hector's favourites and could always be relied upon to spark many a fond memory. He would see his parents sitting around the kitchen stove in winter with some of the older people who had come to visit. With hands joined, their arms swung back and forth as song after song poured from them. It was such a happy time. Now, there were so few of them left but at least the songs continued to be sung. It was important to sing them, to maintain the connection, to remember.

As they finally ventured across to the side in order to hang their coats, Hector and Sarah noted that the milling table had been set up in its customary place. Made of long unplaned planks, it stretched some twenty-five feet along the left-hand wall. Earlier in the evening, the wood had been wet in preparation as had the damp cloth that was left soaking in a large tub at the head of the room. It had since been wrung out and now lay rolled up on the table, like a gigantic *marag*, ready to be devoured.

The table was fairly low, strategically placed close to lap level, and encircled with chairs occupied by people with faces that were very familiar and, at the same time, strangely different. Their neighbours and friends, the Grants, the MacGregors, the Erskines and others, were all willingly caught up in this whirlwind of movement and sound that ironically brought a sense of peace and contentment. You could see it in the eyes and in the smiles, especially the eyes that were, more often than not, focused on the ceiling or the far wall as they sang. From the distance, Hector continued to watch and listen. He sensed that with their singing, they were making a connection back and remembering. He crouched over and whispered in Sarah's ear: *"Bidh è 'na cheòl do m' chluais agus aoibhneas do m' shùil a' bhi còmhla ri mo chàirdean."* (It is music to hear and joy to my eyes, to be joined with my kindred.) Sarah understood all too well; no further explanation was needed. In addition to Hector's memories, she had her own.

Margaret MacGregor sat at the far end of the table, and all hands were on the *marag*, raising and lowering it back and forth before them. It swung up and down, hitting the rough wooden table as it created the musical beat. It was scrubbed back and forth on the surface and, just as quickly, slammed down in front of the person to the left. Each one in turn grabbed another two handfuls as the *marag* travelled around the perimeter of the table through some twenty pairs of hands. Rachael looked into the faces and saw a joy in each one as they languished in the beauty of the language, the fluidity of the motion and the communion with something far greater than themselves. The hall was bursting with life and Sarah eagerly wanted to be a part of it. She waited for a place at the table.

It had not taken long, perhaps three or four minutes, for the song to end. With a rousing cheer, people sat back, laughing and chatting to each other during the well-deserved respite. The cloth also rested, laying silently on the table waiting patiently for its journey to begin once again. Some rose from their chairs, expressing thanks to Margaret and making their way to the front doors to take a bit of fresh air or to the tea table to refresh their throats. Both Sarah and Kristy saw their opportunity and quickly moved forward, seating themselves on either side of Margaret. Soon, Duncan appeared with a small bucket of water and proceeded to once again wet the boards. Shortly thereafter and almost by instinct, all hands were placed on the cloth as Margaret began to sing the first verse of *Air fal-la-lal-o ho-ró air fal-la-lal-lé* — another familiar milling song. It was then the turn of everyone around the table to sing the chorus together, all the time milling the cloth and pushing it on its way.

Sarah looked across at Kristy and saw the happiness on her face as her voice blended so beautifully with those around her. She really did belong here and perhaps, with a bit of the Almighty's help and a great deal of human compassion, the Erskine family would be all the more blessed. It was obvious to all that Kristy loved the milling tunes for many reasons. However, none was more important to her than the fact that they reminded her of her promise to her father to keep the Gaelic — *Cum a' Ghàidhlig suas!* Her eyes were looking beyond Sarah and fixed on an arbitrary point on the far wall. *Tha m'inntinn trom, chan eil mi sunndach. Chionn 's gun do chuir mo leannan cùl rium. 'Is trom an cuideam a tha mi a' giùlain.* (My heart is heavy. I am without joy because my beloved has left me behind. Heavy is the burden I bear.) Regardless, she was keeping her promise.

The milling continued for several hours more, with new precentors at the head of the table and singers around the sides coming and going in turn. Several pieces of cloth had been milled into a fine nap and, beyond the many songs that had been interspersed with riotous laughter and story telling, there was an obvious sense of contentment. Something was being passed down; something lived on. There was also a feeling of comfort in knowing that the cloth, which would soon be transformed into a wide variety of items, would forever carry the lingering Gaelic melodies woven among its threads.

More often than not, there was a price to be paid for milled cloth: strained voices and sore arms, as well as the odd splintered finger and bruised knuckle. However, there was always compensation that came in the form of a hearty meal and a *céilidh* that began later on the far side of the hall. Jamie MacInnes or *Mac an Fhìdhleir* was now seated in his wooden chair on the raised platform at the front of the room as the milling table was finally dismantled by Angus Grant and Neil Erskine. Both men were appreciative of the fact that the space would soon be needed to accommodate the ever-increasing number of square sets that were beginning to appear on the floor. By the time Jamie took a well-deserved break a half hour later, Daniel had eventually "warmed himself up" and soon occupied the same wooden chair as he played several dance tunes on the pipe. James and Margaret MacGregor's oldest boy, Peter, had shown great agility as a step dancer from his earliest days and was on the floor "stepping it off" as Daniel played a medley of jigs and reels. If Gaelic was the language of Heaven, then this was surely its music. The wee Peter never missed a step.

Throughout the evening, Archie MacDonald had been a constant fixture at the milling table; he knew and greeted each song as if it were an old friend. However, he would not allow himself to be coaxed onto the dance floor, even by Tina, saying that some things were best left to the younger people. As he chatted and watched the dancing from the side, Archie reminded himself of his conscious decision to stay to the very end. He wanted his neighbours and friends to know that, even with the recent loss of Andrew, the MacDonalds remained strong and would continue on. Was not their clan motto: *Tha mo dhòchas daonnan annadsa?* (My hope is constant in thee.) And so it would be for him and the others. Still, John and Ida were not up to such gatherings, not just yet anyway. Nothing was ever said. Everyone understood.

Later that same night, as the crowd eventually streamed out through the large double doors, Archie was well pleased with himself for having come and actually enjoying the music and company of others. In particular, he had taken great pleasure in the milling songs and Daniel's selections on the pipe. Now, heading through the darkness towards the horse and wagon, Archie cast his mind back to the time when some of the older more-religious people in the old country would refer to the pipe disparagingly as *croinnghàil dhubha an diabhail.* (the black sticks of the devil) He was appreciative of the fact that this had never been his view. His thoughts took him back to that day last February when he had heard the pipe being played in John and Ida's house, or so he had thought, just prior to Andrew's death in South Africa. As a man of great faith, he had never been a believer in the *taibhsearachd* (the second-sight) and would not start now. He had not shared the story with another living soul and had no intention of doing so. Why should he? He would not question his own faith or, even worse, cause others to do so. It was everything to him. Besides, what good could come of it? Poor Andrew was gone.

For the first time in a very long while, Archie was reminded of the gnawing pain that both he and Hannah had endured at the loss of three of their own children during the devastating epidemic of 1853 - 1854 that swept across the loch. Whether it be forty-six years or nine months, the emptiness never completely leaves those who are left behind to mourn. As he drove past the Kirk, he looked up at the steeple and beyond into the black expanse of the heavens. *"Sìth dha d'anam m'ogha ghaolaich."* (Peace to your soul my dear grandson.)

It was an extremely heart-wrenching sight and an equally difficult experience to endure. And yet he always knew it had to come to this. Even though the land was slowly slipping from sight on the horizon, he had promised himself that he would remain standing there until it was gone, totally consumed by the waters. Rod stood on the stern of the ship as it sailed for home, away from this place that would forever cause him pain.

South Africa would not be remembered as the land where battle honours had been won; it would always be the land whose very soil had been enriched by the presence of his brother.

Rod recalled so vividly his last visit to Andrew's grave before the order had come for the troops to make ready to move out. It was in early morning, well before the camp came to life, that he had made his way down to the river's edge. As the first light of day slowly crept into the eastern sky, the grave looked so different, even with the passage of only a few days. There was a permanence to it now that had somehow escaped him before. This was Andrew's dwelling place never to be visited by his family. Where would his mother and father go to grieve? How could they accept the fact that their son would never again be near them? What could he do to help bring some closure to this wound that seemingly would not heal? Not unlike the pain, the questioning never ceased.

Rod sat by the grave and talked to his brother about playing at the mill by the loch, exploring the fishing boats in New Carlisle, fidgeting in the Kirk pew, teasing poor Elizabeth in school and a hundred other things they did as one. It was then that he came to the stark realization that this would be the last thing they would share together, this bit of ground and these words, these memories. And now it was only he who would have this remembrance of where Andrew rested forever, separated by a vast ocean from everyone who loved him. He rose and placed his hand on the grave as if to feel a heartbeat. He then gently scooped a handful of the parched red soil that was Andrew's blanket and slowly poured it into his pocket. Finally, he bowed his head and spoke his final words to his brother. *"Bidh mo bhriathran do chumha. Fanaidh do chuimhne 'nam chridhe. Beannachd leat Anndra."* (With my words, I will lament you. Your memory will live in my heart. Farewell Andrew.) With that, Rod left him for the last time and returned to camp.

Eight months had gone by and the 2nd (Special Services) Battalion of the Royal Canadian Regiment of Infantry had completed its tour of service, with battle honours intact. The first Canadian contingent was being readied to sail home. Throughout this time, Rod had stayed close to John MacDonald and George Buchanan and they had forged a special friendship that he knew would stand the test of passing years. It would be a tribute to Andrew who had always been the one to bring them together and was the first to break into a milling song. Rod knew that, in time, his parents would want to know that.

The horizon was now completely empty as Africa slipped from view, engulfed by the deep blue waters of the South Atlantic Ocean. It was a long journey home, much longer than the journey there for now Rod was not only alone but consumed with preparing himself to meet his parents and relive the pain all over again. Although he had written to them with the news shortly after Andrew's death, they would want to hear it from his own mouth and heart. When that time came, Rod realized that the wounds would be as fresh then as they had been on that terrible day in February. How could it be otherwise? He would have to be strong for them even with his own very personal grief, and guilt. *Tha m'aigneadh cràiteach trom.* (My spirit is pained and heavy.)

The troop ship docked in Halifax on December 23 and, even with the approach of Christmas, a large crowd had gathered down at the harbour to welcome their victorious heroes. The three boys realized that they would not truly be home in Cape Breton until after the New Year, what with the official documentation that had to be processed, the medical examinations completed and the difficulties of booking train passage during the holiday time. Christmas was spent in barracks near the Citadel and the ladies from the local churches took time away from their own families to provide a full meal with all the trimmings. The soldiers were indeed appreciative of the food, especially after a full year of army cooking. Still, the three longed to be back in Cape Breton and the time seemed to creep by, minutes into hours, hours into days. And yet, the time had not been completely squandered; Rod knew that he must be prepared and ready to go home.

It was a blustery day in early January when the boys left the train in Grand Narrows and proceeded to Baddeck by horse and sleigh. Even with the cold wind on their faces, it felt good to be in the fresh air after the long and stuffy train journey from Halifax. It was refreshing and somehow reassuring to feel the tingle of life on their skin and only when they finally reached Baddeck did they realize just how cold they had become. The *strùpag* that awaited them at the armory, especially the mugs of hot tea, was most welcomed. They would spend the night there and depart early the next morning for St. Anns and *Cobh a' Gheòidh*. It would be another day's journey up the North Shore to *Loch Dubh* and Rod realized that he could put the time to good use to once again collect his thoughts, alone.

John MacDonald's parents lived just past the Presbyterian Church at South Gut St. Anns, near the bridge that crossed the back of the bay. There had been a hearty reception for all three boys and, after dinner, Mr. MacDonald had gone off and reappeared with a bottle of the finest Jamaican rum. He said that there would never be a more-special occasion and a dram would certainly be in order even at such an early hour. The boys were not about to refuse such hospitality and several glasses had been poured and emptied before all three were properly welcomed back to Cape Breton. Eventually, Rod and George were to share long good-byes with John, promising they would get together once all had returned home and were well and truly settled.

From St. Anns, it was a much shorter trip to *Cobh a' Gheòidh*, where the welcome at the Buchanan home was every bit as warm. After supper, they all lingered around the kitchen table telling stories and getting caught up on the local intrigues or the *sgainneal* (gossip) as young Margaret called it with a disdainful tone of voice. She was far more interested in learning about the South African adventure and the soldiers' heroic exploits. At sixteen years of age, Margaret wanted to hear of far-off places and not about the mindless goings on down the road at *Drochaid Na h-Aibhne a Tuath* (North River Bridge), *Cobh an Easgainn* (Eel's Cove) or *Tairbeart*. She was not to be disappointed. Yet, with the seemingly endless number of stories recounted that night, no mention was ever made of Andrew.

It was only by chance that Rod learned that Margaret knew Elizabeth Urquhart from the academy. Over the kitchen table, they shared stories of life away from home in Baddeck. For the first time in quite a long while, Rod thought of Elizabeth and realized that he would have to prepare himself to meet her as well. That too would not be easy for him knowing, as he did, that she had always kept a special place in her thoughts, if not her heart, for his brother. Rod also knew only too well that this meeting would be yet another test of personal strength.

With thanks to the Buchanan family over breakfast the next morning, Rod prepared to head up the north road to New Carlisle and home. George made him promise that they would meet again soon; maybe at springtime they could rendezvous half way at *Sgeir Dhubh* (Black Rock) and spend a few days fishing. Margaret was quick to add that she hoped he would return to *Cobh a' Gheòidh* to visit. It would be much more interesting for him there and offered many other things to do. Rod promised them that he would write and that arrangements would be made for a reunion, perhaps once the planting was in the ground. With that as well as a flurry of handshakes and good wishes, the horse and sleigh departed *Cobh a' Gheòidh* and moved down the winding road, the one that he had yearned to see for so long and that now troubled him.

It was a moment that he had anticipated and for which he thought he was prepared. However, the sudden blurring of his vision proved him wrong. As the horse and sleigh rounded the final bend in the road at the top of the bluffs, he saw once again the majestic lofty mountain, the same one in the song that he had sung to Andrew that night so long ago in South Africa. *Chi mi na mórbheanna.* (I See the Great Mountains) Even as a child, his brother had always loved this mountain and spoke of it as if it were his very own. He would say that it gave him a sense of comfort and security to be in its protective shadow that felt much like being wrapped in a thick woollen blanket on a cold winter's night. Rod stopped the horse and stared down the length of the frozen loch, to the Kirk and up the slopes of *Beinn-mo-Mhulaid.* "*Anndra. Is tric a bhios dùrachd ort air son tìr d'àrachd. Bidh aig fois.*" (Andrew. Often you must long for the land where you were raised. May you be at rest.) With that, he turned the horse to the right and proceeded home.

The welcome was certainly something for which Rod was not fully prepared. As he entered the kitchen through the back porch, the initial deafening silence was soon replaced by screams of joy from his brothers and sister who ran to embrace him and whose faces beamed with a combination of joy and pride in finally laying eyes on him once again. The wee Daniel, Murdoch and Catherine were no longer so small. How they had grown over the past year. In a more measured fashion, his father rose from his chair at the end of the table and shook his son's hand for a long while but was not able to look into his face. John was equally happy and proud to have his eldest son back. It was just that he never looked into eyes; it was simply his way. But it was his mother's reaction that had proved most difficult of all. At first she stood motionless in the doorway to the pantry, looking at him from a distance, almost looking through him. Was it really her son? Had he truly come back to her? What should she say? What should she do?

For what seemed like ages, they simply stood across from each other as everyone else in the room remained silent, in anticipation of what they did not know. It was Rod who finally crossed the floor, throwing himself into her and caressing her head as it buried deep into his chest. For several minutes, neither could speak; they held onto one another and felt an incredible sense of completeness. Rod heard her muffled sobbing as he stroked her hair and continued to slowly rock her into reassurance that it was him — her son. It was all so ironic; he realized that he was a child again, he was in the safe arms of his mother and in the comforting cradle that was his home. At that moment, Rod felt that he had surely run the complete gamut of emotions. However, later that evening, Archie came to visit and welcomed his grandson the only way he could. The family bowed in prayer.

Over the next few days, very little was asked and even less was said about the war and the loss of Andrew. The focus was on the living and it was clear to Rod that the MacDonald house was more complete with his return. Still, it could never be totally whole again and the void within its walls as well as the one in their hearts would always be there. Yet he had been mercifully brought back to them and they, under Archie's guidance, committed to offering up thanks for this rich blessing of life restored.

Neighbours soon learned of Rod's return and the house was busy for several days with numerous visits complete with long chats over tea. Rod went so far as to joke that his back and fingers were beginning to ache from the hugs and handshakes that came in great measure. Even the Reverend Fraser showed an unusual familiarity in expressing his pleasure at seeing this son of *Loch Dubh* safely returned to them. However, of all the events of those first days, there was one in particular that he knew would remain fixed in his memory.

It was shortly after supper on the third or fourth day that the Fergusons, Norman, Rachael and family, had come calling. Rachael carried her young son, who was barely three months old, and positioned herself in a chair at the end of the table close to the kitchen stove. During the course of the visit, the baby had woken from his deep sleep and began to fuss. It was Rod's mother, sitting across in the rocking chair, who asked if she might hold him for a bit. Cradled in her arms, young Andrew Kenneth Ferguson looked up into the strange face, full of uncertainty as to who she might be. Ida rocked him ever so gently and, unknowingly, began to hum an all-too-familiar tune. Even with the large number of people in the room, Rod was suddenly and completely alone, alone with his thoughts as he looked off to the west, through the window across from him, into the face of the great lofty mountain.

She knew that she must concentrate. The next hour would surely seem like an eternity even though she had been preparing herself for as long as she could remember. Years of diligent study in the school house, at the small desk in the front parlour and now here at the academy had all come to this moment. It was such an important time and yet her mind was elsewhere. It appeared to be nowhere and everywhere at the same time, anywhere else but with her here in this waiting room. She prayed a silent prayer that the MacGregor blood in her veins would help her through the traumatic ordeal that was about to unfold. She could not allow herself to be distracted; she must concentrate.

Elizabeth had known of her appointment for several weeks. A room had been reserved in the Court House on Baddeck's main street by education officials from Halifax in order to conduct interviews with the prospective candidates whose names had been duly advanced for consideration. She would be examined to determine her aptitude and qualifications for accreditation of licence as a teacher in the Province of Nova Scotia. Elizabeth knew full well that she was one of the privileged, one of only five students whose grades had been consistently high and who had received a strong recommendation from the academy staff. This was her opportunity to do what she had dreamed of for so long, teaching and nurturing young minds. Her father had always pointed with pride to a crest of Clan Urquhart that hung prominently on the parlour wall. He always maintained that its motto — Mean, Speak and Do Well — would guide the family in its daily life. Both he and Sarah had no doubt Elizabeth would heed these words and make a fine teacher indeed. And with all that, here she sat, unable to concentrate.

Elizabeth still felt betrayed by the story presented to her by Andrew and Rod. How could she have been so foolish as to believe that they were actually going off to build a barn? She had been terribly used and initially, had vowed never to speak to either one of them again. But had she only known the truth, perhaps she could have done something, perhaps she could have stopped them. Perhaps she could have saved them — him. But had she interfered, maybe she would have been seen as nothing more than a meddling or, worse, a love-stricken girl. After all, they had been friends, just friends.

In all the turmoil of the past year and a half, Elizabeth still could not fully explain, even to herself, how she felt when first told that Andrew and Rod had actually gone overseas. Nor could she fathom the emptiness she experienced upon learning the subsequent news five months later. She was forced to wonder if people grieved the loss of friends with the intensity she grieved for Andrew. At times, she hoped they did so as to reassure herself that it was indeed normal; it was to be expected; no one should be surprised. Clearly, she was not surprised; she was forced to acknowledge, at least to herself and often in the stillness of the night, that Andrew had not merely been a friend. Her grief for him was much much more.

The last fourteen months had all been a blur, not only in terms of the passage of time, but also because of the tears that she had shed. In many respects, her life had followed its prescribed course: summer time in *Loch Dubh*, fall studies in Baddeck, Christmastime in *Loch Dubh*, resumption of studies in Baddeck. And so it was. It was a routine but it was now so blurred, as if she were climbing a mountain shrouded in mist, moving towards the sun-drenched summit that never seemed prepared to reveal itself. Perhaps the reality was that it never would. He was gone from her and it was too late to say good-bye or even to tell him how "Little Elizabeth" really felt about him. It was all too late.

As she sat in the drab waiting room of the court house, she glanced through the high narrow window and recognized the bench where she had met Andrew on that beautiful spring day just over two years ago. She had been gazing out over the lake towards *Beinn Bhreagh* and Boularderie when he had startled her. His hand had come to rest on her shoulder and she recalled turning and looking up into his blue eyes. She wanted to be angry with him for his reference to her as *Ealasaid Bheag* but she could not. They hadn't spoken for long; it was only a brief meeting since he was rushing off. She could see him still, those gangly legs running down the street and the blonde hair being tousled by the wind coming off the lake. As he entered the shop, he had looked back and waved her good-bye. It all came to this; this was the one memory that would stay with her and haunt her forever. Andrew was gone from her life with the wave of a hand and she never told him all the things that were in her heart. Perhaps after all, she had been a child and he had been more than honest in referring to her "Little Elizabeth." Perhaps. All that aside, she was left with one stark reality — he had waved her good-bye.

She had often tried to distract herself from such lingering thoughts and knew that she must go on — with her career and life. The task was made somewhat easier by the endless array of events in Baddeck that occupied her time beyond her studies and household obligations to the MacRae family. She had made a special effort to attend the several memorial services held in tribute to the Queen who had passed away in January. Had her death not come only a matter of a few weeks following Rod's solitary return from South Africa? So much sadness to bear all at once. It truly seemed as if she had already been tested.

"Your test, Miss Urquhart. Are you ready for the examiner?" The receptionist now had her hand on Elizabeth's shoulder as if attempting to waken her from a dream. "Mr. Sutherland will see you now."

"Oh yes, thank you ma'am. I am prepared." The receptionist gave her a quizzical knowing smile and asked that she follow her. Elizabeth left her chair by the window and was led down a long drably painted corridor towards a door at the far end marked "Ministry of Education". She hoped that the mist around her would finally be gone, that she would walk into the brilliant sunshine of the mountain top. As the door opened, she prayed for concentration and, most of all, for sun.

It was early afternoon as Iona and little Kenneth drove up the road to Daniel and Tina's house on the far side of the water. The mild breeze coming down from the hills and the warmth of the June sun had made the trip along the loch road a luxurious time for both of them. At the same time, Kenneth was always so full of excited anticipation in seeing his grandparents who made such a fuss over their only grandchild. No doubt, Tina would have some treats ready for him and Daniel would once again take him out to visit with the geese, pigs and other farm animals. *Coinneach Bàn* was forever coming back with fascinating stories and equally imaginative names for all the barnyard creatures. It was so predictable and yet so wonderful to see him happy and healthy. It was a mother's prerogative to believe that a small tad of spoiling never did any great harm.

In rounding the corner of the house, Iona and Kenneth were soon conscious of the fact that Daniel had obviously finished his dinner. They spied him busily working off in the distance cutting the high grass along the edges of the wagon house with his trusty scythe. Everything had grown so quickly what with all the rain, drizzle and fog that had descended upon them in late April and early May. The older people always referred to it as lambing weather because it signalled the time when the *uain bheaga bhrèagh* (beautiful little lambs) first began to appear on the hillsides. Although the raising of sheep was a necessity of life, given both the wool required for the making of cloth and the equally tasty meat, Daniel had always expressed a strong aversion to the animals calling them the *bàs geal* (White Death). Had it not been the sheep, with the aid of the English crown, that had been the cause of the highlanders' clearance and exile from their homeland as well as the eerie stillness that descended upon the glens, except for the incessant bleating? Over time, the people of *Loch Dubh* had learned an important lesson: it was always best to avoid any unnecessary references to sheep, lambing weather or anything even vaguely associated with these creatures in his presence.

Iona gave him a wave as she and Kenneth entered the house where they found Tina zealously clearing the table after the noon meal. The partial remains of a platter of blood pudding, a bowl of curds and a bun of freshly baked bread were still in place. She beckoned them to be seated on the large wooden settle just inside the door as she hurriedly carried the dishes across the room to the wash basin in the pantry. In her haste, a fork suddenly escaped her clutches and dropped to the floor with a loud clang. It gave Iona cause to laugh aloud and to assert that it most surely meant that a lady, other than herself of course, would be coming to visit. Tina was quick in replying quite emphatically that it would not be just any lady. Were not Lord Minto, the Governor General of the Dominion, and his Lady soon to be coming to Cape Breton? Tina had read in both the Sydney papers, **The Record** and the **Cape Breton Post**, that the vice- regal couple would be sailing down the north-east coast to dock at Sydney and Glace Bay. The papers also said that their vessel would skirt the North Shore so that as many inhabitants as possible of the communities that dotted the proposed route could have a good gander at them as they passed, albeit from a certain distance. No doubt, the government wharf in New Carlisle would be a busy place in a few weeks time. She had observed firsthand the excitement that abounded in numerous homes and was aware of the fact that many a family was already putting plans in place with great eagerness and anticipation. It put her to mind of the frenzy that had led up to the old Queen's jubilee celebrations four years past. Where had the time gone?

Iona had brought along the broad strips of long white cloth that Tina had requested earlier in the week. Actually, it was Daniel who wanted them for some reason or another, perhaps as bandages for cuts on the horse's legs. Sometimes it was best not to ask for an explanation. One always ran the risk of being met with either dead silence or a lengthy lecture, depending upon his mood. And as if she did not already have enough to do, he had instructed her to take a perfectly good, bed sheet and dye it to his specifications. Was it not even now in the wagon house soaking in a big tub of herbal dyes? Never one to tolerate waste, Tina had finally screwed up her courage and inquired as to what the need might be. To no one's great surprise, she was summarily dismissed with a wagging finger accompanied by an emphatic *"Nach agadsa tha an t-annas, a' bhean uasal. Se seo mo ghnothaich sa."* (Aren't you the curious one, gentle woman. This is my affair.) Tina knew better than to pursue the matter further and proceeded to do exactly what had been requested of her, waste or no waste. If nothing else, she knew that it was most certainly not to celebrate the election results of last November. The Dominion was still Liberal red under Sir Wilfrid, whether Daniel, Archie and the other blue Tories still in mourning much liked it or not.

Over the final few weeks of June, Tina had busied herself helping Kristy get her things in order for her summer return to Christmas Island. Both women had grown increasingly close in so many ways and not the slightest trace of surprise was betrayed on Tina's face when Kristy informed her, in passing, that she would also be travelling to Halifax. It has been planned for quite some time as a brief vacation of sorts. Tina smiled, hugged her close and whispered in the young woman's ear. They were only a few, carefully chose words but, for Kristy, they spoke volumes. *"Och, a Chairistìona. Tha mi cho toilichte. Bi aoibhinn ri d'bheatha!"* (Oh Kristy, how glad I am. May joy be always with you!) Nothing more was said because it had all been so well understood as they returned to the work at hand. Tina knew that Daniel would not approve of her sentiments and that, if she were to tell him, she would be reprimanded and forced to abide by his word. But then, what he did not know would not harm him. *"Ni sealbh an rud as còir!"* (Providence will do justice!)

The last two Saturdays in June saw Daniel spending more and more time alone in the company of his grandson. He would pick the boy up with the horse and wagon and off they would go. It was never for more than two or three hours at a time and Tina noted that he was always careful to take along several items strategically placed or "hidden" under a tarpaulin in the back of the wagon. Among other things, she had observed him loading a block and tackle, a ladder and an axe. What it was for she had no idea and would not dare ask. If he were to keep such things from her then she could surely do the same. She thought of the long-anticipated reunion in Halifax and smiled.

It was a beautiful sunny day in mid-July that excitement spread all along the coast and up the bluffs to the loch. This was the very same day that would have Lord and Lady Minto "visit" *Loch Dubh*. Right enough, they would only sail by without the slightest inkling as to what it was they were passing. Yet, it would be fine enough just to see them. In each and every home, the best clothes had been laid out as if in preparation for service at the Kirk. The only difference was that even James MacGregor would be with them, no doubt with a little something tucked into his back pocket for good measure in marking the occasion. Tina thought that it would be far better for him to visit Prince Edward Island where prohibition had been brought in by the provincial legislature just last year. No doubt, if he were ever to make the journey across the gulf waters, he would soon shrivel up like a prune. She found herself speaking out loud *"Plumbas tioram a' Phrionnsa Iomhair"* (Prince Edward's prune) and laughed at the strange imagery she had so wittingly conjured up in her mind. This day, the only person missing from the wharf would be her own Daniel who scoffed that he would not even bother going to the wagon house to see *fear-brèige an rìgh*. (The Puppet of the King) He had better things to do with his time, even fishing for trout in the brook would be time better spent.

At 2:00 p.m., the government wharf in New Carlisle was crowded with people from up and down the length of the North Shore, including almost everyone from up on the bluffs. Many acquaintances would be made again; they were all agreed that it had been far too long a time since the last *céilidh* or milling frolic. As still more people arrived and took their places on the broad planking, they were soon aware that a number of fishing boats had already departed the wharf and gone out to greet the vice-regal vessel as it passed by. Tina noted with a chuckle that the *Banrigh Shalach*, Annabelle Calvey, had travelled out on her namesake. Everyone from *Loch Dubh* silently hoped that both their bottoms had been well and truly scrubbed to meet the Mintos.

When the appointed time finally arrived, a cheer went up from the crowd and several Union Jacks, even some homemade ones left over from the Queen's jubilee celebrations, were dutifully waved as the vessel first came into view. Although still a goodly distance off, the people knew that the couple on the stern, the gentleman in uniform sporting medals and sword glistening in the sunlight and the woman engulfed by a large hat with gloved hands resting on the handle of a large blue parasol, were the Lord and Lady themselves.

The cheering suddenly subsided and all waving ceased as, from high up on the bluffs, the sound of the great highland pipe could be heard flowing down the hill, over the town and across the water. All eyes turned upward. There in the distance stood the solitary figure of Daniel Erskine playing *Scotland the Brave* as, behind and above him, an enormous Cross of St. Andrew flag floated in the breeze from block and tackle afixed to a large red spruce. The tune was a piece of the *cèol beag* (little music) or *"cèol crìon"* (very tiny music), a term that Daniel himself had coined to describe the "contrived" musical form that was always dismissed with the greatest disdain. However, on this occasion, he was prepared to swallow his pride and play it for no other reason than to ensure that the *fear-brèige an rìgh* recognized and received the message that he wished to convey in so blatant a manner.

Tina looked up at her blue sheet with Iona's broad strips of white cloth that had been crudely stitched into place. It was now all so clear as to what had occupied Daniel and Kenneth's time over the past few weeks. She could not help but chuckle aloud as did several others standing nearby. Had she been close by her husband, she would have heard much more than the flapping of the cloth once the tune had been completed and its remnants spirited away by the lingering breeze. Indeed, she would have heard Daniel's very personal and emphatic statement intended for the ears of Lord and Lady Minto. *"Suas Alba!"* (Long Live Scotland!)

☒ Chapter Six ☒

Gheibh thu càirdeas, blàths, is mùirn,
Is chi thu caoibhneas, anns gach sùil,
Tha iochd is bàigh a'snàmh an gnùis
Gach dùil tha'n tìr nam beanntan.
                    An Téid Thu Leam, A Ribhinn Òg? (òran)

You can receive friendship, warmth, and respect,
And you can see kindness in every eye.
Compassion and affection swim in the countenance
of every person who lives in the land of the mountains.
                    Will You go with Me, Young Maiden? (song)

The letter was beginning to show the signs of wear. Since it had first arrived by Royal Mail in late May, the envelope had been opened and reopened numerous times in order to offer up its contents. Jennie was now in the habit of carrying it in her apron pocket and reading it over and over to herself, once Duncan had gone off on his regular visitations to parishioners or other church-related duties. She did not want him to think that she had somehow become preoccupied with it although, in some respects, she knew she had. Young Matthew was now accustomed to entering the kitchen unexpectedly only to find his mother pouring over the folded piece of paper. He had jokingly come to call it *iolaire mhamaidh* (Mamma's Eagle) because of the large taloned eagle that featured so prominently on its postage stamp. The name would be a special code between the two of them. His father would never know the significance of the reference or, more importantly, be aware of the fact that she doted over it so.

When the envelope had first been collected down at the post office, Jennie noted that the seal had been clumsily reglued. It was obvious that the postmistress, with tea cup at the ready, had been equally intrigued by its contents. The letter was postmarked Roxbury, Massachusetts and turned out to be the long-awaited note from Effie, her first cousin from Sydney Mines, who had gone off to the Boston states some twenty years ago to take up domestic service. She had done well for herself and had always been faithful in sending both money and a goodly supply of used clothing home to her parents. They resided just a bit east of the town towards Lloyd's Cove and were so proud of their home, located as it was in "the cove" that had gained a fair degree of notoriety for having been visited many years back by the Prince of Wales now King Edward VII. Jennie's aunt and uncle, Alexander and Murdina MacKenzie, were also grateful for the goodly distance between their home and the mine with its recently opened coke ovens and coal-washing plant. The MacKenzies were even more content with their proximity to the sea and its cleansing breezes given that the Nova Scotia Steel and Coal Company was about to further expand operations and was even now building a new blast furnace. Jennie completely understood why they should be so pleased to be away from all the foul air; she was constantly reminding herself of the glorious winds of the broad Atlantic that bathed *Loch Dubh* with fresh new life every day. Of course, she would be the first to recognize that progress was a good thing, especially as it gave work to the young people and kept them here in Cape Breton. However, for young women, such as Effie, even the mines did not offer much personal hope for the future. Like so many others before her, she had reluctantly moved away to earn a living and find a new life.

Initially, Effie had been engaged in service by a wealthy Boston family and, after several years, had met a young Irishman whom she was later to marry. At the time, it seemed so strange to have an O'Sullivan in the family. But so many things were different now. She had a new life in America where change was an everyday occurrence and the old ways were not always kept. Jennie wondered to herself where she might now find herself had she not, all those years ago, met young Duncan Fraser, the newly appointed theology student at Saint Andrew's Church in Sydney Mines. Had she deprived herself of all the colour, excitement and riches that now filled Effie's life by becoming a minister's wife? Perhaps she would be living in a grand house somewhere far away from *Loch Dubh* with servants of her own at her beck and call. As she sat at the kitchen table rubbing her hands across the surface of the envelope, Jennie knew that her clinging to this small piece of paper was a subtle way of rekindling all those old questions, all those uncertainties. Did she really and truly want to keep them alive? Why should she bother? What purpose could they possibly serve? Was she not happily married to this God-fearing man who had given her such a beautiful family? Had God not been good to her? What more could she desire? Duncan never knew of these lingering thoughts and it would be best if he was not aware that she dwelt so much on the letter. At least for the time being, the secret of her eagle would be safe with Matthew.

Effie and Liam were making plans to return home to Cape Breton in late July on a summer sojourn to visit family and friends. They had written with the hope that they would also be able to come and visit Jennie and her family in *Loch Dubh*. As children, Jennie and Effie had been extremely close — almost like sisters — and, over the years, both had grown to mind the distance that had developed between them, less by choice than by circumstance. Besides, the Frasers had not yet met Liam who, from all reports, was now terribly excited by the prospect of finally meeting his wife's "country family." After some lengthy discussion with Duncan, it was agreed that Jennie would craft a reply indicating that a visit would be viewed as acceptable. Duncan had chosen his words carefully and it was therefore somewhat ironic that, unbeknown to him, the words Jennie committed to paper were a bit less staid; they both would be so pleased to welcome Effie and Liam into their home.

There was much to be done in preparation for the long-anticipated company and Jennie was determined that everything would be in a state of complete readiness. Shortly after Sandy's return home from the academy in Sydney, all three children had been quickly pressed into service. With a lengthy list of daily chores, he, Matthew and Emily had soon learned to fear the dreaded word *ùireach* (clean up) that was frequently used by their mother to cover all manner of duties. Sandy was forever complaining about the fact that he was now on vacation and should more properly be in the company of his friends and not wash cloths. One afternoon, as all three children were busily engaged in cleaning the front windows, Sandy quipped to Emily that they would probably end up whitewashing the barn stalls and the livestock so as to make them presentable for the Boston cousins. A child of the manse, Emily had learned early on to mimic her father's oratorical prowess and equally penetrating use of imagery. *"A Shandaidh, a'bhó as miosa 's a'bhuaile is i as àirde geum!"* (Sandy, the worst cow in the shieling gives the loudest bellow!) A somewhat less-than-subtle form of judgement had been dispensed and, for effect more than anything else, she shot him a look as if to kill . It was clear that the sentence passed had had the intended affect. Noting more was said as all three reluctantly returned to the work at hand.

Although miffed that his attempt at inciting humour if not sympathy had fallen on unreceptive ears, Sandy cared even less for his sister's analogy. Still, he was clever enough to recognize that compassion for his plight would be in short supply. In any case, the visitors would come and be gone soon enough; surely it would be best to keep peace in the family by doing what was asked of him. Perhaps like Abraham Lincoln, the Americans would come to free them from their shackles — *"Creutairean bochda — tràillean Loch Dhuibh!"* (Poor creatures — the slaves of *Loch Dubh*!) The boys laughed as they continued on with their polishing. Emily could only respond to their impertinence with a subtle *"Ud. Ud."* (Tut. Tut.) While adept at mimicking her father, she was so like her mother.

Jennie and Duncan had driven down to the New Carlisle wharf to greet the steamer when it arrived on its mid-week voyage up the coast from Sydney to Ingonish. From the corner of her eye, Jennie took note of the fact that Annabelle Calvey had positioned herself in the window of the post office taking stock of all the goings on. No doubt, she was also taking copious mental notes that would provide sufficient fodder for stories to be recounted around town for the better part of a week. *"Ach tha mi ag ràdh ruibh, gu'n toir daoine cunntas ann an là a' bhreitheanais air son gach facail diomhain a labhras iad."* (But I say unto you, that every idle word that men shall speak, they shall give account thereof in the day of judgement.) Jennie spoke softly to herself as she cast her mind back to the image of a certain resealed envelope and the postmistress' well-known fondness for a good cup of steamy tea. With that, she turned her back on both Annabelle and the post office to watch the vessel as it pulled up alongside the wharf.

"*Có ris a bha thu a' bruidhinn anns a' Ghàidhlig?*" (To whom were you speaking in the Gaelic?) Jennie was caught completely off guard; she was surprised that Duncan had actually heard her and was somewhat embarrassed by the sudden predicament in which she found herself. Her natural tendency was to make light of it, even though she knew full well that she had just quoted scripture.

"*A ghaoil. Ris a' bhanrigh. Có eile?*" (Darling, to the Queen of course. Who else?) She knew that he would not understand and held her breath in the hope that he would deem it to be nothing more than idle foolishness on her part and not pursue the matter further. Fortunately for her, his thoughts were directed elsewhere. He was now taken up with watching the passengers as they began to disembark from the steamer and make their way up the wharf's lengthy stretch of planking. He took a moment to remind his wife that they should now speak in the English owing to the fact that, in all likelihood, Effie would have lost most of her Gaelic and the *Èireannach nan Stàitean* (the American Irishman) would have only the King's English, albeit spoken with an American tongue.

Jennie nodded knowingly as she strained her neck in searching the faces of the passengers who continued to proceed towards her. It did not take her long; she recognized Effie the instant she set eyes on her. She had aged a tiny bit alright but you could never mistake the MacKenzie features. Boston may well have taken much away from her but it could never ever rob her of that; it was of the bone and in the blood. Effie looked radiant in a bright green bonnet and cream-coloured frock as she, in turn, searched the waiting faces. They raced to each other and Effie greeted her cousin warmly, in English. They had been so long apart and they would have so much to talk about. There they stood for several minutes holding hands and babbling together, all the while oblivious to everyone and everything around them. Suddenly realizing that she had forgotten herself, Effie turned to introduce both Jennie and Duncan to Liam, who had been standing off to the side almost as if he was nothing more than an observer intruding on a private moment. Duncan shook his hand in welcome and was somewhat captivated by the shocking-red hair and matching gaggle of freckles that decorated the broad smiling face of the rather tall and lanky Irishman who stood before him.

"I am delighted to finally meet you 'Father Duncan'; Effie has told me so much about both you and Jennie. Thank you for having us. I am very much looking forward to making your acquaintance and know that we will enjoy being out here in the country. It will be such a change from the heat of Boston." It was only a matter of seconds into Liam's words of greeting that it became all too apparent that his idle chatter had all been lost on "Father Duncan", who knew that Mr. O'Sullivan would indeed come to make their acquaintance soon enough. Whether he liked what he came to know of them or not, that would be an entirely different issue altogether.

The three-day visit sped by quickly especially for the children who were constantly treated with stories by Liam about the exciting life of the big city with all its teeming colourful life. You would have to drive several hours from the Boston Common to see mountains and little villages such as these. He knew that they would love the motor cars that were now beginning to appear on the downtown streets; they were a great deal faster and much more fun than horses and wagons. Sandy, Matthew and Emily were enthralled by the accounts and accompanying imagery of fascinating sights and sounds completely unknown to them. They thought him a most compelling character who not only regaled them with interesting tales but spoke with such an amusing accent. It was the children who kept him most occupied with treks across the high hills, explorations down tunnel-like paths cut through the woods by the cows and fishing expeditions to the babbling streams that flowed into the loch. Often they disappeared after dinner and did not reappear until just shy of the supper hour. It was apparent that Liam loved being in their presence, almost becoming a child himself. For his part, Duncan was more than content with this arrangement given that he was able to concentrate on his work, which included preparation of the Sunday sermon. He had already settled on the text that would be taken from Saint Peter's First Epistle, Chapter 5, Verse 5: "Likewise, ye younger, submit yourselves unto the elder. Yea all of you be subject one to another, and be clothed with humility: for God resisteth the proud, and giveth grace to the humble." He thought it a shame that Effie and Liam would be returning to Sydney Mines on the Saturday morning steamer. He was more than willing to make a special exception and preach most of the sermon in the English, simply to accommodate them.

On those occasions when they could steal a few moments away from daily household duties, Jennie and Effie occupied much of whatever time was left to them with long walks together down by the loch and shared stories of their lives spent apart. It was during one of these talks that Effie had confided that it had been twelve years since her doctor had broken the news that she could never bear children. Jennie could see her cousin's eyes welling up with tears as she struggled with each painful word. It was shortly after a brief silence that Effie gazed out across the loch, almost as if she were transfixed, and suddenly reached for Jennie's hand. She admitted that, even with all the fineries that Liam had given her in America, she could never be as fulfilled and happy as her cousin. It was as if the still-ness of the water and mountains had finally lulled her towards this greater realization; Jennie had seen it in her eyes and now heard it in her voice. It was on a similar outing the very next day that Effie reached deep into her pocket to retrieve a small blue box that was presented to her cousin on the pretext that it was to ensure that they would remain close even with the distance. Inside, on a cushion of white cotton, lay a tiny gold locket in the shape of a heart that, when opened, held space for three small photos. Effie confided that Liam had given it to her many years ago as an engagement present with the idea that it would eventually be filled with pictures of their children. She wanted Jennie to have it as a constant reminder of blessings received; it would mean a great deal if she would accept it. They would remain close.

For Jennie, the three-day visit had come and gone all too quickly as if it had been nothing more than a blur. Initially, she had admired, perhaps envied, Effie's gracious life in Boston with all the beautiful clothes and other luxuries that she had always dreamed about over the years. Yet her cousin, with the sharing of her heart and the presentation of another, had opened her own eyes to the reality of her wealth here on the shores of *Loch Dubh*.

The entire family had travelled down to the wharf to see Effie and Liam off and, quite unexpectedly, it became a particularly difficult time for the two women. Something told them that, in all likelihood, it would be many more years before they would meet again. As they embraced in parting, Effie looked deep into Jennie's eyes. *"A Shìne, beannachd Dhé leat, mo ghràidh."* (Jennie, may the blessings of God attend you, my dear one.) Jennie suddenly realized that not all the Gaelic had been lost; obviously, it was still an important and reassuring link across time and distance. She felt a comforting warmth that pleased her immensely.

The Frasers stayed there on the wharf until the steamer had passed from view, even though the blustery wind off the water had a distinctly sharp chill to it. Jennie's arms encircled her children and it was only when the steamer was well and truly out of sight that she and Duncan led them back to the horse and wagon and home. *Is blàth anail màthar.* (Warm is a mother's breath.) Jennie's sudden maternal thoughts caused her to reach into her pocket where the letter had once rested. It was no longer there, having now been replaced by a small gold heart. She grasped it tightly in her hand and smiled.

There really had not been sufficient time to sit down and sort out what words would be spoken, even if the decision had been taken to share such personal thoughts and emotions. After all, it had only been a matter of a few days since her return to *Loch Dubh* and much of the time had been taken up with preparatory work for the coming academic year. The last days of August found Kristy busily planning the course outline for her students in each of the nine grades from kindergarten to level eight and cross-referencing the prescribed curriculum with material in **The Royal Reader**. She would be prepared for the first day of class and hoped that the students would be pleased to see her back once again. For her part, she had missed them terribly during her time away in Christmas Island and Halifax. In their innocence and acceptance, they offered a comforting reassurance about her place in their community and lives. She realized that *Loch Dubh* was beginning to have a sense of home about it, almost.

She brought the papers in her hands to rest on the small writing table, beside the pot of tea and plate of ginger cookies that Tina had carried up to her room earlier in the afternoon. Dear Tina was forever saying that a wee *strùpag* would help with the work; a good cup of tea would solve any problem. Kristy smiled as she placed her elbows on the table's edge, cradling her chin in the bridge of her hands. Her eyes eagerly escaped the confines of the room as they gazed out the bedroom window eastward towards the Urquhart house, the mill and beyond to the broad Atlantic. She thought of Halifax. As she stared at the endless blue water, it brought to mind the inherent Scottish trait of longing for something that had been lost, for what had been taken away far across the sea and now, far across time. Was not so much of their traditions, culture and even way of thinking based on this pining for what was, for what was forever beyond reach? She knew the feeling well; it was also part of her. But now, her mind was focused on something much more immediate and personal. For far too long she had coveted that which had been lost to her and was now, thankfully, restored. She slid her hand up to her high-necked collar and felt the gold chain that rested beneath, intentionally concealed from sight by her white blouse. Kristy closed her eyes. She thought of Halifax.

From their very first meeting five years ago, Kristy knew that there was something quite special about Alasdair Erskine. She remembered the uneasiness she felt during the ride up from the New Carlisle wharf on that late-August day with his father and mother. She had asked all the wrong questions, especially about the times of mass at what she thought was the Catholic church. A chuckle resounded off the glass as Kristy found herself looking into the window and back over the years at her own youthful innocence. *"A chaileag ghòrach!"* (foolish girl!) At the time, she could not have been expected to understand the significance of Daniel's hasty desire to pay an unexpected visit to the manse. She was thankful for the gifts of youth.

She had been captivated by the smiling face of the young man to whom she was presented on that summer day long ago. Alasdair stood in the kitchen gulping down a final cup of tea before returning to the stacks of hay that awaited him in the back fields. Even with the soiled coveralls, he was a terribly handsome sight — very tall with windblown sandy-brown hair and the greenest eyes. As Tina and Kristy first entered the room, he smiled at her as if not knowing what words of greeting would be most appropriate. His timidity had even precluded his eyes from meeting hers. She could not help but see this nineteen-year-old man as an innocent boy; there was such a simplicity and gentleness about him. *Is duine foghainteach a tha ann.* (He is a handsome person.) She would keep her thoughts to herself but knew somehow that the transition to her new home would be made much easier by this man. *"Na sùilean maiseach uaine!"* (The beautiful green eyes!)

During the long autumn evenings that were to follow, Kristy would remain at the kitchen table well after the supper dishes had been cleared away. Under the golden light of the kerosene lamp, the large table became an ideal workplace for her to review the children's schoolwork that would be spread out before her. The heat from the stove, which was routinely well-banked for the night, blanketed the room with its warmth while the wind off the loch, screaming under the eves of the house and around its corners, seemed to forewarn winter's advent. Not without notice, it had also become Alasdair's habit to linger at the table with either a newspaper or book in hand, long after the completion of evening worship and the customary *strùpag*. It had not taken Kristy long to feel a comfort in the house that only a few weeks earlier had seemed so foreign to her. Seated here at the kitchen table under the dim light, she realized that it was more than the whimsical drawings that the children had made for her in the margins of their lessons, or the absolute contentment of the dog curled up on a blanket and snoring away behind the blazing stove or even the dawdling aromas of freshly made bread and bottled preserves that permeated every nook and cranny of the room. No, it was something more. Looking up from her work, Kristy found herself staring into two translucent pools of green. She smiled as Alasdair quickly lowered his head as if to resume his reading.

It was the love of Scottish music, the fiddle and great highland bagpipe, that had finally brought both Kristy and Alasdair together at the *céilidhs* and milling frolics that filled many a weekend. Time and again, they could be found on the dance floor and it was there they had finally come to realize that something special had now developed between them. They delighted in the dance and in swinging around the square sets with little regard for the passage of time. Then, they would join in the laugher and chatter with other couples once the music had died away, at least until the fiddle began "to speak" once again. But most of all, they simply revelled in being in each other's arms.

It had not taken Tina long in realizing that Alasdair and Kristy were falling deeply in love. It was more than the lingering walks by the loch or the prolonged evenings at the kitchen table. Her motherly instincts told her that her bairn was finally finding happiness and it pleased her beyond all measure. On more than one occasion, she had encouraged them with the favour of her wisdom as she stood suggestively by the open door, sporting a broad knowing grin. *"Cha mhisd sibh sgrìob a ghabhail."* (You are none the worse for taking a walk.) A mother's advice was seldom to be ignored. Such prompting would frequently result in lengthy saunters and Tina delighted in the fact that they were sharing laughter and the sheer enjoyment of life abounding all around them: the crispness of an autumn day, the first crocuses of spring, a goose with her brood of goslings, a snowflake on the top of a nose. Still, a part of her was terribly and secretly troubled by the sure and present knowledge that Daniel would never approve of such a relationship. Kristy was not of the faith and, regardless of the love that might bring them together, such a union would never receive his blessing.

It was a day in early October of 1899; Tina remembered it well for she was in the midst of fall house cleaning and all windows had been opened for her customary *a' gabhail na gaoithe* (airing) — a final cleansing by the Almighty as she always called it. Daniel and Alasdair had come in from the fields for dinner and talk around the table quickly centred on the need to harvest the last hardy vegetables still in the ground before the arrival of the first major frost. She recalled how Alasdair had suddenly turned and asked her to join him and his father at the table. He said there was something that he wished to discuss with them. As she slowly wiped her hands on the apron and resumed her place, Tina had good reason to suspect what it might be that he was about to raise. Once seated, she firmly grasped the arms of the chair and stared down the length of the table into Daniel's unsuspecting face. She waited.

Looking back, the discussion was now all a disjointed blur to Tina. She could recall bits and pieces of the words that had been spoken but it was the raised voices more than anything else that haunted her still. *Is i rùn mo chridhe.* (She is the love of my heart.) *Is è pàpanach a tha innte.* (She is a papist.) *Is cha toir mise gaol do thé eile.* (I'll not love another.) *Chan eil mo bheannachd agad.* (You do not have my blessing.) It was a violent combative storm that raged around her and she remembered sitting in absolute silence almost as though she were invisible or, at best, a distant observer. Her knuckles went white as she continued to clench the arms of the chair tightly while her mind raced in disbelief of the scene being played out before her. *A Thighearna. Is e seo àm dòruinneach. Cuidich mì! Cuidich iad!* (Oh Lord. It is a tormenting time. Help me! Help them!) Her next recollection was of Daniel rising abruptly from his place and storming from the kitchen in anger. It was only then that Tina finally released her grasp from the wooden arms and reached across the table for Alasdair's hand.

The mother looked into her son's eyes and, for the first time in her life, spoke against her husband to one of their children. *"Alasdair, bidh cron duine cho mór ri beinn mu'n léir dha fhéin e. Chan e maith chàch tha air aire. Nì sealbh an rud as còir."* (Alasdair, a man's faults will be as large as a mountain before he perceives it. It is not the interest of another he has in mind. Providence will do justice.) His only response was a terribly subdued smile as he stroked her hands, looking deep into her eyes. Then, he rose and slowly left the table with not a word passing between them. She sat there all alone, except for the emptiness that now filled her very being. The next day it was Alasdair who was to leave, less in anger than in pain. Tina hugged him in parting and spoke through a flood of tears. *"Mur till thu rium tuilleadh bi mo shùilean ri snighe. Och Alasdair, Alasdair."* (But if you do not return to me any more, my eyes will remain tearful. Oh Alasdair, Alasdair.) Alasdair's own eyes met his mother's and after, much silence, he gently rubbed her cheek with his hand.

"Mo Mhamach ghaoil, ni sealbh an rud as còir." (Dear Mamma, providence will do justice.) His intention had been to quote his mother's own often-used expression as a form of reassurance. The words came slowly and with some degree of resolve even though his voice began to quiver with emotion. It was then that he realized that he could not go on; words failed him. With that, he forced a smile, kissed her on the forehead and was gone. He did not want her to see his tears. She had attempted to speak, she had, even if it was only to address the kitchen door that now confronted her with its own silence. But, as with her son, the words would not come; they remained encased somewhere deep in her heart. *Alasdair. Gu'm bi Dia nan gràs daonnan maille ruibh!* (Alasdair. May the God of grace be always near you!) At that moment, she felt totally helpless and absolutely alone. Seldom before had her kitchen seemed so cold.

Alasdair's absence was everywhere Tina looked and haunted everything she did. As days turned to weeks and weeks to months, she suffered quietly in the knowledge that she had not uttered a single word in defence of her son on that terrible day. *"Bha mi balbh tosdach; bha mi balbh tosdach!"* (I was silent; I was silent!) She was forever admonishing herself. There was a realization that these painful words were her personal cross to bear and that they would never leave her. They were especially troublesome in the cruel irony of silence that so often cloaked the house. She had been placed between her husband and her son. What could she have possibly done then and, more importantly, what could she do now? She felt powerless to reclaim him and to make her family whole again. *"Is iad iobairtean Dhé spio-rad briste. Is e seo fàth mo bhròin. Tha mo chridhe briste."* (The sacrifices of God are a broken spirit. This is the cause of my sorrow. My heart is broken.) The words were spoken often but only softly when she was alone in what now struck her as a cavernous lonely house.

Alasdair was faithful in writing to his mother every month; he was fine and had found steady work in the Halifax shipyards. Tina knew her son well and could sense by his carefully chosen words that he desperately wanted to be home with his family and Kristy. He constantly asked after each of them in turn, even his father, and hoped that his absence had not created hardships on the farm or undue friction between Daniel and Kristy. Tina was always reassuring in her letters, even though it was obvious that things could never be as they once were. On several occasions, Alasdair's brother, Neil, had attempted to persuade his father to reconsider his position. It was as though a member of the family had been taken from them and they wanted him back. Yet, they were powerless against the iron will that was Daniel. More times than one wished to remember, Neil had been dismissed out of hand. It was simply not a matter open for discussion.

Kristy had felt an emptiness that was hard for her to express. Had it not been for Tina and her students, she surely would have resigned her position and returned to Christmas Island. No doubt, her parents would demand an explanation and she realized that they would be as displeased with her as Daniel had been with Alasdair. Many nights, she prayed in her bedroom beneath the crucifix with her rosary, asking God for compassion to find its way into the hearts and minds of men. Several times, she left the crucifix and beads in the closeted carpet bag and prayed under the plain Protestant cross above her bed. She prayed to her God, *"Aon Dia agus Athair nan uile"* (One God and Father of all), to bring light where there was darkness and understanding where there was ignorance. Throughout these dreadfully long days, it was Tina who was constantly nearby to provide much-needed company and quiet comfort. Often it was without a word being spoken, sometimes nothing more than a smile, a pot of tea or an arm around the shoulder. But always her actions instilled a sense of hope. *"Ni sealbh an rud as còir."* (Providence will do justice.) Kristy held onto those words with the fervent hope and prayer that it would. She would be the first to admit, however, that she had no real way of knowing.

Alasdair had also corresponded regularly with Kristy and she had gone to Halifax on numerous occasions to spend time with him. The depth of their love grew stronger even with the space of time and distance. It had been in mid-August, just before her departure for Cape Breton, that they had gone for a long walk along Spring Garden Road and in the Public Gardens. On a park bench facing a small lake, Alasdair presented her with a tiny box containing a gold ring and chain. As he slipped the ring onto her finger, she looked into his eyes and quickly responded to the question he had posed in an almost timid manner. *"Alasdair, gaoil mo chridhe. 'S gu'n dean mi do phòsadh, cho cinnteach ri' m'bheatha."* (Alasdair, you are the love of my heart. I will marry you as certain as my life.) That moment would remain locked in her memory — the image of Alasdair's smile, not only on his lips but in those beautiful green eyes. He then lovingly placed the chain around her neck, knowing that she would want to wear the ring on it until such time as they were prepared to announce the engagement to both families. It was shortly thereafter that they left hand in hand, with the understanding that they would remain strong for each other and for the many challenges that surely lay ahead.

Shadows were beginning to lengthen among the trees in the garden below her window and Kristy forced herself to return to the paper work that rested on the table. She leaned forward to pour a cup of tea from the pot that Tina had brought up earlier. Dear Tina, such a woman of profound faith and patience. Kristy's other hand reached up and held the ring close to her heart, still well concealed by the pure-whiteness of the blouse. Through the window, she noticed that Tina had suddenly appeared and was walking slowly among the beds of her beloved flower garden. Kristy looked down upon her and smiled. *"Och Tina mo banacharaid ghaolach; gu dearbh, ni sealbh an rud as còir."* (Oh Tina my dear friend, providence will do justice indeed.)

They formed part of a routine that was well known to Rod and, indeed, all the young people of *Loch Dubh*. They would first appear during spring ploughing, almost by magic, as if thrust up like perverted fruit of the moist dark soil of winter. As young boys, he and Andrew had the task of following their father, who drove the horse and plough back and forth down the length of the field. They were to pick the bigger stones and pile them in the centre of the field. Over the years, the pile had continued to grow and now formed a long serpent-like spine amid the blossoms of the potato plants, which would flood the field with colour several months later. Indeed, the lengthy stone pile had soon become the adopted home for numerous garter snakes that would bask on its glorious summer warmth. It explained why Rod's younger brothers, Daniel and Murdoch, often visited there to catch them and watch them slither over their hands and up their arms. The boys likened themselves to a latter-day Moses; if he could raise up serpents then so could they. It also explained why their sister, Catherine, was always nervous about wandering anywhere near the potato field, especially if the boys were about. Practical jokes were never beyond them. *Bràithrean anabarrach dona!* (Very bad brothers!)

Rod took great pleasure and comfort in being at home with his family, having been parted from them for the better part of a year and a half. The past seven months had been a time of great personal healing for him. His brothers and sister had accepted him back unconditionally and delighted in having him as part of their lives once again. His father had gone on with his work and had never once mentioned Andrew's name; nor had his mother, although with her it was different. Rod could always sense that she still grieved in silence, not being able to give tangible form to her expressions of sorrow and longing. He noted how she had reacted when the Fergusons had given their new son the name Andrew Kenneth. Rod knew his mother well enough to appreciate the fact that she would be honoured by the gesture. The name lived on and that was a good thing. But her son did not. Andrew was more than a name; he was her flesh and blood. Her son had been taken from her and she had no place to grieve.

There had also been that incident last June that had been the cause of some considerable anxiety in the MacDonald home. It had been mid-afternoon, while he was out weeding in the potato field with Daniel and Murdoch, that Rod was suddenly approached by Catherine. More by intuition than anything else, he knew that the drawn look of concern awash on her face was due to something other than simply her proximity to both her younger brothers and the infamous stone pile. Her words to him were uncharacteristically clipped and very much to the point: he should go to the kitchen without delay. With a gut-wrenching combination of uncertainty and fear, he ran with all his strength only to find a hushed house with his mother seated at the end of the table, her eyes fixed on two tiny specks of white.

Earlier in the afternoon, Archie had visited in order to deliver the mail that Jessie had collected at the New Carlisle post office. There were two small white boxes, one addressed to Pte. Roderick A. MacDonald and the other to the father of the late Pte. Andrew R. MacDonald. Rod could see that one of the boxes had been opened and, even with the distance between them, could make out the shiny silver form of the Queen's South Africa Medal with its striking ribbon of orange, blue and yellow stripes. He noted how his mother was slowly running her finger across the upper of three bars that were affixed to the ribbon — Cape Town, Johannesburg, Paardeberg. Rod moved closer to the table and, as he did, Ida raised her head slowly and turned in his direction. Mother and son looked into each other — faces, eyes and something deeper. Although no words were spoken, a slight smile appeared on her face as she calmly folded her hands in her lap and bowed her head, almost as if pronouncing a benediction. A few moments later, Rod quietly and discretely retrieved the box addressed to him and placed it at the bottom of a drawer in the upstairs bureau. It was never opened.

Rod continued to live with his own very personal pain about Andrew and desperately tried to make room in his heart to now fully understand his mother's. He would watch her from a distance, knowing that what she needed most was consolation. On numerous occasions, he had wanted to reach out to her but realized that she would want to come to terms with her loss in her own way and in her own time. Still, Rod was conscious of the fact that, as a mirror of his brother, he was a visible reminder of what had been taken from them and felt such anguish and guilt for having brought this tribulation upon his own family. He desperately sought a way to allow them to end the suffering he knew they all shared. The distant look in his mother's eyes told him he must try.

The idea had first come to Rod on a Sunday in early July following service at the Kirk. Having been greeted by the Reverend Fraser at the front doors, members of the congregation stood outside speaking with one another in the warm summer air, enjoying the company of others before departing for home. As his parents exchanged pleasantries with Daniel and Tina Erskine, Rod had been temporarily distracted by the smaller children who were engaged in an impromptu game of chase near the cemetery gate. Although many a stern glance of disapproval had been thrown their way, he looked beyond them, past the white stones into the dark green heart of *Beinn-mo-Mhulaid*. It was then that he decided that he should speak with his grandfather.

After dinner, he had changed out of his church-going clothes and walked over to see Archie. No doubt, Jessie would be busily cleaning the kitchen and the children would be off into the hills or over to the bluffs in search of fun and adventure before the evening supper and worship. It was the Sabbath and any thoughts of playing games in or near the house, or even whistling for that matter, would never be tolerated. Public displays of enjoyment would not be seen as either honouring the day or keeping it holy. Still, the younger ones would be gone from sight. It pleased Rod to know that he would be able to spend some time alone with his grandfather who most certainly would be following his normal routine — sitting on the front veranda smoking his pipe and reading his Bible. As children, Rod and Andrew had become accustomed to seeing the permanent fixture of their grandfather at the front of the house every Sunday afternoon with Bible in hand. They had often jokingly referred to him as *Seanair Naomh* (Holy Grandfather) as they escaped to the woods or the loch as a diversion from the solemnity of the lengthy church service and family dinner as well as the eery quiet that fell over the house. It was only now that Rod came to realize the importance of finding a sustaining peace and strength like that which always seemed to blanket Archie on that veranda. Perhaps he and Andrew should have been more conscious of spending time with their grandfather. Regrets aside, at least Rod would now have an opportunity to speak privately with him and to gauge his response to the idea, not only as *Seanair Naomh* but also as an elder and clerk of session.

The entire family had always looked to Archie for advice and, regardless of his final pronouncements, respected his counsel unconditionally. Was it not for this very reason that Rod and Andrew had made reference to their grandfather in the letter to their parents, explaining their decision to go off to the South African War? They both recognized they had used him for their own purpose and, several years later, it now fell to Rod to deal with his conscience. He would sit with his grandfather and hoped that their talk would be as healing for him as the realization of his idea might be for the family. In walking up the laneway towards the house, Rod noticed that Archie had obviously heard him approaching as he looked up from his reading and proceeded to give him a hearty wave of the hand. Warmth of greeting aside, it would not be an easy conversation but Rod realized that he would have to do this for his family, particularly for his mother and, of course, for Andrew.

Although it had never been done before, a memorial cairn would be constructed high up on the hill at the top of the cemetery. The chat had gone well and Archie had agreed to at least carry the idea forward to session for consideration. During the meeting held the following month, Archie was adamant in the view that he would abstain from voting and in any way influencing the final decision owing to the direct family involvement. Propriety aside, the tone was soon set by Duncan Fraser who believed it to be a fine idea and could see no reason why any objections could or should be raised in any quarter. Andrew was a God-fearing man and a valued member of the congregation who had made the supreme sacrifice for

God, Queen and country. As minister, he would be honoured to take part in any such service of dedication. With Daniel and Angus' concurrence, it was to be a unanimous decision. Archie would take great pride in informing Rod of the end result and took a moment to thank session for both the honour and blessing of memory by quoting a passage of scripture. "...*agus cuimhnichidh iad ormsa ann an dùthchannaibh fad as; agus mairidh iad beò le 'n cloinn, agus pillidh iad a rìs.*" (...and they shall remember me in far countries; and they shall live with their children, and return again.) There was also concurrence; life would surely go on and, even though separated by great waters and time, Andrew would be remembered by his family and his God in the far-off country that was now and forever his place of rest.

In late afternoons, before milking and supper as well as on Saturdays, the four MacDonald children worked diligently in gathering up the stones that would give form to the cairn. Many of them had been taken from the pile in the potato field behind the house. Catherine continued to keep her distance, still not completely trusting her two younger brothers to restrain from undertaking their biblical antics. Rod had also gone off on his own to personally gather a few stones from other places that held special significance: the mill bridge down by the loch where they went fishing together, the New Carlisle shore where they dreamed of sailing off together, the schoolyard where they played games together and the bluffs where they talked and grew from boys into men together. Rod recalled how those many months before he had insisted on preparing Andrew's grave by himself as a form of personal duty to his brother. The circumstances and the need were now completely different. The building of the cairn would be a personal honour to be shared by all the MacDonald children.

With water hauled up from the loch in large buckets by Daniel and Murdoch, Rod took charge of mixing the lime and sand that would bring these stones and their stories together. Like a lightening bolt suddenly cutting across a darkened sky, Rod's mind flashed back to that final day of parting so long ago when, for some unknown reason, he had grasped a handful of soil from Andrew's grave and placed it in his pocket. Later that evening after much searching, he found the small brown bag among his military things that had been stored away well out of sight and, until that moment, out of mind. It was the next day that Rod carried the bag to the work site and proceeded to pour half its contents into the mortar mix. The soil of South Africa that now held Andrew in its keeping would also hold together his cairn here on the slopes of *Beinn-mo-Mhulaid*.

During the two-month process of constructing the mound of stones, the four children had worked diligently as a team and found themselves growing closer together in common purpose. They were doing this for Andrew. Even their mother had smiled in approval when first learning of the decision taken by session. No words were spoken but Rod knew that its construction would be a source of great pride and, hopefully, some comfort for her. Its presence would be a visible reminder of her son and of his life. But most of all, he hoped and prayed in the belief that it would finally give her a place to grieve.

Sunday, October 27, 1901 was a day that Rod knew he would remember in the most minute of detail. Indeed, there were only two other such days that would be set apart in his mind and heart forever: the day in October two years ago when he and Andrew had taken the ferry from Baddeck and the day the following February when he had stared into his brother's distant blue eyes for the last time. Today, Andrew was returning home to *Loch Dubh* with the dedication of a cairn that would symbolize his own presence on these hills and along these shores. It was immediately following regular service that the Reverend Fraser invited the entire congregation to proceed up the cemetery hill to the cairn that sat bathed in glorious sunlight. They slowly encircled it as a flock offers protection to a new born lamb and then quietly stood there awaiting the minister's invocation. After a momentary lull, the strength of the words sliced through the silence like a sword: *"Fheara agus a bhràithrean, bithibh làidir sa' chreideamh. Cumaibh cuimhne an drèam a bha 'nan suinn."* (Men and brethren, be strong in the faith. Keep the memory of men who were heroes.) Very intentionally, Duncan Fraser continued the theme from his earlier sermon that had focused on Christian duty and service. The passage of scripture had been chosen purposefully from the Second Epistle of Paul to Timothy, Chapter 2, Verse 3: Thou therefore endure hardness, as a good soldier of Jesus Christ. Several moments later, as he began the prayer of dedication, he placed his right hand of the top of the cairn and raised his head Heavenward facing the eastern sky. Everyone knew from the tear in his voice that this would be the closing prayer.

Immediately prior to the benediction, Duncan asked John and Ida to come forward and join him at the side of the cairn. As they first began to move to the front, Rod retrieved a small bag from his coat pocket and discretely passed it to his mother. At the foot of the memorial, Ida opened it and lovingly sprinked the powdery red ground at its base. The soil of *Beinn-mo-Mhulaid* that cradled her dear Andrew in birth and the soil that now caressed him in death were finally brought together. *"Anndra, mo mhic ghràdhaich agus deagh shaighdear Iosa Criosd, leig t'anail. Beannachd Dhé leat."* (Andrew, my dear son and good soldier of Jesus Christ, take your rest. May the blessings of God attend you.) Ironically, her soft almost-whispered words carried like thunder on the shocking stillness and quiet of the air. With very few exceptions, eyes quickly welled up with tears and many a handkerchief was withdrawn from both handbags and back pockets. Among all those assembled, there was an understanding and appreciation that Ida could now come here to grieve and, in so doing, go forward with life. Rod noted that Elizabeth Urquhart, who had made a special trip home for the service, was staring off to the east, in the direction of *An Toiseach* and *An Deireadh*. As he looked into her face, he wondered whether Andrew's death was an end or a beginning for her. So many things had been left unanswered; still, it would be best to leave her in peace alone with her thoughts.

A gentle breeze blew up from the loch as people slowly began to disperse and proceed back down the hill towards the Kirk. As they went, it appeared as though they were forming a chain between something past, present and future. Around them, the autumn-coloured leaves on the slope of *Beinn-mo-Mhulaid* created a frame that spoke of the passage of life, while the canvas it held in place spoke of life yet to come. Rod smiled at his mother, noting the tiny white box that she held in her gloved hands. He went to her, took her arm and looked into her eyes that now appeared less distant. The scene and thoughts that day were not of death but of life. Under the shadow of his beloved mountain, Andrew had come home.

A faint hint of spring was certainly in the air. You could almost smell it. Although snow still enshrouded the fields, its icy fingers were even now slowly clawing their way back to the shadowy security of forested retreats, where they would be safe from the sun that rose ever higher and stronger in the eastern sky. The March winds off the Atlantic continued to carry the chill of the drift ice that was always driven to these shores. And yet, there were signs and talk of spring and the miracle of new life that would soon burst forth in every direction. In time, the snow would be replaced by the white lambs that would take its place in covering the fields, not in a mournful shroud of death but in a playful dance of life itself. This was Seumas MacDonald's favourite time of year.

Since his father's accidental death six years ago, the task of running the farm had fallen to his grandfather Archie and his mother Jessie. It had not been an easy time for the family, especially for his younger sisters Murdina and Mary. They continued to speak fondly of their father as if he were still with them; they said it made them feel safe knowing that he lingered close by. Yet there was a stoic realization that life must go on and a resolve to accept the will of God. For their part, Seumas and his older brother Duncan had spent their free time after school and on weekends working with their grandfather to help with the many chores around the barn, with the livestock and out in the fields. It was clearer to them now that their grandfather was an old man whose days of active work were quickly drawing to a close. At eighteen years of age, it fell to Duncan to assume responsibility for the farm that he would inherit as the eldest son. It would be a daunting challenge but he was confident of his abilities. More than anything else, he was proud of the fact that he would live in the house built by his grandparents and continue the MacDonald presence here on the land that surrounded and was nurtured by the waters of *Loch Dubh*.

Upon completion of their level eight studies at the local school, both Duncan and Seumas had, in turn, made a conscious decision to not go away for higher education. They had no need of an academy training when their responsibility was clearly here where they were most needed. Their grandfather and mother were tired; you could see it in their faces and in their movements. They had laboured long and hard to keep the family together through difficult times and were now in need of well-deserved rest. It was reassuring for Duncan to know that his Uncle John and Aunt Ida were close by to offer counsel. He was immensely thankful for the gift of family. Even with the untimely death of his father and, more recently, his cousin Andrew, the MacDonalds would continue to occupy and work this land. He liked to believe that both of them would look down upon him and be pleased.

Seumas had been a constant help to his older brother even with the knowledge that soon he would have to make an important decision as to his own future. He had often discussed ideas with his good friend and classmate Allan Urquhart, who found himself in quite a similar situation. The Urquhart farm would be passed to Donald who, as the oldest boy, was now devoting all his time and energy to learning agricultural techniques and procedures from his father. It was quite apparent that, with the exception of the logging camps, there was little prospect for the two younger boys should they decide to remain in *Loch Dubh*. It was during one of their many discussions about the future that Seumas, for some unknown reason, recalled listening as a child to his grandfather's colourful accounts of the hardships during the early days of settlement. *"Cha soirbh a bhith òg 's an àm seo!"* (It is not easy to be young here!) Seumas thought back to Archie's telling comment that, for some reason, had stayed with him all these years. There was a sudden sadness that came with the realization that he would never have the opportunity to find out for himself. He had slowly reconciled himself to the fact he was to leave this place to make his way in life, even though he had known no other. *Rugadh mi anns an àite seo agus tha tide bhi falbh. Is mór am beud e.* (I was born in this place and it is time to go. It is a great loss.). And so it was.

The two boys had met the Irishman from America during his visit with the Fraser family the previous year and, for a time, had talked about booking passage on a steamer to Boston. They heard tell that there was a great demand for carpenters and other tradesmen in the States and the boys were confident that they could make a living if they were earnest in applying themselves. However, it was Seumas who finally decided against travelling so far afield. His cousins, Rod and Andrew, had gone abroad several years back and nothing had ever been quite the same again. Although his situation was quite different from theirs, he would not consciously take any risk that might inflict further pain or sadness upon his family. Surely, there were other choices to be considered.

It was more by accident than by design that, one evening in late March, Seumas had picked up a copy of **MacTalla**, the weekly Gaelic newspaper published in Sydney. His grandfather had been reading it after evening worship and had inadvertently left it on the rocking chair in the kitchen. Seated by the roaring stove, Seumas read a front-page article on the first of four new blast furnaces that had been built in Sydney by the Dominion Iron and Steel Company the previous February. The article reported on the bustling nature of the industry and the fact that additional able-bodied young men would be needed in order to keep pace with the growing demand for high-quality Cape Breton steel. On the inside cover page, Seumas also noted a letter to the editor from a Daniel MacKillop, originally from Judique, who had found work in the mill and was now seeking out others to form a Gaelic sports club. He reread both the article and the letter carefully; he would speak with Allan.

The decision had not been an easy one. Sydney was unknown to them, every bit as much as Halifax or Boston or anywhere else. However, it was just a few hours down the coast by steamer; they would still be Cape Bretoners after all and, judging by reports, be able to speak the Gaelic if they so chose to. Seumas could not explain it, even to himself, but this was an important consideration. If the Sydney option were to be chosen, he had already promised himself that he would track down Daniel MacKillop once he and Allan had gotten settled. No doubt, they would be in good company; they had heard tell of other men from along the North Shore who had gone away and were doing quite well for themselves. It would be a fine opportunity and, if nothing else, the two boys from *Loch Dubh* would have each other for company.

For both the MacDonald and Urquhart families, it was difficult to accept the fact that their sons and brothers were going away from home. Everyone understood that, as young men, Seumas and Allan had to make their way in life; this was a certainty. But for Jessie and Sarah, this realization had come far too quickly. They were not prepared to say good-bye to their sons, at least not yet. They were losing their young to far-away places and it pained them to think that they would no longer have them near by, to hear their laughter, to wipe away their tears, to see them grown into manhood. Things would never be the same. *"Gu'm bheil caochladh mór 's an àite!"* (How much the place is changing!)

Seumas and Allen's last Sunday in *Loch Dubh* was a time of mixed, almost convoluted, emotions. The Reverend Fraser, who had written a letter of introduction to the Minister of St. Andrew's Church in Sydney on the boys' behalf, preached on the topic of God's gift of family using scripture taken from the twenty-eighth chapter of the book of Genesis. "And thy seed shall be as the dust of the earth, and thou shalt spread abroad to the west, and to the east, and to the north, and to the south; and in thee and in thy seed shall all the families of the earth be blessed." As always, there was a tear in his voice during the closing prayer that left no doubt that he shared the sadness of the entire community in the loss of these fine young men. *"Gun gléidh Dia thu . Is fo a sgàil-san gu'm biodh bhur dòchas."* (May God preserve you. And in His shelter may your confidence be placed.) It was a most fitting benediction. It was an even sadder good-bye.

Looking back, Jessie and Sarah were to refer to it as *an latha a' sileadh dheur* (The Day of Tears). It was a warm day in May and the vast majority of the families from *Loch Dubh* were present on the government wharf to see the two boys off. Indeed, many tears had been shed before they boarded the steamer that would take them down the coast to Sydney and into manhood, far removed from their youth. In addition to the well wishes of family and friends, they took with them a large basket of home baking and preserves that had been specially prepared for them. The women had made certain that the boys would be well fed and fortified on their voyage. It was one of the few tangible gifts that they could offer and they did so lovingly and in great abundance. Judging by the sheer size and weight of the basket, the boys could easily endure a voyage of forty days and nights before next experiencing the slightest of hunger pains!

The steamer had long passed from view as Jessie and Sarah finally turned and walked back down the rough planking of the wharf in the direction of their families, who waited in front of Dunn's store. Arm-in-arm, the two figures proceeded slowly and in total silence as if the cries of the gulls overhead were sufficient in speaking of the pain in a mother's heart. Although she created an appearance of being somewhat preoccupied with clutching her long black frock as it billowed in the gusting sea breezes, Sarah gave expression to the lingering anguish that was so apparent among the people of *Loch Dubh*. *"A Sheasaidh, gur muladach sinne an seo gun duin' idir. Tha caochladh mór 's an àite."* (Jessie, how sorrowful we are with many gone from us. The place is not the same now.) It seemed as though *Loch Dubh*, and indeed the highlands of Cape Breton, was being slowly and methodically ravaged, robbed of its young people, much as the highlands and islands of Scotland had been previously and so despicably cleared . Off in the distance, the two women could see the islands of *An Toiseach* and *An Deireadh* that had once guided their own banished families to these very shores many years ago. The beginning and the end — it had all been so simple then. Now it was different, so terribly different.

It appeared as though little could be added to Sarah's simple yet telling comment. As they finally stepped from the lengthy wharf, Jessie took a moment to quietly compose herself as she carefully tucked her handkerchief back inside the cuff of her frock. As if part of the same fluid movement, she turned and gently patted Sarah on the arm. *"Och, ma tà. Aig Dia tha brath air mulad mhàthraichean."* (Oh indeed. God alone knows the sorrow of mothers.) Nothing else needed or could be said. In the sky high above, the gulls continued their plaintive cries.

At first, it seemed quite strange that, of all things, it should be water that she would miss the most. She came to the realization that there was something calming about walking along its edge or looking out over its broad expanse. It was always transforming itself and yet, somehow, always remaining the same. Elizabeth wondered what it was that she was truly seeking in life — the ever changing or the ever abiding. She likened her life to a boat without a sail, drifting aimlessly on a sea of unresolved issues and unanswered questions. She was tired and longed for a safe harbour. For her, there was still so much to think about.

It was now a full year since Elizabeth had taken her examination at the court house in Baddeck. The month that followed had been an excruciating time as she waited for the envelope to arrive from the Ministry of Education in Halifax. It was odd then that, with such an air of ever-increasing expectation, she could not bring herself to open it when it was finally placed in her hands. She stared at it for several minutes, knowing that her entire future would be shaped by this one small sheet of paper. The letter of congratulations, personally signed by the Minister, was accompanied by an accreditation of licence certificate. Her dream of becoming a teacher had been realized and, for the first time in many months, she felt that her steps were truly being guided. There was now a sense of contentment about her.

She was to receive several offers for teaching positions and, by mid-July, she had managed to narrow the selection down to two: a large school in the town of North Sydney and a one-room school house on Boularderie Island. After much thought and consultation with her parents, she decided in favour of the latter given that she would be the only teacher for the approximately forty students from kindergarten to level eight. It called to mind her own days in the tiny *Loch Dubh* school and the firm foundation that she had been fortunate enough to receive there. What she had been given, she would now offer to others.

Bail'a'Mhuilinn (Millville) was a scattered farming community near the eastern end of the island, mid way between Little Bras d'Or, located on the southern channel, and Big Bras d'Or on the northern. It had first been settled in the 1820s and 1830s primarily by highland Scots from the islands of Harris, Lewis and North Uist. The family names were all so familiar to her: Fraser, Patterson, MacAulay, MacLeod, MacKenzie and many others. She recalled the long drive by horse and wagon from St. Anns, across to Boularderie by dory at Ross Ferry, down the north coast road that skirted the Bras d'Or Lakes, past Knox Presbyterian Church that sat almost precariously by the water's edge and, finally, inland to *Bail'a'Mhuilinn*. At several points, the road had been transformed into an enormous green tunnel as the trees arched over the travellers in forming a graceful leafy canopy. Frequently, the sun would forcibly break through and dance among the shadows on the road. Elizabeth was enraptured by the play of light and colour that first surrounded and then engulfed this most willing of participants. In some ways, it was all so reminiscent of her walks down a similarly canopied path that led to the bluffs back home. She had quietly reassured herself of the wisdom of her decision to teach at a rural school; she felt so at home and at peace with the beauty of nature that caressed her senses at every turn.

The Patterson family, with whom she was to be billeted, was assembled at the road in eager anticipation of her arrival. The three children appeared to be especially excited by the prospect of having the school mistress living under the same roof. Little Mary stood with a bouquet of wild flowers and it was only with some reluctance that she was finally persuaded to offer them up to the young woman to whom she was introduced. It so reminded Elizabeth of the Reverend Fraser's daughter Emily who, as a small girl, was always off exploring the hillsides in search of floral wonders. The two boys, John and James, were content to simply extend their hands. It was painfully obvious they were anxious to return home and rid themselves of their Sunday clothes, which both literally and figuratively had been forced upon them for this special occasion. Elizabeth empathized with their plight and smiled, knowing that she would get on well enough with the Pattersons. She was certain that the children would see to that.

Her students were drawn from the farms along the main road as well as down the smaller side roads that led to *Loch a'Mhuilinn* (Millpond) and *A'Choille Mhòr* (The Big Woods) — two tiny groupings of farms in clearings carved from the forest to the east. The school house was a fine wooden structure with high windows on the north and south walls that offered a panoramic view of the neighbouring hay fields. During her first preparatory visit, Elizabeth was struck by just how similar it was in design and composition to the school in *Loch Dubh*: the pot-bellied stove in the centre of the room, the water tank along the side wall, the wooden pegs for coats on either side of the double doors. She had almost been tempted, as if on impulse, to check the back corner to see if the MacDonald boys' initials would be there, carved into the bleached pine boards — R. & A. MacD.

Standing there in the school's doorway, Elizabeth could sense that a change had taken place; she was growing stronger. She could actually think of Andrew now without having that agonizing piercing feeling well up inside. It was more than two years since his death and she found it increasingly difficult to call to mind all the memories that she had once promised herself she would safeguard forever. Many had come flooding back during the dedication of the cairn in *Loch Dubh* last October. But it had been different then. Quite unexpectedly, the ceremony had provided her with a sense of tranquillity and closure. She recalled looking off to the eastern horizon, towards *An Toiseach* and *An Deireadh*, as the Reverend Fraser pronounced the benediction. With the final blessing came the sudden realization that, while she would heed the minister's petition to keep Andrew's memory alive, she would no longer live for him.

Scanning the broad expansiveness of sea and sky from high atop the Kirk hill, Elizabeth remembered her visit to the bluffs some five years earlier as she first prepared to leave her home to attend the academy in

Baddeck. Many things had been so unclear to her then. Standing there at Andrew's cairn, she realized it had taken his death to lift the mist that held the islands captive in its haunting clutches. *An Deireadh* was the end of her youthful innocence that had, in so many ways, included Andrew. Now *An Toiseach* appeared from the mist as the beginning of her new life as a woman with an eagerness to go forward to live and find happiness. While Andrew would always have a special place in her memory, she could admit that finally there was room in her heart for others and, possibly, for love. Gazing out upon the ever-changing yet ever constant water, she smiled knowing that Andrew would surely be happy for her.

Each Sunday, Elizabeth attended Kirk with the Patterson family at St. James Presbyterian Church in Big Bras d'Or. During the lengthy forty-five-minute drive by horse and wagon, she would delight in sitting in back with the children, reading stories from the Bible. Each child had a favourite that, with time, had been read over and over again to the point where each one could recite his or hers from memory word for word. The boys identified with Daniel in the lion's den and Jonah in the whale's stomach. For her part, Mary much preferred the imagery of Zaccheus sitting aloft in his sycamore tree. While it helped make the trip pass more quickly, Elizabeth also hoped that this time together would help instill in them a love of the written word. Every now and again, Mrs. Patterson would turn around to smile at Elizabeth in thankful recognition of her patience with the children. She obviously loved having the small ones around her; she was an excellent teacher and would no doubt, in time, make a wonderful mother.

From the very first moment after passing through its large black-spruce doors, Elizabeth was taken aback by the similarity between St. James and her own church in *Loch Dubh*. Although St. James was a bit larger, it was virtually identical in its simplicity and design, with prominence given to the raised pulpit at the front and the seating immediately below for the eight elders. Even the congregation itself seemed strangely familiar. Elizabeth had taken special notice of an older woman who always dressed in black and whose head moved incessantly from side to side throughout the service, as if consigned to a life of perpetual inventory. Had she not known better, Elizabeth would have thought that Flora Grant was still in their midst. She had made a mental note to inform her parents about her "vision" that would most probably provoke a goodly chuckle. The scene caused Elizabeth to cast her mind back to the time when her lilac dress had caused such righteous indignation among certain members of the *Loch Dubh* congregation. Dear Flora; how quickly her generation and its thinking were passing from sight and mind. *Chan eil sinn cho diadhaidh ris na seann dhaoine còire.* (We are not now as pious as the kindly old folks of yore.) Indeed, they were not and so much was changing so quickly.

It was on a sunny Sabbath in December that Mrs. Patterson had first introduced Elizabeth to Calum MacLeod as they stood speaking in a circle outside the Kirk following service. Elizabeth was quick in recognizing his son Stewart from her grade one class and reached out to playfully tousle his hair in greeting. At twenty-six years of age, Calum had been a widower for three years, having lost both his wife and second child at birth. It had been a tragic loss, especially for Stewart, and Calum was grateful that his sister had agreed to come and live with them as housekeeper. He felt strongly that a woman's presence was important, especially for the boy. It was apparent by his actions that Calum was a protective father who took great delight in his son and valued their time together, even with the heavy demands of the farm that so often kept them apart. It was for this reason that the Sunday drive from the MacLeod house in *Loch a'Mhuilinn* to St. James and back was such a special time for them both. Now, with introductions made, Calum smiled down at Elizabeth and expressed thanks for the extra time and attention she was dedicating in helping Stewart with his writing practices. She looked up into the blueness of his eyes and simply returned the smile. If nothing else, Mrs. Patterson was perceptive enough and knew full well that she would most probably have a willing travel companion when next she had cause to visit *Loch a'Mhuilinn*.

Over the course of the following months, Elizabeth was drawn to this man and quite intentionally found reason to speak to him each Sunday after service as well as the weekly prayer meetings that were held alternately in the halls in *Bail'a'Mhuilinn* and *Loch a'Mhuilinn*. There were several times when she had need to visit the MacLeod home, on the pretext of providing additional exercises for Stewart. On one such occasion in early spring, she and Calum had gone off for a walk up into the fields behind the house. From this elevated location, she could see the Bird Islands off the eastern coast and, in the far distance beyond Cape Dauphin, the North Shore as it wound its way towards Cape Smoky. For a moment, she even thought she could discern the faint outline of *An Toiseach* and *An Deireadh*. She knew it to be more wishful thinking than anything else. Yet, as Calum took her hand in his to return to the farmhouse, she had no need to actually see the islands. She believed that, at last, she had found a safe harbour. There was a new abiding sense of happiness about her if for no other reason than she could once again see the water and it pleased her.

⌘ Chapter Seven ⌘

*Uime sin ma tha neach sam bith ann an Criosd, is creutair nuadh e:
chaidh na seann nithean seachad, feuch, rinneadh na h-uile nithean
nuadh.*

II Corintianach V: 17

Therefore, if any man be in Christ, he is a new creature: old
things are passed away: behold, all things are become new.

II Corinthians V: 17

For most residents of *Loch Dubh* and indeed New Carlisle, the "musical episode" on the bluffs had quickly passed from memory, although at the time, it had made a dramatic impression on everyone standing on the wharf. It remained to mere speculation as to whether or not there had been any similar impact on Lord and Lady Minto as they sailed past. Later, Tina often joked with Daniel that he might have good reason to expect to be sent off to the tower at any time, the tower of the Parliament Buildings in Ottawa! For his part, Daniel always rejoined, in his somewhat whimsical manner, that he would sooner captivity in hell than the Dominion's capital. At least there would be less hot air with which to contend.

The sight of the Scottish flag and the sound of the great highland bagpipe had made a lasting impression on one person in particular who had felt an exhilarating sense of pride. The wee Kenneth or *Coinneach Bàn* had earlier helped his grandfather with the limbing of the tree and the installation of the block and tackle that were to hold the flag in place. Daniel could still do many things but scrambling up a tree at the age of seventy-eight was not one of them. Kenneth had taken satisfaction in assisting his grandfather although, at the time, not fully appreciative of the significance of the event that was about to unfold. Later, as he stood on the government wharf with his parents and grandmother, he felt a tingling up and down his spine as the music flooded down the bluffs towards them. It was as if a babbling brook had finally broken free from the constraints of its banks and was rejoicing in its new-found freedom. *Tha sibhse, a shruthan bhrasa ciùil, a' ruith gu luath gu cuan!* (Swift streams of music, you are running swiftly to the ocean!) And so they had.

In the days and weeks that followed, Kenneth spoke often of his grandfather's exploits and the glorious sound of the pipe that had stirred him. Neil and Iona had seldom before seen their son so animated and it was only after some lengthy discussion that they made a point of approaching Daniel on the matter. It was a surprise to no one, except perhaps Kenneth himself, that the long cylinder in his Christmas stocking that was hung on the clothes line in the kitchen had concealed his grandfather's practice chanter. A more-treasured present could not have been chosen and the joy was evident on the boy's face as he somewhat awkwardly moved his hands over its well-worn holes, attempting to mimick his grandfather's fingering. Both Neil and Iona had thanked Daniel for his generosity knowing only too well that he was offering up the very chanter that had been given to him by his father and on which he first learned the ancient music of the Celts some seventy years before. What he offered up was so much more.

Daniel had always lived with the hope that one of his sons, Neil or Alasdair, would take up the great highland pipe after him and keep alive the musical heritage of the Erskine clan. It troubled him that neither one had ever shown the slightest inclination and, although he had not forced the issue, he was adamant in not wanting to let it die with him. It was too important a part of who he was, of who they were. It was in this context that *Coinneach Bàn's* interest in the pipe rekindled a special feeling in Daniel, almost a saving grace that he appreciated would leave a mark long after he was gone. His practice chanter was a symbolic passing of something greater from tired old hands to youthful ones full of life and the future. Never before had the presentation of a gift brought him such happiness and sheer contentment.

Following the Christmas vacation, Kenneth began to accompany Kristy home from school each Tuesday afternoon. It soon became part of the family ritual; Daniel would be seated at the kitchen table with his cup of tea, while Tina busied herself with the preparation of the evening meal. Both she and Kristy had been put on notice that noise during the lesson must be kept to a minimum; the fewer distractions the better. There was much to learn. The boy would have to concentrate.

The weekly one-hour lesson always preceded supper and, as it turned out, Kenneth looked forward as much to the meal with his grandparents and Kristy as the lesson itself. Tuesday evenings became a special time for him and it seemed to pass far too quickly given that his father would arrive all too soon at the back door to collect him. From the corner of her eye on the far side of the kitchen, Tina found great delight in watching Daniel and Kenneth together at the table. At ten years of age, the boy's hands were certainly large enough to allow his fingers to cover the holes of the chanter and, from the outset, Daniel impressed upon his grandson that one did not hold the instrument as much as caress it. Several cushions would be retrieved from the parlour and placed under the boy to allow his elbows to rest on the table in order for Daniel to diligently monitor each finger movement. Soon enough he had developed a keen agility in sounding the notes clearly without even the slightest slurring as his fingers moved effortlessly up and down the chanter.

In little time and with much faithful practice, Kenneth had progressed beyond the basic movements and was grouping notes together in what seemed to form the rudimentary sounds of some of the old tunes, albeit at a much slower tempo. Daniel had fashioned a makeshift chanter for himself out of a long kindling stick so that he could demonstrate more-detailed fingering for Kenneth who held the chanter, diligently watching and then attempting to copy his grandfather's movements. There was a real sense of accomplishment and pride around the table when Daniel announced that his student was sufficiently prepared to learn a tune in its entirety. For his part, Kenneth still dreamed of the day when he would actually graduate to the pipe and play on the bluffs like his grandfather had for Mr. and Mrs. Minto. Kenneth would do it as much for his grandfather as for himself. He knew from the broad smiles and normally soft words of encouragement that this would please his *seanair* more than anything else.

It was a warm day in mid-June that Kristy and Kenneth had walked home together from school. Daniel was seated at the table as the breeze from the open window gently played with the long yellowed curtains and sent them billowing in his direction on the far side of the room. Tina had a stew simmering on the back of the stove and, having properly greeted the boy, quickly abandoned her kitchen with the knowledge that her self-imposed exile would be well appreciated by Daniel. Besides, there would be sufficient time to make tea biscuits before the supper hour and, in the meanwhile, Kristy could make good use of her help sorting out her things in anticipation of the upcoming departure for home. As she climbed the stairs, Tina hoped that Kristy would once again make the kind offer of serving as courier for a letter destined for Halifax. The King and his Dominion government would survive quite nicely even without her postage fees just this once, she had no fear. For her part, Kristy's thoughts were already focused on how and when she and Alasdair would finally discuss the sharing of news with their families. It had to be done soon; the separation was becoming unbearable for both of them.

In going about their business folding various items of clothing on the bed, the women could hear the sound of the chanter as Kenneth began to plod his way through the introductory bars of the tune that Daniel had selected with some considerable care. It sounded quite halted but Tina knew that, in time, the lad would master it well enough. The wee one might have the blondish hair from her side of the family but the bull-headed determination was definitely an Erskine trait. It would be a blessing in furthering his musical education but, in other ways, it seemed as though it was a curse. She realized that she might not like it but this too was of the Creator. *Och, is olc an airidh, a chrannchur.* (Oh, it is a pity; his lot in life.) Invariably, she would mask all such seemingly deep concerns with a hearty chuckle.

The sudden silence of the chanter was not totally unexpected; from time to time, Daniel would interrupt Kenneth's playing with temperate words of correction and guidance. Yet this time, something seemed different; something was different. This was a protracted stillness that hung eerily in the air. *"A Sheanamhair, trobhad gu luath!"* (Grandmother, come here quickly!) The fearful tone of the young voice pierced the stillness and, without even making eye contact, pieces of clothing were tossed onto the bed as the two women abandoned their work and swiftly descended the stairs. It was with fearful anticipation that they finally entered the kitchen. There, they found Kenneth standing next to his grandfather, who sat slumped in the chair with his head drooping to one side.

"A Thighearna. A Thighearna!" (Oh Lord! Oh Lord!) In a flash, Tina had crossed the room and, gently encasing Daniel's head with her hands, slowly lifted it towards her. She looked into his face and saw a distant look in the eyes, as if he were desperately trying to communicate with her from a far-off place. She could not help but note that his body had gone completely limp except for his right arm, which trembled uncontrollably. It was only then that Kenneth broke into tears as Kristy quickly folded him into her and held him close. All the while, Tina spoke softly to Daniel with words of comfort but there was no response; he looked hopelessly at her from an unfathomable distance.

It fell to Tina and Kristy to carry Daniel into the front bedroom. Although she was reluctant to leave Tina alone, Kristy took Kenneth and raced to the far side of the loch to alert Neil and Iona. Later that evening, Neil drove to Ingonish to notify and collect Dr. Osborne who, after an extensive examination, informed the family that Daniel had suffered a stroke of some sort. He had seen such cases before but could not be completely certain as to its cause, possible duration or lasting effects. What was most important was the fact that, in all likelihood, it would not be life threatening. However, experience and professional judgement led him to the conclusion that the next three days would be critical with the patient demanding constant observation and attention. There would be signs to look for and word should be sent to him if and when they developed. It was at a very late hour, once the doctor had left them, that Tina called both Neil and Kristy to her side in the bedroom. As she looked down at Daniel, Tina advised them that she wanted Alasdair informed of his father's illness and, in her heart, wanted him home. *"Is cuimseach dha sin."* (It is proper that he should be.) It was both a statement of fact and desire; she had already decided. She so desperately needed the entire family with her — with Daniel. Not once during her pleading did Tina's eyes leave her husband's grimaced face.

Over the next three days, Tina, Kristy and Iona took turns sitting by Daniel's bed and applying cool cloths to his forehead as a safeguard against the dreaded fever. Kristy would stay at his side during the late night to allow Tina a few hours of well-deserved rest, after a lengthy and exhausting day. Although seldom one to question her faith, Tina found it difficult to understand what was happening to Daniel and to her. One afternoon, Kristy had approached the bedroom door and inadvertently overheard her as she sat with her husband, holding his hand. *"A Thighearna, ciod is àill leat? Is ann dhuit as léir mo chàs. Is è carraig mo neart."* (Oh Lord, what is your will? You see my distress. He is the rock of my strength.) Tears were never far away; they were already in her voice. For the first time, Kristy felt completely helpless; she could not even begin to comprehend the pain that Tina was enduring. All she was able to do was leave them with their thoughts as she quietly returned to the kitchen. At that moment, she did the only thing she could; she make Tina a cup of tea.

On the third night, as she sat by the bed in soft lamplight looking down at this person who had always seemed more powerful than life itself, Kristy saw a man who, in so many ways, had intentionally separated her from happiness. Now, he lay there helpless, reduced to a mere shell of his former being. For Kristy, there was no sense of vengeance, just a desire for God's will to be done. She prayed that He would bring Daniel back to health for the family, the entire family, that still desperately needed him.

With head bowed and eyes closed, Kristy softly began to recite Psalm VI, which had always been one of her favourites. As the words flowed from her in an almost reverend hushed tone, she was struck by their appropriateness given that they spoke of healing both a broken body and spirit. Suddenly and without notice, these very words became transfixed in the air before her. The deafening silence forced her into the somewhat bewildering realization that Daniel had actually reached out and ever so gently laid his hand on her arm. In the faint light, she could see the eyes carefully studying every facet of her face. Slowly and labouriously, he began to speak in garbled tones that required Kristy to bend down close to him. *"Beannachd Dhé leat, a' bhanacharaid."* (God bless you, dear friend.) That was all he said; that was all he could say. The moisture in his eyes attested to the fact that, while the words had been a struggle and had pained him physically, they comforted him in a completely different way. Kristy remembered peering into those very eyes not knowing what to say in response. She cried and smiled at the same time in taking his hand and rubbing it against her cheek.

It was the first time that Alasdair had seen his home and family in more than a year and a half. Although he had envisaged this moment a hundred times or more, it still seemed so terribly strange in actually coming to pass. He had returned; he was back where it had all begun — the memories of that final day in the kitchen were still fresh in his mind. Tina was at the back door to greet him, the exact spot where she had earlier stood to bid him a tearful farewell. Now the reversal was as staggering as it was complete. Her lingering sadness was replaced by indescribable joy; her family was whole again. Alasdair was led to the dimly lit bedroom where he found Kristy seated by the bed. She rose as if to leave but it was Daniel who signalled with his left hand for her to stay. The old man, with tears now welling in his eyes, extended the same hand in reaching forward for his son. The words were ardious and spoken in a faint whisper. Yet they carried a determination that encompassed both sincerity and urgency at the same time. *"Alasdair, an tu tha seo? Faiceam do làmh. Bi gu math dhi...; tha mo bheannachd-sa agad."* (Alasdair, is that you? Let me see your hand. Be good to her...; you have my blessing.) Daniel took his son's hand and, in turn, passed it to Kristy. Now, having done what he wanted to do and with exhaustion once again claiming him, he slowly returned his head to the pillow.

Alasdair and Kristy continued to hold hands and smile at one another as he seated himself on the side of the bed next to his father. There was such a calmness to the moment as Daniel slipped into sleep and, with it, seemed to offer a long-awaited grace. Moments later, Alasdair and Kristy heard Tina's faint prayer of thanksgiving being offered just outside the bedroom door. *"Och sealbh, deanaidh thusa an rud as còir."* (Oh providence, you do justice.)

⁑⁑⁑

The rocking motion of the train was not unlike a cradle lulling the young into sleep. Indeed, many of the passengers were deep in slumber as the clacking beneath them created a rhythmic beat, much as a mother's heart offers a sense of comfort and security to the child resting on the breast. Rod was conscious of his desire to remain awake in order to catch the first glimpses of the mighty river as the train finally emerged from the safekeeping of the brooding forest. He was riding into his future while, at the same time, being held captive by these memories of his past. Flooding past the open window, the early morning August air was as fragrant as it was cool. It delighted in playing with his blond hair as it rushed on its way to another still unknown destiny. With the St. Lawrence now in full view, Rod was aware of the irony that the scene evoked and, more importantly, the fact that this too was part of his moving forward. The tune *Highland Laddie* ran through his mind.

The last year had witnessed a number of changes in Rod's life that eventually led him to this moment and to this journey, taking him far from *Loch Dubh* and even farther from the only existence he had ever intended to know. Looking back now, he was appreciative of the fact that, in many ways, the building of the cairn had been the first step of that journey. He had recognized that something of great worth and importance had been accomplished for his family and for Andrew. He could sense the difference, especially for his mother. But there was still a gnawing feeling deep within him that spoke about the uncertainties of his own life, the changes to come and the choices that they would cause him to make.

Following the dedication of the cairn, Rod's decision to return to Baddeck to finish his studies had been met with a certain degree of surprise. The idea of his leaving home again was painful for his mother to contemplate, even if it was only down the way to the county seat. Yet he was strangely certain of the wisdom of his decision. His younger brother Daniel had always expressed an interest in farming and he would be well suited to eventually take over from their father. Having discussed it with everyone at great length, Rod knew that there were other ways to serve his family and to feed the sense of fulfilment that he so desperately sought.

During his time at home over the holidays, he had made a special trip to the cairn early on Christmas Day morning, well before anyone else in the house had stirred. It was there, in the dark quiet of the moment with Andrew, that he first came to the realization that his brother's death and his own search for something greater were inextricably linked. Looking up at the looming whitened face of *Beinn-mo-Mhulaid*, his mind was filled with the grandeur of God. In a matter of a few short months, these frozen slopes would awaken into life with the miracle of rebirth that would again envelop *Loch Dubh*. It was then that Rod experienced a lingering sense of his own rebirth as a man. With it came a sense of rejoicing and a corresponding message of duty that was now becoming even more apparent.

Immediately prior to his return to Baddeck in early January, Rod had approached the Reverend Fraser after service at the Kirk and asked if he might meet with him privately on a personal matter. It was later the same week, in the front parlour of the manse, that Rod first broached the issue of his call to ministry. It was difficult for him to put into words what he felt was on his heart. He wanted to be certain that he was properly interpreting these signs and, if this be the case, that he was indeed worthy of the call to service. It was only right that he seek guidance from the man who, for him, so personified the qualities of the Good Shepherd.

Duncan Fraser showed no surprise; indeed, his face remained quite expressionless throughout the meeting as he allowed Rod to pour out his inner-most thoughts and feelings. It was only after some considerable time that the minister finally spoke, thanking Rod for his candour and explaining that the Lord calls people in different ways to different forms of service. He suggested that Rod spend more time in prayer to seek guidance as to the path that was being shown him. The faintest hint of a smile finally appeared as he offered Rod the assurance that, should he continue to feel so called to ministry following careful and considered reflection, session would be approached with a request for the congregation to support his application for admission to theological training. The meeting ended with prayer and the understanding that, with greater clarity of mind and heart, Rod would eventually advise him of his decision one way or the other.

The winter months in Baddeck often found Rod walking along the shores of the Bras d'Or Lake by himself, deep in thought. He desperately sought confirmation of what he was to do while appreciating that, in the end, the decision would not be totally his to make. On one particular outing, as he rounded the point into Baddeck Bay, he came upon a group of black-coated men standing out on the ice. It did not take long for him to conclude that Alexander Bell was yet again testing one of his new inventions for which he had gained considerable renown among the local residents. With an unexplainable need to witness, Rod seated himself on an outcropping of rocks to watch the genius of this bearded and quite burly man as he continued to test the limits of knowledge and perseverance.

Rod looked off, out towards *Beinn Bhreagh* with Boularderie Island in the distance. For some unknown reason, he thought of Elizabeth and the new life she was creating for herself. A warmth came over him as he sat there with the harsh winds of the lake still buffeting his face. It was then that Rod felt an undeniable calm descend upon him and he knew that a new path towards a new life lay ahead for him as well. *Iarr dhuit féin comharradh bho an Tighearna do Dhia; iarr anns an doimhne, no anns an àirde shuas.* (Ask thee a sign of the Lord thy God; ask it either in the depth, or in the height above.) In some strange way, Elizabeth had helped to confirm that a sign had been given. Rod could not recall a time when the mountains and the lake before him had held more beauty than they did at that very moment. All the while, the blackened figures on the ice continued on with their work, unknowing.

As clerk of session and a man of great personal faith, Archie was thankful to God for his grandson's decision. Indeed, the entire family beamed with pride given that that they would have a man of the cloth drawn from their very own midst. This feeling was certainly shared by the entire congregation that most joyfully supported Rod's admission to studies at Presbyterian College in Montreal. "The Reverend Roderick MacDonald" from *Loch Dubh*; it all sounded so fitting and grand as it rolled off the tongue, especially when the 'from *Loch Dubh*' reference was added for effect at the end as it invariably was. They had every confidence that he would do well and serve his Lord with diligence and piety. At the same time, everyone knew that he would always remain one of John and Ida's young boys who fished off the mill bridge.

Rod had completed his final exams at the academy and returned to *Loch Dubh* in early June to spend two months at home with family before departing for Montreal. His arrival had come shortly after newspaper reports of the signing of the *Treaty of Vereening*, officially ending hostilities in South Africa. Rod's sister Catherine had fashioned a wreath out of the mayflowers that grew high on the hill behind the Kirk, near the edge of the woods. It was the first time that the entire family had gathered together, alone, at the cairn since its dedication. In that private moment, there was a genuine sense of peace that surrounded them in seemingly drawing both this conflict and one man's life to a close. As they left the cemetery for home, Rod noticed a wilted bouquet of mayflowers on Flora and Duncan Grant's graves that had obviously been placed there some days before. For *Iain Beag*, and indeed all the people of *Loch Dubh*, it was important to honour the memory of lives lived and lives loved. *Och nach falaicheadh tu mi anns an uaigh . . . nach suidhicheadh tu dhomh àm àraidh, agus gu'n cuimhnicheadh tu mi.* (Oh that thou wouldest hide me in the grave . . . that thou wouldest appoint a set time, and remember me.) It was all so much a part of them. They would remember.

For many different reasons, Rod felt so alone as he made his way from Windsor Station up the mountain towards Presbyterian College on McTavish Street. Even compared with Halifax, the city was all so new and big that he thought he surely would be lost in this wilderness of large buildings and bustling streets that teemed with life on all sides. It was not long, certainly not the forty years that Moses had endured, before he found himself standing outside the Gothic building with its beautiful, limestone rock face and touches of Scottish baronial architecture. Had it not been for the arms of the college displaying the burning bush over the main entrance, Rod could have easily taken it as the residence of one of the many railroad or lumbers barons for which Montreal had become renowned.

There was both an apprehension and an appreciation that this would be his home for the next three years as he was to begin the new life that he had craved and that now rose up before him. He was certain that his steps had been guided from *Loch Dubh* to this place; where they would lead from here was still unknown to him. Wherever that might turn out to be, he took comfort in knowing that he would most assuredly dwell in the house of the Lord. He was reminded of the closing verse of Psalm XXIII and the pastoral scene with the Good Shepherd. *Loch Dubh* would never be far from his thoughts, especially his family and the graceful slopes of *Beinn-mo-Mhulaid* that loomed over its still waters. *"Aisigidh e m'anam, treòraichidh e mi air slighibh na fìreantachd air sgàth ainme féin."* (He restoreth my soul; he leadeth me in the paths of righteousness for his name's sake.) Rod gathered himself as he climbed the stairs and entered through the large wooden doors.

There was certainly no question but that the bees knew, only too well, what it was they were doing. As Margaret peered out the dining-room window towards the back of the house, she was reminded of the episode last fall when they had swarmed in the branches of the crab-apple tree under which she was sitting. She noted that they were busily building a hive on one of the uppermost branches that, according to the older folk, was always a sure sign of a harsh winter ahead. Even now, in early January, the winter had already gone on for so long and Margaret had increasingly grown to detest the snow and cold. She enjoyed the change of seasons right enough; it was just that she yearned to be among her beautiful flowers. In looking out on the shrouded plot of land that was her garden-in-waiting, she reached forward and touched the glass as if, in so doing, it would somehow will the snow to magically disappear. She felt the sharp pang of winter's chill as it pointedly reminded her of its complete control over everyone and everything that dared venture near its glacial domain.

There was the sudden and very clear realization that so much of her life was based on nothing more than the hope of better things yet to come. *"Tha an t-slighe fada agus tha mise sgith."* (The journey is long and I am tired.) The warmth of Margaret's words fell on the frosted pane and quickly disappeared into an expanse of nothingness.

Margaret remained there for several minutes, almost oblivious to the passage of time. In her mind, she sprinkled the white field with a multitude of colours that would once again constitute her garden and her joy. The sting of winter's frigid grave would, in time, be vanquished by a simple crocus, forcing its way through the deadly white mantle. The brave flower's determination would signal not only the rebirth of life but also the resurrection of hope. Did she really live her life through her garden? Was it this that gave her a sense of attachment to something greater than herself, that gave some meaning to her existence? It was both the chill on her hand and the thumping in her ears that finally brought her back from the garden. How foolish it was for her to daydream as if she were a child again. And yet, ironically enough, Margaret found it difficult to remember her childhood; it was as if she had quite intentionally banished it from her mind, as if it had never really happened. She longed for a sense of security about who she was and what relevance her life was to have. Perhaps this was why, seated among the flowers of her garden, Margaret always experienced a contentment and peace that otherwise escaped her.

Saturdays in the MacGregor home were anything but peaceful. As with all households in *Loch Dubh*, very little work was to be undertaken on the Sabbath. All chores, with the exception of only the absolutely essential ones such as the milking of cows, were to be completed the previous day. Even the children came to appreciate the fact that, on this one day at least, their unmade beds would be tolerated. Young Betty was a great help and seemed to be aware of the heavy demands that were placed on her mother. In once again bringing the butter churn to life with an invigorated thumping that was not unlike that of a love-struck heart, she watched as Margaret entered from the dining-room, crossed the creaking floor and returned the bread pans to their drying hooks behind the stove. She moved much more slowly now as though a heavy burden had been placed on her shoulders. Perhaps it was the pressures of the holiday season. Betty knew that her mother worried so about having a few small presents for the children to open on Christmas morning. It was for this very reason that Margaret made a special effort to produce extra prints of butter and quarts of buttermilk; she could use them as barter at Dunn's store down in the town. On several occasions, she had even sold several rabbits caught in the snares set by the boys in the back woods. The ten cents that Mr. Dunn offered for each of them was most welcomed by Margaret who desperately wanted Christmas to be as special a time for her young ones as it was for all the others in *Loch Dubh*. A few trinkets would ensure that they experienced the spirit of the season and make it all the more meaningful for the entire family. As was always the case, Margaret would be content to merely wait for her garden. This would be present enough.

The house was completely empty except for mother and daughter as they began to prepare both the Saturday and Sunday meals. Earlier in the morning, James had taken the three boys off for a walk in the woods. At fourteen and twelve, Peter and Charles looked forward to these woodland forays and had no trouble keeping up with their father. It was Albert, her *righ beag*, who frequently trailed behind and whose short legs oftentimes had difficulty navigating the deep snow drifts. Margaret always encouraged the boys to spend time in each other's company; it was important for them to learn and grow together as a family, not unlike the flowers in her garden. She took tremendous pride in her children and oftentimes wished that her parents had lived long enough to witness their nurture in heritage and faith. *Is mór mo chall ris.* (Great is my loss by it.) She still saw her father and mother in her dreams and somehow their presence, even there, was strangely comforting. As much as the future was unknown to her, the same could not be said of the past.

At eleven years of age, Betty was quickly becoming a stunningly attractive, young woman. Her long hair was as black as night and was beautifully contrasted by her milky-white skin. Beyond her physical features, it was her musical proficiencies that most pleased her mother. Margaret knew that her daughter came by her talents honestly as singing was second nature to all their women; it was in the family as her own mother had confirmed years before. It was a truth that came down through the generations. Margaret began to peel the large bowl of potatoes that had been brought up earlier from the root cellar and glanced over at her daughter, who continued to methodically raise and lower the handle of the churn as if to a prescribed musical beat. It reminded Margaret of the milling frolics down at the hall when the cloth was swung up and down, hitting the rough wood on its endless journey around the table. With the sound of the churn beating in her ears, she began to sing to the potatoes before her.

> "'S a' mhaduinn Di-Luain nuair bheòthaich a' ghaoth,
> Bha mise 's mo luaidh a'dealachadh."

(On Monday morning when the wind got up,
Myself and my love were parted.)

It was shortly thereafter that Betty joined in on the chorus and the two women smiled at each other across the kitchen. It was as though the room itself rejoiced as the haunting lyrics of this familiar North Shore milling song first bathed and then echoed off its walls.

It was in the middle of the third verse that the singing came to an abrupt and quite unexpected halt as a loud clap of thunder reverberated across the loch. Margaret peered out the kitchen window towards *Beinn-mo-Mhulaid* and thought it somewhat strange that there should be thunder with hardly a cloud in the sky. But then, winter weather was so unpredictable what with the storms that frequently came in so quickly over the highlands or, worse still, off the open Atlantic. She only hoped that James and the boys would stay warm and dry. She did not, of necessity, want to nurse colds by spending hours over the stove warming goose grease to be applied to aching necks and chests. There was so much else to occupy her time.

Albert had little trouble keeping up with the others since his father and two brothers were each carrying a heavy bag on their backs. He always joked with his father that the shack in the woods was his personal *tigh-fuine* (bakery) since it smelt just like the kitchen whenever his mother baked bread and rolls. Well-hidden by brush strategically placed against its weathered walls, the crudely constructed hut was barely large enough to accommodate the prized *caora chrom* (the "sheep with the crooked horn"/a still) with a fire warming its sooted bottom and an assortment of pots decorating its sides. Once the new supply of sugar had been duly stored in the corner in anticipation of work yet to come, James placed a few additional logs on the fire and lovingly checked the flow of liquid that percolated through the metal tubing and into the tin bucket. Judging by the smirky grin that now enveloped his face, the boys knew that their father was well pleased with his handiwork.

James had decided that it would be best to leave Albert by the warmth of the fire as he, Peter and Charles went off to quickly check the snares that had been set throughout the nearby woods. It was more than obvious that the boy was beginning to feel the effects of the cold damp air that lingered on his bones. The fact that he did not object to being left behind for a bit was proof enough that they should most probably make their way home in short order before he became too tired or, worse still, caught his death of cold. James knew that he would never hear the end of it from Margaret.

It was less than five minutes later that the sudden blast had shattered the stillness, rebounding through the trees and causing an eery silence to blanket the entire woods. James stopped dead in his tracks and was overcome by a chilling numbness as, abruptly, he turned and began to run back in the direction of the shack screaming over and over again, as if possessed: *"A Dhia, ma's è do thoil è!"* (God, please!) Somehow, he knew; he already knew but the pleading continued. In approaching what remained of the crude structure, James and the boys searched for and eventually found Albert lying beneath the scattered bits of lumber and apparatus. He was bleeding profusely from a wound to the head, resting motionless on a pillow of now-crimsoned snow. James hovered over the motionless body and leaned close to the face; mercifully, there was a faint breathing. Unbuttoning his jacket and removing his shirt, he fashioned a tourniquet around Albert's blood-matted hair. James had the presence of mind to order the other boys to race home to alert their mother to be prepared.

With tears trailing down his cheeks onto his young son's face, James gently gathered the limp body in his arms and ran as he had never run before. It was all a blur except for the stillness of the tiny face and the words that seemed to come from deep within him in enveloping them both. *Mo mhic, mo mhic. A Dhia, ma's è do thoil è!* (My son, my son. God, please!)

Margaret was standing, expressionless, at the door to receive her boy. She and Betty had prepared the bedroom off the dining-room and took him there straight away as the deafening silence that had earlier fallen over the forest now blanketed the house. James and the young ones remained in the kitchen and their only access was through Betty who raced back and forth between the two rooms to replenish the basin with hot water and a bowl with flour that was to be applied to help stop the bleeding. After several hours, she was able to tell them that her mother's efforts had been successful; thankfully, the pressure of the tourniquet and the clotting around the flour had stemmed the flow of life from Albert's small body. He was conscious but barely able to speak as a result of his weakened state. Margaret would not leave his side.

Over the next few days, Margaret and James never discussed the cause of the accident. There was no need; it was all too apparent from the pungent smell that had permeated the boy's clothing. Well into the night, the two of them watched over their son as he lay sleeping peacefully before them. The shroud-coloured bandages were a stark reminder not only of the frailty of the body but of life itself. Looking down on his son, James spoke aloud not to Albert but to something deeper within himself. *"Ciod è a' bhochdainn a rug orm, aig Dia tha brath. Is buan nàire na gach nì. Is e seo fàth mo bhròin."* (What mischief came over me, God alone knows. Shame is more lasting than anything else. This is the cause of my sorrow.)

It was Margaret who, in the quiet of the moment that followed, offered an icy response that was clearly intended to cut to the bone. *"Am fear nach amhairc roimhe amhaircidh e 'na dhéidh."* (He that will not look before him will look after him.) The words were more than successful in conveying a poignant message that was as simple as it was brutal. There was not even a need to look at each other. It was all so well understood by both. With that, she finally left the room as much to allow her husband time alone to ponder his life as it was to make herself a pot of tea. She also needed time on her own, to think.

It had seldom been the case that James MacGregor was the topic of conversation in the homes around *Loch Dubh* except, of course, for his fondness for the drink. Yet, in the weeks and months following the accident, three significant changes had occurred in James' life. The shack was not rebuilt and the woods were returned to their natural sobriety. The monthly inventory of sugar at Dunn's General Store was dramatically reduced in very short order. Finally, the MacGregor pew in the Kirk remained a source of idle conversation, but now for quite a different reason; it had one additional occupant. On more than one occasion, the words *Is mór an t-atharrachadh a thàinig air* (There is great change in him.) had been spoken around many a kitchen table, ironically enough often with a wee dram in hand. For Margaret, no explanations were needed. As James gazed into the face of his son who grew in strength day-by-day, she would stare out the dining-room window at her garden-in-waiting. In time, the first crocus would appear from beneath the snow, signaling the rebirth of life, the resurrection of hope. Her *rìgh beag* had been returned to her. For the first time in the deadly depths of winter, she felt the contentment and peace of her garden.

Thankfully, the room had been well aired and all traces of winter's musty encampment had been evicted with a vengeance. By their very nature, front parlours were always such dour proper places — retreats of solemnity and reflection. It was no wonder that evening worship services were held in these rooms around the family Bibles that continued to occupy a prominent place in the homes if not the hearts of their inhabitants.

Kristy stood at the door leading into the parlour and dutifully noted the care with which Tina had so meticulously prepared the room. Indeed, it would have been virtually impossible to do otherwise. One would have thought that her garden had been systematically uprooted and somehow magically transplanted into the various receptacles that adorned every available space. Late June was such a beautiful time of year, especially for Tina, since it was then that her garden exploded into its most vibrant fullness of colour and fragrance. It was this bountiful beauty of creation, enrapturing both the sense of sight and smell, that now sanctified the room with its incense. The analogy was not lost on her. Late June would also and forever be a beautiful time of year for Kristy for this would be the day that she wed the man of her love.

As she stood alone in the doorway, Kristy called to mind another door, in another place and time. The previous Christmas, she had returned to her parents' home to be with her family, to join in the joyous celebration of the season and to explain. In her heart, she knew that, while there would never be a good time to inform them of her decision, it would be best delayed until the end of her vacation time. She would not deprive her family, especially her parents, of what she believed could well prove to be their last Christmas together.

It was during midnight mass that Kristy first found herself coming close to tears. Kneeling before the majestic altar that had been lovingly constructed by her people years before, she sensed an ironic foreboding of death at a time when the entire world rejoiced with the good news of birth. Soon enough all of this, including her family, might be gone, lost to her forever. It was within these sacred walls that she had been baptized, offered her first confession and received her first communion. This was her heritage and her life and yet she could sense it slipping from her as blood seeps from an open wound. There, before the great altar, she realized no one could possibly know her pain but that soon enough it would no longer be hers alone to bear. She bowed her head. *"A Thighearna, an ainm an àigh, ciod is àill leat?"* (Oh Lord, in the name of goodness, what is your will?) It was nothing if not a rhetorical question; she had an appreciation of what it was and what it would mean. There, in the majesty of her surroundings, she prayed for guidance and understanding.

Over the preceding two months, Kristy had been meeting with the Reverend Fraser at the manse on a weekly basis to prepare herself. Alasdair would be her husband and *Loch Dubh* would be her home. The reality was clear; as she claimed her husband and home, she would also claim a new faith. The decision to convert, or "turn", had been even more difficult than her long separation from Alasdair. The church of her youth was so much a part of who and what she was. During many sleepless nights, she cast her mind back to the time several years past when she had first asked God about His purpose for her here in *Loch Dubh*. Was this truly His will? If He was the God of love, would He continue to embrace her as she began this new life that was founded on love? Now under the plain Protestant cross above her bed, she prayed to her God for comfort and direction in preparing herself for the journey ahead. But most of all, she prayed that compassion and understanding would surround her family.

The Reverend Fraser was fully appreciative of the severity of Kristy's decision and the pain that it would bring her and, by extension, her family in seeking fulfillment and love. He had asked Jennie to have a pot of tea ready. He felt it would help make their discussions less rigid and place her more at ease, not only with the subject matter but hopefully with him as well. As he first presented and then brought to life the principles of the Reformation, Duncan emphasized the use of the word "catholic", meaning universal, in Protestantism. Indeed, the **Westminster Confession** used it to refer to man's oneness in Christ. For her part, Kristy had always associated the names of the reformers, Luther, Zwingli, Calvin, Knox and others, with outcasts from Christianity. Now, after several weeks of diligent study, she came to appreciate the central tenet of their courageous acts of reforming — the desire to reaffirm man's very personal relationship to God. In reclaiming the Apostolic Gospel, they asserted the word of God as the final authority for life and faith — not a system of beliefs about God but rather God Himself. Man would stand free before his God upon whom his eternal welfare rested.

Now Kristy stood before her parents, siblings and extended family in the kitchen with the news of her imminent marriage and conversion. Without warning, she was quickly confronted by the stark reality that any attempt to offer a more complete explanation would be futile. In a matter of seconds, expressionless faces had suddenly blanketed the room combined with mournful sobbing and disbelieving stares. The first words spoken came eventually from beneath her mother's hands that covered her face. *"Och carson? A Chairistìona, ciod e an dùnaidh a thàinig ort? Bidh thu air do sgrios. Carson?"* (Oh why? Kristy, what mischief has come over you? You shall be damned. Why?) Except for her mother's continued wailing, there was a silence as no further words were spoken from any quarter. Finally, it was her father who rose slowly, as if in a trance, and stood impassively in his place at the head of the table. He then walked towards her where he remained for the longest time looking down into her face, speechless.

"Mo nighean, bu chòir dhuit a bhith glic. B'e sin car t'aimhleis fhad 's a bhios tu anns an t-saoghal. Is buan nàire na' gach nì . Mach as mo làthair!" (My daughter, you ought to be wise. That would be your ruination while your earthly pilgrimage lasts. Shame is more lasting than anything else. Get out of my presence!) Kristy could never recall having seen such a savage look in her father's eyes or heard such a harsh, cold tone in his voice. She had returned home as a beloved daughter and was now faced with the reality of departing as a banished vilified orphan. Her excommunication would be even more complete and lasting than she could have ever imagined.

She left the kitchen and, shortly thereafter with carpet bag in hand, returned to the still hushed room and approached the side door — the *dorus-siar* (west door/door facing the wind) that now marked the death she had so feared. She passed through both the room and door without so much as a final word being uttered, not even a wave of the hand. As she walked plaintively down the laneway, away from her home and family, she prayed aloud through her own tears. *"Aon Dia agus Athair nan uile, tha an latha a' tighinn gu crìch. Falbh còmhla riumsa ma tha sin an dàn."* (One God and Father of all, the day comes to a close. Be with me if that be ordained.) She sensed only too well that the road back to *Loch Dubh* would now become the longest journey of her life. It was less a prayer and more a plea for the company and strength that she knew she would so desperately need along the way.

The pain was in her. A woman's intuition told Tina that Kristy was enduring great sorrow; it was on her face and in her eyes. And yet, Tina sensed that it would be best not to raise the matter. They would continue to put all the necessary arrangements in place for a June wedding in the front parlour. Kristy hoped that, with time, her parents would come to accept her decisions for her new life. She wrote to them shortly after her return asking for forgiveness and understanding. At the same time, she had learned from experience and was thankful for the fact that, unlike the practice of the Roman church, most ceremonies in *Loch Dubh* were conducted in the home. A ceremony in the Erskine house would be easier for her parents to endure than one in the Kirk. As the months passed, she continued to pray for the letter of response that never arrived.

It was in March that Kristy held her final meeting with Duncan Fraser. Based on her profession of faith, he would approach session with a recommendation for receipt of full membership in the Presbyterian Church. Several weeks later, Kristy entered the Kirk for the first time with the Erskine family. After some seven years in *Loch Dubh*, just this simple act of entering through the double doors was somewhat strange yet welcomed. The sanctuary was all so new, so plain, so very different. As she took her place in the family pew, she recalled the earlier words spoken to her by the Reverend Fraser. Here, in the simplicity of this house, she would stand free before her God upon whom her eternal welfare would rest.

Kristy would later recall hearing the invitation from the minister to come forward. Although she was convinced that her legs would surely fail her, she rose and walked down the aisle to stand before him and the presiding elder — Daniel Erskine. While gaining in strength daily, Daniel had not yet fully recovered from the stroke and it was for this reason that Alasdair had taken over the running of the farm. Yet no physical infirmities would keep Daniel from this place and this moment. Following Kristy's public profession of faith before God and the congregation assembled, the minister placed his hands on her bowed head. The Gaelic words flowed over her like a babbling brook and it was only then that she realized she was being blessed in the language of her ancestors for the first time in her life. *"O gu'm beannaicheadh tu i da rìreadh . . . a chionn gu'm bu toigh leis an Tighearna do Dhia thu. An' ainm an Athar, a Mhic, agus an Spioraid Naoimh. Amen."* (Oh that Thou wouldst bless her indeed . . . for the Lord thy God loveth you. In the name of the Father, and of the Son and of the Holy Ghost. Amen.) Duncan Fraser prayed the words as he always did, looking up towards the ceiling of the Kirk with eyes firmly shut. Near the end of the devotion, he had suddenly paused as his eyes opened and he gazed down upon Kristy. Initially his words were addressed to the Almighty but then, in a very deliberate way, he had spoken directly to the young woman before him as the prayer proceeded to its eventual close. Ever so slowly, Kristy opened her eyes and found herself looking into the face of Duncan Fraser, who was smiling down at her, and Daniel, who was wiping away tears with his handkerchief.

Oblivious to the white curtains billowing in the open window, Kristy entered the parlour for the second time that day. She walked slowly and confidently to a spot immediately before the minister, with Alasdair and Neil to the right and Iona to the left. Off to the side stood the other members of her family, Daniel, Tina and Kenneth. Earlier that morning, Kristy had made a conscious decision to commit every detail of the ceremony to memory as one would place a photograph in a locket for safe keeping. Years later, she would look back and recall two remembrances of that day: the beautiful simplicity of the ceremony and the light that danced in Alasdair's green eyes. As they kissed, Kristy Erskine was conscious of the fact that she could never know a greater happiness than this. After all these years, she was finally home here on the shores of *Loch Dubh*.

⬚ Chapter Eight ⬚

An Ceap Breatuinn chaidh m'àrach eilean àluinn nan gleann,
Far dh'ionnsaich mi Ghàidhlig 's mi 'nam phàisd' aig an àm;
Air glùinean mo mhàthar chàidh mo thàladh 's a' chainnt,
'S nach leig mi air dìchuimhn' ged is liathghlas mo cheann.
> Dan Alex MacDonald
> *Òran Do Chéilidh Cheap Breatuinn* (òran)

In Cape Breton where I was reared, lovely isle of the glens,
Where I learned the Gaelic in the time of my youth;
On the knee of my mother I was lulled in that tongue,
And I'll not forget it though my head turns to grey.
> Dan Alex MacDonald
> *Song to Cape Breton Ceilidh* (song)

It was nothing more than an unfortunate accident that was bound to happen sooner or later. Archie recognized this but for some reasons could not take his eyes off the broken blade that lay in the tall grass at his feet. As he rested his arm on the handle of the scythe, he felt as though he was looking down upon the body of a dearly departed friend. In some ways, it was not dissimilar to his final farewell to Flora in the front parlour of the Grant home some four years ago. The scythe had been with him for as long as he could remember and had witnessed so much change over the years. The thin sliver of metal was so nondescript and, yet, so powerful in its testament to his work and, yes, to his life and time on this land. He raised his eyes to look over the fields, past the house and down to the loch in the distance. Was it not just a few short years ago that the trees had ruled this vast domain, flowing from the summits of the beinns to the very shores of the loch like some regal mantle of green?

He reached down and lovingly retrieved the broken piece of metal, resting forlornly near the partially hidden field stone that had been the cause of its demise. The signs of toil and wear that had weakened its once-strong body over many years were all too apparent. Archie could not help but draw the obvious analogy. This farm that he and Hannah had carved from wilderness, which was so much a part of his life, was now slowly being lost to him. As his grandson Duncan took over greater responsibility for its operation, things were being done so differently. Even the language being used, the "rotation of crops" and other such fancy-sounding terms, was like a foreign tongue to his ears, every bit as strange as had been the English.

Archie's mind was flooded with a host of memories of those early days now so long past. Initially, many things had been strange for him, Hannah and, indeed, all the other early settlers. At every turn, their senses were confronted by a litany of experiences that had all been unknown to them in the old country. They were subjected to the incessant torment of mosquitoes and black flies, cajoled into sleep by the cadenced croaking of frogs, enraptured by the fragrant scent of pine and spruce forests, bewildered by the sight of unfamiliar wildlife and birds, scorned by the oppressive drifting snows and bitter cold — all this and so much more. It was so terribly new but still they adapted and moved on with life and with living as best they could. And even with everything that had gone before, here he stood, alone with nothing but memories and a broken sliver of metal.

Archie found his farm tasks now limited to the immediate area around the house and the out buildings. He kept the high grass back from the orchard and Jessie's garden as well as seeing to the needs of the chickens each day. These chores had become part of his regular routine every bit as much as the frequent naps throughout the day. As the strength seemed to lapse from his eighty-three-year-old body, Archie had increasingly questioned his own usefulness on the farm and his own purpose in life. This was just such a time.

"Och a Dhia nam feart, is ann dhuit as léir mo chàs. Ciod is cor domh? Tha mi a'fannachadh mar sgàile a'claonadh sìos. Is mairg a dh'iarradh aois." (Oh God of wondrous deeds, you see my distress. What is become of me? I am getting more feeble like a shadow declining. Woe to him that wishes old age.) In looking down to the loch with *Beinn-mo-Mhulaid* in the background, Archie slid his hand over the fractured blade in reassuring himself that he was indeed old but not yet broken. The Almighty still had a use for him and he promised himself that he would soldier on as long as there was breath in his earthly body.

It was later over the dinner table that Archie, in passing, informed his grandson about the mishap earlier that morning. Duncan listened attentively and, from his grandfather's voice, knew somehow that this was more than merely a story being recounted or a blade in need of replacement. Over the past year, it had become increasingly apparent that Archie was still reluctant to relinquish control of the farm even though his body told him he must; it was inevitable. Duncan appreciated the symbolic importance of the scythe to the old man and, on the pretext of having to conduct other business, suggested that he and Archie drive down to the town following the noon meal. Allan Dunn carried a good supply of blades at the general store and a new one could be easily purchased. The broad smile on Archie's face was confirmation enough that he would gladly forego his afternoon nap.

Even from afar, Archie and Duncan could see that the town was more active than normal. One reason was immediately evident from their lofty position on the road leading down to the community as they noted the steamer, off in the distance, rounding the islands on its final approach to the government wharf. The second reason became obvious a bit later as they tied the horse and wagon outside the general store. The fisherman had profited from a plentiful catch and were even now in the process of unloading mounds of fish from the decks of their boats. Duncan's first stop would be at the post office to pick up any mail for his family as well as John and Ida. Archie stayed behind; he always sensed that the Calvey woman disliked him and he had no desire to be put ill at ease in her presence, queen or no queen.

Archie mounted the front steps and passed through the store's double doors only to find an animated conversation already in full flight in what had jokingly come to be known as "speakers' corner." At the centre, rested the black pot-bellied stove that now stood stone cold, serving only as a receptacle for the numerous matches that lit the many pipes encircling it. The large windows facing the harbour were open and willingly admitted the cool sea breeze that flooded in to cleanse the room of smoke. As he took his customary place on the side bench, Archie thought it a pity that the breeze could not as effectively cleanse the room of pomposity. The Englishmen were already on about the many changes that were unfolding of late and the effects on their lives, arguing the case for and against. He would listen to their rantings and ravings; if nothing else they provided enjoyable and free entertainment. From where he was seated, Archie noticed Diarmid MacInnes, father of James or *Mac an Fhìdhleir*, tucked in the corner on the far side of the room and mouthing the words *Ciamar a tha thu?* (How are you?) in greeting. Archie nodded his head and waved a hand as if to reply; there would be no sense in trying to compete with this racket.

A few moments had passed before Duncan finally entered the store. In approaching the counter, he managed to take quick inventory in assuring himself that his grandfather was well and truly ensconced in the other "MacDonald pew." He knew that Archie loved nothing better than a good argument, or discussion as he was invariably wont to call it. Either way, Duncan was pleased by the realization that there was still a great deal of life left in the old man. With the benefit of distance, he stood for a few moments and watched Archie sitting in the corner as he first lit his pipe and then lovingly caressed it in his hand. He proceeded to blow smoke towards the ceiling as if consciously steering clear of the conversation that now completely surrounded him. If the truth be known, he sat there hanging onto each and every word, biding his time. It was then that Duncan appreciated that this moment would surely be one of the strongest memories he would always carry and cherish of Archibald Drummond MacDonald. There before him sat Daniel in the lions' den. The only difference was that this Daniel entered the den willingly and would invariably take the greatest pleasure in tweaking as many feline noses as possible.

"This man Marconi has the gumption to use the heavens to send messages across the seas. Who does he think he is, an angel or God Almighty Himself? And these horseless motor carriages that they are after constructing in Upper Canada, they can move swiftly right enough but will never give the farmers fertilizer for their fields. I see no sense in any of it, at all at all." John Rogers was in his glory, expounding his virtuous wisdom to a captive audience that he knew full well would be enthralled by his insightful brilliance. What followed was a temporary lull that was filled only when the unexpected invitation to beard the lion in his own den came from the far corner.

"Agus Eàirdsidh MacDhòmhnuill (And Archie MacDonald), what is it that you yourself would be making of all this now?" The slow buckish inflection of voice indicated that it had to be none other than Diarmid MacInnes who was well known up and down the length of the North Shore as *an seann chleasaiche.* (The Old Trickster) Many a practical joke had been played on the unsuspecting by him and he had quickly developed a stronger reputation as a man of tall tales rather than one of hard work. Regardless, Archie would thank him later for having quite deliberately created the opportunity for him to respond in such a mischievous yet masterful manner.

All eyes were turned to Archie who had remained silent in his pew, quite craftily glancing out the adjacent window as the steamer made its final approach to the wharf. Turning in the direction of Rogers, he slowly removed the pipe from his mouth and proceeded to use it to advantage by prodding the air before him as if to emphasize his point. "There is an expression in the Gaelic — *Dearg-amadan Sasunnach, is trom an t-eallach an t-aineolas* (For a perfect English fool, ignorance is a heavy burden.), which means wait upon the Lord for He will provide you with all things." With the exception of the snickering coming from the far corner and, of course, the smothered chuckle from Duncan who stood by the counter, there was a silent consensus in the room as nodding heads confirmed the validity of such a thoughtful interjection. Certainly, no one was more pleased than the puffed-up John Rogers who smiled smugly, knowing well enough that even the old Scotchman was bound to recognize his powerful and bounteous gifts of knowledge.

The road up the bluffs towards *Loch Dubh* was strewn with laughter as grandfather and grandson relived the episode in "speakers' corner." While Archie sat contentedly holding onto the new blade lying across his lap, Duncan glanced over at him knowing that, humour aside, he had made no real attempt to actually answer the question. He was intrigued to know what Archie's views might be and proceeded to ask him directly. Looking down at the blade, Archie chose his words carefully. *"Och, ma tà!; cor an t-saoghail. Is mór an t-atharrachadh. Is è freasdal Dé."* (Oh indeed!; the state of the world. There is great change. It is God's providence.)

Duncan was not entirely certain as to whether Archie had finally given an answer or not. But then, it did not matter. His grandfather would have his scythe and, with it, a sense of purpose. Duncan smiled as he once again conjured up the image of Daniel in the lions' den, only this time he was proudly leaning on the handle of a scythe. Unbeknown to Duncan, Archie's thoughts were focused not on the blade but on his grandson, not on the past but the future. It was now Archie's turn to look over at Duncan. *Is tu an t-aobharrach ciatach.* (You are a youth that promises well indeed.) The old man had every confidence in the future and, in a carefully measured tone, expressed it aloud in his own indelible way. *"Tha an latha a' coimhead brèagh."* (The day is looking beautiful.) And so it was.

At every turn, there were even more nooks and crannies that offered up delights for all the senses. The old mill stood tucked into the east end of the loch like some old family trunk that had been shoved aside in the far corner of the attic for safekeeping. Once remembered and opened, it and its contents smelled pungently of must brought on by their years of exile from both air and light. The odours rose to enfold the nose as if vainly attempting to grasp the intruders in their clutches and spirit them off to a previous time and place. They reeked of things past.

The soft winds of early October rustled the leaves on the maple trees that stood higher up on the hills in the company of the ever stoic and inalterable evergreens. Peter Campbell took note of the beautiful hues, the red, oranges and yellows, that appeared as indiscriminate dabs of paint on a constantly changing canvas. He sat in the front of the wagon as he transported a load of wheat and oats to the mill to be ground into the winter's supply of flour and oatmeal. He was confident that the numerous burlap bags imprisoned in the back were being well guarded by the wee Campbell "soldiers" who were on active duty. At six years of age, Lachlan had assumed the role of regimental sergeant-major and took some considerable degree of pride in drilling his brother Colin and sister Moira. One and three years younger respectively, his siblings were normally willing to play the game at least for a time. If the most recent military exploits of Clan Campbell were any indication, Lachlan would once again have to deal with a disgruntled mutinous rabble.

The brief trip down the road to the blackened stone mill was as refreshing as it was timely; the threat of insurrection had thankfully passed by the time the horse and wagon drove through the main gate, into the protective custody of the mill grounds. James MacGregor was in the process of returning home with his three boys, having overseen the grinding of the family's own supply of flour and oatmeal. Peter was especially pleased to see the young Albert who had been nurtured back to full health following the accident in the woods some eight months ago. Thankfully, his life had been spared as had his father's soul. James himself was the first to admit this and the increased attention paid both to his farm and family had not gone unnoticed by others around the loch. Was it not Tina Erskine's habit, every time James' name was mentioned, to recite the Psalmist: *Is dlùth an Tighearna dhaibh-san a tha briste 'n an cridhe; agus saoraidh e iadsan a tha brùite 'n an spiorad.* (The Lord is nigh unto them that are of a broken heart; and saveth such as be of a contrite spirit.) Even though he did not know his scripture as well as some of the older folk, Peter was still grateful for James' generous offer of assistance in unloading his cargo and carrying it inside. Now, with no prisoners left to guard, the soldiers of Clan Campbell left the field both in disarray and in search of greater adventure elsewhere.

Once inside the darkened confines of the mill, Peter was greeted by George Thompson from down in New Carlisle. Thompson had inherited both the mill and the role of miller from his father who had constructed it here on crown land back in the 1870s. After the passage of some thirty years, there was still the odd reference made to the monies that had obviously crossed the palms of certain provincial officials in Halifax for an exemption to construct this commercial building. It was not that the people of *Loch Dubh* chose to believe such devious and totally unsubstantiated accusations. Heaven forbid that it should be so. Nonetheless, it had been noted with a certain degree of interest that, following the increase in mill rates imposed by the miller a few years back, the old Gaelic expression *Cluinnidh am bodhar fuaim an airgid* (Even the deaf hear the clink of silver/money) was suddenly returned to more-common usage. Even though actual payment to Thompson normally took the form of a certain percentage of the load milled and money seldom if ever actually exchanged hands, the phrase still slipped easily off the tongue. If nothing else, the *Loch Dubh* people prided themselves on being fair-minded.

Having completed the bartering particulars of the transaction, Peter returned outside to find the children positioned behind the mill adjacent to the sluice gates. There was great excitement and anticipation as Thompson eventually emerged from the mill to open the barriers, permitting the water in the mill dam to cascade through and bring the giant wheel into motion. Little Moira threw several maple leaves into the water and watched attentively as they floated through the gates towards the ravenous teeth of the wheel that eagerly devoured everything offered up to them in sacrifice. She suddenly felt a tremendous pang of guilt for having sent them off to such a tragic end. It was for this reason that the solitary orange leaf resting in her hand was quickly returned to the high grass on the slope behind her. She did not want the boys to see or hear her for they would surely make fun of her sentimentality. As she gingerly placed it down, Moira stroked its smooth surface and softly blanketed it with her comforting words. *"Cha bhi beud dhuit 's an àite seo."* (You will be quite safe/well here.) Only then did she run to rejoin her father and brothers who were preparing to return to the mill in the company of Mr. Thompson.

From the corner of his eye, Peter had kept a sharp watch on Moira to ensure that she did not stray too close to the water's edge. It was with some considerable interest that he observed the committal of the leaf given that he understood her actions all too well and the possible motives behind them. She was so much like her mother; they both had the ability to see the majestic entirety and beauty of God's universe in the smallest of His works. At that moment, Moira had seen it in a single maple leaf. She was far too young to appreciate the fact that, in their magnificently hued mantle of death, the leaves were a sign of life departing and life still to come again. His eyes began to moisten as he thought of Ismay and the coloured leaves.

Immediately upon setting foot inside the mill, the children were off in ten directions at the same time. Peter found a seat on a bag of coarse oats and watched as Thompson enticed each of them with a handful of groats — the grain with the shells peeled off. They loved to chew it and, whenever they returned home from a visit to the mill, Martha was forever checking their teeth and, with mock surprise and horror, referring to them as *mo bhà acrach.* (My Hungry Cows). She delighted in her children and their laughter. It was for this reason that any thought of being separated from them was always met with nothing short of sheer anguish. In this context, it had been difficult for her last October when she had been placed in isolation for a period of two weeks. She had come down with the German measles when she herself was early with child. In time, the rosy-coloured spots that had quickly covered her entire body disappeared and eventually, with Dr. Osborne's approval, her children were returned to her bedside. Such delight Peter had seldom seen from such a simple act. Now, with the huge stones grinding before him, he smiled in remembrance of that reunion. The children were truly her soul.

In so many ways, Ismay's birth in early May was reminiscent of Lachlan six years ago. How he and Archie had waited so anxiously in the kitchen for news. And when it finally came, there was such joy in their hearts. Even then, he realized he would never be able to find words to express what he truly felt. It had been the same at the birth of each of their children. Looking back over the past several months, there had never been any reason for concern; Martha had made a complete recovery from the measles and was looking forward to the imminent arrival of their fourth child. None were more thrilled at the prospect than Lachlan, Colin and Moira, who drew pictures of what they thought the baby would look like and presented them ever so proudly to their mother. Even during art time at school, Kristy Erskine encouraged the Campbell students and took a particularly keen interest in their growing excitement.

She was a beautiful child and the spitting image of her sister Moira as an infant. Had it not been for the passage of three years, they would have most assuredly been taken for twins. Martha delighted in the fact that she had another girl and joked that, for the first time since their marriage, there was an equal number of men and women in the house. More importantly, Archie would have one more grandchild to spoil with peppermints from the general store in New Carlisle. And while all her children were baptised in the same cream-coloured gown made by Peter's mother, only she, Archie and God Himself knew of the tiny bow of MacDonald of Clanranald tartan that remained pinned inside, just over the heart. So it had been with Ismay.

It had not taken Martha long to appreciate, as only a mother could, that something was not quite right with Ismay. There was a distance in the tiny blue eyes that never seemed to change. Indeed, with the passage of weeks into months, there was no ability to focus, only a dependence on hearing that appeared to grow ever stronger. Martha fought to deny even her own suspicions and took steps to intentionally hide them from Peter and the children, as if excuses or outright denial would somehow remove the fear and correct the situation. It did neither. In early September, she had taken the morning steamer to Ingonish to have Dr. Osborne examine the child. Later the same day, the return to *Loch Dubh* was perhaps the longest and most painful journey of her life. Her tears, flowing from eyes that could see, fell on those that could not, would not, ever. *"Och a Dhia, an diugh an nuair a dhorchaicheas na speuran, bi ad cheann mhath dhi fhad 's a bhios i anns an t-saoghal. Is e an Tighearna mo sholus."* (Oh God, on this day when the heavens darken, be good to her as long as her earthly pilgrimage lasts. The Lord is my light.) Through her tears, she pleaded for understanding and, most of all, for hope. It was well past dusk when Martha finally arrived home and put Ismay to bed. Late that night, in the darkness of her room next to her dear mother's cradle, Martha prayed for guidance in determining how best to share the troubling news with her family. Most of all, she prayed for strength and for light.

Seated on a bench near the mill's main door with his thoughts elsewhere, Peter was suddenly aware of Moira who now stood in front of him and proceeded to place her hand firmly on his knee. As the "wee coo" continued to chew on a mouthful of groats, she took great delight in producing a blue jay's feather from behind her back that she had discovered high up in the loft of the mill. She had decided that it would be given to her baby sister because it was such a beautiful colour and would be a perfect match for her eyes. For the second time that day, his daughter had unknowingly demonstrated that the magnificence of God's creation was to be found in the least of His works. He smiled down at her with gratitude and the knowledge that a small child had brought him closer to the true majesty of Someone, of something, far greater than he could ever hope to fully comprehend. It was not that his child was blind; it was that his family was so truly blessed.

How anyone could possibly call it a mountain, in whatever language, was totally beyond him. He was accustomed to looming masses of green that soared up to touch the sky. *Beinn-mo-Mhulaid* was truly a mountain while this one, royal or otherwise, was nothing more than a wee *cnoc*. (knoll) Not that it mattered a great deal; he was not here to climb the hills like the sheep of his childhood days. Rather, his purpose was to become a shepherd of men, to gather them up and watch over them. *Am buachaille maith; bithidh iad ann dìdein glaic a làimhe.* (The Good Shepherd; they shall be safe in the hollow of His hand.) The image was an apt one and his thoughts were now of Duncan Fraser and the tender care that he rendered to his own flock in such a selfless and consummate manner. No, what lay before him was certainly not a mountain. But then it did not matter for, in time, his sheep would be found on far different hillsides.

As he looked northward up the length of McTavish Street, Rod's eyes were drawn to the elegant mansions that had been built by two of the most prominent commercial barons who were so closely associated with the development of Montreal as a thriving mercantile city. In the foreground was the residence of Simon McTavish who had died well before its completion a good century ago. Some of the local residents claimed that, late at night, his ghost could be seen sliding down the street on the lid of his coffin. Rod was thankful that the gas lamps in the college dormitory were extinguished at 11:00 p.m. He had no inclination to make Mr. McTavish's acquaintance, sailing down the street or otherwise. And farther up still, built into the side of the mountain, was Ravenscrag, the home of Sir Hugh Allan who had amassed such immense wealth in the shipping trade. Rod could not help but see both mansions as glorious testaments to man's vanity. In attempting to leave their mark on the landscape, they immortalized their dwellings as if they were to stand as grandiose tombs. In a hushed tone, he spoke the compelling words from John 14: 2: "In my Father's house are many mansions: if it were not so, I would have told you. I go to prepare a place for you." They were both so different from the homes on other more-distant hillsides known to him. It seemed so fitting that these *tighean loinnear gun bhrìgh* (elegant homes without meaning), as he came to call them, should stand in such pale contrast with the natural glory of the treed slopes that rose up behind in such an unassuming yet majestic manner.

Rod continued to sit at the desk in his dormitory room, looking down onto the street and across to the central lawn of McGill University. He found it passing strange that he felt somewhat at home here, far from the shores of *Loch Dubh*. The second year of his studies was quickly drawing to a close and, with the exception of a brief visit home last summer, he had not seen his family in almost two years. So much had changed since the late-summer day when he first passed through the large wooden doors of Presbyterian College.

On that particular day, Rod had a chance meeting that would bring him to the greater realization that *Loch Dubh* would never be far away. In the main foyer of the college, he encountered a number of other first-year students milling about in front of the reception desk. No doubt, some would have been on the same Grand Trunk train that had arrived earlier that afternoon at the station in Dominion Square. It was as he proceeded across the foyer towards the besieged receptionist that he was suddenly taken aback by faint mutterings emanating from a sheltered alcove off to the side. With curiosity upon him, Rod diverted his path until he found himself standing before a seated figure with bowed head. The young man was obviously self absorbed as he rifled through a piece of baggage that rested innocently on the floor before him. *"Mallachadh! Càit' a bheil na litri-chean?"* (Damnation! Where are the letters?) Rod smothered a laugh as he reached forward and touched the man on the shoulder.

"An téid mì 'n ad chobhair?" (Can I help you?) Rod's question startled Angus MacKinnon, from Hunter River, Prince Edward Island, who was equally surprised to meet another Gaelic speaker in the midst of this large, Lower Canadian city. Once proper introductions had been made, Angus was able to return to the task at hand and was eventually successful in lo-cating his letters of credentials and acceptance — an obvious prerequisite for admission. Of still greater consequence, he had even then begun to forge a close friendship that he believed would last a very long time.

Rod and Angus registered together and were allocated rooms next to each other on the second floor of the adjacent college building, which housed the convocation hall, library, dining-room, and dormitory facili-ties. Of the twenty-five students enrolled for the first-year theological pro-gramme, they were the only two from the eastern provinces. There again, there were three students from the neighbouring colony of Newfoundland. However, their accents were so different, as thick as buttermilk on a cold day, much like some of the others from the United States, Britain and, es-pecially, Ireland. Still other students, in the French-language course, could speak English only haltingly at best. Rod and Angus often boasted that, should the student body ever be charged with the building of a latter-day Tower of Babel, at least the two of them would be able to communicate with the Almighty in His own language. The others never seemed to grasp their particular humour in quite the same way.

It was not long before Rod had adapted to the regular daily routine that all students were expected to follow: morning bell at 7:00 a.m., breakfast at 7:30 a.m., morning classes, dinner at 1:00 p.m., afternoon classes, tea, or supper as he still called it, at 6:30 p.m., evening studies and to bed with the compulsory extinguishing of gas lamps at 11:00 p.m. Throughout, his constant companion was the long black robe that now lay lifeless, draped across the foot of his bed. Jokingly referred to as the eleventh command-ment, it was prescribed that all theological students would wear them to every class and Rod had soon come to the conclusion that, in all likeli-hood, it was as much to prepare the future men of the cloth for the feel of the clerical robes as it was to ensure a degree of sobriety in the classroom. Regardless, Angus was forever chuckling about how their families back home would scoff at the daily parade across campus of the *caoraich dhubha*

Mhontreal (The Black Sheep of Montreal) as they were dutifully herded off to their classes.

With the passage of weeks and months, Rod remained faithful in writing home regularly and had offered his family some insights into the various subjects that he was now pursuing. In addition to Greek and Hebrew that were given across the way at McGill, he was submerged in the study of the Old and New Testaments, pastoral theology, church government and history, sacred rhetoric, and still other courses. On more than one night, long after the lamps had been quenched, Rod stared at the ceiling in search of strength and wisdom in making his way through, and actually fathoming, the myriad of material that was all so new and unfamiliar. It was apparent that the transformation from a black sheep to a caring shepherd was not to be an easy one, even here in the shadow of a "royal mountain."

The first year had been particularly difficult for Rod, yet he had applied himself and received acceptable grades. With the rigorous challenge before him, there had been very little free time for any activity other than his studies. Exploring the city was a fairly rare luxury, although both he and Angus made a conscious effort to attend services, in turn, at the four Presbyterian churches that were in close proximity to the College. It had been in late November that they had first met the Sinclair family at the Erskine Church on La Gauchetière Street. James Sinclair was a well-known physician in the city whose highland ancestors had originally settled in the Eastern Townships near East Angus. The old farm house was still there, although now used only as a summer retreat from the oppressive heat of the city. It was in the Sinclair house on Sherbrooke Street that both Rod and Angus had enjoyed Christmas dinner for the past two years. Although the good doctor still had the Gaelic, his wife and children did not. Consequently, it was later in the evening, over glasses of port in the mahogany-panelled library, that the three men would converse about all manner of things including theology, philosophy and classical literature. Rod's thoughts were frequently of the Reverend Fraser and how, with the exception of the spirited libation, he would surely feel at ease and would delight in such discussions.

For his part, Dr. Sinclair revelled in these all-too-infrequent gatherings. It was not just because of the challenging nature of the debate or even the special bond that seemed to develop so naturally between them — there was something more. These two men, so full of youth and the future, spoke in the language of his own childhood that was now so much a part of his family's distant past. While his throat delighted in the smoothness of a fine port, his ears luxuriated in the sweetness of something far more intoxicating. There was such a joy about it all.

The late-April sun had just taken its leave from the western sky as Rod returned from supper in the dining hall. There would be an examination on homiletics in a few days and he knew that he would have to make a special effort to apply himself. However, his mind was preoccupied with the mission field that he would soon be assigned for the upcoming summer months. He hoped that he would be fortunate enough to return to a congregation in Nova Scotia or even Prince Edward Island. He still missed being by the water. Almost subconsciously, he had retrieved a topcoat and was now proceeding down McTavish towards St. Catherine Street. Even at this hour, there was a fair bit of activity as the electric tram cars jostled along steel-ribbed highways with their cargos of nameless faces peering out in silence. For the first time, Rod carefully noted the multitude of electrical, tramway and telephone lines that criss-crossed above his head and appeared to dissect the sky into hundreds if not thousands of different puzzle-like pieces. How different it was from *Loch Dubh* where faces were known to each other and the majestic expanse of the heavens extended unbroken over the mountains and sea into infinity.

Rod proceeded south along Beaver Hall Street towards the Saint Lawrence. In Victoria Square, he stopped for a drink of water at the stone fountain that carried the noble inscription "Fountain of Health." Several months earlier, ironically enough with a glass of *uisge beatha* in hand, Dr. Sinclair had informed Rod and Angus that the fountain had been erected by the Montreal Temperance Society in the hope that its subtle evangelizing message would be heeded. It made Rod think of James MacGregor and a flood of memories of home streamed across his mind as he approached the river and turned into de la Commune Street. With the twin towers of Notre Dame Church and the dome of the Bonsecours Market building in the distance, Rod stood for a brief time admiring the paddle-wheeled steamboats tied up along the dock. Their presence signalled the reopening of the harbour and the certain arrival of spring. It was lambing time on the hills back home.

As he proceeded down the wooden walkway, Rod was oblivious to the two figures standing in the shadows on the opposite side of the street. "Hé, beau blond, t'aimerais pa ça t' faire réchauffer un p'tit peu?" (Hey, handsome. Wouldn't you like to be warmed up a bit?) The high-pitched voice cut the tranquil evening air as if it were a knife in search of an unsuspecting victim. Although caught somewhat by surprise, Rod turned and was quick enough to know what these darkened figures were and, more importantly, to whom their remark had been addressed.

"Tha mi duilich. Chan eil Fraingis agamsa." (I am sorry. I do not speak French.) With that he walked on at a faster pace, back in the direction of the College. In so doing, it suddenly occurred to him that he had turned his back; he had abandoned his future. He had abandoned two lost sheep in need of a shepherd. If only he had taken the time. If only he was able to speak their language. If only. He could have at least spoken with them and, in the process, made an attempt to put his limited knowledge of homiletics to good use.

Rod quickly passed from view and would not have had any way of seeing the faces of the two women being illuminated as a match was struck to light a much-needed cigarette. *"Ça doit être un matelot polonais. Y sont toujours tellement cheap avec leur argent."* (He must be a Polish sailor. They are always so cheap with their money.) They chuckled to themselves. It seemed as though the cigarette would sustain them at least for the moment; business was bound to pick up. Now well out of sight, the Polish sailor was never given a second thought.

The seed had been planted and allowed to germinate for quite some time. Indeed, it was almost three years ago that it had first taken root and was now nearing maturity. Back then, Emily had still been the young girl who found such enjoyment in picking wild flowers and going for long walks on the hillsides high above the loch. In some respects, those three years felt like a lifetime ago and now her life was moving forward far too quickly. Things were different; changes that could never have been imagined had either come to pass or were on the verge of doing so. She knew that they could have been different, perhaps should have been. But what did it matter? Was this not her destiny of her own choosing? She still had the presence of mind to realize that, increasingly, the reality of her situation could not be ignored.

Initially, the visit of her mother's cousin and husband from the Boston states had been a source of some disquiet among the children. Certainly Sandy had complained bitterly about the work that he was being asked to do in preparation for the family reunion. In stark contrast, Emily had taken to the tasks of cleaning, polishing and sorting given that they added to the sense of imminent excitement that was so seldom felt at home. Her American cousin was coming "from away" and suddenly the visit represented something terribly intriguing if not compelling. Emily shared her mother's tendency to muse about where her life might lead and, of equal importance, what influences might be brought to bear. Or was it all predestined as she had been taught from the **Westminster Confession** and the works of Luther, Calvin, Knox and others? Even with their beautiful colours, shapes and fragrances, the wild flowers no longer held her captive the way they once did. How quickly they and their beauty wilted, died and passed from both sight and mind. Somehow she knew that there was so much more beyond the floral hills of *Loch Dubh* and that, heresy or not, she had a role to play in discovering it and making it her own.

Sandy, Matthew and Emily had spent a great deal of time with Liam, showing him all their secret places that were oftentimes linked together by the many cow paths that dissected the woods like an arboreal maze. They extolled the pleasures of what their visitor liked to call the "simple country life." He demonstrated a genuine interest in each of them by asking all manner of questions about life in *Loch Dubh*, surrounded as it was by nothing but dark waters and high mountains. He found it all very quaint and, on several occasions, had suggested that they should come visit him in the big city. There would be so many other things for them to see and do. Emily was particularly captivated by his promise to take her for a ride on the swan boats in the public gardens. She had never seen a swan before and had difficulty imagining herself riding on its back. Just the thought of having one in a garden seemed like such a strange idea. Was not her own mother so protective of her manicured flower beds? Even the odd chicken that dared venture into this particular sanctum was quickly banished with the assistance of a broom and much shooing. She had made up her mind that, one day, she would indeed go for a ride on a swan, regardless of her initial apprehensions.

Not that Emily's attention had been totally focused on the Irishman and his invitations, as enticing as they were. On those occasions when her mother and Effie were not out for one of their lengthy walks, she made a conscious attempt to pass time in the company of her elegant American cousin. Once, in the kitchen pantry, she had shared with Effie the secret to making fluffy baking-powder biscuits. She herself had learned early on that over-kneading the dough would result in something not totally dissimilar to hard rocks. What laughter had erupted when an unexpected gust of wind flooded through the window, blowing flour into Emily's hair and making her look like a *cailleach* at the ripe old age of twelve. Effie had remarked on the striking resemblance between Emily and her own mother; the white hair served only to highlight the strong physical features that ran deep in her family. For her part, Emily could not explain the tears that suddenly appeared in the corners of Effie's eyes and quickly sought to reassure her that a little less flour would make no great difference. She quipped that the biscuits would be every bit as good as manna from Heaven. Laughter was eventually restored to the pantry as Effie used her hand to gently brush the flour from her young cousin's hair and, more discretely, wipe a few tell-tale tears from her own cheeks.

Later that same evening, Effie had invited Emily into the bedroom to try on one of her hats — the glorious straw one decorated with artificial flowers all around the brim. She felt so elegant with her floral crown and stood for several minutes in front of the window, using it as a mirror in admiring her own reflection. She dreamed of life in the city; she became a grand matron of a large stately mansion who took long saunters down the street so as to provide others with the full benefit of her elegant ap-pearance. Effie gently removed the hat from her young cousin's head and returned it to its box, causing the imaginary stroll to come to an abrupt end. Perhaps one day Emily's dream would come true. After all, Effie had invited her to come and visit her in Boston whenever she liked. They would have great fun together, especially visiting the many dress and hat shops along Tremont and Washington Streets. Not unlike the swan ride, she was determined to make it so.

It was difficult for her to believe that it had been three years already.

Still, so much had changed in Emily's life and that of her family. Sandy had graduated from the academy in Sydney and was currently employed as a custom's agent down at the harbour. It was last September that Matthew had also relocated to town to finish his education. The manse seemed so empty and silent without the two of them; it was apparent that she and her mother felt their absence although it was seldom discussed. Even the practical jokes that had been so frequently played out at their expense were now recollected with a fair degree of fondness. Of particular note was the upstairs bedroom that was now so still as if hushed in anxious anticipation of their return. Joseph's coat of many colours looked forlorn as it lay folded across the foot of Sandy's bed, waiting to once again regale someone with its stories. Yet even with the passage of time, the reflection of the girl with the floral crown in the window had stayed with Emily as if it was a photograph that had been lovingly removed from a drawer to be studied, stroked and brought back to life once more.

It had always been assumed by both Duncan and Jennie that Emily would follow in her brothers' footsteps and, upon completion of studies with Kristy Erskine, would attend the academy in the recently incorporated City of Sydney. There had never been any doubt about it or so it seemed; it had all been assumed. For this reason, it came as a surprise to Jennie when Emily first raised the idea of not continuing on to higher studies, at least not just yet. On more than one occasion, she and her classmate, Morag Ferguson, had discussed the possibility of going away to find work in other parts. They would sit on the mill bridge and talk for hours about themselves in the future tense. Invariably, Emily would look into the dark waters below and see yet another reflection of herself wearing an even more-elegant bonnet. There was the sudden realization that dreams could come true. It was then that the watery image before her abruptly changed, as if the ripples were a curtain separating one theatrical act from another. The curtain was drawn back and she saw herself strolling down the streets of Boston wearing the most exquisite clothes and majestic hats. She promised herself that her dream would come true because she would make it so.

During twenty years of marriage, Duncan and Jennie had had many discussions but this was the first serious disagreement. She had never before challenged his position as head of the household and did so only with a great deal of trepidation. But still, she was determined to stand her ground. On this point, she knew that she must, not only for Emily but also for herself. She could not help but reflect back on her own youth and the dreams that she once had, the dreams that she and Effie had talked about, before she had met this man now standing before her. For many long years, she had lived with doubts about what her life was and what it could have been. While Effie and Liam's visit had helped to calm her mind with all its lingering uncertainties, she did not want her daughter to ever feel regret at not having followed her heart. No, she could not let her. She would not.

It was only after the passing of some considerable time and thought that a compromise was finally reached between them. Emily would be permitted to enter domestic service in Boston for a trial period of one year. It was further understood that she would travel in the company of Morag and that the two girls would be settled under Effie's watchful supervision. Even before her discussion with Duncan, Jennie had written to her cousin asking if it would be possible for the girls to stay at the O'Sullivan residence for a brief period, at least until such time as gainful employment could be found. The response was not long in coming; Effie and Liam were delighted with the notion of having company and would most surely take the girls into their care. At the end of her letter, Effie made a special point of indicating her pleasure at the prospect of finally having "family" in Boston.

It was at Easter time that Duncan and Jennie shared their decision with Emily. As evening worship in the front parlour ended with everyone kneeling, Duncan offered a prayer for God to watch over and guide their daughter as she embarked on a new journey along a different pathway. With head still bowed, Emily opened her eyes and raised them high enough to catch a glimpse of her mother smiling across at her. It was only with the final Amen that Emily quickly rose to her feet and raced across the room to embrace her mother and then her father. Jennie watched with intense interest as Duncan held his daughter. She knew him well enough to appreciate that he would be terribly uncomfortable with such open displays of affection. For his part, Duncan could seldom remember tears flowing so freely as they did now, except for the times when he rocked on the front porch with thoughts of his own youth, his own parents, his own mother. Alone in the rocking chair, his tears were for the innocence of youth and the grievous parting from his past. Now, in the arms of his child, his tears were for the imminent separation from his daughter. For the first time, he was forced to accept the realization that Emily had made the transition from mere child to young woman. He slowly broke the embrace and smiled into her face; how much she resembled her grandmother.

Sitting alone on the mill bridge, Emily felt the warm June breeze play with her hair as she gazed down the loch towards the manse. In a matter of a few weeks, she and Morag would be on a steamer bound for Boston and this place would soon become nothing more than a distant memory of her past. It was then that she looked down into the water and, for the first time, saw nothing. There were no floral crowns, no leisurely strolls, no shops on Tremont and Washington Streets. Thee was only the blackness of the deep water. She knew that the departure date could not come quickly enough. However, it was not *Loch Dubh* or her parents that she was so anxious to leave behind. It was her shame.

As she began to walk in the direction of the manse, her thoughts travelled back to her parents on that evening in the front parlour several months ago. She had found herself in her father's arms before she realized what it was she was doing. There were tears in his eyes; she had seen them. He loved her. He must; he embraced her and looked longingly into her eyes and face. Would he love her now? Would anyone love her again? Even Peter MacGregor, who had so sweetly and convincingly professed his love to her in the barn loft, now kept a discreet distance. It was not the chirping of the birds or even the wind playing through the trees that now filled her ears; it was the ridicule of the voices that came to her. *Mac dìolain — rugadh an diolanas e! Beannachd a seud is a siubhal leis. Bidh i an aire sin ri beò. Is fhasa deagh ainm a chall na chosnadh. Is buaine na gach nì an nàire.* (An illegitimate son — he was born in fornication! May she fare as she deserves. She shall feel the evil effects of this during her life. It is easier to lose a good name than to gain one. Shame is more lasting than anything else.) Emily felt the sudden chill of the breeze coming off the loch, wrapped her arms around herself and quickened her pace.

Her parents must never know; she would see to that. *"Fàth an duilgheadais. An nì nach cluinn cluas cha ghluais cridhe."* (This would be the cause of their sorrow. What does not reach the ear cannot affect the heart.) She found herself whispering these words over and over again to reassure herself while conscious of the fact that her impending exile was to be as complete as it was lasting. Soon, these waters and mountains would be gone from her as would her family. Was this also part of her dream? With a thousand thoughts racing across her mind, Emily unconsciously ran her hands down to her stomach and spoke aloud as if to comfort. *"Tha thu am falach an dràsda. Bi cho sàmhach ri uan — m' uan bhrògach."* (You are well hidden for now. Be as quiet as a lamb — my black-faced lamb.) The young woman would bear her child in silence but now the young girl was forced to cry out in a desperate attempt to be consoled, to be understood. *"Tha mi am aonais."* (I am all alone.)

The cool breeze subsided and Emily proceeded at a slower pace down the winding road leading to the Kirk and home. Her eyes followed the lines of the white steeple as it pointed heavenwards against the broad expanse of green that was *Beinn-mo-Mhulaid*. For all these years, she had looked out her bedroom window upon this mountain and never once questioned its name — The Mountain of My Sorrows. As she grew closer, it loomed larger, higher and more ominous as though her sorrows were somehow growing more burdensome with each passing step.

"Mo ghòraich as coireach rium; is mó an diùbhail! Tha tìde bhi falbh. Mar cheathach air na beanntaibh, is amhuil mo bheatha is aisling." (My own folly is my fault; it is a great pity! It is time to be going. As the mist on the hills, my life is like a dream.) Emily was aware that she was not simply walking down the loch road towards *Beinn-mo-Mhulaid*. She had already embarked on a journey that, even now, was leading her into the dream-like mist that was her future.

🔯 Chapter Nine 🔯

Aig gach nì tha tràth, agus àm aig gach rùn fo nèamh:
Am gu breith, agus àm gu bàs fhaotainn; àm gu suidheachadh, agus àm
gus an ni a shuidhicheadh a spìonadh suas;

Eclesiastes III: 1 - 2

To every thing there is a season, and a time to every purpose
under the heaven: A time to be born, and a time to die; a time to
plant, and a time to pluck up that which is planted;

Ecclesiastes III: 1 - 2

It was hard to believe that she had been gone from *Loch Dubh* for such a long period of time. In some odd way, it was as if she had never been away. It all looked as it was; so unchanged. As a child growing up here, she had always wanted things to happen, anything to happen, that would bring some sense of excitement to her life. It struck her as being strange that she now felt such relief in returning to this place where the word change held such little relevance. Here in the hollow of the mountains, life continued on as it had. And yet, for some reason, beyond her ability to explain, she was grateful.

As the horse and wagon rounded the final turn in the road at the top of the bluffs, the loch stretched out before her as it sat majestically reflecting the brilliant blue sky of the late-August afternoon. A slight breeze rose up from the water to gently stroke her long hair and then, every bit as quickly, to mischievously send it in a flurry of different directions all at once. Perhaps it still remembered her as the little girl who would walk down the road in her ever-so-stylish lilac-coloured dress and who loved the feel of the cloth caressing her slender limbs. Even the wind remained the same; it was as wicked as ever. But the reality was that two years had passed and, if nothing else, her life had changed. Even now, it was changing. As she reached up to reclaim her hair and restore it to some semblance of order, Elizabeth was suddenly thankful for her childhood here in the shadow of these mountains and by the edge of these waters. It did not matter that it was forever the same, forever unchanged and unchanging. She had come back for a special purpose that would, in so many ways, finally draw this chapter to a close. She allowed the breeze to once again ravish her hair and do with it as it pleased. After all, there would be plenty of time to make herself presentable before the wedding.

"Am pòsadh; mo phòsadh." (The wedding; my wedding.) Elizabeth repeated the words slowly as if she were savouring some delectable morsel at a sumptuous banquet table. After all these years, she would finally prove her brothers Donald and Allan wrong. As small children, they would constantly refer to their older sister as either *maighstear-sgoile* (School Mistress) or *se-ann mhaighdeann* (Old Maid), whichever one might succeed at that particular moment in aggravating her the most, depending on the circumstance. Now Allan was making a special trip home from Sydney to be with the rest of the family for the wedding of their very own "school mistress." At twenty-one years of age, Elizabeth's spinster days were finally drawing to a close and she was delighted that her parents and two brothers would be there to share her happiness. *Seadh gu dearbh, Domhnall agus Ailean. Cha bhi: cha bhi mise 'n am chnagaid. Bràithrean anabarrach dona!* (Yes indeed, Donald and Allan. No; I will not be an old maid. Very bad brothers!) She laughed to herself at the thought of calling her eighteen and nineteen-year-old brothers *na seann fhleasgaich.* (The Old Bachelors) Although the days of her childhood were well past, such amusing and hopefully embarrassing revenge on the boys would be wonderfully sweet.

It was precisely two years ago that Elizabeth had first travelled to Boularderie to take up her duties at the Millville school. From the outset, her responsibilities at the school and in the Patterson household were incredibly demanding on her time and energies. Yet, she felt a tremendous sense of fulfillment in being the teacher that she had always dreamed of becoming. It was only several months later, once she had settled into a regular routine, that Elizabeth slowly came to the understanding that something was still missing from her life. Her fondness for Calum MacLeod had continued to grow and, for the first time since that spring day many years ago in Baddeck, she was able to profess her love. The difference now was that she was no longer reticent; she would freely and willingly stand before this man and say those simple words that had always evaded her lips, if not her heart. *"Tha gaol agam ort."* (I love you.) It was only with considerable reflection and the passage of weeks and months that Elizabeth had come to appreciate that Andrew had taught her a valuable lesson about life and living, even though he may not have known it at the time. She hoped that he would now. She felt a need to thank him.

Calum had proposed marriage on a late-October evening the previous year as he drove Elizabeth home from prayer meeting at the Millville hall. Years later, he would clearly recall that night when the stars in the heavens paled in comparison to the light in her eyes. She had accepted his proposal of marriage almost matter-of-factly and then parted from him with a brief embrace. For her part, Elizabeth had committed to memory the scene of his passing from sight down the tree-lined laneway and her speaking softly to the night air. *"Is tù m'annsachd — an duin' òg is mùirneach agamsa."* (You art my best beloved — the young man I so dearly cherish.) She was never more certain of anything and entered the Patterson house through the kitchen door with the promise of a new life and the realization that she would never fully comprehend her own heart. She thought of her dear mother and the commonly-used saying that was forever on her lips — *Och ma tà; aig Dia tha brath.* (Oh indeed; God alone knows.) Elizabeth could not help but think that perhaps it was true after all.

The engagement was officially announced to both families at Christmas. The festive season was made all the more joyous with the news that filled both the Urquhart and MacLeod homes. Yet no one was more pleased than young Stewart who, at eight years of age, could never remember seeing his father happier than when he was with Elizabeth. Totally unbeknown to either Calum or Elizabeth, Stewart had already made the three of them a family, at least in his own mind. Soon it would actually happen for real and he was finally to have a mother once more like everyone else. The house would never again have an emptiness about it; he was to have a whole family after all this time and he was incredibly happy for both his father and Elizabeth. But, most of all, he was happy for himself.

The wedding was to take place in *Loch Dubh* in late August, carefully timed to fall between the end of hay making and the beginning of the school year. At Christmas, Elizabeth had met with the Reverend Fraser and hand delivered a personal letter addressed to him from the Reverend David Drummond, minister of St. James. Duncan read it carefully as Elizabeth sat across from him in the stark silence of the manse's front parlour. The letter introduced Calum MacLeod as a God-fearing man whose love of family was surpassed only by his love of his God. He would make a most deserving husband for Elizabeth Urquhart and, together, they would enrich both the community and Kirk with their family life. Duncan read each word intently and, after several minutes, refolded the paper, carefully placed it back in its envelope and committed it to an inside pocket of his coat without a single comment.

It was Elizabeth's thoughts, not those of another minister, that now most preoccupied Duncan Fraser's mind; she was of his flock. They discussed the sanctity of marriage and the preparation for the service that he was being asked to conduct. As they spoke, he could not help but think of dear Flora Grant and the righteous indignation that had swept over her about a certain brightly coloured frock worn by a certain youthful congregant several years ago. As she spoke of her love for Calum and his for her, Elizabeth was at a loss to explain the tell-tale traces of a smile that appeared on Reverend Fraser's otherwise stoic face. How Flora had pointed her finger and preached to any and all wanton sheep who might be tempted to stray from the fold. *"Och Dhia! Tha thu ruith air t'anraidh. Is e ailleantachd maise nam ban."* (Oh God! You are courting disaster. Modesty is the ornament of women.) In her long black and terribly modest frock, Flora became John Knox preaching to Queen Mary from the lofty pulpit of the High Kirk of St. Giles. *Loch Dubh* had indeed changed, even in the few years since Flora had been called to her eternal rest. Duncan's faint smile was in recognition of the fact that she was now mercifully free from the tribulations brought on by the many changes of this world. It was also with the certain knowledge that the "Queen of Scots" was even now growing more accustomed to fiery sermons delivered from the pulpits of Heaven.

At first, she thought the light streaming through the bedroom window was the first sign of dawn, the dawn of this her wedding day. Elizabeth soon realized that it was nothing more than the shimmering moon that so illuminated the room. On the far wall, beyond the foot of the bed, hung her white dress that now appeared as if it were a vacuous spirit in search of substance and form. She knew that she had been awake for several minutes and that, in all likelihood, excited anticipation would continue to keep her from sleep. In the silence of the room with the ghostly figure watching her every move, Elizabeth dressed and quietly left the house through the kitchen. She walked down by the loch as the moonlight danced on its surface, like the flickering flame of a candle attempting to lick the blackness into submission. The "candle light" guided her steps and she proceeded on through the solitary silence of the early morning. She had never before fully appreciated the beauty that was to be found under the cloak of night that would soon be disrobed and then ravenously possessed by the approaching dawn. It was as if the stillness enhanced the senses and awakened them to splendours that were overwhelming in their intensity. It was almost too great to comprehend all at once and so she did the only thing she could. She walked on, allowing it to simply enfold her.

A few moments later, Elizabeth found herself seated on a cushion of soft dew-mantled grass as she watched the first rays of sunlight amble slowly into the eastern sky. They apppeared somewhat reluctant if not fearful of the looming stoic figures that stood guard before them. Against the light, the stony silhouettes of *An Toiseach* and *An Deireadh* looked so strong, so constant and foreboding. These watchmen had always been with her and were truly a source of comfort, as was the cairn against which she was now resting. She convinced herself that she had come here to watch the sun rise on her wedding day. And yet, she knew that it was as much to witness the dispelling of darkness as it gradually retreated into nothingness. As she rose to return home in order to ensure that her absence would not be noted and questions put to her, Elizabeth picked up a tiny stone and gently placed it on the crown of the cairn. Then, before descending the hill towards the cemetery gate and the loch road beyond, she lovingly placed her left hand, the one soon to be ornamented with gold over the pebble and looked into the face of *Beinn-mo-Mhulaid*. "*Is e seo an làtha 's brèagh nam bheatha. Tapadh leat Anndra.*" (This is the most beautiful day of my life. Thank you Andrew.)

Although somewhat unusual, the wedding ceremony was to be held in the Kirk, which was filled with all the families of *Loch Dubh*, some from up and down the North Shore and even a smattering of people from New Carlisle. In addition to Calum, the MacLeods of Boularderie were represented by his parents and Stewart. Tillie sat next to her grandson who played continuously with his MacLeod of Harris tartan tie, the one that Elizabeth had given him as a present at Christmas. It was a prized possession that he had insisted on wearing on this important day when the clan would gain a new member and he a long-sought-after mother. An errant breeze from the open windows played mayhem with his hair while the fragrance of freshly harvested hay wafted through, as if to sanctify the Kirk with its perfume. But it was not this that preoccupied his mind. Stewart wanted a short service; he had never before been to a wedding and silently hoped that there would be no sermon.

Faith in the power of positive thinking was rewarded as Stewart soon found himself in the company of his immediate and expanded family as they returned to the Urquhart home. Mercifully for him, a sermon had not been delivered; his hunger was for something far more tangible and satisfying. Indeed, it was here, at home in her own kitchen, that Sarah had spent many long hours in preparing a special meal of celebration. With the myriad of details that occupied her time, she had gratefully accepted the offer of assistance from the Erskines. Tina and Kristy would make the cake while Iona, even though heavy with child, insisted on doing up several plates of sweets for the table. It was important to Sarah to have everything just so for the MacLeods and for Elizabeth, Elizabeth MacLeod. It all seemed so strange, so much change all at once. But then, it was just a name; Urquhart or MacLeod, it did not matter. Sarah smiled to herself knowing full well that MacGregor blood would always flow in her daughter's veins.

Later that same night, the residents of *Loch Dubh* gathered in the community hall for the wedding *cèilidh*. Calum and Elizabeth, along with their parents and Alasdair and Kristy, were given the honour of forming the first square set. Everyone else made a circle around them and clapped their hands in time with the beat of Jamie MacInnes' fiddle music. It was not long before several other sets had formed and the entire floor was flooded with whirling circles of colour. It was approximately a half hour later, during one of Jamie's well-deserved breaks, that Elizabeth took advantage of the relative quiet to properly introduce Calum, his parents and Stewart, to everyone present. Peter Campbell, whose mother was a MacLeod from Boularderie, was delighted to discover they were second cousins. Archie MacDonald made a point of telling them that his dear wife Hannah had been a MacLeod and that he had often incurred her wrath by reminding her that the MacLeods of Lewis had once been vassals of the MacDonalds. If the sense of righteous and somewhat vehement indignation that quickly poured from her was any indication, there was truly no doubt but that she was a MacLeod, as strong headed as the bull on her clan's badge. Much laughter ensued and Elizabeth basked in the joy of the moment, knowing that the MacLeods felt so at home with her people. She tousled Stewart's hair and held him close. *Mo mhac.* (My son)

It was also during the break that Margaret MacGregor and Kristy had finally been convinced that it was incumbent upon them to offer up a song in honour of the newly married couple. Once the women had finally agreed upon what they considered to be an appropriate selection and the words of introduction properly made, a hush fell over the hall as the two melodic voices broke into the chorus of the well-known love song *Ho Ro 'S Toigh Leam Fhein Thu*. (*Ho, Ro, How I Love You*) Margaret and Kristy took turns singing the verses and it was several moments later that Kristy's voice suddenly began to waver. From the distant look in her eyes, it was as if she were singing to someone or something well beyond the confines of the hall's wooden walls.

> *"Toil d'athair 's do mhàthair,*
> *'S do chàirdean mar chòmla.*
> *'S gu 'n cluinneamaid gar n-éubhach.*
> *'S an teampull Di-Dòmhnaich."*

> (With your father and mother,
> And kindred to join us.
> Then our banns they'd be proclaiming
> In church upon Sunday.)

Amid the loud cheers and applause that followed the singing of the final verse, Kristy glanced over and smiled at Elizabeth who stood off to the side surrounded by her family. It was all so abundantly clear; the pain had never completely left Kristy MacNeil Erskine.

The Monday morning steamer would take the MacLeods down the coast to Sydney Mines, from where they would make their way home by road to Boularderie. Over the past few years, Elizabeth had been seen off from this very wharf on occasions too numerous to recount. But this was different; there was a greater sense of finality given that she was beginning a new life beyond the Urquhart home and *Loch Dubh*. Sarah and Hector stood with Donald and Allan in waving to Elizabeth, Calum and Stewart who had positioned themselves on the prow of the steamer. Elizabeth realized that it would be a difficult moment for her family, especially her mother, and wanted somehow to break the awkwardness of the moment by reassuring them that she would never be far away.

" *Athair agus a mhàthair, an ainm an àigh, bithibh cùramach air na seann fhleasgaich!*" (Father and mother, in the name of goodness, watch over the old bachelors!) The laughter that erupted on the wharf and flooded over all those gathered together told her that her parents would be fine knowing that their daughter would always be their child and in need of them. As for Donald and Allan, revenge of the *maighdeann aosda* was indeed sweet. Calum placed his arm around Elizabeth's waist as they continued to wave to the figures that now grew smaller and smaller with the distance. *Rinn mi an deagh phòsadh*. (I have done well in marriage.)

Her flower garden it most certainly was not. With the first snowfall now blanketing the hillsides, it was difficult to even conjure up images of the beautiful flowers that had earlier graced her garden let alone call to mind their lingering bouquet. Her entire kitchen, even the wooden walls, reeked of beef fat and Rachael would not have been surprised to see every dog and cat in *Loch Dubh* lining up outside the back door of what they surely would have taken to be *feòladaireachd Ferguson*. (Ferguson's Butcher Shop) From previous experiences, the entire family was all too familiar with the ritual of candle-making, as well as the resulting and quite hideous odours that would descend upon the house. Not surprisingly, Norman had taken advantage of the opportunity and gone off to the woods with Stuart and Andrew. There were still several sleigh loads of hardwood to be transported back to the house to be sawed, split and piled in order to feed the voracious appetite of the kitchen stove over the long winter months. It was with the first appearance of this particular cast-iron kettle, the one always used for boiling fat, that the three had made their furious dash for coats and eventual freedom. All Rachael could remember was the sudden reappearance of Norman's grimacing face from the other side of the door. *"A Raonaid m' eudail, meal an gàradh cùbhraidh!"* (Rachael my darling, enjoy the fragrant garden!)

"Falbh!" (Away with you!) Her faint-hearted yelp soon passed as she chuckled to herself and went about her business of filling the kettle with large chunks of fat that had been stored in a milking pail in the far corner of the pantry. She promised herself that she would reciprocate his mischievous behavior in her own time and way. *"Mo ghàradh; och ma tà."* (My garden; indeed.)

The steaming kettle had eventually been coerced into offering up sufficient amounts of tallow to make eighteen good-size candles. With the pantry window now wide open, Rachael looked down at the three moulds sitting at the end of the counter as she carefully repositioned them for cooling closer to the back wall. While the process demanded a great deal of her time and energy, to say nothing of patience, Rachael knew that the occasional use of candles helped reduce the amount of expensive kerosene needed to fuel the lamps. For some reason, her eyes were drawn away from the moulds to the open window. Eighteen candles, eighteen years of marriage.

The invading cold air caused her to wrap her arms around herself for warmth and, in so doing, to reflect on the fact that those years had been equally demanding of her time, energy and patience. Still in all, she had never complained. She had been blessed with four beautiful children who, like these very candles, were the light of her life. Even though Harris had been taken from her, she was now even stronger in her resolve and faith. There was a peace in knowing that God, the creator of all things, had moulded her life and would continue to do so. In staring off in the direction of the Kirk, Rachael looked into the darkness then beginning to blanket the evening skies over *Beinn-mo-Mhulaid*. *"Éirich, dealraich; oir thàinig do sholus, agus tha glòir an Tighearna air éirigh ort."* (Arise, shine; for thy light is come, and the glory of the Lord is risen upon thee.) She slowly lowered the window to a crack and turned back into the kitchen to light the kerosene lamp and begin preparation of the evening meal.

Norman and the boys were to eventually return from their self-imposed exile with hearty appetites and made quick work of the meal placed before them. It was not only the delicious taste of the food that brought smiles to their faces but also the fact that the aroma of freshly baked beans and cornmeal cake had been victorious in driving the dastardly bovine odours from their midst. Begun with grace, conducted in silence and ended in prayer, the supper brought a quiet to the kitchen that seemed to invite grateful thanks for yet another merciful favour. All the while, Andrew's angelic face masked the fact that his thoughts were more concerned with things temporal than spiritual. He desperately wanted someone to read the letter to him again.

Later that evening as she tucked him into his bed, Rachael withdrew the folded letter from her apron pocket and read it aloud under the dim light of the kerosene lamp to the most captive of audiences. Morag has arrived safely in Boston by steamer where she and Emily had been met by Effie and Liam. The O'Sullivans have a wonderfully large house located several miles away from the harbour. There are many motor cars on the streets that are so fascinating to watch but oftentimes scare the poor horses half to death. Both Effie and Liam are very kind and have already taken them on trips into the the city and the outlying areas, sometimes using the tram cars that are such fun to ride. The buildings are terribly big and their parliament has the most glorious gold dome unlike anything she had ever seen before. She has entered domestic service in the household of a friend of Liam's parents, which is close by to the O'Sullivans. The Kennedys are very kind to her. She can visit Effie, Liam and Emily whenever she wishes. Emily will be staying with them a bit longer since she herself has not yet found gainful employment, not terribly surprising since she and Effie tend to while away so many hours speaking of family! For her part, she will send money home before Christmas so that everyone will be certain to think of her. She misses them all a great deal and hopes that we will keep both her and Emily in our thoughts and prayers. She would write again soon and sends her love.

It had been four months since the girls had departed for Boston and it was Andrew, in particular, who had found it difficult to deal with Morag's absence. It was fortunate that, over the past few weeks, he had been kept busy with his school work and helping his father on the farm with small chores. Still, Rachael knew that he desperately missed his sister. *"A Mhamaidh. Nithear ùrnuigh air a son a ghnàth; geallaidh mi sin dhut. Cha bhi beud dhi."* (Mamma. Prayer will be made for her continually; I promise you. She will be quite well.)

"Dìreach, a mhic mo ghaoil. Tha e dìreach mar a thuirt thu. Dùin do shùilean an dràsda agus dean do chadalan." (Just so, my dear son. It is just as you said. Now close your eyes and go to sleep.) Rachael placed a kiss on his forehead and then left him in darkness as she struggled to remove the lump from her throat. She could not explain why she was so near tears as she waited outside the bedroom door composing herself before returning to the kitchen. She did not want to lose Morag the way she lost Harris; it was just that she was so far away with no one to care for her. Why was it that more and more young people were forced to move away from these shores to make a living, forced to cast families asunder? But then, after all, perhaps Andrew was right. Perhaps Morag would be quite well, right enough. Descending the stairs with her conflicting thoughts and emotions, she purposefully made her way towards the kitchen. Rachael's mind had gone back in time almost five years; her thoughts were of *Coinneach Bàn* playing in a snowy field at Hogmanay and of *Iain Beag* placing a spring bouquet of mayflowers on his grandparents' graves. The wisdom of the children.

Rachael entered the kitchen to discover that, in her absence, company had arrived. Norman was in his rocking chair by the stove engaged in conversation with Angus and Isabelle Grant who had dropped by for a bit of a *góbaireachd.* (chit-chat) As winter began to settle over them, the people of *Loch Dubh* quite willingly resumed the custom of conducting visitations to neighbouring homes. Other than services at the Kirk, prayer meetings and the occasional *céilidh* and milling frolic, the visits offered an enjoyable way of staying in contact with each other over the long dreary months. They also helped to keep everyone attuned to the latest gossip although Heaven forbid that it would ever be referred to as such. Seated on the cushion-ladened settle, or *seise* (bench) as the older folk still called them, the Grants greeted her warmly as she first appeared through the doorway. Rachael was most grateful for the faint fragrance of baked beans and cornmeal cake that continued to linger in the room. She hoped that the long line of dogs and cats outside the back door would have disappeared well before Angus and Isabelle's arrival. Och well, if nothing else she still had eighteen candles to show for her efforts.

It was not long before Norman and Angus had finally exhausted their discussion of deer hunting and, without the slightest pause, moved on to the ever popular issue of politics. The ballots of the Dominion election were only two weeks cold and already the campaign had been relived many times over in the homes around *Loch Dubh*. Sir Wilfrid had been handily re-elected despite the fiery and eloquent oratory of Robert Laird Borden who, after three and a half years as leader of the opposition, had been well broken in and was seen to hold such promise for the Tories. It had not gone unnoticed by everyone in the congregation that, on the Sunday immediately prior to the voting, Duncan Fraser's sermon had not so discretely included brightly hued references to the tormenting red fires of Hell and the calming blue tranquility of Heaven. The kitchen erupted in laughter as Norman conjured up images of poor Jennie Fraser being forced to dye her husband's clerical robes a deep Tory blue. She might as well; he wore his politics on his sleeve for all the good that it did him. *"Gu dearbh."* (Yes indeed.)

As the laughter subsided, Angus recounted his meeting earlier in the week with Archie MacDonald whose objectivity and insights into political matters were certainly well known throughout the community. He had no doubt but that the increased Liberal vote in and around Ingonish was the result of what he referred to as *airgiod grod Laurier* (Laurier's tainted money) buying votes while the strong Conservative showing further down the North Shore was most assuredly *deanar toil an Tighearna.* (The will of the Lord be done.) With as much sarcasm mixed with a modicum of devilment as he could muster, Angus had asked him at the time if he would be hanging black crepe around his door for poor Mr. Borden. *"Och Aonghais, is mór am beud e. Is doimheadach an nì e — staid an t-saoghail. An dall a'seòladh an doill!"* (Oh Angus, it is a great pity. It is a troubling thing — the state of the world. The blind are leading the blind!) It was obvious that there would be no consoling poor Archie. At least in his mind, the crepe was even now draped over the MacDonald door.

Throughout the discussion, the women were ungraciously relegated to the status of interested bystanders. Politics was not of any great concern to them since they did not have the vote, not that they necessarily wanted it mind you. Both Rachael and Isabelle sat quietly, skillfully feigning attentiveness even though they could not have been less interested. It was only when Archie's name had been raised and humorous comments made at his expense that Isabelle was finally provoked into making a stand. *"Ud. Ud, Aonghais. Na biodh cùram ort. Leig dha — an duine bochd."* (Tut. Tut, Angus. Never you mind. Leave him alone — the poor man.) Having clearly noted the stern edge to her voice, the men knew enough to let the matter lie and, as they replenished their pipes, a temporary and welcomed quiet fell over the room.

With smoke now belching forth in billowy clouds of self-indulgence, the conversation picked up once again and soon turned to the recently announced appointment of the Earl Grey as the Dominion's new Governor General. Norman had no doubt but that he was an honourable man and would serve King and country well. It was just that his present title was so unfortunate. With a proven fondness for colours, the Reverend Fraser would most certainly have even more material for his renowned sermons of impartiality. The hearty laughter that once again filled the room was cut short, this time by Rachael who obviously had had enough of all such political pronouncements. *"Och, an ainm an àigh; gum bu fada beò an rìgh! Théid tea a bhreothadh."* (Oh, in the name of goodness, long live the King! We will put on the tea.) With that, Rachael and Isabelle rose and crossed the kitchen floor to the pantry while both Norman and Angus looked across at each other in silence and even began to feel some sympathy for dear old Mr. Borden. In terms of defeats, the men had been trounced at their own game by those who were not even permitted to enter the polling station. Talk quickly turned to other less controversial matters; it would be best to keep the peace.

It was not long after the serving of the *strùpag* that Angus and Isabelle had decided to make their way home. Later, as Norman banked the kitchen stove for the night, Rachael cleared the table of dishes and returned them to the pantry. Her attention was clearly focused on carefully placing the left-over pieces of cornmeal cake, molasses biscuits and sugar cookies back into the tins on the shelf before her. It was only then that she was once again able to detect the faint odour of the candles that were slowly taking form in their moulds at the far end of the counter. Her mind was cast back to the scene earlier that afternoon when she had stood by the open window and looked off into the evening skies over *Beinn-mo-Mhulaid.* *"Och a Dhia, tha móran dhiùbh air cùl a chur ri tìr nan craobh 's nan àrd-bheann. Tha m'ìnntinn trom a'smaointinn air Mórag... Bidh mo ghaol oirre gu sìorraidh. Bidh mo ghaol oirre gu sìorraidh."* (Oh God, many have left the land of trees and mountains. My spirit is sad thinking of Morag... I will always love her. I will always love her.)

And then, Rachael turned and quietly left the pantry. The only sound was the wood crackling in the stove as it was enfolded by the rampant flames. She was glad for the light from the lamp that now guided her footsteps across the broad floorboards of the darkened kitchen. With the still-forming candles behind her, Rachael walked silently towards the front bedroom and rest.

Judging by the way his hands softly glided over the slender pieces of darkened wood, it was as if he were stroking a new-born kitten for the first time. There was love in the movement and one could sense, even from a distance, that a bond was already being formed. Of course, to refer to them as pieces of wood would have been met with a look of absolute horror; even heretics of the early church would have received a more-sympathetic countenance from the disciples. These were not mere pieces of wood but rather treasured fragments of living history. They were part of a spirit that transcended time, encompassing the broad spectrum of human emotions. They were the joy of birth, the pain of death and everything in between. No, these most certainly were not simply pieces of wood. These were the drones of the great highland bagpipe.

It had been just over two years since Daniel's stroke and, in that time, he had made a remarkable recovery. For all intents and purposes, he was back to his former self except for the slight limp and the fatigue that now overcame him much more quickly than before. Tina would jokingly claim that it was due to the fact that he was now almost as old as Methuselah himself, nothing more. *"Is thu mo bhodachan gun teagamh sam bith."* (You are my little old man without any doubt.)

"Beir uam thu, a'bhean nìgheadaireachd!" (Away with you, washer-woman!) She would always wait for the admonishment that would surely come, accompanied by the waving of an arm for greater effect. However, each time she quietly gave thanks for both her husband's return to health and her family's return to completeness. There were so many reasons to be thankful . Alasdair and Kristy had brought a joy of life to the house that was oftentimes infectious and Tina had no doubt but that much of Daniel's progress had been his will to live and see his family prosper.

As much as he may have wanted to resume his music, Daniel knew he no longer had the strength to play as he once had. In a strange sort of way, it forced him to relive the terrible confrontation with Alasdair and the parting that had occurred as a result. A son had been lost for the better part of two years and, while the issue had never been discussed in the house, he had grieved mercifully alone and in his own way. Now Alasdair had been returned to him and never again would he allow his family to be broken apart. And yet his pipe was like family; he had grown into manhood with it and knew its characteristics and peculiarities as well as those of any child. The drones were to be blown in slowly and allowed to find their own pitch that could be adjusted only after they had settled themselves. The chanter reed was to sit straight in a goodly bed of hemp or it would warble like a caged bird at the most embarrassing of moments. And the bag — if it didn't have its occasional seasoned drink of molasses and warm water, it would sulk and leak air like a stray cow after a good feed in the turnip field. In so many ways, he was losing a child and the grieving was no less painful.

Saturday, June 25, 1904 had not only been Kenneth's twelfth birthday, it had also been one of those rare times when details of an event are forever committed to memory. Once Daniel, Tina, Alasdair and Kristy had arrived at the house, Iona appeared from the pantry carrying a beautiful birthday cake that was then positioned in the centre of the kitchen table. Daniel had brought with him a tiny tin box wrapped in white paper that he carefully retrieved from his coat pocket and, with the broadest of grins, placed on the table before his grandson. Kenneth's initial expression of curiosity at seeing the box was soon replaced by one of even greater bewilderment as he unwrapped the container only to find a small tarnished key. Iona explained to her son that it belonged to the linen trunk in the dining-room and that the present from his grandparents was to be found inside. Kenneth was followed into the adjoining room and all eyes were fixed on him as he turned the key and gently raised the whale-backed lid. For several seconds, there was absolute silence as Kenneth gazed down upon his grandfather's pipe that lay on a white muslin tablecloth. Slowly, he turned to look back in something akin to disbelief. Daniel walked forward and stared into his grandson's face. *"A Choinnich Bhàin, tha e agadsa a-nis. Cluich air a' phìob gu sona gu sòlasach agus gu daonnan."* (Fair Kenneth, it now belongs to you. Play the pipe happy, contented and always.)

Daniel soon found his waist completely encased by Kenneth's arms with his chest caressed by the boy's head as he leaned into him. *"A Sheanair, tapadh leibh. Geallaidh mi dhuibh. Och ma tà!; cuiridh mi geall ort."* (Grandfather, thank you. I promise you. Indeed, I promise you.) Kenneth returned to the trunk and lovingly picked up the pipe. Even at such a young age, he understood the look on his grandfather's face, a look that told him that this was much more than a musical instrument. He knew that it was a sacrifice for Daniel to relinquish it, even to his own grandson; he could see it in the eyes that were welling up with faint tears. Kenneth's mind was flooded with memories of that day, several years ago, when Daniel had played this very pipe high up on the bluffs overlooking New Carlisle. He had been so proud of his grandfather then and was even more so now. This pipe was part of what his family had been and, of equal importance to Daniel, what it would become. Kenneth had made a promise to his grandfather and, on that day in the dining-room in front of the linen trunk, he swore that he would honour it above all else.

The cold winter air needed no invitation. It had brazenly taken refuge in the root cellar, lurking beneath the floor boards as if waiting to reclaim the entire house as its very own. Descending the stairs, Iona had been cut by its severity as if it were a knife, slashing any warmth that dared cross its path. The potatoes and turnips had been dutifully stored in the wooden bins in the far corner and she would be quick in filling the basket before retreating to the comfort of her balmy kitchen. As she felt her way along the chilled stones of the foundation walls for support, her hand tingled with life. Because she would not be long, she was reassured that the bairn inside her would be none the worse for this brief exposure to the savagery of winter. Iona thought it ironic that these ghostly stones would soon support new life and new happiness in the Erskine home. *Is è mo theaghlach carraig mo neart.* (My family is the rock of my strength.) The imagery seemed so appropriate but, still, she must not linger. It was so bitterly cold.

Above her, Iona could hear the creaking of the floor boards as Kenneth marched back and forth across the kitchen playing the pipe. He was so determined to make his grandfather proud and was practising three, old Jacobean-inspired tunes that he would play for Daniel as a special surprise at Christmas. Over the past few weeks, Iona had heard the melodies so often that she was convinced that even the Bonnie Prince himself would cry out *Fóghnuidh so!* (This is enough!), assuming of course he had enough of the Gaelic to say as much. Even with the God-forsaken cold, humour was not lost on Iona and she chuckled to herself while setting the empty basket down on the chilled earth.

It was as she was stooped over the retaining rails of the bin, reaching for the turnips, that she was shattered by the most excruciating pain. She caught herself just in time and clung to the thin wooden bars for support. A piercing torment engulfed her as she fought desperately to catch her breath. She attempted to cry out for Kenneth to come and yet the only sounds were of the boards groaning under her son's weight and the pipe — the pipe! *"A Thighearna, ma thoilicheas tu. A Choinnich, cluinn m' éigheachd; cuidich mi!"* (Oh Lord, if you will. Kenneth, hear my cries; help me!)

It had not been long, perhaps ten minutes or so, before Kenneth had finally taken note of the lengthy absence and gone in search of his mother. Having found her lying motionless on the cold damp ground and with panic upon him, he ran from the cellar to search out his father who was eventually found splitting wood behind the wagon house. Neil carried Iona to the bedroom off the front parlour with Kenneth close behind. Shortly thereafter, he went off in desperate search of Tina, leaving the boy to watch over his mother. Now terribly alone and afraid, Kenneth remained by her side. It was the first time in more than two years, since the day of his grandfather's stroke, that he actually broke down and cried. He knew that he shouldn't but it was all too much for him to understand, too much to believe. He looked into the unmoving expressionless face of his mother, the one person more than anyone else who had always given meaning to his life and substance to his love. Now there was no feeling, only a strange sense of being separated from her as she lay before him so incredibly still. He clutched her hand in confirming that she was still there. It was cold, terribly cold. At that moment, Kenneth did all that was in his power to do — he held his mother's hand while, through his tears, he prayed a silent prayer.

Both Tina and Sarah Urquhart were now with Iona, who was conscious but whose pain had grown even more intense. Her labour had begun much earlier than had been expected and with a severity that, for the moment, was inexplicable even for the two experienced midwives. Neil remained in the kitchen with Daniel and Kenneth as the hours crept by with no news. Except for the frequent appearances by Sarah in search of hot water and clean towelling, the fifteen foot distance between kitchen and bedroom became an excruciating eternity of space. Alasdair and Kristy arrived several hours later with a large basket containing the evening meal that was soon laid out on the kitchen table. Their efforts were greatly appreciated but, more than anything else, it was their presence that mattered most, especially to Kenneth.

It was well into the night, long after Kenneth himself had been sent to his bed, that Tina returned to the kitchen. She wilted into a chair at the end of the table as Kristy quickly put the kettle on the stove to make a much-needed pot of tea. It had been an extremely difficult birth; the cord had been wrapped around the bairn's neck and there was fear that he would be stillborn. After the birth, it felt like a lifetime that she and Sarah had worked on the child attempting to coerce it to take its first breath, a breath that seemingly would not come. Tina had looked down into Iona's anguished face and realized how badly this child was wanted, with how much love it would be blessed. If only it would breathe.

Both women frantically continued their efforts, refusing to believe that this child was not to be. *"Mallachadh! Tarruing d'anail. Tarraing d' anail!"* (Damnation! Draw your breath. Breathe!) A faint plaintiff gurgling was eventually heard that, at least, offered some hope that life had not yet completely escaped them. Drenched in their own sweat, Tina and Sarah almost willed the child to breathe, for air to be taken and life to be grasped. Finally, a piercing cry echoed across the room that spoke of life given and life restored. In her weakened state, Iona looked into Tina's face, seeking an answer to a question that she did not know how to put even if she had had the strength. *"Och Iona, is ciatach am balach e. Tha sgamhanan móra aige; tha an dara pìobaire agad."* (Oh Iona, he is a handsome lad. He has good lungs; you have another piper.) With that, Iona attempted to force a smile and knew that she could now seek rest; she was tired, full of pain and, strangely, very cold. It was as if she were lying on a bed of icy foundation stones.

Several days were to pass before Iona found sufficient strength to actually hold her son. Tina had not left her side and watched over the wee one much as a sheep tends its own lamb. The men were permitted in for brief periods. Kenneth, in particular, had desperately wanted to see his mother. He needed to dispel those images of a lifeless face that lingered in his mind and continued to haunt him. He could not endure the idea of his life without her and he had to reassure himself that she would be there. *"A Mhamaidh, tha mi duilich. Cha bhi sonas ach far am bì thu; tha mi duilich."* (Mamma, I am sorry. There is no happiness but when you are here; I am sorry.) Iona reached out to rub his cheek as she held her second son close to her breast.

"A Choinnich, chuala mi ceòl na pìoba; chùm e suas mi. Is tu Mac mo ghaoil — mo laochan. Bidh mi nad fhreasdal." (Kenneth, I heard the music of the pipe; it sustained me. You are my beloved son — my little hero. I will be depending on you.) As Neil smiled down on his family, Tina sat off in the corner, watching the scene unfold and, all the while, reminding herself of the miracle of life that had been restored to her family twice in as many years. Silently, she thanked God for blessings received.

Ni sealbh an rud as còir. (Providence will do justice.) Now, with something close to total fatigue upon her, Tina finally allowed herself to drift into sleep.

For as long as she could remember, it had willingly offered her tremendous peace and solitude. With the possible exception of the flower garden, it was the one place that always brought a sense of serenity and lent perspective to her existence. And now, with the warm June breeze drifting through the branches high above her, she was content enough just to sit and watch life play itself out before her. Not that the speed was at all brisk here in *Loch Dubh*; indeed, it moved as the seasons, at a measured pace with predictable results. It was so reminiscent of her own life, so consonant and prophetic.

This place gave Jennie a sense that she was in a divine presence. It was this that made the orchard so special, in some ways more so than her beloved flower garden. She had often seen photographs in books of the great cathedrals of Europe with their striated vaulted ceilings and high buttressed walls. In particular, she had been intrigued by the photographs illustrating the rosette windows with their multitude of shapes and colours. Yet Jennie felt a grandeur here in the orchard that she knew could never be replicated by human hands. From where she sat, the trees soared majestically towards the heavens with an awe-inspiring power and sense of sanctity. Overhead, the branches intertwined into a canopy of lacy arches whose design would most surely humble the mortal brilliance of even the most renowned artist. And the infinity of blossoms — the magnificent mantle of white, pink and crimson wove an intricate tapestry that beguiled the senses. *Is e àrd eaglais bhrèagh Dhé nan dùl an gàradh ubhall. Tha mo dhìol agamsa oir seo m'òr 's m'ionndas.* (The beautiful orchard is the cathedral of the God of nature. I have my satisfaction for this is my gold and my treasure.) For so many reasons, Jennie was frequently drawn to and delighted in the natural glory of this most unassuming place.

The sudden sharp pain jolted Jennie back to the reality of her grassy pew. Lying peacefully on her mistress' lap, *Rionnag's* claws had inadvertently penetrated the cloth of Jennie's skirt and provoked her into breaking the quiet reverence of the sanctuary. *"A Rionnag! Is tù chuir am bior annam. Cha ruig thu leas ciùrr a thoirt dhomh."* (*Rionnag*! What a start you gave me. You need not hurt me.) The sudden outburst had startled *Rionnag* who quickly turned her head and looked quizzically into Jennie's face. Her ears had been accosted and her peace disturbed unnecessarily by the high-pitched voice. There appeared to be no good cause for such intrusive behaviour and, having taken a moment to confirm that indeed it had been totally unwarranted, *Rionnag* first lowered and then slid her chin back across the dark cloth. As she resumed kneading the fabric with her paws, her thoughts were of a time when she herself had been a kitten seeking nourishment from her mother. How she so desperately wanted to nourish her own young. Her beautiful kits had always disappeared, somehow taken from her so suddenly. She had grieved for them; they had been so beautiful and so dependent upon her. Now, she had nothing; she was alone. The kneading seemingly brought her close to her mother and these memories soothed her troubled mind. With the sun caressing her black fur, *Rionnag's* front paws finally lay still as sleep claimed her.

Jennie looked down on this creature that had been a member of the family for so many years. It seemed impossible that eleven had already passed since they had adopted the wee thing, or was it the other way around? She recalled the late-summer evening when Duncan had heard a faint mournful cry outside the open kitchen window. In the darkness, it had taken several minutes for him to eventually locate the culprit, a bit of black fur that had obviously become separated from its mother and was in desperate need of sustenance. The next morning, there was tremendous excitement as the children appeared in the kitchen to find something of much greater interest than oatmeal porridge. Emily gravitated to the wooden box by the stove where the kitten had been placed on a tea towel used for a bed. The child gently took the tiny animal up into her arms and began to speak to it in soft motherly tones. With all the wisdom of her four years, she proceeded to put everything in context by explaining the entire story, all quite matter-of-factly, to her parents. *"Is teine-biorach i — is e seo tiodhlac Dhé. Buinidh i dhuinn a-nis."* (She is a shooting star — this is God's gift. She belongs to us now.) Not one person in the house, not even Duncan, could find the courage to refute either Emily's view of the world or sense of ownership. While considerable discussion had ensued among the children following the morning meal, a consensus was finally reached that would have the shooting star officially named *Rionnag*. (Little Star) Even though Duncan had gently dismissed Emily's request for a service of baptism, the Frasers would look back on that day as the time when they had been blessed, unwittingly, with their fourth child.

All these years later, Jennie found herself sitting quietly in the orchard with her wee black bairn curled up in her lap. Yet her thoughts were of her other children, Sandy and Matthew in Sydney and Emily in Boston, who were now grown and gone from her. She had often chided herself for the motherly torment that, seemingly, would never leave her. There had been many sleepless nights as her thoughts went out to them, especially to Emily whom she had not seen for almost twelve months. The letters may have come fairly regularly but they did not bring her daughter closer. Jennie felt so helpless. She looked down at the slumbering *Rionnag* and was consumed by sadness in the realization that she could not reach out and hold her daughter.

Emily's letters were filled with odd bits of news and, from time to time, small amounts of money. Effie and Liam were paying her a reasonable salary, especially since their adoption of a newborn child in January. They maintained that, with the additional responsibilities, another pair of hands would be most welcome around the house. Effie had first written with the news in mid-February and it was apparent that she was thrilled with the prospect of finally having a family of her very own. It was her desire to have the baby christened Murdina Jennie, to honour both her mother and cousin. She hoped that Jennie would not mind and had indicated that it would mean a great deal to her if Jennie would find it in her heart to agree. A letter was quickly posted containing congratulations from both Duncan and her as well as the wish that God would watch over Murdina Jennie O'Sullivan and grant her a long and happy life.

In her heart, Jennie was delighted for Effie and knew that her cousin would be a doting caring mother. Finally, she had been blessed with a child and there was no doubt but that it would be the object of much love and attention. The irony of timing had not been lost on Jennie as she reached down to stroke *Rionnag's* shiny black coat that blended so beautifully with the colour of her own skirt, making them one. The joyous sounds of childhood would ring throughout the O'Sullivan home at a time when the silence of the *Loch Dubh* manse was almost deafening. Jennie so wanted to have her children back; they were still so young, especially her Emily. With the prescribed year drawing to a close, she hoped that Emily would indeed return home, even if it was only to Sydney to complete her studies. At least she would be with her immediate family; there was no good reason for her to stay in far-off Boston. Perhaps both she and Morag Ferguson would return together and everything would be as it was. *"Agus ge b'e air bith nithean a dh'iarras sibh nur n-ùrnaigh, ma chreideas sibh, gheibh sibh iad."* (And all things, whatsoever you shall ask in prayer, believing, ye shall receive.) It seemed so appropriate to offer up a prayer aloud her in this place.

The sound of Jennie's voice was yet another needless disturbance that *Rionnag* could have easily done without. Still, she was thankful that it was only Jennie with whom she had to deal. Duncan was almost never to be seen and all the children, especially the diabolical *Sandaidh an driuga ghil* (Sandy of the White Comet), had long since and quite thankfully taken their leave of her. With them gone, peace had been restored to her life. Now, she could actually lie beneath the kitchen stove or on the sun-drenched floor of the pantry, which was one of her favourite spots to lounge. She could luxuriate wherever and whenever she liked without fear of distraction or torment. How fortunate Jennie was to be free of the entire lot. Her thoughts once again turned to her own mother and, lowering her head to Jennie's lap, she resumed her kneading.

"Cat aimhleasach!" (Mischievous cat!) The words rang in *Rionnag's* sensitive ears as she suddenly found herself abruptly and quite rudely plopped in the adjoining tall grass. She watched as Jennie strode briskly back in the direction of the manse, dusting bits of grass from her frock as she went. *Rionnag* sat there for a long while looking down towards the loch and thinking about the multitude of things that were seemingly sent to torment her. Eventually, she would forgive Jennie's rudeness, but only in time. Several bowls of warm milk and a good deal of attentive stroking would be required; she would insist on that. Even with the weight of years upon her, she still had her pride.

Jennie returned to the kitchen with a sense of guilt for having squandered the better part of the afternoon in the orchard when other things awaited her hand, especially the evening meal. Duncan would be home from his visitations soon enough and would expect to have a hot supper on the table. She dutifully prepared the vegetables and placed the meat, accompanied by a thick blanket of sliced onions, in the cast-iron frying pan. It was well known that a goodly feed of liver would enrich the blood and Jennie was thankful for the fact that the MacGregors had recently butchered a pig. She had asked young Peter to be certain to thank his parents for their generosity; the Frasers were indeed fortunate to have such generous and thoughtful neighbours.

With supper preparations well underway, Jennie crossed through the dining-room and entered the front parlour. She opened the drawer of the corner table to retrieve the letter that had been carefully placed in a neat pile with all the others and tied together with a red ribbon. Now seated in the rocking chair on the front veranda, she read Effie's letter once again. "Murdina Jennie O'Sullivan." It sounded so distinguished as it rolled off her tongue. She conjured up images of the young girl growing up in the big city and taking for granted all those things that her mother and cousin had only dreamed about all those years ago in Sydney Mines. How much things change; how unpredictable life is. Well and truly lost in thought, Jennie was understandably taken by surprise as something abruptly rubbed against her ankle. *"Och, nach tu mo leanabh dubh fhéin!"* (Oh, is it not my own black child!) Chuckling aloud, Jennie placed the letter back in the envelope knowing that Duncan's arrival was imminent. As she rose and entered the house through the large screen door, a now deferential *Rionnag* followed close behind. A bowl of milk and a small piece of liver would do much to restore her faith in the Fraser clan, at least for the time being.

Na fiaclan gorma. (The blue teeth) Martha cringed at the very thought. It was that time of year when the blueberries began to ripen and the small ones would most certainly appear in the kitchen in search of receptacles suitable for picking. At eight years of age, Lachlan had several years of experience and considered himself quite the expert at the harvest. Colin and Moira would always settle for a small cup, knowing their limitations in battling the rough undergrowth where the blueberry bushes tended to thrive, to say nothing about their penchant for eating more than they saved. A small cup would do them nicely while Lachlan boastfully laid claim to a much larger bowl. Regardless of the size of their collections, Martha would always tickle them unmercifully upon their return just to see the colour of the teeth. Without exception, they would be as blue as the heavens. Yet there were always a few token berries left in the cups for good measure and Martha would make such a fuss over them.

The three children had been dutifully outfitted with containers from the pantry cupboard and were making their way to the edge of the forest to begin the picking. Peter was working in the vegetable field in the back corner of the farm and would keep an eye on them to ensure they did not stray too far into the woods. They would certainly mind him and do as they were told. When it came to parenting, he was more the disciplinarian even though, deep inside, he was seldom able to bring himself to admonish the children without breaking into a broad grin. He was a gentle soul and the three Campbell lambs, now crossing the pasture with such determination, were all too aware of it.

Martha sat on the back step, almost lost in thought, as she watched the small ones round a wooded corner and disappear from her view. She quite suddenly felt a tug on her sleeve and glanced down on Ismay who stood by her side. In so many different ways and for equally different reasons, it was difficult for Martha to believe that her bairn was already two years old. She had always been a beautiful child and, as she grew taller, Martha had lived with the hope that those small blue eyes would also grow and somehow be made to see. At the same time, she was ravaged with guilt for having done this to her own flesh and blood and for praying to God to undo something that He, in His ultimate wisdom, had bestowed upon this child. Initially the question had lingered: was it a bestowal or an infliction that had been given? Martha had watched Ismay grow and, in a strange sort of way, experienced an enhanced understanding and acceptance. There had been so many times when she thought she had come to terms with Ismay's condition only to find herself suddenly awash with new questions, new doubts, new sorrows. Ismay's condition! She could not even bring herself to think the word 'blind' let alone say it aloud as if to do so would somehow make it irreversible. But why, why now as she watched Lachlan, Colin and Moira disappear from her sight, did she start to grieve anew?

Martha repositioned herself on the edge of the step and reached for Ismay, cradling the child in her lap. She stroked the ringleted black hair with her hand and watched intently as the young one spoke to the distance in front of her. *"A Mhamaidh, a bheil sinn a'dol do'n ghàradh? Is toigh leam fàile cùbhraidh nam flùraichean agus a bhith gam faireachdainn. Tha mì air son tadhal air mo charaidean."* (Mamma, are we going to the garden? I enjoy smelling and touching the flowers. I want to visit my friends.) Ismay broke into a gale of giggles at the thought of calling the flowers her friends. Martha looked into her tiny face and saw a sparkle in the eyes. Perhaps it was more than just the maniacal mischievousness of the Campbells. Perhaps, as she grew in body and faith...just possibly.

"Bheil iad aig baile an diugh? Leig dhuinn falbh agus faighean a mach. Thig leam." (Are they at home today? Let us go and find out. Come along with me.) Martha took her daughter by the hand and slowly walked towards the garden. Ismay was very conscious of the soft crunching of the stones beneath their feet and the feel of the invigorating freshness of the breeze on her face. As they first approached and then entered the garden, the child's excitement seemed to rise accordingly as she eagerly pulled her mother by the hand. It was Ismay who somehow guided her down the rows of flowers to be reacquainted with, in turn, *maighistir dearg, bana-mhaighstear*

bhuidhe agus maighdeann purpur. (Mr. Red, Mrs. Yellow and Miss Purple.)
She had come to know the flowers by their fragrances and had given each
one a name as her mother had first described them to her. It was only now
that Martha came to realize that the descriptions and the florid surnames
held absolutely no relevance for her daughter. They were empty words that
carried no beauteous images of life, a life that for her was an eternal night,
bereft of even its starry jewels. She had never seen a sky of crimsoned
clouds, a field of ambered oats or a sea of heathered waves. *Is truagh mo
chor. Mo ghràdhag aig am bheil sùilean gu faicinn ach chan eil iad a' faicinn. Och,
brat dorch na-h-oidhche!* (Sad is my condition. My little darling who has eyes
to see and does not see. Oh the dark mantle of night!) Even in the beauty
that was her garden, the sorrowful thoughts would not leave her.

From a short distance, Martha watched as Ismay's tiny fingers stroked
the face of each friend in proceeding down the pathway, calling them all by
name. It was Ismay who first drew her mother's attention to the increased
rustling of the leaves. Martha looked over at the tall silver birch trees that
sheltered the garden and noticed how the leaves were continually changing
colour from green to white as the wind persisted in savagely turning them
about, over and over again. Off on the horizon, she could see the dark
clouds rolling in from the north-east over *An Tòiseach* and *An Deireadh*.
It was a sure sign of a bad storm brewing. She would take the wash in
from the line before it was sent flying over the mountains like so many
phantoms, ending up in St. Anns or God only knows where. She could
even now hear the screams of absolute horror from the far-off residents:
Tha am f-àile làn bhòchdan! (The air is full of ghosts!) As she reluctantly
bid farewell to her garden friends after an all-too-brief visit, Ismay could
hear the ever-increasing voice of the wind and smell the briny scent of its
breath. She hoped that her friends would be safe from the storm. She so
enjoyed passing time with them.

The storm had reached its height later that evening and, by next
morning, had long slipped inland over the highlands. From the moment
of her waking, Ismay desperately wanted to return to the garden to ensure
that her friends had indeed weathered the dreaded winds that had howled
around the house for hours. Martha was so grateful that her daughter
was not able to see the multitude of petals that lay scattered under her
feet or the broken stems that bowed down before her as if paying some
sort of mournful homage. Ismay once again caressed the flowers and was
well pleased that the salty winds had not violated the beautiful lines and
fragrance of their faces. In the glorious sunshine of the new day, Martha
closed her eyes and opened her mind to the wonders of life that were so
reflected in the laughter of one so small, so innocent, so wise. She hoped
that, in time, she too would grow in such wisdom.

It was later that same morning that the news had first reached the
homes around *Loch Dubh*. The storm had been much more severe along
the coast where the full fury of the high winds and equally high seas were

most intense. It had seemingly come out of nowhere and struck in mid-afternoon when a number of fishermen were out on the water tending to their nets and traps. The dark clouds on the horizon had been a foreboding of approaching trouble and most boats had taken advantage of the rising winds in making a hasty retreat to harbour before the full brunt of nature's anger could be felt.

Worry had first begun to set in by late evening as darkness began to fall. The storm continued to buffet the coast with no sign of letting up while the white caps continued to increase in size and quantity. Some likened it to a field of drifting snow that enshrouded the water as far as the eye could see. The *Annabelle* had not returned to port and there was a widely held hope that, as a seasoned fisherman, George Calvey would have made for another safe haven further up the coast. The postmistress was reassured by neighbours that, in all likelihood, he had guided his boat into Ingonish Harbour where he was even now passing a peaceful night. No doubt, he would return before the noon hour the next day to scoff at any doubts about his seamanship.

It had been the jagged cliffs of *An Deireadh*, and not the safety of Ingonish Harbour, that had called the *Annabelle* out of the storm and into its ultimate destiny. The vessel had been driven onto the rocks and, even then, there had been no rest from the incessant onslaught. Its bowed sides showed the signs of the constant battering of the waves that licked over its broken frame in much the same way that a predator devours its prey — slowly, meticulously and with the greatest sense of accomplishment. George Calvey was found floating in the waters between the two islands. His open eyes were transfixed on the sky above as if willing the sea to lull him between these two rocks, these two solitudes — the beginning and the end. Even with the deafening stillness of the wind and water or perhaps because of it, it would be a long and difficult voyage back to New Carlisle for the other fishermen who reverently lifted him from his watery cradle in order to finally take him home.

The shock and grief that surrounded Calvey's tragic death were shared by the people of both New Carlisle and *Loch Dubh*. His wife, the *Banrigh Shalach* or *Meachranaiche Rìoghail* (Royal Meddler) as she was sometimes titled, had always been viewed with some disdain and sometimes avoided at all cost. However, George Calvey was regarded by everyone who crossed his path as a decent kind man. He was forever taking time to share a story or two and to treat the children to a tour of his beloved Annabelle. Unlike his wife, he genuinely seemed to like the people from up around the loch and took time to speak with them. This included "that old MacDonald man," even though he knew that the wife could not abide the sight of him. There was some comfort in knowing that this well-respected man had finally found the rest and peace that he so richly deserved. *Làimh ri uisgeachaibh ciùin treòraichidh e mì. Aisigidh e m'anam....* (He leadeth me beside the still waters. He restoreth my soul... .)

The funeral service was held on an overcast Saturday afternoon in early August. Seated high on the point of land, the Church of England was filled to capacity with those who had come to pay their final respects, including many from *Loch Dubh*. Martha and Ismay travelled down to the village with Archie, who felt it a duty to honour the dead with his presence. The other three children would stay at home with Peter who had never much cared for wakes and funerals. He always maintained that he preferred the company of the living and that the only such service he would attend would be his own. Martha had instructed him to mind the children well otherwise his attendance at a funeral, albeit his very own, might well be required much sooner than he could ever imagine.

Some considerable time had passed since many of the people from *Loch Dubh* had last been inside the church. Immediately before the service was to begin, they took a few moments to reacquaint themselves with the richness of the sanctuary: the marbled altar, the gilded candles, the en-crusted cross, the stained-glass window and the clareted candle suspended from the ceiling. It was all so different from their Kirk where the plainness compelled the mind to focus more on matters spiritual than temporal. Was not their gawking just such a case in point? As Archie sat quietly in the pew next to Martha and Ismay, his mind went back in time to his own Hannah's death so many years ago and the pain that had been inflicted on him and his family. At that moment, he was consumed with sympathy for Annabelle.

Later, as Calvey's body was carried and committed to its grave in the cemetery behind the church, Archie looked across at Annabelle and found himself using his handkerchief to clear his blurring eyes and snif-fling nose. In slowly leaving the grave side, it was Ismay who quite unex-pectedly offered words of consolation to her grandfather. *"A Sheanair, chan fhaod sibh a bhith a' gal. Tha mo charaidean an seo; bidh iad an urra oirnn. Cha tig cron oirnn."* (Grandfather, you must not cry. My friends are here; they will watch over us. No harm will come to us.) The bouquets of fragrant flow-ers that encircled the grave had reassured the child that the committal of a loved one was not to be feared; her friends were there to lend comfort. Archie recalled looking down into her tiny face. In her innocence, she saw so much more than they. He took his granddaughter by the hand. Unknowingly, she had opened his eyes to the fact that their paths were truly being guided.

As they slowly descended the hill, Archie looked over to the horizon with *An Toiseach* and *An Deireadh* rising up from their watery dwelling. For some reason, he whispered the evocative words of David the Psalmist. *"'S an fhairge bha do shlighe, agus do cheuman anns na h-uisgeachaibh móra; agus cha do dh'aithnicheadh luirg do chas."* (Thy way was in the sea, and thy path in the great waters, and thy footsteps were not known.) It was then that Archie felt compelled to rededicate himself to follow in Another's footsteps, hav-ing faith in the path wherever it might lead. With that, he smiled down at

Ismay and felt her tiny hand resting so lovingly and securely in his own. Archie continued to smile knowing that, in the innocent and compelling manner that was hers alone, his granddaughter had felt and now offered genuine comfort. *O linn gu linn.* (From generation to generation)

⬚ Chapter Ten ⬚

'S e mo ghuidhe 's mo dhùrachd
Gu'n tigeadh sibh 'n taobh seo,
'S gu'm faic mi le m'shùilean sibh bèo.
> Ailean MacAlasdair
> *Tighinn Do America* (òran)

It's my wish and my desire
That you will come across to my side,
And my own eyes will see you alive once more.
> Allan MacDonald
> *Coming to America* (song)

It had not been as easy a task as she had first thought. After all, it was to be a simple straightforward letter that was a matter of form, a letter that had been written by many before her and, no doubt, would be by many after. But if it was so routine a chore, why then did she find it so difficult to commit pen to paper? Why did she feel as though something was about to die when, in actual fact, she knew only too well that it was just the opposite? Why now, two months after her letter of resignation as school mistress of the *Loch Dubh* Public School, did it still trouble her so greatly?

The first suspicions of her condition had come in late May. Kristy had spoken to Tina in confidence, choosing not to discuss it with Alasdair for fear of raising his expectations, especially if it was proven not to be true. On numerous occasions, he had made it known that he desperately wanted a child. One evening as they lay in each other's arms in the large maple bed, Alasdair once again became a child himself when explaining how a bairn would bring so much joy, not only to them but to the entire Erskine home. The image of his father at Kenneth's birthday party and the presentation of the pipe had made a lasting impression on him. It was all so difficult for him to explain, even to himself. Yet, if nothing else, he had a natural sense that it was more a matter of the heart than of the mind. It was not something he thought but, rather, something he felt. As he stroked Kristy's soft hair, Alasdair looked up at the roughly hewn boards of the ceiling and remembered how, as a child, his eyes would follow the lines in the grain of the wood, imagining them to be intricate roads beckoning him to exciting far-off places. He had often dreamed of where those roads might take him but here, with Kristy in his arms, he realized that his voyage ended where it had begun. He had never known such happiness and peace as he did now back in *Loch Dubh*, under this charted ceiling, in these loving arms.

Having been separated from his family for over two years, Alasdair had come to a greater appreciation of its importance in forging his own sense of identity. Increasingly, he recognized that he was unquestionably the embodiment of his parents — a person whose identity was forged by the place that was *Loch Dubh*. He had always belonged here with his family and was now thankful that his father's illness had, in some strange and unexpected way, guided his footsteps back. At the same time, his heart went out to those young people who were being forced to leave this place, forced to leave their home and a part of themselves behind to find a living in distant cities. One day, he and Kristy would bring life into the world as a testament to their love for each other and as an affirmation of their presence on this land by these tranquil waters and under the watchful sentry of these mountains. He and his family belonged here and, God willing, always would belong. The more he thought, the more he came to the stark realization that he had indeed become his parents. *Is iomadh linn a chuir thu romhad.* (You put many a generation before you.) As he lay there, Alasdair was suddenly conscious of the broad smile that had crept across his face and was certain he had seldom before felt such contentment with his life. He held Kristy close.

It had not taken Tina long to confirm that, indeed, Kristy was with child. She knew the signs all too well. As a young woman, she had hoped and prayed that she herself would experience them more often. With every birth that she had attended over the years, the questioning was never far away. Her mind would go back in time and she would relive the pain once more. But that was all past and the joy she felt for Kristy and Alasdair was confirmed by the undeniable twinkle in her eyes. It now fell to Kristy to share the good news with her husband at a time and in a circumstance of her choosing. Tina's own beautiful son was to be a father. She sat in the rocking chair knitting, smiling to herself and realizing that all those old hopes and prayers could be put to rest. There was a sense of relief, as if a heavy burden had finally been lifted from her shoulders. *"Tha mo dhiol agamsa. Dìreach. Dìreach."* (I am satisfied. Just so. Just so.)

Tina and Kristy had spoken together in mid-June, just prior to the end of the school year. At the time of Kenneth's birthday party, Kristy knew of her condition but had not yet shared it with Alasdair or anyone else. She would not have it detract in any way from Kenneth's special day, especially given that they were covert conspirators with regard to the special present that had even then been secretly stored in the linen trunk. But now, she relished the idea of choosing her time carefully so as to maximize the impact. After all, it was certainly not beyond her to be playful with Alasdair. How he enjoyed her mischievous nature and loved, at least in a joking manner, to put her on notice. *"'S e m' uan beag mear a th' annad — maothar na treuda. Is mise an cù chaorach agadsa. Bidh mi an urra ort."* (You are my playful, little lamb — the young of the flock. I am your sheep dog. I will protect you / keep you safe.) At times such as these, he would mimic her Christmas Island accent by slowly and very intentionally elongating the words, which succeeded only in producing a hopping mad lamb. In actual fact, Alasdair was anything but domineering; he would never have been successful in controlling her even if he had wanted to. When all was said and done, he would succumb to her enchanting smile and equally alluring eyes.

"An ann a'coinne riumsa a tha thu? Nach bu tu an t-each!" (Is it imitating me you are? What a brute you are!) Without exception, Kristy's words were as predictable as was her tone of voice. Although he bore the battle scars of many a *sgleog* (a box on the ear), Alasdair could never resist teasing her and took great joy in doing so whenever the occasion presented itself. He sensed that they would always remain young lovers.

It was in the early morning of July 1, Dominion Day, that she nuzzled up close to him in bed and, in her most provocative voice, asked how he intended to celebrate the day. With the smell of the summer breeze and the sound of lowing cows wafting through the open window, Alasdair was being called to the barn and the milking. Yet he found himself caught in the fearsome clutches of the little lamb who refused to relinquish her possession of him. She recalled how those beautiful green eyes turned towards her and how he so swiftly and ruthlessly assaulted her with the only effective weapon at his disposal. He tickled her unmercifully as he cooed in her ear. *"Molaidh mi thu, mo bhean bhreagh."* (I will celebrate you my beautiful wife.) He kissed her on the forehead and, sensing her weakening grasp, quickly rose from the seductive prison that was their bed.

Against the light flooding into the room from the window, Kristy could see the rays of sun turn his silhouetted form as black as night while illuminating the fringes of his tousled hair, making it appear as though it was on fire. It was while he was attempting to slip into his trousers that she abruptly propped herself up in bed and, almost in a whimsical manner, made him aware of her own plans. *"Och ma tà! Molaidh mise thusa, mo chéile bhòidhich — a tha gu bhith nad athair a dh' aithghearr."* (Oh indeed! I will celebrate you my handsome husband and shortly a father to be.) The room went quiet, as even the breeze seemed to hold its breath in anticipation of what would come next. Alasdair slowly turned and looked at her in silence for several seconds; initially the look was one of surprise mixed with uncertainty and disbelief. This was quickly followed by the acceptance of an obvious realization and, with that, all thoughts of escape had left him. On this morning at least, the cows could wait a bit longer to be watered, fed and milked. He returned to her eager clutches and another form of celebration that, if the newspaper accounts of his extramarital exploits were to be believed, would undoubtedly receive royal sanction from King Edward himself. *"Gum bu fada beò an righ!"* (Long live the King!) He quite willingly fell back into her waiting arms.

"Alasdair, bi modhail. Thoir an aire! Tha thu a'labhairt air an righ." (Alasdair, behave yourself. Be careful! You are speaking of the King.) Even though Alasdair's reference to His Majesty made no sense to her at all, it was hard for Kristy to scold him further. On this occasion at least, she would allow him to be the sheep dog or for that matter anything else that he wished to be. She loved him with an unconditional love that simply made her want and need to hold him close.

As the weeks progressed, Kristy became more radiant and content with her ensuing condition and burgeoning size. She intentionally spent as much time as possible outside in Tina's flower garden, taking the fresh summer air. So many times in the past, she had looked down from her bedroom window as Tina strolled leisurely among the precisely laid-out beds. She always appeared to draw such enjoyment and peace from these excursions. Now, as she wandered the very same paths, Kristy began to appreciate the fact that the garden was something much greater than a carefully delineated floral repository. There was a sense of nurturing here, a satisfaction in seeing the glorious beauty of life envelop you at times when other things seemed so harsh, so forlorn, so beyond any degree of control. This was truly the one place where Tina held sway, where she ruled completely. *Seo an rìoghachd aice.* (This is her kingdom.)

Kristy had seldom before stopped to think about it but it seemed to explain why the woman in each home took such pride in her own personal dominion. In so many other ways, their lives were not their own; they were fragmented into a myriad of tiny slivers of existence like the clouds of a mackerel sky — fragmented yet tenuously whole. Here on this modest quilted square of earth, each life was restored to completeness and somehow miraculously joined together, one to the other. The women were worthy and had some semblance of command over their lives, even if it was only in the smallest of spaces for the briefest of times.

The September sun was undaunting in its desire to blanket everything beneath it with its warmth, as if refusing to accept the inevitability of autumn's chilling advent. Its rays streamed across Kristy's face as she positioned herself on the soft green grass under the crab-apple tree. Sitting there, she was reminded of two other memorable garden moments: Alasdair's proposal of marriage in the Halifax Public Gardens almost four years ago and her wedding in the "floral" parlour created by Tina now two years past. Perhaps, unbeknown even to herself and in its own subtle almost metamorphic ways, the garden was now assuming a special place in her heart and life as well.

She reached down and placed her hands on her enlarged stomach and spoke aloud. *"Seadh, a lùr. 'S gu maith a dh'éireas dhuit; Saoghal fada 's móran slàinte. M'eudail — 's gil' thu na sneachda nam beann."* (It is so my jewel. May goodness be always yours; a long and healthy life. My treasure — you are fairer than the snow on the hills.) Positioned as she was in the middle of a broad expanse of colourful vegetation, she laughed aloud at her own choice of rather untimely, wintery descriptor and sense of exuberance. Kristy also harkened back to her own unique celebration of this year's Dominion Day. She thought Alasdair truly naughty in invoking the name of the King and hoped that, if nothing else, Queen Alexandra would be understanding. Given Edward's propensity for frequent and well-known meanderings, it was clearly in her nature to be so.

On her lap was placed a pine baking board taken from the kitchen pantry to serve as a makeshift writing table. The preliminary letter to education officials in early July, notifying them of her intention to resign, had not been a simple or easy affair. Indeed, it had not taken long to prove the point. The pen had remained positioned over the paper, hovering as if it were a gull soaring over a blanched sea. Her thoughts were of all the students who, in her few short years here, had passed through her care. Her first memories were of Elizabeth Urquhart, who was now herself a teacher, and the MacDonald twins. How she had prayed to Matthias and the other saints to watch over them. And now, poor Andrew was at rest in a far-off land with only a cairn to stand witness to his all-too-brief passage on this land. And Rod was now a minister of the Church. She had influenced these and other lives and wondered if she had truly made a contribution, if she had made a difference. There was, at the same time, a quiet discernment that she was not, in fact, relinquishing this enlarged family; they would always be a part of her — a part of this place. It was only then, upon careful and considered reflection, that the gull descended to its watery rest. The words flowed like a babbling brook and the letter was signed with a genuine sense of contentment and pride. All doubts were quickly dismissed by the mounting realization that she had indeed made a difference.

It was the second letter on that July afternoon that had been far more difficult for Kristy to first ponder and then actually compose. Over the past two and a half years, her correspondence to Christmas Island had been diligently posted on a regular basis but, sadly, was consistently greeted with a deafening silence. The pain of separation never really left her and, if nothing else, the process of writing in itself seemed to somehow lessen her grief by drawing them closer in a strange sort of way. Looking out over the garden, Kristy noted that there were many buds that were yet to bloom, still to add their radiance to the floral carpet that stretched out before her. There was an eternal cycle of beauty in the garden that beguiled the senses with wonder and amazement. Here, in the deep green shadow of the mountains, the garden was a treasure trove of jewels nurtured by the earth's warm womb. Her child would be just such a jewel and she hoped that her parents would one day gather this new life up in their arms as their own, that one day they would also gather her up in their arms. She thought of her mother abiding in her own garden. For now, it was all she had.

As Kristy sat there in her solitude, she heard the back door slam as Daniel and Tina first appeared and then slowly walked off, arm-in-arm, towards the back pasture. It had become Tina's subtle way of coaxing her *bodachan* (little old man), as she was now in the habit of referring to him, out for a therapeutic walk and, at the same time, a few quiet moments alone together. It was something that she had undertaken daily after his initial recovery from the stroke. There was an appreciation of the somewhat tenuous gift that had been given her, of something restored, and she was determined to relish each moment. *"Cha ruig thu leas a bhi toirt meathadh dhòmhsa. Bidh do mheirglas sgìth!"* (You need not be taunting me. Your jaws will be tired!) Even with the distance, Kristy could hear Daniel's feigned admonishment and see Tina's laughing face as she leaned into his shoulder. Regardless of the passage of years, they still gave the impression of being so much in love.

With the fragrance of new life surrounding her, Kristy lowered her pen and began to write. She longed to see and feel her parents' love, for herself and her child. Even with sadness upon her, Kristy was sustained by the knowledge that the Almighty would decide. He would continue to guide her as He had from her first day here in *Loch Dubh*. She looked off towards the loch as the first shadows of *Beinn-mo-Mhulaid* began to appear at the far end of the water. Here there was such peace and fulfilment. This was her home. This was where her family would be raised. This was where she and Alasdair would grow old, walking arm-in-arm like Tina and Daniel, through green pastures surrounded by the love of children and grandchildren.

Tina and Daniel disappeared from view as they passed over the crest of a hill. One day, they would be truly gone as would her own parents. Yet, through the passage of the years and generations, Kristy knew that she would remain secure in a love and faith that found expression in those brief but compelling words of Tina: *Ni sealbh an rud as còir.* (Providence will do justice.) Tina's legacy was so much greater than this garden. She lowered the pen and the blanched sea was quickly restored to its azured beauty as the script of her words began to appear with a heightened sense of confidence. There in Tina's garden, surrounded by the fullness and beauty of life, Kristy smiled with considerable contentment as she completed the letter.

From a distance, the community hall gave every appearance of being a child that had been well disciplined for some terribly mischievous deed. It sat quietly and sedately in its place looking out over the darkened waters of the loch. It no longer had a boisterous sense about it; its once joyous songs were long gone like an echo rushing over the mountains in search of a new resting place before it exhausted itself into oblivion. Indeed, the only visible signs of life were the eyes that continued to glare out into the night, aimlessly seeking out anyone or anything to offer consolation and, perhaps, confirmation that its behaviour had not been so wicked after all.

The tall windows on either side of the large central doors now appeared as two candles cursing the darkness that enveloped the hall. From the far side of the loch, Norman and Rachael Ferguson could see tiny blackened figures being devoured by the light as they entered through the doors and quickly passed from view. While several horses and wagons were already tied to the nearby trees, the warmth of the October evening was an incentive for some of the younger families to proceed on foot, much as they themselves were doing. Indeed, the slight breeze coming over the bluffs from the broad Atlantic below was invigorating to the skin and the eyes were enraptured by the light of the first stars that were even now beginning to appear in the north sky.

"A Stiùbhairt! Anndra! — luidein mhaolach. Greasaibh oirbh agus falbhaibh leinn." (Stuart! Andrew! — foolish rascals. Hurry up and come along with us.) Norman's somewhat less-than-temperate words pierced the air that up until that time had been dominated by the lapping of the water on the loch's shore. Rachael turned and smiled at the boys as if to take the harshness out of their father's rebuke. She knew that boys would be boys and, as such, would sooner be anywhere else tonight, anywhere else but at prayer meeting.

Although such meetings were held on a weekly basis, the boys had come to associate the hall with the raucous sights and sounds of music and dance that came with its *céilidhs* and milling frolics. Like most young people, Stuart and Andrew regarded the hall as the heart of the community. It invigorated *Loch Dubh* with a sense of life. Of course, they would never dare refer to it in this way in the presence of their parents or any of the older people. Had they not been taught from youth that it was the Kirk that was the foundation, the rock of their salvation, the sure and constant sign of meaning in their lives? There was an acceptance, albeit reluctant, of the fact that, this night at least, the rough wooden walls of the hall would not rejoice in fiddle music, square dancing or laughter over tea. Rather, they would be dutifully washed with hymns of praise, smoothened by prayers for the forgiveness of sin and polished with the assurance of faith restored. Their father's reprimand notwithstanding, Stuart and Andrew knew they had better behave.

At the double doors, Norman and Rachael were met by the Urquharts, Hector, Sarah and *Domhnall Òg.* (Young Donald) It was well known throughout the community that Donald had been extremely interested in pursuing their Morag before she up and ran off to Boston with Emily Fraser in search of fame and fortune. Initially, his dejection had been a cause of some concern for his parents who knew full well that, at twenty years of age, he was eager to settle down. The resilience of the Urquharts was more than apparent as he wasted no time in taking up with Sadie Grant, who at nineteen, was still at home and seemingly desirous of any outward demonstrations of affection and, by extension, offers of marriage.

For his part, Donald liked her well enough and appeared hell bent in his determination to prove his sister Elizabeth wrong. Soon enough God willing, he would no longer be *an seann fhleasgach*. (The Old Bachelor) It was not by chance then that, on this night, Donald strategically guided his parents to the wooden chairs immediately behind the Grants who had seated themselves near the centre of the hall.

The Erskines were just entering through the doors as Norman and Rachael turned to take their places. Kristy was certainly showing that she was fully six months with child but still looking so radiant standing next to Alasdair. Rachael hoped that she would be relieved of a healthy bairn. Was it not oftentimes the first born that was most problematic? But then, one should never question the will of God; she had learned that herself after much soul searching. As they were seated, Rachael could see Ismay Campbell standing on her mother's lap up near the front, ironically creating the impression that she was attempting to look about the room. The girl was now well over two years of age and had grown into a strikingly beautiful child. But more than anything else, it was always the magnificent blue eyes that drew Rachael's attention to the tiny porcelain face. There, in the dim light of the kerosene lamps, she thought of her own blindness following Harris' passing and prayed that this small child would be blessed in other ways. It was the prayer of one mother for another. *Och ma tà. Aig Dia a mhàin tha brath.* (Oh indeed. God alone knows.)

The small riser at the head of the hall, so often occupied by Jamie MacInnes and his fiddle, had become the domain of Archie MacDonald and his Bible. In his capacity as one of the three Kirk elders, Archie took his turn leading the meeting as he had done so many times before. Holding the Bible close to his chest, he read scripture from both the Old and New Testaments. It was not uncommon for the clerk of session to read with his eyes firmly fixed not on the text before him but rather on the wooden rafters of the hall, as if seeking divine guidance. Most people knew differently; the Bible had always been his security and constant companion. He knew its pages well and its words were like friends that guided, that sustained, that comforted. Far less known was the fact that Archie was somewhat timid about public speaking, which was for him an unfortunate prerequisite for the role of clerk of session. As he glanced up the length of the hall at Archie, Angus Grant was reminded of his own dear father who, like Archie, had no need of a Bible to quote chapter and verse. The only difference was that Archie could read, at least in the Gaelic. And so he did to the silent rafters. *"Chum gu'n cuireadh e 'na làthair féin i 'na h-eaglais ghlòirmhoir, gun smal, gun phreasadh, no ni air bith d'an leithidean sin; ach chum gu'm biodh i naomh, agus neo-lochdach."* (That he might present it to himself a glorious church, not having spot, or wrinkle, or any such thing; but that it should be holy and without blemish.)

The practice was well known and respected by all the men who had come prepared with the understanding that they might well be called upon at any time. It was following the singing of the first hymn and presentation of the word that Archie asked several individuals throughout the hall, each in their turn, to join in fellowship by leading in prayer. Among the first to be singled out was Hector Urquhart who stood at his place with hands firmly planted on the back of the empty chair before him, rocking slowly back and forth, lulling himself as if somehow coaxing forth the words. All heads were bowed and eyes closed as he skilfully wove in references to Archie's choice of scripture and evoked the Almighty's mercy in cleansing them from all stain of earthly sin. Indeed, all heads were bowed and eyes closed except for at least one nonconforming individual. Young Andrew Ferguson had taken a quick inventory of the room and was reaching deep into his jacket pocket to retrieve a handful of freshly picked cranberries. His sights were set on Moira Campbell who was ever-so-piously seated near the front with her family. Andrew was of the view that perhaps her haughty airs would be much better reflected in a glowing crown of red hair. He would be the one to do the honours and this, please God, was the moment.

Hector was not to be dissuaded from concentration on prayer even by the persistent badgering of the pesky flies that could be so bothersome even at this time of year. It was fortunate for the wee Moira that Andrew's aim was as green as his years. Positioned halfway between aggressor and intended victim, Hector's neck and right cheek had begun to assume a ruddy hue as he prayed on, oblivious to the fact that he was even now a soldier on the front lines of battle.

It was only at the completion of the lengthy prayer that Sarah, upon opening her eyes, bore witness to the red blotches on her husband's body and clothing. The discharged shells were scattered on the floor about them, giving evidence to the fact that the enemy had positioned himself somewhere to the back, from where the rear-guard action had obviously been orchestrated. Heads were turned with glaring eyes that fell on a field of absolute innocence. Certainly none would have pointed an accusatory finger at the angelic face of Andrew, whose hands remained tightly clasped together in prayer, reflecting his piety and ever so conveniently concealing his "bloodied" fingers.

Across the way, the lengthy service had been made more bearable for James MacGregor by the comforting gift of chewing tobacco. Was it not always safely committed to his coat pocket for just such emergencies? He was seated in his customary chair off to the side of the hall, just down some ten feet or so from the pot-bellied stove near the front. It was during Hector's protracted prayer that James' eye ceased to be "on the sparrow" and was actually on the blackened comets that erupted from his mouth en route to their intended destination in the wood box. There was a certain safety in undertaking artillery practice at this time of year; he knew well enough just how perilous it could be during the winter months. He was suddenly reminded of the meeting last March when his trajectory was scuttled by a sudden poke in the ribs from Margaret. The sullen wad had landed on the red-hot stove and both the ensuing guttural sizzle and pungent odour had quickly blanketed the room. For the most part, it had not gone unnoticed or uncredited when, later in the fresh air of the hall's front steps, James had thanked Daniel Erskine for his powerful message focussing on the need for a pious and humble heart. As they exchanged greetings, Daniel recalled the prophetic words of Isaiah when he spoke of the judgement to befall the House of Israel for its flagrant vanities. *"Agus an àite deagh fhàile bidh bréine..."* (And it shall come to pass, that instead of sweet smell there shall be stink...) For his part, James professed that he had been terribly moved by the message and would surely ponder it in his heart. As he bid a final farewell, James' left hand reached into his coat pocket to ensure that a sufficient supply still remained to sustain him on the return journey.

It was on their own way home that both Norman and Rachael became somewhat impatient with Andrew's dallying. There was no good reason for them to know that it would be the only opportunity the young warrior would have to remove the stains of his sinful action before arriving at the kitchen door. He quickly dipped his hands into the cleansing forgiving waters of the loch, wiped them on his trousers and raced to rejoin his family as they passed in front of the Kirk and the manse further up on the hill. In the days that followed, his parents were somewhat amused by the fact that Stuart took to calling his younger brother *Anndra an saighdear.* (Soldier Andrew) They certainly did not understand the significance but did not seem to mind; the bestowing of such nicknames was a common enough practice among the Scots and this one would most probably disappear as quickly as it had come. For Rachael, it was a timely reminder of another Andrew who had been a true and valiant soldier. Hearing the name spoken aloud pleased her and called to mind a powerful message about life that she had learned earlier: the wisdom of the children. She would make a point of visiting Andrew MacDonald's cairn before the first snow.

It was not so much a case of things not changing for indeed they were. There was change all around. You could see it in the large framed houses that replaced the small squat cabins of the early settlers. You could hear it in the blending of English words with the Gaelic as the younger people gathered to talk down by the river on their way home from school. You could even smell and taste it in some of the food seasoned with the array of spices that was available in town or from the Lebanese peddlers who sold a multitude of items from the backs of their wagons during their summer treks through the highlands. People still chuckled about the incident last year involving Angus Matheson and the peddler family that appeared at the end of his laneway. Had not the blood drained from Angus' face when, in turning to his wife, he quite disdainfully told her in the Gaelic that these people had no business here. They were not their kind; they were from away. As she gingerly climbed down from the wagon with her stout elfin figure, Mrs. Hamoud quite intentionally took a moment to dust off her skirt with her hands before glancing up, smiling covertly at Angus. Even with the distance that rested between them, one could almost see the twinkle in the eyes. *"Och, is e seo dùthaich nan Gaidheal? Rugadh agus thogadh mi an Cheap Breatuinn. Gu dearbh is e Canadian a tha annam coltach ruibh féin!"* (Oh, is this the country of the Gaels? I was born and raised in Cape Breton. Indeed I am as Canadian as are you!) The elfin figure now assumed a stance bigger than life as she stood her ground. Later, as shock turned to embarrassment, Angus cursed the road that brought such change to their very door steps.

"Tha Gàidhlig aice. Is mó an diùbhail; tha dragh anns an t-saoghal. Aig Dia a mhàin tha brath." (And she speaking the Gaelic. It is a thousand pities; there is trouble in the world. God alone knows.) It took all in her power but Ena Matheson finally succeeded in smothering her laughter. She knew that it would be best. Her husband was, after all, a proud man.

With the December winds now in full assault, the kitchen windows rattled as if they were so many teeth chattering uncontrollably in the frigid air. The Reverend Rod MacDonald sat by the stove sipping a most welcomed and comforting cup of tea. He chuckled to himself as the peddler episode sprang to mind. He had overheard the story being recounted with great hilarity at MacKinnon's General Store on a Saturday afternoon in early August. As was the custom, the local farmers gathered for a chat in the far corner while they waited for the women to complete their transactions at the counter. Certainly their discussions could never be mistaken for gossip. That was clearly something that only the women engaged in when they came together over quilting or knitting, creating a clacking of tongues not unlike a hen house under attack by a ravenous fox. No, they were merely educating themselves as to the news of the day and sharing useful information of common interest. It was most unfortunate for them that, on that particular day at least, they had their backs to the door and had not taken notice of the arrival of the new minister. At the same time, it was all most fortunate for Rod who learned yet another whimsical story about the members of his congregation, albeit at the expense of poor Angus.

The narrow road north from Baddeck, which was often travelled by the peddlers on their seasonal rounds, had led Rod to *An Abhainn Mheadhonach* in early July, shortly after the celebration of Dominion Day. It had always been in his mind that, upon completion of studies in Montreal, he would return to Cape Breton. It seemed so appropriate that he be ordained into the ministry and inducted into a church on this island. There was never any doubt that his years in Montreal had been a learning experience, academically and otherwise. In that time, he had come to a greater appreciation of the simple beauty of his heritage, even with its all-too-numerous quirks and foibles. But most of all, he had come to recognize how one could become invigorated by the sheer strength of one's faith. Rod was forced to admit that he also wished to be close to his family, especially his grandfather who was now getting on in years. Rod knew that there was much he could still learn from *Seanair Naomh* but that, in all likelihood, there was not a great deal of time left to them.

An Abhainn Mheadhonach, or Middle River as some of the younger people were now calling it, had been without a minister for almost two years and the congregation was eager to make Rod feel at home. Tucked back in a field well beyond the shadowy reach of the imposing Kirk, the less assuming manse had earlier been the scene of a beehive of activity with people coming and going at an almost frantic pace, as preparations were made to receive the new minister. It had been aired, painted, scrubbed and polished to within an inch of its life. Even the kitchen cupboards had been well stocked by the neighbouring families with every conceivable requirement so as to ensure that the minister's body would be well fed for the task of nurturing the souls of his flock. *Mo chaoraich.* (My Sheep) Sitting alone in the manse kitchen on that first afternoon in July, Rod realized that his commitment had been made, his ambition had been finally reached and his task was now at hand. Something told him that there was no need to be afraid. Somehow, he would be guided through these green pastures and beside these still waters.

The service of ordination and induction had been held on an evening in late July and was well attended. Even most of Rod's family had travelled down from *Loch Dubh.* Only his brother Daniel and cousin Duncan were forced to remain behind to take care of the milking and other essential chores on the two MacDonald farms. Few occasions held such importance in the life of a family and faces quite freely reflected the tremendous sense of pride and thanksgiving that was felt but, as was the nature of the highland Scots, so seldom expressed. It was at the invocation of the service that Archie watched his grandson proceed into the sanctuary wearing a dark blue suit that would soon be concealed by the black robes and white tabs of the ministry. Even as the congregation stood, Archie bowed his head in prayer. It was Jessie who glanced up and noted the tears streaming down his face as though refusing to follow the deeply wrinkled pathways that had been etched there with the years. She put her arm through his and patted it gently. It would not be appropriate to speak and, even if she could find words, Jessie knew that they would be a vain attempt to comfort. This was a matter of the heart and she would simply leave him be.

Later, well after the close of the service in the Kirk and subsequent reception in the community hall, the MacDonalds returned to the manse for a cup of tea, alone. Everyone was seated around the kitchen table as Jessie and Ida busied themselves by placing yet more plates of sweets before them. Rod was speaking with his father when, from the corner of his eye, he noticed Archie quietly leaving the room only to return shortly thereafter with a small package wrapped in brown paper. Rod recognized the creased paper and rough twine as coming from Dunn's General Store in New Carlisle; like so many others, his grandfather was never one to abide waste. The package was lovingly placed before Rod as Archie once again resumed his seat at the head of the table.

"Gabh so. Seo tiodhlac dhuit. Tha e agad a-nis." (Take this. This is a present for you. It belongs to you now.) As he spoke, Archie pointed to the package down the length of the table and motioned to his grandson to open it. Rod slowly removed the twine and paper as everyone at the table sat in silence, watching his every move with great interest and even greater curiosity. It was obvious that only Archie himself was aware of the contents; it had been his idea and quite properly his alone. The paper was finally peeled back to reveal a black leather-bound Bible that bore an inscription to Archibald MacDonald and already showed the wear of frequent use over five and a half years.

"A Sheanair, cha ghabh mi seo. Cha dealaich thu ris." (Grandfather, I will not accept this. You will not part with it.) Rod was looking down the length of the table as Archie rose from his place and came round to stand at the side of his grandson. He placed his hand on Rod's shoulder and smiled down. At that moment, Jessie could not help but look deeply into the old man's face and marvel at the range of emotions that this day had brought, was bringing, to him. With the exception of the melodic chirping of birds being carried into the kitchen on the night breeze, there was an absolute stillness. It lingered for what seemed like a very long while. At the same time, there was a well-founded appreciation on the part of the family that Archie was never one to waste his words and, as was the case with his coins, obviously chose them carefully and sparingly.

"Tha e agad a-nis. Tha an latha a' tighinn gu crìch agus chaill mi mo shealladh. Tha mi buidheach agus làn uaill, a Mhinisteir MacDhomhnuill. Beannachd Dhé leat do ghnàth." (It belongs to you now. The day comes to a close and I am losing my eyesight. I am contented and extremely proud, Reverend MacDonald. May the blessings of God attend you always.) With that, he returned to his seat, asked for another cup of tea and smiled. There were no more words. There were no more tears. This day was cause for quiet celebration.

The past four months had witnessed such a breadth of change for Rod. He recalled visiting the grassy field on the MacLean farm where he, Andrew and the other young men had received their initial training and parade drill almost six years ago. So much had happened since, both to him and his family. In some strange way, he felt closer to his brother in that broad expanse of field than he had in a long while. He thought of the cairn back in *Loch Dubh* on the slopes of Andrew's beloved *Beinn-mo-Mhulaid*. Now here in *An Abhainn Mheadhonach* as he looked off to the mountains rising up to the north, Rod reached down and ran his hand across the soft warm grass, just as he had done across the parched red earth of Andrew's grave on that final day. *"Seo cridhe Dhé. Agus Anndra mo bhràthair ghràdhmhoir, thug thu mo bheatha dhomh air ais nuair a thug thu air ais chun àite seo mi. Tapadh leat."* (This is the heart of God. And Andrew my dear brother, you brought my life back to me when you brought me back to this place. Thank you.)

It had not taken long for the congregation to take note of the stark silence that fell over the solitary manse once the other members of Clan MacDonald had returned home. Numerous congregants ever so discretely availed themselves of every possible opportunity to ensure that the minister was introduced to their granddaughters, daughters, sisters and nieces. In ways subtle and sometimes not, Rod was made aware of their glowing qualities, especially their prowess around the house and strapping physical features. At times, it seemed as though several of the principal proponents had mounted personal campaigns of their own. Still in all fairness, they had no way of knowing that their minister had maintained a four-year correspondence with George Buchanan's sister, Margaret, in *Cobh a' Gheòidh*. Nor did they have any reason to suspect that Rod agreed most heartily with their view that the manse was in need of company or that he had every intention of rectifying this situation himself in the very near future.

Rod felt both challenged and invigorated by the work ahead and quite intentionally sought inspiration from the pastoral setting that surrounded him at every turn. One evening as he walked down by the river, a memory abruptly began to flood back across his mind. It was spring 1904 and he was strolling along de la Commune Street, down by the St. Lawrence. Although he could not recollect or even understand the actual words that had been spoken, he clearly remembered the intent in the young women's voices. He was uncertain as to whether he should feel greater shame for recalling the incident or for having thought of them many times since. Was it not that he saw them only as lost sheep that had strayed from the flock? Why then had he not attempted to speak with them, to save them? Why were their shadowy faces now so firmly engraved in his mind? As he made his way back to the manse in the fading light of day, he was reminded of the words from Jeremiah: *Agus bheir mi dhuibh aodhairean a réir mo chridhe féin, agus beathaichidh iad sibh le eòlas agus le tuigse.* (And I will give you pastors according to mine heart, which shall feed you with knowledge and understanding.) Rod prayed silently that he might be filled with both.

The sharpness of the frigid arctic wind was lost on her. It came from the south-west, from the direction of St. Peter's through the Barra Strait at Iona and around the Washabuck Point, screaming across the ice-covered lake as if it were an eagle in full flight. There was a savagery to it, an unrelenting assertion that it was in control, that everyone and everything before it would fall victim to its wrath. And yet she stood there on the shore looking off in the direction of Boularderie Island and beyond, oblivious to the merciless wind. She was numb, not from the cold, but from the knowledge that she was alone and powerless to act. The cold and wind be damned; she was so completely alone.

January 14 was an inauspicious day in the life of Baddeck, almost like any other. It was a Saturday and many of the farming families had journeyed into town from the outlying areas to shop for household goods. The main street was crowded with horses and sleighs as blackened figures raced from store to store as much to find shelter from the biting cold as to acquire the much-sought-after provisions. There would be many a cup of hot tea or cocoa consumed before the sleighs would be filled and the horses once again directed homeward. Even from their vantage point further up the hill on main street, no one would have taken the slightest notice of the solitary figure standing down by the shore. In so many ways known and unknown, Emily was truly alone.

Today was her baby's birthday; Murdina Jennie O'Sullivan would be one year old. Emily did not much care for the name but then she had not chosen it. It was Effie, her mother, who had. Her mother! No, she could not and would not abide the thought. Effie would never be her child's mother; she never could be. With the wind in her face, Emily knew she was even then becoming the ship on storm-tossed waters, battered by a sea of emotions. It was not the first time she had been so troubled. Sure enough, she was grateful to Effie and Liam for giving her child a good home with all the accompanying promises and hope for the future. Still, she hated them for taking her child away from her and claiming her as their own. Did she not still have the scars to prove that she had carried this child and given it life? Did she not still have the longing to go to her and give nourishment? Without fully realizing what she was doing, Emily had raised her arms to feel the warmth of her child against her breast. Instead, all she felt was the deadly biting cold.

The parting on the Boston pier in early August had been much more difficult than she had at first thought it would be. At seven months, the tiny being was already exhibiting discernible characteristics that gave her such a distinctive personality. Emily was not leaving behind a baby, she was leaving a child, her child. She sought consolation in the belief that the voyage, first to Halifax and then on to Sydney, would be a time for her to reflect and collect her thoughts in preparation for the reunion with family. She would be alone, given that Morag had earlier made the fateful decision to stay on in Boston. Most certainly there was romance in the air and her friend would no doubt make a new home and establish a family for herself far from the shores of *Loch Dubh*. The solitary figure standing on the ship's bow hoped that the trip back to Cape Breton would mark a new beginning for her as well, that the salt water would somehow magically cleanse her of both the shame and loneliness she felt so deeply. Still, she realized that, in many ways, she was sailing directly back into her past. The briny waters were a preservative that kept things as they were and would not help change them into things that she might wish them to become. "She was my future, all that I had, and now *thréig mi i. A Thighearna, tha mi am aonais.* (I abandoned her. Oh Lord, I am all alone.) She is gone from me. I have nothing but memories." Emily's tears fell to the waters below where, like her hopes and dreams, they blended and then quickly dissolved into oblivion.

Duncan and Jennie made the journey to Sydney to join Sandy and Matthew in welcoming Emily home. There was much excitement on the wharf as the steamer first appeared off in the distance, coming ever so slowly down the length of the South Arm. A throng of people had gathered and were eagerly awaiting a first acknowledging glimpse of an expected loved one. As the ship slipped towards its berth, Emily looked off to the approaching landscape before her and thought how frightfully small and drab Sydney seemed compared to Boston or even Halifax. It was all so small, so terribly drab. The cheering on the dock quickly brought her back to the task at hand and it had not taken her long to spot her family standing in the middle of the crowd. Her father's clerical collar stood out like a beacon guiding her into the safety of the harbour. At that moment, Emily realized that the voyage had not totally prepared her for the reunion that was about to take place. Spontaneously, she did something that she had not done in a very long time. She prayed.

There was genuine rejoicing in seeing their daughter and sister once again, especially for Jennie who had, on so many occasions, yearned to hold her. She held Emily close for several moments as if to reclaim all the opportunities that had been lost over the past year. Yet with all the joy and laughter of meeting, the motherly instinct to express a certain concern was not to be contained as the all-too-knowing embrace was finally broken. *"Mo chaileag, is tu an t-aog dhuainidh! Is tu chuir am biorgadh annam. Tha feum agad air suipear mór. Gu dearbh!"* (My girl, you are a miserable-looking skeleton. What a start you gave me. You are in need of a good supper. Yes indeed.)

Both Sandy and Matthew broke into raucous laughter as their mother continued to fuss aloud. Matthew put his hand on his sister's shoulder in offering sage words of advice. "Emily, I would be careful if I were you. She will have you fattened up, like a pig to the slaughter, in no time. Why do you think it was we escaped to Sydney?"

"Ud. Ud.. Na toir aire air ciod a their e. Nach b'e an t-olc iad! Is gliocas neart mhàithrichean." (Tut. Tut. Pay no attention to what he says. Are they not evil ones! Wisdom is the strength of mothers.) Jennie proceeded to poke them both in the chest with her finger in making her point and in subtly asserting that they were not yet too old for a scolding, if not a spanking. At well over six feet in height, both Sandy and Matthew were forced to admit some things were well beyond their power and comprehension. In their mother's eyes, they would always be her wee ones.

It was the next day that Duncan, Jennie and Emily departed Sydney by steamer for the trip north, first to Baddeck and then up the North Shore to New Carlisle. By this time, Jennie was most eager to hear of her daughter's experiences in the Boston states as well as news of Effie, Liam and the bairn. She and Duncan had been so pleased for them both now that they were truly a family. She knew that Effie would be a wonderful mother and hoped one day to meet Murdina Jennie in person. Throughout the trip, Emily smiled and nodded a great deal, feigning fatigue from the longer voyage the day before. She assured them that she would be in a better frame of mind to talk once she was truly home and had time to rest, to think.

Surprisingly, Emily's return to *Loch Dubh* and the manse had been made much easier than she could have ever imagined by the oddest of circumstances. Upon first entering the kitchen, all three took note of *Rionnag*, spread across the entire length of the pantry window sill as she basked in the glorious warmth of the late-afternoon sunlight. At first, she raised her head quizically as if attempting to confirm the identity of the phantom that now stood before her in the open doorway. Within seconds, *Rionnag* was at Emily's feet, emitting a purr that, according to Duncan, would surely rattle the dishes in the side cupboard. Emily gently picked up the *teine-biorach* (shooting star) that she had first encountered in this very room some twelve years ago. *"Och a phiseag; mo ghràdhag! Tha thu fhathast 'n ad leanabh as òige d'an teaghlach. Bha mi aonaranach ás d' aonais."* (Oh 'puss'; my dear little one! You are still the baby and youngest of the children/family. I have been lonely without you.) Emily held *Rionnag* lovingly in her arms as both Duncan and Jennie noted the slightest of tears forming in their daughter's eyes. All the signs told them that she was happy to be home and it was good to have her here where she truly belonged.

During the course of the first week, Emily kept herself busy with visitations to neighbours and friends who lived around the loch. She spent the better part of an entire day with Rachael Ferguson, sharing news of Morag and delivering a special package of used clothing and other gifts that she had been instructed to carry home safely. Quite intentionally, she did not visit the MacGregor household, although she did see the entire family at Sunday service. Emily made a special point of speaking with Peter and Martha Campbell; Ismay had been only a wee thing when she left and had now grown into a beautiful child. She also spoke with Neil and Iona Erskine who proudly carried eight-month-old Aulay in their arms. Iona had asked Emily if she would like to hold him for a bit but the kind offer was politely declined. Emily feigned humour by maintaining that she would, in all likelihood, drop him. In actual fact, she could not bear the thought of holding another baby close to her.

It had not taken Emily long to notify her parents that it was her preference to not attend academy in Sydney. She had given it a great deal of thought and wished to complete her studies in Baddeck, where she might feel more at ease. She had had enough of big cities and knew that both

Sandy and Matthew would not take offence at her decision. Indeed, they had lives of their own and did not need a younger sister about to annoy them. Emily attempted to make light of it by recollecting their youthful days of teasing in the manse. She hoped that no further arguments would be made and that her use of such levity would be all that was needed to end the discussion. Judging by their somewhat demonstrative facial expressions, both Duncan and Jennie were obviously taken aback by their daughter's strident insistence on the point. Still in all, they were pleased that she had committed herself to furthering her academic pursuits wherever that might be. Baddeck was much closer to *Loch Dubh* than was Sydney so they would, in all probability, see a great deal more of her.

Emily settled into a routine with a family in Baddeck, arranged by her father with the minister at Greenwood Presbyterian Church. She was well accepted by the other students at the academy and regarded as exceedingly bright by her instructors. Her only problem seemed to be one of concentration. Consistently, the comments on her performance report referred to the fact that she needed to apply herself and be more attentive to her studies. Also, it had not gone unnoticed that she never seemed to be interested in developing any close friendships, although several of her fellow students had been extremely diligent in their attempts. More often than not, she could be found, at the end of the school day, sitting alone down by the edge of the lake or further along by the bay. A few of the older fishermen had commented on how sorrowful a scene it was, as if she were mourning a loss. In such a small community, most everyone knew soon enough that the Reverend Fraser's daughter had just returned from a year in Boston and surmised that she likely needed nothing more than a bit of time to readjust to the slower pace of life. She was a mere child; in time, she would adapt. She would be fine.

"Cha bhi meadrachd ach far am bi thu." (There is no jollity / happiness but where you are.) The instant they had struggled from within her in an attempt to find life on the crisp air, the words were savagely clutched by the wind and whisked away. It was only then that Emily, robbed of even the warmth of her own plaintive words, finally felt the chill sting on her face, turned and slowly walked back towards the town.

The floral pattern was like the face of an old friend that had not been seen for a very long time. As with people, it too had aged somewhat and showed the ravages of wear and tear that come with the years. It had rested peacefully in its solitude for all this time and now seemed almost reluctant to be held. It had transformed its exile into a type of cloistral retreat, where it was constantly looking inward, contemplating its own existence. Here in its glorified seclusion, time had stood still simply because it ceased to have relevance.

It had taken Kristy several minutes to retrieve the carpet bag from the far reaches of the closet. Her immense girth made bending over virtually impossible. After a number of futile attempts, she finally braced herself against the door frame and extended the tip of her shoe through one of the brown-leather handles, hooking it like a fisherman jigging for cod. She was thankful that Tina and Daniel were downstairs in the kitchen and not able to witness her antics. It was less her contortions and more the motivation for them that might prove troublesome or, at least, bothersome. There was no need or reason for them to know and it would probably be best to leave well enough alone.

Kristy placed the bag at the foot of the bed and carefully opened it as though not fully aware of what agitated spirits might escape to reek havoc and exert revenge for this sudden and thoughtless disruption of their repose. There was a faint smell of must as she picked up the two small packages and gingerly relieved them of their shroud-like wrappings. For several minutes, she stared down at the crucifix, uncertain as to whether she dare run her fingers over its contours as she had so often done in the days of her youth. It had held such symbolism for her as a child; it brought to life the excruciating pain of death that was endured for the salvation of man. Yet now she had come to look upon the plain wooden cross that hung in her bedroom as an even more-powerful symbol. Its simplicity and emptiness spoke of the miraculous resurrection of the body from both the cross and death, and the ensuing gift of eternal life. As she sat there on the edge of the bed, her hands came to rest on the life that was soon to come from within her. The crucifix and rosary beads would not be for her child; they were for her mother.

The letter had arrived just after the New Year, even though the postmark had been registered as December 12. Still, the date was of no consequence to Kristy. She had finally received a response to her many letters that had been dutifully written over the past three years. Her initial reaction was to simply hold and look at the envelope with the small delicate scrolling that was so unmistakably done in her mother's own hand. She pictured her mother sitting at the kitchen table meticulously writing the words "Cairistìona Erskine." Had it pained her to do so? How had her family reacted to the news of the impending birth? Did they even care? Would this letter be the final severance? She had waited so long for this moment to arrive and now, with a mixture of joyous anticipation and fearful trepidation, all she could do was clutch it in her hands and wonder.

It was clear from the short note that Bernadette MacNeil had every intention of travelling to *Loch Dubh* in late January against the wishes of her husband. Even in the Gaelic, the words were brief and extremely clipped in a precise sort of way. She would make the journey alone. She would be with her daughter; she would be in attendance for the birth of her grandchild. The choice of words was not lost on Kristy who read them over and over again, savouring each one like a parched meadow rejoicing in the first glistening droplets of rain. She knew that it was in her mother's nature to never speak ill of her father or ever contemplate going against his will. In all likelihood, she had demonstrated great courage in taking the decision she had and in sharing it with her family. Kristy recalled the chill that had befallen her that day at home in Christmas Island when she passed through the *dorus-siar* of the kitchen that had, in so many ways, marked a death. As she folded the paper and carefully returned it to the envelope, she hoped that her mother would pass through quite a different door on her way to *Loch Dubh*.

Soon thereafter, Kristy shared the news in passing with Alasdair, Tina and Daniel over the supper table almost as if she were doing little more than commenting on the day's weather. Even with excitement and anxiety upon her, she was appreciative of the fact that she was the only one present who had knowledge of the woman who would soon enter this house. The others had never met her and should, in fairness, be given time to ponder, to respond and to prepare themselves. Few words were spoken as she looked into their faces searching for reaction and hoping for some sign of approval. Kristy stood as she was approached and then embraced, in turn, first by Alasdair and then Tina. Their faces were awash with the joy they felt for her. They knew only too well the heartbreak of a severed family and the terrible emptiness that it brings. For his part, Daniel remained stoic and quiet as he stayed seated at his place. It was only after his wife and son had returned to their chairs and silence was restored that he gazed across into Kristy's face. *"A Chairistìona, seo sonas mór ort. Deanar toil an Tighearna. An aile! An aile!"* (Kristy, there is great happiness on you. The Lord's will be done. It is so! It is so!) In his own and very understated way, Daniel told her that he too shared in her gladness. It was his house; he was pleased with the notion of the long-anticipated visit.

It was later that week that a horse and sleigh were seen proceeding up the laneway from the loch road. Having come to rest at the back door, the driver rummaged through an assortment of boxes and bags in the back of the sleigh for several minutes. Finally and ever so slowly, a slight figure rose from the ordered chaos wrapped in a thick buffalo rug that made her look twice her actual size and older than her years. She had been enticed from the shelter of the corner, behind the driver's seat, where she had nestled herself for the past two days searching for relief from the harsh elements. The first day's journey from Christmas Island to Englishtown had been bitterly cold but, for the most part, slow and uneventful. In an attempt to make up valuable time on the second day, the driver had charted a course on the ice, skirting the coast all the way up the North Shore. Hearts had quickened on more than one occasion when the ice cracked and groaned under them like a giant aquatic bear awakening from sleep with an insatiable hunger. It offered a logical explanation for the presence of rosary beads wrapped around Bernadette MacNeil's gloved hands as the driver lifted her from the sleigh and gingerly placed her, as though she were a china doll, on the back step of the Erskine home.

Looking back, those first few minutes were nothing more than a blur for Kristy, both in terms of her vision and memory; who said what, to whom, when? All Kristy could remember was being in her mother's arms again, except this time it seemed as though it was her mother who was in hers. It was as if she had grown smaller and much more frail in so short a period of time. And the embrace, was it not somewhat awkward owing to the baby that came between them? Yes indeed. But that would all change soon enough. As they entered the kitchen, Kristy held closely to her mother, vowing to herself that nothing would come between them ever again. There was a genuine sense that something had been recaptured, hopefully never to be relinquished. They were soon to be caressed by the warmth of the large stove and, with introductions made and coats put away, Mrs. MacNeil was given a place of honour in the rocking chair next to the roaring fire. It was only then that Kristy took note of the fact that her mother had quietly, and quite skilfully, removed the rosary beads from sight.

For Bernadette, the initial unease of the first hours, brought on by the uncertainties of a strange house and household, was soon dispelled by the care that the Erskines took to make her feel welcome. Kristy would never forget the moment when she had finally escorted her mother upstairs to her room to settle. They were chatting, in the midst of placing garments in the chest of drawers, when Bernadette abruptly and for some unknown reason broke into uncontrollable sobbing. Kristy went to her and held her close, not knowing the cause but desperately wanting to offer a comforting presence. Her mother reached for the side table and gently picked up the rosary beads that she and her husband had given their daughter so many years ago. She looked at the crucifix over the bed and turned to face Kristy directly. *"Cha robh sinn riamh air son gu fàgadh thu e. Aig Dia a mhàin tha fios. Bha sinn air son gum biodh tu sàbhailte sona ann a' creidimh. Rinn sinn ùrnaigh gu daonnan a h-uile làtha."* (We never wanted that you should be parted from Him. God alone knows; we wanted you to remain safe and happy in faith. We prayed every day always.)

"A Mhamaidh, mo riar fhéin, tha mi sona an seo, làidir ann an gràdh agus creidimh. Creidibh mi, bidh mo chridhe agus m'anam fo dhìdean an Tighearna fad mo làithean. Cha dealaich mi uaithe gu bràth mar nach dealaich mi uaibh fhéin." (Mamma, upon my word of honour, I am happy here, deep in love and strong in faith. Please believe me; my heart and soul will be with Him forever. I will never be parted from Him as I will never again be parted from you.) There, under the crucifix, they languished in each other's arms with the realization that their tears of sorrow were even now being transformed into tears of joy. Kristy looked into her mother's eyes and once again became her wee bairn. *"Och ma tà, rinn mi ùrnaigh air ur son a ghnàth, mhàthair ghaolach, agus a-nis tha mi air freagairt fhaighinn."* (Oh truly, you were always in my prayers, my dear mother, and now my prayers have been answered.)

They continued to hold each other close.

"Cruaidh mar an darach agus buan mar am fraoch — mo nighean bhòidheach." (Hard as the oak and lasting as the heather — my beautiful daughter.) Bernadette whispered the words in Kristy's ear, as if to make light of her earlier and quite visible display of emotion, and then kissed her softly on the cheek. There was a sense that nothing else need be said on the matter and it was not. They spoke of a whole host of things as they continued on, basking in each other's company and, all the while, committing clothes to the waiting chest of drawers.

In the week and a half before Kristy's labour began, it was the kitchen that brought Bernadette close to her daughter's new family. She, Tina and Daniel spent hours in conversation about anything and everything, including the posing and answering of riddles, a game often played by parents with their children following the evening meal and before family worship. They delighted in their different accents, expressions and songs; they learned from each other and found joy in the experience. Entering the kitchen one evening as he returned from the barn, Alasdair observed the three of them sitting around the stove engaged in story telling, the women clicking their knitting needles and Daniel drawing on his beloved pipe. With the devil upon him, he addressed them with the straightest of faces as he removed his coat. *"Gabh iolla! Nach iad na trì sgeilmeachan? Bu laibhir na cearcan!"* (Just look at it! Is it not the three prattlers? More noise than the cackling of hens!)

It was at that very moment that Kristy entered the room from the direction of the front parlour to find both Tina and Bernadette reprimanding Alasdair, in perfect unison, with a feisty *"Ud! Ud! Nach e a tha dona?"* (Tut! Tut! Is he not an evil one?) She watched as the two women suddenly leaned forward, joined hands and broke into broad laughter. Kristy simply stood there and smiled. Never before had she felt such warmth in the kitchen and it struck her as being nothing less than pure luxury on the bones.

Thankfully, the actual birth was relatively easy when it eventually came. The labour had gone on for the better part of two days and all three women wore the signs of absolute exhaustion. Tina and Bernadette never left Kristy's side, except for taking short turns to rest in the rocking chair in the far corner and to check on the hot water, clean towelling and anxious men who waited in the kitchen below. It was in the early morning hours that Kristy was finally delivered of a healthy and quite vocal girl. With fatigue upon her, she held the baby briefly, marvelling at her beauty and smiling up at the two women who now sat on the edge of the bed next to her. It was only then that she entrusted the child to their care and allowed herself to fall into the deepest of sleep. Alasdair and Daniel were woken and advised of the news by Tina. Moments later, she returned to the room to find Bernadette had cleaned the child and wrapped her in a small woollen blanket. It was then that Tina was summarily sent off to rejoin her husband and son; Bernadette would remain to watch over the two of them. As much as she too wished to stay with Kristy, Tina realized that this was a special time to be shared by a mother and daughter. She would respect it.

Bernadette languished in the chair with the newborn slumbering in her arms while Kristy slept soundly in the bed across, the very same bed whose love had produced the miracle of life that now rested on her breast. As the first light of morning slowly streamed into the room, she looked up at the plain wooden cross that rested on the wall high above her daughter's head. She dimmed the kerosene lamp and began to rock. *"Och, seadh. Cha dealaich iad uaithe gu bràth. Tha mi buidheach."* (Oh yes. They will never be parted from Him. I am satisfied.) The broad smile that crept across her face was confirmation enough.

In nomine Patris, et Filii, et Spiritus Sancti. (In the name of the Father, and of the Son, and of the Holy Spirit.) Amen.

ᨕ Chapter Eleven ᨕ

March 1906 – July 1907

Is fearr deireadh ni na a thoiseach: is fearr esan a tha foighidneach 'n a spiorad na esan a tha àrdanach 'n a spiorad.

Eclesiastes VII: 8

Better is the end of a thing than the beginning thereof: and the patient in spirit is better than the proud in spirit.

Ecclesiastes VII: 8

Senator's Corner it certainly was not. He was only on the other side of the island but, in actual fact, he may as well have been on the other side of the world. It was all the more strange since, as a youngster, he had often visited the fishing boats down at the public wharf and could see the North Shore way off in the distance to the north east. The Atlantic winds always blew the belching crimsoned smoke from the Sydney blast furnace inland, over the Bras d'Or Lake and the highlands, leaving him with an unobscured view up the coast. In those days, there had been a sense of security in being surrounded by all the shops and houses that ran down from Commercial Street towards both the pit and ocean, clinging to the coast like so many small children huddling around a warm stove for comfort on a cold winter's day. Now standing on the edge of the bluffs, he looked to the south-west, out over the seemingly endless breadth of water with the coastline serving as a thin frame against the massive canvas of sky. Still, he was never able to discern any particular features that could confirm that he was indeed looking back in the direction of his home in Glace Bay. Even now, there was probably another small boy standing on that very wharf staring north towards Cape Smoky. It seemed so ironic; in that boy's eyes, any persons standing on these bluffs would not exist. They would be totally consumed by the mass of blue and purple that, from a distance, was nothing more than a line on the horizon that trailed off into infinity.

Christopher Hickman had already been in *Loch Dubh* for seven months and, for the most part, the adjustment had been fairly painless and uneventful. The time had passed relatively quickly and he was forced to admit that he was truly enjoying his new role as master at the public school. Even with all the wisdom of his nineteen years, it was a new and enlightening experience for him to be in a position of authority that carried such status throughout the community. This was certainly one aspect of the job for which his academic training had not fully prepared him. Had he not possessed such a strong recall of his own formative years growing up in "the Bay", Christopher would have surely thought that he had somehow or other been elevated to full sainthood. The patron saint of travellers he certainly was not, nor of anything else for that matter. Initially, he was of the view that he might quip with the Reverend Fraser that it behoved the *Loch Dubh* apostolate to undertake a recruiting drive so as to identify an additional ten godly men. Even though he was coming to know the minister a bit better with each passing week, he still thought better of making any such evangelical pronouncements.

The oppressive silence of the manse, which had so troubled Jennie since the departure of her children, was mitigated by the presence of this young man "from away." In the context of availability of space in the homes around the loch, it was so logical that he be lodged with the Frasers. At least this was the argument used by Jennie when first discussing the subject with Duncan. Her tactful approach had been that it would be such a fairly effortless yet meaningful way for them to give something back to the entire community. It took some doing on Jennie's part to eventually convince her husband but, in the end, her appeal to the minister's sense of social conscience finally prevailed. Jennie had been careful never to make mention of the fact that the young man's presence would also benefit the Fraser household, by bringing a sense of life back within its walls. Nor did she ever mention that she was terribly lonely. *"Tha mi 'n am loman aonrachd. Tha mi 'g an ionndrainn gu dearbh."* (I am absolutely alone by myself. I am truly missing them.) After many years of marriage, she had learned that some things were best kept to herself.

There was no doubt that, initially at least, Christopher felt the bleakness of the land and the solitude of his new life in the country. However, his misgivings were soon dispelled, primarily by Jennie and his students who were eager to make him feel welcome and wanted. True enough, it was unfortunate that he did not have "the Gaelic." His family had originally come to Cape Breton from Newfoundland and Gaelic was never a part of their cultural upbringing at home, given that his father's people were English and his mother's Irish. As a consequence, the one noticeable problem that he had encountered in *Loch Dubh* was with some of the younger students who only had had limited exposure to the English at home, if any at all. His predecessor, Kristy Erskine, had taught in English as was the prescribed ruling from the Ministry of Education in Halifax. However, it had not taken Christopher long to determine in his subtle way that Kristy had indeed conducted some of her work in Gaelic. That would all have to change now of course and it was a cause of some genuine concern for him as to how it would impact on the general perception of the school master as well as on his actual effectiveness in the classroom.

It was not that he necessarily wanted to be a devout servant of provincial education officials on the mainland — quite the opposite, if the truth be known. They gave the impression of being overly stuffy and always guided by this, that or some other innocuous or outdated rule. It was simply that he did not speak the language and was too old to even make the effort. It certainly was not unusual for him to hear it spoken outside at recess and as the children made their way to and from school along the loch road. On numerous occasions, he had observed them from a distance as they slipped so quickly back into their native tongue. There was an ease, a comfort, a joy that was plainly obvious on their faces and in their actions. Christopher likened it to the feeling of absolute exhileration when finally ridding one's feet of a pair of tight-fitting new shoes. Learning English was a matter of progress and the head; speaking Gaelic was a matter of identity and the heart. He could and would appreciate the importance of the distinction between the two.

The front doors of the school were buffeted by the early-morning winds and created an incessant rattling that was tempered only by the chatter and laughter of the children, who were revelling in the warmth that embraced their bones as they busily removed boots and placed coats on the wooden pegs at the rear. Across the room, Christopher sat at the desk beneath the large blackboard and watched as they raced down the centre aisle to the pot-bellied stove. Here, they gathered together absorbing the heat as it finally cast off the last remnants of the March chill. He checked his pocket watch and noted that eight o'clock had already come and gone. It was of no real consequence; he would allow extra time for them to comfort and settle themselves.

As was the custom, the school day was begun with the singing of *God Save the King*. All the children dutifully stood at attention and gazed up at the portrait of Edward VII that occupied a position of prominence high on the central wall at the front of the room. Christopher faced the King from the side of his desk where, from time to time, he was also able to glance out of the corner of his eye at the younger students in the front row. It had often been difficult for him to stifle laughter as he watched some of them struggle with the words and sounds that forced their tongues and mouths into the queerest of shapes. It so reminded Christopher of his first session with them last September when he had discussed the news of the admission of two new provinces into the Dominion. The small ones had made a valiant attempt to pronounce Alberta. On the other hand, Saskatchewan became a complete disaster. Now, he glanced over and still saw remnants of that same look of puzzlement in their eyes and on their faces as they devoutly stood and paid homage to their sovereign, all the while attempting to mouth words that they obviously did not completely understand.

For some reason, Christopher's eye was drawn to something else that intrigued him even more — something quite odd that he had obviously not taken notice of before. It was quite puzzling and caused him to wonder if it were nothing more than an aberration. There, at the rear of the room where the older students were placed, stood young Kenneth Erskine with head held high, facing the front in absolute silence. With imperialistic harmony ringing throughout the room and blanketing everything in its path, it seemed to suddenly fall on one set of deafened ears. More out of curiosity than anything else, the school master was determined to seek clarification of, if not a complete answer to, this unexpected intrigue.

The request for Kenneth to remain behind at recess was made in passing, almost casually, so as not to draw undue attention. Christopher was careful to wait until the room had been vacated by the other children before addressing the young man who stood before his desk, under Edward's constant and vigilant gaze. The school master looked up and smiled, knowing he would have to choose his words carefully. It was only after several seconds of stark silence that they finally came forth tinged with an odd blend of curiosity and expectation. "Kenneth, I noticed earlier this morning that you were the only student who did not join in the singing of the anthem. May I ask you why this is? Is it that you do not know the words?"

It was all too apparent that Kenneth had been completely caught off guard. Christopher saw it in the boy's face and in the fact that he paused for a long while before even attempting a response. It was as though he was about to undertake an exam, knowing full well that every word would be graded as if it was being written in gigantic lettering on the blackboard for all the world to see. Yet, when it did come, his voice was as strong as it was mindful. A now more-confident look seemed to indicate that he had succeeded in finally collecting his thoughts. "I mean no disrespect to you, Mr. Hickman. But I cannot say with my mouth that which I do not believe in my heart. He is not my King and I will not be asking God to save him. My requests to the Almighty will be saved for better things. He is King of the English and I leave such singing to them."

It was now Christopher's turn to be caught off guard as he suddenly found himself both shocked and bemused at the same time. In what was done for both strategic and dramatic effect, he rose slowly from his chair, allowing himself time to gather his own thoughts in order to formulate an appropriate reply. He looked into the blank resilient face across from him. A reply was certainly required and Christopher felt compelled to choose his words with some considerable care. "I would suggest, Kenneth Erskine, that you give this matter some careful consideration. I cannot force you to sing if you choose not to. However, you might wish to ponder your decision and the reasons for it. You may go now."

As Kenneth donned his coat at the far end of the room before rejoining the others outside, Christopher watched the young man with great interest. Although he had lived in *Loch Dubh* only for some seven months, it was obvious that, in more ways than one, Kenneth or *Coinneach Bàn* was truly Daniel Erskine's grandson. He had heard the stories as well as the amusing tales of the old man and "his wee sheep." It was not as though Christopher agreed with him for indeed he did not. Yet he could not help but respect the strength of convictions of this fourteen-year-old child, be they ever so misguided and misplaced. He would learn. He was still young.

With curiosity abounding, it had not taken long for the other children to determine why it was that Kenneth had been asked to stay behind. During the noon break, the prodding questions had come fast and furiously from several quarters and, as was his manner, Kenneth was forthright in dispelling the taunts and insinuations that he was the school master's *sgoilear iomlan* (Perfect Pupil). Not only was he not Mr. Hickman's favourite, but he was also, in all probability, not held in the highest of royal esteem. But then, it was of no consequence to him.

Shortly after the sounding of the afternoon bell, Kenneth began to make his way home in the company of the other students. As he turned right onto the loch road, he suddenly became the unwitting recipient of an unceremonious alpine greeting from one Albert MacGregor who had enthroned himself precariously on a snow bank high above the others. "Well, well. Is it not Kenneth Erskine, the most famous loyalist in *Loch Dubh*!" The laughter cascaded down onto the road where everyone suddenly halted, awaiting the victim's response to such an audacious challenge. They all knew that it was bound to come, most probably sooner rather than later and in fairly strong language. Initially, the rejoinder took the form of a silent stare in the direction of the insolence. Now in the company of his peers, Kenneth would obviously have no choice but to once again choose his words carefully for the second time that day.

"*Bruidhinn Gàidhlig! Chan eil agad ach a bhi a'bruidhinn, agus rud eile dheth, chan eil mi nam rìoghaire. Moladh càch an rìgh; leanadh mo theanga ri mo chiobhal. Chan eil mi bonn 'n a eisimeil. Amadan!*" (Speak Gaelic! You have only to talk and moreover I am not a royalist. Let others praise the King; may my tongue stick to the roof of my mouth. I am not a whit obligated to him. You idiot!) And then, the silence returned as damning glares continued to shoot upwards in the direction of Margaret MacGregor's now somewhat deflated *Righ Beag* (little king). Kenneth was well pleased that he had said his piece and, more importantly, that he had set the record straight for the benefit of those gathered around him. Standing there at the foot of the snowy crag, he thought of his grandfather playing the pipe high on the bluffs those many years ago. Somehow he knew that Daniel would be proud of his grandson for having so publicly and effectively demonstrated the strength of his convictions. It was all over as quickly as it had begun; Kenneth turned and headed down the road in the direction of home with the others trailing behind. He promised himself that, after supper and evening worship, he would be even more diligent in practising his music.

Each piece was not unlike a person anxiously waiting to share his or her own story. Without doubt, they had distinct identities that spoke of their personal experiences and the messages they wished to convey. And yet it was not so much their individual stories or colourful appearances that set them apart one from the other. What was most striking and intriguing was the very act of coming together, in all their diversity, to create something much larger than themselves. One could not look upon them without realizing that here was a greater identity that evoked a sense of community and belonging.

The small piece of cloth had been cohersed into life ever so slowly and methodically with the stitching that was as intricate as it was colourful. Rachael held it in her hands gazing down on the unique pattern, remembering what thoughts had gone through her mind on those many occasions when she had sat by the kitchen stove, diligently bestowing a personality upon it. Of late, she often found her thoughts fixed on Morag in far-off Boston whom she had not seen for almost two full years. She knew only too well how difficult it was to explain the emptiness in a mother's heart when a child is taken away. In so many ways, one had been. Rachael could never bring herself to discuss the matter with Norman; it was his way to simply keep busy.

Morag's letters came, sure enough, on a regular basis and Rachael was glad for both the news and money that were contained in each one. For the first year at least, she and Jennie Fraser had been able to commiserate with each other. Now, praise God, Emily had returned home, even if it was to Baddeck. Rachael remembered a time not so long ago when she would have referred to the county seat as *Baddeck fhada*. (far-off/distant Baddeck) What she would give now to have her own daughter there. If only this small piece of cloth were her child; it seemed so odd that she should find comfort in holding it close.

"Seo poit-thì ùr. Cha bhi am pathadh oirnn ag obair. Ni i ola mhór do ar sgòrnain feadh cracaireachd." (Here is a fresh pot of tea. We shall not be thirsty as we work. It will be good ointment for our throats as we talk.) Isabelle's joviality was infectious as always and, for obvious reasons, Rachael had no wish to be maudlin or dampen the genial mood around the table. She returned the cloth to its place among the others almost as quickly as she recommitted thoughts of Morag to the back of her mind. She, Isabelle Grant and Sarah Urquhart had spent the better part of six months working on their respective quilted squares that were gathered up and assembled every few weeks. It was as if pieces of a puzzle were being brought together. Indeed, there was great interest in seeing not only the individual squares but also the larger tapestry that, collectively, they were in the process of producing. In making room on the table for the tray carrying Isabelle's tea pot, cups and plate of sweets, Rachael looked over at "Morag's square" now resting as one amongst many, waiting patiently to be chosen and grafted into place. She couldn't help but wonder if this quilt would eventually come to reflect their own lives here on these shores and in the shadow of these mountains. Would the completed puzzle tell them something that,

through their individual pieces, they did not already know or were not yet able to see? Rachael could not help herself; her mind was flooded with thoughts of a young girl who was so far away from her, far away from the puzzle that was *Loch Dubh*.

Through the dining-room window, Rachael could now see tiny bits of brown thatch that timidly poked from beneath the broad sea of white. The fields had such a mottled look about them, teetering between the cold of winter and the warmth of spring that could even now be felt on the April air. There was a sure smell of spring's advent; soon it would be lambing season.

"*Och ma tà. Bha an geamhradh an-iochdmhor ach cha robh e cho dona ris an uiridh. Tha cuimhn' agam air sneachda cho domhainn 's gun d' ràinig e mullach an taighe. 'Se "an dallchor mór" a ac' air. Aig ar n-aois chan eil feum againn air anaoibhneas mar seo.*" (Oh indeed. The winter was cruel right enough but not as bad as last year. I remember the deep snow as high as the roof of the house. They are after referring to it as "the big snow." At our age, we have no need of such trouble.) Rachael continued to look through the window and, in the reflection, watched as Isabelle spoke aloud to the cups while dutifully pouring the tea. Perhaps it was just the distortion of the glass but did she not look a bit more stooped and did not her hair seem to be a tad whiter than before? She allowed her gaze to encompass a broader reflection and the image now before her was of three women at the table, three women who had grown old. Perhaps it was a phantom or even the *bòcain* weaving their evil magic across her eyes. Or, perhaps it was true. At that moment, all Rachael could think of was *Floiridh Aosda* and the possibility that they were all becoming Floras. Now, with the exception of the sound of tea filling the cups, there was only quiet.

"*A Raonaid, blàthaichidh cupa teth do cholann gun teagamh sam bith, nas fheàrr na Tormad gu fìor.*" (Rachael, a hot cup will warm your body without doubt, truly better than Norman.) Sarah was always so full of mischief and had often been jokingly chastised for having "ten devils in her." It was obvious that today would be no different. There was a contrived expression of shock on Rachael's face as she waved her hand in mid air in Sarah's direction as if the movement said it more clearly than words ever could: "Tut. Tut." The reprimand was given and received in good humour. Indeed, all three women laughed aloud as they tucked into the strùpag before once again buckling down to the work that lay in front of them.

The quilting *céilidh* was as much a time to weave together the news or gossip of the community as it was to sew together a new piece of bedding. Indeed, there had been more than one off-colour comment made about the good uses that the quilt could have been put to if only the women had spent more time working like bees and less time clucking like hens. The last four months had seen three weddings involving the young ones of *Loch Dubh*. Duncan MacDonald, Jessie's boy, had taken the hand of young Mabel Taylor from down in the town last January. *Domhnall Òg* Erskine, "the old bachelor", had finally rid himself of the infamous nickname given him by Elizabeth, by marrying Sadie Grant in March. And the Reverend Rod MacDonald had just recently wed Margaret Buchanan down the shore in *Cobh a' Gheòidh*. By all accounts, the latter had been a grand affair, certainly one befitting a man of the cloth. It was Isabelle who, washing down a mouthful of sugar cookie, put the matrimonial affairs in their proper context. *"Chan eil sinn a'fas sean. Bha sinn 'n ar mnàthan-bainnse — cloinn a mhàin. Gu tric tha mi a'smaoinicheadh gum bu chòir dhomh a bhith air fuireachd car na b'fhaide anns an sgoil."* (Most assuredly, we are not getting old. We were young brides — mere children. I often wonder; I should have stayed in school longer.)

"An sgoil. Och ma tà! Ruaig thu na gillean a ghnàth. Gabh truas ris an sgoil. Cha robh e comasach thus a cheannsachadh." (School indeed! And you the one always chasing the boys. Pity the school. It was not capable of subduing you.) With a mocking shriek made at Isabelle's expense, Rachael provoked gales of laughter around the table as needles came to rest and the women once again found such simple joy in each other's company and, subtly, at each other's good-natured expense. During the long months of winter, their *céilidhs* had been a welcomed respite from the many chores around the house and farm that occupied so much of their time. In some respects, the get togethers were their winter gardens — places where they found comfort and peace, even with the torment of the ten devils that Sarah always brought along for company and entertainment. As the laughter subsided, Rachael once again picked up the squared cloth and thought of Morag, not as a piece of a puzzle but as a flower in a garden. Whether consciously or not, the women were creating a bouquet of the most beautiful and fragrant flowers that symbolized something much greater. Although she could not hold her daughter close, she could almost smell the fragrance of her hair, of her beauty. Soon enough the final lingering traces of winter would pass from view and other bouquets would be gathered up to be rejoiced in.

The women settled back to their work as needles and thread gracefully swooped up and down from their laps like gulls over *An Toiseach* and *An Deireadh*. For some reason, Isabelle thought of the pillow that had sat for so many years in dear Flora's room directly above them at the top of the stairs. She recalled the stitches that had so lovingly brought the two worn and faded pieces of tartan together in the shape of a heart. That pillow had gone with Flora to her eternal rest and, even with the passage of some seven years, she still felt the old woman's presence. It was like a scent that lingered in the air, embedded in the timbered body of the house. But what did it matter? Those days were long gone and was not the true legacy of Angus and Flora to be found in their children and grandchildren? Still, Flora lingered, there was no doubt. So few of the older people remained — only Archie, Daniel and Tina who were well advanced in years. Although she did not know her Bible as some of the others did, Isabelle brought to mind the words of the Psalmist David. *Agus a nis, nuair a bhios mi sean agus liath, a Dhé, na tréig mi....* (Now, also when I am old and grey-headed, Oh God, forsake me not....) She promised herself that she would make a special point of speaking with these three after service on Sunday and creating a bit of a fuss over them.

It was as the women were in the throes of finishing up their work that they first heard the sound being carried on the wind coming up from the loch. Young Kenneth was practising the pipe in the back field, which was itself as much a sign of spring as were the lambs on the hills. There had been a fair bit of talk about the incident last month at school involving Kenneth, Mr. Hickman and the singing of the anthem. Most people around the loch had thought the boy's actions rather foolish and many a conversation had invariably ended with quite similar words of admonishment: *"Is e seo ar dlighe; bi dileas do'n rìgh."* (It is our duty; be loyal to the King.) In their minds, it was an obligation and a privilege; it certainly was not an option. However, there had still been numerous chuckles and sighs of relief when the Governor General, Lord Grey, had chosen to not follow the same route as his predecessor when he had visited Cape Breton last July. Perhaps he had been forewarned about Clan Erskine and its penchant for cameo recitals on the bluffs. Regardless, it was all too obvious that *Coinneach Bàn* was cut from the same cloth as his grandfather and maybe, just maybe, the tune he now played was to celebrate the recent departure of the last British troops from the garrison at Halifax. There was no question that Daniel would be delighted to see the tail end of them as they finally sailed from *Alba Nuadh*. ("New Scotland" — Nova Scotia) Each would have a tail as white as a lamb — *an bàs geal*, whose clearance from the province could be viewed as the just and highly symbolic retaliation of history. But still, everyone knew well enough never to raise the issue with Daniel and now, in all likelihood, Kenneth. *O linn gu linn.* (from generation to generation)

The wild rose bushes, which shadowed the side of the house like a rank of ever diligent soldiers, seemed to intentionally droop towards the kitchen window as if reconnoitering the battlefield before overpowering it with their magnificent bouquet. It was late June and the blossoms had come somewhat early, as had spring itself. With memories of the harsh winter of 1905 still fresh in their minds, the people of *Loch Dubh* had welcomed the early demise of the dreaded snows that first powdered and then cloaked everything that dared stand beneath them. Resting at the open window, Jessie wiped her hands on the long white apron and took a deep breath of the fresh, wonderfully fragrant air. It was with the greatest relief that all recollections of winter's deadly grip had been banished from memory.

The three pans of bread baking in the oven were billowing forth like gilded clouds and dispersing their own savory aromas throughout the room. Jessie turned from the window and slowly returned to the pantry to continue her work. All the while, she was conscious of the two glorious fragrances that struggled for control of her senses. Mabel was still busily engaged in washing up the dishes from the noon meal with her back to Jessie . From a distance, Jessie watched her daughter-in-law and so admired the lovely sandy-coloured hair that trailed down the middle of her back. Duncan had done well in taking her as his bride and the five months of their marriage had already settled him considerably. Only a mother would be astute enough to note the slight changes in the son and only she could discern when the boy had finally become a man. For the first time in a very long while, Jessie thought of her own dear Malcolm and the pride he would obviously feel looking down upon their eldest child. Like his children, he had never been one with the words. On such matters, his lips were always silent; he spoke with his heart. It was the MacDonald way.

The presence of another woman in the house had not created any noticeable difficulties, at least none that had been contemplated by Jessie when Duncan first announced the happy news to his mother and grand-father last November. Poor Archie; he liked the girl right enough, there was no question of that. However, what troubled him was the fact that he was now increasingly forced to speak the English in his own home. Jessie knew that it had been even more troublesome for him than had the issue of Martha's engagement to *an Caimbeulach Dubh* (The Black Campbell) eleven years ago. At least he had the Gaelic . But that was now so long ago, even before Malcolm's accident.

Still, Archie had accepted Mabel as a valued member of the MacDonald household, realizing that she brought joy and laughter to his grandson. Jessie knew full well that, with the years upon him, Archie found increased strength and comfort in the belief that the true source of all wisdom was the fear of God. Of late, as more of the English fell upon his ears, his failing eyes turned more frequently to the Gaelic in the family Bible. She had no doubt that he had taken the words from the Book of Proverbs to heart: *A mhic, biodh eagal an Tighearn agus an righ ort: riu-san aig am bheil atharrachadh giùlain na biodh gnothuch agad.* (My son, fear thou the Lord and the King: and meddle not with them that are given to change.) At the same time, it had been many years since Archie had spoken so frequently and fondly of his dear Hannah and those early days of settlement in the thick dark forest. He did so now. So much had changed; so much was changing. There was a comfort in the past.

Jessie returned to the pantry where a large mound of dough, slumber-ing under a make- shift blanket of dish cloths, lay resting on the counter next to the baking board. With one quick movement, she swept back the covers and her hands tore at its edges as she methodically fashioned the rolls and laid them out on the flat blackened pan. She stood there for a moment looking down, admiring her work. Although she was never one prone to day-dreaming, Jessie envisaged a large sheet of doughy eggs and chuckled to herself in picturing a chicken brooding over them in utter frustration. *"Giùlain thu féin!"* (Behave yourself!) The words of admonishment had slipped out almost without her being conscious of what she was doing. Such nonsense for a woman of her age. She felt compelled to silently scold herself for such silliness and for dawdling when other things were demanding both her attention and time.

Fortunately, Mabel had already vacated the kitchen. She was still a young lover and often went off to visit Duncan at his work in the vegetable fields behind the barn; they would have more privacy there. As she crossed the room, Jessie was grateful that her comment had not been overheard and was relieved that the couple would have other things to discuss beside the dotage of the *cailleach*. She quietly moved from the kitchen and entered the front bedroom to wake Archie from his afternoon nap. As the door slowly creaked opened, she was taken by how absolutely peaceful he appeared. It would be a shame to disturb his rest but, from experience, she knew that he would be annoyed if he did not return to his "work," tending to the encroaching grasses around the garden and orchard with his trusty scythe.

Now, standing at the foot of the bed, Jessie remained there for several minutes simply looking into the open eyes. The scythe would remain still. For some reason, she did not cry and it troubled her as she sat on the edge of the bed next to him. Without thinking, she leaned forward, lovingly folded the arms across the chest and closed the eyes for the final time. She thought about his eyes and the fact that they had borne witness to so much life, so much change. Jessie rested there awhile with her chin resting on her hand, looking down at the serenity of Archie's face. Finally, she reached for the Bible on the side table and placed it under his hands. *"Sìth dha a' anam agus beannachd Dhé leat, Eàirdsidh MacDhòmhnuill."* (Peace to your soul and may the blessings of God attend you, Archibald MacDonald.) Wtih that, she left the room and, almost reverently, looked back one final time before closing the door behind her.

A genuine sense of shock and loss quickly swept across the community as the news of Archie's passing was carried from house to house. It was not long before Duncan Fraser arrived to minister to the needs of the family. His task was made all the more difficult owing to the fact that he felt the loss as deeply and personally as anyone. It was not only the death of a member of the congregation, an elder, or a clerk of session but it was also the death of a dear friend. Word had been sent to *An Abhainn Mheadhonach* and it was presumed that the Reverend Rod and Margaret's arrival would also be imminent.

There was not a single house around the loch that had not been touched by the death. Each one had special reminiscences that were soon brought to mind and willingly shared. This too was an essential and very conscious part of their grieving, as if the act of remembrance would somehow mitigate the immediate sense of loss. The Erskine home assumed a special importance as, once again, the honour of constructing the coffin fell to Daniel. Years before, he had carefully stored a number of broad white-pine boards in the loft of the wagon house. Although he would be the first to deny it, there had been tears in his eyes as he ran his hands over the grain and began the solemn task of providing Archie with his final earthly bed. It was not by accident that, as he worked, Daniel took stock of the fact that there would be sufficient lumber for one more such receptacle. He and Archie were of the same approximate height and size. The second one would also be built and placed for safe keeping in the loft until such time as it too was needed. There was no moroseness, no sadness for either Archie or himself as he went about his work. Indeed, the tears had dissipated and were replaced with a quiet contentment and sense of calm. As he slowly and methodically moulded the boards into a recogniz-able shape, Daniel's thoughts were of *An Toiseach* and *An Deireadh,* those craggy bits of land that had first greeted the early settlers as they searched for a new place where they could truly feel they belonged. The beginning and the end — the course had been run. Archie was finally home.

Over the next two days, the MacDonald home received a steady stream of visitors wishing to pay their final respects to Archie whose re-mains were waked in the front parlour. In addition to the neighbouring families around the loch, many residents of New Carlisle and others from up and down the length of the North Shore crossed the threshold of the black-creped door. More than a few heads were turned on the first night when Annabelle Calvey, the postmistress from down in the town, arrived not only to personally pay her respects in the front parlour but also to extend condolences at the *strùpag* served by the ladies in the kitchen. Few people were aware of the fact that, even in the midst of her own pain, she had noted Archie's presence and witnessed his genuine display of sorrow at her own George's committal. She would do no less.

Rod and Margaret arrived on the second day of waking and were greet-ed warmly in a rather measured way. There was a sincerely felt belief that his presence would do much to offer comfort to the family as well as to all those who mourned this beloved man. It was only later that night, with the departure of the final visitors, that Rod made it known to his parents and Jessie that he wished to conduct the final vigil before the funeral. He could see the lingering fatigue in the faces of his father and cousin Duncan from the previous night. Milking and a host of other chores still awaited them and they would need their rest. No, on what would be a terribly long day that lay ahead, he would conduct the vigil by himself. It was something he wished to do, not as a minister but as one man for another. He would do it for his *Seanair Naomh*. He would do it alone.

It was the following morning, the day of the funeral, that the immedi-ate family gathered in the front parlour to say their final private farewells. It was particularly difficult for Martha who entered the room supported by Peter and the children. The three oldest, Lachlan, Colin and Moira, proceeded forward ever so timidly with their parents, occasionally looking up into their tearful faces for assurance. But it was Ismay, holding her mother's hand, who walked with a serenity that transcended her four years. As they stood before the coffin, time fell still and yet, in some unfathomable way, every action and every word were blurred with speed.

Peter promised himself that, for all the remaining days of his life be it long or short, there would be two memories of that moment that would never leave him. He could not explain them and sensed that, for whatever reason, he should not ask. Martha took Ismay up in her arms as she looked down at Archie and placed a small tartan bow inside his jacket, laying it lovingly over his heart. It was then that she cried openly for the first time and it was Ismay who quickly offered words of comfort. *"A Mhamaidh, chan fhaod thu a bhith a' caoineadh. Tha seanair ann an gàradh Dhé. Tha e tèaruinte agus sona am measg a luchd-dàimh."* (Mamma, don't cry. Grandfather is in God's garden. He is safe and happy among relatives.) Through her tears, Martha looked into the small face and silently prayed that Ismay was truly able to see what she could not.

The funeral service at the Kirk, which Archie had helped build with both his hands and heart, held such beauty in its simplicity. Duncan Fraser had invited Rod to assist by reading the scripture, which he did from a black leather-bound Bible. Daniel led in the singing of Psalm XXIII with eyes fixed on the back wall of the sanctuary high above the heads of the mourners. And later Duncan Fraser prayed, while his voice continued to quaver with the tears of profound sorrow. As with all the times before, there was no doubt; the entire congregation knew that this would be the closing prayer.

Archie was laid to rest in the MacDonald plot in the cemetery, beside his beloved Hannah and just down from Malcolm and the other three children who had preceded him years ago. Rod stood to Duncan's right as the body was committed to the waiting grave. It was so different from another burial that came to his mind, another internment from somewhere across the years and over the seas. It was then that Rod looked up the hill in the direction of the cairn and beyond, into the dark green heart of *Beinn-mo-Mhulaid*. It seemed so terribly strange that here, at this open grave and in the looming shadows of the mountain, he should experience a heightened sense of the majesty of life.

Rod's eyes then returned to the faces of those whose heads remained bowed, as Archibald Drummond MacDonald was lowered and placed to his final rest. *Ged gheibheadh iad bàs, bidh iad beò.* (Though they were dead, yet shall they live.) With that, Rod slowly turned and walked from the grave, with Margaret and the other members of the family as they proceeded down the loch road for home. He held the Bible close.

Thankfully, quiet had finally been restored. For a time, it was as though he was surrounded by never-ending distractions that kept him from his work and thoughts. It was not that Duncan minded conversation for, indeed, so much of his life was spent in speaking with and listening to others. Yet there was a peace in the silence that enabled the mind to reflect on those things that were truly important. It was not unlike sailing into a safe haven away from the onslaught of a ravenous storm; in many respects life was a tempestuous sea that battered both the body and the soul. In quiet solitude, there was a serenity and a peace that passed all understanding. *Agus gabhaidh mo shluagh còmhnuidh ann am fàrdaich fhoistnich, agus ann an ionadaibh-còmhnuidh tèaruinte, agus ann an àitibh-tàimh suaimhneach.* (And my people shall dwell in a peaceable habitation, and in sure dwellings, and in quiet resting places.) The manse had once again reverted to a quiet resting place, much to Duncan's relief — and Jennie's chagrin.

As was so often his habit, Duncan Fraser sat in the rocking chair on the veranda. Here, the shade provided a cool refreshing respite from the mid-day sun that danced over the lengthy surface of the loch, leaving a thousand twinkling stars in its wake. Except for the occasional creaking of the floor boards beneath him, he was enfolded and enraptured by absolute stillness. Christopher Hickman had mercifully returned to Glace Bay for the summer months at the close of the school year. How he and Jennie would discuss everything and anything under creation! Even though he was not half as well read as he thought himself to be, it never once prevented the school master from offering an opinion and, from time to time, a lengthy dissertation. Indeed, it often seemed as though he had more opinions than the Psalmist had hairs on his head. And Jennie was only encouraging him all the more with her incessant prodding questioning. As he continued to rock, Duncan was content in the knowledge that the timing was most fortuitous given that there would still be another week before Emily's anticipated return from Baddeck. Here in the stillness of the veranda, he would relish and give thanks for the peace that, at least for the moment, had been restored to him. He had found a quiet resting place.

The sudden wild squawking caused Duncan to turn his head in time to discern the sleek movement of the blackened hunter as it prowled through the tall grass along the fringes of the orchard. It was apparent that *Rionnag* had veered far too close to the apple trees that cradled several nests of birds that were nurturing their young high above. He allowed his gaze to wistfully climb the graceful slopes of the mountains, much as a shepherd goes off in search of his sheep. His eyes passed over the cemetery and the white silhouette of the majestic Kirk as it proclaimed its vigilance against the rich green hues of *Beinn-mo-Mhulaid*. He pondered the appropriateness of the mountain's name as his eyes moved on, finally coming to rest on the small community hall. It still pained him to witness his congregants passing through its doors to attend the all-too-numerous milling frolics and *céilidhs* that were held within its walls. It was not so much the laughter, music and dancing that so troubled him, although they were certainly cause enough for concern. No, it was the fact that the evil drink was invariably present and the cause of raucous and, from time to time, savage fighting. Had he not himself borne witness to the scrapes, scratches and odd blackened eye that appeared on sheepish faces in the pews on the Sabbath? *"A Thighearna, fhuair mi teinn agus bròn."* (Oh Lord, I found distress and sorrow.) He continued to rock.

Duncan's eyes moved on, sweeping past the now-silent school house as they wound their way along the road towards the *muileann dubh* (black mill), passing over the Campbell, Erskine and Urquhart homes en route. With some difficulty, he could distinguish the form of a woman carrying a bundle in her arms down by the water's edge. It was undoubtedly Kristy, with the wee Grace, out to take the fresh invigorating air that streamed over the surface of the loch. He had baptised the child only last month and been taken with the name, given that it was not terribly common in highland usage. In the customary and understated manner for which she had become known, Kristy had only ventured that, beyond the glorious birth of her first child, there was much for which to be grateful and the name seemed so appropriate. For Duncan, her comment had evoked memories of his meetings with the young woman several years ago as she prepared for admission into membership of the Kirk and marriage to Alasdair. He had taken special interest in her personal growth in faith and it pleased him beyond all measure.

Duncan's attention was abruptly broken by the directness of the implied question that was now being put to him, almost as if it were a challenge. Having escaped the demoniac heat of the afternoon sun for the invigorating coolness of the shaded veranda, *Rionnag* was puzzled by the fact that Duncan's eyes were transfixed as if he were about to pounce on some unsuspecting prey. The fact that he did nothing more than smile down at her made Rionnag realize that even he did not have the common courtesy to respond to her genuine expression of concern. She would leave him in peace or wherever it was he might now find himself. Given such insolent behaviour, she wondered why it was she had even bothered.

As if continuing down the pathway of some obscured pilgrimage, Duncan's eyes began to travel down the north side of the loch, passing each household in its turn — MacGregor, Ferguson, Erskine, Grant, MacDonald and MacDonald. There was a genuine sense of gathering up the sheep from the hillsides, gathering them up for safekeeping in the fold and in the faith. The pastoral analogy had always had a calming effect but now Duncan was forced to admit he could not escape one realization; he still mourned the loss of one taken so suddenly from his flock. He still mourned Archie. The death had devastated him like no other. Not even the passing of Archie's own son Malcolm, who had passed at such a young age, had evoked such a response. He would never say as much but he knew that, in so many ways, Archie had been like a father to him.

The rocking chair fell silent. Duncan could not move; he had unwittingly brought himself back to this. As much as he had deliberately buried it again and again, it rose from the recesses of the grave to haunt him. Over the years, it had always been the memory of his mother's voice that dispelled his anxieties and cleared his mind. Yet something now challenged him like never before and he was forced to accept the fact that the ultimate battle, which he had avoided for so long, now lay directly before him. Finally, he would have to confront his tormentors, alone. Archie was no longer nearby.

In the stillness of his mind, three scenes came racing forward as if they were acts in some nefarious play that had waited a lifetime to string themselves together. They had their own story to tell. Scene one: he was back in the small rudely made bed in the croft on the slopes of *Ben Gulicanthe*. The picture was of a mother attempting to lull her bairn into sleep as the flickering candle light illuminated the tiny face before her. *"A Mhamaidh, cuin a tha ar n-athair a' tighinn dhachaidh?"* (Mamma, when will father be coming home?) The singing ceased as she looked into his eyes and found her own slowly filling with tears. He wanted to reach out to comfort her but did not. He was frightened by the tears, by the uncertainty of their message. At that moment, he would have no way of knowing that, within the year, fear would once again consume him. This time, it was not the tears. There were none as he experienced the devastating loss of his mother. She was taken from him quickly as the ravenous epidemic swept through the glens and up the mountain sides, indiscriminately snatching life to satisfy its evil voracious appetite. Even at her graveside, he did not cry. He was still frightened by tears but, strangely, could not explain why.

The second scene was of a home where the young boy had been taken and was to live for several years. The Reverend and Mrs. Carmichael willingly accepted him as one of their own. They had known his mother well and often, between themselves, spoke of the terrible hardships of her life on the desolate croft. It was on one such occasion, late into the evening, that the young boy had quietly slipped downstairs and overheard them in the kitchen. There was a reference to *am Frisealach Peacach* (the Sinful Fraser) followed by the most savage of words that slashed at his ears and his heart: *"Dh' fhàg e iad."* (He abandoned them.) He turned in fearful silence and, still, he did not cry. He returned to his bed where memories of a lullaby on the slopes of *Ben Gulicanthe* blanketed him as he desperately sought sleep. His thoughts were of the one person in his life who had been a constant presence, who had ever truly loved him. He thought of his mother.

The third and final scene was of the very same boy escaping to the crags high above the Carmichael house where the air was fresh, cool and hushed. It was only in the distance, far removed from the multitude of clamouring voices that seemingly surrounded him at home, that he could find peace. It was only here, in the thundering quiet, that he could hear the unmistakable sounds of his mother's beautiful voice on the soft breeze. The stillness brought her close to him, so close that he could actually feel her presence. He also felt her reassurances that he was deserving of the love that he now so desperately craved. In some ways, she continued to rock him.

The boy rose from his grassy seat atop the crags as, with the movement, the chair slowly rocked itself into silence on the veranda. Duncan walked towards the screen door with its gingerbread scrolling and grasped the handle as if to enter. He turned and, almost timidly, lifted his eyes in order to look down upon the cemetery where Archie slept. "*M'athair, beannachd leat.*" (Farewell my Father.) Duncan wept.

O short is the time until the day fades, when night falls, and I ask
for rest.

> Angus MacLellan
> *The Happy Island* (song)

O, 's gearr an ùine gu'n teirig là, thig an oidhche 's gun iarr mi tàmh.
> Angus MacLellan
> *An Innis Àigh* (òran)

It was not like her to dote. There was never any doubt that she was a
most attentive mother and always diligent in nurturing her children with
the support and love they required. Still, she had a strong desire to instill
in each of them a sense of independence, an ability to think and fend for
themselves, be it making hay in the back fields, plodding through blinding
snows on the loch road or exploring the fringes of the uncharted woods.
Herself a child of *Loch Dubh*, she knew only too well the importance of
engendering a sense of rugged individualism. This was not to denigrate the
significance of community; it was to recognize and appreciate the innate
character of the highland people.

Martha sat at the kitchen table finishing a cup of tea. Through the
screen door, she could hear the squealing of the children as they played
in the back, enjoying the last few days of freedom before the school bell
would sound once again. Over the last several weeks, she had been reluctant to let them out of her sight and she found it hard to explain. Certainly
the children had not minded the additional attention, except of course for
the time she had caught them behind the barn in the throes of shaving
off the cat's whiskers with a butcher knife. She could still see the relief
on the face of the *piseag chloimheach* (mangey puss) as it scurried for cover
under the stone foundation. The other faces had quite another story to
tell, albeit a feigned attempt at a logical explanation. Martha realized that
she had arrived just in the nick of time to avert a major feline catastrophe.
Later that night, she and Peter convulsed in laughter as they lay in bed,
imagining the righteous indignation of the clean-shaven cat and the utter humiliation resulting from the ridicule that would surely have been
heaped upon it by its barnyard companions.

During the two months since the death, Martha had visited her father's grave numerous times. Often, it was late in the evening when the

children had already been settled in their beds. She wanted to be alone, perhaps to speak with him and say those things that she always meant to but never quite found sufficient time or just the right occasion. As she sat by her father and mother, surrounded by MacKinnons, Fergusons, Grants, MacAulays, Urquharts and others, she came to the conclusion that perhaps her reluctance to speak, to be demonstrative in expressing her love, was also part of the highland character. She looked down the length of the loch at her home set back from the road with its rigid squared frame placed against the fluid curvaceous images of the mountains. The house was more than her home; it was a box of jewels containing those things that she valued more than anything else. But why now, sitting here, did she feel so horribly alone? Martha stood and dusted the soil from her skirt. As she began to depart, she looked down at the two graves. One was blanketed in a deep green while the other was even now being purposefully woven with grassy threads as its reddish-brown cover slowly passed from view. *"Tha mi am dhilleachdan."* (I am an orphan.) In the fading light of day and with some considerable reluctance, she left them and slowly walked down the road that now seemed so incredibly tiring and terribly long.

It was later that same week that Peter had gathered up the brood and headed down to the town in search of school supplies. Lachlan, Colin and Moira were always so excited by the prospect of picking out their new pencils and pens, ink and copybooks. They delighted in choosing different colours so as to ensure the safeguarding of ownership later on. Ismay loved the feel of the salted breeze on her face, the sound of the gulls over the wharf and the smell of spicy fragrance in the general store. In so many ways, Ismay was already in school.

Peter and Martha had often discussed how their youngest child would eventually be educated. The local school and teacher were certainly not appropriately equipped or capable of dealing with her particular needs. They had heard of the Halifax School for the Blind and an initial letter of inquiry had recently been forwarded to county officials in Baddeck. The written response was received on impressive-looking letterhead with news that was so matter of fact as to be painfully blunt. The education of their blind child at the Halifax institution would be at no personal cost to the parents as was the case with all public education in the province. However, it would obviously necessitate an extended separation of the child from the family. On more than one evening, Martha had read the letter, and particularly this phrase, over and over again. "An extended separation of the child from the family." Even the words had a coldness to them that chilled her. From the outset, it was all too clear that the issue was never money. It was the pain that would come with the severing of family, if that were ever to be contemplated or permitted. Ismay had just marked her fourth birthday. Mercifully, they would have a year to ponder the implications of their ultimate decision.

It was something that Peter had given a great deal of thought to but, quite intentionally, had not shared with Martha. It had been his idea and his alone from the very beginning. He was painfully aware of the fact that the letter from county officials had been tucked into a corner of the pantry for safekeeping but, more often than not, rested in his wife's hands and before her eyes. On several occasions, some known to her and still others not, he had chanced upon Martha as she simply stared at the words on the page. There was so little he could do to relieve the anguish that troubled her, so much was beyond his or their control. It was for this reason that he had spoken in confidence to Martha's sister-in-law Ida who agreed to meet him down in the town at the appointed hour.

With a kaleidoscopic array of school supplies spread out on the counter, Peter settled the bill with Allan Dunn who returned from the till with a few coins of change as well as four small sticks of peppermint. The shopkeeper knew that the gesture would be appreciated, especially by the young ones who always stood in awe with their faces practically glued to the large glass jars of candied treasures positioned on the counter. It was several moments later that Ida and John's horse and wagon rounded the final turn in the road and proceeded down to the store. There, they found Peter surrounded by the children as they sat on the front steps, looking over towards the fishing boats and eagerly devouring their prized gifts. Ida would watch over Lachlan, Colin and Moira as he and Ismay went off to undertake a personal matter. In so doing, Peter assured her that he would return within the hour and, as he lifted Ismay into the wagon, put the other three children on notice that they were to mind their aunt. With a goodly portion of peppermint remaining in their now sticky hands, it was most likely that the town cats would be able to continue their meanderings wherever they wished in relative safety, free from any barbarous attacks from Clan Campbell.

Martha was finally able to breathe a sign of relief as, several hours later, the horse and wagon made its way up the loch road from the direction of the bluffs. They had been gone for a terribly long time, certainly longer than she had anticipated. Like all mothers, she was fully aware that the combination of childish curiosity and deep waters along the wharf was a cause for genuine concern. Subconsciously, she counted heads as the horse and wagon wound its way up the length of the laneway. All four children seemed content enough and she would take time to sit with them and be royally entertained by their animated accounts. There was never any shortage; going to town was always such an adventure.

From her vantage point on the back step, she watched as Peter gently lifted the four children down from the wagon. Lachlan, Colin and Moira immediately ran to her, proudly displaying their colourful supplies and recounting the story of Mr. Dunn's special gift. With exuberance abounding, Moira inadvertently made reference to *an t-ioghnadh aig boban*. (Pappa's surprise) No sooner had the words slipped from her lips than she was summarily slapped on the shoulder by Colin with the admonition: *"Dùin do chab, òinnseach! Seo an t-ìoghnadh aig Ismay.*" (Shut your mouth, idiot! This is Ismay's surprise.) Martha's curiosity had been aroused by the jousting that continued to play itself out before her. It was only further heightened as she watched Peter cross the yard towards the house, leading Ismay by the hand and carrying a small crate in the crook of his arm.

Her name was *Taghta* (Choice/Chosen); Ismay had decided on it because the pup had chosen her master as much as Ismay had her. At first it seemed like an unusual name for the small ball of black and white fluff that one day would grow into a Border Collie. As they drove into the MacKinnon farm just up the shore road from New Carlisle, Peter had told himself that it was to be Ismay who would make the decision from among the five pups in the litter. He could not begin to imagine how she would do so but that was for her to determine. He knew her well enough to know that she could, that she indeed would.

Once inside the barn, Peter and Douglas MacKinnon watched carefully as Ismay crouched down using the pups' yapping as her guide. She then proceeded to pick each one up in turn and brought it close to her face. She undertook this methodical process three times before finally making her final choice known. It was the second one. Only then did her father reach down, pick up the pup and place it in her arms. "*A bhobain, chan e seo .*" (Pappa, this is not the one.) Peter and Douglas looked at each other in amazement and soon enough realized that the highly animated pups had indeed reshuffled themselves as they frolicked about on the bed of soft hay. Peter placed another pup in her arms, hoping against hope that he would not embarrass himself further by repeating his error. As Ismay caressed the tiny thing, it began to lick her face with wild abandon. And amidst the resulting giggles, she was still able to reassure her father. "*Seo am fear 'taghta'.*" (This is the "chosen one.") Even though he could not fathom how it was that she had known which one was which, Peter did not feel it appropriate to ask her. This was certainly not the first time that, in Ismay's presence, he felt that some things were best left to themselves. *Taghta* would be a fine name indeed.

Later that night as they prepared for bed, Peter began to explain to Martha why it was that they were in need of a dog. It would be of great assistance in the daily herding of the cattle and sheep, especially around lambing time. The more he expounded the many "obvious" benefits for the operation of the farm, the more Martha smiled at him dubiously with ever-increasing amusement. Finally, she reached over and placed a finger across his lips as if extinguishing the flaming wick of a candle. "*A Pheadair Caimbeul, tha thu breugach agus tha gaol agam ort.*" (Peter Campbell, you are a liar and I love you.) There was a shared understanding and appreciation that Ismay and *Taghta* would grow together and hopefully learn from each other. Clearly, it was not an attempt to resolve the issue of their daughter's future education, something that still greatly troubled them both. The intent was simply to provide Ismay with another friend, a friend who would be with her for all seasons, even in the depths of winter when the garden and its flowers had long passed away. It would be a life for which she would be responsible, a life that would undoubtedly bring additional meaning to her own veiled existence.

Martha had every confidence that her daughter, regardless of all else, would develop the traits of rugged individualism that she knew to be in the blood of her people. She thought of Archie and how he and Ismay had come to share a special appreciation of friends. Ismay and *Taghta* would grow together and perhaps, in some strange way, they had indeed chosen each other. As she rested her head on the pillow, Martha thought aloud: *"Bithidh Eàirdsidh MacDhomhnuill làn uaill gu dearbh."* (Most assuredly, Archie MacDonald would be proud.) She knew that she would sleep contented.

⧟⧟⧟

"A'mhuileann bhàn." (the white mill) The words bounced off the pane of glass as Sadie stood there looking into the near distance. The reverberating sound startled her somewhat given that she had not even been conscious of the fact that she was speaking aloud. Her surprise soon turned to amusement with the realization that white was not a word normally used to describe the grist mill tucked into the eastern corner of the loch. Indeed, black had always seemed the most appropriate term for the darkened tones of the stone that deepened with each passing year. For as long as she could remember, it had simply sat there like a gigantic crow diligently waiting to pounce upon some poor unsuspecting victim.

How odd it seemed that the brooding somber crow had somehow, as if by magic, transformed itself into a graceful spirited gull. Yet she knew it was not completely unheard of for the first frost to make a reconnaissance visit by the middle of October — a portent of things still to come. It had spun a thin layer of crystal enchantment on the mill's rocky walls that only served to mask its own demonic face. As much as she hated to see its precocious return, Sadie knew that it was a useful reminder that the advent of winter would soon be upon them. The pungent odour that now engulfed *Loch Dubh*, emanating from many a vinegared pot with its treasure of chow-chow and other pickled preserves, was every bit as much a sign of the change of seasons as was the frost. For many, these acrid vapours were also symbolic of their state of mind. As was too often the case, the winters could be as long as they were harsh.

Sadie continued to look at the bleak stoic walls of the mill and found her mind flooded with memories of her grandmother. Had not these same walls been altered as in the twinkling of an eye from black to white, much like the hair on dear Flora's head? As children, she and Iain had often likened *Floiridh Aosda* to the black mill. One seemed as dour and eternal as the other — both simply sat there like unwavering sentries guarding, for whatever reason, the waters and mountains. And how she and Iain would trick little John into seeking out the *cailleach*, knowing full well that he would receive a blast that would surely reverberate up and down the length of the North Shore. *Sgread i ann de thoirm' na dhùisgeadh na bha ann an Ingonis.* (She yelled with enough noise to wake those in Ingonish.) The thought made Sadie chuckle to herself as she imagined the look of absolute horror that must have enveloped poor John's innocent and unsuspecting face. She hoped that he had long forgiven them for their devious mischief and, with that, finally turned from the window to return to her work in the kitchen.

With the exception of the wood crackling in the stove in the far corner of the room, the kitchen was strangely silent. Both Hector and Donald had gone off to the barn after the morning meal to tend to the animals, leaving her alone in the still vacuous house. She had no way of knowing just how much it would bother her. Sarah had been gone only for the better part of a week and, already, her absence was so noticeably felt. Sadie was fully appreciative of the fact that her mother-in-law wanted to be with Elizabeth for the birth of her daughter's first child. Still, Boularderie seemed such a terribly long distance away. She hoped that Sarah would return soon. Her presence would take another type of chill off the house, a chill settling on her very bones that was not unlike the frost that now encrusted the mill's craggy face.

"Na creagan, na creagan. Carson a chaidh mi an sin? A Thighearna, maith mise. Maith mise." (The rocks, the rocks. Why did I go there? Oh Lord, forgive me. Forgive me.) Sadie now found herself standing before the front window of the kitchen, overlooking the fields that sloped gently down to the loch. On the far side of the water, she could see the two MacDonald houses as well as that of her own parents, further along to the left. She was glad that the Kirk was at the far end of the loch, out of view from where she stood. Its very image was unsettling to her; she felt so unclean, so undeserving. She wrapped her arms around herself as if the action would somehow reassure her by bestowing a sense of value and worth. Sadie imagined the arms to be those of her mother, whose warm embrace had always been so consoling, so comforting, so understanding. She was suddenly shocked into the realization that they were not her mother's. They could not be; these arms were eerily cold.

It was only a matter of seven months since she and Donald had been united as husband and wife. She would be the first to recognize that the two of them had been eager for marriage and that they already knew each other extremely well. After all, had they not both been born here and raised together along these shores? With the benefit of the passing years, Sadie also knew that *Loch Dubh* was not the type of place where secrets could be kept for long, especially with the chatter from the incessant wagging tongues that reverberated like a fart in a church pew. How then was it that she had been able to keep her secret for such a long time? How much longer could she keep it buried inside her? How much longer could she go on living with this painful chill on her bones?

The announcement last December of the forthcoming marriage of the Reverend Rod MacDonald to Margaret Buchanan had been greeted with great excitement and happiness throughout the community. Although the bride-to-be was not known to them, the residents were more than confident that Rod would have chosen wisely. It was obvious that no one, especially those attached to the wagging tongues, had taken note of the fact that the joyous news had not been unanimously welcomed. Sadie had long lived with the hope that her feelings for the MacDonald boy would slowly become evident to him and that, somehow, her dreams would be fulfilled. With the December announcement, she was finally forced to accept the reality of her situation. All these years, she had been so childish and terribly foolish. And yet, in the midst of her sadness, she was thankful for one small blessing. It seemed as though her secret would be hers and hers alone.

Donald's attention, while flattering and mildly reassuring, could not begin to fill the void she felt rested within her. And yet, their marriage had taken place so quickly. Looking back, it was as if she had been carried along by a fast-moving stream with no sense of control, no say in the matter. She was watching her own life unfold before her from a far distance, encased in mist. Still, was this truly her life? Was she not merely doing what was expected of her? Everyone was so terribly pleased and happy for her. He was a good man with much promise. He would be a dutiful provider and a loving husband. She would be blessed with much happiness and, God willing, many children. On one point, everyone assured her over and over and over again. In marriage with Donald, she would be happy and quite contented.

"*Gu sona sòlach!*" (Happy and quite contented!) Sadie drove the knife through the bun of bread on the counter before her as she prepared a platter of sliced meat and reheated baked beans for the noon meal. The men would be in soon enough accompanied, as was their predictable habit, by appetites to rival that of Giant MacAskill. She had better put the tea pot on.

"*Ciod e am prannadh a th'ort, nic-chridhe? Agus, cò is annsa leat?*" (What are you muttering about my dear lassie? And, who do you love above all others?) She had not heard the door open behind her. Donald had crept up behind her and, even now, had his arms wrapped firmly around her waist. She could smell the barn as he first nuzzled and then gently kissed her neck.

"*Och Dhomhnaill, chlisg thu mi! Thà thu cho làn tèachd. Giùlain thu féin; tha d'athair an seo.*" (Oh Donald, you startled me! You are so full of romancing. Behave yourself; your father is here.) From the far corner, Hector smiled at his son and daughter-in-law. He was not so old that he could not remember the early days of his own marriage to Sarah and their spontaneous romantic interludes, some of which had actually taken place in this very kitchen. His son had the distinct advantage of having married a Grant. In contrast, his own wife had the MacGregor blood in her veins and, although he would never admit it to her or anyone else, he enjoyed Sarah's feistiness. Rob Roy would never be dead as long as she lived and breathed!

During the meal, conversation turned to the events that, in all probability, were unfolding in the MacLeod house on Boularderie. There was a tremendous sense of anticipation around the table. This would be Hector and Sarah's first grandchild who, from Hector's point of view, would be all the more special given that it would be a gift to them from their own *gràdhan* (Little Darling), a name he always used for his daughter. Still, given the circumstance, this particular sentiment would be best kept to himself. Before he and Donald rose to return to their work, Hector eased his own mind by raising his tea cup as if it were a goblet filled with a dram of the finest whisky. *"Leigibh dhomh deoch-slàinte 'òl d' ar cloinn agus do na h-oghaichean."* (Allow me, a toast to our children and grandchildren.) With all three cups raised, Hector looked into the eyes of the young woman who sat across from him. *"A Mhòrag, is ionann sin is mar a thachras dhuit mo chaileag."* (Sadie, just so shall it happen to you my girl.)

"'Se, a'ghaolaich." (Yes, my darling.) Sadie could see the gleam in Donald's eyes. She smiled at him, lowered her own eyes and slowly sipped the tea.

Alone once again with her work, Sadie gathered up the dishes and crossed the kitchen towards the side pantry. As she passed through the narrow doorway, she felt the chill return to her bones. It was as if she had unwittingly entered a grave. The Urquhart talk of life still rang in her ears as she quickly escaped the frigid tomb for the more-welcoming warmth of the stove. In looking about the room, she realized that it was not so much the cold of the grave as it was its silence that now enshrouded her. The quiet was so terribly frightening and she was desperate to fill the vacuum with anything. Please God, the stillness. Please, make it stop!

"Tha mi anns an tigh chaol gun chàil. Is trom an t-eallach am peacadh." (I am in the narrow house / lifeless. Sin is a heavy burden.) As the words spilled out and flooded over the floor of the hushed room, Sadie found herself once more standing before the front window looking out over the fields. She had always known that Donald desperately wanted a child; was it not reconfirmed even today? Why then had she gone to the rock pile that summer evening when every fibre of her being told her that she was with child? What drew her there to struggle in lifting the large rocks? Why had she purposely killed the life that was even then living and growing inside her? Why, oh dear God, why?

Words were no longer needed. The silence was awash with her sobbing as she stood there with her head bowed. *"A Thighearna, seo buileach nàire. A'bhean choite."* (Oh Lord, this is most shameful. The cruel woman.) With these plaintive words spoken aloud, Sadie ever-so-slowly turned from the window that continued to frame the rock pile, the image resembling a tragic painting of dashed expectations now presented in exaggerated, almost monumental, proportions. She dried her eyes with the hem of the heavily soiled apron and moved on. The dirty dishes waited for her in the pantry.

Seldom had the house ever been more festive in appearance and atmosphere. The spruce boughs and evergreen vines that earlier had been gathered up in the woods were now hung over every doorway. They beckoned you from room to room, like emerald stars guiding footsteps on an epic journey in search of a manger. It was in the front parlour that the main star came to rest with its sparkling light that had once been confined to the small, metallically papered packages of tea. There it sat crowning the large fir tree decorated with its mantle of acorns, coloured buttons and silvered spools. It seemed somewhat odd that, of all rooms, the parlour should be the focus of such festivities. For so long, it had abided only the most solemn and ponderous of matters. At least for now, all that had changed and the transubstantiation from gloom to cheer was greeted with a tremendous sense of relief.

Christmas in the manse was always a special time for Jennie given that it was truly the one and only occasion throughout the year when she felt totally empowered to act on her emotions with her entire family. Over the years, she had received more than one raised eyebrow from Duncan as he sat by the kitchen stove reading while, all around him, Jennie and the children created a whirlwind of movement and laughter. Sandy, Matthew and Emily were only small and could not yet read their father's face, to say nothing of his mind, the way she could. But then, it did not really matter to her. What mattered, what was important was that she bring the family together in a spirit of joyous revelry. It was important for the children; it was Christmas.

Jennie slowly descended the stairs carrying a large bundle of linen in her arms that billowed up before her like a mischievous cloud intent on keeping her pathway hidden from view. Earlier in the day, there had been pangs of sadness in seeing Sandy and Matthew leave for Sydney and now it bothered her that the stripping of the beds gave the appearance of being a conscious act of cleansing the house of every trace of their presence. Clearly, nothing could be farther from the truth but, still, the room must be prepared before Christopher's return from Glace Bay. No, she would not be sad, at all at all. It had been a glorious time having all three children home and there were still several days remaining to enjoy Emily's company before her own imminent departure for Baddeck and her studies.

As she crossed the dining-room towards the doorway leading to the kitchen, she could hear Duncan and Emily speaking at the table in the far room. It was not so much the subject of their discussion that brought her to a standstill as it was the fact that Duncan was taking the time to engage his daughter in conversation as, indeed, he had done with his two sons while they had been home. Jennie could not fully fathom why it was that he now spent more time in the kitchen speaking with his children than in the parlour reading his Bible, as had always been his tendency. Seemingly, there was no explanation for the change even though there obviously had been one. *Is mór an t-atharrachadh a thàinig air. Rùintean dìomhair rìoghachd nèimh!* (There is great change on him. The mysteries of the Kingdom!) Even with her ponderous attempts to understand the reason for change, she could not find one. But then, Jennie was more than content to simply accept it as a blessed gift.

She sat for a moment at the dining-room table convincing herself that her bones were in need of a brief rest. In actual fact, she had no desire to enter the kitchen, to disturb the conversation, to undo something that might drive Duncan back into the sacrosanct lure of the parlour. She remainded motionless as the cloud slowly slipped from her lap onto the floor like the mist creeping down the slopes of *Beinn-mo-Mhulaid*. It was so apparent that he was enjoying this time with his daughter who had now grown into such a beautiful young woman. While Jennie might think it a shame that Duncan had not passed more time with the three children when they were younger, she was not about to tempt fate; not now.

Jennie reached for the Christmas card that sat on a crochet doily in the centre of the table. The festive scene on its cover was of a man in a long black coat and sporting a top hat lighting a street lamp with a long-handled pole as passers-by gazed into a shop window. Her hands were once again drawn to the small evergreen wreath that hung on the lamp pole. The velvety texture of the card was so incredibly soft to the touch, so much softer than the washboard that she would soon be stroking in quite a different manner. The feel was so sensual to her fingers and she smiled knowing that Effie would have chosen this card especially with her in mind. The enclosed letter was so detailed and full of accounts of little Murdina Jennie who was now on the verge of marking her third birthday. The photo of her had been taken on an autumn outing to the farmers' market in the south end of the city. It was one of Effie's favourites of her daughter who was pictured standing in front of a vegetable stall holding a large bouquet of the most wondrously shaped flowers. Jennie recalled how Emily had poured over the letter and photo for several minutes. There had been a bit of a tear in her eyes and Jennie could not help but think that her daughter still missed some things about her time with Effie and Liam. But still in all, this was where she belonged, here in Cape Breton with her family. She would be fine enough.

It was several hours later that Jennie found herself admitting that she had seldom before seen such a beautiful present in her entire life. As she lifted the china teapot from the gift-wrapped box on the table, her broad smile reassured Christopher that it had been well chosen indeed. He had wanted to return to *Loch Dubh* with a special gift for the whole family and, with not a single flash of brilliance in sight, had quickly recruited his mother for the task. It was now more than apparent that a woman's wisdom and knowledge of the workings of a household had saved the day for young Mr. Hickman, school master or no. "We shall christen it now with a good cuppa to warm your bones after your long journey. Thank you Christopher and welcome back. We have missed you."

Although unaware of it at the time, Jessie's sentiments were keenly shared by the other two members of her family seated at the kitchen table. Emily had come to admire the good looks and dry sense of humour of the man whom she had seen only fleetingly during the brief periods of time when their paths crossed, before he returned to Glace Bay and after she arrived home from Baddeck. She looked forward to these occasions; she loved how he spoke with a heavy English accent and how he smiled. It always seemed to light up the room. And over the past four months, Duncan himself had made a conscious attempt, whenever he was at home, to join in the conversations with Christopher and Jennie. More often than not, the topics were as disparate as they were eclectic. One evening, it was Canadian athletes: William Sherring had won the Olympic marathon in Greece the year before while Tom Longboat had been the first runner across the finish line at the Boston Marathon, in record time mind you, just this past year. The next evening, it was good old, Cape Breton ingenuity: the first radio message had just been transmitted across the Atlantic from Port Morien, just down the coast from Glace Bay, while Mr. Bell was still flying bigger and more intricate kites over the frozen lake at Baddeck. Surprisingly enough, Duncan found it to be a learning experience and actually began to look forward to their chats, with or without Jessie.

It was several days later that Christopher and Emily had gone for a walk down the loch road, on the pretext of taking the air to settle bloated stomachs after what was a particularly hearty meal. As they returned, it was Christopher who first spotted the dark blot on the snow near the side of the barn . With time to spare and the opportunity to remain in each other's company a bit longer, they decided to investigate and approached slowly, more out of a sense of idle curiosity than anything else. *"Mo Thighearna! Chan eil e fìor, mo Rionnag ghràdhach."* (My Lord! It is not true; my beloved *Rionnag*.) Emily's shriek of absolute horror sliced the air as if it were a knife piercing her own heart. Through her tears, she was not even conscious of the fact that her words were falling on Christopher's unfathoming "English" ears. But then, it did not really matter. He understood all too well as he crouched down and lifted *Rionnag's* frozen body from its bed of snow. From somewhere beneath the stone foundation came the cries of kittens eagerly awaiting their mother's return and much-needed sustenance. It seemed painfully obvious from her torn body that, in her weakened state, *Rionnag* had left them to find nourishment and had crossed the path of a vicious enemy. In all likelihood, it was the MacGregor dog next door that had a well-known reputation for killing not for food but for mere sport.

Under the soft glow of a kerosene lamp, *Rionnag* was buried in the soil of the root cellar beneath the manse later that same evening. As Duncan said a prayer over the animal's still body, Jennie recalled how, many years ago, he had gently dismissed his daughter's request for a service of baptism for the wee bit of black fur. Now her tears were of sadness for the passing of their beloved friend mixed with those of happiness for the humanity that now filled her husband's heart. Something had died; something had been born. As Christopher's shovel filled the shallow grave, Emily leaned her body into her father who stood motionless, watching the scoops of earth take *Rionnag* from their sight. He put his arm around his daughter's waist. *"Tha i anns a'ghàradh bhrèagh làn eunlaidh."* (She is in a beautiful garden full of birds.) Even in her grief, Emily sensed that his words had seldom before been so heartfelt and comforting.

The five kittens had been rescued from beneath the barn and placed on a blanket behind the kitchen stove. With eyes barely open, they huddled together listening to the reassuring sound of each other's heart beats. One of them so reminded Emily of *Rionnag*. She was completely black like her mother with the exception of a small white spot in the centre of her forehead. Duncan and Emily crouched down to stroke the tiny bodies and it was then that Duncan promised his daughter that, this time, good homes would be found for the wee ones. They would not meet the same watery demise as had all their brothers and sisters that came before. Emily reached forward and picked up the small black kitten. *"A bhobain, is teine-biorach cuideachd i. Buinidh i dhuinn a-nis."* (Pappa, she is also a shooting star. She belongs to us now.)

Jennie watched this scene unfold and listened attentively from the discrete shelter of the pantry. As Emily placed the tiny kitten in Duncan's arms, there was an additional warmth about the kitchen. She smiled with the certain knowledge that, somehow, *Rionnag* had miraculously come home.

Even as a child, he had been fascinated by the delicate interplay of the pink and white colouring of the blossoms. It had always seemed so strange that, though the last snows of winter nestled by the edges and in the moist areas of the forest, these colourful and fragrant bits of life would suddenly appear as if returning home after a long journey. John felt the smooth texture of a tiny petal as he ran it gently between his fingers. It was only then that he realized he had come to a greater appreciation of this fragile blossom in his hands because he too had just returned from an equally trying, if not epic, trip. Unlike the mayflower, his was a passage of distance, of time and of understanding. A mild May breeze made its way down the length of the loch and began to play riotously with his hair. John turned to face it, not as a combatant to confront but as a friend to greet. It was here that he truly belonged, not in the pit.

At sixteen, *Iain Beag* Grant seemed to be much older than the years that were actually upon him. It was not only his bearing although, in itself, his tall lanky frame conveyed the appearance of an older age. At six feet three inches, he towered over both Angus and Isabelle who continued to refer to him as "the bairn." It was still not beyond both Iain and Sadie to taunt their younger brother about his preferred status in the family. Had he not always been the first to get a taste of the oatcakes or molasses biscuits hot from the oven? And, as a matter of form, did he not always receive the most colourful set of newly knitted mitts under the Christmas tree? It explained in part why it was they had mischievously sent him off, long years ago, in search of grandmother and her wise counsel. They knew all too well that Flora never seemed to like anyone, especially children. She would humble the *peata bèag* (little pet/little spoiled child) in a way that they never could, at least not without ending up on the receiving end of a severe scolding or, worse, the dreaded kindling stick.

John now looked down the length of the loch towards the bluffs and beyond to the open Atlantic. He chuckled to himself as he recalled the reception that had awaited him that day long ago in his grandmother's bedroom. He could now look back upon it as an amusing tale to be safe-guarded and eventually passed on to his own children as an interesting bit of family history. It was important to remember. As his eyes scanned the shores of the loch, he glanced up at the Urquhart house where Sadie was now happily married to Donald and then across to his parents' home that would one day become Iain's. Everything seemed to fall into place as if it was somehow ordained or predestined. Or was it? Is that what brought him back to *Loch Dubh*? If it was all so predestined, what was its purpose and what was to be his lot in life? The questions were nothing if not rhe-torical. But even then, John always seemed to know the answers.

What made John appear older was not so much his physical stature but rather the fact that he had been away for what seemed a lifetime, albeit only two years. It had taught him things that one could never learn from the pages of a book or the surface of a blackboard. He meant no dis-respect towards Kristy Erskine who had been his teacher for many years, or even Mr. Hickman who occupied the same position for his final year of studies at the *Loch Dubh* school. Both had been extremely kind, dedicated and responsive to the needs of those in their charge. His recollections were now of the years he had passed within the walls of the school. He remembered the map of the world with the Empire coloured in bright red; he remembered the rows of desks on either side of the pot-bellied stove; he remembered the school bell on the edge of the teacher's desk. As much as he enjoyed the fun and camaraderie that was shared within those boarded walls, he always found greater joy in escaping its clutches on a warm spring day for the exhilarating freedom of the open hills. It now struck him that, for the past two years, he had been imprisoned in a blackened school where there was never a bell to be stared at, never to ring, never to signal an escape to freedom. There was no bell in the pit.

Even the terminology could lead one astray. Management referred to it as the colliery or the mine; the working men always called it the pit. Of one thing there was never any doubt. It provided the principal source of employment and livelihood to the residents of Sydney Mines. So much depended upon the operations that sat precariously along the shore at the end of Pit Street. John had originally been drawn to "The Mines", as the town was affectionately called, not only because of the plentiful amount of work but also for the sense of excitement that living in a big municipality offered a boy from the country. A lad could stand and watch the world go by at Thompson's Corner, with its large fountain in the middle of the intersection. In addition to the continual coming and going of shoppers, the junction was often congested with numerous horses being given relief for their parched throats as their owners went about their important business further along the street. Sydney Mines was a booming and exciting place to be. And people were so boastful about their town that carried numerous distinctions: the first dial telephones in the Dominion, one of the first towns to have electric street lights and now the first store of the British-Canadian Co-operative Society up on Fraser Avenue. The shops along Main Street provided a colourful and fascinating place to see and be seen. Still, it was only a facade facing the street with its back to the winds coming off the Atlantic. It had turned its back; it was a facade with its back to the pit.

Initially, it had not taken John long to find lodgings with the Matheson family, who lived in a company house just down Main Street from St. Andrew's Church. Edward Matheson was a colliery supervisor, whose father had worked there before him for many years and where, no doubt, his three sons would work when they were of an appropriate age. Only fifteen-year-old Christine would escape the pit's eager grasp. She, at least, could remain in school; girls were of no use in mining coal. In time, John would come to appreciate the fact that it was not so much that going underground was in the blood; it was simply that there was little else.

From the very first day, John was not at ease with his new trade. He remembered looking back over his shoulder as the box cars carried the men deeper and deeper into the bowels of the earth, far out under the ocean floor. It reminded him of a candle. Looking back, all he could see was a tenuous flickering of light that grew increasingly faint until it was totally consumed by blackness. It was always the same; almost without warning, the candle light that was Sydney Mines passed from his view as he descended into what, over time, became his living Hell. As a child, this was how he had imagined it to be; it was all here with the possible exception of the flames and the cloven-footed devils. How was it that these men around him could abide the water, the cold, the dust, the rats? In slowly working their way down the length of the shafts, John began to note the blackened faces of nameless boys positioned at the gateways, slowly opening and closing the doors as if in an eerie demonic trance. In their eyes, he saw young Albert MacGregor, Andrew Ferguson, Lachlan and Colin Campbell running through the hills high above the loch. And now, he realized that these eyes would always stay with him. They were so white against their blackened skin against the blackened walls of the pit. And yet, the boys did not run in the open air. They stood frozen in suffocating black haze. It was all so sad, so predictable and, for John, so troubling. *Mar sgàile a' claonadh sìos, chan eil leus soluis an seo.* (Like a shadow declining, there is not a ray of light here.) He spoke not only of the pit. John knew that he was also referring to his life here in this place.

In standing at the foot of the loch, John looked up into the blue skies along the eastern horizon and thought of the black walls. They never stopped falling; it never ended. It was like the bedroom of a child waking up from a bad dream in the middle of the night. There is a pitch-black curtain that is drawn before the eyes. He wants it to go away but it doesn't, it wouldn't. It simply lingers for no apparent reason other than to instill fear. Yet, amid the anxiety, there is always the certain knowledge that, in time, the morning light will stream through the window and shred the somber curtain into so many tiny strips of oblivion. It was all so different in the pit. The wall of black coal would fall and the men would scamper to load its fragments into the wooden cars to be hauled by the ponies to feed the candle high above. From the outset, it all seemed so futile; there was always another wall to take its place. The only saving grace came on pay day when he would proceed directly to the bank to deposit his money while many of the other men would follow their circuitous routes home by way of the tavern. On those days at least, he could console himself. It would only be with time and money that he would be able to break free. Only then could he return to the land of trees and mountains where his spirit could soar free. The days seemed to crawl by.

It had not taken the other men long to lay a nickname on the Grant boy. He would not be Grant or even Johnny. He was labelled "Scotty" by those who found his accent so amusing. "You are real Scotchie my boy and that is what you will remain. Just keep your head down and your nose clean; you will do well with us Scotty." John took no offence at George Sutherland's remarks. Clearly none was ever intended and, if anything, they reflected a paternalistic concern; they would look out for the lad. In actual fact, John did not mind the nickname, given that such titles had forever been an integral part of one's identity growing up in *Loch Dubh*. Sometimes one would stay with you for a week while another might endure for a lifetime. Regardless, the granting of special names was oftentimes elevated to a heightened art form, to say nothing of comic relief, and always taken in good humour.

No, what bothered "Scotty" more than anything else was the fact that the very men who mocked the influence of the Gaelic on his English tongue, were themselves from Gaelic-speaking families. The gibes would come from MacKenzies, Stephensons, Pattersons, MacQueens and others who fancied the English to be the way of the future. Their children would not be learning the old language; of what use would it be anyway? Better to get on with the future and leave the past where it belonged — in the grave. It was then that John came to appreciate that their future was itself a grave; it was the colliery; it was the mine; it was the pit. Whatever the term, John vowed that it would never be his grave. *An sloc-ghuail . . . cho dubh ri finichd, mar dhubhar na h-uaighe.* (The pit . . . as black as jet, like the shade of the grave.) For now at least, he would bide his time.

It had been the previous August, on the steamer down the coast on the return voyage to Sydney Mines from vacation time, that John had first heard tell of the MacPhee property located two miles north of New Carlisle on the shore road. Seated inside the cabin sheltered from the strong north-easterly wind, John had overheard a conversation between two *bodaich* who were bemoaning the changes to the face of the land. Was it not a tragedy that Dougal and Sarah had died alone, childless as a result of "the terrible sickness" that had claimed all five children some fifty three years ago? Their solitary passing would surely banish their legacy from the soil of Cape Breton every bit as much as they themselves had been banished from the old country. It was indeed a pity for both the MacPhees and these two passengers who now mourned their loss. But for John, it was not a time of sadness. He had never heard of them before, let alone known them. No, for *Iain Beag*, it was providence.

Inquiries were made in writing with county officials at the court house in Baddeck. The one hundred and fifty acre farm would be sold at public auction in the spring once assessments had been undertaken of its true value and the process of public notification had been put in place. In John's absence, his father would act on his behalf. At the end of the day, the bidding had gone over John's predetermined limit of $250.00, over by some $50.00. Still, the property would pass to John Grant who would never be told of the true price paid. Angus and Isabelle would find the extra money somewhere, somehow. It was not a great sum to pay to have their son back home on the North Shore.

John continued to feel the smooth textures of the petal between his fingers as, once again, he turned to the bouquet lying on the ground before him. Last spring had been the one and only time in several years that he had not come to Flora's grave to present her with mayflowers. To his mind, these words seemed so strange to think, let alone say — to present her with mayflowers. Yet, it was something that he wanted to do for her and for himself. No one else need know; no one else did know. He was glad to be back home, far away from the pit. For some reason, he thought of the eyes of the boys with the blackened faces standing diligently at the gateways. He had escaped this living Hell, this grave that continued to call so many young men away from the farms. As with Flora, his grave would be prepared one day. He hoped that it was many years off and that, when the time came, it would be dug here in the shadow of *Beinn-mo-Mhulaid.* *"Beinn-mo-Ghàirdeachais."* (Mountain of My Joy)

He would find time to return to "The Mines" soon to speak with Christine. For some reason, he knew she would be happy enough here in this place with him at her side. *"Anail nan speur, anail na beatha . . . ann an tìr nam beò."* (The breath of the skies, the breath of life . . . in the land of the living.) — the land of the living where somethings were yet to come to pass. Of this, he was most confident. However, for now he was content just to be home in the freedom of the open hills.

Chapter Thirteen

July 1908 – May 1909

Behold, I shew you a mystery; we shall not all sleep, but we shall all be changed.

I Corinthians XV: 51

Feuch, tha mi a' labhairt ni dìomhair ruibh; cha chaidil sinn uile, ach caochlaidhear sinn uile.

I Corintianach XV: 51

"*Mo Thighearna anns na speuran shuas!*" (My Lord up in Heaven!) The scream could be heard ringing around the loch; in the forested fringes of the higher hills, even the birds were likely frozen in absolute fear. All the while, the reaction in the kitchen was somewhat different. Aulay laughed with great delight as Iona struggled to catch her breath and made a futile attempt to compose herself after such a ghastly start. Her heart was still pounding as though it was about to leap from her chest; her hands were pressed firmly against her breast as if to prevent it from doing so. She stood there quieting herself and finding some degree of consolation in the fact that this was not the first time that the bairn had surprised her and that it most probably would not be the last. Regardless, her heart continued to beat at a quickened pace.

Never before had the three piglets heard such a horrific noise, with the possible exception of the crows that were known to occasionally fight over bits of scrap out behind the barn. The fright was evident in their beady eyes and drooping tails as they beat a hasty retreat in the direction from which they had been so deviously lured. The squealing was nothing more than an added protective measure that offered some assurances of safety in numbers as long as they could continue to hear each other. They would quickly return to the pen and their mother's side. There, at least, they would find both the sustenance and the relative safety that she always seemed to afford them. Aulay chased after the trio and opened the screen door to allow them to complete their escape from what would surely come to be known, at least in barnyard circles, as *an taigh-cuthaich*. (The Mad House) They had all learned a valuable lesson in that they would never again trust the wee one who always spoke so sweetly to them. It was more than obvious that, all the while, he had simply been up to no good and the kitchen escapade was the only proof that was needed. Next time, they would know better than to be tempted by his gifts, tasty morsels or no.

Aulay returned to the kitchen and the doorway leading into the pantry where he found his mother still standing, holding her hands over her heart. The only visible difference from before was that a foreboding scowl had now appeared on her face as she stared down at him. From experience, he knew the expression well and realized that it would take all the wisdom of his three and a half years to extricate himself from the situation. He would have to placate her without delay, well before any thought was given to recruiting his father and the dreaded *maide* (stick) as a suitable form of punishment. Aulay quickly collected his thoughts and proceeded to offer what he believed to be a perfectly sound explanation as to why it was the three little ones had ventured into the kitchen and, quite unintentionally, scared his mother half to death.

With hands now firmly planted on his hips, Aulay looked up into the face of judge and jury with all the confidence of a barrister standing before the High Court of King's Bench. The situation was thus: it was not a question of their being bad or even of their having barged their way in. In fact, he had willingly invited *Creideamh, Dòchas* and *Coibhneas* (Faith, Hope and Charity) to come into the house. It was only Aulay himself who knew that the original intention had been to name them *Athair, Mac* and *An Spiorad Naomh.* (Father, Son and Holy Ghost) The three names had often been used in Kirk and, initially at least, that seemed good enough reason for him to use them. However, upon reflection, he had finally thought better of it; he would not tempt God's wrath by evoking these names, especially in the Gaelic. It would be fine in the English if that was the language he chose to speak; the Gaelic was an entirely different matter. He had heard "bad words" being spoken by the English fisherman down at the wharf and felt not the least bit reluctant in using them, as long as he was out of earshot of his parents of course. If he spoke such words in the English, God would not have the foggiest idea what it was he was saying. He had respect for God and would never use His name or, indeed, the language of Heaven in vain. That would be a sin or, in this case, a criminal act worthy of the stick.

The three virtuous piglets had been lured into the kitchen with bits of bread that had been strategically placed in a trail leading from the barn, across the yard to the back door. Once inside, they continued to root along the wooden floor in search of even more-delectable titbits. All the while, their presence had gone unnoticed by Iona who was in the pantry busily removing a freshly baked batch of sugar cookies from a long black tray and placing them on a cooling rack on the window sill. A few stray crumbs near her feet was all the enticement needed. It was *Coibhneas* that had quizzically nuzzled Iona's ankle in the hope that it might provoke even more manna to descend from on high. To their utter amazement, the only thing to rain down upon them was the ungodly high-pitched scream that was anything but heavenly. Their sensitive pink ears were still ringing and flapped unmercifully as eyes were focused on the back door and the freedom that lay beyond. All this and more was now admissible evidence before the High Court as it fell to Aulay to plead his case.

"Chan eil cuilean no piseag agam mar chàch. Tha cù aig Ismay, eadhon a' chaile-ag dhall. Is iad mo pheatachan. Bha mi airson gu'm faiceadh iad mo dhachaidh.. Chan eil cobhartaich no crònan ann. Ach. Ni iad gnòsail nas fheàrr na cù no cat. Och ma tà, ghràdhaich iad thu, a mhamaidh." (I do not have a puppy or a kitten like the others. Even Ismay, the blind girl, has a dog. They are my pets. I wanted to show them my home. There is no barking or purring. But they grunt better than a dog or cat. And indeed, they like you Mamma.) The last remark was clearly meant to clinch the case once and for all. There he stood awaiting judgement. With the initial fright now passed and a more-regular heart beat finally restored, it was difficult for the judge and jury to silence the demure barrister, especially when his arguments flowed so flawlessly and with such utter conviction of innocence. But silence him she must. With hands folded across her chest, Iona realized she had no alternative. If not, she would surely burst into laughter and this case, as with previous ones, would soon be lost.

"Amhladh, seo mo annlan agus chan eil mi a' fuiligeadh mucan r' m' annlan. Dèan deifir, cluich agus gabh beachd. Droch bhatt thu gu dearbh." (Aulay, this is my kitchen and I will not be having pigs at my feet. Rush back to your play and pay attention. You are a mischievous one. Yes indeed.) She passed him a warm cookie and placed her hand on the crown of his blond head as if steering him to the back door. He had the presence of mind to gladly accept both the peace offering and the verdict while making his escape with almost as much speed as had "The Trinity" moments before. The only difference was that the piglets may have had a sense that perhaps they had done something wrong. Aulay did not. Iona stood looking through the black mesh of the screen door long after he had disappeared from view.

She returned to her baking and her thoughts in the pantry. Aulay was a good bairn, as caring and loving as any little boy. How she and Neil had tried for another child for so long. Kenneth was her first born and would forever be her pride and joy. Still, she always envisaged herself with a large brood of young ones around her feet. Chicks, maybe, but not piglets! *"Taigh nam muc."* (The House of the Pigs.). Without fully realizing it, she had managed a small chuckle at her own expense as the words spilled out over the counter. She had wanted more children so desperately and, with Aulay's arrival, all her prayers seemed to have been answered. Even with the difficult birth, or maybe because of it, he was every bit as beautiful as Kenneth had been as a baby. And as Aulay grew, the resemblance to his older brother became even more pronounced: the blue eyes, the lanky legs, the blond hair, the strong nose. It was almost uncanny how two individuals, separated by some twelve years, could be so much alike. Iona stopped and looked out the side window, seeing nothing. It was as though she were gazing through a much tighter, blacker mesh. She could not allow her thoughts to become lies to herself in the hope they would somehow right everything. The window allowed her to come to a greater realization; she recognized that her two sons were so similar physically and yet so different in other ways. There was a problem. *"A Dhé chaoimh. Carson mise? Carson m'Amladh beag?"* (Oh dearly beloved God. Why me? Why my little Aulay?)

Iona left her baking behind as she walked through the dining-room, turning right into the long hallway that led directly down to the front door. The hinges slowly creaked open as if expressing anguish over her imminent departure from the house. With door open and freedom assured, she passed through the archway onto the front veranda. There, a chair awaited her as well as her thoughts. She could have gone to the flower garden in the back as was so often her habit. However, today she wanted to be alone; she needed to be alone, away from Neil and Kenneth working in the back fields and Aulay playing God knows where. She wanted and needed to think.

The panoramic view that greeted her eyes was something she never tired of — that is, whenever she could find the time to indulge herself in such luxuries. It took occasions such as this to remind her of the magnificent beauty that surrounded her and, indeed, everyone who called this place home. It always made her feel so humble and somewhat insignificant to sit there pondering the breadth and magnitude of this living canvas. If for some reason it was not possible to see the richness of colour, how could it possibly be described or imagined? The blues of the sky, the greens and purples of the mountains, the yellows of the oat fields, the blacks of the water, were all from a palette that truly defied belief. If it were not possible to see! Iona's thoughts turned to Ismay and the colourless lifeless canvas that descended before the young child's eyes. She closed her own eyes and tried to imagine life with this hideous eternally black veil that for some five years had separated the small girl from the coloured canvas that was *Loch Dubh*. Yet she was such a happy child who had seemingly come to deal with her blindness. In a way that was hers and hers alone, Ismay was obviously content and terribly bright.

A joy always pervaded the community with the birth of another child. Of late, it was reassuring to know that, in time, these homes and farms would not be deserted even with so many of the young people still leaving for the towns and cities. The sadness was felt but so seldom expressed; it was simply the way. It was different with a birth; there was a sign of hope. Such happiness had been evident two and a half years ago with the arrival of Alasdair and Kristy's little girl Grace. And even with the distance, the same exhilaration was felt around the loch with the news, nine months ago, that Elizabeth MacLeod had been delivered of a healthy baby girl. Iona thought the name Naomi to be such a beautiful choice — a link to the past. With all the talk of the future, the mines of Cape Breton, the docks of Halifax, the industrial factories of Toronto and the prairies of the Canadian west, it was important to remember and honour what had come before. Iona had not yet seen the MacLeod child but pictured her as already possessing a full head of her mother's reddish-brown hair. No disrespect to the MacLeods, but would it not be a fine gift from the MacGregor side of the family? Och, it was perhaps a bit silly and it would probably sound a tad queer so she would think it only to herself. Iona slowly opened her eyes and, sitting there on the veranda with Boularderie many hours away by horse and wagon, hoped Naomi would have Elizabeth's colouring.

It had first become evident to Iona over the past few months when the entire Erskine family gathered together, for birthdays and at holiday time. Grace and Aulay would play together and, through a mother's knowing eyes and ears, she realized that her son was not as advanced as his much younger cousin. She heard it in his talk; she saw it in his actions. It was not that Grace was a gifted child, although she was as clever as any. She was developing at a normal rate. Aulay was not.

"Tha thu nad amadan! Tha thu nad dhearg-amadan! Tha easbhuidh ort!" (You are an idiot! You are a perfect fool! You are crazy!) Iona could already hear the taunts of the children in the school yard. Her eyes moved across and down the loch where they came to rest on the school house and there they remained. She found her thoughts so muddled and became increasingly frustrated by the fact that they had assumed a life of their own; she had no control. Would he grow out of it? Would he learn to read and write? Would her child be called "the fool"? Would God give her patience and strength to cope? Would Kenneth care for him after she and Neil were gone? There on the veranda, as she faced the beautiful painting that sat before her, Iona realized that there was never any shortage of questions. It was just that there were never any answers.

She rose from her chair in as much an attempt to clear her mind as to stretch her cramped leg. Without thinking, she wiped her hands on the long white apron as if to rid them of something undesirable. Across the loch, she could faintly make out the tiny figures of Kristy and Grace walking hand-in-hand down the pathways of Tina's flower garden. She smiled at this placid scene that had so beautifully and effortlessly worked itself onto the surface of the larger canvas. With that, she rounded the corner of the house and proceeded towards her own garden. There was still a bit of time before she would have to return to the kitchen. She could pick a few blossoms so as to place a fragrant arrangement in the centre of the supper table. Aulay would be pleased and make such a fuss.

At first, Iona had not taken notice of the fact that, with the exception of the bawling of the cows in the front pasture, a silence had settled over the yard. Especially here in her garden, it was so colourful, so peaceful, so reassuring. All the while, the mild breeze of the July afternoon tugged at her long aproned skirt like a child demanding attention. She languished in the sheer joy of the moment and it had not taken long for a small bouquet to gradually take form in her left hand as she took time to admire the varied array of shapes and colours. A few blades of grass would provide the perfect emerald frame for the masterpiece once it was placed in the empty preserves bottle that would serve as a vase. It was then, as she reached into the grassy fringes of the garden, that the prattle first settled on her ears, robbing them of their all-too-brief interlude.

"I will kick your bejeesis arses to the moon if you don't behave — scaring my dear *mamaidh* so! Rush back to your play and pay attention. You are rascals indeed." Leaning on the rails of the pen at the side of the barn, Aulay was in full flight as he admonished the piglets for their earlier foray into his mother's kitchen. Iona knew him well enough to know that the coarse lecture could be delivered only in the English in order to ensure that God could not hear. It would be later that night, as bedtime prayers were dutifully being said in the Gaelic, that God would, none-the-wiser, look down and smile upon "Saint Aulay."

As she departed the garden for her kitchen and the preparation of supper, Iona glanced over in the direction of the barn with the hope that the Almighty would forever look down and watch over him. *"Mo ghràdhag, beannachd Dhé leat a ghnàth."* (My dear little one, may the blessings of God attend you always.) Even if she had wanted to say something more, she would have been prevented from doing so by the large lump that had formed in her throat. With that, Iona entered the house with her flowers, leaving Aulay to complete his lecture to the three wee ones in private. Clearly, he had not yet finished laying down the English law. But then, it was of no great consequence; God might well be listening but clearly would not understand a single word.

She was doing nothing more than leaning against the doorway of the bedroom and yet she could not recall a moment when she had been filled with as much peace and love. The early afternoon sun flooded through the open window and the white curtains gently billowed up and down as if keeping beat with the melodic lines of some mysterious sea shanty. She was pleased that this particular shanty was as inaudible as it was invisible. On more than one occasion, she had overheard the fisherman talking among themselves down on the wharf as they went about repairing the vast array of nets and traps. Their salty stories and turns of phrase would surely have caused many a righteous head to turn as white as snow. An image of poor Archie came to her mind.

Grace would be three years old in only four short months. Kristy's wee one was now a little girl and, in the twinkling of an eye, would become a young woman before her mother's very eyes. Where had the time gone since the day when she was born? It was all such a blur, a blur of absolute joy. As she continued to lean against the doorway, Kristy was thankful for the miraculous gift of birth and life. This was her child, her own flesh and blood, her own beautiful Grace who now slept so soundly on the small bed, oblivious to her mother's presence. She thought back to those early days in 1896, twelve years ago already, when she had first arrived in *Loch Dubh* and had sought some sense of what it was God intended for her in this place. As she looked down into the tranquility of the tiny face before her, the words came in a soft whispered voice. *"Tha freagairt agam; seo gràs an Tighearna."* (I have my answer; this is the grace of the Lord.) With that, she turned to go back downstairs to her work in the kitchen. She stopped herself and gazed back into the room in order to complete the thought. Kristy's words flowed lovingly beyond the billowing white sails into the broad expanse of blue sky. *"Tapadh leibh."* (Thank you.)

The booklets and paper had already been placed on the kitchen table ready to receive their student. Kristy had not minded the idea of returning to her old vocation; indeed, there were many things about it that she had truly missed. And there could not be a more ideal time for the class than early afternoon, following the noon meal. At that time of day, the house was always so terribly quiet. As she seated herself at the table, her hands reached out to rearrange the papers. She knew only too well that the shuffling was unnecessary and that it was nothing more that an attempted distraction that did not succeed.

Kristy did not want to think about it, but there seemed to be little choice; it was the stillness that often evoked such thoughts that could be so troubling. It was now an accepted routine that, once the noontime dishes had been cleared from the table, Alasdair would return to his chores in the fields or the barn while Kristy would resume her work in the kitchen. For everyone else, it was time to nap. At first it seemed somewhat strange but Kristy was forced to accept the fact that Tina was also getting on in years. This woman who had always been her sure foundation was growing old and tired. It was difficult to even imagine life without Daniel and Tina, whose waning bodies required more and more rest. For Kristy, this reality was thrust before her eyes and her ears as their absence and the accompanying silence seemed to grow in intensity. The thoughts were terribly painful.

She rose from the table, humming a milling tune to herself as a further distraction in attempting to dispel any sense of gloom. She could not allow herself to become maudlin, especially with the school bell about to ring. She would wear a smile when her charge arrived, of that she was certain. It was strange to think, let alone to say, but it was as though Ismay could read the expression on her face. In less than six weeks of passing time together in study, Kristy came to the realization that this child was perhaps one of the most perceptive persons she had ever known. She was not handicapped, crippled or deprived because of her blindness — quite the contrary. It was because of her capacity to recognize and revel in the life that had been given to her that, at least in part, made her truly gifted.

Even with the slight chill on the October air, Kristy would not miss the opportunity to once again witness the scene that she never tired of

seeing unfold before her eyes. It was so natural and simple yet so powerful in the emotional response that it always evoked. She grabbed Tina's
woollen shawl that had been left draped over the rocking chair and passed
through the front door where she would wait patiently on the covered
veranda. Kristy was strangely oblivious to the wind that buffeted the edge
of the shawl up and down as if it were revelling in its own mischievous
milling frolic. Fortunately, it was not long before the figures came into
view, appearing from behind the brooding spruce trees, as they slowly
made their way along the loch road. Ismay walked with such determination that an unknowing observer would never have reason to suspect that
she was without sight. But that same observer would also have every reason to marvel at her self-effacing companion. As Ismay walked on, *Taghta*
followed a short distance behind watching her master's every move. The
instant the girl's step showed the slightest sign of veering too closely to the
side ditch, the collie would take up a position beside her. Ever so gently,
Taghta would lean into her leg and apply subtle pressure until such time as
the course was corrected. Given her breeding, *Taghta* would then race in a
circle around her "flock" as if to reconfirm and celebrate; the instinct was
simply too strong.

It was obvious that, in so many ways, *Taghta* had become Ismay's eyes.
Even to that same unknowing observer, it would have soon become apparent that Ismay had become *Taghta*'s heart. Kristy took great delight
in watching the relationship between the two unfold as they proceeded
down the road. There had been more than one occasion on this very veranda that she had felt the tears run down her cheeks. She was grateful for
the fact that she was alone. Some things could be described and explained
while others were better left unsaid; they simply spoke for themselves.
Kristy knew this to be just such a time.

Over a cup of tea earlier that month, Martha had shared with Kristy
the story of how the procession of two had initially come about. From
the very first day of school, Martha had routinely taken Ismay's hand and
walked her to the Erskine home for her afternoon lesson. *Taghta*, the in-
separable companion, trailed behind and always remained on the Erskine's
back step until such time as the lesson was completed and Martha reappeared to accompany the child home. Not even an errant cat crossing
the back yard could dissuade *Taghta* from leaving her post. It was in late
September, three or four weeks into the routine, that Martha had left her
kitchen through the back door with Ismay in hand en route to the lesson.
Only then did she realize that she had once again forgotten to bring along
a long-promised recipe for Tina. Martha was determined that she would
not be chastised for having the memory of a *cailleach*, even if it was only in
fun. With that, she stroked Ismay's hand and told her to remain there on
the step with *Taghta* until her return.

It could not have been more than a minute later that Martha emerged
to find the back steps completely deserted. With both fear and despera-

tion, she raced to the corner of the house only to realize that she had arrived just in time to observe the two figures making their own way down towards the loch road. Her first instinct had been to call out to them but something made her think better of it. Strangely enough, it was now her turn to trail behind in silence. She shadowed them down the hill and up the road to the point where they turned right into the Erskine laneway. Martha returned home that day with a broad smile and the full realization that her fondest hopes and prayers were being answered. Her daughter was already demonstrating the sense of independence that she and Peter so wanted to instill in all their children. Of equal importance, she recognized that Ismay and *Taghta* were indeed growing together and learning from each other. *Och Taghta, is beannaichte do shùilean.* (Oh *Taghta*, blessed are your eyes.)

It had been the previous March that Martha first asked Kristy and Christopher Hickman if she might meet with them both in private to discuss an important personal matter. In the front parlour, she informed them that she had been in correspondence with the office of the county warden in Baddeck. He was prepared to assist the Campbell family in whatever way he could to facilitate Ismay's admission into the Halifax School for the Blind. There was no doubt but that she would receive a fine education from the instructors who were specially trained in such matters. Martha attempted to explain to the two teachers, oftentimes with a lump in her throat, that it was not a matter of money, for indeed the school, board and transportation to and from Halifax were all made available at no cost. There was even a ladies auxiliary that made clothes for any needy students. No, the issue was not money. It was that she and Peter could not bring themselves to accept the thought of their daughter being taken from them and left alone in far-off Halifax, away from everyone and everything that she knew and loved. It soon became abundantly clear that Martha had asked for the meeting in order to propose an alternative course of action.

Both Kristy and Christopher noted the look of sheer desperation in Martha's eyes. Kristy imagined it to be the same fear that would have been in Rachael Ferguson's as she watched over Harris' sickbed all those years ago. It was the fear of having something precious taken from you, of watching it slip away as you sit by helplessly. At that moment, it was as if Martha's eyes, and not Ismay's, were setting the context for the discussion that was about to unfold. It had not taken long for the three of them to develop a detailed proposal that, in time, would be presented for approval. And as it was to turn out, education officials did not have any objections with Ismay remaining in *Loch Dubh* and being instructed there on the well-understood condition that acceptable arrangements be put in place. As a result, Ismay would attend public school in the morning with the other children. It was deemed important that she not be removed from them completely; she was as integral a member of the community as were the others and should not be isolated. As much as possible, Christopher would ensure that the morning sessions focused on spelling, verbal interaction and other non-visual aspects of the curriculum to which Ismay could relate. In the early afternoon following the noon meal, there would be a two-hour private session at home with Kristy when the Erskine house was otherwise quiet and most conducive for instruction. For Kristy and Christopher, Martha's words of thanks were not necessary. They both regarded teaching as much more than a profession. That aside, the look in Martha's eyes was more gratitude than words could ever hope to express.

Kristy had no illusions about the challenging task that she now presented to herself. She was an accredited teacher but had never before taught a blind child. She had no idea of the prescribed learning materials to say nothing of techniques that should be brought to bear. During the months of April and May, she was in frequent correspondence with Mr. Lamond, the county warden. Through his good offices, she was eventually given a referral to the superintendent of the Halifax School, the eminent Dr. Frederick Fraser. Within three weeks of her writing, a large brown envelope was received in the post that included course books and a curriculum guide for elementary levels. The covering letter, while fairly congenial in tone, was clear in its underlying message. Beyond the wide range of courses offered in the literary, musical, technical, gymnastic and kindergarten departments, the school provided rigorous standards of education and discipline at all times throughout the six-day school week. Miss Campbell's presence would be most heartily welcomed at the school where she would receive both diligent attention and care. In the interim, the materials were enclosed with the compliments of the board of managers. Subtle pressures aside, Kristy had unknowingly crossed paths with what was to become the first of Ismay's two guardian angels.

It was a chance meeting on the streets of Baddeck that led Mr. Lamond to mention the case of the *Loch Dubh* girl to an acquaintance of Mabel Bell. As a deaf woman and person as well known for her philanthropy as her husband was for his eccentricity, Mrs. Bell began to take a particular and almost personal interest in Ismay's welfare. Kristy was soon to receive a host of packages from schools for the blind in Boston and Washington as well as the Ontario School for the Blind in Brantford. The vast majority of the printed material was produced using the New York Point System, a series of raised points on paper that were read in a horizontal manner. Over the summer months, while the children of *Loch Dubh* basked in their freedom from the confines of the school house, Kristy remained at her own classroom desk in the front parlour learning a new alphabet as well as the writing techniques involved with grooved cards and pencils. She was a diligent student determined to be prepared for the grueling tests that lay ahead.

Apart from her difficulties with the new alphabet, Kristy found her sessions with Ismay to be tremendously gratifying. She had almost forgotten how rewarding it was to feed young minds with knowledge while nurturing their spirits with an eagerness for learning, an eagerness for life. Ismay was a naturally inquisitive child, forever posing questions and asking Kristy to describe people, objects and places. At first, Kristy was reluctant to use colour as a descriptor but soon realized, as had Martha herself several years before in the garden, that the girl had developed her own interpretative system and was totally content in assigning particular meanings to words. On more than one occasion, the teacher found herself looking into those small blue eyes and trying to imagine a rainbow in a darkened sky. School was becoming as much a learning experience for Kristy as it was for Ismay.

Given that Christopher Hickman's classes were conducted in English and that all the printed materials available to Kristy were limited to that language as well, she made a conscious attempt to use the Gaelic every now and again, especially when offering words of encouragement. She had no doubt that these efforts were appreciated as, ever so softly, Ismay would invariably respond with a soft whisper to herself *"Dìreach. Dìreach."* (Just so. Just so.) It was on one such occasion that Ismay had lifted her hands from the nubbly surface of the paper and allowed them to follow Kristy's voice. Then, ever so gently, they began to stroke the teacher's cheeks. It was all too apparent that Kristy had been taken by surprise as, for a brief moment, a hush fell over the room that was to be broken only when Ismay finally posed one of her more-inquisitive questions.

"A Chairistìona, an urrainn dhuit gnùis Dhé fhaicinn?" (Kristy, are you able to see God's face?) For the second time in a matter of mere seconds, Kristy found herself completely taken aback. It seemed like an eternity that she sat there in silence, wondering what could possibly have prompted such a question. All the while, the tiny hands continued to gently stroke her teacher's cheeks. Finally, Kristy collected her thoughts and attempted a response, still uncertain as to the workings of this young mind.

"Chan urrainn mo ghràdhag. Tha Dia ann an àirde nan nèamh." (No, my dear little one. God is in the height of Heaven.)

It did not take Ismay half as long to find her words as it had Kristy. And indeed, when she spoke, it was with a conviction that transcended the wisdom of a five-year-old child. *"Tha Dia ann an gnùisean na h-uile. Tha mi a' smaoineachadh."* (I believe God is in everyone's face.) Kristy did not respond, indeed could not, because no words seemed appropriate or sufficient. As she sat gazing down into the tiny face and struggling to stop the tears that were not far away, she was conscious of the fact that all she could do was smile and that, in so doing, Ismay would surely see it in her own indelible way.

What possible difference would it make anyway? Regardless of what the true circumstances may have been, why should anyone want to reopen something that could well cause nothing but anguish and pain? Even if that something was the truth, was it honestly worth knowing especially now after all these years? Jessie returned the Bible to its customary place on the side table in the front parlour and, in the same movement, parted the curtains of the window that looked out and down towards the loch. It was now five months since Archie's passing and still the house held an abiding sense of his presence. It was strongest in this room where he had last lain before being taken to the Kirk and the grave. It was here that Jessie now felt him linger and, in some strange way, she wished that she was able to speak with him. It would make a difference, at least for her. There was little doubt but that both Archie and Hannah had gone to their graves knowing. Jessie vowed that she would do no less. She would speak with Daniel Erskine.

Of the original group of settlers, Daniel and Tina were the last ones to still be among them. Grants, MacAulays, MacDonalds, MacGregors, Fergusons and Urquharts — all the older people had long passed. Daniel was the strongest and perhaps only link back to that time. There was no doubt that Daniel would have knowledge and, as with everything else, remember even the most minute details. Although his body had been temporarily affected by the stroke of several years back, both his mind and memory were still as clear as a bell. Once more, Jessie looked down at the Bible that over those many years had been dutifully opened and read by Archie every day of his life. There was never any question, especially on the part of those closest to him, that it spoke to his heart in a way that no other person or thing ever could. Now, Jessie wished that it could speak to her in quite a different way albeit for a different reason. *"Ar peacaidhean diomhair."* (Our secret sins.) She would speak with Daniel.

The clomping of hooves gradually intensified in frequency and volume as if it were the ticking of a clock, coercing Jessie out of a deep troublesome sleep. In continuing to peer through the window, she could now see Mabel in the seat of the wagon laughing uproariously while Duncan held tightly to the reins. It certainly should not have come as any great surprise; the old mare always picked up speed as she turned into the long laneway up to the house. A vision of a stall of oats and a bucket of cold water obviously flooded her mind and quickened her step. Jessie watched with great interest as her son quite skillfully brought the mare under control both with his words and pressure on the reins. With calm restored, he turned to Mabel and folded her into his arms. Jessie saw the love in their faces and, for a fleeting moment, she was taken back to the early days of her own marriage to young Malcolm MacDonald. In some respects it seemed like yesterday and yet, in others, it was a lifetime ago. Was it not already eleven years since the tragic accident that took him from her to an early grave? And yet the grave would never be victorious. Malcolm lived on in his children, especially the boys who resembled him so. There was now for Jessie only one lingering doubt. Had her husband gone to his grave not knowing? If nothing else, she owed it to him. She would speak with Daniel soon.

By the time Jessie had made her way down the hall and entered the kitchen, the large pot of chow-chow on the stove had already begun to bubble over. The smell of vinegar clung to the room as though it were conspiring to preserve much more than the green tomatoes, onions, cucumbers and beets that had been amassed from the fall harvest. It was this heavy pervading odour that had first prompted her to suggest to Mabel that she accompany her husband on the short trip down to the sawmill. It was never any mind to her; years of putting up preserves had made her practically immune to the sharpness of the tart vapours. On the other hand, it was different for the young girl and a drive in the fresh air would do her all the good in the world, especially for someone in her condition.

In so many ways, it was a ritual of the season. The harvest was gathered, the first frost brushed the grasses outside the window; the preserves were put up, the first flakes of snow cascaded over the fields; the banking was put around the house, the chilling mantle of winter settled in over the entire landscape. The homes around *Loch Dubh* were banked each fall with sawdust taken from Angus Wright's mill just down the shore road from New Carlisle. The drive to and from was not long, just an hour or so, and the shoveling was light work. The old timers, who were raised with heavy chores, always likened it to shoveling mist. All the families were grateful for the fact that there was always a sufficient amount to insulate every home, keeping the root cellars and their contents free from the deadly frost. It was yet another time when the residents of *Loch Dubh* gave thanks for the differences between themselves and their neighbours at the bottom of the bluffs. The houses of New Carlisle were normally banked with the more-plentiful and easily accessible kelp or seaweed found all along the shore. It never took a great deal for the distinctions, sometimes real sometimes only imagined, to be accentuated. The two communities were so completely dissimilar in this and many other ways.

Mabel passed through the back door of the house and entered the winter porch with its ceiling festooned with an aromatic and colourful array of herbal icicles. From amid an inverted forest of mint, savory, thyme and rosemary, there appeared small bouquets of delicate blossoms: the purples of the chive, whites of the parsley and yellows of the dill. She stood there for a moment, taking a deep breath and allowing the fragrances of this upside down garden to cascade over her like a warm spring shower. She knew well enough that, as soon as the kitchen door opened, she would once again be awash in a sea of biting noxiousness. Almost reluctantly, she placed her hand on the knob and entered the room.

"Och Mabel, there is such lovely colour in your cheeks. The ride did you good, I can see that." Jessie had her hands in a deep pan of soapy water as she busily washed a multitude of bottles that were being lined up on the kitchen table and looking ever so much like an enormous flock of chicks eagerly waiting to be fed. The pungent air had wasted no time in streaming through Mabel's hair, sweeping away any lingering sweetness of the herbs that continued to rest unsuspectingly on the other side of the door. She quickly resigned herself to the duties at hand; before receiving their feed of chow-chow, beets and mustard pickles, the bottles must first be sterilized in the well-prepared oven. Work awaited her.

"Jessie, it was such a wonderful drive, especially down the bluffs. I was afraid that there would be a chill but there really wasn't. The air off the water was so beautiful on the skin and it played with my hair so. I do miss the sea breezes down in the town." As she combed her hair with her fingers, she suddenly caught herself, not realizing at first that her comments might well be misconstrued as homesickness for New Carlisle. "Still, I much prefer to walk along the quiet waters of the loch and up into the hills. It is so beautiful here." She waited expectantly to see just how effective her attempted recovery might prove to be.

Mabel's comments were greeted with nothing more than a knowing nod of the head and a broad smile on Jessie's face. From the corner of her eye, the older woman watched the young girl as she carefully placed her coat on a hook fastened to the back of the door. It was soon replaced with a long white apron as she began to place the bottles on large cooking sheets. The unsuspecting flock had no idea that it was, even now, being prepared to embark on a voyage of purification that would ensure its longevity through the long winter months to come. With the clanging of bottles resonating in her ears, Jessie found herself reflecting on her own two daughters who were only slightly younger than Mabel. At twenty, Murdina was completing her second year as a nursing assistant at the Baddeck hospital. The youngest, Mary, had just recently decided to join her brother Seumas in Sydney, where she had found gainful employment as a housekeeper to a wealthy Arab family living just behind Charlotte Street. Jessie realized that, even with the sounds of Mabel's work, she could not conceal the fact that the large house now seemed terribly empty. There was just the three of them and, for the first time, Jessie imagined the feeling that must have swept over Archie following Hannah's death. He was the older generation making way for the younger one. Had he felt as lonely as she did now? Had he felt that he still had a purpose, that he still belonged? Jessie thought of his beloved scythe and the comforting reassurance that it always seemed to bring. *Bheir do shlat agus do lorg comhfhurtachd dhomh.* (Thy rod and thy staff, they comfort me.) For the second time that day, she contemplated the Bible and the folded piece of brittle paper that it had safeguarded if not concealed for all these years. She looked through the kitchen window across the loch to Daniel and Tina's place.

When the darkness came, it appeared so suddenly that there was virtually no time to prepare oneself. It was as though the moon had passed before the sun as the world had gone so black, so quickly and without the slightest warning. *"Cuir uisge anns a' choire. 'S bidh mi dèonach air tì!"* (Put water in the kettle. I will be wanting tea!) If nothing else, Jessie knew that it was not the voice of God or even a *bòcan* for that matter. Her vision had remained fixed and her mind wandered aimlessly to the point that she had not taken note of her son as he proceeded down the side of the house, filling the box at the foot of the stone foundation with shovelfuls of sawdust from the wagon. It was never beyond him to play a practical joke and even Mabel was growing somewhat accustomed to his surprising and oftentimes whimsical antics.

"A Dhonnchaidh, chuir thu eagal orm!" (Duncan, you scared me!) While Jessie's words bounced off the glass, there had still been sufficient volume to carry them to her son's ears on the other side. Little proof of the culprit's identity was required as he proceeded to press his face into the pane to create a smudged image, obviously intent on placating his mother by quickly lightening the mood.

"A Mhamaidh, tha thu ann an cèo. Dh' fhuirich thu ro fhada anns an taigh-chòcaireachd. Tha thu a' fàs 'nad phicill mar chàch!" (Mamma, you are in a mist. You stayed too long in the kitchen. You are becoming a pickle like the others!) Mother and son soon found themselves laughing at the ridiculousness of the situation to say nothing of his analysis of her state of mind. *"Gabhaidh mi cupa tì a dh' aithghearr."* (I will take a cup of tea shortly.) If nothing else, he was intent on having his refreshment and Jessie knew that the impish one had become as much a "tea granny" as had his father before him. She smiled and shook her finger in his direction as a begrudging form of acknowledgment and then turned inward towards the stove and her work.

"Mabel, himself will soon be in for a cuppa. We had better make room for the pot on the stove. I do not believe that a cup of vinegar would sit well with him right now although it might do wonders in straightening out his mischievous face!" The clanging of bottles was replaced by laughter as the two women went about their business with renewed vigour in putting the kettle on and making up a small plate of sweets for a *strùpag*. For the first time, Jessie noticed that Mabel was finally beginning to show and thought how much it suited her. She was a strong young woman and would carry the bairn well; there was no doubt of that. Jessie's thoughts once again returned to Archie and how wonderful it would have been to watch as he held his first great grandchild in his lanky arms. Would that child not continue to proudly carry the MacDonald name?

The brisk autumn wind was the first thing to greet the members of the congregation as they approached the main doors in departing the Kirk following morning service. It was there even before the Reverend Fraser who stood on the front step with his clerical robes swirling about him and the white tabs bobbing up and down around his neck. In waiting her turn to shake hands and exchange pleasantries with the minister, Jessie thought how grateful he must be for the tight weave of the woollen robes. She mused that, today of all days, he would be thankful to be a man not only of the cloth but also a man of the tightly woven cloth. As she scanned the heads of the people now gathering to chat below at the foot of the steps, she hoped that she would be able to have a brief word with the clerk of session.

Daniel Erskine had been elected the new clerk at the October meeting of session. The previous month, the congregation had undertaken the important task of first nominating and then electing a new elder to fill the vacancy created by Archie's death. Hector Urquhart would join Angus Grant and Daniel in guiding the work of the congregation and in offering leadership to its members. It was on this basis that Jessie now approached Daniel, as he stood with Tina who was engaged in an animated conversation with Margaret MacGregor concerning her latest batch of *maragan dubha*. (blood puddings) This time, she had decided to use a bit less onion and they had turned out exceptionally well. She would bring a few samples around later in the week to prove her point and had no doubt but that she would be on the receiving end of many a rave compliment.

Daniel had shown no surprise when Jessie tapped him gently on the arm and asked if she might have a moment with him. Her first words were of congratulations for his recent election. She was proud that, of all the men in the congregation, he should be the one chosen to succeed Archie. Daniel smiled knowingly and thanked her for her generous words. And then, almost as if in passing, she inquired as to the possibility of making arrangements for a private time with him at some point during the week to discuss a matter that had arisen from her study of the Bible. It would not take long and she was eager to gain his insights so that she might better understand. Daniel was only too pleased to accommodate the request and they agreed to meet in the late afternoon of the following Wednesday.

As she proceeded down the loch road three days later, Jessie knew that her arrival had been well timed, even though she and Daniel had not set a precise hour for the meeting. In the distance, she saw Ismay and *Taghta* walking away from her in the opposite direction on their way home. It was apparent that the class was completed and that, in all likelihood, Tina, Kristy and Daniel would now be gathering round a fresh pot of tea on the kitchen table. She assured herself that she would not disturb them for long; her questions would be brief. She prayed that her anguish would then be over. She prayed that, with Daniel's understanding and hopefully his answers, she would at least know, finally.

After initial pleasantries were exchanged with Tina and Kristy including an offer of a cup of tea that she gratefully declined, Jessie was taken by Daniel into the front parlour. Daniel noted the family Bible in her hands and knew that she had indeed come prepared to discuss her biblical quandary in earnest. *"A Dhomhnaill, tha feum orm air cuideachadh. Tha feum orm mineachadh air seo."* (Daniel, I need your help. I need an explanation of this.) She had opened the Bible to retrieve the folded piece of yellowed paper and proceeded to pass it to him with care. She remained standing in front of him, waiting in silence as he first looked at her quizzically, unfolded it and then strained to read its faded text:

July 12, 1840

> I, Captain John Moyer, by the powers invested in me as captain of the vessel *Elizabeth Anne*, do hereby place in the custody and safekeeping of Archibald and Hannah MacDonald an infant boy orphaned this day at birth by a passenger in my charge. May his body and soul be forever in their care and that of Almighty God.
>
> signed: John Moyer

July 12, 1840, was the date of her husband's birth. She had a right to know.

Daniel looked up from the paper and stared into Jessie's waiting eyes. It was as if clouds had parted and the sunshine had fallen on a sombre dark place. He knew everything all at once: he realized he was obliged to speak; he must address the matter put to him; he was compelled to relieve the anguish in her voice. It took but a second for Daniel to appreciate that it would no longer be a betrayal of the promise given to Archie and Hannah. It was a matter of honour; he would not lie to Jessie or deny her the answers she sought. He respected her far too much for that and perhaps it was truly God's will and providence that she should now know. He motioned to her to be seated.

The *Elizabeth Anne* had set sail from Tarbert, Isle of Harris and Lochmaddy, North Uist in June of 1840. Among her passengers were the cleared families of Scalpay, the MacAulays, MacDonalds, Grants, MacKinnons, MacGregors, Urquharts, Erskines and Fergusons, who came to settle on the land around *Loch Dubh*. One of the passengers was Hannah MacDonald's younger sister, Catriona, who was with child and bore the disgrace of being unwed. Some saw her death in childbirth as the retribution of sin although none who looked into Hannah's eyes on that day, as the body was committed to the deep, would have allowed such words to flow from their lips. All that was known was that the bairn's father was a philandering rogue by the name of Fraser who had come down from the hills and had departed as quickly as he had first appeared. The wee one would be named Malcolm after the girls' father who, along with his wife, had mercifully been taken to eternal rest several years before and thus spared the humiliation and shame.

"*Och, a' Sheasag, b 'e am mac fhéin e. Thog iad e. Ghràdhaich iad e. Bha Calum mar mhac aig Eàirdsidh agus Anna gu dearbh. Leig dha mar sin.*" (Oh Jessie, he was their own son all the same. They raised him. They loved him. Malcolm was truly Archie and Hannah's son. Leave it thus.) With an almost quiet reverence, Daniel folded the paper and motioned to Jessie for the Bible. Her eyes never once left his face as he carefully recommitted the paper and its story to sacred repose among the pages of scripture. She rose slowly as he came forward in returning the Bible to her care. There was only the faintest trace of a smile on her face as Jessie expressed her thanks for both his recollections and for his words of advice. With that, she shook his hand and departed for home.

Jessie was glad to finally be alone as she walked down the loch road with the growing darkness and silence blanketing her every step. Duncan and Mabel would be waiting and, no doubt, had begun to worry after her. Och indeed, her questions had been answered all too truthfully and, for the first time, she wondered if she had really wanted to know. Jessie was now faced with her own troubling dilemma. She must decide whether the family Bible, which she continued to carry closely, would be the final re-pository for the faded words that had been brought back to life. There was so much to think about all at once. She would need time. That much she owed to her children, to herself and to Malcolm.

From her vantage point on the back steps, it appeared as though they had positioned themselves in a straight line like tiny soldiers, all of them with official head-dress now dutifully removed. Every April, she would look out to find that their white peaked hats had been doffed as if prescribed by some longstanding regimental tradition and put away for another year. There was almost a sense that they were paying homage to the arrival of spring. But then, she certainly would not complain; she much preferred the sight of their flat black heads. It was good riddance to the *curraicean geamhraidh* (wintery caps) or toques as some of the people down in the town called them. Thankfully, winter was a spent force that had come all too quickly, lingered and departed begrudgingly. Was it not about time for it to beat a hasty retreat from these hills? After all, it was lambing season and soon enough the flower garden would be in full bloom once again. She looked over towards the soggy plot of land beneath the apple trees that even now awaited the warm caress of the sun. *"Brisidh am fàsach a mach agus thig e fo bhlàth. Chum aiseirigh na beatha; chum aiseirigh an dòchais."* (The empty place will blossom and bud. To the resurrection of life; to the resurrection of hope.) Spring was always such a joyous time of year. Even the battalion of stoic black-headed fence posts seemed to delight in the warmth.

Margaret watched as James and the two boys, Charles and Albert, made their way towards the back field in the horse and wagon, shadowing the straight line of fence posts as they went. The harsh winter weather was forever damaging a number of them and it had become a yearly routine to reposition, and sometimes replace, those that had been mangled by the emerging frost. The ground was still a bit too wet for the planting of crops so the time was opportune for the mending of fences and other prepara-tory work in the fields and out buildings. For his part, Peter had gone off to the barn to build some much-needed new stalls. Two of the cows would soon freshen and extra space for the calves would eventually be needed.

With all her men accounted for, Margaret left the fresh crisp air behind and reluctantly returned to the kitchen where the forlorn-looking butter churn eagerly awaited her warm grasp.

As she entered the room through the back door, Margaret noted that Betty was already busying herself with the clean up of dishes from the morning meal. She was scraping the last bits of porridge from the bottom of the pot on the stove and unceremoniously shoveling them into an old cracked bowl that was often used to mix poultices. Its white surface now bore a jaundiced look from the numerous preparations of mustard plaster it had produced over the years. For now at least, looks did not matter. The scraps would be fed to the dog that, given the speed with which he always devoured them, was obviously more focused on the quality and quantity of the food than the appearance of the dinner ware.

Margaret positioned herself to the side of the churn while watching her daughter go about her business. She was ever mindful of the blessing of family. She and James were indeed fortunate to have all their children around them. Peter was working hard to hone his skills on the farm given that it would one day fall to him. Charles spent his winters cutting timber in the woods and, for the rest of the year, had a good job down at Angus Wright's sawmill. His money was dutifully saved in order to support his goal of becoming a carpenter's apprentice and eventually establishing himself as a tradesman in his own right. Betty was a big help around the house but Margaret increasingly sensed that these days were already numbered. She had been seeing a good deal of Jamie MacInnes the fiddler and, if her motherly instincts were correct, it was only a matter of time before her daughter would be a married woman. Albert, her sixteen year old "bairn," worked part time as a clerk at the Bank of Nova Scotia down in the town and hoped to be taken on as a permanent employee. Unlike Peter, he did not have the makings of a farmer and most definitely, unlike Charles, had absolutely no love of the woods. Even though it was almost seven years since the incident out back, Margaret understood the lingering fear. Yet this anxiety paled in comparison to the pain that had engulfed her at the mere thought of losing a child. She was indeed fortunate for the blessing of family.

So much had changed over those seven years. *Loch Dubh* had lost so many of its young people. With the exception of the Erskines and Grants, all families with older children had bid tearful farewells to loved ones down at the wharf. Through the side window, she looked over towards the manse and reflected on Jennie's loneliness without her children. Sandy and Matthew were now established in Sydney and Emily, following her graduation from the academy last spring, had been offered a steady job at the Baddeck Public Library. Although the county seat was a goodly distance away, it still provided many topics of conversation to the people of *Loch Dubh*, especially on long winter nights when they would gather around the stoves with tea, or perhaps something a bit stronger, in hand. There was talk, in jest of course, of renaming the village "Belldeck" in honour of Mabel Bell, who continued to do such wonderful things for the community, and Alexander, who persisted in playing with his kites and other such toys. There was a consensus that, while she would be sorely missed, Emily would indeed do well for herself elsewhere. As was the case with so many others, it was simply the way.

Margaret continued on a tour around the loch in her mind and considered the number of young people who were now gone from them. As she placed her hands on the slender wooden pole and brought the churn to life, she was struck by the cadence of the thought: they have gone away. The words sounded so terribly sad as if they were a lament, carrying a sense of passing. Elizabeth Urquhart was now married in Boularderie with a family of her own while her brother Allan was at the steel works in Sydney. The Reverend Rod MacDonald was in *An Abhainn Mheadhonach* while his sister Catherine was working in Baddeck and brother Murdoch had gone off to the western plains on the harvest trains in search of fame and fortune. The other MacDonald family, Jessie's brood, had Seumas in Sydney at the steel works, Murdina in Baddeck at the hospital and Mary in Sydney in domestic service. And finally, Morag Ferguson was still in Boston and, from all the most recent accounts, about to be married. It was as if a battle had taken place on these shores. True enough, blood had not been shed but it may as well have been. The young people were gone from sight and would, in time, be gone from memory. For the first time in a very long while, she thought of Andrew MacDonald. The younger children were growing up not having known him. He was just a name to them, a pile of stones at the top of the cemetery hill. Margaret felt consolation in the thought that he was with Archie and Hannah.

"A Mhamaidh, tha e dà uair dheug. Cuiridh mi poit tì air an stòbh. Bi na fir a' tighinn air ais gu luath." (Mamma, it is twelve o'clock. I will put the tea pot on the stove. The men will be returning soon enough.) Betty had gently and somewhat reluctantly placed her hand on her mother's shoulder to remind her of the passage of time. She had seen that look before and realized that Margaret was deep in thought. Sometimes it was best not to disturb her but, still, the others would indeed arrive soon with large appetites requiring a full spread on the table.

It was not long thereafter that James and the two boys returned from the back fields with their work completed and so terribly pleased with themselves. A number of posts had been in need of replacing and there was a sense of accomplishment and confidence that the repairs would ensure that the natural traipsing tendencies of the cows would be offset by their masterful work. Betty cast a playful knowing glance in Margaret's direction. *"An irioslachd; chum gu'n dean iad beagan uaill' asda féin. Ach, nam b'urrainn dhaibh poit tì a dhèanamh!"* (Their humility; that they may boast themselves a little. If only they could make a pot of tea!) She could not resist the temptation and both mother and daughter broke into spirited laughter at the expense of the three, dutifully humbled men standing in front of them in the doorway.

Albert was sent to summon Peter from his work in the barn as his father and brother were relegated to the wash basin in the porch. James had just playfully splashed water over Charles' head and was in the process of wiping his hands dry when Albert suddenly appeared on the back step looking at them through the gray meshing of the screen door. Only once before had he seen his son's face so drained of life and now the memory of that time, which had been banished from his mind as surely as the bottle from his hand, was upon him. Albert stood before him gasping for breath and struggling for the words that fought to stay locked within him. Finally and plaintively, they somehow managed to escape from him. *"A Thighearna. A bhobain, thig gun dàil. Is e Peadair a tha ann."* (Oh Lord. Pappa, come quickly. It's Peter.)

James found his son lying in a massive pool of blood. There was never any doubt about the cause; the answer was apparent from the dark crimsoned stains on the bull's horns. It was so much like his son to never fear, to always be so trusting. James lovingly retrieved Peter from the stall and proceeded to carry him across the yard towards the house. There was no urgency, unlike the episode nearly seven years ago in the woods when he had frantically borne a bloodied Albert in his arms. This time, there were no tears or pleading with God. There was nothing but him and his beautiful eldest son. There was nothing else. In that brief period of time that lasted an eternity, James cradled Peter in those very same arms and walked the fairly short distance to the back door that now seemed so terribly terribly far away.

Peter was buried three days later. During the weeks that followed, the people of *Loch Dubh* spoke quietly among themselves about the event and commented on the tragic circumstances that had taken someone so young, someone with such promise. Yet what stayed most with them was Margaret's strength. Not one person could recall seeing her shed a single tear throughout the entire ordeal. She held herself with a stoic dignity that belied the tremendous grief of her loss, a grief that was evident in the faces of the entire family, everyone except her. So many of the women wanted to reach out to their friend but felt restrained by the look in her eyes. It was as if she quite intentionally did not seek or desire comfort. Only Rachael Ferguson and Ida MacDonald could commiserate in silence and relate to a mother's loss. The age of the child was of no consequence; a part of you died. As with the body, it was also all too easy for the spirit to die. It was as much a natural response as a Christian duty. Rachael and Ida would pray for Margaret and for the resurrection of her broken spirit. What more could they do? Feelings of absolute helplessness surrounded them all but, unlike their shawls, they provided no warming comfort. There was nothing but a numbing chill on their bones.

With time and the increasing sultriness of the late-spring sun, the soggy bit of land beneath the apple trees was transformed into a vibrant colourful swath of life. The garden remained solitary as if it were an illusion waiting for an unsuspecting person to walk into its midst only to discover that it was nothing more than a self-induced deception. May 28, 1909 was the day that would have marked Peter's twenty-first birthday. It was also the day that Margaret first returned to her garden.

She sat there for the better part of an hour under the crab-apple tree, in the exact same place where she had rested so many times before. Yet it was different now. She was not there to feast her senses. Her eyes were not flooded with colour, her nose was not enraptured with fragrance. She was there to speak. During the wake, the funeral, the committal and the endless expressions of sympathy that followed, she had forced herself to be a pillar of strength, of courage, of resignation. Now she looked over, beyond the cemetery where Peter lay, up the darkening slopes of *Beinn-mo-Mhulaid* and into the expansive blue skies that stretched beyond. *"An robh mo chionta cho olc? An e mo dhìoghaltas? A mhamaidh 's a bhobain, na càiricheabh mo pheacadh air. Bithibh gu math dha; is dleas sin dhà. Is dleas sin do mhac mo ghaoil."* (Was my transgression so evil? Is it my punishment? Mamma and Pappa, do not lay my sins to his charge. Be good to him; that much is due him. That is due my beloved son.) With that, Margaret stood as if about to leave, having said aloud what had remained trapped deep inside. Once more, she looked into the sky but this time the words did not come. *Tha mi 'g a ionndrainn. Is ann a tha tìde bhi falbh.* (I miss him. It is time to be going.) Then, with words having been both spoken and pondered, she left her garden as quickly as she had come.

For Margaret and the rest of the family, each day became an eternity. There was a void that was always felt and yet seldom spoken about. It was simply understood. Life would go on and grieving, even within the family, would be done in private. Each had their own way. In the seclusion of the many kitchens around the loch, people commented on how the MacGregors were seen going forward with their lives. Yet in the confines of each MacGregor heart, they were walking through a dream. To the eye, the daily routines went on as before: meals were prepared, cows were milked and crops were tended. To the heart, the pain came and lingered. It would not leave.

It frequently happened that Margaret found herself waking in the middle of the night and unable to fall back to sleep. She would invariably escape to the front veranda to watch the moonlight dance over the surface of the loch, illuminating the stark porcelain-like profile of the Kirk as it sat under the brooding gaze of *Beinn-mo-Mhulaid*. From a distance, the lone seated figure in the long white nightdress would have been easily mistaken for a *bòcan* resting momentarily from its mischievous exploits. *Is amhuil mo bheatha is aisling eadar cadal is faireachadh. An ceò-éideadh mar cheathach air beanntaibh.* (My life is like a dream between sleeping and waking. The shroud of mist as mist on the hills.) For the first time in her life, Margaret truly came to realize just how appropriate the mountain's name truly was.

There were two developments that, in quite different yet symbolic ways, reflected the dreadful sadness that had descended upon the MacGregor household. The old cracked bowl, which had so often held scraps of porridge, was placed back on the top shelf of the pantry. Its use would once again be limited to the mixing of poultices and mustard plaster. The day of Peter's death was the day that the dog had gone missing. Something told them that he would not return; in his own way he had gone looking for Peter; he had gone to be with Peter. The second change had a more visual and lingering impact. James' hair began to turn white, almost overnight it seemed, and he took on the appearance of a *bodach* well before his time. Margaret would never refer to him as such even on the odd occasion when she attempted to force a smile in the presence of the children. She knew that, if she were to be truthful, she would be compelled to call him a *bodach uisge beatha*. (Old Man of Whisky) It was as though she was looking back through time. She watched as he carried the bags of sugar across the fields and into the solitude and consolation afforded him once again by the woods.

Margaret peered out from behind the curtain that draped the dining-room window as the figure was finally consumed by the thick evergreen trees. *"A Thighearna! Có is urrainn oidheam sam bith a thoirt as?. . . Mo mhac mùirneach."* (Oh Lord! Who can bring any sense out of it? . . . my dearly-beloved son.) She then did something that she had promised herself she would not do. For the first time in a very long while, Margaret cried.

🖾 Chapter Fourteen 🖾

July 1909 – July 1910

When I was young I truly loved
To be among the hills,
And others thought that I was silly;
John MacDonald
Song to America (song)

Thug mise cion nuair bha mi òg
Do bhith an còir nam beann,
Is saoilidh càch gu'n robh mi gòrach;
John MacDonald
Òran Do America (òran)

An air machine. It remained so difficult to imagine a man flying through the heavens like a sparrow, even though she had actually seen it with her own eyes. Still, the contraption may have been many things but a graceful sparrow it most assuredly was not. Its wings looked so big and bulky in proportion to the size of its body. Even from the safety of her vantage point on the frozen shoreline, it appeared so clumsy in its reluctant ascent into the blue skies over the bay with the snow-capped trees on the slopes of *Beinn Bhreagh* as a background. Everyone had become so accustomed to Mr. Bell's cluttering the sky with an endless array of kites. Indeed, one of the old farmers from the outskirts had nicknamed them *"eòin Bhell"* (Bell's Birds) and the term had rapidly fallen into common usage throughout the town, in the English at least. But now, this was quite a different matter altogether. There was a sense of importance about it and she wondered if it would be something that would be looked back upon and remembered as a memorable moment in time. Still in all, this was not the Thames of London, the Seine of Paris or even the Ottawa of the Dominion's own capital. It was Baddeck Bay. It was difficult to fathom how anything of any great significance could ever happen here.

Emily looked out the side window of the library and stared across the calm waters towards the Bell residence on the peninsula that protruded out into the Bras d'Or Lake like a slender green finger pointing at Washabuk across the way. Both the extremity of land and the grand mansion that was perched upon its craggy face were known as *Beinn Bhreagh* and had, following numerous and protracted real estate wranglings, become the private fiefdom of Alexander and Mabel Bell. From her vantage point at the window, Emily could see only the western tip of Boularderie Island off in the background. Concealed behind the mansion and the adjoining robe of evergreens was the North Shore of Boularderie as it wound its way eastward towards the open Atlantic. This was the route that she had taken so many times before by steamer as it proceeded down the great Bras d'Or Channel, passing Cape Dauphin and turning left in the direction of the North Shore and New Carlisle. She thought how interesting it was that, from where she now positioned herself, the way home was hidden from her view. In some respects, it was symbolic. It would be a passage less frequently travelled.

Emily's thoughts were now of her father and mother and how they would have enjoyed the scene that had played itself out on the frozen surface of these waters only five months ago. There had been nothing but admiration for Mr. McCurdy and the bravery he had shown in allowing himself to be committed to the seat of the flying machine, not once but twice in as many days. The second day, the Wednesday morning, saw an even larger crowd, in sleighs, on skates and just standing about, that watched "John A.D." climb into the contraption that he himself had designed. Perhaps he had been lured back by the heightened anticipation of the assembled audience or perhaps it was the enticing name that had been purposefully bestowed upon it — *The Silver Dart*. The moniker had been the cause of much laughter given that the machine was anything but silver in colour or dart-like in either appearance or speed. Emily chuckled to herself as she conjured up an image of Mr. Bell coercing Mr. McCurdy to be seated in *The Grimy Snail*. There simply would not have been the same appeal. Perhaps McCurdy had also taken a hearty swig of the medicinal *uisge beatha* as much to instill confidence in his mechanical contrivance as to fortify himself against the raw February chill. Regardless, he had flown over the frozen surface of Baddeck Bay and made history in the Dominion as well as the entire Empire. It was possible that she had indeed witnessed something that she would one day recall with excitement and pride for her children.

It was as if the warm July breeze was pushing her away from the open window, with its panoramic vista, towards her chair and the administrative duties of the reference desk that awaited her. Her children. For the first time in several days, she thought of Murdina Jennie in far-off Boston. Her daughter would now be four and a half years old and the only remembrances she had were those of a tiny infant. She was a little girl who, judging by the photos that were dutifully forwarded each December with Effie and Liam's Christmas card, had the angular facial features of the MacGregors, to say nothing of the gangly legs. Emily was now seated across from the main doors of the library and intentionally busied herself with processing the stack of returned books that was neatly piled on the corner of her desk.

She still found it so terribly difficult to grasp the reality of Peter's death, killed so tragically in a senseless barn accident — a barn not so dissimilar from another where they had ironically enough created life together.

Emily could remember, as if it were yesterday, how she had opened the letter from her parents, read the news about Peter and did not cry. Even for her, it would be difficult to describe what it was she had felt. It was everything and nothing all at the same time. There was sadness and yet an odd feeling of relief. There was loss and, God have mercy, a pang of vindication. Yet all these thoughts coalesced in evoking both guilt and shame that resurrected a dreadful sense of unworthiness. Was it not precisely the same feeling she had borne during those terrible spring days exactly five years ago when she had prepared herself for exile in Boston? Now, in just a few short weeks, she would take the steamer and return to *Loch Dubh* to spend vacation time with her parents. She would make a point of visiting the cemetery. If nothing else, that at least was due Peter.

It had not taken Emily long to adjust to the routine of her position as assistant librarian. She enjoyed meeting the local townsfolk who crossed the library's threshold with increased regularity. There was a certain predictability about her job and her life in Baddeck that was quietly comforting and made her feel worthy of the respect that was shown her. In just the past twelve months since her graduation from the academy and acceptance of the current position, she had come to the realization that a great deal about her home in *Loch Dubh* was slipping from her memory as it was from her in other ways. It was neither an unconscious development or a result of circumstance; she willed it to be so. Still, she could not deny that she had always looked forward to sleeping in her old room, to visiting with her parents and to making a fuss over her *Rionnag*. Most of all, she had looked forward to seeing Christopher and spending time with him in long walks down by the loch and far up into the hills near the woods where some of the loveliest wild flowers bloomed. Now all that was about to change as a result of her own choosing. Quite deliberately, she indeed willed it to be so.

It was something that had slowly developed over time, unlike the plot of some classical novel that so often portrayed it as an instantaneous, almost magical, flash of recognition. Not so; Emily and Christopher had fallen deeply in love. There had been no magical spark when they met that day in late August 1905 upon his arrival in *Loch Dubh* to take up duties as school master. Emily could look back now at those earlier times and realize that neither of them had ever conceived of the possibility. Perhaps they couldn't have, given that they both had been so much like children, uncertain as to their own emotional maturity. But as with all children, they had grown and come to the understanding that they were much more than merely close friends. A defining moment had been *Rionnag*'s death and the way Christopher had comforted her. It seemed so ironic that something so wonderful should be born from the death of something so dear to her.

Emily's decision a year ago to accept the position at the library had far-reaching consequences in *Loch Dubh*. Christopher had always felt somewhat hesitant about pursuing Emily while living with her parents. The watchful eyes, especially of the Reverend Fraser, seemed to be ever present. There was a concern, if not preoccupation, as to whether it would destroy his relationship with Jennie and Duncan. Increasingly, they seemed to enjoy his company as a boarder under their roof. But would they continue to enjoy it, or even tolerate it, if they were aware of his true intentions towards their daughter? Christopher had never before felt such an array of emotions and, with each passing day, was convinced that a proposal of marriage would soon be on his lips. Perhaps the time was not right; maybe the circumstances were not yet appropriate. In any event, Emily's decision to take up residence in Baddeck did much to distill his thinking and make the choices open to him all the more clear.

It had been shortly after the resumption of classes the previous September that he first wrote to education authorities inquiring after possible vacancies for the next academic year in and around the Baddeck area. Early April saw the arrival of a letter notifying him of an upcoming position at the Baddeck Academy and inviting him to apply should he wish to receive consideration. An intensive interview followed several weeks later that eventually resulted in an offer of appointment based on the assumption of his continued interest and availability. For him, confirmation would be a clear indication of the choice he had made, a choice that went well beyond his more-immediate career aspirations. That same night at his desk in the manse, he drafted a letter of acceptance with the realization that, with every stroke of the pen, the course of his life was about to reveal itself. Years later in looking back at that defining moment, he would appreciate that it had not really been so terribly difficult a decision to make. Even though he knew it to be the right and only one, what troubled him still was how he was to communicate this decision to others.

One thing that he had never fully taken into account was the predicament he would have in sharing the news with the students and parents of *Loch Dubh*. This he did as a courtesy before returning to Glace Bay at the end of the school year. It was heart-wrenching for him to say good-bye to everyone, but especially the little ones, whom he had come to know so well after four years in their presence. In many ways, he had been made to feel a part of their families, of their lives. This was yet another aspect of the teaching profession for which his training had not prepared him.

He would miss everyone but there were particular individuals, other than Jennie and Duncan of course, who had grown especially near and dear to him. He thought of Ismay Campbell and Kristy Erskine. Over the past year, they had formed a unique bond that broadened his appreciation of what it meant to be a teacher in ways that he could never have imagined. It also enhanced his knowledge of the perseverance of the human spirit that was now brought into even greater focus in the most unexpected of ways.

Both he and Kristy had decided that they would sit with Ismay to inform her personally of his decision and, thereby, lessen the fear of change that would be brought to her life. The news was broken at the completion of the class seated around the Erskine's kitchen table with both Kristy and Christopher taking turns in gently offering assurances that all would be well. There was a momentary pause as the tiny blue eyes stared off in space as if formulating a response with the greatest of care. "I will miss your words and laughter but I am surrounded by smiling faces. I will still have Kristy and *Taghta* to guide me. I can hear your happiness and know that God will watch over you for us." Then there was silence. She was finished; she was content with her response. It was how she held her head and quietly folded her hands in her lap that signalled further words of explanation were not required. Ismay had spoken so briefly but, in so doing, had said so much. It was the first and only time that Christopher was moved close to tears during his entire four years with, as his mother continued to refer to them, "the Scotch people up in the mountains."

Christopher had been caught completely off guard by the girl's comments and had difficulty in finding words to formulate a reply, if indeed one would have been appropriate. The quiet was finally broken as Kristy slowly leaned down towards Ismay, stroked her hair and then whispered in her ear. *"Tha thu a' faicinn móran mo ghràdhag."* (You see many things my dear little one.) When it came, the response was once again uttered in a way that was as soft as it was confirming, not only for herself but for the two teachers who sat before her. *"Dìreach. Dìreach."* (Just so. Just so.) Christopher did not want to ask; he would not inquire as to the meaning of the words. He felt he had already heard and been given far more than he deserved.

Christopher would also miss Duncan and Jennie. They had been such gracious hosts to him, having welcomed him into their home and hearts with unconditional warmth. He decided that one of his first duties upon returning to Glace Bay would be to purchase a set of six cups and saucers, to match the tea pot, as a parting expression of thanks and gratitude. Jennie would like that and he would promise to return for a *strùpag* so that the cups could be properly broken in as had been the pot with laughter and good conversation. On that late June morning, it was not a tearful farewell, at least not for him, when he departed the Fraser household for the wharf and the voyage south. Something told him he would be in their presence again but not, in all likelihood, as an acquaintance. God willing, it would be as family and, if he had any say in the matter, it would be sooner rather than later.

Emily had now processed the incoming books and placed them on a small table behind her desk. They would be recommitted to their places on the shelves just as soon as a quiet moment presented itself. There was still a mound of paperwork demanding her attention, including numerous requests for the recently published novel, **Anne of Green Gables**, by that

Montgomery woman. All the while, from the corner of her eye, she could see Roderick Matheson from *Beinn an t-Sealgair* (Hunter's Mountain) reading his cherished newspapers. He was an old widower who had been taken off the farm as a result of failing health and now lived in town with his married daughter. Emily could always sense his longing to be back on the land where he was raised and where he belonged. Baddeck was where he resided; it was not his home. Having lived so long with the rhythmic flow of the hours of the day and the seasons of the year as his guide, he needed a sense of continuity in his life. It was for this reason that, every Monday, Wednesday and Friday, he would arrive and spend several hours reading **Mac Talla**, Cape Breton's own Gaelic newspaper. It did not matter that it had ceased publication five years earlier. He would read and reread the local and world reports, history, proverbs and correspondence from back issues. Emily could see that he found a comfort in the words, as if sitting under a lilac tree in full bloom with its bouquet cascading down like a fragrant blanket. She smiled over in his direction. The only thing missing from the picture before her was a good cup of tea. At that moment, she wished she could make him one.

The tranquillity of the library was abruptly shattered as three very matronly looking women swept through the main doors and proceeded to engage in an impromptu and rather clamorous conversation just inside. The talk was of poor Mary Patterson whose husband had been taken in the cholera epidemic that had spread across the town during the winter. With thirty deaths in all, most families had been touched in one way or another. Today's topic happened to focus on poor Mary and the fact that she no longer had a man to do the heavy chores around the house and provide other services. It was indeed a tragic loss; you could see it on her sullen face that was ageing so with each passing day. Poor dear.

At first, Emily was mildly amused by the boisterous comments that reminded her of the barkers she had seen and heard several years ago at a travelling carnival in Boston. It was only after a most lenient lapse of several minutes that she finally screwed up her courage to interrupt the midway festivities that continued on unabated. "Excuse me ladies, but might I ask you to lower the fullness of your conversation just a bit? I am afraid it may serve as a distraction for the people using the library." As was ever her way, Emily held herself gracefully and spoke softly as befitted the circumstance.

Silence immediately descended upon the library once more but not without a price. Even so, it was not destined to last long; others were more than determined in seeing to that. "Young lady, I do not know from where you come. However, you obviously have no idea as to whom you are speaking in such rabid tones. I will have you know that I am a personal acquaintance of Mrs. Bell and that I shall inform her of the insolent behaviour of the staff at the very library that she herself helped establish. Whatever next!" Shocked by the vehemence of the woman's rage, Emily could not image Hades having more flames than what now shot from the eyes of Mrs. Rose Clarke. The young librarian knew full well that she had just been summarily dismissed out of hand and that, in all likelihood, she and Rose would probably never be close.

Emily quickly busied herself with the papers on the desk and her head remained bowed as the flames continued to be discharged in her general direction. She knew it to be a fact for indeed she could feel each and every one against her skin. It was because of this distraction that she had not taken notice of the person who now stood directly in front of her. Roderick Matheson placed his hand over hers and, in raising her head, Emily could see an unmistakable twinkle in his eyes. His voice was strong and confident as he proceeded to speak, quite intentionally, to a much wider audience. *"Mar mhèilich nan caorach! Bha mi air an ais air an fhearann car tiota. Feumaidh iad lomairt math gu beachd. Sealbh agus latha math dhuit."* (Just so much bleating of sheep! For a moment, I was back on the farm. All they need is a good shearing, most assuredly. Good luck and good day to you.) He winked at her and, with that, shuffled past the three onlookers who stood in silence and complete ignorance of the indignities that had just been showered upon them.

A subtle grin of absolute satisfaction appeared on the face of the assistant librarian as Rose Clarke and her entourage finally departed in a huff. Emily was grateful to the old man for teaching her a valuable lesson in a way that all the books surrounding her could not. There was something about *Loch Dubh* as there was about *Beinn an t-Sealgair*. It was in the air as well as the blood. It was in her still. She was forced to accept the fact that it always would be and she was thankful for it as well as the way in which the truth had been revealed to her. She returned to the window and stared into the vastness of the blue skies over *Beinn Bhreagh* and Boularderie. *"Tapadh leibh."* (Thank you.)

It was one of those rare late-September evenings when one could sit outdoors and bask in the sensuous beauty of both seasons. It was as though Mother Nature herself had taken a brief respite from the pickling pot that perked away on the stove with its mixture of the lush savours of summer and bitter tangs of autumn. The warm breeze encircled the loch and softly rustled the leaves high up on the hills that even now had begun to change colour, proving that a mischievous and somewhat premature frost had already undertaken at least one nightly visitation. It was one of those evenings to simply sit and allow the beauty to envelop each one of the senses. Mother Nature would return to her pot soon enough and this interlude would most assuredly disappear as quickly as the mist from the hills on a sunny day.

Sarah had brought out some kitchen chairs after supper and was now busily positioning them on the front veranda. If it had not been for the fact that they were placed in a large semi-circle facing the loch, one might have thought that an impromptu prayer meeting was being held outdoors. It certainly was to be nothing of the kind, at least on this Saturday evening anyway. Sarah relished time together with family and friends; perhaps it was nothing more than a factor of age, of growing old. Still in all, she enjoyed the singing of the old songs and the sharing of tales from yesteryear, be they based on historical fact or were just so much concoction. Her Hector was terrible at spinning a yarn and seldom did the truth have a role to play. He was forever taking great delight in scaring the young ones half to death with his stories of the *bòcain* and ghoulies. On more than one occasion she had jokingly threatened to notify the Reverend Fraser that one Hector Urquhart, of late duly elected elder of the Kirk, had many more than the proverbial ten devils in him. He would only laugh at her and continue to make eerie noises and strange faces as his self-professed *sgeula beag fìor* (true little story) invariably played itself out to a frightful climactic end.

Her Hector was so much like his father, God rest his soul. The old people had been pious right enough but they still found time to gather together, to chat and yes to laugh. Was not laughter also a gift bestowed upon them by the Almighty? She glanced over her left shoulder as the sun began almost reluctantly to disappear from the western sky behind the crest of *Beinn-mo-Mhulaid*. Her eyes fixed on the now shadowed Kirk at the far end of the loch and she knew she had answered her own question. *"A Thighearna, an lànachd aoibhneis. Thug thu dhuinn a nasgaidh e."* (Oh Lord, the fullness of joy. You gave it to us as a gift.). The reassuring words pleased her.

As she rounded the corner of the house, Sarah could see both Hector and Donald up at the barn readying the animals for the night. She stopped there for a moment to indulge herself before returning to the kitchen. Without question, Donald was his father's son. He resembled him so and, although she would never admit it to another living soul, she was pleased that he had the stories in him as well. Was he not a picture of the handsome young Hector who had taken her hand in marriage all those years ago and given her three beautiful children? For the moment, she chose to ignore all thoughts of the kitchen that beckoned her to return. Sarah would sit on the back step for a wee bit longer. This too was a gift she would give herself.

For one of the few times in her life, Sarah was immensely grateful for the fair distance between the house and the barn. How would she possibly go about explaining the riotous laughter that suddenly erupted from her as she sat there by herself? Perhaps Hector would act on his own veiled threat to have her committed to what he called the *taigh-cuthaich* (madhouse) in Sydney. She never knew if in fact there was such a place but, at the same time, was determined to not tempt fate by inquiring further. It would be equally difficult to account for the vision that had so suddenly crossed her mind: Queen Victoria sitting majestically at the kitchen table, in the presence of Elizabeth, Donald and Allan, as they all enjoyed a wee *strùpag*, complete with golden-crowned bread. The days of their youth were long gone and now only a scant memory as were the days of Victoria's reign. Yet Sarah was content in the knowledge that her children had a happy upbringing and had wanted for very little. Most of all, they had been raised surrounded by unreserved displays of affection and love, unlike herself. Never once did she bring to mind a memory of her mother.

It was all too obvious that the laughter had subsided as quickly as it had come, almost as if it had been banished to a far corner or recess of a darkened attic. Sarah had unwittingly conjured up an image of that day long ago when she had watched Elizabeth proudly stroll down by the loch in her lilac-coloured frock. There had been no doubt; Sarah had seen her mother in the window. Right enough, it had been nothing more than a reflection distorted by light and shadow. As if to reassure herself of her present state of mind, Sarah reached out and plucked a blade of grass growing by the edge of the step. She gently stroked it with her fingers and found herself speaking aloud. *"Cha mhi mo mhàthair. Tha i 's an ùir ma's math mo chùimhne. Cha till i a chaoidh."* (I am not my mother! She is buried if I re-member well. She will never return.) The thoughts were brought to life in a clear booming voice as if the increased volume would further assert their validity. She could not allow such foolishness to trouble her, especially this evening with company coming. Sarah hoped that Hector would not tell his stories about the *bòcain*. Sometimes they were all too real, even for her.

The kitchen was strangely still as Sarah entered through the back door to find the dishes still in their places on the table, eagerly awaiting her arrival. *"Chan eil mi sibh a' smaoineachadh air a' chuid as lugha. Tha sibh fìor gu dearbh. M'obair, m'obair."* (At least I am not imagining you. You are real indeed. My work, my work.) She chuckled to herself as she gathered them up and proceeded to pile them on the counter to await their cleansing, like the removal of so many sinful stains. *" 'S còir dhan bheatha a bhith cho furasda. Bhiodh mo theaghlach naomh gun teagamh sam bith."* (Life should be so easy. My family would be saintly without any doubt.)

"A Mhòrag, ciod e am prannadh a th'ort?" (Sarah, what are you muttering about?) From behind her, Sadie had appeared in the doorway leading from the dining-room holding the fussing child in her arms.

"Och neoni a ghràidh. Cha robh mi ach bruidhinn rium fhìn. Mar sin, cha bhi mi ag argamaid a chaoidh." (Oh nothing my dear. I was merely speaking to myself. In that way, I never get into an argument.) Both women laughed aloud as Sarah busied herself with the dishes while Sadie placed herself in the rocking chair by the stove. Sarah was so pleased for the girl and Donald; she knew that they both had wanted a child ever since their wed-ding day. They had tried often enough but it all seemed to be to no avail. It had been during Elizabeth and Naomi's visit a year last summer that

Sarah's heart had gone out to Sadie. It had not escaped her notice how Sadie held Naomi, perhaps picturing the day when she herself would give birth. Nothing had been said; would it not have caused only more pain and anguish? Sarah would faithfully keep them in her prayers. It was not as though she took any personal credit, but clearly Sarah found joy in the fact that God in His goodness and mercy had blessed her son and daughter-in-law with a child within the year. Now as Sadie sat stroking the tiny head of Blair Angus Urquhart, Sarah could only imagine the tremendous sense of fulfillment that was in the mother's heart. But then some things needed no such power of imagination. It was all so very real to her. She could see in the wee face, even at the tender age of four months, the likeness of her Donald as a bairn. So much had changed and yet nothing had. As she placed the dishes in the waiting pan, Sarah promised herself that she would not look out the window into the fading light of day. She would not tempt fate. She did not wish to dwell on her mother and the past. The future was her true happiness.

Luckily the house was straightened away, especially the kitchen, by the time the Fergusons arrived at the back door. Rachael and Norman were accompanied by Andrew who, at nine years of age, was beginning to take a great interest in the old tales. The reality was that Hector Urquhart's storytelling had become almost legendary among the children of *Loch Dubh* who began to refer to him affectionately as *Eachann nan Sgeul.* (Hector of the Stories) In fact, Andrew had looked forward to the visit all day, unlike Stuart who had remained home to do some pressing chores around the barn. However, the truth of the matter was that he and Kenneth Erskine would soon be heading down to the town. A social time was being held in the Church of England hall and there would be several young ladies who might well be in need of company.

The chairs on the veranda, which had sat forlornly empty for the better part of an hour, were once again caressed with warm bodies as discussion quickly focused on Morag's recent marriage. Although Norman and Rachael had been unable to travel to Boston, they were pleased that there had been a Cape Breton presence: Effie, Liam and Murdina Jennie had attended the ceremony. There had been great excitement in the Ferguson home just last week when a large brown package arrived, containing a treasure trove of used clothing, a lengthy letter and several photographs of the June wedding. From previous correspondence, they knew that the groom was a Cabot from, as Morag put it, an "old Boston family." He was a barrister and a prominent member of his father's legal firm. They had a lovely home tucked in behind the legislative building and not far from the Public Gardens. Andrew had laughed when he saw the return address on the large package — Louisbourg Square. He insisted that his sister must be living in a house with big holes in the walls, just like the pictures he had seen in school of the fortress ramparts down the coast in Louisbourg. Rachael had given him a loving slap on his backside and told him not to trouble himself about Morag or her house. The letter had gone on to say that she and Elliott hoped to travel to Cape Breton the following year for a lengthy visit. Rachael had already spent a considerable amount of time going through the newly arrived garments and was terribly preoccupied with concern, even then, as to what she would wear for their eventual arrival. After all, it would be important to make a good impression.

"*Bithidh fàite air do ghnùis. Fóghnuidh seo airson an t-seann teaghlaich am Boston.' Nì iad naill as d' fhàite gu dearbh. Ach faicill ort. Cuir ort rudaigin eile!*" (You will wear a smile. This will be sufficient for "the old Boston family." They will indeed adore your smile but be careful to wear something more!) Norman's comment was greeted with great gales of laughter from Hector and Daniel as all three men continued to puff on their pipes. Rachael shot her husband a look that, had they not been in the presence of company, could have easily resulted in serious bodily injury. It was Sarah who finally diffused the somewhat awkward situation.

"*A Thormoid Mhic Fhearghuis, nach tu an t-olc! Giùlain thu féin; tha an gille 'nar làthair.*" (Norman Ferguson, are you not an evil one! Behave yourself; the laddie is in our presence.) All eyes turned to Andrew who sat in front of them on the edge of the veranda oblivious to the fact that he had just been used as a lightening rod for pious rectitude. He was much more interested in hearing Hector's stories and was tired of their silly talk, which he hoped would soon end.

Much to Andrew's chagrin, the discussion soon turned to the topic of the new school mistress, Miss Massey from North Sydney, who had just recently assumed her duties. She was residing with the Reverend and Mrs. Fraser, as had her predecessor, and word abounded that she was even more devout than Duncan Fraser himself. The expression *maise gnùis a' bhiorain-ghriosaich!* (the beauty of the poker face!) had been used frequently to describe her, as much by adults in the kitchens around the loch as by children on the playground beside the school. "She is a crotchety *cailleach* who does not like us!" Andrew had quite suddenly and unexpectedly turned his head and joined the conversation as he recounted how the mistress had, on more than one occasion, forbade them from uttering a word of the Gaelic, even outside during recess. Less than four weeks into his academic training, young Aulay Erskine had already provoked a major incident by advising Miss Massey, who had most unwisely ventured onto the playground, to "*thoir ifrinn ort!*" (go to Hell!) as he stood adamantly before her with hands firmly planted on his hips. He had broken his own rule by using profane language in the Gaelic but was quickly bolstered by the fact that the other children had snickered quietly in approval. God had heard but surely would also have understood the extenuating circumstances of their predicament. Miss Massey's many subsequent attempts to discern the meaning of Aulay's words had been met with numerous and fairly consistent confirmations from all the others that it was nothing more than a traditional highland greeting. A consensus was formed on the playground that day that they would never tattle on one of their own, especially one so young and brave.

"*Nì eagalach! A' chnagaid choite. Bruidhneadh iad Gàidhlig an taobh a muigh na sgoile. Có is urrainn oidheam sam bith a thoirt as? Tha bànrigh againn anns a'bhaile mu thràth.*" (A dreadful thing! The cruel old maid. Let them speak the Gaelic outside the school. Who can bring any sense out of it? We already have a queen down in the town.) Ever the diplomat, that was as close as Sarah would come to actually accusing the school mistress of abusing the powers that had been invested in her. Sarah had not yet had the pleasure of meeting Miss Annie Mae Massey and decided that she would not go far out of her way to do so. "*Tha an aibheis uile làn bhòchdan. Cor an t-saoghail — is mór an t-atharrachadh beagan is beagan. Aig Dia a mhàin tha brath.*" (The whole atmosphere is full of hobgoblins. The state of the world — there is great change, little by little. God alone knows.) The temporary silence that followed the uttering of such profound words, complete with many a nodding head, spoke volumes about the unanimous agreement with which they had been accepted.

The evening turned out to be a complete disaster, at least for poor Andrew who never did get to hear the eagerly anticipated ghoulish stories. The arrival of the *strùpag* had put a quick end to that as a wee cuppa was always a clear sign that the visit was drawing to a close. As the Fergusons made their way home along the loch road, Andrew gave serious thought to Sarah's words — a queen down in the town. He had no idea that such a royal personage lived nearby and promised himself that he would be certain to bring it to Miss Massey's attention. No doubt, she would surely be impressed with this bit of news and perhaps, as a result, be a little less strict with them. Regardless, they would continue to keep an eye out for Aulay. He was, after all, one of their own.

It was all so reminiscent of another trip taken in the dead of winter. Little had changed along the road that skirted the coast as far as the eye could see. In some respects, it seemed appropriate to believe that it somehow had all been frozen in time. The harsh north-east wind coming off the open Atlantic only served to heighten this perception when, in actual fact, a great deal had indeed changed. It was not just the landscape that reminded him of that other time. The jingling of the horse bells was also familiar and soothing; it offered a constant rhythmic pattern as the snow and wind continued to swirl around him.

Memories of that trip some nine years ago came back to Rod as he steered a course north towards Cape Smoky, which loomed far off in the distance like a herculean giant slumbering under an immense white sheet. The bells were indeed comforting but, at the same time, strangely hypnotic. The sound lulled him into a sense of security that he knew was not really there. It was certainly something that he could not feel, even if one were to discount the numbing cold of the wind. How could it be otherwise? His recollections were of another time when he had desperately struggled to collect his thoughts and to prepare himself. It had been perhaps one of the longest journeys of his life or so it had seemed at the time, certainly longer than either the voyages to or from South Africa. And yet, with so much having changed in his life and that of his family, he was back where he had been. The only difference was that Andrew was now with him.

Margaret was in the back of the sleigh with the boy, bundled up beneath a thick rug. Andrew Archibald MacDonald had been born six months after his great grandfather's death and had just recently marked his second birthday. The idea of undertaking such a lengthy trip with the young lad had been a source of very real concern for both Rod and Margaret. In his three and a half years of ministry in *An Abhainn Mheadhonach*, Rod had conducted six funeral services for children under the age of eight. At least three had succumbed to the dreaded pneumonia that slowly sucked the life from their tiny lungs as parents looked on helplessly. The pictures were still so vivid in his mind, how he would stand over the tiny coffins knowing that he was there as shepherd to comfort the bereaved with his words, words that fell silently in the unforgiving winter air like so many flakes of snow. *Is mise an aiseirigh, agus a' bheatha: an ti a chreideas annam-sa, ged gheibheadh e bàs, bidh e beò.* (I am the resurrection, and the life: he that believeth in me, though he were dead, yet shall he live.) Yet shall he live. For Rod, this was a test of his own faith and, undoubtedly, the hardest part of his ministry.

The February winds were always brutal, especially along the open and extremely vulnerable coastline, requiring a more measured pace with frequent stops along the way. It was for this reason that Rod had requested an entire week's leave at the last meeting of session. They had driven to Baddeck the first day and spent the night with his sister Catherine. The second night saw them with Margaret's parents in *Cobh a' Gheòidh* where the young Andrew quickly became the focus of much attention and admiration. Although Rachael Buchanan had been present for the birth of her grandson, her husband had not yet laid eyes on him. As he watched them together, Rod thought of Archie and the important role that *Seanair Naomh* had played in his grandchildren's lives. With such reflections upon him, Rod made a conscious decision to leave them alone in the kitchen, just the two of them, with the hope that they would come to know one another, each in their own way, and begin to forge their own lasting memories. The timing was fortuitous; he wanted or perhaps needed to take the air down by the water, alone. Walking along the frozen shoreline, he looked across the cove and St. Anns Bay with St. Anns Mountain rising majestically in the distance. For a brief moment, none of it mattered, not even the sharp dampness of the wind that sliced across his face. It did not matter because he was not there. He was standing on the far side of the Modder River gazing across at a grave. Sunday, February 27 would mark the tenth anniversary of Andrew's death. *"A Thighearna, na biodh 'ar cridheachan fo thrioblaid."* (Oh Lord, let not our hearts be troubled.) As the wind whistled around him, it was all too apparent that his words were yet again falling in the unforgiving winter air like so many flakes of snow. This too was becoming a test of faith.

It was the next day, in late afternoon, that Rod sat in the kitchen of his own parents' house in *Loch Dubh* and realized that he could not recall another time when it had offered as much warmth as it did then. In some respects, it was not unlike the exhilarating feeling that he and Andrew had experienced when they would arrive at the cracking stove after an early morning scuttle down the stairs and through the frigid house. It had always been so difficult to leave the sultry warmth of their bed. The long drive from *Cobh a' Gheòidh* to *Loch Dubh* had been so similar to those childhood days. The wind had clawed at their faces and the cold had penetrated to their very bones. Now as he sat beside the kitchen stove, Rod was grateful for the warmth that brought colour back to their lifeless skin and laughter back to their muffled voices. The tea pot was on and the supper would be ready soon enough. There was such a genuine comfort in being home with family. And more than anything else, he wanted Andrew to feel it, to experience it as a sure foundation for his life. Rod knew that, should his father ask him to lead them in offering grace, he would make reference to the miraculous gift of life that reappeared as surely as spring follows winter. *Beannachadh an teaghlaich o lìnn gu lìnn!* (The blessings of family from generation to generation!) There was indeed a special comfort in being home with family, especially at this time.

The large wooden table that had so lovingly and patiently nourished three generations of MacDonalds would certainly rejoice as it was once again the focal point of a family gathering. John and Ida had invited Jessie, Duncan and Mabel to join them for supper so as to bring the entire family together. Jessie proudly carried her granddaughter of ten months into the room and, after welcoming pleasantries, shooed John out of the rocking chair. It was the first time that both Rod and Margaret had seen Catriona and the choice of name had been actively inquired after. Duncan and Mabel recounted that they had discussed the matter at some length and decided to call their child Janet in honour of Jessie. However, it was Jessie who quite discretely suggested the name Catriona. It was a name she had always loved and one that was in the family. Malcolm would have liked to have a granddaughter with that name, she was certain. The entire family, but especially Jessie, was well pleased as the bairn, Catriona Janet MacDonald, slept on oblivious to the attention being paid her. Jessie smiled down into the tiny face silently recalling how, on the day of her baptism last autumn, she had gone to the family Bible and removed a folded piece of yellow paper. No one except the Almighty had seen her place it into the flames of the kitchen stove. *"Tha mo chuimhne cosmhuil ri luaithre. Caidil gu sunndach, fhir mo rùin.*" (My remembrances are like ashes. Sleep well, my loved one.) She had spoken to the lid on the stove as she closed it with a finality that was not unlike the filling in of a grave. Jessie shut her eyes and promised herself that she and her family would go on with life.

Rod had indeed been called upon to say grace over the supper table and to lead worship later in the evening before Jessie, Duncan, Mabel and Catriona departed for home. It was only then that the conversation reverted to the Gaelic. Margaret had taken Andrew off to settle him in bed and Daniel had gone down to the town to see Agnes Bain who was obviously of some growing and considerable interest to him. Rod sat in the kitchen with his parents and they spoke of the many changes that had taken place in *Loch Dubh* even in the two and a half years since Archie's death. They spoke of the untimely passing of Peter MacGregor as well as the birth of two new children — Catriona MacDonald and Blair Urquhart. Undoubtedly, there would be more wee ones appearing like lambs on the hills given that both the engagement of Emily Fraser to Christopher Hickman and that of John Grant to a Matheson girl from Sydney Mines had been announced at Christmas. Everyone agreed that it was good to have *Iain Beag* back on the North Shore where he belonged. So many other young people had gone away and not even come back to visit. *An ainm an àigh, is mór am beud e.* (In the name of goodness, it is a great pity.) For the people of *Loch Dubh*, it was not an uncommon sentiment.

There was a momentary lapse in the conversation as Ida rose to fill the kettle with water in order to make a fresh pot of tea. Rod took advantage of the pause, as well as this time alone with his parents, to ask if, as a family, they might visit the cairn the following day. There was no need to explain why or even to point out the significance of Sunday, February 27. John looked into his wife's face and, as if reading her mind, answered Rod in a subtle way that was his own. " '*S fhada bho nach robh mac ar gaoil an seo. Is e so ar dlighe agus tha seo cubhaidh.*" (It is a long time since our beloved son was here. This is our duty and it is proper.) It was so obvious that he was not only a man of few words but was also one who had dwelt on the matter and, as a result, formulated his response with some care. There was a sense of closure to them. After so long a time, perhaps finally an inner peace would be restored.

It was late the following day, immediately following an early supper, that the entire MacDonald family made its way down the loch road to the Kirk. As he walked arm-in-arm with Ida, John could not help but see their steps through the cemetery as a walk back through time. The graves of the *sinnsirean* (ancestors/the fathers) were first to be passed as the hill rose up with those of later generations. And so it would no doubt continue like so many pages being added to a book, thus prolonging the story of their lives in this place. They paused at Archie and Hannah's graves with its rounded white stone. Carved into the top was the image of a sheep lying down with a Celtic cross rising up behind. It was so appropriate given the text that appeared at the bottom of the stone, beneath the names and dates. *Is mise am buachaille maith, agus is aithne dhomh mo chaoraich féin, agus aithnichear le m'chaoraich féin mi.* (I am the good shepherd, and know my sheep, and am known of mine.) John had read it many times in the past but it was only now that it struck him as being such an appropriate testament to their lives — a testament carved in stone and now engraved in memory. He also noted the names of his two brothers and sister who had died as children in the early years of settlement well before his own birth. They were so young, mere lambs themselves: Roderick 1844 - 1853, Kenneth 1847 - 1853, Catriona 1846 - 1854. It had not been lost on John and Malcolm, even as children, that their parents had seldom made reference to the others. Perhaps it had continued to be all too painful even with the passage of the years. As a child, John could never understand. It was only now that he could.

John and Ida turned to see Jessie standing in front of Malcolm's stone with Duncan and Mabel at her side. No words were spoken; such visits were normally as still as the graves themselves. It was always a time for quiet thought. There was a power in the silence that was as difficult to explain as was the need to visit. A link to the past was being maintained and it seemed so appropriate that Andrew and Catriona were with them. Regardless of age, it was important to reflect, to remember, to honour.

The family slowly climbed the hill where they eventually gathered on the far side of the cairn and, as with all the gravestones, faced the eastern sky. There had been no predetermination as to what would occur or who would speak if indeed anyone would. It was only after a few minutes that the silence was ultimately broken by Rod's words of invitation: *"Dèanamaid urnuigh."* (Let us pray.) What came next was a prayer that spoke of a youthful spirit, a kind heart and a steadfast faith in God. It spoke so simply and yet so eloquently of Andrew and his all-too-brief earthly pilgrimage. It was a prayer for the celebration of a life.

As the stillness once again flooded back to reclaim its dominion, Ida slowly left John's side and moved forward where she lovingly placed her gloved hands on the cairn. It was as though she were completely alone with her thoughts in gazing down upon the snow-encrusted body of stones. All eyes were upon her as the family simply waited, not knowing. The silence continued for several seconds more and then departed as quickly as it had come. *"Chan e seo clach-chinn; seo carraig mo neart. Dia nam feart, thug thu dhomh a nasgaidh e. Beiridh bean mac, ach 'se Dia ni nèamhach. Tha thu rèidh a nis mo nèamhach mùirneach. Beannachd leat Anndra."* (This is not a headstone; this is the rock of my strength. God of wonderful deeds, you gave him to me as a gift. A woman may bear a son but God alone can make an angel. You are at peace now my dearly-beloved angel. Farewell Andrew.) It was the first time in his life that Rod saw his father cry.

Ida turned and smiled knowingly at all the others. It was done; it was finally over. She took John's arm and together they began to walk back towards the Kirk as the darkness totally enveloped the slopes of *Beinn-mo-Mhulaid* like a raven mist. Rod, Margaret and Andrew were the last to depart. As he looked at the cairn that had been so tenderly caressed by his mother's hands and words, Rod reached down and took Andrew up into his arms. *"Anndra, thoir dhomh geall gun cuimhnich thu an là an diugh."* (Andrew, promise me that you will remember this day.) With the black leather-bound Bible still firmly in his grasp, Rod knew that it would be important for his son to reflect, to remember, to honour. Now, with the darkness almost completely obscuring the cairn from their sight, the three of them left it and proceeded down the hill towards home.

There were actually some people who had the audacity to believe and actually write that coal was the heart and soul of Cape Breton. Had he not himself read such foolishness in the Sydney papers? Indeed, the entire island had often been portrayed as a rock perched precariously on the summit of a black mountain that rose up from the very floor of the Atlantic Ocean. Clearly, a great deal of the economy depended on the pits that dotted the eastern coast of the island and burrowed out under the water like the warren of a gigantic black rabbit. There was no doubt that the mining industry was important to the livelihood of both Cape Breton and Nova Scotia but it certainly was not a heart or a soul. Such people would be well advised to avoid such naïve musings in the future and leave matters of the spirit to those who have been so entrusted. Duncan Fraser was glad that the pits of Sydney Mines, Florence, Glace Bay and a host of other communities were as far removed from his thoughts as they were from the highlands of Cape Breton. Distance was oftentimes a good thing, it was oftentimes a saving grace.

The mild July breeze rustled the newspaper and, from where she was seated on the veranda, Emily could see the look of sheer determination on her father's face as he struggled with the wind for ownership. She smothered a chuckle at the thought of the papers breaking free from his clutches in order to float wild and free over the loch like so many of Alexander Bell's kites over *Beinn Bhreagh*. It always struck her as humourous that her father so eagerly awaited the arrival of the **Cape Breton Post** and **The Record** that came by steamer and then, having read them in their entirety, would complain bitterly about the overly sensational nature of the reports that always appeared as feature articles: the coal miners in Springhill still on strike after eleven months; Campbellton, New Brunswick burned to the ground leaving only four houses standing; people still feeling the effects of the smallpox epidemic of the previous summer. And yet if the truth be known, there was the odd bit of good news. Even with the sorrow surrounding the death of King Edward two months earlier, there were interesting accounts of the new King and Queen as well as of their six children. They were all so young, even the future Prince of Wales was just sixteen years of age and held such promise. One day, God willing, he too would follow in his grandfather's and now his own father's footsteps and become a great king. There was a general sense of optimism about King George and Queen Mary that was shared by everyone. Well, almost everyone; Daniel Erskine and *Coinneach Bàn* would have their own views and, unquestionably, it would be best to leave them to themselves.

Duncan carefully folded the papers and tucked them under his arm. Even though Emily continued with her sewing, she was strangely distracted by the fact that the papers had ceased their rustling. She looked over at her father in profile as he gazed out over the loch and the mountains beyond. At that moment, he seemed so serene and at peace with himself. What had caused Duncan's sudden reflection was the realization that he had been born the very year that Victoria had become Queen. Now it was her grandson who sat on the throne. For one of the few times in his life, he contemplated his own mortality; he was growing old. His eyes were now turned and focused on his daughter who sat contentedly on a side bench, putting the final touches to the dress that she would wear tomorrow at Kirk. His *gràdhag* (dear little one) would soon be married and gone from him. She was most certainly a beautiful young woman who, unbeknown to her, bore a resemblance that was strikingly familiar as if from another time and place. *Rè linn do sheanamhar.* (During the time of your grandmother.) His thoughts were centred on something across time and space; they were of *Ben Gulicanthe*. He was indeed growing old.

The screen door creaked open, almost begrudgingly, as the quiet was broken by Jennie's arrival from somewhere inside the house. There was a large meal to be prepared for the extended family supper and she had already been held captive by the kitchen for the better part of the day. Her visit to the veranda would afford her a well-deserved respite from the stove, which would be most welcomed. However, it would also provide her and Duncan with one of the last opportunities they would have to be alone with their daughter before the entire family descended upon the house and this private moment was lost forever.

As she sat down beside her daughter, Jennie looked over at Duncan and smiled. Earlier in the week, the two of them had discussed the matter between themselves and had agreed that it would be most appropriate. In fact, Jennie had been somewhat taken aback by Duncan's further response. He had gathered his wife up in his arms and caressed her gently as he thanked her for the three gifts of life that she had bestowed upon him. Of all the words preached by this man of God over some forty years of ministry, none had touched Jennie's heart more than those that had come forth at that moment. Duncan slowly released her from his embrace and looked deep into her eyes. *"A Shìne a ghràidh, tha mo rùn ort gu dearbh."* (Jennie my dear, I truly love you.) Suddenly, she was appreciative of the fact that, as life moved ever nearer to its close, some things were in need of saying while others were not. These particular words were not but, still, she would be forever grateful for having heard them spoken again after such a lengthy period of time.

Now seated next to Emily with Duncan looking on attentively, Jennie reached into the pocket of her apron and retrieved a small package beautifully wrapped in flowered paper. She offered an explanation although none seemed necessary. *"Is tu ar n-annsachd. Sonas ort a ghnàth agus tha sinn a'toirt dhuit e a nasgaidh fa-chomhair an là màireach."* (You are our best beloved. Happiness to you always and we give this to you as a gift in view of tomorrow.) Emily had placed her sewing on her lap and now proceeded to carefully take the present from her mother's hands. She smiled at both her parents and, even with curiosity upon her, slowly and meticulously removed the paper. The elegant blue box revealed a small locket in the shape of a heart that hung on a length of matching gold chain. Emily gently lifted it from its bed of white cotton and opened it to discover three, tiny heart-shaped frames. In one of the frames was a photograph of Murdina Jennie O'Sullivan as a baby, the very first photo that had been forwarded in the Christmas card from Boston. Years earlier, Jennie had placed it in the locket for safekeeping with the knowledge that, in time, it would be replaced with pictures of other children. The tears that Emily shed were proof enough to both Jennie and Duncan that they had chosen well. It would be fitting for their daughter to wear this golden heart on her wedding day as a symbol that she would always remain in theirs. Duncan and Jennie were thankful for this quiet moment alone with her. In terms of both gift and timing as well as Emily's tearful response, they were content in the knowledge that they had indeed chosen well.

The steamer arrived later that same afternoon carrying Christopher and his family — his parents, brother and sister. Jennie had made arrangements for the Hickmans to be lodged with the Bain family in town who often let rooms to people travelling up and down the North Shore. Christopher and his family would be content enough there for the duration of their three-day stay on the North Shore. As planned, Jennie, Duncan and Emily were at the government wharf as a greeting party not only for the Hickmans but also for Sandy and Matthew who were passengers on the same vessel. Even though Sandy was himself now engaged to a young woman from Sydney, it was soon apparent that it would not preclude him from making humourous comments at his sister's expense. It was later that evening around the supper table that he stood with tea cup in hand to toast *an naoidhean*. (The Little Child) *"Deoch-slàinte Emilidh — chum caithream a dhèanamh nad shonas. An deireadh ri tighinn is an toiseach ri falbh!"* (A toast to Emily — to rejoice in your happiness. The last to come and the first to go!) The entire Fraser Clan, including Emily, broke into laughter as cups were dutifully raised and clinked in fine style.

Shortly thereafter, Sandy made a special point of going around the table to give the *naoidhean* a big hug. She willingly accepted his embrace and, in the process, took advantage of the situation by grabbing his ear and setting the record straight with an amusing statement made at his expense for the benefit of everyone seated before them. *"Ud. Ud. Tha e a'buannachadh orm!"* (Tut. Tut. He is getting to me!) It was several minutes later that the laughter finally subsided, allowing Jennie to replenish both the pot of tea and the plate of sweets that sat in the centre of the table. Quite unexpectedly, it was Duncan who eagerly and with an uncommon flourish stood and proceeded to top up the cups. He wanted this time of fellowship to continue; it was obvious that he so enjoyed having his family back together again. It had certainly not escaped the watchful eyes of Emily who, on more than one occasion, had taken note of her mother smiling down the length of the table at her father. Her family was so very important to her, including the *bràithrean anacuibheasach aingidh*. Even with the abundance of laughter and talk that surrounded her, Emily thought of her wedding the next day surrounded by family and friends; she thought of the gold locket; she thought of Murdina Jennie.

It was nothing if not a fine day for a wedding. A flock of wispy clouds offered intermittent shelter from the heat of the early afternoon sun while an invigorating breeze made its way up and over the bluffs to flood the farms encircling the loch. The Kirk pews were filled with the residents of *Loch Dubh* as well as a host of people from New Carlisle and still others from up and down the North Shore who knew Duncan Fraser and his family. At the appointed hour, there were more than a few gasps of amazement as Emily slowly made her way down the aisle towards the front of the sanctuary where her father and Christopher stood waiting. It was not the beautiful cream-coloured dress or even the gold locket around her neck that caught their attention and peaked their interest. Most had never before seen Emily with her long chestnut hair swept up and pinned to the back of her head. More than that, they had never before witnessed someone wearing flowers in their hair, especially in the Kirk. Yet, it was so like Emily. In the few brief seconds that passed as she slowly proceeded towards them, Duncan Fraser's mind was flooded with a multitude of memories. He thought of how, as a child, she would conjure up distinctive names and personalities for the flowers in her bouquet. And always the questions and stories that would flow from her! She had changed so much but still this floral crown was testament to the fact that, in some respects at least, she had not changed at all. The flowers, the stories and so much more of her youth were still very consciously a part of her as she now stood before him. Duncan glanced over and smiled at Jennie and the boys. At that moment, he ceased to be the presiding clergy. He was nothing if not a proud father.

The ceremony was conducted in English, for the benefit of the Hickman family, and was relatively short in duration as was the custom. Yet many would agree, as they recollected later, that it was most memorable because of one thing other than the flowers — the benediction.

With vows exchanged, Duncan led the congregation in a final prayer. He invoked the blessings of God on the couple and, almost without thinking and certainly without notice, continued on in Gaelic. *"Gràdhaich sibh a chéile le gràdh sìorruidh. Feuch, bidh Dia a' ghràidh agus na sìthe maille ruibh. Mo chlann, beannachd Dhé leibh a ghnàth. Amen."* (Love one another with an everlasting love. Behold, the God of love and peace will be with you. My children, may the blessings of God attend you always. Amen.) Those who spoke the Gaelic and knew the minister well could recognize the faintest of tears in the voice. However, unlike so many times before, this time it was unquestionably a tear of immense happiness.

For the second time in as many days, the manse's dining-room table was resplendent with a bounteous evening meal. The plate of sweets had been replaced by an enormous fruit cake smothered with thick wispy icing that was duly apportioned by Emily and Christopher as both sides of the family looked on. Earlier that day, Jennie had been presented with not six but twelve cups and saucers to match the tea pot that Christopher had given her as a Christmas present some two and a half years ago. They looked lovely on the white muslin cloth she had borrowed from Iona Erskine and Jennie was confident that she had set a good table for the Hickmans. They seemed to be lovely people and most appreciative of every little thing that was done for them. In observing the varied social interaction that unfolded so effortlessly around the table, Jennie was perceptive enough to see both Christopher's gentle manner in his mother and quick wit in his father. She promised herself that she would find a quiet moment alone with her daughter before the evening was out. *Tha e 'na dhuine aithnichte. Och mo chridhe, fhuair thu an deagh phòsadh.* (He is a remarkable man. Oh my love, you have done well in marriage.) Och indeed, some things were still in need of saying.

Leading up to the actual wedding, it was something that had been debated for days if not weeks on end in each of the farm houses around the loch. And still people found it somewhat difficult to believe even when it finally came to pass before their own eyes. The Reverend Duncan Fraser was not only at the wedding *céilidh* but on the dance floor more often than not. In *Loch Dubh* and elsewhere, such celebrations in the hall were very much community events. It was often said in jest that a bride and groom were not really needed to ensure a successful wedding *céilidh* — just a good fiddler and plenty of dancers with lively feet. In fact, there seemed to be tremendous merit in this adage as *Mac an Fhidhleir* was well and truly ensconced in his wooden chair at the front with the fiddle speaking the Gaelic like never before. Betty MacGregor, his bride of only two months, was off to the side speaking with Morag Ferguson and her American husband who were home from the Boston States. It was Betty who finally coerced Elliott onto the floor and the natural reserve of the Cabots, be they an old Boston family or no, soon dissipated amid the music and laughter. It was all too apparent that the Cabots were not renowned for their dancing but, like everyone else, knew a good time when they saw it. The music and dance continued on as did the laughter.

Iain Grant and Daniel MacDonald could be seen in the far corner near the tea table, spinning their charm on Alexandra Dunn and Agnes Bain from down in the town. It was one of the very few areas of the hall that was not awash in colour and movement, thus allowing them a more-private time. Immediately in front of them, the bride and groom had joined Duncan and Mabel MacDonald, Donald and Sadie Urquhart, and Alasdair and Kristy Erskine in a lively square set. The older people would not be easily pushed off the floor and there was a goodly amount of guffawing as bodies bumped into one another, oftentimes quite intentionally, in claiming floor space and always with raucous good-natured comments abounding. Sarah Urquhart had come accompanied by Hector as well as his "ten devils." Still, no one seemed to mind, including Duncan and Jennie, if they had even bothered to stop dancing long enough to take note.

At times, it seemed as though the music, the dancing, the singing and the laughter would never end. But end they did. The community had provided Emily and Christopher with a fine send-off that would undoubtedly linger in memories for years to come, among them the unforgettable sight of the Reverend Duncan Fraser "stepping it off" on the dance floor. And, all too soon, it was simply nothing more than that, memories. The Monday morning steamer had taken the newly-weds down the coast, back to Baddeck and a new life far from the mountains of *Loch Dubh*. Sandy and Matthew were also on board and so, as a consequence, that afternoon saw the manse returned to a more tranquil state with the now stark absence of the children's voices and laughter.

The sun had just begun to set off to the right behind the face of *Beinn-mo-Mhulaid* as *Rionnag* curled herself up into a velvet ball on the very bench that Emily had occupied only three days ago. Duncan looked down upon this image of absolute contentment and smiled. *"Och Rionnag, ar pàisde. Tha mi a' fannachadh lìon beagan is beagan ach is buaine na gach nì an gaol. Éirich ròscal mo chridhe. Tha mo dhìol agamsa."* (Oh *Rionnag*, our little child. I am getting more feeble little by little but love is more lasting than anything else. Joy springs up in my heart; I have my satisfaction.)

Gazing out over the loch and the mountains, Duncan could not remember a time when he was more at peace than at this very moment in his rocking chair on the veranda. As she stood silently in the frame of the archway separated only by the mesh of the screen door, Jennie had overheard the evocative words spoken by her husband to their slumbering black child. A smile came to her face as she softly repeated the words to herself. *Tha mo dhìol agamsa gu dearbh.* (I truly have my satisfaction.) With that, Jennie turned and quietly returned to the work that awaited her in the kitchen.

For ye were as sheep going astray; but are now returned unto the
Shepherd and Bishop of your soul.

I Peter II: 25

*Oir bha sibh mar chaoraich a' dol air seacharan; ach philleadh sibh a nis
chum Buachaill' agus Easbuig 'ur n-anama.*

I Peadar II: 25

Had she been asked to explain how it came to be that they were standing where they were at that particular moment in time, the answer
would have most assuredly included the word nuptials. At first blush, it
would not have appeared to make a great deal of sense. There did not seem
to be any obvious connection, be it tenuous or otherwise, between the joy
surrounding a wedding ceremony and the uncertainty that now obscured
the laneway every bit as much as the fading light of day. The previous four
months had witnessed three marriages involving the young people of *Loch
Dubh*. Betty MacGregor and James *Mac an Fhidhleir* MacInnes had been
married in May, Emily Fraser and Christopher Hickman in July and, just
of late, *Iain Beag* Grant and Christine Matheson from Sydney Mines. The
children, as she still continued to refer to them, had grown up before her
eyes all too quickly without her even taking the time to realize it. It was
only now that she did.

Yet, in some strange maternal way, Kristy was certain that she would
always think of them as wee. They had been so terribly young and full of
innocence in those first days following her arrival at the school in 1896.
Both Emily and John had been all of seven years old while Betty was just
five. She thought back to the Friday afternoon readings from **Robinson
Crusoe** and the expressions of concern that had crossed their tiny faces
when picturing poor Messrs. Crusoe and Friday on *An Toiseach*, or was it
An Deireadh. Had she not taken the time to reassure the children, the
mothers of *Loch Dubh* might still be baking for the poor unfortunates out
there on their lonely island. And soon enough, these very children would
have young ones of their own and the cycle of life would continue on like
the turning of the ever vigilant water wheel of the *muileann dubh*. As with
generations before them, grandparents would take such joy in enfolding
new life in their arms. In so doing, it was here that they would bide for a
time and see something recaptured from their youth, something that gave

testament to their own earthy pilgrimage. One day, they would be called home with the sure and present knowledge that they had willed a legacy that would continue on long after they were nothing more than so many names on weather-beaten gravestones.

As much as they might attempt to deny it, Daniel and Tina doted on their granddaughter whenever the opportunity presented itself. And at four and a half years of age, Grace was not adverse to seeing a few extra peppermints slipped into her pocket down at Dunn's General Store, having *seanair* or *seanamhair* cuddle with her in bed when the frightful wind howled around the corners of the house, or laughing uproariously as all three mimicked the antics of a butterfly flitting through Tina's flower garden. Kristy took such delight in the happiness that they shared together. But still, it was not enough; something was missing. In her mind and in her heart, she knew that she owed it to her own parents and, most of all, she owed it to Grace.

Even with the distance, it was possible to see the soft yellow glow of the Aladdin lamp that always hung in the kitchen window. Dusk had already begun to slowly wash down the laneway like an encroaching dark wave as Kristy and Grace stood at the road looking up at the MacNeil house. Behind them, a soft August breeze floated off the lake and stroked their backs as if gently nudging them forward, encouraging them to walk into the wave, to proceed the short distance that would take an eternity to cross. It had all come to this. She had not laid eyes on her home or her father in seven and a half years. It struck her as somewhat odd that, from where she stood, the scene seemed so unchanged, so familiar, so welcoming. Yet all she saw was the look on her father's face that day long ago and his parting words that still echoed in her ears: *Is buan nàire na gach nì. Mach as mo làthair!* (Shame is more lasting than anything else. Get out of my presence!) She was faced with the reality that, for the first time since the May 1903 ceremony in the *Loch Dubh* Kirk, she now doubted her own resolve to place one foot before the other. Yet it had been a full day's journey, and even with all the novelty and excitement of the steamer and coach rides that had brought them here, it was obvious that Grace was tired. Kristy grasped the tiny hand as they began to walk towards the house and into the unknown.

The initial barking had alerted Bernadette to the arrival of company. As Kristy and Grace drew closer, *Dìleas'* (Faithful) initial utterances were quickly abandoned as her entire body seemed to convulse with a genuine sense of pleasure and excitement in seeing her old friend once again. Kristy reached down to caress the dog's head and rub her ears, as much in greeting and acknowledgement as in dispelling her own guilt at having almost completely forgotten this most devoted family member. The temporary pangs of guilt she felt were for having never thought to ask after her during her mother's visit of almost five years ago or in the frequent letters that had since passed between them. Kristy looked up and could now see her mother standing at the side door with her hands tucked into the pockets of her long apron. She simply stood there gazing down towards the road. Mother and daughter walked on as *Dìleas* continued to bound from side to side. Kristy prayed that the reception that awaited them inside the house would be every bit as loving and heartfelt.

The reunion on the step was all that Kristy could have expected and more. Bernadette had longed for the day when her daughter and now granddaughter would be reunited with her family. It was for this reason that she had suggested that they come and it was for the very same reason that she had not informed Joseph of the impending visit. Over the course of the preceding weeks, she had gone to mass every day and, in the shadow of the central altar, lingered to say special prayers. She prayed that God would temper contrite hearts and allow compassion and understanding to enter where bitterness and intolerance had resided for far too long. She hoped that the candles that had been lit in faith would flame a spirit of reconciliation. It brought to mind her own parting words to Kristy many years ago when her daughter had first left on the long journey that would take her from them to *Loch Dubh* and into a new life. *Is tìm dhomh bhith nas tric ann an ùrnaigh agus leanadh dlùth ri Dia.* (Now is the time for frequent prayer, keeping close to God.) There before the magnificence of the main altar, she would do no less.

As Kristy and Grace entered the kitchen behind Bernadette, Joseph rose silently from his place at the head of the supper table. After several seconds of blank stare, it fell to Kristy to break the stillness that brought such an eery chill to the otherwise warm room. *"M'athair, is math a mhéinn a tha ort. Is math leam sin. 'S fhada bho nach robh mi an seo agus tha mi a-nis an seo romhaibh. Thàinig mi dhachaidh airson an teaghlaich, air ar sonsa."* (Father, you are looking well. I am glad of it. It is a long time since I have been here and I am here now before you. I came home for the sake of the family, for us.) As she glanced down at the child standing by her side clutching her hand, Kristy realized that her words seemed so cold, so terribly matter of fact. It was as if she were speaking to some inanimate object, someone or something that wasn't quite real. Still, it was her father's face, a face that held no expression — a face that, for the first time in her life, she could not read.

The silence persisted as Bernadette remained close to the door with her hands clasped together over her chest, knowing that both her husband and her daughter were in God's hands. She waited and prayed quietly. It was all she could do. *"A Mhamaidh, cò e? Ar seanair?"* (Mamma, who is he? Is it grandfather?) Peeping out from behind the deep folds of her mother's long skirt, Grace had unwittingly bridged both the silence and the schism with an olive branch of inquisitiveness and innocence. Still, there was safety by her mother's side as she continued to peer from behind the cloth into the old man's expressionless face, searching for some hint of recognition that was not there.

Joseph slowly returned to his seat and, with ponderous eyes, sought out the face of his granddaughter. When the words finally came, it was as though they were first torn from his heart before flowing from his lips. *"Och is mi seanair gu beachd. Tha thu de Chlainn Nèill gun teagamh sam bith. Tha sin soilleir — an gnùis agus am faighneachdas. Trobhad an seo a chagair gus am faic mi thu."* (Oh yes, it is me "grandfather" most assuredly. You are a MacNeil without any doubt. That is obvious, the face and the curious nature. Come here dear so that I can see you.)

Kristy led Grace by the hand and closed the distance that had rested between them for so many years. She looked down on her father who leaned forward and spoke kindly to the child as he slowly retrieved a small paper bag from his pants pocket. Kristy imagined it to be the very same bag of peppermints that had always been passed down the pew to the children at mass to induce quiet for a few more minutes, at least until the priest had finished his homily. Now with this one simple gesture, Joseph had acquired a new friend. As Grace savoured her treat, he looked up into Kristy's face. No words were spoken. With that one simple gesture, he had also reclaimed his daughter.

"A Sheanair, a bheil thu ruith dearbadan-dé anns a' ghàradh, mar a tha Tina agus Domhnall?" (Grandfather, do you chase butterflies in the garden like Tina and Daniel?) Joseph did not fully understand the question but, given the circumstance, felt no need to ask for clarification. Joseph simply smiled at the child as he reached for Kristy's hand, motioning for her to sit beside him at the table. In the same movement, he gathered Grace up in his arms and placed her on his knee. It was only then that Bernadette finally moved from the door and busied herself by bringing more cups to the table and retrieving the tea pot from its resting place on the stove. In approaching her husband and daughter, she whispered a prayer of thanksgiving for blessings received. She promised herself an additional novena would be said at bedtime.

Over the course of the following days, there was less and less silence as the grievous separation was put to rest. It was never discussed and, for both Joseph and Kristy, there was a tacit understanding that they would speak about only the present and the future. The closest he came to broaching the subject was one evening as they sat at the kitchen table, long after Grace had been put to her bed. He felt a need to speak. *"Och Chairistìona. Tha Giorsal bheag gu sona sòlach, mar thu-fhéin. Gun dèanadh Dia faire ort. Tha e ceart. 'S tusa mo nighean, mo ghràidheag, agus na mo chlainn, chì mi Dia."* (Oh Kristy. Little Grace is happy and contented as are you. May God watch over you. It is right/just. You are my daughter, my beloved, and in my children I see God.)

Kristy reached across the table and took the wrinkled old hands in hers. The only thing that touched Joseph more than this subtle embrace were the words that flowed from his daughter so freely. *"M'athair ghaolaich, dh' ionnsaich sibh móran dhomh ach gu h-àraidh gun éisdinn ri mo chridhe. Tha ròscal mo chridhe ag éirigh an dràsda chum caithream a dhèanadh nad làthair. Mo riar fhéin, cha dealaich mise ris a rithist."* (My dear Father, you taught me much but you taught me to listen to my heart. Now joy springs in my heart to rejoice in your presence. On my word of honour, I will not be parted from it again.)

"Tha e mar sin. Tha sinn rèidh a nis mo nighean bhòidheach. Tha mo dhìol agamsa. Tha e mar sin." (It is so. We are at peace now my beautiful daughter. I have my satisfaction. It is so.) Joseph smiled at Kristy and enfolded her hands in his. Bernadette, who had quite intentionally busied herself out of sight in the adjoining pantry, now entered the kitchen and put the tea pot on in preparation for the evening *strùpag*. A cup of tea would be fine for the time being but Joseph promised himself that he would toast his prodigal daughter with something a bit stronger when the right moment presented itself. Kristy's thoughts were of dear Tina and her philosophy that there was nothing better than a good cuppa to resolve any problem. *Seadh, seadh gu dearbh!* (Yes, yes indeed!)

The Saturday night saw the MacNeil house filled to overflowing with Kristy's seven brothers and sisters and their families who came from all along the coast, from Shunacadie to Castle Bay and several points in between. Two of her brothers, Vincent and Francis, were fiddlers of some renown and it had not taken long, once the supper dishes were cleared away, for the lingering aromas of baked beans and corn bread to be replaced by the melodic strains of jigs, strathspeys and reels. The large kitchen table was soon pushed up against the wall to create room for the dance floor. And how it was put to good use. On several occasions, Joseph quipped that Father MacIsaac in the glebe house down the road would surely be woken from his sleep by the racket, only to thank God for what he believed to be the thunder that would bring much-needed rain. He would be none the wiser that the "thunderous" MacNeil *céilidh* had gone on well past midnight. As the revellers finally made their way to their beds in the small hours of the morning, Kristy was certain that memories of this time would never leave her. More than the music, the dance, the singing or even the spinning of tales, it was the laughter and the sense of fellowship that would stay with her. This was truly the essence of home and, after all these years, it was finally hers once again.

If Father MacIsaac had been surprised the following day by the absence of rain, it was not apparent in his homily or greeting at the main doors of the church. The entire MacNeil family went to the late-morning mass and was warmly greeted by fellow parishioners who had not seen several of "Joseph and Bernadette's bairns" for quite some time. As they walked down the central aisle to the pew, Kristy felt a strange feeling in the pit of her stomach as if she were travelling down a familiar yet darkened road. She knew where everything was but it was all somehow lost from her sight. It was difficult to explain. She looked up at the radiant crucifix high above the altar that dominated the chancel and compelled all eyes to its intense graphic form. Kristy thought of the plain wooden cross above her bed in *Loch Dubh* as she closed her eyes and quietly folded her hands in her lap.

At that same moment, Grace was also travelling down a road, albeit a completely new one that was as interesting as it was puzzling. What was the meaning of the statues of people wearing night clothes? Why did people kneel down as if saying prayers at bed time? Why was the reverend wearing a white gown and not a black one? What language was he speaking? Why did everyone, with the exception of her mother and herself, make a sign by touching their foreheads and chests? Kristy knew her daughter like the back of her own hand and, as she turned to her father, noted that he was already reaching deep into his coat pocket. Having raised eight children, Joseph could still detect the early stages of a fidget. There would be no need for answers to the multitude of questions that Grace would have, at least not for now. A peppermint would see to that. Joseph smiled down the pew in the direction of his granddaughter. *'S ann de Chlainn Nèill a tha thu. O lìnn gu lìnn.* (You are a MacNeil. From generation to generation.)

Having played it all out in her mind a million times before, Kristy was still surprised by the fact that the departure from Christmas Island was much more painful than the arrival. Certainly it was more tearful. There were many hugs and loving words of parting as the coach pulled up at the end of the laneway. Joseph crouched down and promised his granddaughter that soon they would indeed find a butterfly in the garden and chase after him like there was no tomorrow. Grace giggled with excited anticipation of that time still to come. He rose and, in facing Kristy, asked that she promise him one thing, that she would return soon with the wee one and also with Alasdair. The tears were still in Kristy's eyes as she leaned out the window of the coach, waving to the two figures that grew smaller and smaller until they were completely lost from her sight. The coach would take them to Sydney and, from there, they would board the steamer for the journey north to New Carlisle and home. She looked to the left, out over the broad expanse of the Bras d'Or Lake towards the Washabuk point and Baddeck further back. Although she could not explain it, it was at that moment that Kristy smiled with the realization that, for as long as she lived, she would always associate the precious gift of family with the words nuptials and peppermints.

An empty tea crate. It seemed a most unlikely item to treasure as it sat there in the back of the sleigh looking ever so much like some forlorn orphan being spirited away from the safety of its home. It was only a matter of a few days ago that it had sat resplendent in Dunn's General Store with its aromatic cargo of black tea. Given the insatiable highland thirst for tea as well as *uisge beatha*, it had been quickly relieved of its contents and now sat there as nothing more than a forsaken shell of its former self exposed to the biting cold of the December air. As the horse and sleigh glided up the road towards the bluffs, Margaret could not help but draw an analogy between the vacuous crate and the pangs of emptiness that still lingered inside her. This would be the second celebration of Christmas since Peter's death and she prayed that it would be a more joyous occasion than last year. Her eyes moved slowly from the empty crate, surrounded as it was by several bags of sugar, to the profile of James who sat silently in the seat beside her. Something from deep within told her that, in all likelihood, this holiday time would be little different from the last one.

Sure enough, all three children would make a fuss and, in their own indeterminable way, do their best to compensate for the absence of Peter and his infectious laughter that had always blanketed the house with its warmth. Charles had abandoned both his job at Angus Wright's mill and his plans to become a carpenter. He was now the eldest son and, as such, had taken over where Peter had left off on the farm. Betty was an "old married woman" of seven months and would spend the better part of the Christmas time with her new extended family at the MacInnes farm down the coast road. From the vantage point high up on the bluffs, Margaret looked off to the south and imagined she could actually pick out the house as it sat upon the expansive patchwork quilt of spruce green and snowy white. And her *righ beag* had just been taken on full time at the bank as a teller with his very own wicket. Albert had proven himself and got along with the other two employees, including the new manager — a Robertson from Sydney. And indeed Albert enjoyed working down in the town. He would do well; did he not always have a mind for sums and figures? Above everything else, there was still a strong aversion to the woods.

It was Kristy who had first approached Margaret in early November about the possibility of directing the children's choir at a Christmas concert to be held in the community hall. It had taken tenacious determination on Kristy's part to break through Margaret's reluctance and reverse her resolve to politely decline. There were so many other things to be done, including the baking of fruit cakes and plum puddings that were so demanding of her time and energy. But even with the litany of tasks that awaited her cleaning, sorting, knitting, sewing and baking, Margaret realized that they were nothing more than excuses masking her own fear. To work with the wee ones would mean that she would see Peter in the mischief of their twinkling eyes, his innocence in their dishevelled hair and his spontaneity in their sheepish looks as lyrics momentarily escaped them. From years of revelling together in song over the milling table and elsewhere, the two women had forged a close lasting friendship. More by intuition than fact, they knew each other's thoughts without a word being spoken. It was for this reason that when the assertion *"Tha feum aca ort."* (They need you.) came from Kristy's mouth, both women fully appreciated that it was a plea that arose from her heart: *Tha feum agad orra.* (You need them.) Margaret had finally agreed but only after some considerable soul searching. She would do it for the children, for the love of song. She would do it for Peter.

Over a period of three weeks, Margaret had travelled to the hall every Tuesday and Thursday afternoon to conduct choir practice. The children came directly from school and were more than eager to participate on stage for the entire community to see. Moira Campbell had visions of her own stellar performance in the tradition of Dame Emma Albani, a farm girl herself from Lower Canada who was the Dominion's first opera singer to gain international acclaim. She was truly blessed with a beautiful soprano voice and had been given the distinct honour of performing at Queen Victoria's funeral in London. Moira promised herself that she would sing as if she were standing before the Prince of Wales, the old Queen's great grandson. She thought him terribly handsome and had even clipped his picture from the Sydney paper to be placed on her bedside table. Although it was the *Loch Dubh* community hall and not the Royal Albert Hall, it would still be a command performance for her and perhaps even for the other students should they decide to behave themselves.

Margaret had taken the tea chest and, with the greatest of care, removed the paper lining affixed to the inside walls. The reverse side revealed large sheets of silver that would suit her purposes just fine. In addition to the choral presentation, she planned a nativity scene for the finale that would be acted out on stage as a large luminous star descended from the heavens, assisted by a lengthy piece of twine attached to a hook in the rafter. It would be a moving sight with the choir singing *Silent Night* and the placing of the Christ child in the manger. The members of the choir had been asked to select a boy and a girl from their own ranks to serve in the roles of Mary and Joseph. It had not taken long for a caucus to be formed and, eventually, a consensus reached. Aulay and Grace would be the Holy Couple, at least for this night. Even Margaret was confident that, with several rehearsals and strict words of guidance, they would do well. It would be a fitting way to end the concert before the Reverend Fraser bestowed the benediction. It all seemed so right.

Mixed with the warmth percolating from the pot-bellied stove, the pine boughs that decorated the face of the stage cast a lingering fragrance throughout the hall on the December night as people first began to arrive. Some had come early in order to be assured of a good seat near the front. It would be a proud moment for many a mother and father who might well imagine their child to be completely alone on stage and singing with the beauty and clarity of an angel. True enough, this was not the Royal Albert Hall in London or even the Lyceum Theatre in Sydney. It was only *Loch Dubh* but, no mind, it would be a wonderfully entertaining evening. Their child and the others would see to that.

At precisely seven o'clock with the assembled audience in place, Duncan Fraser left his seat and stepped onto the stage where Margaret and the choir had already taken up their well-rehearsed positions. He quickly took note of the substantial crowd that now completely filled the hall with the exception of a small area immediately in front of the tea table at the rear. As was the custom, the concert was opened with prayer and it was one of great thanks for the gift of music and of fellowship at a time when they gathered to celebrate the most wonderful gift of all. He intentionally kept the prayer short conscious of the fact that, more than anything else, this was an evening for the children. He smiled knowingly at Margaret and quickly resumed his seat next to Jennie in the front row.

The choir performed beautifully, or so was the view of each and every parent who thought their bairn's voice carried the others so wonderfully. A rousing round of applause followed each selection as Margaret took them through their paces and softly offered a reassuring *"math sibh féin"* (well done) to the choir members as the clapping slowly subsided. She had surprised even herself with the sudden realization that she was smiling broadly throughout the evening. She knew that she had glimpsed Peter's innocence in their sheepish looks as, on more than one occasion, lyrics had indeed eluded them as tiny hands were waved in the direction of family members seated down below. It was then that she knew that the pangs of emptiness in her heart were being replaced with joyous song. *Tha feum agam orra.* (I need them.) Kristy had known it all along and Margaret would make a special point of thanking her later.

Immediately before the intermission, Margaret turned to the audience and made the announcement that a special song would be performed. No further explanation was offered and a sense of puzzlement soon fell over those assembled as Kristy slowly rose from her seat in the middle of the hall, proceeded down the centre aisle and onto the stage. She went over to Ismay Campbell, who stood in the first row of the choir, and took her by the hand to a spot in the centre of the stage. Most residents of *Loch Dubh* knew from attending services at the Kirk that Ismay had a beautiful musical voice. What they did not necessarily know was that she had also developed both a love of and aptitude for poetry. After their regular afternoon sessions in the Erskine kitchen, it had become Kristy's habit to read to her from the works of the great British poets — Tennyson, Burns, Keats, Byron and others — and, as she did, one could almost see the intensity with which Ismay absorbed each and every word. There was a love of language that often took the form of poems that she would compose, most often in Gaelic but from time to time in English, and share from memory with her teacher. Now, as she crouched down with her hands encircling Ismay's tiny waist, Kristy whispered into the child's ear. *"Mo ghràdhag, seinnidh sinn an dàn iongantach agad."* (My dear little one, we will sing your wonderful poem.) Throughout the hall, there was a growing sense of anticipation.

Kristy remained focussed on the blueness of Ismay's eyes as the child stared off into the absolute silence that continued to blanket the hall. Ever so softly, the two voices began to flow together as the Gaelic poem came to life.

"Nach fhaic thu, nach fhaic thu
Glòir na h-oidhche seo?
Fosgail do shùilean, fosgail do chridh'
Dhan t-solus-latha nach tig gu crìch."

(Oh can't you see, can't you see
the glory of this night?
Open your eyes, open your heart
to the light that knows no end of day.)

Kristy sensed that her hands, which continued to rest on the small waist, were all the support that the little one needed. Somehow the child was living the words that flowed from her so effortlessly and melodically. It was Ismay's composition and it would be her voice to fill the room with its beauty. In much the same way that dear Archie MacDonald would read scripture, Ismay seemed to look off to the rafters as she now sang on alone.

"Tha mi a' cluinntinn tuiteam an t-sneachda
'S e a' suaineadh nan craobh buachailleach na phlaide.

Tha mi a' làimhseachadh lainnir nan reultan
'S iad a' treòrachadh nan ceuman seasmhach.

Tha fàileadh an t-sabhail nam bheul
'S a' cniadachadh an luchd-turais sgith.

Tha taom a' ghràidh nam shròin
'S e a' dòrtadh air a' leabaidh fheuraich.

Chi mi aghaidh Mhaireannach Dhé
'S i a' soillseachadh mo cheum san dorchadas.

Nach fhaic thu, nach fhaic thu
Glòir na h-oidhche seo?
Fosgail do shùilean, fosgail do chridh'
Dhan t-solus-latha nach tig gu crìch."

(I hear the falling of the snow
as it blankets the shepherding trees.

I touch the glimmering of the stars
as they guide the resolute footsteps.

I taste the scenting of the barn
as it caresses the weary travellers.

I smell the pouring of love
as it cascades over the grassy bed.

I see the everlasting face of God
as it lights my darkened path.

Oh can't you see, can't you see
the glory of this night?
Open your eyes, open your heart
to the light that knows no end of day.)

As the final words trailed off into the hushed confines of the room, the audience remained eerily still. There was no applause. As Tina wiped a tear from her eye, both she and Daniel likened it to hearing a recently discovered psalm for the very first time. There was almost a reverence to it that defied explanation. After several seconds, it was Duncan Fraser who was the first to clap his hands together and soon it spread down the rows and across the length of the hall. Ismay smiled as Kristy led her back to her place with applause now resonating in her ears. Kristy brushed the child's long black hair back over her shoulder with her hand and, in turning to return to her place below, heard whispered words of self-assurance being spoken. *"Dìreach. Dìreach."* (Just so. Just so.)

The tea table did a brisk business as cups were poured and buttered scones consumed with great delight during the break. Both Peter and Martha Campbell received numerous rave compliments about their daughter and her powerful use of language. While Martha took comfort and pride in the accolades that were so generously bestowed upon her child, there was even greater comfort and pride in the confirmation that Ismay was not handicapped. Indeed she was a terribly gifted child. *Beannachd Dhé a tha thar gach uile thuigse.* (The blessing of God which passes all understanding.) Seldom before had she been so proud of her daughter, her truly blessed child.

The concert resumed and the children sang with increasing fervour as the end drew ever near. It was as the first verse of *Oidhche chiùin* (Silent Night) echoed off the walls that Andrew Ferguson, positioned off to the side, unfastened the long piece of twine that saw a silvery star slowly descend from the heavens to hover over the stage like a divine beacon. Mary and Joseph, dressed in flowing robes made of old bed sheets, reverently appeared from behind the choir carrying the infant doll to the manger, which had been strategically positioned on the corner of the stage during the tea break. As Mary stepped forward to lay her child lovingly on the bed of hay, Joseph looked down upon her and spake in a thunderous voice saying *"A Mhàiri, gluais do thòn! Tha thu 'nad sheasamh air mo chois."* (Mary, move your arse! You are standing on my foot.)

Almost instantly, the beckoning star crashed to the stage as young Andrew, now doubled over with laughter, lost his grip on the twine. He was certainly not alone for indeed the entire audience, including Duncan and Jennie, laughed uproariously knowing that Aulay was neither quoting scripture or making light of the serenity of the moment. Indeed, the only sign of indignation was on the face of poor Mary who finally succeeded in placing the bairn in His manger. With laughter still ringing throughout the hall, He would surely not get a wink of sleep.

In finally mounting the stage, Duncan Fraser stood between Mary and Joseph with a hand on each of their shoulders as he pronounced the benediction. While it referred to the gift of a child born in a stable, the prayer made special reference to the gift of life and laughter. This too was part of the joy of Christmas. Much to Mary's chagrin and Joseph's relief, the baby slept on oblivious to the kerfuffle that had just played itself out with such unexpected drama. Sleep in heavenly peace; sleep in heavenly peace.

The bulbous nose. It was all that she could focus on as she looked at the picture of the tiny face that seemingly had come to represent so much history. The lines were not etched into the skin perhaps the way they should be if one were to care one iota about historical accuracy. Yet the most blatant detail, no doubt unintended, was the broad nose that dominated the face. In some respects, it reminded her of Sir John A.'s features as well as his fondness for the drink that had apparently coloured his nose a deep Liberal red. She laughed at the thought of the righteous indignation that the Dominion's first prime minister would surely feel in being associated in any way, shape or form with either the Grits or the physical attributes of the disloyal American general — later first president or not.

Jennie gently rubbed her finger across the stamp affixed to the envelope that depicted George Washington in military uniform. He did indeed have a grand and amusing nose but still it did not bring her as much pleasure as the memories of *iolaire mhamaidh* (Mamma's Eagle) — the name that Matthew had given the letter from Effie and Liam some ten years ago. She wondered where the time had gone; it slipped by as if little had changed and yet she knew otherwise. As she sat in Duncan's rocking chair on the veranda, she reflected on the transformations to her own family: Sandy married in Sydney, Matthew contemplating an offer of employment in Halifax with a legal firm and Emily expecting her first child in Baddeck, all of them gone from *Loch Dubh*. Yet she and Duncan would finally be grandparents; how she had longed for the day. With the warm breeze of the June afternoon carrying the fragrance of the apple blossoms up from the orchard, Jennie knew that it would be a memorable summer. In addition to everything else, she would also make the acquaintance of her namesake, Murdina Jennie O'Sullivan, for the very first time.

The letter had arrived from Boston in mid May. Effie's parents were now in failing health and the O'Sullivans had decided that a trip to Cape Breton was not only desirable but necessary. It would be important for Murdina Jennie to know her grandparents and, at the age of six and a half, she was now old enough to understand the significance of her extended family. As was the case with the previous letter, the O'Sullivans made a special point of expressing a desire to include a visit to *Loch Dubh* as well. For Jennie, the only difference this time was that there had been no need for discussion or coercion. In his own way, Duncan now looked forward to the visit almost as much as she did.

In the days leading up to the arrival, Jennie busied herself with cleaning and sorting out the manse. Her concentration was on the upstairs bedrooms where the three would stay. From money sent home on a fairly regular basis by Sandy and Matthew, she had eventually saved enough to order several rolls of floral wallpaper from the Eaton's catalogue, which now brought new colourful life to the rooms. In some strange way, the paper transformed the bedrooms in a totally unexpected manner. They were no longer her children's but those of guests. Initially, it had been disquieting for her and extremely difficult to explain. Quite intentionally, Duncan lightened the moment by joking that, given his wife's fondness for flowers, he would not be surprised to wake up one morning to find that their guests were none other than a swarm of bees that had taken up residence. Never at a loss for words, Jennie took it all in good form. *"Ud. Ud. Tha thu 'nad aoghaire agus bithidh thu nis nad fhear-coimhid bheachan. Feuch creutairean Dhé. Tha iad mar sin uile."* (Tut. Tut. You are a pastor and now you will be a beekeeper. Behold God's creatures. They are all thus.) Duncan knew enough not to push his wife further. Family was important to her as was a good impression. He had made his point by lightening the moment and, now, would let her be.

On the afternoon that the steamer docked at the government wharf, Jennie could not help but harken back to the first visit. Now, as she held Duncan's arm tightly, she waited with eager anticipation as the passengers began to disembark and make their way along the long expanse of planking . Her gaze was suddenly drawn to the small girl with tartan ribbons in her long nut-brown hair who anxiously scurried down the boarding ramp. Effie and Liam soon appeared and were quick in their attempts to follow close behind their daughter. From where she stood, Jennie could tell that they had aged a bit but Effie's elegant manner and Liam's crop of fiery-red hair could never be mistaken. Still, it was something else. It was the small one's face that so captivated her as they drew closer. There was something oddly strange now that the pictures in the Christmas cards came to life before her. Murdina Jennie looked so terribly familiar.

The first few days saw the O'Sullivans settled nicely into their upstairs "garden." During the day, Liam was off with his daughter retracing many of the same paths that he had trod years before under the capable guidance of the three Fraser children. At the same time, Jennie and Effie made a conscious effort to find time away from the kitchen for the occasional stroll down by the loch. It was on one such outing that Jennie, from the corner of her eye, finally commented on the radiance that so dominated her cousin's face and entire demeanor. It was all so clear that Murdina Jennie had truly been a blessing to her.

"Effie, it has been far too long since we have sat together and there have been changes with the years. How happy I am for you and Liam; now you are truly a family. God has watched over you and answered your prayers as I knew He would. There will be much joy for you both in the months and years to come. Och, there will be grandchildren and you will be even more happy if you can imagine that to be possible. I have not told you as yet but Emily is now with child, our first grandchild. Duncan and I are like a newly married couple full of blissful expectations as was the case with Sandy's arrival. It is all so glorious."

For what appeared to be several long seconds, Effie simply looked into Jennie's face as the breeze off the loch played with their hair. Finally, she reached out and joined their hands together. With only the sound of the water lapping against the shore, there was a sense of expectancy about the moment. "My dear Jennie, we have both seen and experienced so much since the days of our youth though our lives have gone in quite different directions. You will never know how close we will always feel to you and Duncan even with the distance between us. *Bidh Cheap Breatuinn nam chridhe agus ann a'cridhe mo theaghlaich. Tha e ceart. Cumaidh ceanglaichean an teaghlaich mi agus gléidhidh mi thu nar smaointean agus iomadh ùrnuigh. Tapadh leat a Shìne.*" (Cape Breton will always be in my heart and in my family. It is proper. The ties of family will sustain me and keep you in my thoughts and many prayers. Thank you Jennie.)

Jennie clearly remembered being taken aback not only by the fact that Effie had spoken in the Gaelic but also by the words she had apparently chosen with such care. There seemed to be so much that Jennie did not understand and yet, at the same time, so much that she did. "*Sin beannachd teaghlaich o linn gu linn. Faodadh e bhi mar so a ghnàth.*" (It is the blessing of family from generation to generation. May it always be so.) Jennie's words were as heart-felt as they were brief. It seemed as though nothing else need be said, and it was not. They chose to simply sit in silence holding hands and admiring the broad vista of water and mountains that rested before their eyes.

It had never been Jennie's practice to share such personal conversations with Duncan. Yet that night, as they prepared for bed, she confided in him that Effie had a special reason for returning to *Loch Dubh*. As her parents faced their own mortality, Effie was intent on reaffirming the ties that bound her larger family together. Duncan's only response was to nod in silent understanding. No explanation was needed. It was apparent, even to him, that Murdina Jennie had indeed been a blessing.

It was the following Friday evening that Emily and Christopher arrived from Baddeck. Emily had notified her mother in advance of their intended visit, if for no other reason than to ensure that Jennie would have sufficient time to prepare the bedroom off the dining-room for them. Jennie understood and appreciated the fact that her daughter wished to see the O'Sullivans during their brief stay. They had been so kind to her during her year away in a strange land far from home. It was only proper that they should spend a few days together in each other's company and perhaps reminisce. It would close a chapter and certainly no harm could come of it. After all, Cape Breton was truly her home.

Having arrived late in the afternoon, Emily and Christopher were just in time for a sumptuous supper of codfish hash fried in bacon grease, which had been a favourite of hers since childhood. Around the table, the traditional silence was broken on numerous occasions as Murdina Jennie regaled her audience with stories of her studies at the Immaculate Heart of Mary School and the fact that she had recently done an oral report on Cape Breton in front of all her classmates. She was very proud of her mother's Nova Scotia origins and had even gone so far as to include a few words of Gaelic that Effie had practised with her. She recounted how the other children had laughed uproariously at the strange sounds coming from her mouth and how Sister Kathleen O'Reagan had quickly and quite sharply called all her students to order. Once peace and quiet had finally been restored, none of them were perceptive enough to see the tears welling up in their teacher's eyes as her thoughts were cast back to another land across the seas from where her own family had been exiled by blight. There was a bond.

With elbows on the table and chin cradled in the bridge of her hands, Emily was totally captivated as she listened intently to the child's exuberance. Her attentiveness did not go unnoticed by Effie and Liam who quite willingly allowed this special moment to continue for some time. However, there were limits. "Murdina Jennie, that is enough. Let us eat our supper before it grows even colder. There will be plenty of time later for your stories without keeping everyone from their meal. You are so like your father!" Liam shot his wife a whimsical glance as the entire table erupted in great gales of laughter. Even Duncan joined in though he had taken careful note of the name of Murdina's school. The issue was never raised, even the following morning when the child presented Jennie and Duncan with a recent photograph of herself in her first communion dress. In expressing thanks, Jennie made a great fuss over it and asked Duncan if it was not beautiful just. He agreed that it was. Nothing else was said on the matter.

The next day, Liam and Effie lingered over tea with Jennie and Christopher in the kitchen while Duncan repaired to the parlour to put final touches to his Sunday sermon. With all the adult talk now dominating the table, Murdina Jennie had been more than receptive to the idea of a walk down by the water when Emily first suggested it. It was far too lovely a day for a child full of life and curiosity to remain cooped up inside. Effie's knowing smile was confirmation enough that a walk would be just the thing. As they strolled hand-in-hand down the laneway and onto the loch road, it was not entirely by accident that their meanderings drew them first towards the Kirk and the cemetery that stretched up the hill beyond. There, they lingered for a time before a simple white stone. It was the small girl who finally looked up into Emily's face and asked why it was that they had stopped at this place. "This is a good friend of mine, little one, who would have liked to have met you. He would have so enjoyed you, especially your wonderful stories and laughter." Murdina Jennie was not yet able to read the name on the stone and certainly not the Gaelic inscription at its base. The significance of the visit was completely lost on her. She pretended to comprehend although it was quite apparent that she did not. Without such understanding, she would never be cognizant of the fact that this was to be the only time that she would make the acquaintance of Peter MacGregor. It was something that Emily knew she had to do for the child as well as her father. With that, they quietly turned and left the cemetery, allowing it to return to its natural state of rest.

With the exception of the call to worship and the benediction, the entire service was conducted in the English. Few seemed to mind, even the older people, given that it was common knowledge that the Frasers had company visiting from away who were in their presence. As she sat in the pew of a Kirk that seemed so familiar to her, Effie's thoughts were of her own childhood in another place of worship with her parents who would likely be taken from her all too soon. The words of the hymn *How Firm A Foundation* came to her mind as her eyes began to moisten. Beside her sat Murdina Jennie whose own mind was flooded with a multitude of questions. Where was the altar and the crucifix with the figure of our Lord sharing His suffering and sacrifice for our sins? How could you possibly do the stations of the cross when there were no stations? Where were the kneeling rails? Why was Father Duncan dressed in a somber black cassock with those two white strips of cloth falling from his collar? And where was the font containing the holy water? There were other questions as well but she knew better than to ask any of them to anyone other than herself, at least for now. It would be a sin to speak during the mass even though this one was so different and puzzling. To talk would mean a long visitation to the dark recesses of the confessional booth, something that still upset her. She could not see one here and it was this, more than anything else, that pleased her most.

As it slowly glided into its mooring alongside the government wharf, the Monday morning steamer assumed a symbolic significance that defied words. The time for departure had come all too quickly. Of greater consequence was the unstated belief that this most probably would be a painful moment, a parting perhaps never to be repeated. There was a poignancy to it that was lost only on Murdina Jennie who skipped along full of excited anticipation about yet another boat ride. As much as such thoughts were banished from their lips, tears flowed freely. Emily crouched down and hugged the little girl who once again had tartan ribbons streaming down the back of her hair. The words were as hushed as they were simple. "Murdina Jennie, remember our walk together and those who never had the joy of knowing you as have I. *Is tu m'annsachd.*" (You are my best beloved.)

The speck on the horizon was not simply the fading shape of a steamer of the Bras d'Or Steamboat Company. On that day, it was so much more. As the figures remained on the wharf waving into the distance, one more than the others realized that a cherished part of *Loch Dubh* had been recaptured and then grievously lost forever. "*Is tu m'annsachd. Beannachd leat a ghaoil.*" (You are my best beloved. Farewell my dear one.)

"*Gum bu fada beò an rìgh!*" (Long live the King!) It seemed like an odd and somewhat untimely thing to say just then. As he leaned on the handle of the hay fork, Alasdair looked up towards the lofty walls of the barn whose uneven boards allowed the afternoon sunlight to stream through the numerous oddly-shaped cracks. From a distance, it reminded him of a series of shooting stars across a darkened sky. All the while, the fragrant smell of freshly cut hay permeated the air as he savoured the brief and quite unexpected break from committing the wagon load of hay to its wintery bed in the depths of the mow.

The rich heavy perfume of the hay brought to mind Kristy's comment a few weeks past when she recalled her encounter with several young women from Upper Canada who were visiting New Carlisle as part of a sailing excursion up the coast. She mimicked their stroll along the main street using the old broom as a makeshift parasole handle in guiding her path across the kitchen floor. She sauntered on, all the while offering what she thought to be a fitting parody in her best, toffee-nosed, English accent. "There was such a reeking of perfume and toilet water that it reminded me ever so of a French brothel the morning after pay day!" Amid the laughter, Alasdair had been sorely tempted to jokingly inquire as to the circumstances by which his wife had come to acquire such first-hand knowledge. However, with both Tina and Daniel present, he thought better of it. Playful jesting only extended so far and he dared not incur the wrath of Kristy or his parents.

Alasdair also called to mind the memories of some six years before when, in the privacy of their bedroom, he had first evoked the reference to another King. Kristy had, in her own endearing way, informed him that she was with child, their first. Grace was now five and a half years old and truly her mother's daughter. They were so much alike in so many fascinating and oftentimes surprising ways. Always a man of few words, Alasdair was pleased that his child now knew the love and held the adoration of both sets of grandparents. It was important for her as it was for them, especially Kristy. But of even greater import was the fact that they would soon be parents again. As he quietly resumed spreading the hay across the broad expanse of mow and tromping it down under his feet, Alasdair felt special satisfaction in knowing that his family was growing. He had every confidence that *Loch Dubh* would be enriched by this new life every bit as much as would the Erskine home.

The week before, Kristy had finally come to the realization that it was more than just the sweltering August heat that brought her such physical discomfort. Her body told her that it was in turmoil; changes were occurring that she recognized from past experience. Alasdair had always dreamed of a large family and she was delighted with the prospect of bringing another life into the world. She seldom admitted, even to herself, that she had been all too preoccupied over the past few years with raising Grace, continuing her instruction of Ismay and assuming responsibility for the day-to-day operations of the household. At seventy-three years of age, Tina was growing more feeble and, although it grieved her to watch it happen before her very eyes, Kristy knew that it was her duty to carry on. It was all tacitly understood. It was simply to be.

In that same period of time, Kristy had shared in the joy of several other births to families around *Loch Dubh*. Betty and James MacInnes had been blessed with a baby boy, Diarmid, in April. June had seen the arrival of Sadie and Donald Urquhart's second child, Ewan. The following month witnessed the addition of Hannah to Reverend Rod and Margaret MacDonald's family in *An Abhainn Mheadhonach* as well as Malcolm to that of Duncan and Mabel MacDonald. At the same time, other families were eagerly awaiting their first child. Emily and Christopher Hickman in Baddeck, John and Christine Grant up the shore road and Morag and Elliott Cabot in Boston. *"Clann an cloinne!"* (Their children's children!) Kristy had once again caught herself dwelling on the passage of years since her first arrival on these shores. But just as quickly, a smile came to her face. It would no longer be her child but rather her children who would appear like the first crocuses of spring, bringing new colour, new life and new meaning to this place. She was immensely content knowing that, from the very first day she looked into them, Alasdair's green eyes had seldom before danced with the joy of life that now filled them to overflowing.

Late August was traditionally a time of endless tiring work on the farm. Beyond the many routine chores, the harvesting of the hay fields and the garden demanded long hours under the grueling heat of the late-summer sun. Like all the women of *Loch Dubh*, Kristy knew that her tasks were not limited to the kitchen or even the house. She worked alongside Alasdair in the fields and garden and, from time to time, allowed Grace to lend a helping hand, more to include her than anything else. Even in her expectant state, Kristy knew that her help was now required more than ever to complete the extensive work on time. Although she and Alasdair had never discussed it, they both knew that Daniel and Tina had changed. As the naps grew in duration to feed feeble bodies, so had the dependency. In some respects, Kristy and Alasdair were now expecting their fourth child. On more than a few nights, she remained awake gazing up at the roughly hewn boards of the bedroom ceiling, the same ones whose imaginary roads Alasdair had travelled down as a bairn. Now as she looked over at her sleeping husband, she was eternally grateful for the road that brought her to this place from Christmas Island. She smiled as her thoughts then went to her parents and the visit that she and Grace had made a year ago. Comforted and contented with her reflections, sleep would not be far off.

Latha a'dhuibheid. (The Day of Blackness) This was how Kristy would come to refer to the next day. Her hands were completely black from the dark rich soil of the field behind the barn. Kenneth and Aulay had come after the noon meal to give their aunt and uncle a helping hand with the potato picking. The field was completely awash with plants that hovered over their concealed riches like so many rows of chickens brooding over their eggs. Soon enough, the earthly gems would be deposited in the bins of the root cellar to help sustain the family through the long winter months. But for now, both Alasdair and Kristy were grateful for the extra sets of hands that would quicken the work but seemingly not lessen the wrenching back pain. Thankfully, a large bottle of horse liniment was already in the kitchen porch awaiting the washing of hands and the soothing of tired aching muscles.

Although Kristy was seldom adverse to allowing Grace to assist her parents with the farm work, the arrival of Kenneth and Aulay had precluded it on that particular day. Kristy never considered herself a prude, certainly not like the school mistress, Miss Massey, whose scowling face had now become synonymous with the vinegary aromas of pickling time. It was Aulay who first referred to her as "Mistress Chow-Chow" behind her back and the name quickly fell into common usage, even among the adults. One never quite knew what might come out of Aulay's mouth next, be it in the Gaelic or English depending upon the circumstance. His comments, while frequently humourous, were often as off-colour as they were spontaneous. Today at least, Grace would stay behind at the house with her grandparents. She would be content enough and, no doubt, entertain Tina and Daniel following their routine afternoon naps.

The sun was beginning to crest in the western sky as Kristy straightened out the crook in her back and excused herself from the others in the field. Her attention was now focused on the preparation of supper and, with the two boys joining them later at the table, a much larger amount of vegetables would be required to accompany the pork roast cooking in the oven. As she walked back to the house, Kristy began to brush off the dark soil that completely covered her hands and even worked its way up to her elbows. *"An talamh dubh! Cùis mhaise dìreach mar chaora bhrògach!"* (The black earth! An object of beauty just like a black-faced sheep!) Even with her sore back, she still managed to chuckle to herself as she approached the back step of the house, leaving a lengthy trail of clotted earth behind her like a colossal spotted tail.

At first the voice was so soft that Kristy had almost not heard it over the meandering breeze working its way up from the direction of the mill. There in the garden sat Grace reading a story to Tina, who had positioned herself against the crab-apple tree, a place that she always referred to as *mo shuidheachan iongantach talmhaidh.* (My Wonderful Earthly Pew) Kristy gingerly walked over to better observe the scene that brought her so much pleasure. Grace read on with enthusiastic determination even though Tina had obviously fallen asleep as the warmth of the late-afternoon sun embraced her body beneath the folds of her long dark dress. At her side was a small bouquet of flowers from the garden that she had obviously gathered up shortly before in order to place on the supper table. Dear Tina and her flowers; her garden was so very special to her.

The cracking of a small twig under Kristy's foot finally alerted Grace to her mother's presence and served as a temporary distraction from her eloquent delivery. *"Och Mhamaidh*, I was reading to *Seanamhair* but she fell asleep even before I completed the first page. Should I finish it now or wait until later when her nap is over?"

"There is no need to trouble your wee head *mo ghràdhag*; you have read that very same story to *Seanamhair* a hundred times before. We should start getting ready for supper; it is growing late. Come along now." Kristy then crouched down and gently placed a hand on Tina's shoulder to wake her. Even with the seductive warmth of the sun on her aching back, Kristy went suddenly and terribly cold. "Grace, run to the field and bring your father here. *Siuthad, greas ort mar choinean, mo chaileag.*" (Go on, be quick as a rabbit my girl.) Even with a look of absolute puzzlement on her face, the child did as she was told and ran off leaving her mother and grandmother alone in the garden. Kristy looked down at the small bouquet that rested at Tina's side, the last bouquet that she would pick from her beloved garden. Kristy ran her still-soiled fingers through Tina's neatly pinned, gray hair and leaned into the woman who had been her anchor for so many years. As the words *Ni sealbh an rud as còir* (Providence will do justice) and the memories came flooding back, Kristy could see no justice in a cherished life now taken from her. She knelt down and began to rock Tina back and forth in her arms as the tears streamed down her face.

Even from a distance, it was all so painfully obvious. As he raced around the corner of the barn, Alasdair knew that there was no further need to hurry or even to ask for explanations. He sent Grace to the house as he told his two nephews to return home to bring Neil and Iona without delay. They too did not dare ask questions or seek an explanation. It was only then that he went to Kristy, bending down to place his hands on her quivering shoulders. *"Och, a Chairistìona, bha i an sìth anns a' ghàradh aice a ghnàth. Tha i an sìth gu beachd an dràsda. Leig dhi falbh."* (Oh Kristy, she was always at peace in her garden. She is now truly at peace. Let her go.)

"A Thighearna, chan eil e ceart. Chan eil e ceart. Ghràdhaich mi i gu mór. Och Alasdair, dé nì sinn as a h-aonais?" (Oh Lord, it is not right. It is not right. I loved her so. Alasdair, what will we do without her?) The sobbing continued but her words did not. She now wept uncontrollably as he finally encouraged her to her feet. He embraced her as he looked down upon his mother. Even as tears appeared in his own eyes and began to blur his vision, Alasdair was strangely at peace knowing that, finally, Tina had indeed found rest.

"Gléidhidh sinn i nar cùimhne agus cuidichidh e sinn. Creid mi. Fóghnuidh seo." (We will keep her in our memory and that will sustain us. Believe me. This will suffice.) It was now Alasdair's turn to gently rock his wife in his arms. He knew that he had to remain strong for her and Grace, which he wanted to so desperately while realizing that it would be a test unlike all others he had been subjected to in the past.

Several minutes later, Alasdair found Daniel seated at the kitchen table with his Bible in front of him conducting afternoon devotion. He sat to the side of his father at the very same table that had driven them apart some eleven years ago. Now he hoped, he prayed, it would show compassion in allowing them to come together as never before. When the words finally came, Daniel sat motionless for several interminable seconds with his eyes fixed on Alasdair's face. Initially, it was a blank expression as though he did not fully comprehend their meaning. It was only then that he looked down at his Bible and closed it slowly. There were no tears. He rose and looked at Alasdair, Kristy and Grace, although an observer could not have been faulted for thinking that he was actually looking through them to something farther removed. *"Tha e dèanta. Feuch, is freasdal Dhé e."* (It is done. Behold, it is God's providence.) No one in the room could ever recall having heard such softness in the old man's voice. As they remained there in silence, Daniel picked up the Bible and walked quietly to the bedroom. The only sound was the soft clicking of the door into place as it closed after him. There was an obvious need to be alone in grief.

With the eventual arrival of Neil and Iona, the two sons lovingly carried their mother to the bedroom off the dining-room so that Iona and Kristy could begin to prepare her body. It was only when the door was securely closed behind them that Neil and Alasdair went to their father to offer what consolation they could. Daniel's eyes had reddened; he had expressed his sorrow privately in the confines of the room that he and Tina had shared since their marriage, the very same room that now seemed so empty. His words to his sons were very matter-of-fact and came in the form of a request for help. The three men went to the loft of the wagon house where they lowered the coffin that Daniel had prepared for himself at the time of Archie's passing. There was a strange irony that surrounded their work as the two sons carried the empty receptacle to the house for their mother, under the watchful gaze of Daniel who followed close behind. It was only then that Alasdair openly broke down in tears.

During the two days of waking, Tina rested in the front parlour that was stripped of all decoration with one exception — the flowers from her garden that dotted the room. Custom aside, Tina was to remain surrounded by the colours, shapes and fragrances that she had so loved to nurture throughout her life. Before neighbours and friends began to arrive to pay their final respects, the family gathered together in front of the coffin to bid their own personal farewells. It was Daniel who prayed aloud. It was Alasdair and Neil who stood by stoically. It was Iona and the three children who fought back tears. It was Kristy who walked forward and placed a gold chain around Tina's neck — the very same chain that had carried her engagement ring around her own neck those many years ago. She recalled savouring the same floral fragrance in this very room on the day of her wedding. Kristy looked down into Tina's face and whispered softly. *"Thà, a' lùr; leig t'anail. Gu' m bi Dia nan gras daonnan maille rubh. Beannachd leat a ghaoil."* (Yes, my jewel; take your rest. May God always be near you. Farewell dear one.)

A sense of genuine shock had spread throughout the community as the news of Tina's untimely death was carried from house to house. Although it was never said in so many words, most people had been of the view that Daniel would surely be the first in the Erskine household to be called home. Regardless, a *strùpag* was prepared and served in the kitchen as people continued to pass through the door from the front parlour. The women brought endless amounts of baked goods to be served with endless cups of tea poured from the pot that was always at the ready. Amid the hushed discussions, it was only James MacGregor who was brazen enough to produce a flask in order to partake in a *deoch*. Everyone else it seemed had more respect for Daniel's position, not only as a member of session but also as its clerk. While they all might sympathize with Margaret's plight, there was little else that could be done.

On the final night of the wake, *Coinneach Bàn* took his grandfather aside as the last visitors departed. It had nothing to do with the night vigil in the parlour since both Alasdair and Neil had made it abundantly clear that they would undertake the responsibility, sparing their father and other family members any further anguish. It was only on the day of the funeral, following the service in the Kirk, that the purpose of their discussion became known. As Tina's mortal remains were lowered into the grave and the first handful of soil covered the broad white-pine boards, Duncan Fraser spoke the words of committal. His voice fell silent and only then did Daniel look up from the grave, up the hill in the direction of Andrew MacDonald's cairn. The mournful sounds of *The Flowers of the Forest*, one of the most beloved laments of the highland Scots, began to cascade down towards the grave and beyond as Kenneth played a final tribute for his grandmother. It did not go unnoticed that it was the first time that Daniel removed a handkerchief from his pocket as tears flowed freely down his craggy cheeks. Everyone stood motionless as if to breathe would somehow shatter the sanctity of the moment.

Coinneach Bàn dared not look towards the grave for fear of losing control of the instrument. Instead, he set his eyes on *An Toiseach* and *An Deireadh* in the far distance until they too became obscured by his blurred vision. He knew his *seanamhair* would be proud, not only for his will to play or even for the tune that had been chosen. Rather, she would be proud because he had decided to follow where others had led. There was consolation in the continuity that would live on even when the flowers of her own garden had wilted and passed from sight.

As the last note was sounded and the music evaporated on the cool August wind, *Coinneach Bàn* removed his right hand from the chanter and stood rigidly still. *"A Sheanamhair, tha mi gad ionndrainn mu thràth. Aig Dia a mhàin tha brath. Och mo shùilean ri snighe ged bhios tu nam chùimhne a ghnàth mar fhlùraichean breagha."* (Grandmother, I miss you already. God alone knows. My eyes will remain tearful although you will always be in my memory like beautiful flowers.) He promised himself that it would be so for as long as he lived.

"Beannachd leibh."

CHAPTER SIXTEEN

Oh, it's the golden summertime that's come again;
Robins now are singing on every tree;
Oh, it's the golden summertime that's come again.
Dan Alex MacDonald
The Golden Summer (song)

Gur bheil an samhradh òrgheal air tighinn mu'n cuairt;
Ceilearadh nan smeòrach air barr gach bruaich;
Gu bheil an samhradh òrgheal air tighinn mu'n cuairt.
Dan Alex MacDonald
An Ceitean Orgheal (òran)

It was not so much the crispness on the air that signalled the changing seasons. Rather, there was something in the air that made the transformation even more apparent. As looms once again resumed their lyrical clacking rhythms, *Loch Dubh* was as much enfolded by the melodious strains of jigs, strathspeys and reels as it was by the rich colours of the autumn leaves. It was as if the resonating sounds from the hollow of the mountains brought new life to the hillsides that, even now, were preparing themselves for the cloaking bereavement of the wintery snows. However, amid the many changes coming to pass, there was one constant affirmation of the joys of life that would nurture and sustain — the community hall would once again reverberate with the swirling sights and pulsating sounds of milling frolics and *céilidhs*.

It was not as though Jessie were too old to show the younger ones how a square set was to be danced properly. There was still plenty of life left in her old bones and, even with the weight of fifty-seven years upon her, she loved nothing better than to make the broad boards of the hall's floor sing under her feet. She could still remember a time when she and Malcolm would laugh uproariously in each other's arms as the spirited music of the fiddle propelled them with ever-increasing speed round and round. It was yesterday and yet it was already fifteen years since he had been taken from her. For some strange reason, she suddenly thought of the letter in Archie's Bible. *Tha na seann nithean air dol seachad. Na cuimhnean; is iad seo an chùimhnean agamsa a mhàin.* (Old things are passed away. My memories; they are only my memories.) She knew they were; she knew they had to be.

There was such an overwhelming sense of comfort in the kitchen.

Perhaps it was the warmth of the fire or the sweet mell of freshly baked bread that still lingered having been taken from the oven earlier in the day. Or perhaps it was something else. Jessie looked down into the tiny face of her three-month-old grandson, who had been well fed and now slept blissfully cocooned in his blanket in the crook of his grandmother's arm. *"Calum Beag."* (Little Malcolm) She smiled in admitting to herself that she found joy in just hearing the name being spoken aloud. And there, across from her at the kitchen table, sat Catriona busily engaged in drawing a picture under the amber light cast by the kerosene lamp. While the artist softly nattered away to herself, Jessie continued to smile. In the two and a half years since Catriona's birth, Jessie had quite unexpectedly come to a greater appreciation of family. As with poor Tina, would they not all soon enough be nothing more than engraved names on stones cascading down the slopes of *Beinn-mo-Mhulaid*? With the passage of the years, each of them would be drawn to the mirror and forced to look into it only to discover that they had suddenly grown old; they had all become *Floiridh Aosda*. And yet, Jessie sat in her rocking chair by the kitchen stove and continued to smile, into the very face of life itself. It was much more than mere names. Catriona and Malcolm would remain as part of her testament to this place long after her body was committed to the ground and her name to stone. Once more, she brought the chair to life as, ever so softly, she began to hum an old milling tune to herself.

Mabel entered the kitchen and stood over Catriona who remained totally engrossed in her artwork. "You will be a good girl and go to bed when you are asked now won't you my darling? Your beautiful dress is all laid out in your room for Kirk in the morning. It will be an important day for the family and I want you to be well turned out and rested." What she meant to say was that she wanted her daughter to be rested and on her best behaviour, which was never a certainty even at the best of times. Mabel glanced over at Jessie and smiled; it was all too apparent that Catriona was totally consumed by something of far greater significance than her mother's suggestive words. The fact that Malcolm would be baptized at the morning service was of no real consequence to his sister, none at all. The stubbornness of the MacDonalds aside for the moment, Mabel smiled as she gathered up the child's long auburn hair from the edges of her face and laid it down the length of her back. She then leaned forward and kissed the tiny cheek knowing that her words had indeed fallen on deaf ears. "You are truly your father's daughter."

Jessie smothered a laugh, conscious of not waking the wee Malcolm in her arms as she continued to rock him into deeper sleep. "The bairns will be fine right enough. You two go along and enjoy yourselves. The fresh air and dancing will do you nothing but good. Off you go and, should anyone ask after me, tell them that the *cailleach* is getting too old for such merriment." Duncan had just entered the room as Jessie completed her self-depreciating commentary. He turned to retrieve the coats from the hook on the back of the kitchen door and skillfully offered his own words of parting that were as much intended for the benefit of his mother as his daughter.

"*A Chatriona, mo lurag, giùlain thu féin an nochd agus gabh beachd air a'chaillich.*" (Catriona, my little darling, behave yourself tonight and pay attention to the old woman.) Although Duncan seldom spoke the Gaelic around his wife, he could not resist the temptation to tease his mother. Mabel at least knew the meaning of the word *cailleach*, which was as often used in a playful manner as it was in a slightly derogatory one. She looked over at Jessie with a sense of expectation as Catriona remained oblivious to the scene around her and continued to concentrate on her work. As was seemingly the case with all MacDonalds, the words would not go unchallenged for long.

"*Cha ruig thu leas a bhi toirt meathadh dhòmhsa! Nach tu a tha dona, a Dhonnchaidh Mhic Dhòmhnuill! Siuthad, greas ort.* (You need not be taunting me! Are you not a mischievous one, Duncan MacDonald! Go on; hurry up.) Mabel, keep an eye on him. He is an evil one, *och ma tà.*" (Oh indeed.) Jessie continued to chuckle to herself long after her son and daughter-in-law had departed for the *céilidh*. He was so much like her Malcolm years ago. While the heat from the stove continued to soothe her arthritic bones, it was this continuum of family that warmed her even more. Seldom could she remember being so content with her life.

It was obvious that the *céilidh* was already in full flight as Duncan tied the horse and wagon to a tree at the side of the hall. The music and laughter percolated through the double doors and windows as he and Mabel hastily made their way up the stairs. They were soon on the dance floor as *Mac an Fhìdhleir* took to full flight in spinning his magic that even the four walls could not contain. The tall windows had all been opened to allow a cross breeze to flood the room that was already seething with the whirlwind of activity, covering its floor like a gigantic, undulating patchwork quilt made from a myriad of shapes and colours. The quilt was actually more like a kaleidoscope that changed forms and hues as the dancers wove themselves into intricate patterns that were as spontaneous and captivating as the music itself.

Several minutes and square sets later, the fiddle ceased its singing for a time as it came to rest and now luxuriated in the still-warm seat of the wooden chair at the front of the hall. Jamie was taking a well-deserved break as he eagerly crossed the room to join his wife who stood talking with her mother at the tea table. At the same time, Duncan found himself soaked in perspiration and left Mabel in the company of several other women, including Sadie Urquhart, who were eager to compare stories about the wee ones. Although he could never quite understand this female need to discuss the state of the children outside the home, Duncan was most grateful for the respite it now afforded him from the sweltering heat of the hall. From the corner of his eye, he caught sight of his cousin

Daniel going through the doorway to join the other men outside for a breath of fresh air and whatever else might be on the go. While there were few certainties in life, there was little doubt but that James MacGregor would yet again be holding spirited court in the shadowless darkness that was his domain.

Once outdoors, Duncan could see that the younger men, Albert MacGregor, Lachlan Campbell and Stuart Ferguson among them, had positioned themselves at the foot of the stairs. As Duncan and Daniel made their way through, it became clear that the lads were taken up with determining who would escort which young lady home at the end of the evening. A cigarette was passed among them as if it would somehow temper the competitive spirit that made it all seem like a ritualistic game. At the grand old ages of twenty-seven and twenty-five, both Duncan and Daniel were grateful that the onerous concerns and preoccupations of youth were long gone from them. *"Mèilich nan caorach. Tha iad cho làn rò is a theachdas iad. Feuch! Àilgheas nan òigearan."* (The bleating of sheep. They are as full of romance as they can be. See the pride of the young men.)

Daniel laughed at Duncan's feigned paternalistic remark as they now headed off to the side where the other men had gathered together in a series of clusters near the edge of the trees. He grabbed his cousin's arm as if to guide his faltering path across the darkened ground and then patted it as if offering a consoling motherly comfort. *"Och seadh! Is doimheadach an nì e. Falbh còmhla riumsa a Dhonnchaidh, mo bhodachain."* (Oh yes! It is a troubling thing. Now come along with me Duncan, my little old man.) Suddenly both broke into riotous laughter that caused the entire group of young men to turn all at the same time and look with puzzlement in the direction of the two figures walking arm-in-arm and passing from sight into the pitch-black fringes.

Although it took several seconds for their eyes to adjust to the darkness, both Duncan and Daniel had little difficulty in identifying the somewhat imposing figure that stood before them with his back turned. Clutching a tin flask in his hand, James MacGregor was surrounded by a gaggle of men whose objective was clearly to feed his ego so that he, in turn, would feel obliged to quench their seemingly insatiable thirst. It appeared that numerous trips had already been made throughout the evening to the auxiliary supply of liquor that sat in the back of the MacGregor wagon just off to the side. Already, the elixir had obviously succeeded in loosening many a tongue and, even from a distance, Duncan and Daniel could sense the makings of a heated debate.

Indeed, the discussion had turned to the recent Dominion election that saw Sir Wilfrid and the Liberals given the boot and replaced by Robert Borden and his Conservatives who had wandered in the political wilderness almost as long as poor Moses and the children of Israel had in the desert sands. "It is nothing short of sheer stupidity for us to have elected that rag-tag crew. Laurier gave us good government in Ottawa just like George

Murray does up in Halifax. The Tories will not govern us as much as rob us blind with more of their scandals. It has always been their way. You mark my words." Duncan recognized the voice as it suddenly brought back a flood of memories. It was none other than John Rogers from New Carlisle whom Archie, with the help of Diarmid MacInnes, *an Seann Chleasaiche*, had playfully ridiculed for his pomposity several years back. Duncan could still see his grandfather, "Daniel in the lions' den", taking such delight in tweaking the unsuspecting feline noses as he sat in the corner smoking his cherished pipe. On that occasion back in the summer of 1903, Duncan remembered looking over at the old man and promising himself that that scene would always remain a special memory of his dear *seanair*. He was pleased that it had.

"My grandfather was Tory blue until the day he died and he would not agree with your flippant comments. If he were here, he would tell you so to your face." Duncan had walked around James' big frame and now appeared in the circle where he stood before Rogers in order to confront him directly. There was a brief silence as the other men now fixed their attention on the two figures who glared across at each other. Finally, it was Rogers who attempted to break the awkwardness of the moment with a remark meant as much to further bolster his own image with the other men as it was to belittle the comments of the "young boy" who stood before him.

"Well your grandfather is not here and that is one less Tory vote for which we can all be most thankful. He can cast his ballot for the devil himself now for all I care. Perhaps that's where his polling station is located anyway." One could sense that Rogers' next order of business was most probably to break into a hearty chuckle to further reinforce his dismissal of the MacDonald rejoinder as being frivolous if not downright trite. However, all this soon became just so much speculation as the cracking of fist to jaw intervened to reinforce a far different point of view. The circle suddenly opened wide as the two men fell to the ground with jabs being landed on both sides. The sudden turmoil brought the younger men scampering over to observe, having temporarily discarded all thoughts of romantic interludes. Only after the passage of several minutes did a few men step in to break the two combatants apart, thus allowing sufficient time for each to glare at one other and, by so doing, feel that his actions had been vindicated and pride now properly restored. The sounds of a fiddle being tuned and the sight of inquiring women appearing at the top of the steps, like so many chickens first emerging from the hen house into the light of day, were well noted and heeded. It was all that was necessary to encourage the men to quickly return to the hall, which most of them did in very short order. The temporary excitement had passed but the *céilidh* continued on. There were still two good hours left before the arrival of the Sabbath; the time was not to be wasted.

During the long drive home, Duncan experienced more aches and pains in his arm from Mabel's disapproving slapping than from the cuts and bruises to his face. The next morning, Catriona took great delight in her father's blackened eye, thinking it made him look so much like the Urquhart's Holstein heifer that was about to freshen. Such amusement was certainly not shared by Mabel and Jessie as the family departed for the Kirk in almost total silence. To his credit, the Reverend Fraser made no comments about Duncan's blatant wounds either before or after the service, even though he had carefully searched the faces of both parents during the baptism as was his practice in posing the prescribed questions to them. In spite of the odd snicker coming from the pews, there was a sense that some things were best left unsaid and so they would be, at least for the time being.

With the passage of several weeks, the bruising, swelling and discolouration around the eye dissipated and soon there was no evidence of the battle honours awarded so unceremoniously on that fall evening. Still, Duncan would always take great pride in knowing that he had stood his ground in defence of his grandfather. From that day onwards, he could never again look up into the sky without thinking of Archie. In some strange yet quite comforting way, the heavens appeared to be a bit more blue because of his presence. It was on that drive home from Kirk that Duncan promised himself that one day he would share the story with Malcolm when the lad was old enough to understand.

A Sheanair, cuiridh mise clach ad chàrn-sa. (Grandfather, I will put a stone on your cairn/I will not forget you.) As he gazed off into the endless expanse of sky over *An Toiseach* and *An Deireadh*, Duncan smiled knowing it to be yet another promise he would surely keep.

The scene was nothing if not ironic. Here, on a bitterly cold, February evening, Iain Grant sat and watched as the woman lovingly presented a rosebud to a young man whose interests seemed to be focused on far more-sensual gratifications. You could see it in his eyes and the manner in which he seductively leaned over her shoulder, as if fully expecting to be rewarded with something of much greater physical pleasure. In quietly observing the scene play itself out on the garden bench, Iain thought it possible that the presentation of the flower was her way of subtly professing her love for the amorous suitor. On the other hand, it might be nothing more than a desperate attempt to maintain a respectful distance between them, at least for the moment. Iain realized that he would never know the final outcome of this touching encounter and, at the same time, admitted that he frankly did not give a tinker's damn one way or the other.

The romantic scene was frozen forever in time as it lay imprisoned on canvas in a heavily gilded and somewhat overpowering frame. The large painting completely dominated the wall above the mantle on the far side of the formal sitting room. For Iain, it was far bigger than life and more than a bit unnerving as was the house itself. Even by New Carlisle standards, the Dunn home was seen as exceedingly grand with its high ceilings and elegant furniture that had been specially ordered and shipped up the coast from Halifax. Although the Eaton's catalogue occupied a prominent place in the corner of their store down on the main street, it was obvious that the family was above certain things such as purchasing furnishings in so common a manner. It did not matter that Iain had known John Dunn for several years; indeed, Dunn had hired him on as a helper for a time at the store some fifteen years earlier. *Iain an dealanaich.* He still found himself cringing at the mere mention of the words that some of the old timers continued to use in referring to him even after all this time. But more than that, he now found himself cringing in the presence of John Dunn.

The light from the kerosene lamps bathed the ornate carpet in the centre of the room that separated the two men who sat a goodly distance across from each other in faint shadow and almost complete silence. It was widely held by Iain and many others that the shop keeper, even with his obvious fondness for James MacGregor's elixir, looked down on the people from *Loch Dubh* as being little more than boorish. Did he not create the impression that they were somehow not up to the standards he had set for his own cherished family? It had always been more than language, even though he was still known to make the occasional derogatory comment about the Gaelic and those who chose to speak it. No doubt, his impression about their "uncivilized behaviour" would have only been reinforced by stories, such as the most recent accounts of Duncan MacDonald and John Rogers' altercation last fall at the *céilidh*. The vast majority of people around the loch agreed that Rogers deserved to have the daylights beaten out of him to say nothing of his lofty pretensions and airs of superiority. It was not that the *Loch Dubh* people were clannish — no no. Still in all, the beating looked good on the Englishman from down in the town. Duncan had done well for himself and for poor Archie. Nothing more needed to be said although it often was, over and over again around many a kitchen table and with the greatest of glee.

Undoubtedly, John Dunn would consider "the Scotsmen" of *Loch Dubh* as just so many hooligans from up in the hills, regardless of the fact that they were also paying customers. This would certainly explain the deafening stillness of the room as he sat there stoically in the overstuffed chair near the roaring fire. How Dunn could tolerate a "wild man" in his house, and calling upon his beloved Alexandra to boot, was beyond Iain who had quickly and quite strategically placed his right foot over his left to hide the gaping hole in the toe of his sock. Poor Dunn, not only did he have to abide a hooligan in his midst but an impoverished one at that. Iain's natural inclination would have been to laugh out loud but he suddenly thought better of it. It was best to leave well enough alone and not tempt fate. If nothing else, he was grateful for the crackling fire that warmed the room and softened the deadly silence.

After what seemed like several hours of excruciating torture, the door leading to the front hall slowly creaked open as Alexandra and her mother entered the room. Iain had always found the Dunn girl extremely attractive, especially with the long blond hair that framed her oval face and drew attention to her crystal-blue eyes. He rose from his place and smiled sheepishly; she had been a pretty child who had now been transformed into a stunningly beautiful woman. He had known for quite some time that he was smitten with her and now hoped that her parents would eventually come to see him as an acceptable suitor for their daughter. Most of all, he hoped that they would not take notice of the toe that protruded out of his sock for all the world to see. *A Thighearna, tha thu 'gam chiabhadh. Chan eil cothrom air. Mo chrannchur!* (Oh Lord, you are teasing me. There is no help for it. My lot in life!) He was surely tempted to chuckle aloud at his own plaintive thoughts but somehow knew better. This was a serious moment.

"Iain, it is so good to see you again. I trust that the ride down from the lake was not too difficult on you; is it not a terribly cold evening? Some might say almost too cold for the sleighing social. But then as long as you both are bundled up well, you will be fine I suspect. Oh just listen to me prattling on so." Edith Dunn tittered aloud as Iain took her extended hand and smiled knowingly into her face. He knew her to be a genuinely lovely and considerate person. Even as a boy, Iain remembered having that impression of her; she always made time for people. In this regard, she was so like poor George Calvey who loved to speak with everyone, but especially the children regardless of where they came from, *Loch Dubh* or no. It was only now that he saw so much of her in Alexandra and that pleased him immensely. What she had of her father, he did not know and cared even less. He was simply thankful to be heading towards the front door to escape both the house and the watchful gaze of John Dunn who, throughout, remained seated by the fire with drink firmly clasped in hand.

Iain and Alexandra walked the short distance up the road to where other young people from the church were gathering for the sleigh ride. Under the ever watchful supervision of the Reverend and Mrs. Johnston, the youth group's winter social was always so predictable: take the coast road down to the point, sing songs and drink cocoa around the bonfire, ride back up to the church, join in a prayer of farewell and finally depart for home. Still, there was so little else to do on a dark winter's evening that even a church outing was much more preferable to staying inside with family. Alexandra and the others would make of it what they could; a simple distraction would be created for the benefit of the minister and his wife in order to allow everyone a bit of free reign. After all, the Johnstons were never inclined towards suspicion and invariably there would be a social note from the pulpit the following Sunday to the effect that it had been a stellar example of young people sharing and enjoying Christian fellowship together. It was all so very fortunate for Alexandra and the others; there was never any inclination towards suspicion.

The four sleighs departed from the church at precisely 7:30 p.m. Initially, there had been a mad dash as bodies darted about in search of a place in the last three. Those who had not been as fleet of foot as the others had unwittingly and begrudgingly relegated themselves to the clerical sleigh in the company of George and Mavis Johnston. Such was not the case with Alexandra and Iain who had been quick off the mark and were already nestled in the hay of the last sleigh as others continued to scamper about. With the most subtle of moves, Alexandra placed her hand on Iain's leg and gently squeezed it. "You should know that I was never afraid of lightning, even as a child. Perhaps we will see some tonight if we are lucky." Alexandra smiled knowingly into Iain's face and winked. For the first time in a very long while, *Iain an dealanaich* was actually grateful for the nickname that had been bestowed upon him many years ago by the old farmer. Even with the chill of the night air on his face, he felt a growing warmth inside that pleased him.

Iain had no idea that a sleigh ride could be so incredibly enjoyable. With hay now playfully strewn all about, the others were oblivious to the fact that Alexandra's romantic advances continued on with some degree of determination. Judging by the broad smile that now filled Iain's face, everyone thought him to be a most affable young man even if he was one of the *Loch Dubh* people. Later, as the group sat on logs positioned around the perimeter of the fire, Mrs. Johnston began to take an interest in the boy who was so accommodating in prompting the others into song. Although it had been noted with genuine good humour, few of the young people seemed to mind when Iain began to lapse into Gaelic as he sang on, alone, with great delight. Alexandra sat close by with the knowledge that, unbeknown to him and everyone else, Iain's cocoa had been fortified by her father's finest reserve, which was securely hidden from view in a flask deep inside her coat pocket. She looked up at the full moon that reigned over a cloudless sky and illuminated the fields of snow that encircled the ghost-like figures of the spruce trees looming off in the near distance. She remained confident that there would be lightning before the evening was over.

Other than the glimmering moonlight, the only thing to appear in the sky that night was the bitter wind of disappointment. Mavis Johnston had insisted that Iain and Alexandra ride back in their sleigh as she sat in back with them, all the while peppering him with a host of mundane questions and a barrage of equally frivolous comments. The scowl on Alexandra's face spoke volumes about the absolute frustration that she was enduring. The one and only saving grace was that the minister and his wife would speak glowingly of Iain to John and Edith Dunn; she would see to that make no mistake. There would be other opportunities and Alexandra had no intention of loosening her hold. After all, she realized the only other option would be to order a man from the catalogue if she was ever to satisfy the expectations of her parents, especially her father. At twenty-one years of age, she was old enough to know what it was she wanted and, in time, she was adamant that she would have it. With hay conveniently scattered about, she gripped Iain's leg tightly.

With the drink upon him, Iain was now thankful that the horse knew its own way home. The reins lay at his feet on the sleigh's floorboards like a pile of slender browned *maragan*. For some reason, he couldn't quite remember the final prayer and words of farewell that had been spoken at the church. Indeed, the ride up the bluffs became a bit of a blur as had the latter part of the social outing itself, including the sleigh ride back to New Carlisle. However, he was able to recollect that Alexandra had positioned herself to one side while Mrs. Johnston had rather unceremoniously plunked her wholesome body on the other. Oh yes, the minister's wife had sat next to him in the hay on the way back to town and now he could vaguely remember that he had caressed her leg with his hand, somehow and quite foolishly thinking it to be Alexandra's. *"Och Iain, ciod e an dunaich a thàinig ort? Pàidhidh tu sin fhathast; Aig Dia a mhàin tha brath. Bidh e na sgeula beag àbhachdail!"* (Oh Iain, what mischief came over you? You shall suffer for that yet; God alone knows. It will be an amusing little tale!) As the horse and sleigh glided down the loch road towards home, he shook his head and laughed aloud. He pictured the look of utter shock that must have surely crossed Mrs. Johnston's face at that amorous moment. Poor woman, how sad to be loved only to be abandoned so quickly. *"Iain an dealanaich, nach tu a tha dona!"* (Lightning Iain, are you not a bad one!) They continued on at a quickened pace and not once did the horse acknowledge the raucous laughter that continued to blanket its backside.

Later, as he lay under the thick warm covers of his bed, Iain's thoughts were of family. He saw his sister Sadie with her two wee bairns, Blair and Ewan, as well as *Iain Beag* and Christine who had just recently been blessed with a beautiful *gràdhan*, Flora Isabelle. At twenty-eight, it was time for him to finally decide on a wife and settle down to raise children of his own. It was seldom discussed but still he knew that it was of no small concern to his parents. He would pursue Alexandra and, God willing, spirit her off to the "back woods" that was *Loch Dubh*. He hoped that, in time, it would come to pass. For now though, he realized that he would have to remain focused on the more-immediate issues that faced him. He raised his head from the pillow and looked down at the foot of the bed where he had carefully laid out the pair of grey woollen socks. Iain smiled. In the morning, he would ask his mother to search out her darning needles in order to make them whole once again.

The "unknown child." Rachael Ferguson spoke the words aloud once again in an attempt to confirm that she had indeed read and understood the English text correctly. She was conscious of being quick in closing the door behind her as she departed from the warmth of the manse's kitchen. She knew she wanted time alone to think about it all. It was so much and so difficult to grasp at the same time. The cool rawness on the early May wind that now greeted her penetrated her bones and made the words sound all the more chilling. As she took a moment to wrap the dark woollen shawl tightly around her shoulders, she noted that the snow high up on the hills had finally receded to the very edges of the forest. Its disappearance was always so welcomed as it signalled the arrival of the small lambs that symbolized the true advent of spring. Yet today, of all days, there was no sense of birth or rebirth in the air, only a deadly chill. There was little question as to the cause; the drift ice was in.

Rachael made her way down the laneway to the main road, her feet picking up speed as the wind continued its flagrant assault on her face and clothing. It howled up from the bluffs and cascaded over the loch like a gigantic wave. And yet her thoughts were elsewhere. Was it truly possible that a child could be laid to its final earthly rest without even so much as a name to identify it on a stone? As if death itself was not enough pain to endure. It was all so terrible; it could not be God's will. The tears rolling down her cheeks surprised her as she found herself looking off into the distance. It had been some time since her thoughts had last gone to Harris and this realization caused a sudden pang of guilt to come over her. But at least there was a name over his tiny grave. In years to come, people would know that this wee one had been given life by Norman and Rachael Ferguson and that God, in His infinite wisdom, had taken him away at an early age. If nothing else, there was a name to signify that he had lived among them, albeit for far too short a time, and brought them such joy. The tears now blurred her vision as she faced the frigid wind and walked through it. At least there was a name.

Stopping in the centre of the road, Rachael suddenly turned and looked back towards the Kirk and the slope of *Beinn-mo-Mhulaid* that rose up behind. From the distance, the small white stones appeared as so many flakes of snow that had been methodically sprinkled on the ground from a great height. It was here that the comparison ended for she knew there to be one haunting difference: these flakes would never disappear, even in the nurturing warmth of the summer sun. As much as time tempered the pain of grief, so too did it dilute the beauty of memories. Still, in a mother's heart, the child would always be loved and remembered; the child would forever be known.

The road had a beckoning effect on Rachael who quite inadvertently found herself walking past the laneway leading up to her own house. The cool air now felt strangely invigorating on her face and made it tingle with life. It was such a contrast to the heat of the kitchen stove that would hold her captive soon enough as the supper hour approached. There was time for a brief respite from the chores and she would not feel the least bit guilty for allowing herself this luxury that some others might consider frivolous. But then, their views were of no consequence to her. In some ways, did it not seem as though she had lived over the stove for the past month as had all the women of *Loch Dubh* in ensuring that a proper provision of cooking and baking was placed in the manse kitchen? Jennie's extended stay in Baddeck and absence from them had been truly felt by most families in one way or another. Yet no one would begrudge the extra work or hours spent away from their own family duties. It was, after all, a time of celebration.

The arrival of Emily's baby was the cause of much rejoicing — the first grandchild for Duncan and Jennie who had waited so long and, near the end, so eagerly for the time to finally arrive. There had been a twinkle in the mother's eyes when she first placed Duncan Christopher Hickman into the waiting arms of his grandmother. It was not until the following week, with the arrival of Jennie's letter from Baddeck, that the news of the safe arrival and the choice of names were made known. For the first time in a great while, the minister was grateful for the solitude of the manse. He cried as he read the letter, conjuring up memories of his daughter picking wild flowers and recounting each of their stories in turn. And then, his thoughts were elsewhere, of another boy, in another cradle, place and time. Duncan eventually forced himself back to the present, to the knowledge that his grandson, his namesake, would be surrounded by assurances of love throughout his life. The Reverend Fraser's greatest joy was not only in the birth of this child but also in the realization that something painful had ended. The chains that had enslaved him, and by extension his family, had finally been broken and cast aside. His tears were soon replaced by a broad smile as he purposefully committed the letter to the pages at the back of his Bible, indeed to a very particular and well-known passage: Revelations 21: 5. *"Feuch, tha mi a'deanamh nan uile nithean nuadh."* (Behold, I make all things new.)

There was never any doubt but that Duncan, with the ongoing pressures of ministry upon him, was truly grateful for the meals that the women of the congregation dutifully brought to the manse kitchen on a daily basis. In fact, he used it to full advantage as he welcomed his wife home with uncharacteristic mischief. He greeted her as *"mo bhoireannach shocair"* (My Lady of Leisure) and insinuated that she would surely have to be retrained in order to maintain the high culinary standards set by the other women during her absence, standards to which he had now become quite accustomed. Jennie brushed him off with a hearty *"Ud. Ud."* (Tut. Tut.) and made a veiled threat to the effect that his supper might well consist of nothing more than a large bowl of left-over porridge if he did not mind himself. It was not so easy to brush off the other member of the family who had also raced to her side in welcome. *Rionnag* refused to leave Jennie's lap, looking up into her face whenever the stroking of her black fur would cease. One could almost sense the subtle understanding that existed between them. Each one was reassured by the other's presence and doting attention. They were a family again.

As was the case with all the *Loch Dubh* women, Rachael was genuinely pleased to see Jennie and to have her back after such a lengthy absence. At the same time, she was terribly envious of the privilege that had been given to her friend to be at her daughter's side for the birth of her first grandchild. Her own Morag had been delivered of a boy in Boston in February and she was not able to be there. Oh, it has been suggested often enough by both Morag and Elliott who had gladly offered to pay the cost of the train passage. But how could she possibly go? It was such a terribly long journey and, everything else aside, she had responsibilities to the other members of her family as well as the farm itself here in *Loch Dubh*. Although it was not quite the same as being there, Rachael was constantly pouring over the photo of her daughter and grandson that had been included in the letter delivered just two weeks ago. Rachael was pleased that Morag had developed the habit of taping her letters closed and realized that such security precautions would surely drive Annabelle Calvey to distraction. While the cups of hot tea might continue to quench her thirst, on these occasions at least, they would be powerless in satisfying her insatiable curiosity.

Rachael had brought the photograph along with her on her visit to Jennie and it had only taken a matter of a few seconds for the oohing and awing to drive Duncan from the kitchen to the far recesses of the front parlour. *"Faoin-chainnt nan seanamhairean. A Thighearna, saor thu mi."* (The prattle of grandmothers. Oh Lord save me.) Both women laughed aloud as Duncan feigned torment in leaving them to their own devices around the table. Jennie was not to be outdone and, although there was no picture, there may as well have been given the detailed imagery that she drew of her own beautiful grandson. On that day at least, humility was in short supply unlike the rampant pride that illuminated the faces of the two women.

It was several minutes later that Jennie rose to put the kettle on the stove in order to prepare for a much-needed pot of tea. Rachael dutifully removed the lid from the tin of molasses biscuits that she had carried over with her and placed it in the centre of the table. A wee *strùpag* was always just the thing to keep the tongues wagging and, with the passage of a month, there was much for them to prattle on about. Inevitably, the discussion returned to the issue of the bairns as Rachael recounted for Jennie's benefit the visit of Mr. and Mrs. MacNeil a few weeks back when Kristy had given birth to her second child — a son, Fergus. It was well understood by everyone at the time, including the MacNeils, that the loss of Tina had affected Kristy greatly. There was never any doubt but that both Joseph and Bernadette would be there for their daughter and, although they had remained only a few weeks, it was not the length of their stay that mattered. Never before had Kristy had her entire family together. Still, it pained her to realize that the one person who had made it possible had not lived to rejoice in it with her. It was strangely ironic that on the day the MacNeils departed for Christmas Island, Kristy and Grace had taken them for a short walk down the laneway towards the loch. On the way back to the house, it was Grace who first noticed the purple and yellow heads of the crocuses struggling through the thin yet lingering blanket of snow along the edge of the garden. *"Och a Thina, tha thu an seo fhathast."* (Oh Tina, you are with us still.) Kristy whispered the words softly to herself. It was at that moment that she decided that it was no longer necessary to grieve Tina's loss. It was also the day for which, upon reflection, many people in *Loch Dubh* would be thankful. After seven months, Kristy had been returned to them.

Jennie and Rachael were so engrossed in conversation that they had not taken notice of the fact that yet another member of Clan Fraser had escaped from their presence. *Rionnag* quickly found a spot behind the butter churn where the afternoon sun bathed the smooth spruce boards of the pantry floor. The wooden vessel also served to muffle the voices that continued their nattering refrain. True enough, she was glad to have Jennie home but surely there had to be certain limits. After all, an afternoon nap was not a luxury; it was a necessity. The nightly prowl up into the hills would soon be upon her.

For their part, the two women discussed any number of issues affecting the families around the loch, including Albert MacGregor's successful career as a banker, Iain Grant and Daniel MacDonald's courting of Alexandra Dunn and Agnes Bain respectively from down in the town, and Elizabeth MacLeod's upcoming summer stay with her parents. Jennie was pleased to hear there had not been any further fighting since the *céilidh* of last fall, at least none that had become common knowledge. As their talk continued on covering a multitude of topics, both women were confident that their discussion could never possibly be misconstrued as gossip, certainly not here in the manse. No no. It was just a way of keeping up-to-date on the goings on. But still in all, such talk was trying on the throat. Another cup of tea would be just the thing.

Jennie crossed the room to the stove and the tea pot that awaited her. The floor boards creaked mournfully under her feet and, unknown to her, *Rionnag's* ears were folded back in subtle annoyance even though she did not bother to open her eyes. If nothing else, she remained thankful for the warmth of the sun that blanketed her rich black coat. Jennie had not taken notice of the slumbering child even when she had peered into the pantry and through the side window in the direction of the Kirk. She picked up the pot and made her way back to the table and her waiting company. With some considerable difficulty, the child attempted to resume her sleep.

"A Raonaid, sgrìobh Mata litir thugainne bho Halifax. Ràinig i an dé. Fhuair sinn an naidheachd eagalach agus ro bhuaireasach." (Rachael, Matthew wrote us a letter from Halifax. It arrived yesterday. We got the dreadful and disturbing news.) As she approached the table, Jennie retrieved the letter from the side cupboard and placed it on the table next to the steaming pot of tea.

Rachael picked it up and, with Jennie's encouragement, proceeded to read the note, albeit haltingly; she so seldom had occasion to read, especially in the English. The letter dealt primarily with the horrible aftermath of the recent disaster at sea. Matthew recounted how, from his office window overlooking Pier 4, he had witnessed the removal of the Titanic victims from the MacKay-Bennett, which had been one of several ships contracted by the White Star Line to aid in the gruesome rescue. At the time, it seemed like such an odd word to Matthew — "rescue." He reported how a strange hush had fallen over the city as the vessel glided down the length of the harbour, which had been completely cleared of all ships as a mark of respect. Once the MacKay-Bennett had been secured at its mooring, the almost 200 bodies were brought down the gangway and laid upon the cold slabs of planking according to their status on the ill-fated vessel: first-class passengers placed in coffins, second-class and steerage passengers sewn into canvas bags and, finally, crew piled in a large heap. The scene graphically exposed the true horrific face of the tragedy. From the pier, they were systematically and collectively taken to the Mayflower Curling Rink for processing. In death, class no longer had relevance.

Matthew had not lingered long at the window. He sensed that to do so would be undignified, not so much for himself as for the "rescued" victims. As a barrister's clerk, he had learned over time to always choose his words carefully, not unlike Sarah Urquhart's spending habits with her pennies as she luxuriated in flipping through the pages of the Eaton's catalogue for hours on end down at Dunn's store. Even so, the words of Matthew's letter could not mask the fact that he had been terribly troubled by the ordeal.

Attached to the last page was a newspaper clipping from the **Halifax Herald**. It detailed the services that had been conducted to date in the various churches and the three cemeteries designated to receive the victims. It was then that Rachael had first learned of a small child of approximately two years of age with fair hair who could not be identified and remained unclaimed. The article said that he would be committed to an earthly grave paid for by the very seamen who had rescued him and that he would now be known only to God. When she had finished, Rachael looked up and across at Jennie who sat silently with her hands folded in her lap. As the letter was slipped back into the safekeeping of its envelope, the two grandmothers sat drinking their tea and silently reflecting on two tiny lives recently given and another taken away. It was a poignant moment as only the melancholy whistling of the wind and the soft clinking of cups on saucers could be heard. *Rionnag* slept on, grateful for the warmth and otherwise stillness that had finally settled over the room.

Rachael now found herself standing on the road at the point where it veered sharply to the left before descending the bluffs to the town below. She looked out over the expanse of drift ice that shrouded the water as far as the eye could see. She felt the bitter cold on her face but still there was a sense that standing there, even for a few minutes, was a way of paying tribute to the hundreds of souls that had perished. Even with the distance, Rachael could distinguish the many slabs of white that were thrust up hither and yon across the endless field of jagged ice stretching off to the horizon. They so reminded her of the much smaller slabs that rested on the hill behind the Kirk. On the slopes of *Beinn-mo-Mhulaid*, there was a stone inscribed with the name Harris Ferguson. In Halifax, there would soon be another bearing the words "an unknown child." Once again, Rachael could sense the tears welling up in her eyes as she reluctantly turned and slowly walked back down the road to her home and the warmth of her kitchen.

Soon enough, the school bell would ring for the last time. It was difficult for her to believe that her child was already fifteen and now stood more as a man than the boy she imagined him to always remain. Like so many before him, Lachlan had decided his future was in ploughing through the fertile soil of the farm and cutting through the tightly woven timbers of the surrounding woods. No longer would he be in the company of a multitude of books that spoke only of life away, far from these mountains and waters. With these poignant thoughts as points of reference, it begged the question: who was she to convince him otherwise of the wisdom of his decision? After all, this was where her heart had always been and where it would forever stay. He would be no different.

Martha sat on the fresh new grass just off to the side of the front steps leading to the veranda. Her eyes were focused on the mountains across the loch as they gently sloped up behind Neil's and Iona's house and, in the process, assumed a blackish-green mantle that contrasted so strikingly with the endless expanse of pale blue sky. So often, she tended to take these things for granted and it was only in quiet moments such as this that she realized just how important they were to her and to the people of *Loch Dubh*. They were a blanket that enfolded them and offered a soft warm comfort against the chilling realities of their lives. And yet, so many of the young people had gone away, more out of the sheer necessity of life than a buoyant desire for adventure. The same scene had played itself out down at the government wharf on any number of different occasions. How well she knew the personal pain that was brought to families. Were not all her own nieces and nephews, with the exception of Duncan and Daniel, now living elsewhere? Martha wondered if they missed this place because she believed there was a lingering sense that it missed them, their promise of the future but especially their laughter. It was the same wrenching feeling she had experienced several years back when she sat by her parents' graves, a feeling of loneliness, of something forever lost. In so many ways, some subtle and others not, *Loch Dubh* was slowly being orphaned with the loss of these young people. She smiled as she thought of Lachlan's decision.

Who was she to convince him otherwise indeed.

The sun glistened off the loch as it slowly made its way towards the western horizon where *Beinn-mo-Mhulaid* stood stoic watch over the Kirk and cemetery. It was then that it suddenly struck Martha that her quiet time in the soft May air had stretched into the better part of an hour. Soon enough, supper would be on the table to feed the clan hard at work in the back fields. The three older children, Lachlan, Colin and Moira, had quickly changed out of their good clothes after school and quite willingly gone off to help their father with the potato planting. As much as Peter would enjoy both their company and assistance, Martha knew that the novelty would soon wear thin for at least one of them. Moira's constant insistence on being treated as an equal was exceeded only by her almost prissy dislike of dirt. It so reminded Martha of the little girl from Prince Edward Island, Anne, in the Green Gables book that her daughter so loved to read at night in her bed before sleep claimed her. Just maybe this explained in part why it was she had been so determined to help in the potato fields. Perhaps for a few fleeting moments, Moira became Anne, at least until such time as her hands began to assume a horrid earthly hue. Even for a child, these flights of fancy had their limits.

"Och mo chaileag, nach ann de Chlainn Domhnaill a tha thu!" (Oh my girl, are you not a MacDonald!) As she rose and meticulously dusted the bits of grass from her long black skirt, Martha spoke these words aloud. In so doing, she conjured up an image of the tiny bow of MacDonald of Clanranald tartan that had attended all her children at their baptism and now rested over another heart. A broad smile suddenly appeared on her face and, with her skirt now in an acceptable state of appearance, she looked up into the eternity of sky and added a whimsical comment for good measure. *"Mo bhobain ghaolaich. Nach tu a tha dona!"* (My dear Pappa. Aren't you the naughty one!) She had consciously spoken of him in the present tense and was pleased that she could think of Archie without having to blot a stream of tears from her cheeks. All her thoughts of him now were happy ones and she continued to smile as she relived the story of the tartan bow while making her way down the laneway towards the loch road.

There were few certainties in life but Martha was quite confident that one would surely await her as she rounded the corner of the Erskine home. The sound of her shoes on the coarse gravel caused *Taghta* to raise her head from where it had rested on her paws, drooping as they were over the edge of the step. The kitchen door was chilled in shade as the main structure of the house blocked out the fading rays that now sequestered themselves off in the western sky. Intriguing sounds or not, *Taghta* would never leave her chosen spot close to the door where she diligently waited for her master to reappear.

It was the delirious wagging of tail and prancing of paws that now welcomed Martha and beckoned her onward. *"Bi cho bìth ri uan mo ghràdhag. Cha bhuair sinn an leasan. Bi sàmhach tacan."* (Be quiet as a lamb my dear little one. We will not disturb the lesson. Be still awhile.) As she softly whispered the words, Martha slowly sat herself down on the top step, knowing enough to allow *Taghta* to encircle her several times. The instinct to herd was simply too strong. Martha watched with great delight realizing so well that the animal's desire to love was every bit as great. It was only after she had been well herded that Martha grabbed hold of *Taghta* and laid her across her lap. The rubbing of ears was always a sure fire way of lulling the collie into heavenly bliss. With calm restored, the two would wait patiently in silence.

As she looked out over the backyard towards the barn and wagon house, Martha allowed her thoughts to wander as her fingers continued to pacify the now docile *Taghta*. The act of granting comfort extended well beyond the collie as she unwittingly brought to mind a host of memories: Lachlan's birth on a spring evening with the scent of apple blossoms in the air, Peter's proud confidence in saying his wedding vows in the Gaelic, her mother's lilting humming as she churned butter in the pantry, Dr. Osborne's almost reluctant revelation about her daughter's blue eyes, the dedication of Andrew's cairn and a beautiful man too soon taken from them, Archie's infectious laughter as he was tickled unmercifully by his grandchildren. Her musings were everywhere and no where all at the same time. Had she not known better, she would have thought that the *bòcain* themselves had woven a spell to lull her into some malicious trance. Indeed, had this been the case, it would have all been to no avail. Martha would have none other than Robert Burns himself to thank for ensuring her safety from such mischievous deeds.

> "Gie me ae spark o' Nature's fire,
> That's a' the learning I desire;
> Then tho' I drudge thro' dub an' mire
> At pleugh or cart,
> My muse, tho' hamely in attire,
> May touch the heart.

Kristy's voice carried softly through the screen door as the poetry reading signalled that the lesson would soon be completed for the day. All thoughts of the *bòcain* were cast aside and Martha was content to simply sit there as the bard's words continued to spill out over her and the now completely docile *Taghta*.

Several minutes later without Martha realizing it, Ismay stood motionless in the kitchen doorway. She remained there in silence as, behind her, Kristy lifted Fergus from the cradle that she had brought down earlier from the upstairs bedroom. When Ismay had first arrived, Kristy encouraged her to hold the baby for a bit and watched with delight from across the room as the girl first held him somewhat nervously and soon enough began to gently stroke his head and explore the detailing of his tiny hands with her own. Kristy sat back and observed the scene, carefully sensing that Ismay was coming to know her child in ways that others could not appreciate or even begin to understand.

Now Ismay stood in the doorway seemingly reluctant to leave the kitchen. There was a quizzical look on her face as she raised her head slightly to one side. The breeze cascaded through the netting of the screen door and played with her long black hair as if it was enticing her outside to play in its freedom. *"A Mhamaidh, an tu tha seo?"* (Mamma, is that you?) Both Martha and *Taghta* were obviously surprised as they suddenly looked around in the direction of the door that now framed the tiny figure. There was a distinct impression that the scene was in fact a photograph from a bygone era, somehow made older by the meshing that seemed to age if not distort the detail.

"Is mi gu beachd, Ismay. Bha feum agam air sràid a ghabhail agus thàinig mi mar seo: gabhaidh sinn sgrìob dhachaidh còmhla — an triùir againn: mi-fhìn 's tu-fhéin is Taghta." (It is me most assuredly, Ismay. I needed to take a walk and I came so that we could walk home together — the three of us: you, me and *Taghta*.) As Ismay slowly opened the door and passed through, *Taghta* ran to her side and leaned into her in conveying the reassuring message that she too was present. Martha stood and took a few steps forward where she caressed her daughter's head with her hand and called out a greeting to Kristy. Ismay's face radiated with a broad smile as she first searched out the collie to pat her head and then extended her hand in search of her mother's. It was only then, with reassurances made, that the three set out for home and supper.

Initially, *Taghta* was somewhat confused by the fact that her charge was being led by another as they proceeded down the laneway. She was nonetheless content knowing that all was in order. With the luxury of time upon her, she raced ahead and then back, circling the two figures as they walked on hand-in-hand. They were safe enough but a bit of guidance would do no real harm. After all, it was what she did best and enjoyed the most.

Now making their way down the loch road, Martha and Ismay spoke of the poetry that had been read and the little one expressed delight in how Kristy had used her voice to imitate a broad Scottish brogue. The pronunciation of the words seemed terribly strange and yet so delightful to Ismay's ears. She loved the flow of language, even if some words escaped her understanding, at least for the time being. She savoured them as if they were fresh tea biscuits from the oven, topped with molasses and served with ice-cold milk from the can in the spring.

Martha chuckled to herself at Ismay's innocent and compelling joy of learning. If only she had been half the student her daughter was when she herself had been in school those many years ago. But then, she was appreciative of the fact that Ismay's brothers were not maniacally evil like the two with whom she was forced to contend. How Malcolm and John had loved to pester and tease her unmercifully. So much was different now; so very much. As her thoughts wandered off yet again, Martha was suddenly brought back to reality by a gentle tug on her hand. It was Ismay's way of ensuring that she had her mother's total attention.

"*A Mhamaidh, beiridh mi naoidhanan, mo naoidhanan-féin, 'nuair a bhios mi 'n as sinne?*" (Mamma, will I have children of my own when I am older?) For the second time in a few short minutes, Martha found herself completely taken aback by her daughter. A mother's natural tendency would have been to stop and take a few moments to absorb both the reason for the question as well as its timing, to say nothing of an appropriate response. The hush in the air was terribly noticeable as they continued on with Martha attempting to quickly collect herself and her thoughts.

"*Tha gu dearbh, a' lùr. Is ionann sin is mar a thachras dhuit. Bithidh thu 'nad mhàthair iongantach air son móran chloinne. Ach c'airson tha thu a'faighneachd?*" (Yes indeed, yes my darling. Just so shall it happen to you. You will be a wonderful mother to many babies. But why do you ask?) Martha had quite intentionally saved the most penetrating question for last as she looked down not knowing what sort of answer she might expect. With Ismay, there was only one certainty — there was never any certainty.

"*Sireadh mi iad mo gnùis fhaicinn agus do ghnùis sa. Aisling, sin a mhàin. Ach cudthromach.*" (I want them to see my face and yours. It was a dream that is all. But important.) The little girl strode on as if she had done nothing more than comment on the weather, the warmth of the air or the freshness of the breeze. Martha continued to look down upon her daughter trying to understand the workings of a mind so young and yet so wondrously complex. What was left of the journey home was embraced by silence as the fading sunlight flooded their faces with a radiance that, for a mother, was both luxurious and comforting.

Martha began to give thought to the setting of the table and the ravenous crew that would surely await them at the kitchen door. All the while, *Taghta* continued to encircle her charges as they turned into the laneway leading up to the house. Martha knew that, like the loch and mountains, the collie was surrounding them with another blanket of security, equally warm and comforting. The instinct was simply too strong.

These my wishes I am sending –
May your life be long and healthy,
May the lovely Gaelic *céilidh*
Always grace the land of bens!
Song to the Gaelic Mod of Cape Breton (song)

Seo mo dhùrachd leibh an dràsda,
Saoghal fada 's móran slàinte,
'S gu'm bi céilidh grinn na Gàidhlig
O gu bràth an tìr nam beann!
Òran Do Mhòd Gaidhealach Cheap Breatuinn (òran)

"*A chlachan mhóra. Nam b' urrainn dhuibh labhairt. Na sgeòil ri innse.*" (Oh great stones. If only you could speak — the stories to be told.) The words were hushed, spoken almost as a prayer, as her hand stroked the rough texture of the greyish-brown stones. Elizabeth sat on the arch warmed by the summer sun and was struck by the incredible irony. She had never ever taken the slightest interest in fishing. Yet she had always loved the water, watching the sun illuminate its furrowed brow and listening to its rhythmic voice as it greeted the shoreline. While it was not something that she dwelt on, Elizabeth often thought that there was something intrinsic in the Celtic character that made it necessary not only to see but also to experience the broad expanse of water and the soaring heights of mountains. It was less a longing for the old country and more a sense of defining one's place amid the vastness of time and space. In some ways, they offered a constant perspective to life. Whether gazing out over an endless floor of cresting seas or up at a boundless wall of mountains and sky, you knew where you stood — at home on the edge of infinity. It was for this reason that she felt so humble sitting there on the arch of the mill bridge overlooking the loch with *Beinn-mo-Mhulaid* rising up at the far end. In so many different ways, *Loch Dubh* would always be her home. Still, she was thankful that the little one had not heard her words about the stones.

The quiet was restored only to be broken several minutes later by the most unexpected and pensive of questions. "*A Mhamaidh, càit a bheil na h-éisg?* (Mamma, where are the fish?) Do you think that they are all taking a nap and don't know that we are here?" Elizabeth turned towards

Naomi who, up until that point at least, had sat diligently holding the switch with its length of string and hook that her grandfather had hastily fashioned and baited for her. It was obvious that, even with all the wisdom of her five years, her expectations far exceeded the ten minutes that she had already invested in a sport that was clearly becoming increasingly frustrating. There was a genuine look of concern on her small face as her legs dangled above the still dark water. Just the same, Elizabeth dared not laugh knowing full well that it would only upset her all the more. What the wee one might lack in patience was made up tenfold in determination. A mother's intuition told her all that was needed was a subtle word of encouragement.

"*Tha iad an seo. Gabh foidhidinn mo ghràidh. Thig iad agus tha ùine gu leòr againn a bhàrr.*" (They are here. Just be patient my darling. They will come and besides we have plenty of time.) With James snugly placed in the crook of her left arm, Elizabeth reached out and gently caressed Naomi's shoulder with her right hand. It was a simple act of reassurance that was greeted with some degree of relief. Perhaps before the day was out, she would yet place a grand fish before her *seanair*. If only she knew when the aquatic nap time was over; it would make her life so much easier and perhaps then she could finally be free to go off to play high up in the hills.

There was only the slightest hint of a breeze and, except for the constant churning of the mill's water wheel behind them, the only sound was the crying of the gulls that carried up and over the bluffs from the wharf down in the town. With Naomi once again contentedly focused on the task at hand, Elizabeth reached down and rubbed James' cheek as he slept placidly in her arms. It was difficult for her to believe that it was already fourteen months since she had given him life. She would always remember the look on Calum's face as he was eventually permitted into the room following the birth. Both grandmothers, Sarah and Tillie, placed the baby in his arms and quietly closed the door behind them as they left. As he smiled down at the small ruddy face, Calum's voice suddenly began to quaver. "*Ar mac. Och Ealasaid, ar mac bòidheach. Tapadh leat. Tapadh leat.*" (Our son. Oh Elizabeth, our beautiful son. Thank you. Thank you.) As sleep finally claimed her weary body, Elizabeth recalled seeing her husband's tears and never before experiencing such an all-encompassing feeling of contentment and fulfilment at the same time. She knew that she would sleep soundly.

Now, here on the bridge looking out over water and mountains, Elizabeth's thoughts were of Calum and Stewart at home in Boularderie working the hay fields. At seventeen, Stewart was a strapping young man who was of great help to his father on the farm. Calum often quipped that his boy would surely break any number of hearts with his handsome good looks and mischievous sense of humour. For her part, Elizabeth would always see him as the little boy fidgeting with his MacLeod tartan tie in the church pew on the day of her wedding to his father. She looked down at

James and imagined him one day wearing the same small tie that had long since been committed to a trunk in the far corner of the attic. Upon her return, she would make a point of retrieving it for James, for the family. It was so much more than a multi-coloured piece of cloth. It evoked memories of happy times in the past and would, no doubt, contribute to others yet to come. It was so terribly simple and yet so wondrously important. For Elizabeth, it brought her family together in a symbolic way that she knew she could never hope to adequately explain. But then, after all, there was perhaps no need. The thoughts were hers and hers alone.

In the serenity of her surroundings, Elizabeth had no possible way of knowing that something else, other than the lonely cries of the gulls, was about to abruptly shatter the calm. Without the slightest warning, both Naomi's patience and determination had finally run their course. *"A Mhamaidh, fhuair mi mo leòr; is faoin e!* (Mamma, I have had enough; this is silly!) Let the fish stay in their beds all day for all I care." As the girl swung her gangly legs back over the arch, Elizabeth could no longer contain her laughter. It was less a response to her daughter's impatience than it was an observation on how fluidly she switched from one language to the other without even realizing what it was she was doing. In less than a month, Naomi would be off to school in *Bail'a'Mhuilinn* where the Gaelic would not be tolerated let alone taught. Elizabeth's successor as teacher, a Mr. Taylor from Florence, was very similar to Miss Massey down at the *Loch Dubh* school, at least this is what Elizabeth had gleaned from comments that floated around the loch as freely as the fragrance of apple blossoms in spring. In some respects, it was hard to accept the fact that this aspect of their history and culture might soon be lost, all in the name of progress or so the story went. It was still important for Elizabeth to hold onto it. It was a connection to the past even if it might not prove to be one to the future. She was adamant that, at home, they would continue to knead bread in the pantry, walk down by the brook and say prayers at their beds in the old tongue. No one would deprive her children of this; it was still important.

Naomi had now placed the switch on the stone ledge as a final act of defiance if not utter disgust. She would have no further want or need of it. A walk along the loch would be far more productive and interesting. Sensing a genuine mood of anger mixed with disappointment, Elizabeth grasped the tiny hand and together they moved off down the road in the direction of the bluffs. The wild flowers that grew in abundance along the sides proved to be of far greater appeal to Naomi who had quickly resolved that her grandfather would simply have to do without the promised fish. A bouquet of beautiful flowers for *seanamhair* was now the focus of her attention as the look of determination once again crept back across her face.

Naomi ran from side to side harvesting anything that vaguely resembled a flower while Elizabeth trailed behind savouring the fresh salt air that streamed up from below the bluffs. Here in the hallow of the mountains, it blended with the smell of newly scythed hay and created a fragrance that was as soothing on the nose as it was refreshing to the face. Off to her left high up on the far hill, she could see two figures turning hay in the fields behind the MacDonald barn. She knew it to be John and his son Daniel. It seemed odd that her impressions of Daniel were still based on her recollections of the small boy who had constantly wanted to accompany his older brothers, Rod and Andrew, on their fishing expeditions. At twenty-six years of age, he was about to be married to Agnes Bain from down in the town, as was Iain Grant to the Dunn girl. He was no longer "the wee lad" and she was no longer the starry-eyed young woman who had, ages ago, quite intentionally strolled down by the loch at exactly the same time that his twin brothers fished off this very bridge. Upon reflection, there was an acceptance that she had had such little say in the ebb and flow that was her life. The years had seen to that; so much was now completely different from before. Yet this place, these stones persisted, so constant and unchanged.

A sudden gust of wind seemed to come out of nowhere and playfully tousled her long hair around her face. In reaching up to place it back into some semblance of order, Elizabeth realized that the movement had unwittingly caused her to recall a similar incident many years ago. It was the day that she had donned her favourite mauve-coloured dress and strolled down to the mill bridge where Andrew and Rod were seated. Had it not been the very same day that she had first taken note of the fact that her mother's hair was tinged with grey? Now she was forced to admit that her own hair was beginning to reveal the odd strand of pure white. As Naomi continued to run from flower to flower before her, Elizabeth was fully aware of the strange irony of the moment. She had become her mother as she glanced down the road and into a looking glass. Beyond the glass, what she saw was herself running to and fro.

For a brief moment, Elizabeth stopped and turned back in the direction of her parents' house high up on the hill, as if the movement would somehow confirm her positioning both in place and time. It was eight years ago and she could see herself driving down this very road on that warm summer day as she returned to prepare for her wedding. She remembered thinking that *Loch Dubh* had not changed, that in some strange way it would not or possibly could not. But now she was forced to admit that it most certainly had. People you loved were never supposed to grow old but they did. She thought of her parents who were now becoming weary with the years upon them. People you seemingly knew forever were never supposed to die but they did. She thought of Flora, Archie, Tina and poor Peter who rested behind the Kirk. And yet there was also the quiet reassurance of new life being given, of others who had come to take positions left vacant. Things were indeed different, but even with such tumultuous change, there was still a sense of contentment in being in this place.

The day was getting on and now, with a large assortment of flowers mixed with the occasional weed cascading from her tiny arms, Naomi was eager to return home to bask in the glow that would surely fill her grandmother's face as she was presented with the colourful collection. Elizabeth placed her hand on her daughter's shoulder and the three of them walked slowly back in the direction of the house. As they recrossed the bridge, Elizabeth imagined two figures off to the side laughing to themselves as their legs dangled over the stone arch and the wind played with their blond hair. This time, the words did not come; they remained locked somewhere deep within her out of sight but never far from her mind. *A chlachan mhóra. Nam b'urrainn dhuibh labhairt.* (Oh great stones. If only you could speak.) It was all too clear that they could not and that the stories would not be told. The years had indeed changed so much.

"*Hiodroho hodroho, haninen hìechin,*
Hodraha hodroho, hodroho hachin,
Hìodroho hodroho, haninen hìechin,
Hodraha hodraha, hodraha hodraha,
Hodraha hodraha, hodraha hachin."

In his mind, the scene was so incredibly clear. Daniel was seated at the crudely made table positioned near the open fire in the centre of the croft house, or *an taigh dubh* (the black house) as they were then more commonly known. His mother was busily preparing soup for the evening meal in the large black pot that hung over the flames, suspended on a length of roughly forged chain. The cooking smells blended with the sweet fragrance of the freshly thatched roof that cascaded down over them like a gentle spring shower. It warmed him every bit as much as the fire itself whose flames danced up and hungrily licked the very edges of the pot. At the table, his father had just completed the practice chanter lesson and finished, as was always his habit, by singing one of his favourite piping tunes. This day it was *Cogadh no Sìth* (War or Peace / The Gathering of the Clans) — a piece of *ceòl mór* ("big music"/the classical music of the great highland bagpipe) that his own father, in his time, had taught him. Daniel could see himself as the young boy, listening attentively knowing that this music was being carried forward from the far recesses of history, before the turn of the century and well before the hated *Disarming Act*. He thought it strange that this, of all possible visions, should come to him now as a dream that held him captive with both its clarity and beauty.

As he lay sleeping in his bed, the open window flooded the room with the cool air of an early September afternoon. Daniel's mind was full of things past. His grandfather, *Iain an t-òganach* (John the Young Man) as he was known to the end of his long life, had been taught the pipe during the dreaded period following the rising of 1745, when the English came and suppressed the highlands in the most heinous of ways. Their law prohibited the wearing of the tartan and, though not specifically mentioned, the playing of the great highland pipe. Was it not considered an instrument of war and, as such, a very real threat to the English Crown? Who else but the *Sasunnaich* (the Englishmen) would actually forbid the playing of a musical instrument. And oh how the streams of blood poured over the heathered moors and bens as men, women and children fell beneath the cold merciless blades of the foreigners' bayonets. Even now, with the passage of years, it was difficult to believe the extent of the cruelty imposed on the people of the glens, all in the name of securing the rotund German's seat in London. *Is trom an t-uallach an t-aineolas.* (Ignorance is a heavy burden)

Daniel had been taught by his father on the practice chanter and, later, the very pipe that his own grandson, *Coinneach Bàn*, now played with such pride. He had also learned the ancient art of *canntaireachd* (humming a tune/chanting/singing) that consisted of a series of vocals that imitated the sounds of the pipe. Centuries before, it had been invented and widely used as a training tool by at least two of the great highland schools of piping: the MacCrimmons of Boreraig and the MacArthurs of Peingown. It was nothing short of providential that this ancient art form would later become the salvation of the music for it was *canntaireachd* that carried the pipe music of the highland Scots in the throat and in the heart during the time of suppression. It was a saving grace; it sustained the music and it sustained their spirit as well as their sense of identity. It was too powerful a force to die, too strong to be bludgeoned by a cold blade. English laws be damned!

Daniel thought the name of the tune *Cogadh no Sìth* so appropriate. The clans still gathered all these years later and, with the conviction of the young like *Coinneach Bàn*, would surely continue to do so for generations to come. Even though the playing of *ceòl mór* was heard less frequently than before, his grandson would still be a piper of the "smaller" traditional music that had been transported across a vast sea from one highlands to another. It pleased him. And yet, the look of absolute contentment that bathed his face gave way abruptly and quite unexpectedly to one of sheer puzzlement. Had it all been nothing more than a dream, the subconscious reminiscences of an old man with more to look back upon than forward to? If so, why then was it that he saw the ribbed pattern of the ceiling above him? His eyes were indeed open. He was awake and not lingering in a dream across water and time. And still he heard his father's voice. It was the beautiful sounds of *canntaireachd*. It was *Cogadh no Sìth*. But how? Dear God, how?

Rising from his bed, Daniel almost reluctantly made his way across the room to stand before the open window. Even with the years upon him, he still had the presence of mind to know that his ears were not deceiving him. The sound was louder and clearer and coming from somewhere off to the side. But where and who? Who but he in *Loch Dubh* knew *canntaireachd* and who but he had even heard this particular piece of music? He was certain that it would not be *Coinneach Bàn*, given that the tune had never been shared with him over the kitchen table. Where was it coming from? Who was singing it? There was an incredible insatiable need to know and yet, at the same time, a terrible feeling of dread as to what it was he might find. Was he indeed losing his mind? *"A Thighearna, cuidich leam."* (Oh Lord, help me.) The whispered words were more a plea than a statement as Daniel slowly left the bedroom and proceeded out the front door.

The yard was eerily silent as Daniel rounded the corner of the house and walked towards the barn, vainly searching for someone or something that even he was not certain existed. But he had heard it as clear as day. He had! Now off to the side of the building, he came upon Grace and Aulay in the vegetable field, busily pulling carrots from the soil by their green plumes and placing them in a large basket. Aulay had walked home with his cousin after school and had decided to lend a hand when Kristy, presently teaching Ismay Campbell in the kitchen, had asked her daughter to go off and gather up some vegetables for the evening meal. As their grandfather walked down the drill towards them, both Grace and Aulay looked up from their work, smiled and greeted him warmly. *"A Sheanair, a bheil thu an seo airson ar cobhair?"* (Grandfather, are you here to help us?) It was obvious that they hoped he was. They so enjoyed being in his presence, especially if a sweet were to magically appear from his pants' pocket, which happened more often than not.

Daniel placed a hand on each of their heads and mussed their hair playfully. *"Chan eil; 's math a fhuaradh sibh! Ach có bha a'seinn?"* (No, you are doing fine! But who was singing?) Initially, the two children looked at each other as if uncertain as to what their grandfather was asking of them. It was only after a momentary lull and some considerable scratching of head that Grace eventually broke into wild laughter.

"Amhladh. Balach faoin. Sheinn e briathran gun bhrigh." (It is Aulay. He is a silly boy. He was singing gibberish.) She continued to giggle as Aulay's gaze almost sheepishly fell to the ground at his grandfather's feet. Given his growing embarrassment, he could not bring himself to look into Daniel's face. For his part, Daniel had no doubt that Grace was speaking the truth. But how was it possible? How could it have come to be? With questions flooding his mind, he suddenly realized that this was not the time to attempt to extract an explanation from the child, if indeed one was possible. As the boy stood there waiting for some reaction from his grandfather, Daniel stared down upon Aulay's bowed head and smiled knowingly.

"Tha guth iongantach agad fhir mo rùin. Is e seo tiodhlac Dhé gu dearbh, tiodhlac Dhé." (You have a wonderful voice my loved one. It is truly the gift of God, the gift of God.) Daniel continued to look at Aulay not knowing what else to say. Nothing would be more appropriate than these complimentary and

consoling words that had been offered in a soft almost reverent manner. He smiled at them both, turned and slowly walked back to the house. He wished he had brought along the bag of peppermints. Nevertheless, it was right that he should leave them as they were. He needed time alone and did not want the children to see the tears that now began to well in his eyes. It would have been of no use to ask the boy any additional questions or even to ponder it further himself. He was certain that Aulay would not be able to offer an explanation just as he himself could not. It was all so very simple. It was truly the gift of God.

Later in the week, during a visit with Neil and Iona, Daniel inquired in passing as to his young grandson's possible interest in music. Only then, upon reflection, did Iona recount a story that, at the time, had intrigued her but had since been unconsciously relegated to the back of her mind. She scolded herself for not having the presence of mind to share it with Neil but now did so willingly. It had been a few months past that she heard the sound of the practice chanter coming from the boys' upstairs bedroom above the kitchen. She doubted her own sanity, if not her ears, for she knew well enough that Kenneth was in the back fields helping his father with the spring planting. With curiosity upon her, she slowly crept up the stairs not knowing if she might expect to encounter a *bòcan* coming down to meet her. None did, thankfully, but still the sound persisted. She tiptoed across the floor of the landing and peeked around the casement of the bedroom door. There, Iona watched quietly as Aulay sat on Kenneth's bed "playing" the chanter. He stared out the window as his fingers travelled up and down the instrument, all the while oblivious to the fact that he was being observed. The tune was played in a rough slow manner but still Iona could recognize it as one that Daniel had often performed for dancing at *céilidhs*. It was obvious that he had carefully watched his brother practising the fingering and was now imitating it as best he could. It was all too apparent that the music was in him. It was only after several minutes that Iona left him, gingerly returning downstairs to her work in the kitchen. She would never admit it to her elder son or anyone else for that matter but, on that day, the sound of the practice chanter had never settled so sweetly on her ears.

The next visit to New Carlisle saw Daniel posting a letter to John Angus MacDonald in *Drochaid Na h-Aibhne a Tuath* who was a well-respected carpenter and known for having crafted several chanters and pipes from local wood. The intent of the letter was clear: a request was being made for a practice chanter that would be given to Aulay as a Christmas present. It did not matter that it would be a new one in contrast to Kenneth's that bore the wear of so many years. It was of no consequence because Daniel knew that something of a much greater age was in the boy. It would never be his to explain and he would never attempt to do so. There was no need. That evening at worship, a tear came to the old man's voice as he ended his prayer. *"A' toirt buidheachais a ghnàth air son nan uile nithean do Dhia o lìnn gu linn.*" (Giving thanks always for all things unto God from generation to generation.) He thought of Tina and was comforted by the knowledge that she would be pleased in looking down upon them from where she sat in her lofty garden.

A *céilidh* would be just the thing! It was a sentiment that was widely shared around the loch, once the hay had been dutifully committed to the mows and the vegetables to the root cellars. The autumn was always an arduous time of year with all the back-breaking work that was required to prepare for the onslaught of the long dreary winter. It was such a contrast to the invigorating days of summer when life seemed to teem from every conceivable nook and cranny around them like a tea kettle left to boil madly on the stove, sending droplets of water dancing in all directions across the fiery black surface. A *céilidh* would lift their spirits and bring them together to signal their defiance to the drifting snows and bitter cold that were so diabolically intent on keeping them apart.

On more than one occasion, James MacGregor was known to have offered an insightful comment to the effect that the gatherings at the community hall were good sustenance for the soul. Invariably, he would do so from off to the side of the hall steps as he gazed over at the Kirk and the manse that sat a bit higher on the adjoining hill. Many had been left wondering how *Mac na poit-dhuibh* (Son of the Black Pot/Son of the Still) would possibly have the foggiest notion since his attention was continually focused on feeding an appetite for something far less spiritual. There had been more than a few chuckles raised in the houses around the loch when the view was made known, as it frequently was, that the closest MacGregor came to matters of the spirit was the fact that he could see the Kirk from the windows of his house, at least on those days when he was not busying himself in search of other spirits further back in the woods.

"*Tha e fhathast 'na leanabh do Dhia. Is airidh e air saoibhreas agus gliocas agus neart fhaotainn.*" (He is still a child of God. He is worthy to receive riches, wisdom and strength.) As a member of session, Hector Urquhart felt obliged to represent the Christian belief and often chided his wife for passing pointed comments at James' expense, which had become an all-too-common occurrence around the loch. Sarah's own response had been to look up at him from her sewing and ever-so-subtly raise her needle high into the air. With her tongue firmly committed to cheek, she quite deviously asked if her dear husband would mind going out to the barn so as to bring one of the camels in to her. She would have to clarify the matter once and for all. Her sewing could wait while, all too plainly, the laughter that erupted from her could not. It continued unabated as she slapped her knee for good measure. Similar scenes would take place in any number of homes on any number of occasions. On that particular day at least, the phantom camel was never retrieved and so, most assuredly, had not been tested to determine if it indeed could pass through the eye of Sarah's needle. If nothing else, *Mac na poit-dhuibh* was a man rich in "spirits" who gave them much to talk and oftentimes chuckle about.

There was a bit of reluctance in Iona's step as she walked down the loch road that late afternoon in mid-November to speak to James privately. She knew that he would be home and, of greater importance, that Margaret would not. Since Kristy had persuaded her three years ago to conduct the choir at the Christmas concert, Margaret had continued to relish working with the wee ones to produce something special for the community. Iona had watched from her pantry window as Margaret made her way down the laneway and along the loch road in the direction of the hall. On the far side of the water, the children were beginning to appear from the double doors of the school, fleeing the clutches of Miss Massey and racing to the more-enjoyable work that awaited them at the rehearsal. The school mistress had always insisted that everyone in the community call her by her family name in order to show proper respect for her and the position she held. Her first name, Annie Mae, was never to be used and everyone had been more than willing to carefully respect her wishes. In any event, the people of *Loch Dubh* much preferred to refer to her, at least among themselves, as *An Gnùis a' bhiorain-ghriosaich!* (The Poker Face!) And besides, it rolled off the tongue more easily than Annie Mae. If nothing else, they were always more than deferential and, in so being, most eager to show due respect.

Iona found James sitting at the kitchen table sipping a cup of tea that Margaret had obviously prepared for him before leaving for the hall. He welcomed her warmly in offering her both a seat at the table and a cup. Initially, her thinking had been to be quick about the business at hand and return to the comfort of her own home. However, it was the face and eyes that convinced Iona otherwise. For some strange reason, she was reminded of his visit to their home on Hogmanay all those thirteen years ago when he had appeared with a face as black as night. She knew it to be curious but it was the very same look of a man who, with all his possible or probable faults, wanted to feel that he was a member of the community and a friend. Iona graciously accepted his kind offer as she unbuttoned her long black coat and seated herself across from him at the table.

Birthdays. Iona wished to discuss birthdays with James. There were two compelling reasons for doing so; the first week of December would be a momentous time in the life of *Loch Dubh*. Her husband would celebrate his fiftieth birthday on Tuesday the second while Margaret would mark the very same milestone the following Friday. She had come to propose that both families use the Saturday night *céilidh* as a surprise gathering of the entire community in their honour. It had not taken James long to offer a response as his face filled with an immense hearty grin. Iona could not help but see the sullen blackened face of that Hogmanay night now replaced by something so completely different. They would talk again but, for now, they had come to an agreement and the plans would be well and truly put in place. Yet of all the surprises plotted by the two conspirators on that particular day, there was one that had come about quite unexpectedly. Iona had a fleeting glimpse of another James MacGregor, one far less known around the shores of the loch. Her initial reluctance in approaching him was now replaced with a tremendous sense of gratification for having done so. She was grateful for the insight she had gained and was now determined to do whatever might be in her power to ensure that the blackness of his face would be banished forever from the MacGregor home. She had no idea how. She only knew that she should and would try.

The weeks that followed were nothing short of organized chaos with Iona making endless arrangements whenever Neil was out of sight and ear shot. She was thankful for the assistance of Betty MacInnes and her younger brother Andrew. Betty had agreed, given the advantage of distance and the obvious security it afforded, to bake an immense cake that would be decorated with the names of her mother and Neil. Andrew had seen to the ordering of colourful streamers and other appropriate trimmings at the general store. For their part, the women of the community were baking an assortment of cookies, cakes and squares for the tea table that would undoubtedly be richly laid out with a sufficiently high sugar level to sweeten even the face of Miss Massey, although she would in all likelihood not be attending. Some things were still beneath her. Her soured reply would only have offered validity to the title that had been so graciously bestowed upon her.

With the element of surprise carefully guarded, Iona had suggested to Neil in passing that they collect the MacGregors on their way to the hall. Aulay smirked with excitement as he sat in the back of the sleigh with the two MacGregor boys and immediately next to Kenneth who had carefully wrapped his pipe box in a blanket and placed it on his lap. Iona positioned herself beside Margaret and kept her engaged in idle chat as both Neil and James rode up front guiding the horse and sleigh towards its destination. Even from a distance, they could hear the music of *Mac an Fhìdhleir* drifting over the loch on the cold evening air. Although the hall's double doors and windows were well closed to safeguard both the warmth and the surprise that waited within, the music was obviously not to be contained. The horse and sleigh passed the Kirk and, with the distance that still remained, the passengers could not possibly have noted the silhouetted figures of Alasdair and Kristy who stood watch at the side window.

There was certainly no doubt about the element of surprise that had been carefully kept by everyone for the better part of three weeks, although it was somewhat of a chore for the younger ones. You could see it clearly on both Margaret and Neil's faces as, coming through the doors, the fiddle music was quickly halted and replaced by a rousing cheer of *"Là-breith sona, a Mhairead agus Nèill!"* (Happy Birthday Margaret and Neil!) that rang off

365

the rafters now festooned with red and green streamers. Ever the practical one, Iona had had the foresight to suggest the colours to Andrew knowing that they would also add a festive touch to the Christmas concert that was to be held in two weeks time. She knew it would please Margaret.

Once hands had been shaken, backs slapped and everyone light heartedly reprimanded for the mischievous nature of the surprise, the fiddle soon returned to life as a number of square sets were formed and spilled out onto the floor. Many of the younger couples were quick to take their places, including Iain Grant and Daniel MacDonald who were eager to show off their new brides. It did not matter that Alexandra and Agnes were uncertain as to the correctness of all the steps or even some of the more-basic movements. They only knew that the *céilidh* was a great deal more fun than their somewhat staid wedding receptions a few weeks before down at the Church of England hall. Many others sat along the sides of the walls watching the dance as it unfolded and chatting away with one another, or at least attempting to as the hall reverberated with a virtual calliope of sounds. From where he sat elevated on the platform at the head of the hall, *Mac an Fhìdhleir* had the distinct impression that Miss Massey must surely be the only truant person given that the hall was literally filled to overflowing. Even the tea table at the back had become trapped by the onslaught of bodies that surrounded it. Never before had he enjoyed such a large audience and it encouraged him to play all the more. The smaller children had also been allowed to attend, although it would only be until the break that was normally called at around 10:00 p.m. It was too important an event in the life of the community for them to be left out and their running about bore evidence to the fact that they too were delighting in the fun and novelty of the occasion.

It was not by accident that Margaret and James, Neil and Iona were coerced into joining the same set forming in the middle of the floor. As they danced around the circle, Iona could not help but notice that James' back pocket was strangely empty of the flask that normally adorned it at all such events. It gave her all the more reason to smile as she held tightly onto Neil's shoulder. Amid the festive atmosphere, Iona realized that the throats of a few of the men, John Dunn among them, would regrettably be a bit more parched than usual. It made the dance all the more special for her and, no doubt, for Margaret as well who loved to "step it off" whenever she had the opportunity. Tonight at least, her feet would be well travelled on the broad pine boards of the hall's floor.

Mac an Fhìdhleir continued to play uninterrupted for a good hour and a half without a pause right up to the tea break. It was commonly believed that Betty had most probably and skillfully reminded him of her mother's love of the dance for it seemed that this, in his own small way, was perhaps his own special gift for her. It was only at the break that the fiddle made way for James and Daniel who crossed the floor and mounted the platform in order to address the guests of honour. Conscious of the two young brides in the crowd before them, they were mindful of the need to sprinkle their comments with a bit of the English. In so doing, James made reference to a wife and mother's love of family and, in particular, her pride in children. Daniel followed with words that spoke of children and grandchildren who enriched all their lives with the blessings and promise of youth. Not once did he take his eyes off Neil who stood along the side wall next to Iona with his hands on Kenneth and Aulay's shoulders. Although Daniel and James had not discussed the specific details of their comments beforehand, there was a common thread through both that referred to the importance of nurture and the retention of something far greater than themselves. The remarks, as brief as they were poignant, brought a rousing round of applause that was as much a sign of agreement as it was of eagerness to return to the dance floor. It was all so apparent that the message had been duly received as the two men quickly stepped down, making way for Jamie and his fiddle that once again began to fill the hall with its magic.

The dancing and singing continued on unabated and it was during a momentary break between sets that Margaret, Neil and Kenneth had gone forward to speak with the fiddler. Shortly thereafter, Kenneth left the hall briefly only to return in short order with his pipe in position on his shoulder. A silence fell over the crowd, a combination of curiosity and expectation as to what was about to unfold. Now standing in the centre of the platform, it was Margaret who began by indicating that she was taking the liberty of speaking on behalf of both the community's newest *bodach* and *cailleach*. Not unexpectedly, she was then forced to wait a bit for the laughter to subside before continuing. *"A chàirdean ghràdhach, abair céilidh iongantach! Thug sibh dhuinn e — dhomhsa agus do Niall — a nasgaidh. Agus bheir sinn dhuibh tiodhlac a nasgaidh an dràsda."* (Dear friends, what a marvellous *céilidh*! You gave it to us — Neil and me — as a gift. Now, we will give you a gift in return.) Without the slightest pause, Margaret began to sing *Auld Lang Syne* in the Gaelic, having undertaken her own translation of the verses. It was only on the chorus, when she reverted to the English, that both Kenneth and James struck up their instruments to accompany her. A slight wave of her hand served as a subtle invitation for everyone in the hall to join her as she sang the chorus yet again. Arms were linked together and bodies swayed from side to side as the beautiful full sound of voice, fiddle and pipe blended as one and enveloped the hall with a genuine sense of warmth and fellowship that would have surely made the bard proud.

With her love of literature, Kristy took particular delight in the fact that Margaret had taken the time and made the effort to so thoughtfully and skillfully produce a translation of one of Burns' most eloquent and perhaps best known pieces of verse. As she sang and swayed to the rhythm, she happened to look across the room at the two, newly wed couples who were savouring the last bit of revelry before the clock announced the arrival of the Sabbath. Kristy knew that, in a short period of time, these were two homes where the Gaelic would surely be lost, less by design than by necessity. If Alexandra and Agnes were cut from the same cloth as their parents, there would be no interest in learning the "strange tongue" of the people up by the lake or in having it passed on to their children. *Is bochd an gnothuch e agus bithidh mór ar call ris.* (It is a sad affair and great will be our loss for it.) She would keep these thoughts to herself. Tonight, at least, was a time of celebration.

A lingering shadow was absolutely the last thing she expected to see at this time of day. The noon sun was high in the May sky and blanketed the earth with its warmth. It felt refreshing on her face and arms that, for too long a time, had known nothing other than the rough feel of heavy woollens during the bleak winter months. *"Tha an t-earrach air tighinn."* (The spring has come.) How she delighted in just hearing the words spoken aloud, as if the mere act of sounding them would somehow banish winter's cold sting from her bones forever. It was the most glorious time of year with its sense of rebirth. Although she would never admit it, especially to Duncan, Jennie felt a sensuousness on her skin that was almost sinfully wicked. She nonetheless enjoyed it, all the while appreciative of the fact that it would be best to keep such thoughts to herself.

As she walked up the sloping field towards the fringes of the woods, the shadow persisted in following her every move. With the possible exception of her solo forays at night, *Rionnag* had always been most content when in the presence of people — older people. It was more than the stroking of her fur and the odd bowl of fresh milk that she could coerce so easily from them with her pleading eyes and the nuzzling of shins with her head and sleek black body. She genuinely enjoyed watching their movements, especially the swaying of Jennie's long skirts and the swishing sounds that they made. True enough, they could never be as graceful as she was but then they were only human.

On this particular day, *Rionnag* was not to be left behind and would follow Jennie on her walk regardless of where it might take her. It did not much matter. A stroll through the fields was always such an interesting experience for her. She could meander along at her own chosen pace and to her heart's content, nibbling the slender blades of newborn grass and stalking the tiny butterflies that always flitted to and fro. She was honest enough to admit that she was seldom able to actually capture one but then the fun was more in the chase than anything else. She was a natural-born hunter and enjoyed the thrill of the challenge. Most of all, *Rionnag* was pleased to be rid of the dreaded snow; spring was her favourite time of year. It was more than the numerous birds nesting in the orchard trees or the scores of mice scampering across the fields and in the barn's hay mow. No, more than anything else, it was the luxuriating warmth of the earth under her paws that made her feel like a playful kitten all over again.

Jennie's eyes were trained on the outcropping of rocks that poked its nose out from the edge of the woods as if seeking relief from the coolness and suffocating fragrance of the pine and spruce that loomed so prominently nearby. Although she was known to spend time in her flower garden as well as the apple orchard, it was here high up in the hills that she came from time to time to gain perspective and bask in the expansive view of ocean and coastline that wound their way southward, eventually blending together in the most wondrous infinity of blue. It was to this very spot that she had come two weeks ago to witness the pristine skies smudged with dark lingering smoke. The evidence of the tragic fire that struck North Sydney was painfully obvious even from *Loch Dubh*. They were later to learn from accounts in the Sydney paper that a blackened swath had been cut all along the waterfront and across the entire stretch of the town from Archibald Avenue to Caledonia Street on the north side of Commercial Street. From where she had placed herself on the lofty seat on that day, Jennie knew only too well that the darkened horizon spoke not only of the magnitude of the fire but also of the personal suffering that most assuredly followed.

The true impact of the disaster had been brought home to both Jennie and Duncan by Miss Massey, whose sister resided a matter of steps away from Caledonia Street. The first few days following the initial news of the fire were heart wrenching for the school mistress whose concern for the safety of family members was evident on the normally expressionless face. As they sat around the kitchen table, she slowly began to recount memories of the terrible fire that had destroyed much the same area of the town some thirty-two years ago when she had been but a mere child of eleven. The horrible memories of that time never left her, especially the initial look of utter fear that filled her mother's face. It was later the same day that anxiety gave way to grief. From the archway leading into the kitchen, the two girls watched as their mother first greeted the minister at the front door and, shortly thereafter, broke into the most mournful sobbing. Miss Massey would always see her father that morning walking down the street towards work at the marine slip. He had turned and waved good-bye to his two daughters, or his two girlfriends as he so often called them, standing on the front steps. He was gone; he had waved good-bye.

Jennie could see the look of absolute fear in the eyes and she rubbed the school mistress' folded hands in offering comforting assurances that everything would be just fine. She said that she was certain of it although, in her heart, she was anything but. The arrival of a letter a week later had mercifully confirmed the accuracy of Jennie's beliefs. However, the greater news was the fact that those moments in the manse kitchen had shown that Miss Massey, or Annie Mae as Jennie had inadvertently called her at the time, had a greater depth that was all too carefully guarded if not completely concealed from the light of day. The forced smile that appeared on the face told Jennie that, widely held views aside, there was a caring and sensitive person inside the hardened shell that was the school mistress. There was also the realization that, with the crisis now passed, Jennie would revert to the practice of referring to her boarder as Miss Massey. Still, she was gladdened by the fact that she had proved, at least to herself, that Annie Mae was truly inside.

Jennie looked down over the loch as it formed a beautiful sliver of silver lying as it did on a bed of deep-green velvet. The water was almost luminous as the sun danced off its surface and bathed the surrounding hills with its nurturing warmth. Jennie allowed her eyes to follow the contour of the loch's shore as it wound its way from the foot of the Kirk to the head of the bluffs at the far end. Off in the distance, the birds were circling high over *An Deireadh* and *An Toiseach* and dabbing the blue sky with their colours, like so many speckles of paint on an enormous cerulean canvas. It was this sense of overwhelming space that she loved more than anything else. It gave perspective to her life and to her time in this place with these people. She found it difficult to imagine the day when she would no longer sit on these stones, when all this would be taken from her.

The Reverend Duncan Fraser was now in his seventy-fifth year of life and forty-second of ministry, twenty of which had been spent in *Loch Dubh*. It was Jennie, more than anyone else, who knew the extent of her husband's commitment to the Kirk and its congregants. It was so much more than the public face of ministry: the preparation of sermons, the visitations to the sick and dying, the administering of the sacraments and numerous others duties. Duncan himself loved to use the analogy of the Good Shepherd when referring to his ministry among the people who lived in the shadow of these mountains. They were truly his flock and his care of them, while oftentimes trying and tiring, was his true joy in life. But the shepherd was now showing the signs of fatigue. He was no longer the young man that he always imagined himself to be. It was painfully obvious that the spirit was perhaps stronger than the flesh that grew increasingly weak. Even Emily had noticed a change in her father during the Christmas visit. It was all so painful to accept. With a myriad of thoughts streaking across her mind all at once, Jennie continued to look out over the broad Atlantic that stretched as far as the eye could see. *"A Thighearna. Thigeadh do rìoghachd."* (Oh Lord. Thy kingdom come.)

Her eyes now returned to the mountains as they gently sloped down, dotted with the homes of her neighbours and friends, Duncan's flock. At the same time, her right hand rhythmically stroked *Rionnag* who had earlier made it a point of positioning herself in the hollow of Jennie's lap. In their twenty years here, she and Duncan had shared in the many joys and sorrows of these families. It was so much like a quilt being sewn together, as tattered and worn squares of cloth were removed and replaced by new stronger ones. People died and people were born. It was always changing and yet somehow always the same. Jennie smiled to herself well satisfied with the analogy she had drawn, knowing that it was more than the invigorating rays of sun that brought her warmth. She thought of Sandy as a wee bairn with his Joseph's coat of many colours. What lay before her eyes was her very own blanket of security and comfort. It was something that she had always known but only now saw for what it truly was. She was as grateful for these rocks as she was for the perspective that they afforded her.

From somewhere high up in the adjoining trees, the sudden and loud crying of the blue jays startled Jennie, to say nothing of poor *Rionnag* who now saw the birds more as a nuisance than a challenge. She was more than happy to remain where she was and to receive the attentive care from Jennie that she believed she so richly deserved. *"Is iad chuir am biorgadh annam! Ach, tha iad ceart — èisd ri fuaim na gaoithe. Tha coltas an uisg' air; tha gu dearbh. Is ann a tha tìde bhi falbh, math a dh' fhaoidte."* (What a start they gave me! But they are quite right — listen to the sound of the wind. It threatens rain; yes indeed. Perhaps it is time to be going.) For the briefest of moments, *Rionnag* raised her head from her pillowed bed and stared inquisitively into Jennie's face. At the same time, she availed herself of the opportunity to stretch her front paws with the clear intention of promptly resuming her slumber. It was obvious that her preference was to stay precisely where she was, rain or no rain.

"Is thu Rionnag — mo naoidhean dubh agus mo pheata fhéin." (It is you *Rionnag* — my little black baby and my own spoiled child.) As Jennie leaned her head back in wild laughter, she happened to notice a horse and wagon making the turn at the bluffs and moving down the loch road in the direction of the mill bridge. She played a game with herself in attempting to identify who the passengers might be: the Urquharts, the Erskines or the Campbells? A few minutes later, she was somewhat puzzled when all three laneways were passed by and the horse and wagon worked its way along, eventually coming to a final stop at the side of the Kirk. There was a young man holding the reins while beside him sat a woman with a small child on her lap. Jennie could see the man take the child by the hand and proceed slowly towards the cemetery gate. For some unknown reason, the mother remained seated in the wagon with knitting needles at the ready. Now, with ever-increasing curiosity upon her, Jennie carefully observed the drama unfold, paying particular attention to the two figures that leisurely made their way up through the white stones and beyond Andrew MacDonald's cairn. Jennie was intrigued as she looked over at the father and child who were then off to her right, and with the benefit of a small grove of birch trees that lay between, unaware of the fact that they were being watched.

At fifteen months, Flora was absolutely mesmerized by the wondrous carpet of mayflowers that now appeared before her. Although still a bit unsure of her footing at such a tender age, she ran about excitedly plucking the pink and white blossoms from their stems and unknowingly crushing more with her tiny feet than she picked with her nimble hands. John allowed her to run free for a few moments as she giggled with absolute delight before once again being taken by the hand. Together, they collected two small bouquets and eventually began to walk back down the hill. At Angus' and Flora's graves, *Iain Beag* crouched down and lovingly placed the bouquet he had been carrying. Jennie noted he did not linger long. The two figures returned to the wagon where the little girl could be seen proudly showing her mother her glorious floral prize. Christine was now seven months with child and had obviously decided it was best to not even attempt a climb up the cemetery hill. With time permitting, it was quickly agreed they would stop at Angus and Isabelle's house before heading back along the coast road for home. It was at his grandparents' graves that John had first suggested it to his daughter who was most eager to oblige. Her bouquet would be presented to grandmother. As the horse and wagon moved down the loch road towards the Grant house, Jennie could not possibly have seen the huge smile that settled on John's face. He was certain this would be a tradition that he and his daughter, along with *Floridh Aosda* and Isabelle, would share for many years to come.

Rionnag was almost as perturbed with being so unceremoniously plunked down on the ground as she was with the dictatorial order. *"A phiseag, thig còmhla riumsa."* (Puss, come along with me.) It was all so damnably nervy if not downright insolent. She would take her time, and in so doing, make the point quite emphatically that she was not a dog to be commanded to do this or that or anything else. As she watched the horse and wagon leave the Kirk, Jennie had suddenly come to the realization that she had better stop dallying. After the preparation of supper, she would bake a batch of oatcakes to be served later in the evening. Session was to meet in the front parlour and it was her habit to place a pot of tea and a plate of sweets on the table before vacating the room so as to leave the men to conduct their business in private. She had heard the rumour that it might well be Daniel's wish to resign as clerk owing to his age and to encourage either Hector or Angus to assume the duties. Jennie hoped that Duncan could convince him otherwise; it would never be the same without him. He was the last of his generation, the generation that first settled these mountains and gave them life. He was the eldest of the flock; he was the only link back.

For a fleeting second, an image of *Floridh Aosda* flashed across Jennie's mind. There the old woman stood in her long black dress with her cream and white hair pinned up in a bun on the back of her head. Her tall figure had always made her appear so formidable and yet the image in Jennie's mind was now much less intimidating and severe than the woman she remembered. It did not take her long to realize what had caused this scene to be so different. Flora was holding a large bouquet of mayflowers in her hands. They softened her appearance even though the wrinkles on her face, neck and hands were all too evident. What made her seem more welcoming was the look in her eyes, or so it was that Jennie imagined. It was as though Flora somehow knew that she was being remembered with fondness all these years after her passing. There was a legacy that lived on. For the second time that day, Jennie thought of the large quilt that was *Loch Dubh*, ever changing and forever the same. It was a simple gift that she would freely give herself and enjoy; she stood there for a few minutes more basking in the warmth before passing through the screen door and returning to her work in the kitchen.

It was perhaps ten minutes later that eventually saw *Rionnag* sauntering down the hill towards the manse. As was always her habit, her pace was leisurely as she stopped along the way to nibble a few blades of grass and do whatever else happened to come to her mind; she was proud and would take her own sweet time. She would see to that. Come along with me indeed!

⟠ Chapter Eighteen ⟠

These men were all joyful on New Year's Day
When leaving their homeland to go to war;
Though their parents are sad and their friends miss them,
From the Crown they'll receive glory and fame evermore.

> Donald MacMillan
> *Song to the Transvaal* (song)

Siud na fir bha sùnndach air là na Bliadhn' Ùire,
A'fàgail na dùthcha a dh'ionnsuidh a' bhlàir;
'S ged tha 'm parantan tùrsach 's an càirdean 'gan ionndrainn,
Gheibh iad urram o'n chrùn agus cliù gu là bràth.

> Donald MacMillan
> *Òran Do 'N Transvaal* (òran)

"The sick people" and their possible involvement with a race was something simply beyond his comprehension. From the photograph in **The Record**, it appeared as if they were indeed all quite ill. Everyone in the group had bandages wrapped tightly around their heads and looked so forlorn as they sat huddled together on the bow of the ship. Aulay listened attentively in attempting to put the various pieces of the puzzle together as John Rogers read aloud the account of the recent troubles that had erupted on the Vancouver harbour front. It was painfully obvious to everyone that he was yet again enjoying the sound of his own voice. Did it not give him a sense of authority as he read the newspaper article to the group of men gathered around the cold stove, whose only purpose was now to serve as an impromptu table for the many cups of tea that were raised around the room? Nothing, not even the sweltering summer heat, would prevent tea from being consumed in copious amounts, especially if a plate of buttered molasses biscuits was to be had for the taking.

Rogers was standing by the stove that had now taken on the appearance of a pulpit as the gospel according to **The Record** was delivered to the great unwashed. Diarmid MacInnes sat in the far corner of the store snickering to himself with the word *amadan* running through his mind. He wished that Archie was still here because he more than anyone else could always be counted upon to put the Englishman in his rightful place. There was no doubt but that on this occasion Archie would surely call into question the authenticity of the passage being read. It was well known that **The Record** was a longtime supporter of the Liberal Party and that it enjoyed a goodly circulation in New Carlisle. In contrast, the smaller stack of the **Cape Breton Post** that rested on the corner of the counter was primarily reserved for "the Scotch people" from *Loch Dubh* and others further down along the shore. Rogers was in the habit of referring to it as "that Tory rag" and suggesting that it could be put to far better use if placed in the outhouses that dotted the town's backyards. He was as subtle as he was discreet.

The gospel reading continued unabated as Diarmid consciously blocked out the sound by looking through the open windows and focusing his attention on the fishing boats that were approaching the government wharf. The gulls circled high above and cried aloud in wild expectation of the fish entrails that would shortly be cast back upon the water once the catch had been properly gutted and cleaned. Their cries now cascaded through the windows and it was not only Diarmid who thought that the sound had never before settled so sweetly on the ears. In contrast to "the Reverend" Mr. Rogers, the gulls at least served a useful purpose.

Aulay crossed the room and returned to the store counter where Neil and Iona were waiting patiently to be served by John Dunn, who was busily wrapping a parcel for the MacKinnon woman from up the coast road. From the stories, he knew her to be the wife of the man who had sold the border collie to Ismay's father a few years back. Aulay had always wanted a dog but, given his mother's reaction to the piglets, thought it best not to broach the subject again, at least for a while. His focus shifted quickly, as it always seemed to do, and was trained on the spool of string that sat high above the shopkeeper's head on its own small shelf near the ceiling. It hummed with life and whirled about like a mad top as Dunn pulled on its long dangling tail to secure the packet of goods before him. Aulay imagined that the spool was singing a song, much like the couples at the birthday *céilidh* last December as they spun around the square sets on the hall floor. With the fragments of a tune in his head, he promised himself that he would try to finger it on his practice chanter once they had returned home.

On that day at least, prayer was answered. "The Reverend" John Rogers had finally and, from the point of view of many of those present, quite mercifully completed the scripture reading as he folded the paper and tucked it back under his arm. He then quickly filled the momentary silence by gracing them with the most ponderous of looks as he began to share the wisdom and compassion of his own deeply held, Christian beliefs. "These people should never have been allowed into the country in the first place. They do not belong here and will cause nothing but trouble, you mark my words." Of course no one did but that in no way dissuaded him from a tirade about how it was completely understandable that a race riot should have broken out in reaction to the boat load of Sikhs arriving on their shores. After all, there was no place for them here and, in addition to everything else, most could not even speak the King's English properly. Although Aulay saw very little wrong with the last point of the rambling diatribe, it would only be later at home that Iona would explain who the "sick people" were and why their heads were bandaged so. He would still feel sorry for them and saw no good reason why they should not come to Canada, all the more so if John Rogers thought otherwise.

Having received and paid for the carefully prepared list of household goods, Neil carried the large box out to the wagon as he bid the men around the stove a final farewell in passing. Iona took the opportunity to rummage deep inside her handbag to retrieve a few coins that she knew should quite rightly remain where they were, safeguarded and set aside for the purchase of the odd trinkets for the boys at Christmas. However, with Neil safely out of view, she took Aulay by the hand and led him to the large jars of candy sticks that sat so enticingly by the shopkeeper's till. A small treat would do him no real harm even if the fatherly advice had always been to not spoil the child. Still, he was her baby, and besides, Neil would be none the wiser. This was obviously not the first time that Iona had brought a smile to her son's face in such a fashion and Aulay was wise enough to know that the secret should be kept between them. With purchase completed, she placed her hand on his crop of blond hair and guided him towards the door as sweets were dutifully hidden deep in the pockets of his overalls for safekeeping. Iona then turned and wished John Dunn and the other men a good day.

From the corner of the room came an unexpected and almost desperate call as Diarmid took note of Iona and the boy approaching the double doors. *"Boireannach glic! Tha thu fàgail roimh 'n ath shearmon 's a' Bheurla. Dean ùrnuigh air mo shonsa."* (Wise woman! You are leaving before the next English sermon. Pray for me.) Iona chuckled aloud and gave him a wave of her hand as if the movement said it all — Tut! Tut! He so reminded her of Archie except of course for the fact that Diarmid was adverse to work and so seldom darkened the door of the Kirk. Still in all, she knew that his prophecy would prove to be only too true. In all likelihood, it would not take long for John Rogers to return to his cast-iron pulpit for yet more fire and brimstone.

They rode up the bluffs at a slow pace. There was no need to hurry home; Neil knew that Kenneth would already be out in the back pasture coercing the cows towards the barn in preparation for the evening milking. Aulay was always intrigued and impressed by the fact that a good bellow of *"trobhad seo"* (come here) from the gate was all that was needed to produce a stampede of hooves as udders heavy with milk swayed wildly to and fro. Like some magical clock, it was in the animals' nature to return to the barn in late afternoon for the feed of hay and water that awaited them. However, Aulay fervently maintained that they were among the most beautiful of God's creatures with their big sad eyes and why should they not understand the Gaelic? Why not indeed.

As the horse and wagon made its way ever higher along the dusty road, Aulay gazed back down towards the buildings of New Carlisle from where he sat on the open tail-board with his legs dangling over the edge. The town played a game of hide and seek among the trees, at least until the last bend in the road was turned and the buildings were finally lost from his sight. However, it was more than the view that he was now savouring. He knew from experience that, if he managed it well, one candied stick would tantalize his mouth until it finally dissolved as they approached the long laneway up to the house. With his back to his father and mother, his secret would be safe.

Neil glanced back at the boy before placing his arm around his wife's waist. Iona was momentarily caught off guard by her husband's sudden romantic impulses. She playfully slapped his leg in mock retaliation, all the while feigning shock even though she nudged ever closer to him in the seat. Knowing that the horse was more than familiar with the route home, Neil dropped the reins from his hands and brought Iona's face close to his. Although he made a genuine attempt to whisper, his booming voice still resonated on the still air. *"Is mis' am fear-gaoil as fheàrr fhathast — nas fheàrr na 'n dithisd fhear-phòsda, Iain Grannd agus Dòmhnall MacDhòmhnuill. Nach eil thu ag aontachadh?"* (I am still the best lover — better than the two new husbands, Iain Grant and Daniel MacDonald. Do you not agree?) The question was rhetorical if nothing else because he quickly proceeded to tickle her unmercifully in the ribs to coerce a favourable reply to his less-than-humble inquiry.

"A Nèill, giùlain thu fhéin; tha Amladh faisg oirnn. Cluinnidh e thu!" (Neil, behave yourself; Aulay is close to us. He will hear you!) All attempts at maintaining a stern reprimand were soon lost as Iona clutched his hand and held it firmly around her. She had always loved his dry sense of humour, something that he had clearly inherited from his mother. She thought of Tina and her cherished garden that was now so meticulously and lovingly maintained by Kristy in its original state. It was not the small white stone in the cemetery that stood as a testament to her life here in *Loch Dubh*; it was her family. But it was also her garden and the significance it had held for her. It lived on to blossom and fill the air with its glorious swaths of colour and equally intoxicating fragrances. Still it was more than colour and fragrance. It was the fact that Iona knew that Tina was still with them.

She glanced over her shoulder to see Aulay sitting contentedly in the back looking out over the loch. How he had grown over the past nine years, and with each one, brought more meaning to the family. Kenneth would always be her first born and occupy a cherished place in her heart. He would also, in time, bring her grandchildren to rock and cradle in her old age. That time would come even though she wished it to be sooner rather than later. Of all the women of *Loch Dubh*, Rachael Ferguson was the closest to her in age and was already blessed with a grandchild, albeit in far-off Boston. But she still had Aulay who was her baby and would need her motherly care for a considerable time yet. In looking over her shoulder once again, she realized that in so many ways he would forever be her wee one.

Of all the moments over those nine years, Iona was constantly coming back to the infamous encounter with the three piglets in the pantry. The image of Aulay standing in defence of Faith, Hope and Charity would always be as fresh in her memory as if it were yesterday. Perhaps it was because it had given her a special insight into the mind of one so full of innocence and the joys of life. Or perhaps it was because she had come to accept him for what he was, a child different from the others, that made him all the more beloved in a mother's heart. She no longer worried about him and what would face him in the years to come. She could not explain it fully but realized that he would grow into manhood surrounded in this place by people who knew him and cared for him when all that remained of her was a white stone and her own garden.

Agus a nis fanaidh creidimh, dòchas agus gràdh, na tri nithean seo; ach is e an gràdh as mò dhiubh seo. (And now abideth faith, hope, charity, these three; but the greatest of these is charity.) Just the thought was comfort enough and Iona felt no need to look over her shoulder a third time. She held onto Neil's hand tightly as the horse now turned into the laneway leading to the house. Once the dry goods were committed to their place in the pantry, she would make a point of visiting her garden.

Seldom before had there been such a flurry of activity in the MacDonald kitchen. Ida was busily sorting through the baskets of green tomatoes, cucumbers and onions on the pantry counter, all in a state of readiness for the preparation of preserves that was as certain an indication of autumn's advent as were the coloured leaves on the majestic maples high up on the hills. Soon she would be in the midst of putting up chow-chow in the jars that had been dutifully stored over the summer months in boxes in the corner of the porch. Even with all the bustling to and fro, there was still an obvious sense that she was consciously attempting to keep herself occupied. The movements were almost exaggerated in the scurrying back and forth between the pantry, the porch and the kitchen stove where several pots of water were at the brink of boiling. There was a great deal to be done but still she desperately wanted to be busy, to keep her mind focused on other things. It was a difficult time for her and it would be best to fix one's thoughts on other matters as much as possible.

It was not so much that she was the sentimental type for indeed she was not. Ida always prided herself on her sense of practicality. She had been born and raised on a farm and knew as well as anyone that you quickly learned to deal with life as it was given to you. Even with death, there was an inevitability in accepting God's will. As she passed in front on the kitchen window, she stopped momentarily to gaze towards the far end of the loch, towards the Kirk, the cemetery and Andrew's cairn. It was now more than fourteen years since she had last set eyes on his beautiful face, except of course for the times when she sat with him in her dreams as she did more often than not. Yet she never shared this fact with another living soul, not even John. On this point, she would be adamant; these were private moments that she would guard and treasure for herself. It was her prerogative after all, the prerogative of a mother, as was the insatiable desire to nurture and sustain her young. There was some satisfaction in knowing that Andrew would forever be the boy she had last kissed good-bye on that late-summer day as he and Rod returned to the academy in Baddeck. And still, on more than one occasion, she found herself speaking aloud. *"Och Anndra, mo mhac mùirneach, ciod is ciall do m' aisling?"* (Oh Andrew, my dearly beloved son, what is the meaning of my dream?) There was never any answer but there was also no sadness. Above everything else, there was still something to cling to and that pleased her immensely.

The sound of boiling water cascading over the edge of the pots onto the stove top drew her back both from the window and her momentary distraction. There was a great deal of work to be done well before the supper hour. She would apply herself and ensure that the bottles were sterilized and ready to receive their vinegary contents. She promised herself that she would keep busy and not let her mind wander any further.

Ida's tall frame was silhouetted against the early afternoon sunlight as it streamed into the kitchen through the pantry window. Her hair, with its now noticeable streaks of grey, was all askew as if intentionally defying the pins that earlier had been put in place to keep it from her face. Not that appearances mattered very much at that moment. She was certain that Agnes would not take offence. Daniel had chosen well with the Bain girl from down in the town and their marriage of some ten months had already brought great joy to the house. It had been such a long time since Ida's own daughter Catherine had gone off to Baddeck. She loved having another woman around her even if the young bride's beauty was all the more striking when contrasted with her own greying hair and the tell tale signs of crow's feet appearing at the corners of her eyes. No, Agnes was wonderful company and a great help around the house that one day would be hers to direct. There was much for the young girl to learn but that would come in time. For now, Ida was simply overjoyed in the knowledge that Daniel had finally found both his true love and unbridled happiness. She could freely admit to herself that she was so much like a brooding hen with her chicks. The worries about her young, be they seven or twenty-seven, were still the same. This too was the prerogative of a mother.

From the pantry window, Ida knew that she would be able to see the large double doors of the barn even though she adamantly refused to look in their direction. She quietly returned to the baskets on the counter. *"Och Eideird, m'ablach bochd. Seo latha do chunntaireachd. Is mór am beud e; is bochd an gnothuch e."* (Oh Edward, my poor creature. This is your day of reckoning.

It is a great pity; it is a sad affair.) In fixing her eyes on the cupboards in front of her, Ida was conscious of the fact that John and Daniel were even now in the barn preparing for the slaughter. In the past, she had taken it as a given that she would be present to help the men with the necessary work. After all, she knew the process that was to be followed better than anyone: slit the throat of the animal, raise the body with block and tackle, allow the blood to drain, burn off the hair with buckets of hot water and finally gut the carcass and prepare the meat. She had done it many times before and normally when the moon was on the rise. It was always said by the older folk that such timing would ensure savoury meat. She had indeed done it all too frequently and always without giving it a second thought. Yet today was different. Today she could not bear to see it all unfold before her eyes, not today and not to poor Edward.

Ida recalled how, during Rod and Margaret's visit of last March, two-year-old Hannah had taken the wee piglet into her care and decided that he should be called after the Prince of Wales. It did not matter that the animal was a female. Hannah said "his" ears were big and floppy like those of the handsome prince whose photograph had recently appeared in the Sydney papers. Fortunately for the dapper prince, he would never make the acquaintance of his namesake. Edward she was to be and the child took such pride in having had the honour of bestowing the name. It seemed to make the piglet all the more special. However, what Ida had not reckoned with at the time was that he would become a member of the family.

The green tomato was returned to the basket as Ida placed her hands on her hips and chuckled loudly. She could still see the scene so vividly in her mind as Daniel met her in the barnyard a few weeks back with Edward following her about like a trusty sheep dog. *"A bhantighearna, gabh mo leis-geul. Is mac an rìgh e! Dean lùbadh. Is deas sin dha."* (Madam, pardon me. It is the son of the King! Make a curtsy. This much is due him.) Daniel's expression never flinched as, with tongue firmly planted in cheek, he pleaded in mock sincerity with his mother to do good by her regal companion.

"Na h-abair diog! Cha lùbainn do dhuine 's am bith. Nach bu tu an slaoightire daor Dhomhnaill MacDhòmhnuill. Falbh! Is ion dhuit teicheadh." (Don't say a word! I would not curtsy to any man. What a dreadful rascal you are Daniel MacDonald. Away with you. You have good reason to scamper.) She could still hear the laughter that came from him as he first bowed and then ran off to rejoin his father in the back field. He always had the devils in him for he could plead any farcical case with the straightest of faces. Although she was forever wont to feign annoyance, Ida loved his dry masterful wit. She knew that Agnes would surely have her hands full with this one.

The scene in the barnyard had been a cause of much laughter over the intervening weeks. Even Agnes, in her expectant state, saw the humour and would do her best to bend a knee and offer a "Good day to you, Your Royal Highness" whenever she crossed paths with the rosy-cheeked royal. With the possible exception of Daniel Erskine and *Coinneach Bàn*, all the families of *Loch Dubh* were fervently loyal to the crown. It was no different with the MacDonalds and they meant no disrespect to Their Majesties or the Royal Family. But still in all, it was good fun and no one in London would ever be the wiser. Unless they were terribly mistaken, King George had far more important matters to occupy his mind. If it was not the sabre-rattling Germans, it would be his cherished stamp collection. Either way, Clan Donald was safe from the tower, at least for the time being.

Later that evening following supper and evening worship, Ida motioned both Daniel and Agnes to their bed. She insisted that the washing up of the tea cups and plates from the earlier *strùpag* could wait until morning, even though she knew that it would never be possible for her to sleep if her kitchen were to be left in an unsightly state. What would the neighbours think and how they would surely talk about *an taigh comaidh air a'chnoc àrd*. (The Messy House on the High Hill) She would have none of it, at all at all. With the washing finally completed and dishes once again placed back in the pantry, Ida dimmed the kerosene lamp that hung over the table as the kitchen fell dark and silent. Through the front window, she could see the moonlight dancing across the surface of the loch like an immense looking glass that reflected the face of the heavens. Standing there for the few brief moments of reflection that she did, Ida thought it a fitting way to end a busy and somewhat trying day.

"Thig gun dàil mo ghràidh. Tha feum ort air cniadadh mór." (Come here right away my dear. You are in need of a good hug.) John had waited patiently for her under the covers and now beckoned her to quickly join him in bed. He was conscious both of the fact that Ida had been quieter than normal during the evening and of the probable reason for her seemingly pensive mood. Having washed her face at the porcelain basin and changed into her nightdress, Ida slipped under the covers to her waiting husband and an unexpected surprise. John propped himself up on one elbow as he turned and looked down into his wife's face. Over thirty-three years of marriage, he had come to know every facet of this woman's being. In her eyes he could see a certain vulnerability that was only exceeded by the innocence with which she placed herself close to him. The trap had been laid and it was the perfect time for the devious plot to unfold. With all good intentions and promises of a loving caress now banished from his mind, John proceeded to tickle his defenceless wife until screams of raucous joy washed over the room and the sparkle of life filled her eyes. Even during their early days of courting, he had always maintained she was never more beautiful than when she broke into delirious laughter. The years had changed little and it pleased him.

In the midst of her persistent chuckling, Ida gasped for breath long enough to admonish her assailant for the viciousness of the attack. *"A Iain MacDhòmhnuill, is tu an duine gun nàire gun athadh. Giùlain thu fhéin. 'S làidire am fuaim na fuaim tuinne agus tha eagal orm gun cluinn a'chlann sinn. Dé a smaoinicheas iad?"* (John MacDonald, you are a man without shame. Behave yourself. There is more noise than the roar of a wave and I am afraid the children will hear us. What will they think?) She looked deep into his eyes not knowing if her chiding would be heeded or simply be taken as an even greater incentive for further wickedness. With him, it was always so difficult to tell. The only certainly was that she realized full well from where the ten devils in Daniel had come; he had inherited each and every one of them honestly from the MacDonalds. She continued to look pleadingly into her husband's eyes, knowing that he probably would be a man of his word and soon enough give her a devious wink in finally delivering on his promise. He caressed her lovingly.

"*Na gabh corruich mo chailleach. Ge b' oil leis an-fhortan, tha a' chlann 'nan cadal. 'Na leigeadh Dia gun éisd iad ri do ghàire agus mo shonas. Cha mhisde sinn sin.*" (Don't be angry my old woman. In spite of the mischief, the children are asleep. God forbid that they hear the sound of your hearty laughter and my happiness. We are little the worse for that.) John reached out and ever so gently tucked several loose strands of his wife's hair back into place at the sides of her head, which lay indented deep in the feathered pillow. He was pleased with the fullness of joy that was so evident on his wife's face. For her part, she was simply relieved that her husband's mischief had passed, at least for the time being.

"*Nach eil fhios agad? Liath thu mo cheann. Is e mo chrannchur ach na cuireadh sin campar ort. Tha an uair agad a dhol a chadal mo dhiabhoil bhig — a h-uile gin dhibh.*" (Do you not know? Your conduct has made my hair grey. It is my lot in life but do not let that trouble you now. It is time for you to go asleep my little devil — everyone of you.) She kissed him on the forehead as if he were a wee bairn being put down for an afternoon nap. She watched him for a long while, well after he had drifted into sleep. It was not so much to ensure that the mischief had actually passed as it was to reflect on something much greater. Ida's thoughts were of her family and, in particular, the grandchild who would soon bring new life to the house. She had little doubt but that the presence of the ten devils would continue on down through the generations. Secretly, she hoped that it would although she would never admit to it or say so aloud to another living soul. It was important to see yourself in the faces of your children and grandchildren. There was a serenity in knowing that the link was always so much more than the earthly body and that it lived on long after mortal remains had passed away. Perhaps this was why she still sat with Andrew in her dreams. It was the beautiful face of "*macan mo rùin*" (my beloved little son), forever young and close to her.

Thoughts of poor Edward were now relegated to the far reaches of her mind even though she knew that a full explanation of pig heaven would have to be offered to Hannah at the time of her next visit. Ida knew that she could and would deal with that eventually. For now, she hoped that she would dream that night, that she would sit and talk. This too was the prerogative of a mother.

Even with the distance, Kristy could still make out its distinctive form as it rose up from the straight horizontal lines of the stern as the steamer made its final approach. Aulay likened the shape to the big wart on Miss Massey's forehead just above her right eyebrow. Initially, he had thought that it must surely move about her face depending upon her mood, which everyone agreed was pretty well always severe and cantankerous. He had developed the habit of studying her face each morning at the beginning of the school day to determine the validity of his theory. After several weeks, he concluded that the lump's present location must be the most appropriate spot for a grouchy state of mind. At least this part of his rather unscientific hypothesis would be borne out — she was forever in a foul mood. Still, wart or no wart, he would continue to speak the Gaelic in the school yard.

Theories aside, there was a tremendous sense of expectation building among the crowd that had gathered on the government wharf. The people of *Loch Dubh* had been advised that, once the drift ice had retreated back out to sea and shipping lanes were once more secure, the cargo would be transported from Sydney where it had remained in storage since its arrival from Boston and Halifax in early April. Both Kristy and Iona were pleased that the chill on the air had finally departed from them, even though they had thick woollen shawls wrapped tightly around their shoulders. True enough, the early May air was refreshing enough but they knew only too well that the wind could change at any time, making their teeth chatter uncontrollably every bit as much as Annabelle Calvey's mouth. Was the postmistress not now standing in the post office window gawking at the proceedings as they unfolded? No doubt, she would have more stories to tell about "those people from up by the lake." While the weather was never predictable, there were other constants in life whether one wished for them or not. *Coimhead oirre — cho deil aig a gnothach. Culaidh-thruais.* (Just look at her — so enthusiastic at her business. An object of pity.) Kristy's thoughts followed her eyes as, together, they passed over the post office and quickly returned to the expectant scene that was about to unfold at the side of the wharf. As was her custom whenever considering the peculiarities of others, Kristy would keep her opinions to herself. It was something that clearly separated her from the others who lived around the loch; they were always more than eager to share their views, be they solicited or not.

As the steamer was carefully manoeuvred towards its mooring, Neil and Alasdair backed the horse and wagon down the length of the wharf in order to prepare for the transfer and what would then be a slow drive up the steep hill to the bluffs and beyond. They would be in need of a rest and were grateful for the knowledge that other men were even now gathering to assist with the unloading at the main doors of the Kirk. For many, it was hard to believe that, after all these months and the controversy that had ensued, it was all finally coming to pass. More than anyone else, Kristy found it difficult to contain her excitement as she smiled down on Grace and Fergus who were playfully seeking protection from the breeze in the deep pleats of her long skirt.

For the better part of two years, both Morag Cabot and Effie O'Sullivan had discussed the possibility of the two Boston families honouring their special ties to the small community in the highlands of Cape Breton. It was in the spring of 1913 that this particular idea had first come to Morag almost by way of providence. The Cabot family worshiped at the Old North Church, the historic Episcopal church just down from the State House and a brief walk from their home in Louisbourg Square. It had been the powerful and emotional rendition of Handel's *Messiah* at Easter Sunday service that had given her the inspiration for which both she and Effie had been searching. While listening to the magnificent voices of the choir fill the sanctuary, her true focus was centred on the sounds of the organ that seemed to make the majestic presence of God all the more real. It was then that she decided that the two families should meet and discuss her idea further.

Well aware of Presbyterian church structure and procedures, Morag knew that the proposal should be properly placed before the clerk of session and not the minister. It was for this reason that a letter was forwarded to Daniel Erskine in early July. In it, Morag explained the desire of the two families to present a gift of a reed organ to the *Loch Dubh* Kirk as an expression of their thankfulness for the important role it had played in their lives and that of their families. Even with his own personal repulsion incited by the very idea of allowing a musical instrument to pass through the main doors of the Kirk, Daniel realized well enough that he was bound to carry the request forward to session. It would not be for him to decide but, at the same time, he was confident that the goodwill of the Bostonians could and would be channeled in some other more-meaningful and appropriate direction.

In actual fact, very little of session's time was taken up with Morag's letter at the September meeting in the front parlour of the manse. There was an acknowledgment that, given the far-reaching implications of the proposal, the decision must ultimately rest with the entire congregation and that it would be necessary to call a full meeting. Musical instruments had never been allowed in the Kirk; for most people, the praising of God with human voice was the only proper and dignified way to conduct worship. Yet Daniel and the other members of session knew that they were mere stewards of the congregation and would await the wisdom of its deliberations and final decision. They had every confidence that it would be the correct one.

An announcement was made from the pulpit the following month and a meeting was convened after evening worship on a blustery night in late November as the wind's mournful whistling echoed through the Kirk.

Among those gathered that night, there were many who saw symbolism in the eerie sound. Except for funerals and the odd wedding, the pews had seldom before been so full. Unbeknown to the Cabots and O'Sullivans, their offer had presented the people of *Loch Dubh* with a topic that generated many hours of lively discussion. Indeed, in the days leading up to the meeting, little else occupied the conversations at kitchen tables in the houses around the loch with both sides being argued with tremendous voracity. If nothing else, such discussions had shown that a consensus would not be easily reached and that the debate would certainly rival anything coming out of the House of Commons up in the Dominion's capital. Once worship had been completed, the Kirk would surely become more theatre than church. It would be an event not to be missed.

As the play unfolded, it became apparent that the lines were as well rehearsed as they were closely and evenly drawn. Daniel Erskine presided over the meeting but, as was the case with Duncan Fraser, refrained from offering his own personal thoughts on the matter. Both men knew that their views of opposition would be brought forward more properly and perhaps more effectively by others who sat in the pews before them. The climax of the lengthy meeting, which at times became more debate than discussion, came as Angus Grant defended the current form of worship that had nurtured them and their ancestors for many generations before. The precenting of the Psalms was all the music that was needed and, while no disrespect was intended towards the Boston families, the kind offer should be graciously acknowledged and politely declined. He made a conscious effort to not look over in the direction of Norman and Rachael Ferguson who sat directly across, knowing they were, no doubt, fully supportive of their daughter's proposal.

More than a few people were somewhat surprised when Hector Urquhart rose to make an equally eloquent case for acceptance of the offer. He believed that all music was a gift from God and should be used to further glorify and enjoy Him. He quite craftily elaborated on a point of theology in asking pointedly if they had not forgotten the first question and answer of their **Shorter Catechism**. He also mentioned that Elizabeth's church, St. James on Boularderie, had an organ since 1908 and that Knox, its sister church at Ross Ferry, had just recently voted to obtain one as well. What he did not dare make reference to was the fact that the St. James organ had been slipped into the church under cover of darkness and that, given strong divisions in the congregation, had remained stored in a utility room for several weeks allowing the passage of time to temper emotions. Hector acknowledged that it would be best to remain silent on this point knowing that it would only work against the case he was earnestly attempting to make.

When the vote was eventually called by Daniel after the better part of two full hours, bodies turned wildly in order to see which hands were being raised yea or nay. It reminded many of poor Flora and her ever-pivoting head. If nothing else, the taking of stock would be useful reference and provide fodder for idle chat for months to come regardless of what the outcome might be. It was by the slimmest of margins but the smile on Rachael Ferguson's face belied her pleasure at the wisdom of the decision taken. Later on, she would visit with the Urquharts in order to personally express her thanks to Hector for his eloquence. But for now, it would be important to let the matter settle for a bit. Besides, there would be several months yet before the organ's arrival to ponder the changes that were to take place. *Cha tachair e gu luath ach bithidh e ceart leis an àm. Bithidh e ceart gu dearbh.* (It will not happen in a hurry but it will be well in time. It will be well, yes indeed.) She had every confidence that time would pass and bruised egos would mend.

It had not taken long to determine that the only person in *Loch Dubh* who had received any formal musical training was Kristy, although in her mind two years of mandatory piano lessons at the academy in Sydney many years ago did not qualify her as an organist. With her own doubts set aside, she was determined to not disappoint the congregation once the formal request had been put to her. In this regard, she was grateful for her chance meeting down in the town with Mrs. Harder, the organist at the Church of England, who made the kind offer of a refresher course. Kristy eagerly accepted and, with a copy of the Church of Scotland's hymn book under her arm, undertook a number of lessons over the winter months from the elderly matron. Kristy dutifully practised some of the favourite selections with particular attention being paid to Part I of the hymnal: "Selections from the Psalter." She focused on Psalms XXIII, XXIV, XLVI, C and CXXI, which were five of those most frequently sung by the precentors. She knew that the playing of these might in some small way help the older people, including Daniel, accept the inevitable and realize that it too was intended as a positive reaffirmation of the answer to the very first question of **The Shorter Catechism** — "Man's chief end is to glory God and to enjoy Him forever.". At least she hoped it would help.

As much as the congregation was slowly adjusting to the upcoming arrival of *"Bocsa ceòlmhor Bhoston"* (The Boston Music Box) as it was now called, nothing had prepared them for a far greater change that would befall them and affect their lives in every bit as dramatic a way. It had been pondered for the better part of a year but Duncan Fraser had chosen to announce his retirement from the Kirk and indeed the ministry from the Easter pulpit. It had been his original intention to notify the congregation in January, shortly after the celebration of Christmas. He had discussed it with Jenny and together they had agreed that a delay of several weeks would be appropriate so as not to create the impression that it was in any way related to the issue of the organ. Even though he was still opposed to the presence of musical instruments in the sanctuary, Duncan's belated notice of departure to take effect the following September would allow sufficient time for wounds to heal. He promised himself that he would do all in his power to see that they did.

It was during the announcements, immediately prior to the collection of tithes and offerings and the delivery of the sermon, that Duncan first made the congregation aware of his decision. Between each of his slowly spoken and carefully chosen words, there seemed to be a tremendous gulf of time and silence as the news was first received and then absorbed. Shock gave way to sadness as numerous tears were shed by both men and women. The sounds of sobbing and the sight of handkerchiefs being retrieved from hand bags and back pockets made it all the more difficult for Duncan to complete his words. For years to follow, he would maintain that it was Jennie who willed him to go on. Not once did she take her eyes off her husband and not once did she doubt the suffering that his words brought to his own heart.

Earlier in the service, Duncan had chosen and read the New Testament lesson from II Corinthians, the apostle Paul's personal letter to the Corinthians whom he regarded as his children. While the verses spoke of Paul's difficulties and hardships in mission, Duncan's selection was far more telling for the message it carried. He began his sermon by once again quoting the apostle's stirring words from the eleventh verse of the thirteenth chapter. *"Fa dheòidh, a bhràithrean, slàn leibh: bithibh coimhlionta, bithibh subhach, bithibh a dh' aon inntinn, bithibh sìochail; agus bidh Dia a' ghràidh agus na sìthe maille ruibh."* (Finally, brethren, farewell. Be perfect, be of good comfort, be of one mind, live in peace; and the God of love and peace shall be with you.) Although he had not intended to do so, Duncan preached the entire sermon in Gaelic. Of all those seated before him that day, it was only Jennie who recognized the subtle difference in the intonation of his voice. For the first time in his many years of ministry, her husband was no longer the shepherd standing before his flock. He was now the father speaking to his children and this, more than anything else, explained why the tear in his voice came not in the closing prayer but the concluding words of the sermon. *"Fheara agus a bhràithrean, deanaibh gàirdeachas anns an Tighearn' a ghnàth oir tha mise maille ruibh a ghnàth. Amen agus amen."* (Men and brethren, rejoice in the Lord forever for I am with you always. Amen and amen.)

It was several weeks later that Kristy finally found herself seated at the organ that had been placed beneath the pulpit with the precentors now seated on either side. To her own amazement, she had grown accustomed to the feel of the two keyboards as well as the peddle board at her feet. She looked over at Lachlan, trusting that he would do his part as he sat to her left with his hand at the ready close to the cranking mechanism. She still marvelled at the rich walnut grain that stood in such contrast to the lighter spruce and pine wood of the Kirk's interior. She had even caught herself rubbing her hand over the raised gold lettering — Mason and Manlin, Boston, Massachusetts — that appeared over the upper keyboard. It did not have an intricate crown like the organ at the Lyceum

Theatre in Sydney but then this after all was a chapel model that was more modestly suited to a house of worship. With her focus now back on the order of service, Kristy waited patiently for the minister to pronounce a final prayer over Daniel and Agnes' wee lad who had just been baptized John Murray MacDonald. The baby slept quietly and was as oblivious to the water that trickled down over his tiny cheeks as he was to the fact that he would forever occupy a special place in his Kirk's history.

Duncan climbed the stairs to return to the pulpit and it was only then that the organ came to life. At that very same moment, Margaret MacGregor rose and stood behind its rich cabinetry with the pulpit fall forming a scarlet halo over her head. As Lachlan cranked his heart out, the sounds of the organ began to blend with Margaret's beautiful voice and filled the sanctuary to overflowing.

> "See Israel's gentle shepherd stand
> With all-engaging charms;
> Hark! how He calls the little lambs,
> And folds them in His arms."

Kristy looked up and studied Duncan carefully as, ever so softly, the music evaporated into silence across the sanctuary. Something told her that the trace of a smile that now appeared on his face was not so much due to the fact that the baptismal hymn was based on scripture, but rather because it spoke of the faithful shepherd, something that he would always be to the flock on the hills surrounding *Loch Dubh*. It was only then that the benediction was given and the service drew to its eventual close.

"Amen agus Amen." (Amen and Amen.)

"Nach eil latha brìagha blàth ann gu dearbh?" (Is it not just a beautiful warm day?) It was more a statement than a queston as Martha stood at the kitchen window looking out at Moira and Ismay who were playing near the rose bush that had been planted ages ago by poor Mrs. MacAulay. For years, it had grown wild in front of the vacant house as though seeking retribution for the total absence of proper attention and care to which it had earlier become accustomed. Yet, since the first day that she and Peter had purchased the old home some eighteen years ago, Martha was determined to lovingly coerce it back into a controllable state. If nothing else, it would be a tribute to the old woman's desire to bring additional beauty to this place. The lush crown of pink blossoms that now covered it reminded Martha of her four children and her own contribution in bringing something of equal beauty to *Loch Dubh*.

Martha knew that she should focus on the work before her. The roast would have to be sliced and the other food prepared without delay given that the gathering was now only a few hours off. And yet, it was the way that she had posed the question to herself that lingered in her mind. The choice of words and the actual inflection of her voice so reminded her of her father who would sit on the front veranda with her mother as the children, Malcolm, John and herself, raced about on the grass and through the orchard to the side of the house. Those days were so long ago and yet the memories were as clear as if it were yesterday. She could still smell the scent of his pipe and hear the clicking of her knitting needles. Perhaps on this of all days, it was timely to remember the past. It would encourage her and everyone else to make today a special time and, in some strange way, help them to accept the impending sadness as well as the inevitable uncertainty of the days ahead. *"Thoir an aire, mo chaileag! Tha móran ra dheanamh an seo."* (Pay attention my girl! There is much to do here.) While Martha laughed aloud at her own words of reprimand, it seemed as if it was now her mother's turn to speak. Her laughter was slowly transformed into a radiant smile as she turned and resumed the work that awaited her on the pantry counter. She sensed a presence.

It did not take a great deal of insight to realize that this was the last weekend of August. The fleeting fragrances of the gardens and the soft breezes wafting up from the bluffs that blended so ingeniously with both the scent of freshly scythed hay and the ever-increasing coolness of the Atlantic winds might suggest it. Still, depending upon the year, these "certain signs" of autumn could frequently carry well into September and even early October. No — what was far more telling and as accurate as any barometer was the exuberance of the children. How they revelled in the last days of summer's freedom before returning to the classroom and *Gnùis a' bhiorain-ghriosaich*. It was always so predictable and amusing.

The yearly ritual of ordering school supplies at Dunn's General Store had been made less complicated by the fact that there were now only two Campbell students to equip. It was the previous June that Colin had joined his older brother in the decision to call an end to his academic training as he passed through the double doors of the *Loch Dubh* school for the last time. It had been a much more difficult decision for him than it had been for Lachlan. Unlike his brother, he did not have the luxury of knowing that he would, in time, take over the farm from their father. Yet Martha and Peter always sensed that the stubborn streak of the MacDonalds was more evident in Colin than any of the other children. It therefore came as no surprise to them that, within three weeks of the final day of school, he had persuaded Angus Wright to take him on as a full-time labourer at the sawmill and lumber camp down the coast road. With an ever-increasing number of Gaelic-speaking farmers working at the camp and mill over the winter months to earn extra money for their families, Wright would put the linguistic and other talents of the young "Gaelicker" to good use. Martha had every confidence that he would do well for himself. Besides, there would certainly be no difficulty in ensuring a goodly supply of sawdust for the winter banking around the Campbell house.

As she stood there, Martha was overcome with the somewhat traumatic realization that her family was growing up. Perhaps it had happened all too quickly because she was left with a lingering feeling that she had not taken enough time to spend with them and to commit those moments to memory the way her dear mother did by always pressing flowers between the pages of the family Bible. *"Mo bhà acrach agus na fiaclan gorma."* (The hungry cows and the blue teeth.) The words seemed to come out of nowhere but, upon reflection, the images of smiling faces with groated mouths and blueberry-stained teeth prompted Martha to realize that it was possible that she had not been such a negligent mother after all. While her Bible was certainly not as flowered as her mother's had been, her mind and heart were resplendent with memories and that gave her a renewed sense of satisfaction. She was well pleased as she bowed her head and placed the last slices of roast onto the large platter.

The people of *Loch Dubh*, especially the women, were bound and determined to make the farewell for the Frasers a happy and memorable event. However, there had been a slight and quite unexpected change of plans. It was not just because Jennie had personally requested it although she had done so for good reason. How she cringed at any thought of a formal reception in the hall that would only make the parting all the more difficult. It was at the June meeting of the WMS (Women's Missionary Society) that she had discreetly asked if the community might also view a picnic as an acceptable format. In no way did she want it perceived as a slight in depriving her friends and neighbours of the more-commonly held reception, especially if planning was already under way. The women listened closely to the almost-pleading tone of her voice and knew her well enough to know that she would be speaking for Duncan as well. It was all duly noted and agreed; a picnic would be just the thing. In fact, it would be easier for everyone.

There were other reasons for making the picnic a fun time. The news of late, particularly that of the past three months, had been all so terribly upsetting. Peter was forever sitting by the stove reading aloud the articles from the Sydney newspaper as if he were a roving correspondent reporting from the scene himself. The seemingly endless series of heart-wrenching events appeared to have had its beginning with the sinking of *The Empress of Ireland* in late May when over one thousand souls had tragically perished in the dark waters of the Gulf of St. Lawrence. Then there was the spectacle of the two railways, the Grand Trunk Pacific and the Canadian Northern, fighting for survival against the bourgeoning massive debts as well as the hundreds of men who were consequently thrown out of work. Of late, a great deal of attention had been focused on the plight of the unemployed in the towns and cities clear across the Dominion, the worst some claimed since the 1890s. The summer had also seen the second consecutive year of drought out on the Prairies. John and Ida's youngest son

Murdoch lived in Calgary and had written home with disturbing stories of farm families abandoning the land only to find even greater hardship in a strange city where no one knew them or seemingly had any inclination to offer assistance. As she once again looked out over the loch and mountains, Martha found it difficult to comprehend the intensity of their pain in having to leave their homes and lives behind. She realized that, as was the case with most people in *Loch Dubh*, her family possessed a wealth that defied description.

And now it was the war. Less than two weeks had passed since the Dominion parliament with Mr. Borden as prime minister had debated the issue of war against both Germany and Austria-Hungary, although for all intents and purposes Canada had been at Britain's side since her earlier declaration on August 4. Martha remembered the date well; it was a Tuesday because she was in town when word had come on the Wednesday steamer from Sydney that Britain had taken the fateful decision at midnight. To his credit, Sir Wilfrid Laurier stood in parliament as Leader of His Majesty's Loyal Opposition and eloquently stated that Canada's rightful place was at Britain's side. The newspaper had reported that he had even gone so far as to use the words "Ready, aye, ready!" Something told Martha that, on this occasion at least, even her dear father would be willing to take the pronouncement of the "Old Grit" to heart.

But still, war was a tragic affair. It was something not to be glorified, for as certain as night followed day, Canadian men would be asked to answer the call, to serve and no doubt to die. While the cause against the Hun was a just one, war would not be kind to or considerate of young lives with dreams of the future and the promise of things yet to come, growing old together with children and grandchildren of their own — to cuddle, to nurture, to take their places. For the first time in a great long while, Martha thought of her nephew Andrew and the waste of one man's precious life. She knew that newspaper headlines were much more than so many words on sheets of paper. They were alluring trumpets that called out and changed lives in sometimes tragic and irrevocable ways. It was now some fourteen years since *Loch Dubh* had last been so touched and affected by war and its horrible consequences. Certainly farming families appreciated the fact that winter snow was all that would be needed to transform these hills into emerald green gems with the coming of the next spring. Martha said a silent prayer in the hope that melting snow would not be supplemented by the tears of grieving parents.

The mid-afternoon ride over to the bluffs was reminiscent of the old Queen's Diamond Jubilee celebrations back in 1897, except for the fact that Rod and Andrew were not there to position and settle the horses in the back field. The opening on the bluffs was so like that time now many years ago although the absence of Union Jacks and the large wooden cone that had frightened poor *Floiridh Aosda* half to death was duly noted. Even with the knowledge that it was to be a picnic, everyone took care and came dressed in freshly washed and pressed clothes, although not necessarily their formal Sunday best. There was only the faintest hint of a breeze coming off the water that thankfully enabled the women to go about their work without having their skirts blown about like sheets billowing on a clothes line. And, as was to be expected, the men had seated themselves in the shade of the spruce trees off to the side where they smoked their pipes and were already comparing notes on the hay crop and other bits of news that they seldom found time to exchange during the hectic summer months, except for hurried discussions following service at the Kirk or prayer meetings and milling frolics in the hall. For their part, the women were not about to complain about the distance between themselves and the menfolk. They could go about their business of laying out the food while still keeping a keen eye on the children who were engaged in various games of chase. There were a few notable exceptions as several of the younger boys, including Andrew Ferguson, had gathered near *Eachann nan Sgeul* and were pleading with him to tell a ghoulish story of the *bòcain*. From the broad smile that filled Hector's face, there was little doubt but that, in time, he would weaken and regale them with one of his most horrifying tales.

Word spread quickly and everyone stood as the Fraser family first appeared from the canopied pathway leading down into the clearing. The three children, Sandy, Matthew and Emily, had all come home with their families to be with their parents and to share in this special time together. Jennie proudly carried little Duncan who was already two and a half years old and, with the round face and inquiring brown eyes, bore such a shocking resemblance to the Frasers. Jennie had let it be known at an earlier meeting of the WMS that both she and Duncan looked forward to caring for the wee one once they were moved into Emily and Christopher's home in Baddeck. The doting grandparents would watch over him during the day now that Emily had been enticed back to work with the promise of a promotion to the position of head librarian. It would make Duncan and Jennie's transition into retirement all the easier although it would in no way lessen the sadness that still clung to the homes that encircled the loch.

Duncan and Jennie quickly began to circulate among the small clustered groups and were terribly obvious in their attempts to maintain a jovial atmosphere. There was a masking of true emotions but everyone recognized that the more-poignant moments of parting would come on the front steps of the Kirk following Duncan's final sermon the next day and on the government wharf Monday morning as the steamer departed southward. There would be ample opportunity then for final good-byes, no doubt complete with misty if not tearful eyes. That was yet to come. For now, it was agreed that they would simply enjoy this time of fellowship together.

With all these activities taking place at the same time and, to a certain degree, competing for attention, few had taken note of the two figures seated off to the side, on the rocks where Elizabeth Urquhart had often gone over the years to think. *Coinneach Bàn* had taken the carefully folded newspaper clipping from his pants pocket and watched intently as Lachlan studied the illustration and the accompanying text. The picture was of a soldier in highland uniform with his rifle and bayonet fixed at the ready. Above the kilted figure appeared the words *"DEAS GU CATH — READY FOR FIGHT"*. Although one would have to look closely, you could ever so faintly discern the silhouette of a piper playing on a far hilltop in the background. The article spoke of the duty of Nova Scotian men to be involved and share in the glory, especially if one was to believe the stories that the fighting would be all over by Christmas. There was already some talk of a Nova Scotia battalion being mobilized to join a second Canadian division for overseas service. *Coinneach Bàn* pointed to the soldier and summoned up all the conviction of his twenty-two years. The cause was not in defence of any king; it was to defeat the marauding Huns who had already shown their true colours by butchering innocent men, women and children as they made their way across Belgium. Canada could not stand idly by and allow such atrocities to continue. As he looked over towards the grouping of men under the towering spruce trees where a huge Cross of St. Andrew flag had once flown, *Coinneach Bàn* was certain his grandfather would surely agree.

A conscious decision had been made in advance that the festivities would come to a close shortly after the meal as the sun first began to seek refuge behind the treed wall of the western mountains. Everyone understood that Duncan would want to spend additional time pouring over his notes as the final sermon was prepared for the morning service. Indeed, the sun had not fully disappeared from the sky by the time Duncan, Jennie and the children finally arrived back at the manse. With few exceptions, their eyes were still reddened as a result of the emotional closing prayer that had been offered. An immense circle had been formed as hands were joined together for a final time with the realization that something of a far greater significance was about to be broken.

As they slowly made their way up the laneway towards the manse, Jennie's focus settled on the now-empty veranda where so much family history had played itself out over the years. It was her suggestion that they sit there for a spell as the fading rays of sun transformed the surface of the loch into, what appeared to be, a magnificent carpet of shimmering candle light. She commented that the twilight was far too precious to waste by remaining indoors; consequently, not one dissenting voice, not even Duncan's, was raised. There was a subtle unspoken realization that, for the second time that day, there would be a memorable form of fellowship together.

Duncan sat in the rocking chair as the others made reassuring small talk about the upcoming move to Baddeck and the exciting new chapter that was about to unfold. Still, with the exception of the wee bairn who seemed intent on terrorizing poor *Rionnag*, all thoughts were on Duncan whose eyes were more often than not fixed on the tranquil vista of the glen that stretched out in front of him as it had for so many years. But this time it was different, so completely different from all the times before. Although it was cause for reflection, the contemplative moment was quickly and quite unexpectedly shattered as a playful tug on *Rionnag*'s tail resulted in a resounding hiss indicating extreme irritation. This combative bit of drama served to remind Duncan that he and Jennie had not yet decided if it would be best to take their *leanabh dubh* (black child) with them or whether it might not be more compassionate to leave her here as a manse cat, free to prowl the fields and hills that she loved. It might yet be another tearful farewell that they would have to endure in the coming hours. Still, some difficult good-byes had already been said. No one on the veranda, not even Jennie, knew that Duncan had spent several hours walking through the cemetery earlier in the week visiting with Archie, Flora, Tina, Peter and many others. On that particular evening, no one realized that his late arrival home was certainly not due to unexpected business in the Kirk. He merely wanted to complete his visitation and, of equal importance, to ensure sufficient time to allow his eyes to dry.

There were many stories recounted on the veranda that spanned the years in this place that had been so much more than a home. While some evoked memories of sadness, most harkened back to the joys of a family growing up surrounded by a much larger family with a love of life and an eagerness to share it with exceeding generosity. Then, as the final fragments of twilight slowly faded into darkness, the women were the first to move inside the house to light the kerosene lamps. The men, Sandy, Matthew, Christopher and the baby, were soon to follow. It was several minutes later that Duncan rose from his chair and moved towards the screen door with its gingerbread scrolling. As the door cracked open, *Rionnag* hesitated and looked up at Duncan who was now staring off towards the eastern horizon where the storm clouds continued to gather over *An Toiseach* and *An Deireadh*. In the stillness of the moment, it was only *Rionnag* who heard Duncan's parting words that night to the waters, mountains and people of *Loch Dubh*. "*A Thighearna. Thigeadh do rioghachd. Deanar do thoil.*" (Oh Lord. Thy kingdom come. Thy will be done.) With that, the door slowly closed behind them as the two figures passed from sight, leaving both the rocking chair and veranda in silence under the watchful gaze of *Beinn-mo-Mhulaid*.

CREDITS

The songs quoted in this book are credited as follows:

Chapter One (page 22) *Cagaran Gaolach*, taken from the compact disc - "*Bho Thìr Nan Craobh*" by Mary Jane Lamond, B & R Heritage Enterprises.

Chapter Four (page 85) *Òran Do Mhac Iain Mhic Sheumais*, taken from Donald A. Ferguson, *Fad Air Falbh As Innse Gall (Comh- Chruinneachadh Cheap Breatuinn)*/Beyond the Hebrides (Including the Cape Breton Collection), Royale Print, Halifax, Nova Scotia, 1977, p. 62.

Chapter Four (page 107) *Chì Mi Na Mórbheanna*, taken from Helen Creighton and Calum MacLeod, Gaelic Songs in Nova Scotia, The Canadian Museum of Civilization, Gatineau, Quebec, 1964, pp. 12 - 13.

Chapter Five (page 114) *'S e Mo Leannan*, taken from Ferguson, *Fad Air Falbh As Innse Gall*, p. 248.

Chapter Six (page 128) *An Téid Thu Leam, A Ribhinn Òg?*, taken from Creighton and MacLeod, Gaelic Songs in Nova Scotia, p. 55.

Chapter Seven (page 162) *Air Faillirinn O, Ho Ri Ho Ro*, taken from Ferguson, *Fad Air Falbh As Innse Gall*, p. 253.

Chapter Eight (page 169) *Òran Do Chéilidh Cheap Breatuinn*, ibid., p. 191.

Chapter Nine (page 191) *Ho Ro 'S Toigh Leam Fhein Thu*, ibid., p. 80.

Chapter Ten (page 210) *Tighinn Do America*, ibid., p. 43.

Chapter Twelve (page 250) *An Innis Àigh*, ibid., p. 221.

Chapter Fourteen (page 290) *Òran Do America*, ibid., p. 47.

Chapter Sixteen (page 335) *An Ceitean Orgheal*, ibid., p. 183.

Chapter Seventeen (page 355) *Òran Do Mhòd Gaidhealach Cheap Breatuinn*, ibid., p. 128.

Chapter Seventeen (page 359) The commencement of the MacCrimmon *canntaireachd* — *Cogadh no Sìth* — taken from Francis Collinson, <u>The Bagpipe - The History of a Musical Instrument</u>, Routledge & Kegan Paul, London, England, 1975, p. 157.

Chapter Eighteen (page 374) *Òran Do 'N Transvaal*, taken from Ferguson, *<u>Fad Air Falbh As Innse Gall</u>*, p. 105.

Chapter Eighteen (page 388) *See, Israel's Gentle Shepherd Stands*, hymn taken from <u>The Presbyterian Book of Praise</u> (Canadian), Oxford University Press, London, England, 1903, hymn 409.

The poems quoted in this book are credited as follows:

Chapter Fifteen (pages 321-322) *Nach fhaic thu?* (*Oh Can't You See?*), original composition by the author. Gaelic translation by Douglas McKercher (Ottawa, Ontario).

Chapter Sixteen (page 352) *Epistle to J. Lapraik* (*The Poet is Born not Made*), poem by Robert Burns taken from Raymond Bentman, ed., <u>The Poetic Works of Burns</u>, Houghton Mifflin Company, Boston, Massachusetts, 1974, p. 45.

Kevin S. MacLeod, C.V.O.

Kevin MacLeod was born in North Sydney, Cape Breton, Nova Scotia, and raised on a farm in nearby Boularderie. He began his public education at the local country school in Millville and went on to study at Boston University (Boston, Massachusetts) and Carleton University (Ottawa, Ontario), where he received Bachelors (History/Political Science) and Masters (International Affairs) degrees.

Following studies at the Université de Dijon (Dijon, France), he returned to Ottawa where he was employed for ten years as an administrative assistant in the House of Commons. Subsequently, he served as Chief of Staff to a Minister of the Crown before joining the then Department of the Secretary of State (now the Department of Canadian Heritage), where he currently serves as Chief of Protocol.

In 1992, Her Majesty The Queen invested him as a Member of the Royal Victorian Order (M.V.O.) for personal service to The Sovereign. A decade later, she promoted him to the rank of Lieutenant (L.V.O.) during the highly successful Golden Jubilee Visit and, in 2005, to Commander (C.V.O.) — the highest level available to Canadians. He is the only Canadian to have been promoted through all three ranks.